THE LOST SWORDS:
THE FIRST TRIAD

THE LOST SWORDS: THE FIRST TRIAD

WOUNDHEALER'S STORY
SIGHTBLINDER'S STORY
STONECUTTER'S STORY

Fred Saberhagen

Nelson Doubleday, Inc.
Garden City, New York

For Joan
As are all the others, whether labeled so or not.

THE FIRST BOOK OF LOST SWORDS: WOUNDHEALER'S STORY
Copyright © 1986 by Fred Saberhagen
ISBN 031-52058-0
THE SECOND BOOK OF LOST SWORDS: SIGHTBLINDER'S STORY
Copyright © 1987 by Fred Saberhagen
ISBN 031-55296-2
THE THIRD BOOK OF LOST SWORDS: STONECUTTER'S STORY
Copyright © 1988 by Fred Saberhagen
ISBN 031-55288-1

Published by arrangement with
TOR Books
Tom Doherty Associates
49 West 24th Street
New York, New York 10010

Printed in the United States of America

Contents

THE FIRST BOOK OF LOST SWORDS:
WOUNDHEALER'S STORY

1

HERE in the green half-darkness an endless melody of water ran, a soft flow that played lightly and moodily over rock. The surrounding walls of dark rock oozed water like the Earth's blood, three clear rivulets that worked to fill a black pool no bigger than a royal bath.

At the single outlet of the pool a stream was born, to gurgle from the vessel of its birth across a rocky floor toward the distant sunlight. What little light inhabited the cave, a dim, funneled, gray-green, water-dappled illumination, came in through the small air space above the tumbling surface of the small outflowing stream.

Now multiple moving shadows were entering from the sunlight, distorting the gray-green light within the cave. Bold, purposeful splashings altered the endless murmur of the water. Rocks in the streambed were kicked and tossed aside, with hollow echoing sounds. The voices of children, pitched to quiet excitement, entered the cave too.

There were three of the visitors. Two of them, a girl and boy in their middle teens, were sturdy waders who supported and guided between them a smaller and much more fragile-looking figure. All three had rolled their trousers above their knees for wading; a useless precaution, for all three were dripping wet from feet to hair. It had been necessary to crawl, half in the cold splashing flow of water, to get in under the low rock at the very entrance.

"We're in a cave now, Adrian," the girl announced with enthusiasm, bending over her small charge. She was perhaps fourteen, her brown hair hanging over her face in long, damp ringlets. Her face was attractive in its youth and health, though it gave no promise of ever being known for its great beauty.

The little boy to whom she spoke said nothing. He was no more than seven years old, with long, fair hair falling damply around a thin, sharp-featured face. His mouth was open just now, and working slightly, the lips rounded by some inner tension into a silent cry. His eyes, remarkably wide and blue, were sightless but active, sending their blind gaze wavering across the rough and shadowed ceiling of the cave.

Now he pulled free his right hand, which the older boy had been holding, and used it to grope in the empty air in front of him.

"A cave, Adrian." The sturdy youth, in a voice that was just starting to deepen, repeated what the girl had said. Then, when the child did not respond, he shrugged his shoulders slightly. He was somewhat bigger than the girl and looked a little older. His hair was of the same medium brown as hers and showed something of the same tendency to curl; and his face resembled hers enough that no one had trouble in taking them for brother and sister.

The girl was carrying three pairs of shoes tied at her belt. All three of the children were plainly dressed in rough shirts and trousers. Here and there, at throat or wrist, an ornament of gold or amber indicated that the choice of plain clothing had not been dictated by poverty.

The explorers had all waded out of the ankle-deep stream now and were standing on the flat sandy floor of the cave. The girl halted after a couple of steps on dry sand, studying the surprisingly large room around her. She frowned into the dark shadows ahead, from whence the sounds of running water had their deepest origin.

She asked: "Zoltan, is this place safe?"

Her brother frowned into the deeper shadows too. Self-consciously he felt for the dagger sheathed at his belt. Then he dropped into a crouch, the better to scan the cave floor in the half light.

"No droppings," he muttered. "No gnawed bones. I don't even see any tracks." He brushed his strong, square fingers at sand and rock. "Ought to be safe. I don't think that anything large can be living in here. Besides, the wizards checked out this whole area this morning."

"Then we can hide in here." The girl's voice returned to the conspiratorial tones of gaming, and she stroked the small child's hair protectively, encouragingly. "We'll hide in here, Adrian; and Stephen and Beth will never find us."

Adrian displayed no interest in the question of whether they would ever be found or not. "Elinor," he said, in a high, clear voice. The name sounded as if he were pronouncing it very thoughtfully and carefully.

At the same time he reached his groping hand toward the girl and touched her clothing.

"Yes, it's me. I've been with you all the morning, remember? So has Zoltan." She spoke patiently and encouragingly, as if to a child much younger than seven.

Now Adrian seemed to be giving her last statement his deepest thought. He had turned his head a little on one side. His round mouth worked, his blind eyes flickered.

Zoltan, standing by with folded arms and watching, shook his head. "I don't think he even understands we're playing hide-and-seek," he remarked sadly. In relation to his young cousin, the Prince Zoltan stood more in the role of companion and bodyguard than that of playmate, though at fifteen he was not too old to slide from one character to the other as conditions seemed to require.

"I think he does," Elinor said reproachfully. "Something's bothering him, though."

"Something's always bothering him—poor little bugger."

"Hush. He can understand what you're saying." Kneeling in dry sand, she patted the cheek of their young charge soothingly. The Princeling slowly patted her hand in return.

Elinor persisted with her cheerful encouragement. "Beth and Stephen are 'it' this turn, Adrian, remember? But we've got a great place to hide now. They're never going to be able to find us, here in a cave. Can you tell we're in a cave, by the way things sound? I bet there are a lot of blind people who could do that. Isn't it fun, playing hide-and-seek?"

The small boy turned his head this way and that. Now it was as if he were tired of listening to Elinor, thought her brother, who couldn't blame him if he were.

"Water," Adrian whispered thoughtfully. It did not sound like a request, but a musing comment.

The girl was pleased. "That's right, we had to wade through the water to get in here. I was afraid the rocks would bother your feet, but I guess they didn't. Now you're out of the water, you're sitting on a dry rock." She raised her head. "Zolty, will we be able to hear Beth calling if they decide they want to give up?"

"Dunno," her brother answered abstractedly. He had turned his back on the others and was facing the cave's single entrance, his eyes and ears intently focused in that direction. "I thought I heard something," he added.

"Beth and Stephen?"

"No. Not a voice. More like a riding-beast. Something with hooves, anyway, clopping around out there in the stream."

"Probably some of the soldiers," Elinor offered. There had been a small patrol sent out from High Manor, in advance of the children's outing. Not that the adults of the royal family, as far as she knew, were particularly worried about anything. It had been purely a routine precaution.

"No." Her brother shook his head. "They're supposed to be patrolling a kind of perimeter. They wouldn't be riding through here now. Unless . . ."

"What?"

Zoltan, without taking his eyes off the entrance, made an abrupt silencing motion with his hand.

His sister was not going to let him get away with becoming dramatic. She began to speak, then broke the words off with a hushed cry: "Adrian!"

The child's eyes were only half open, and only the whites of them were showing. A faint gasping noise came from his throat. He had been sitting bolt upright where Elinor had placed him, but now his thin body was starting to topple slowly from the rock.

Zoltan turned to see his sister catch the child and lower him into the soft sand. But then just as quickly he turned back the other way. Something was now outside the cave that could shadow the whole entrance. The darkness within had deepened suddenly and evenly.

Elinor was curled on the sand, lying there beside the child, and when Zoltan took another quick glance at her he could see that she was frightened. Adrian was starting to have a real seizure, what looked to Zoltan like a bad one. The Princeling's little body was stiffening, then bending, then straightening out again. Elinor had stuffed a handkerchief into his mouth to keep him from biting his tongue—her eyes looking back at her brother were full of fear. Not of the fit; she had seen and dealt with those before. The nameless presence outside the cave was something else again.

Then suddenly the shadow outside was gone.

Only a cloud shadow? As far as Zoltan's eyes alone could tell, it might have been nothing more than that.

But he didn't think so.

He waited. Something . . .

* * *

And now, from out there in the renewed sunlight, in anticlimax, came childish voices calling; shouting imperiously, and not in fear. Calling the names, one after another, of the three who waited in the cave.

Then silence, stretching on, one heartbeat after another.

Zoltan had a strong impulse to return the call. But somehow his throat was misbehaving, clogged with relief and lingering fear, and at first no sound would come out.

But no answer was necessary. Their trail must have been plainer than he had thought. Again the entrance of the cave dimmed slightly, with small, wavering shadows. Two more children entered, splashing.

"We found you!" It was a cry of triumph. Beth, as usual, had no trouble finding her voice or using it, and there was no indication that she had encountered anything in the least unusual on her way to the finding. She was a stout ten-year-old, inclined to try to be the boss of everyone in sight, whether or not they might be older than she, or related by blood to the rulers of the land while she was not.

Clamped firmly in the grip of one of her stout fists was the small arm of Stephen, Adrian's younger brother.

Adrian and Stephen shared a certain similarity in face and coloring. But with that, even the physical resemblance ended. Already Stephen, no more than five, was pulling his arm fiercely out of Beth's grip and beginning to complain that their three rivals in the game had cheated by coming into the cave to hide.

Zoltan grabbed small Stephen suddenly and clamped a hand across his chattering little mouth, enforcing silence. Whatever had shaded the cave mouth before was coming back, just as silently as before, and more intensely. The shadow that now lay across the sunlight seemed deeper and darker than any natural shadow had the right to be.

Now even Zoltan's eyesight assured him that this must be more than just a cloud.

Stephen, awed by the strange darkness and by the seriousness of the grip that held him, fell silent and stood still.

Presently Zoltan let him go, and drew his dagger from its sheath.

Now Adrian, with a grunt and a spasmodic movement, reared himself almost to his feet, then fell back on the sand. Elinor lunged after him, but one loud shrill cry had escaped the boy before she could cover his mouth with her hand.

An echo of that cry, in a different voice, deep and alien and perhaps inhuman, hideously frightening, came from outside.

And with that echo came a noise that sounded like a large number of riding-beasts splashing in the stream outside. Stones were being kicked carelessly about out there, and there were men's voices, rough and urgent, speaking to each other in unfamiliar accents, not those of the Tasavaltan Palace Guard. Zoltan could not make out words, but he was sure that the men were confused, upset, arguing about something.

Now waves of sickness, almost palpable, came and went through the atmosphere inside the cave. The children stared at each other with ghastly faces, pale in the deep gloom. Zoltan had the feeling that the floor was tilting crazily under his feet, though his eyes assured him that the stream was undisturbed in its burbling course. The child in Elinor's arms emitted another pitiful cry; she clamped her hand over his mouth more fiercely than ever.

Beth was standing stock still. Her eyes met Zoltan's, and hers were wide as they could be. But she was biting her lip and he thought there was no sign that she was going to yell.

There was now almost no light left in the cave, and it was difficult to see anything at all, though by now his eyes had had time to adapt. Shadow, imitating rock, bulged and curled where once the entering sunlight had been strongest.

Something, thought Zoltan, is trying to force its way in here. Into the cave. To us.

And he had the inescapable feeling that *something else* was keeping the shadow, whatever the shadow represented, from forcing its way in.

How long the indescribable ordeal lasted he could never afterward be sure, nor could Elinor. Nor were any of the younger children able to give consistent estimates. But eventually, with renewed kicking of rocks and splashing by their mounts, the riders outside withdrew. The shadow moderated. But no component of the threat retreated very far. From time to time Zoltan could still hear a word or two of the riders' talk or the sharp sound of a shod hoof above the constant murmur of the stream.

Beth moved. Almost calmly, though timidly, one quiet step after another, she went to Elinor's side, where she sat down in the sand. Stephen continued to stand rigid, his eyes moving from Zoltan's face down to the useless dagger in Zoltan's hand, and back again.

And once more the sickness came, like an evil smell. It seemed to burrow in and grip, somewhere even deeper than the belly and the bones. A sudden realization crossed Zoltan's mind: *This must be the sensation that people describe, that they have when a demon comes too near them. Quite likely we are all going to die.*

But once more the sickness in the air abated.

Adrian's seizure was growing more intense, but so far Elinor was coping with it somehow. She and Zoltan had both seen some of his fits before that were as bad as this, or almost as bad.

Now a new feeling, curiosity, grew in Zoltan, until it was almost as strong as the fear he felt. Dagger still in hand, he got down slowly on all fours in the sand until he could peer out all the way into the restored sunshine outside the cave.

In the distance, slightly downhill from Zoltan and far enough away so that he could see only her head and pale, bare shoulders above a rock, there was a girl. Black-haired and comely, perhaps his own age or a little older, she appeared to be sitting or kneeling or crouching right beside the stream.

What caught Zoltan's attention most powerfully was that the girl was looking straight at him. He was sure of it. Despite the distance, some thirty or forty meters, he thought that he could see her gray eyes clearly, and he was certain about the finger she had lifted to her smiling lips. It was as if she were trying to convey a message: *Say nothing now. In good time. You and I will share great secrets, in good time.*

The way her black hair fell round her ivory shoulders reminded him at once, and irresistibly, of a little girl he had known, years previously, when he had been but a small child himself. Zoltan had loved her, in the way of one child for another, though until this moment he had not thought of her for years. Somehow his first look at this older girl in the sunlight brought back the vision of the child. And the suspicion, the hope, began to grow in him that this was she.

With a start Zoltan became aware of the fact that Elinor was calling his name in a frantic whisper, that she must have been calling it for some time. He turned his head to look helplessly at his sister.

"He's getting worse!" The words were uttered under her breath, but fiercely.

And indeed, the child's fit was now certainly the worst that Zoltan had ever seen him undergo. Zoltan got to his feet, the girl outside temporarily forgotten.

There was a lull outside, a certain lightening of the shadow.

And then, suddenly, a confused uproar. Whatever was happening out there, the noise it made was for the moment impossible to interpret.

Then Zoltan understood. With a rush, new hoofbeats and new voices made themselves heard in the distance. As if blown off by a sharp breeze, the sickness faded from the air, the darkness lifted totally. Abruptly there began the sounds of a sharp fight immediately outside the cave, the honest sound of blades that clashed on other blades and shields. To Zoltan's ears it sounded like the soldiers' practice field, but in his mind and in his stomach he knew that this was more than practice.

Now one man's voice in particular, shouting powerfully outside the cave, was recognizable to them all. Zoltan's knees, which until now had stayed reliable, went suddenly shaky with relief. "Uncle Mark," he gasped.

Elinor looked back at him. "Uncle Mark," she echoed, prayerfully.

Adrian, twisting his body and pulling with both hands, somehow tore his face free of her grip. "Father!" he cried out loudly, once, and fell into a faint.

2

ON the night following their temporary entrapment in the cave,
Zoltan and Elinor slept soundly at High Manor, in their own beds.
In contrast, it was well after midnight before the Princes Adrian and
Stephen, and their playmate Beth, were returned to their homes in
Sarykam, the capital city of Tasavalta. When Prince Adrian was put to
bed in his own room in the Palace, the fit was still on him, though the
fierceness of it had diminished.

Prince Mark, Adrian's father, had brought his family home himself
because there had seemed to be little or nothing more that he could
accomplish personally at High Manor in the aftermath of the attack.
Next morning's sun was well up before he roused from his own uneasy
and sporadic slumber.

He was alone on waking, but felt no surprise at the fact. He assumed
that his wife had remained all night at the child's bedside, getting such
sleep as she was able in a chair. She had done the same thing often
enough before; and Mark himself was no stranger to such vigils either.

Presently Prince Mark walked out onto the balcony that opened from
his and the Princess's bedroom. Squinting into sunlight, he looked
about him over the city and the sea. The far horizon, which had once
seemed to promise infinite possibilities, was beginning to look and feel
to him like the high wall of a prison.

Having filled his lungs with sea air and his eyes with sunlight, and
convinced himself that at least most of the world was still in place, he
came back indoors to join his wife in the child's room. It was a small
chamber that adjoined their own. Kristin, looking tired, was standing
beside the small bed and listening to the Chief Physician of the Royal

Household. There was visible in her bearing a certain aristocratic poise that her husband permanently lacked. Her hair was blond, her face as fine-featured as that of her older son, and her eyes blue-green, with something in them of the sea, whose sharp horizon came in at every eastern window of these high Palace rooms.

The current Chief Physician—there had been several holders of the office during the seven years since Adrian was born—was a gray-haired, white-robed woman named Ramgarh. She had been in attendance on the Princess and her elder son since their return to the Palace in the middle of the night.

As Mark entered, the doctor was saying, in her calm, soothing voice: "The child is breathing steadily now, and his pulse is within the range where there is no cause for concern. If the history of recovery from past seizures holds for this one, he will probably sleep through most of the day."

It was only what the father had expected to hear. In the past seven years he had endured more of his firstborn's fits and seizures than he could begin to count. But still he put back the curtain from the bed to see for himself. There was Adrian, asleep, looking as if nothing in the world were wrong with him.

Mark, Prince Consort of Tasavalta, was a tall man of thirty. His hair had once been as fair as that of his sons'; but age had darkened Mark's hair into a medium brown, though hair and beard still tended to bleach light in the sun. This morning Mark's face wore a tired, drawn look, and the lines at the corners of his mouth were a shade deeper than they had been the night before.

Princess Kristin had come silently to stand beside her husband, and he put an arm around her. Their pose held more than a suggestion that they were leaning together for mutual support.

The physician, after dispensing a few more soothing words for both the parents, departed to get some rest. Mark scarcely heard the doctor's parting words. They were almost always essentially the same: an exhortation to hope, a reminder that things could be worse. For about two years now there had been no more promises that new kinds of treatment would be tried. The catalogue of treatments that the doctors were ready and willing to attempt had been exhausted.

When the door had closed behind the physician, the Prince and Princess looked at each other, and then both turned their eyes back to the small form in the bed.

She said: "He will be all right now, I think."

Mark's voice was flat and heavy. "You mean he will be no worse off than before."

Before the Princess could answer there was an interruption. A nurse-maid had just entered the room, leading their second child, who had just awakened, his usual healthy self. Stephen was carrying, rolled up in one hand, the hand-lettered storybook that had been with him all during the long ride from High Manor.

Stephen was obviously still somewhat fogged with sleep, but he brought with him an image of hearty normality. Though almost two years younger than his brother, he was the sturdier. And now, in the way that Stephen looked at his sleeping brother, there was a suggestion of his resentment, that Adrian should be getting so much attention just because he had had another fit.

But Stephen, aware that parental eyes were on him, tucked the colored scroll of the book in at the edge of Adrian's bed, a voluntary and more-or-less willing sharing. Then he tugged at his father's trouser leg. "Can we go back to High Manor again today? I want to watch the soldiers."

His father smiled down at him wanly. "Didn't you have enough excitement there yesterday?"

"I want to go back."

"You'll be a warrior." Mark's big hand brushed the small blond head.

The mother stood by, saying nothing, not smiling.

The nursemaid returned to take the energetic child away for breakfast.

Driven by the need to do something, Mark strode out upon a balcony, where he drew a deep breath and looked out over the tile rooftops of the city well below him. From the outer wall of the Palace, Sarykam spread downhill to the sea, which here made first a neatly sheltered bay, then endless blue beyond a thin, curving peninsula of docks and lighthouses and fortifications.

A favorable combination of warm latitude and cool ocean currents made Sarykam a place of near-perpetual spring. Behind the Palace and the western fringe of the city, the mountains rose up, rank on rank, and topped with wild forests of pine. The trees upon the eastern side of the crest, toward the city and the sea, were warped by almost everlasting winds, fierce at that altitude but usually much milder down here near sea level. Six hours' ride inland, beyond those mountains, lay High

Manor, which, among its other functions, served sometimes as a summer home for royalty. And only a couple of kilometers from the Manor was the cave where yesterday's mysterious kidnapping attempt—Mark had to interpret the violent incident as such—had been thwarted.

There was much about that attempt that the Prince still found mysterious. Naturally investigations on both the military and the magical level had been set in motion last night—as soon as the fighting stopped —and were going forward.

Even now Mark could see a winged messenger coming from inland, perhaps bearing news of some results. There, halfway between the highest tower of the Palace and the crest of the mountains, were a pair of small, fine wings beating swiftly. He could hope that the courier was bringing word of some success by the searching cavalry.

Had the attempt been only the impulsive gamble of some bandit chief, reckless enough to accept the risks in return for the chance of a fat ransom? The Prince thought not, for several reasons.

The enemy had come with powerful magical assistance. The small detachment of the Palace Guard that had been stationed, as a matter of routine protection, in the area where the children were playing had been surprised and wiped out ruthlessly. The children had been tracked to the cave where they were hiding.

And then, just when the greatest tragedy should have been inevitable, came inexplicable good fortune. The enemy, for all the competence and determination they had displayed up to that point, had been unable to determine that the children were actually in the cave. Or—and this alternative seemed even more unlikely—the enemy had known they were there, but had simply been unable to get at them. Either explanation seemed quite incredible under the circumstances. It was true that Elinor and Zoltan had both reported the subjective feeling of some protective power at hand, but in Mark's experience such feelings had little to do with the real world.

Of course in this case the feelings could have had some basis in fact. Karel, who was Princess Kristin's uncle as well as her chief wizard, had divined from his workroom in Sarykam that something was wrong out near High Manor and had done what he could do at a distance. Meanwhile one of the winged messengers employed by the military had fortunately witnessed the wiping-out of the Guard detachment and had darted back to its roost at High Manor to report the attack. Mark, who was at the Manor, had hastily gathered a force and ridden out at once.

The children had been completely unprotected in the presence of the enemy for only a few minutes.

Mark and his swordsmen had surprised the attackers—who to all appearances were no more than a group of bandits—at the very mouth of the cave in which the children were sheltering. Fortunately it had been possible to drive off the demon at once. Mark had assumed at the time that the enemy had been on the point of entering the cave, and that his arrival was barely in time to save the children. But the children, when questioned later, insisted that the intruders, including their demonic cohort, had been immediately outside the cave for a long time. The adults took this estimate as an exaggeration—no doubt the time had seemed an eternity to children who were thus trapped.

The fight at the entrance to the cave had begun without any attempt to parley, without even a single word of warning on either side. And it had been conducted to the death. None of the nameless human invaders had shown the least inclination to surrender, or even to run away. Mark had shouted for his soldiers to take prisoners, but even so none of the attackers had survived long enough to be questioned. Two who were only lightly wounded when captured were nevertheless dead, apparently of magical causes, before the Prince could begin to interrogate them.

Now a new figure appeared at the doorway to the balcony. It was Karel himself, come down from his eyrie in the second-highest tower of the Palace to talk to Kristin and Mark. This wizard was not only highly skilled and experienced, but he looked the part—as so many of the really good ones did not—sporting a profusion of gray hair and beard, a generally solemn manner, and a massive and imposing frame clothed in fine garments. Karel departed from the popular image by having red plump cheeks, giving him a hearty outdoor look he did not deserve.

Yesterday, as the wizard had already explained, he had done what he could do at a distance. First in his own workshop, then mounted and driving his riding-beast with blessings and curses through the mountain pass toward High Manor. Grasping at every stage for whatever weapons of magic he could find, Karel had endeavored to raise elementals along the course of the small stream that issued from the cave. He thought now that his try with the elementals had been more successful than he had realized at the time, evidently good enough to confuse and delay the enemy until Mark and his force were able to reach them.

Karel's voice rumbled forth with his habitual—and generally justified
—pride. "Might have tried to produce a hill-elemental right on the spot,
but that could be a problem to anyone in a cave, as I divined our people
were. When you confront a hill-elemental it will tend to keep in front of
you, so that what you're trying to reach is always behind it. It'll tumble
rocks about and tilt the ground beneath your feet, or anyway make it
seem to tilt, so that you go tumbling on what had been a gentle slope, or
even level ground."

"Zoltan reported feeling something like that."

"I know, I know." Karel made dismissive motions with a large hand.
"But that sounded more like a demon outside the cave, the way the lad
described it."

"There was a demon, I am sure of that. And mere bandits do not
ordinarily have demons at their disposal."

"I am sure that you are right in that, Your Highness."

"Go on. You were talking about the elementals."

"Ah, yes. Your river-elemental, now, is distance, length, and motion.
But it can also be stasis. It sweeps things away, and hides them, and
separates things that want to be together. I kept the river-walker on the
scene, and the rock-roller in the background."

"Whatever your methods were, they seem to have been effective. We
are very grateful to you, Karel."

The graybeard brushed the words away, though it was not hard to see
that he was genuinely pleased by them. "Sheer good fortune was on our
side as well. As to our investigation, I want to talk to Zoltan again.
There are things about his account that still puzzle me a little."

"Oh?"

"Yes—certain details. And he's the oldest of the young ones in the
cave; maybe the most levelheaded, though there perhaps his sister may
have something of an edge. Not much that one can hope to learn from
children in a situation like this. Apparently none of them even made an
effort to look out of the cave mouth while the enemy was there."

"Shall I send a messenger to bring Zoltan here? He and his sister are
still at High Manor."

"No great hurry. There are other avenues of investigation I must try
first. I have a strong suspicion now of who was behind yesterday's
atrocity." Karel paused for a deep breath. "Burslem."

Prince and Princess exchanged looks. Mark had the feeling that their
tiredness had frozen them both into shells, leaving them unable to com-

municate freely with each other. And his own tiredness, at least, was not of the kind to be swept away by a night's sleep.

Mark said to the wizard: "Worse than we thought, then, perhaps?"

"Bad enough," said Karel. "Just how bad, I don't know. We can be sure that a man who once headed magical security operations for King Vilkata himself is a wizard of no mean capacity. And there's been no word of Burslem for eight years."

"Where is he now?" the Princess asked.

Her uncle signed that he did not know. "At least he doesn't have an army lurking on any of our frontiers. Those were ragtag bandits he recruited somehow for yesterday's adventure. Having spent much of the night with their corpses I can be sure of that much at least. I think he'll wait to see if we've caught on to the fact that he was behind them."

"And then?"

"And then he'll try something else, I suppose. Something nasty."

"What can we do?"

"I don't know. I see no way as yet in which we can retaliate effectively." And Karel shortly took his leave, saying that he had much to do.

Husband and wife, alone again on the balcony, embraced once more then walked back into the room where their older son still slept. On the walls of Adrian's room were paintings, here brave warriors chasing a dragon, there on the other wall a wizard in a conical hat creating a marvelous fruit tree out of nothing. The paintings had been done by the artist of the storybook, in those happy months before Adrian was born, created for small eyes that had never seen them yet.

Princess Kristin said in a weary voice: "His mouth is bruised as well, I suppose from Elinor trying to keep him quiet in the cave. I never saw a child who bruised so easily."

Mark said nothing. He stroked her hair.

Kristin said: "It's only great good fortune that any of the children are still alive, that that cave was there for them to hide in while Karel's elemental moved the river around outside. Otherwise who knows what might have happened to them?"

"I can imagine several things," said Mark, breaking a silence that threatened to grow awkwardly. "If Burslem is really the one behind it. And in the cave Adrian kept crying out, or trying to cry out, as Elinor told us. You realize it's quite possible that he almost killed them all, betraying that they were there."

His wife moved away from him a little and looked up at him. "You can't mean that what happened was somehow his fault."

"No. Not a fault. But already his blindness, his illness, begin to create problems not only for us, for you and me. Problems already for all Tasavalta."

"It is Burslem who creates problems for us all," the Princess said a little sharply. "I will confer with Karel again, of course, but I don't know what else we can do for Adrian. We have tried everything already. Are you going to make him feel guilty about being the way he is?"

"No," said Mark. "But if we have tried everything, then we must find something else to try. My son—our son—must grow into a man who is able to guard others. Not one who will forever need guardians himself."

"And if he cannot?"

"I am not convinced that he cannot."

Word of the Prince's intentions went out through the Palace within the hour, and within another hour was spreading throughout the city of Sarykam. Prince Consort Mark, determined on an all-out effort to find a cure for the blindness and the strange seizures that had afflicted his elder son since birth, was calling a council of his most trusted advisers. The council was to meet early on the following morning, which was the earliest feasible time for all of its members to come together.

3

ON the morning appointed for the council, Ben of Purkinje was up even earlier than usual.

He was an enormous man, a pale beached whale rolling out from under the silken covers of his luxurious bed. The stout, carven frame supporting the mattress creaked with relief when his enormous weight was lifted from it. Comparatively little of that weight was fat.

Once on his feet he cast a quick glance back at the slight figure of his dark-haired wife and noted with a certain relief that she was still asleep. Then he padded into the marble bath adjoining the bedroom. Presently the sounds of water, flowing and splashing in great quantities, came into the bedroom; but they were not heard by the woman in the bed, who slept on.

The subtler sounds of her husband's return awoke her, though. Her eyes opened as Ben came back into the room, cast aside a towel that might have served as a ship's sail, and started to get dressed.

"I was up late," she greeted him, "with Beth. She was babbling about strange wizards and I don't know what. What happened is catching up to her. You can't expect it not to."

"How is she now?"

"Sleeping. I was up with her most of the night, while you slept like a log."

He grunted, pulling on a garment.

"Why are you up so—? Oh, yes. That council meeting."

"That's right, I must be there."

Barbara rearranged herself in bed, grabbing pillows and stuffing them under her head so she could sit up and talk in greater comfort. "While you're there, I think there are a couple of things you ought to remind the Prince about."

"Ah."

"Yes. It was you who gave him the most valuable Sword of all, before he had any thought that he was to be a Prince. See if he remembers now who his friends were in the old days. See if he remembers that."

"He remembers it, I'm sure."

> *I shatter Swords and splinter spears*
> *None stands to Shieldbreaker*
> *My point's the fount of orphans' tears*
> *My edge the widowmaker*

The verse had in fact been running through Ben's head ever since he had awakened. The recent fighting had brought the Sword of Force to everyone's mind, it seemed. Now Ben whistled a snatch of tune to which he'd once heard someone try to set the Song of Swords, or a couple of verses of it anyway. When Ben was very young he had decided that he was going to be a minstrel. The dream had stayed with him stubbornly for years. By all the gods, how long ago and far away that seemed! He'd be thirty-five this year, or maybe next; he'd never been able to find out for sure exactly when he'd been born. Anyway, there'd be gray showing up in his hair soon enough.

"Yes, Shieldbreaker." Barbara was musing aloud, energizing herself for the day by discovering extra things to fret about, as if she, like everyone else, didn't have enough of them already. "I wonder if he does remember where he got it."

Ben grunted again.

Giving the Sword of Force to his old friend Mark hadn't really been any great act of sacrifice for him, or for Barbara either—or at least he had never thought of it that way. Eight years ago, on that last day in the war-torn city of Tashigang, Shieldbreaker had come into Ben's hands unexpectedly, and his first impulse had been simply to hide it somewhere. But his own house in the city had been in danger of total destruction, the tall structure so badly damaged on its lower levels following the fight with the god Vulcan that it was ready to collapse into a heap of rubble, rooftop gardens smashing down into servants' quarters, then the family rooms, then everything into the weapons shops that had occupied most of the ground floor.

Surrounded by dangers, faced with a multitude of other problems, including their own survival and that of their baby daughter, Beth, neither Ben nor Barbara had been able to think of anything better to do with the Sword of Force than take it to Mark, as soon as they heard he had survived the day, and was in good favor, to say the least, with the victorious Princess Kristin and her generals. Ben, looking back now, thought silently that he'd do the same thing again. The Swords, any and all of them, were too much trouble for anyone to own who aspired to any kind of a peaceful life—yet there was no practical way to destroy the god-forged weapons. And no way to hide them so they'd nevermore be found—the Swords themselves seemed to take care of that.

Dressed and as ready for the day as he could be, Ben said good-bye to Barbara with a kiss, to which she responded enthusiastically for all her nagging. On his way out of the house, Ben looked in on sturdy little Beth, still their only child and twice precious to both of them for that. Beth was, as her mother had said, asleep. Her father stopped off in the kitchen and grabbed himself a fresh pastry to eat for breakfast en route. Later in the day would be time enough to get down to serious feeding.

He was not a vindictive man, and as a rule he detested violence. But if he'd been able to get one of those bandits from in front of the cave mouth into his hands . . .

To reach the Palace from his house required only a short walk through the busy morning streets of Sarykam. High official that he was, Ben made his way there on foot, amid the sometimes jostling throngs of merchants and customers, workers and passersby. In Tasavalta, most people walked unless some physical disability prevented it. Outward display of wealth or position, except by means of certain subtle modes of dress, was considered in bad taste for anyone except actual royalty. Ben and Barbara, as much outlanders here as was the Prince their patron, had adapted. The condemnation of display was another thing that bothered Barbara, her husband supposed, though she could hardly complain about it openly.

Well, Ben and his wife no longer possessed the riches that had briefly been theirs when they dwelt in that great house of their own in Tashigang. Wealth had been lost, along with the house, the business, and the treasury of elegant weapons that for a while had been their stock in trade. But certainly they had done well enough here in Tasavalta, where they stood high in the councils of the Prince and Princess. Well enough, perhaps, for anyone Ben knew except Barbara.

Ben rated a sharp salute from the two guards in blue and green who flanked the small and almost private gate through which he entered the complex of the Palace proper. The guards, who knew him well, took care to look alert while in his presence. Ben's job included a number of duties, all related in one way or another to security, and to the gathering of intelligence in foreign lands. It was a post that had been created for him at Mark's behest, and when Ben was appointed to it there had arisen something of a storm of quiet protest among influential Tasavaltans who did not yet know their new Prince well, and did not know Ben at all. It would have been hard to find anyone in the whole realm who looked the part of intelligence adviser less than Ben of Purkinje did.

The first matter to occupy Ben's attention this morning, once he was inside the Palace, was not the council meeting, but something more routine. He thought it was time that he looked in at the private section of the royal armory, to check for himself on its most valued contents.

To reach the private armory he had to pass two more sets of guards, each more determined-looking than the last. Each of these also saluted sharply when he approached them, and took care to be alert while in his presence.

Now Ben entered a cavelike, windowless room, lighted only by a rare Old-World lantern on one wall, which bathed the whole chamber in a cool, perpetual glow. This room was fenced round with powerful magic as well as with physical barriers and human guards.

Once alone inside the room, Ben approached a large shelf built out of one wall at waist level and opened the first of a series of ornate wooden cases resting on it. Each case had been made, with great craftsmanship, in the shape of an enlarged Sword, with intertwined serpents carved to form the lid at the place where it looked like a hilt. Inside this first case, the Sword Coinspinner had lain for several years following the last war. Mark had fought the last day of that war with Coinspinner in his hand, and it had sent certain of his enemies to death and had kept him alive where no ordinary sword could have. Upon its ebon hilt the Sword of Chance bore as its symbol a pair of dice outlined in stark white.

Today Ben was able to see that hilt only in his mind; for the Sword itself had taken itself away, and the blue velvet of the interior of the case was empty when he opened it. To Coinspinner, the spells of Karel that bound the armory around had mattered no more than had the human guards. Like its eleven brothers, the Sword of Chance disdained all magics lesser than its own.

> *Who holds Coinspinner knows good odds*
> *Whichever move he make*
> *But the Sword of Chance, to please the gods,*
> *Slips from him like a snake*

And quietly, sometime during an otherwise unremarkable winter night, Coinspinner had vanished from its triply guarded case. Where it might have gone, no one in the Palace could begin to guess.

The Palace authorities would have preferred to keep the disappearance of the Sword a secret. But word of it had got out, though in a somewhat garbled version. Now, years later, it was still widely whispered among the people that a gold coin bearing the likeness of the god Hermes had appeared in the place of the Sword of Chance, within its magically sealed case. Actually there had been no such coin on this occasion of the Sword's vanishing, and efforts had been made to set the story straight, though to no avail. The people knew what they knew. Even some who lived in the Palace accepted what most of the populace outside still believed as a matter of course—that the god Hermes, along with the multitude of his vanished peers, was still alive somewhere and likely someday to return.

Ben knew better than that, or thought he did, in the case of the multitude of divinities. In the case of Hermes he was certain. With his own eyes, and with Mark standing beside him, he had seen the Messenger lying dead. In the god's back had gaped a great mortal wound, a mighty stab that they thought could only have been the work of Farslayer.

With a shake of his head Ben put memories away. He closed up the carven case, which some wizards had hoped would be able to confine Coinspinner, and moved on.

Here, a little distance along the stone shelf, was a second protected case, in its construction and decoration similar to the first. And this one, when opened, showed itself occupied. Ben touched the Sword inside, but did not take it out. Stonecutter's blade, identical in size and shape to those of its eleven mates, was a full meter long, and the mottled pattern of the bright steel seemed to extend far below the smoothly polished surface.

The Sword of Siege struck a hammer's blow
With a crash, and a smash, and a tumbled wall.
Stonecutter laid a castle low
With a groan, and a roar, and a tower's fall.

Letting the case stay open, Ben rested his huge right hand affection-
ately for a moment upon the black hilt. His grip covered the symbol of a
small white wedge splitting a white block. Ben could well remember
how this Sword had saved him and Mark, upon one day of danger now
long years ago. Stonecutter had not been much used since that day, but
unlike Coinspinner it was still here, waiting faithfully until it should be
needed by its owners.

There was, as Ben always took care to drill into the armory guards,
one more advantage in having this or any other Sword of Power: As
long as we have it, we can be sure that our enemies do not. So we must
either keep safe the Swords we know about, or destroy them. And no
human being had yet discovered a way of destroying one, other than by
bringing it into violent opposition with Shieldbreaker.

Ben closed the second case. He walked on to the third, which for the
last eight years had been the repository of the Sword of Force.

This case, when he opened it, showed him only its blue velvet lining,
and Ben had a bad moment until he saw the little marker, dutifully
placed there by the Prince himself and signed by him. It was meant to
assure the people of the armory that he had taken Shieldbreaker out
with his own hands.

Ben hurried on to join the council.

Its members were already assembling, in a pleasant room high in one
of the taller Palace towers. Most were in the room when Ben arrived,
but were not yet seated. Ben's first glance on entering the room had
been directed at Mark, in an effort to make sure that the Prince did now
indeed have Shieldbreaker in his personal possession. Mark did have on
a swordbelt, an item not usually worn by anyone inside the Palace. And
there was the unmistakable hilt, its tiny white hammer-symbol visible to
Ben's eyes across the room. A faint suspicion died; being responsible for
security meant that you became ever more imaginatively suspicious.

Standing at the middle of one side of the long table, Mark had Karel
on one side of him and on the other, Jord, the man Mark had called
father all through his childhood and youth. Mark continued to call Jord

his father even now, and to respect him as such, even though the truth of a somewhat more exalted parenthood for the Prince had become known during the last war.

Ben was mildly surprised to see Jord here now. The older man was tall, and still strong, bearing a superficial resemblance to his adopted son. Jord was intelligent enough, and certainly trustworthy, but he was not usually called in to discuss affairs of state. Of course today's affair was a family matter also. Not that Princess Kristin had ever been noticeably eager to emphasize the humble origins of her now-royal husband. Of course, if today's discussion should turn out to be substantially about Swords, there would be another reason for Jord's presence—no one else in the world could bring to it his fund of experience. Of the half dozen men recruited by Vulcan to help forge the Swords some thirty years ago, Jord was the only one to survive the process; and he was still the only human being who had ever touched all of the Twelve.

Next Ben looked around the table for General Rostov, commander of the Tasavaltan army. But the General's burly frame and steel-gray beard were nowhere to be seen. Probably Rostov, as usual, had many other things to do, particularly in the light of recent events. And probably, too, Mark did not count this meeting as having a great deal to do with military strategy.

Also in the group around the council table were several White Temple physicians, several of whom had been in attendance upon Prince Adrian since he was born. During that period a heavy turnover had taken place among Palace physicians; but everyone knew that there were none better anywhere than those of the White Temple.

Present also was the Royal Master of the Beasts, who was in charge of winged messengers, among other things, and therefore was likely to be called in on any council where quick communications or late news were of importance. Completing the assembly were two or three minor magicians, aides to Karel.

Mark had seen Ben come in, and beckoned him over for an almost-private word before the meeting started. "How's Beth this morning?" the Prince asked.

"Sleeping like a small log when I left. And your boys?"

"As well as can be expected."

"It's great to be young, Your Highness." Ben usually favored his old friend with one "Your Highness" every day. He liked to get the formality in early, and made sure to do so always when others were listening, so everyone would know that the Prince did not carry his familiarity with his old friends too far.

"I can remember that being young was pleasant," said the man of thirty, smiling faintly. "And how is Barbara?"

"Fine," said Ben promptly. "But she won't admit it. Sometimes I think I'm married to the Blue Temple." And he made a little money-rubbing gesture with his massive thumb and forefinger.

The faint smile got a little wider. Even that much was good to see on Mark's worn face. He said: "I feel a little better myself. Some hopeful news has just come in—you'll hear it in a minute. I'd better get this thing started now." And he turned away, rapping the table with a hard knuckle.

Ben went to take his seat in the place assigned him by protocol.

As soon as the meeting was in order, Mark repeated to his assembled advisers his absolute determination to find a cure for Adrian's blindness and his seizures—or at the very least, to prove beyond doubt, once and for all, that the illness they represented was incurable.

Having done that, he threw the meeting open to comments and suggestions.

The wizard Karel stroked his gray beard and his red cheeks and wondered aloud, tentatively, if the child's condition might not be the result of some last stroke of vengeance on the part of the Dark King. King Vilkata was almost certainly dead now, but his whereabouts had never been learned with any certainty since he was seen to flee the battlefield where he had stood in opposition to the Silver Queen. The Dark King Vilkata had been Mark's bitter enemy. And he had also been blind.

Karel's suggestion was not a new one to the ears of anyone around the table. Mark had often pondered it. But no one had ever been able to come up with any means of confirming it, or disproving it absolutely. It was plain that Karel only raised it again now because the possibility still tormented him that he might have been so outmatched in magic.

There was a brief silence around the table. Then Jord spoke up, as a grieving grandfather. "Whatever the cause of the poor lad's suffering, Woundhealer could cure him—I know it could." This was not a new suggestion either; the only problem with it was that for the past eight years no one in Tasavalta had known where the Sword Woundhealer might be found.

Mark had paused respectfully to hear both of these remarks yet once more. Now he continued.

"As I see it, when a particular case has resisted all normal methods of healing, magical and otherwise, there yet remain three possible remedies to be tried."

The Chief Physician, frowning slightly, looked across the table at the Prince. She said: "The first of those would be—as Jord has reminded us —the Sword Woundhealer. Second, the God of Healing, Draffut—if it is possible that he has survived what seems to have been the general destruction visited upon the gods." The physician paused. "But I confess that I do not know what third possibility Your Highness has in mind."

Mark sighed wearily. "At the moment it seems to me not a very practical possibility. I was thinking of the Emperor."

"Ah," said the physician. The syllable emerged from her lips in a way that only a wise old counselor could have uttered it, suggesting a profound play of wisdom without committing her to anything at all.

Jord had frowned as soon as the name of the Emperor was mentioned. A moment later almost everyone around the table was frowning, but no one spoke. No one really wanted to talk about the Emperor. Most of these folk had accepted the Emperor's reputed high status more or less on faith, as the basis for granting Mark high birth. That assumption in turn had allowed them to accept him as their Prince. But to most of the world at large, the Emperor, if he was admitted to exist at all, was accorded no status higher than a clown's, that of a low comedian who figured in a hundred jokes and proverbs.

Mark took in the reaction of his counselors without surprise. "I have spoken to him," he told them quietly. "And you have not, any of you. But let that pass for now."

At this point Ben shuffled his feet under the table. He might have had something to say. But he went along with his old friend and let it pass.

The Prince resumed. "Regardless of how helpful the Emperor might be to us in theory, in practice I know of no way to call upon him for his help. Some think that he perished too, eight years ago, with the passing of the gods from human sight and ken. For all I know it may be so."

Mark paused for a long look around the table before going on. "From him—who was my father—I have a power that few of you have ever seen in operation. I know not why I have it; there are others, doubtless worthier than I am, who do not. But for the sake of the majority of you, who do not know about this power, or who have heard about it only through some garbled tale, I want to tell you the plain truth now.

"What I have is the ordering of demons, or rather the ability to raise a shield against their powers, and to cast them out, to a great distance. Yesterday I used this power to drive what I am sure was a demon away from the entrance to the cave."

There was a murmuring around the table.

Mark went on. "Over the last seven years I have repeatedly tried to use the same power for my son's benefit, but to no avail. Whatever ails him, I am convinced that it is not possession by a demon."

There might, Ben supposed in the silence of his own mind, there might exist a demon so terrible, and yet so subtle in its potency, that it could work without being recognized for what it was, and not even the Emperor's son had power to cast it out. The huge man, who had seen demons at close range, shuddered slightly in the warm sunny room.

Or, he thought, it might be that the Emperor, from whom Mark's power derived, was now dead, and all his dependent powers beginning to lose their force. That same thought had probably occurred to others around the table now, but no one wanted to suggest it to the Emperor's son.

Mark was speaking again.

". . . the same objection holds to seeking the help of the Healing God. Draffut is of a different order of being than most of those we called gods—Hermes and Vulcan and so on. Those who have met them both can swear to that. Still, even if Draffut has survived until this day, we know of no way to contact him and ask his help."

"It is so." Old Karel nodded.

The Prince raised his chin and swept his gaze around the table. "We come now to Woundhealer. And that may be a different matter. Here at last I see a ray of hope. Only this morning a report has reached us by messenger—it is a secondhand report and I do not know how reliable—that a certain branch of the White Temple, in the lands of Sibi, far to the southwest, now has the Sword of Mercy in its possession."

There was a stir around the table.

Mark went on: "According to the message we have received this morning, the diseased and the crippled are being healed there every day."

Jord was now gazing at his adopted son with fierce satisfaction, as if the news meant that Mark had at last decided to listen to his advice.

And the Master of the Beasts was nodding his confirmation of the message. It had been brought in shortly after dawn by one of his semi-intelligent birds.

Mark said: "I propose to take my son to that Temple, that he may be healed. The journey, even by the most optimistic calculation, will take months. It may of course be difficult, but the lands in that direction have been peaceful, and we think that Burslem is elsewhere. I foresee no very great danger in the trip."

"How many troops?" asked Ben.

His old friend looked at him across the table. "I don't want to march with an army, which would very likely provoke our neighbors in that general direction, and would at least call great attention to our presence. To say nothing of the problems of provisioning en route. No, I think an escort of thirty or forty troops, no more. And, Rostov may not like it, but I am bringing Shieldbreaker with me, to protect my son. I did not have it with me near High Manor two days ago, when it was needed. I'll not make that mistake again."

4

ON two successive nights following his strange experience in the cave, Zoltan was prey to peculiar dreams. Each morning he awoke with the most intense and mysterious parts of those visions still tangled in his mind—running water, soft black hair that fell in sensuous waves, a beckoning white arm. A certain perfume in the air.

On the second morning, as soon as he was fully awake, it came to Zoltan that he had known this fragrance before, in waking life. It was that of a certain kind of flower, whose name he had never learned, that grew in summer along the course of the newborn Sanzu. In summer and early fall there were many flowers along the banks below the point where the river left the hills of its birth and, already joined by its first tributary rivulet, began to meander across a plain.

Once he had recognized that perfume the dreams no longer seemed strange and new. Rather, they felt so familiar that Zoltan could comfortably put them from his mind. There was no point in telling anyone about them, as he had considered doing. Not anymore.

Sitting up in bed on that second morning, he squinted out through the open window of his room into the entering sunlight. High Manor, though it sometimes served as a royal residence, was definitely no palace. Though very large and old, it was not much more than a fortified stone farmhouse. The view from Zoltan's room on the ground floor was appropriately homely. There was the barnyard in the foreground, then the manor's outer wall, a little taller than a man, and then green and rocky hilltops visible beyond that. Something winged was circling over those hills now. In all probability it was only a harmless bird, but in any case it was too far away to be identifiable.

Many of the hills in the area had caves in them, and the cave where the children had taken shelter, and where the river was born, was one of them. It burrowed into the foot of a hill just beyond those that Zoltan was able to see from his room.

After staring for another few moments at the hills, he jumped up and began putting on his clothes.

In the great hall downstairs, Zoltan found that the usual morning routine had not yet been reestablished. His mother and sister were not yet up, and formal breakfast for the family was not yet ready. He made his way into the kitchen, exchanging morning greetings with the cooks and servants, wheedling and pilfering to assemble a breakfast of fruit, cooked eggs, and fresh bread.

Stowing a second small loaf inside his jacket, he went outside. Summer was showing signs of waning—the leaves and fruit on the nearby trees established that—and the early air was cool. Zoltan gave good morning to the stablehands, who were busy, and saddled his own riding-beast, Swordface. The name derived from a bold forehead patch of bright white hair.

Soft black hair . . . and the scent of certain flowers. They were sharper memories than mere dreams should ever leave in waking life, and during the daytime they kept coming back to Zoltan at moments when he least expected it.

He rode out through the open front gate of the Manor. A soldier was stationed there this morning, and Zoltan waved before heading his mount at a steady pace toward the hills. He had said nothing to anyone about his destination, but he was going back to the cave. When he got there he . . . but he didn't know yet exactly what he was going to do.

Two days ago, coming out of the cave with the other children, all of them shaken and unnerved, he had got a close look at some of the bandits, who of course by that time were already dead. Neither Zoltan nor any other Tasavaltan had been able to recognize any of them. At the time, looking at the corpses, about all Zoltan had been able to think of was that men like that would never have had a beautiful young girl traveling with them. Unless, of course, she were their prisoner. And then she'd have to be tied up, hobbled somehow, to keep her from running away. But he had the impression that the girl he had actually seen had been perfectly free.

Now, two days later, there were moments it seemed to Zoltan strange that he had not yet mentioned the girl to anyone. It was not that he had deliberately decided to make a secret of her existence. It was just that when Karel, and Uncle Mark, and others had talked to him, questioning him about what had happened while he was in the cave, she had vanished from his mind completely. Zoltan had told his questioners that he hadn't even looked out of the cave. Later on, dreaming or awake, the memory of her would pop back, and he'd think: *Oh yes. Of course.* And then he'd wonder briefly how he could ever have forgotten, and wonder whether he ought to tell someone next time he had the chance.

Maybe going back into the cave this morning and looking out again from the exact same spot would help him to fix the whole experience in his memory. Then he could tell everyone all about it. He really ought to tell someone. . . .

That girl, though. The more Zoltan thought about her, the more he realized she was a great mystery. He wasn't at all sure that she was the little dark-haired girl that he remembered from his childhood. Sure looked like her, though. It might take a wizard as good as Karel to figure out who this one really was.

Zoltan's brow furrowed as he stared forward over the neck of his riding-beast, for the moment not paying much attention to where Swordface was taking him. It was more than strange, it was really alarming that he hadn't mentioned the girl to anyone, not even to Karel when the wizard had questioned him. It was very peculiar indeed. Almost as if—

Swordface stumbled lightly over something, recovering quickly. Zoltan raised his head sharply and looked around him. He had the sensation that he'd almost fallen asleep in the saddle, that he'd just been riding, without being able to think of anything, for an uncomfortably long time. Where was he going? Yes, out to the cave. He'd had a sudden sense that there was something . . . watching? Calling him?

What had he been thinking about before he almost dozed off? Oh, yes, the girl.

Maybe she was really an enchantress of some kind, just observing, or trying to help the children, and the attacking villains hadn't been aware of her presence at all. That would explain things satisfactorily. Or maybe . . .

It seemed like one of those great questions about which it was almost impossible to think clearly, like life and death, and the meaning of the universe. Anyway, it was all a great mystery, and he, Zoltan, ought to be trying somehow to solve it. Maybe that had been the message of her eyes.

* * *

Usually it took a little less than half an hour to ride out to the cave from the Manor. This morning Swordface was ready to run, and Zoltan, his own eagerness growing, covered the distance a little more quickly than usual. It remained a fine, cool morning, with a little breeze playing about as if it could not decide which way it meant to blow over the uneven sea of grass that stretched over most of the country between the Manor and the high hills.

And Karel had tried to raise elementals here. Zoltan had never seen anyone raise an elemental, or even try, and he was curious; he had heard people say that particular kind of magic was almost a lost art. And it seemed that the effort must have helped somehow; Karel was very good. The boy wondered if there could be anything left of those powers now, two days later. If today he might feel a hillock twitch when he stepped on it, or find the stream somewhere suddenly twice as wide and deep and full of water as it was elsewhere.

Twice in the next few minutes, as he drew ever closer to his destination, he passed small squadrons of cavalry, and on both occasions the soldiers rode near enough to make very sure of who he was before they saluted and went on with their patrol. Zoltan's growing sense of adventure faded each time as the patrols approached him, then began to grow again. He felt confident that he could avoid being spotted by the soldiers if he tried.

Presently he drew in sight of the cave burrowed into the base of a high, rocky hill. From the low, dark mouth of it the Sanzu issued, and the open place in front of the cave was still torn up and stained where the clash between bodies of mounted men had trampled the rocky soil and littered it with death. There were no graves here—the bodies of friend and foe had all been removed elsewhere for examination and burial.

Now a few more mounted soldiers came in sight, and Zoltan exchanged a few words with their young officer, explaining that he had felt an urge to ride out to see what was happening.

"There's nothing much happening now, Prince." Zoltan as a royal nephew did rate that title, but ordinarily he heard it only on the most ceremonious of occasions. This soldier was one he did not know. The two talked for another minute, and then the patrol moved on.

Zoltan, alone again, sat his mount, listening to the murmur of the stream, and looking at the dark, low aperture from which it issued.

There was no use going into the cave again, he decided. The black-haired girl was not here any longer. She had to be somewhere, though.

For just a moment it seemed to Zoltan that a cloud had passed over the sun. But when he looked up, the sky was clear and empty.

The scent of certain flowers. . . .

The memory this time was as sharp as reality. He thought that it was the same perfume that had come to him in his dreams, and that the flowers grew downstream, not really very far from here. He turned his riding-beast in that direction, following along the bank.

Zoltan had a good idea of the lay of the land for perhaps a kilometer or two downstream from the point where he was now. Beyond that point, if he should have to go that far, everything would be strange and new.

He looked ahead eagerly, feeling ready for some undefined adventure.

There were no soldiers in sight now. The last patrol he had seen had ridden off in a different direction.

The high plain ahead of Zoltan as he rode was dotted with a thin, scrubby forest, and there were very low hills on the horizon, between which, somehow, the Sanzu must find its way.

Half an hour after Zoltan had seen the last soldier, he was still following the Sanzu downstream, without any clear idea of exactly what he expected to find in that direction besides the flowers. He was now entering the region where the land started to turn rough again after the strip of plain, and the stream started trying to get away from the high country in one little rushing descent after another. There were still signs everywhere of the recent passage of Tasavaltan patrols, but he ignored them.

Half an hour after that, and now far out of sight of home, the boy was stretched out on a flat rock beside the tiny river, reaching down to where a patch of tall white flowers grew at the water's edge. The flowers were delicate things with long stems and almost frothy petals, and there was a golden center in each blossom. The perfume was here, all right, but it was still not as strong as Zoltan had expected it would be—he would get only a tantalizing hint, and then another one, long moments later.

A few meters behind Zoltan, his riding-beast was placidly cropping grass.

Somehow, once Zoltan had found the flowers, his craving for adventure was temporarily forgotten. He lay there looking long and long into the pool.

He gazed into the murmuring water until he saw the reflection of white shoulders and black hair.

5

ON that same morning, in the city of Sarykam, there were trumpets and drums at parting: a demonstration by the people of the city for the Prince they had come to love and respect over the last eight years of peace, and during the war that had gone before.

Prince Adrian, his small body clad in plain garments of rich fabric, a scaled-down version of his father's clothing, perched in the saddle of a sturdy riding-beast beside his father's mount. Jord, in the role of grandfather, held one of the Princeling's tiny hands in his huge ones and said good-bye. Mark's mother, Mala, a plain woman in her late forties, was there too, to wish the travelers well.

Adrian had ridden before, briefly, in parades and on the practice ground. Perhaps he thought that this was to be another parade. His parents had told him repeatedly what the purpose of this journey was. But there was no indication that their explanations had penetrated very far into the darkness that sealed his eyes, and more often than not closed off his mind. He held his head now in a characteristic pose, tilted on one side as if he were listening to something that only he could hear. His sightless eyes were busy. And one small hand, when Jord released it, rose and questioned the air ahead of him. His other hand continued to clutch the reins.

Now Karel, on a balcony overlooking the Palace courtyard in which the expedition had assembled, was giving the travelers such blessings as he could, chiefly by invoking the name of Ardneh.

One notable absence from the scene was that of General Rostov. There were plenty of likely reasons for his not being present—the near-success of the apparent kidnapping attempt seemed to require a thorough revamping of some of the defenses, and the General's full attention was required for that. But he had let it be known that he disapproved of Mark's taking Shieldbreaker out of the country. Rostov considered the Swords in the royal armory, like the other weapons, all public property and liable to be required at any time for the defense of the realm.

A short distance away from where Mark and Adrian sat their mounts, Ben, too, was mounted and ready. His wife had come to see him off and to offer him a few last words of advice and admonition.

When he had had what he thought enough of this, Ben excused himself to take a final count of heads. Making sure that everyone who was supposed to be in the train was actually present was really someone else's job, but an independent checkup wouldn't hurt. There were thirty mounted troops under the command of a young cavalry officer, and a handful of skilled wizards and physicians. Cages in the baggage train held half a dozen small winged messenger-beasts, and near them rode a journeyman beastmaster to manage and care for them.

Finally the order to march was given, hard to hear amid the noise and confusion that invariably took over any attempt at ceremonious departures. Tumult passed through the gates of the Palace, and then the city streets.

As Mark passed out through the great main gate of the city onto the high road that led to the southwest, he was engulfed by a last roar of good wishes that went up from people assembled on the city walls and on both sides of the road. In return he drew Shieldbreaker and saluted them all. The sun, exploding on the blade, provoked yet another outcry from the people. Mark felt a brief twinge of conscience for taking the Sword with him on what was essentially a private mission; but then he reminded himself that nothing that affected the royal family could be purely private, especially not a matter of such importance as Adrian's illness. Besides, in his heart the Prince felt that the Sword was his to do with as he wished; it had been given to him eight years ago, and not to Rostov.

Only let young Adrian come back strong and healthy from this pilgrimage; everything else was secondary to that. Apart from his feelings as a father, Mark, who had never felt he had a homeland of his own before this one, saw how important a healthy heir to the throne could be to the land and people of Tasavalta. He had read much history in the last few years, and he realized how important it was to everyone that the firstborn of the royal family should be strong and healthy, with two good eyes, and a keen mind to place at the service of his people. When the eldest child did not inherit this throne, it seemed that a time of trouble, perhaps even civil war, was practically guaranteed.

Twisting in his saddle, Mark looked back. He was far enough from the walls of the city now to be able to see above them. Kristin had evidently returned to other affairs that were demanding her attention; but high on a parapet of the Palace the fair head of little Stephen was still visible, watching intently after his father. As soon as Mark turned, his tiny, distant son waved to him yet once more; and Mark returned the wave.

Some time passed before the Prince looked back again, and when he did it was no longer possible to see who might be on the walls. The city was vanishing piecemeal now, disappearing almost magically by sections in this folded landscape. One piece or another would drop out of sight behind one hill or another, or slide sideways behind an edge of cliff. Then sometimes the walls and towers would move into view again as the road rose up beneath the travelers or carried them through another turn.

Now Mark's gaze kept returning to the small figure that rode—so far in silence—at his side. Adrian's riding-beast had been specially selected, and specially trained, with magicians as well as beastmasters taking part in the instruction. The animal was an intelligent one, for its species—no riding-beast approached the mental keenness of the messenger-birds, some of which were capable of speech. It was also phlegmatic and dependable.

The boy usually sat in his saddle as he did everything, indifferently, when he could be persuaded to do things at all. Sometimes when riding he would forget to hold the reins that had been placed carefully in his right hand. Instead he would extend one arm, or both, groping into the air above the animal's neck. At the moment, one of the young physicians, alert for any sign that the child might be going to topple from his saddle, was riding on his other side.

So far all was well. Adrian's father had already observed that the child looked comparatively well this morning. The boy had spoken several connected words to his mother just before their departure and had seemed to understand at least that his father and he were going on a ride together. Now he was humming and crooning to himself in apparent contentment, and he had not yet dropped his reins.

Mark turned again in his saddle and glanced back toward the rear of the column. Somewhere amid the baggage carried by the train of spare mounts and laden loadbeasts were the components of a litter, in which, strapped to a sturdy loadbeast or slung between two animals, Prince Adrian could ride when keeping him mounted became too difficult. Of late his seizures had increased in frequency, and it seemed inevitable that on this long journey the litter was going to see substantial use.

But only on the outward-bound leg of the journey, his father thought. Mark was consumed with hope that the litter would not be needed on the way back. *Pray Ardneh that on the way home my son will ride all the way at my side. And he'll talk to me. And he'll see me, look at me with his eyes and see me. He'll look at the world, and I'll explain the world to him. We'll talk, every day and every night, all the way as we're riding home.*

At last the walls of Sarykam and the towers of the Palace dropped permanently out of sight among the folds of the mountainous landscape. The journey still proceeded along well-kept roads, past neat villages whose inhabitants more often than not came out to wave. The border was still ahead.

But it was not very far ahead. Tasavalta was not, in terms of geographical area, a very large domain.

Now Mark looked back over his other shoulder. Three or four meters behind him, mounted on the biggest and strongest riding-beast that could be found in Sarykam, an animal of truly heroic strength and dimensions, was Ben of Purkinje.

As soon as Prince Mark caught his eye, Ben urged his mount forward and rode at the Prince's side.

Mark said, in a low voice and with feeling: "Truly, I am glad that you are coming with us."

Ben shrugged his shoulders, beside which Mark's looked thin. "And I am glad to be here, for more reasons than one." He sighed faintly. "Barbara grows a little more shrewish with each passing year."

"I suppose that she still nags you about giving me the Sword?" Mark tapped the hilt of Shieldbreaker at his side. He too had known Barbara for a long time.

"About that, and several other things. So I'm glad enough for the chance to ride out of the city for a time. Besides, I grow fat and immobile sitting there in my office, trying to look to the clerks as if I know what I am doing."

"Or sometimes trying to look as if you didn't. . . . I have no doubt, my friend, that you know what you are doing, in your office or elsewhere. I don't suppose that any last bits of useful information reached your ears before we departed?"

"This morning? No." Ben shook his head. "Were you expecting something in particular?"

Mark gestured. "I hardly know, myself, what I am expecting. Perhaps some news of one of the other Swords."

Ben cuffed at a fly on his mount's neck. "There's been nothing really new about any of them since we heard from that fellow Birch about two years ago."

Mark remembered the fellow called Birch. A poor man, he had come to the rulers of Tasavalta saying he was breaking a long silence and hoping to be rewarded now for his information. Birch's report had been to the effect that once, years even before the battle of Tashigang, the god Vulcan had been seen, by Birch himself, with the Sword Farslayer in hand. Birch even claimed to have seen Vulcan kill Mars with it; in that claim both Mark and Ben were inclined to believe him. But there were no other witnesses to the Wargod's death, or at least none had come forward.

Another minute or so passed in silence, except for the sounds of moving animals, and a faint, contented crooning from Adrian. Then Mark said: "Doomgiver and Townsaver are gone." The statement sounded like what it was: the hundred-and-first rehearsal of the first condition of a puzzle or a riddle, which in a hundred trials still had not been solved—and to which, for all the puzzlers knew, no final answer existed.

Ben nodded. "Both destroyed by Shieldbreaker, in Vulcan's hand. No doubt about that, for either of them. And Shieldbreaker, thank Ardneh, now rides there at your side. Stonecutter's safe in our deepest vault at home. And tricky Coinspinner's vanished from the same place, gone we don't know where."

"That's five of the twelve more or less accounted for."

"Yes. Leaving seven more. Where Farslayer is now, we just don't know. And Woundhealer lies on this road ahead of us, or so we fondly hope."

"That's seven."

"Right. And Hermes once took Dragonslicer from my hand, and as far as we've been able to find out, no human eye has seen it since."

"And Hermes, a moment after taking Dragonslicer from you, also seized Wayfinder from Baron Doon . . ."

". . . so Hermes ought to have been carrying those two Swords when Farslayer struck him down. But none of the three blades were there when you and I came upon his corpse. D'you know, Mark, I've wondered about that. I mean, maybe Farslayer wouldn't have killed him if he hadn't been carrying the other two Swords with him when he was struck. Three Swords at one time! I've touched two of 'em at one time, and so have you. You know how it is."

Mark was shaking his head doubtfully. "You think just touching three Swords would be too much for a god?"

"Hermes wasn't the god who forged them."

"Even so, I think it damned unlikely that he was just overwhelmed by magic. No, I think the simple truth is that Farslayer killed Hermes, regardless of any other Swords, just as we both thought when we found him dead. As the Sword of Vengeance could kill anyone else in the world, god or human being."

"I don't suppose it killed all of the gods."

"No. Not most of them." Again Mark rode for a time in silence before he added: "I think that their time was simply over."

"That's not really an explanation."

But now Mark had turned his head and was looking at his son. The small boy had appeared briefly to be listening to the men's conversation. But now Adrian had tired and wanted to be carried, mewling almost like an infant and holding out his arms toward his father's voice.

Mark picked him up and held him briefly before his own saddle. Presently that grew awkward too, and the march was halted while the litter could be unlimbered and put together. The people handling the assembly had not yet performed the task frequently enough to be accustomed to it, and the process seemed, to Mark, endlessly slow.

Eventually the litter was ready, and the procession could forge on.

6

EVEN as Zoltan watched, the reflection of dark hair, in an eddy where the surface of the stream was almost still, turned into an image of black twigs and branches.

He raised his head; there were the branches, part of a dead bush on the other side of the stream, as real as any objects could be. But no, something was wrong. The color of the vision in the water had been slightly different. And he had seen white skin, too. Hadn't he?

Zoltan jumped to his feet and waded in without bothering to remove his boots, keeping his gaze fixed on the reflected twigs. He reached the other bank in half a dozen splashing strides.

He bent over the leafless bush and examined it closely. What must have happened was that she had been hiding in the other bushes just *here,* and had leaned out . . .

He plunged into the streamside vegetation, searching diligently, ignoring the thorns that clawed at him. But he looked in vain for a clue that anyone had ever hidden there.

Zoltan was about to wade back to the other bank and reclaim Swordface when a changed note in the burble of the water downstream caught his ear. For the space of many heartbeats he stood motionless, listening. It had sounded like a trilling laugh. . . .

He started downstream along the bank, on foot, then made himself go back and get his riding-beast. He stroked the animal's head to keep it quiet. Here near the south bank there was almost a pathway, a game trail of some kind, Zoltan supposed. He had now come beyond the area where the marks of recent cavalry patrols had obliterated all other trails.

The path beside the stream grew easier, and he mounted Swordface again and rode. Before he had ridden fifty meters he arrived at another pool. This one looked deeper, and its depths were even more clear.

Something else caught Zoltan's eye. A few long, dark hairs were caught on a rough bush at one side of the pool. Zoltan dismounted and picked the delicate filaments from the bush. He stood there running them through his trembling fingers; the repeated touch of his hands made the hairs turn into threads of common spiderweb and vanish.

Enchantment. If only—

At a sound he spun around. This time he caught a glimpse of movement along the water's edge, thirty or forty meters downstream, as of pale flesh again, and some tight, silvery garment. This time he did not really see her hair that clearly—what he saw next was more like a pure burst of sunlight, as it might leap back from moving water.

Unthinkingly he shouted: "Come back! I won't hurt you!"

No answer. She was gone. There was a faint sound from somewhere even farther downstream.

He swore and splashed and waded. Then he went back to get Swordface again.

The next rapids were steeper, and the path descending beside them was so steep that Zoltan had no choice but to dismount and lead the riding-beast along.

Presently he was forced to leave the animal behind him, tethered lightly to a bush. The way down through the little rocky gorge had simply become too precipitous. It was easy enough for an agile human to clamber down, using both hands and feet, but the hoofed animal would never have made it.

Beside the next little space of flat land there was no solemn pool, but a continuous sinewed rush of water. Zoltan stood beside it listening, watching, holding his breath as if even that faint sound might interfere with his catching the clue he had to have. *She*, being an enchantress after all, might be able to hear his breath above the rush of water. He thought it very likely now that he would be able to hear hers.

If only he had been able to tell old Karel about her. Karel could have helped him in this search . . . but no, that wouldn't have been right. Because no one else was meant to find her, only he, Zoltan. A deeper understanding of that point was slowly growing in him. And he was going to find her, now. She couldn't be that far ahead of him.

Zoltan went on. Always forward, always beside the rushing, babbling stream, and down.

Presently he came to a place where the stream was behaving queerly. First, without any apparent cause, there were wide swirls across its surface. And then came a much more serious departure from the normal. The whole baby river meandered for several meters sideways across a slope, a steep place where it should have plunged straight down. Staring at this phenomenon, Zoltan pulled out his dagger and looked about him suspiciously. But then he felt foolish and put the useless knife back into its sheath. Probably one of Karel's elementals had really taken shape two days ago and still existed in the form of this disturbance.

Ordinarily Zoltan would have been fascinated and somewhat frightened on encountering this phenomenon. Now it made little impression, except that thinking of the elemental recalled Karel once again to Zoltan's thoughts. But there was some reason, some important reason, why he should not even think of Karel now. . . .

Anyway, it was more enjoyable by far to think about the girl. To speculate on why she had signaled to him so enticingly, and what secrets—and perhaps other things—she might have to share with him when he had won this game by catching up with her. Zoltan no longer supposed that she might be a prisoner of the bandits, or really in need of rescue. She was just being playful with him, that was it.

There were things about that explanation that puzzled him—but somehow it would be inappropriate for him to think of puzzling things just now. Now was a time for action.

He had followed the stream yet a little farther—just how far was not important—when he actually caught a glimpse of the girl again, her head and arms and part of her upper body. This time she was trying to hide from him among the intertwined branches of two fallen trees, right at the water's edge, and holding herself so still that for a long moment or two he could not be sure that he was really seeing her at all. And when, without shifting his gaze away for even so long as a heartbeat, Zoltan had come right up to the place, still by some enchantress's cunning she had managed to slip away, so cleverly that Zoltan had never seen her go. All he could think of was that she must have let herself slide into the water and drift away, gliding downstream beneath the surface.

And then he found one of her garments. The girl must have discarded it when she plunged into the water. But, when Zoltan came up to it and took hold of the fabric, it turned into brown moss in his fingers. Moss, grown long and tinged with gray, as if it had been growing here upon this log and rock for years. But though the cloth was no more than moss when he touched it, and seemed to be fastened in place, Zoltan could not be fooled.

The trouble, he decided, was that he simply wasn't moving fast enough to catch her.

Having reached this conclusion, he began to leap and run. All went for a little while. Then halfway through a steep descent he slipped, stepping on a slippery, angled rock, and fell, striking his chest on another flat rock with a thud that sent a shock of pain all through his rib cage. The breath was knocked clean out of him before he splashed into the next pool down. If the pool had been much larger he might have drowned. As it was, the rushing water deposited him like driftwood upon a narrow fringe of beach.

It seemed like a long time to Zoltan, lying in the grit and mud, before he could be sure that the pain in his ribs was going to let him breathe again.

Now something really strange was happening. Where was all the light?

Then he realized that the sun was going down. In fact it had gone down already. What light there was came from the full moon rising over the highlands, from which he had spent all day traveling.

Some animal off in the distance howled. It was an unfamiliar sound, as if Zoltan might already have reached some part of the world that was completely strange to him.

Groaning, he dragged himself up into a sitting position and decided that, after all, he was probably going to be able to go on breathing. Even though pain shot through his chest every time he drew in air.

It was, of course, impossible for him to get lost here—all he had to do was to follow the stream back up into the hills. Not that he was ready yet to turn back. He would rest here for a little while, and then he would go on. She couldn't be far away.

Something made Zoltan turn his head. There, illuminated by the last sunlight of the western sky and the rising moon high in the east, he saw the top of the girl's head, no more than ten meters away. Her gray eyes, fixed on Zoltan steadily, were looking over the top of a pile of brushwood. Another white spot, at a little distance, might be the top of one of her shoulders. He was much closer to her now than she had ever allowed him to get before.

The last light of day was dying quickly, and for the first time Zoltan began to be afraid.

He thought the gray eyes laughed and beckoned, but still the girl moved away from him, going somewhere farther beyond the brushpile, and disappeared.

He had to go after her. It was simply that he had no choice. Zoltan managed to stand up and follow her. Not only his ribs but his leg hurt, as he discovered when he tried to walk. He went on, with great effort and some pain.

After only a little distance, on an easy slope, he came to a larger pool than any he had encountered yet.

On a flat rock just at the side of the pool he saw her eyes again, and the black hair. But *that* object ought not to be her body. The shape of it was wrong, completely-wrong. It altered further as he looked at it, the bones and skin alike becoming something different. And then Zoltan saw her scaly length, her flicking tail, go writhing across the rock, plunging down into the riverbank slime beyond.

But there were still eyes—other eyes—looking at Zoltan, from another direction.

He turned, raising his own gaze to meet them.

The dark, winged shape, almost man-sized, perched amid shadows on a high ledge of rock. It looked as much like an illusion as the girl had looked like reality. But the eyes that looked down at him from the winged shape did not change. Gradually, heartbeat by heartbeat, he came to believe that they were very real.

7

THE full moon that Zoltan saw above the hills had waned to dark and waxed to full again when a column of about twenty riders approached within a few kilometers of the White Temple of Sibi.

At midday, a mounted scout, the first member of the advancing party to actually come within sight of the Temple and its compound, hurriedly surveyed the scene from a slight elevation nearby, then wheeled his riding-beast and sped away to make his report.

Less than an hour had passed before the scout was back, and the column with him. Halting atop a small hill that gave them a slightly better vantage point than that of the first reconnaissance, they looked over the situation more thoroughly.

At the head of the force as it arrived there rode a bulky, middle-aged man at whose belt hung a Sword, the symbol on the black hilt turned inward toward his body so that it could not be easily seen. Besides the Sword itself, appearances suggested nothing very remarkable about its owner. He was outfitted more like a bandit chieftain than an officer of cavalry, and indeed the clothing worn by his followers was very far from uniform. The men in the group—and the few women who were among them—made up an ill-assorted but well-armed gang, with no sign of any livery or colors, though pieces of the uniforms of several different armies could be distinguished among their garments.

At the leader's right hand rode a woman dressed chiefly in animal skins, and whose face and body were painted in ways that suggested she must be some kind of a minor enchantress. That she was not a magician of overwhelming skill could be deduced from the obvious way that her youth-spells struggled with the years to preserve her own appearance.

From their hilltop these leaders looked out over a dozen buildings and an extensive compound, mostly garden, all centered on the white stone pyramid, at least ten stories tall, that was the Temple itself.

The enchantress was the first to speak. "The Sword, if it is there, is lightly guarded."

The bulky man beside her turned his head. "Are you sure? Do your powers tell you that?" His voice was skeptical.

"My eyes tell me. I cannot be sure."

"Then use your powers," the man grumbled, "if you really have any. And make sure. As for eyes, I have two good ones of my own."

"I have powers," she flared, "and one day I'll make sure that you respect them."

He only grumbled again. Even that answer sounded as if it were merely as a matter of form. His attention had already moved back to the Temple, and the woman's threat, if it had really been that, was disregarded totally.

The enchantress dismounted and got to work. From a bag she carried she extracted fine powders of various colors and blew them into the air in different directions, a pinch at a time, from her hardened and somewhat dirty palm. The men around watched curiously, but for a time no one had anything to say.

Presently the woman was able to promise the bulky man—who waited expressionlessly for her report—that the magical protection of the treasure he had come here to get would be trivial at best; she would be able to set it aside easily. "That last prisoner we sacrificed," she assured him, "was a great help."

The man beside her nodded calmly. He had really not expected much in the way of magical tricks and traps from the White Temple; nor much in the way of armed force, either. His only real worry on his way here to take the treasure had been that someone else might have beaten him to it.

Now he motioned to his other followers and raised his voice enough to be sure that they all heard him. "We'll ride in, then. We will take what we want, but no more than that. And let there be no unnecessary killing or destruction."

Hard-bitten lot that the troopers were, they received that last order without protest. Indeed, there came in response a murmur or two that sounded like approval. There were many people who considered any move against the White Temple to be unlucky. Those who still believed in gods—and what bandit did not, at least on occasion?—were vastly reluctant to risk making enemies of Draffut and of Ardneh.

The Temple people inside the compound, and those few who were outside near the front gate, noticed the approach of the bandits when the riders were still some distance off, but their entrance was unopposed. The two White Guards at the entrance retreated rapidly, not bothering to try to shut the gates.

Extending from just outside those gates into the foot of the pyramid itself, there stretched a line of people who had come here hoping to be healed—the sick and injured, some of them accompanied by their attendants.

With the last admonition of their leader still in mind, the intruders cut through this line almost courteously, giving the lame and the halt time to scramble out of their way. The bandit column halted just inside the compound walls, where, at the sharp orders of their leader, its members dismounted and were rapidly deployed, some to guard their rear, a few to hold the animals. Most of them moved on foot against the pyramid.

The pyramid had one chief doorway, at ground level. Half of the small handful of White Guards who were now assembled in front of that doorway decided at once to take to their heels. The other half were not so wise, and the attackers' weapons, already drawn, had to be used. Blood spilled on the white pavement and on the chalky stones of the pyramid itself.

The bandit leader and others went into the Temple, and shortly afterward another Sword was brought out of the small interior room where it had been enshrined. When the bandit leader had satisfied himself that the object he had just acquired was indeed the genuine one he had been expecting, he left it in the hands of his chief lieutenant—in the case of this particular Sword he was willing to do that—and turned his attention elsewhere.

The Sword that had been at the leader's side when he arrived at the Temple had come out of its sheath, briefly, while the fight was on, though there had been no need for him to use it. Now it was again sheathed firmly at his side; this was one blade that he was not about to hand over to anyone else.

The leader looked about him now. "You, there!" he shouted, and gestured imperiously.

An ashen-faced, white-robed priest came forward, trembling, to learn what the next demands of this robber and murderer might be.

"Bring out some food and drink for my people here. Enough to make them happy. And there's someone I'd like to see. I've been told that she lives here now."

Eight years had now passed since anyone had called her Queen, and when she heard that title spoken by one of the servants chattering and whispering in fear and excitement outside her bower, it required no very quick thinking on her part to suppose that she had at last been over-taken by someone or something from those old times.

Listening to the voices more carefully now, she soon recognized a familiar, careless booming that broke in among the others. No need to guess any further. She could tell that the tones of the familiar voice, even as loud as they were, were intended to be soothing; he already had what he wanted, obviously, and he was trying now to set these harmless white-robed folk at ease. Panic, she had heard him declare many times, was always undesirable, unless you wanted to make things unpredict-able.

Now the familiar voice outside said: "Tell Queen Yambu that Baron Amintor would speak with her."

The woman who had been listening from behind a leafy screen arose and went to the entrance of her bower, so that her caller might be able to see her for himself.

"Amintor," she called out softly. "I had heard that you were still alive."

He turned toward her in the open sunlight, showing her a face and body changed by the eight years, though not nearly so much, she knew, as she herself was changed. He bowed to her, not deeply but still seri-ously, she thought.

He said: "And I had thought, my lady, that you were dead. Only quite recently did I learn that you were really here."

"And so you have come here to see me. Well, you will find me altered from the Queen you knew."

"Aye, to see you. And I had one other reason for wanting to come here, which I thought it better to make sure of first. Now we can visit at our leisure. But you look well."

"Always gallant, Amintor. Come in."

Amintor followed the lady among her trellises into what was more a garden than a house, but even so, apparently her dwelling. Cultivated insects hummed musically among some flowers. In the silence of his own mind the Baron was thinking that she looked about sixty years old now, or fifty-five at the very least, although he knew that in fact she could hardly be much more than forty. Her hair had turned from raven black to silver since he had seen her last, and her face bore deep lines that he had never seen before. Her step was firm enough as she moved ahead of him, but without energy. Her body was still straight and tall, but he could tell little more than that about it because of the loose gray clothing that she wore. That, too, was a considerable change.

They had now reached a roofed portion of her dwelling where there was simple furniture. Here the lady gestured her caller to a plain wooden seat.

"I know what I look like," said the former Queen, seating herself across from him, and in her voice he could hear for the first time a hint of the old fire and iron. "Hold Soulcutter in *your* hands throughout a battle, man, and see what you look like at the end of it. If it were not for Woundhealer, of course, I'd not be here now to talk about the experience. . . . I suppose you've got that one in your possession now; Woundhealer I mean. I thought I heard some clash of arms out there. Well, I could have told them that they'd need more guards. A child could have told them they'd not be able to keep such a treasure here without defending it. But they're impractical, as always. Never mind, tell me of yourself. That's not Woundhealer at your side, is it—? No, it couldn't be. What is this one that you have, then?"

Her visitor had been waiting for an opportunity to reply. When he was sure that his chance had at last arrived, he said: "My lady, you amaze me as always. How d'you know it's not the Sword of Mercy that I wear here? You've not touched it, and I wear the symbol on the hilt turned in."

"Amintor, Amintor." She shook her head a little, as if to rebuke him for his slowness. "The Sword you wear at your side is the one you're going to grab when danger threatens. No fear of your relying upon the Sword of Love for that—you'll want to make some wounds, not heal 'em. What then? It can't be Shieldbreaker, not unless your fortunes have risen higher than the rest of your outfit indicates."

Amintor smiled. His hand brought the bright metal a few more centimeters out of its scabbard and turned it to give the lady a better look at the black hilt. Now she could see the concentric circles making up a small white target.

"It's only Farslayer, my lady. Nothing for you to wince at when I start to draw it in your presence."

"Only Farslayer? And I may be your lady, but I'm Queen no longer; now I can wince whenever the need arises. I'm afraid that any of the Twelve would be likely to make me do so now."

"Even . . . ?" Her visitor inclined his head slightly, in the direction of his own waiting troops. There was some laughter out there; apparently they were being fed and somehow entertained.

"Oh, the one you've just appropriated has kept me alive when otherwise I would have died. But I've had all the help from it now that it can give me. And I won't be sorry to see it go, for it reminds me of all the rest. But never mind all that. While we have a little time here, tell me all that you've been doing. Gods and demons, Amintor, listen to the way I'm babbling on. Seeing you again awakens in me a craving that I had thought was dead. A craving for information, I mean, of course." There was the hint of a twinkle in the lady's eye. "Now that you're here, and no one seems to be pursuing you, sit with me for a while and talk. If one of the servants ever dares to stick her head in here, I might even be able to offer you a drink."

Amintor smiled, gestured to show that he was at her disposal, and settled himself a little more solidly in his seat.

The lady demanded: "First tell me what happened to you on the day of that last battle."

His smile broadened. "Well, to begin with, I was locked up in a closet."

That closet had made him a dark and well-built prison, on the ground floor of the House of Courtenay, within the city of Tashigang. By the time Amintor was thrust into it and the door barred shut on him, the fighting had already broken out inside the city and was getting close to the house. Something even worse impended also—the wrath of Vulcan, more terrible than any simple human warfare. Or so it was considered at the time.

After Amintor had spent some time in a useless trial of his fingers' strength upon the hinges of the closet door, he found himself unable to do anything better than curl up in a corner and try to protect his head from falling bricks. The level of the noise outside his prison was now such that he fully expected the walls to start coming down around him at any moment. The battle had definitely arrived in the vicinity of the house, and the building appeared to stand in some danger of actually being knocked down.

Still, there were some voices out there that occasionally were able to make themselves heard above the tumult. There was one in particular whose roaring the Baron thought could only be that of an angry god. Then, just when it seemed that the din could be no worse, it somehow managed to redouble. Only when part of one of the closet walls actually came down in a thundering brick curtain was Amintor able to do anything to help himself.

When that opportunity arrived at last, he did not waste it. In an instant the Baron had scrambled his bulky body out over the pile of fallen masonry now filling the space where the lower part of the wall had been. Gasping and choking in a fog of dust, he caught dim glimpses of a scene of havoc.

What he had last seen as two rooms on the ground floor of the House of Courtenay had been violently remodeled into one. In this large space there were now a mob of people scuffling, men and women together surrounding the figure of a giant and trying to bear it down. The plain physical dimensions of that central figure, which struggled to maintain its feet, and laid about it with a Sword in its right hand, were little if at all beyond the human scale. But there was something about it all the same that made Amintor at once accept it as gigantic, more than human.

That fact was accepted by the Baron, but it was not of much immediate concern to him. What concerned him first was his own survival. In that first moment of his freedom from the closet the immediate danger that he faced was the mass of staggering, tumbling, rolling bodies, coming his way and threatening to bury him again.

Despite that immediate threat, Amintor's eyes in the next instant became focused upon the Sword in the giant's hand. That Sword, generating from within itself a sound of thudding like a hammer, went blurring about with superhuman speed and power, smashing furniture and knocking down sections of the remaining walls whenever it touched them. But it did no harm to the bodies of the unarmed folk who found themselves in its path.

Unless Amintor's eyes were lying to him, that blade passed through their bodies as through shadows, leaving them unharmed.

But when one man came running with a mace to join the wrestling fight against the god, Shieldbreaker turned in its arc with a thud, shattered his weapon into fragments, and in the same stroke clove him gorily in half.

Only later did the Baron have the time to puzzle out some meaning from all this. At the moment he could only do his best to get himself out of the fighters' way. Doing so was far from easy. He was in a corner with only the ruined closet behind him, and it appeared that he was trapped.

He dodged as best he could.

Just when the crush of struggling bodies was at its nearest to Amintor, threatening to pin him against the wall, he saw at the giant's waist a swordbelt that carried two sheaths. One of them was occupied, and momentarily the black hilt that sprouted from it was almost at the Baron's hand.

Again he did not hesitate. The tempting second Sword came out of its scabbard into his grip. It was still in his hand as he made his dodging, running, cowering, crawling escape from the building. He came out of the place through what had been the back door but was only a jaggedly enlarged doorway now, from which fragments depended on wrecked hinges. Evidently the fighting had indeed been fierce in and around the building even before that little mob of madfolk, whoever they were, had decided that they were going to wrestle a god. The fallen were everywhere, in the street and on the floor, most of them uniformed in the blue and gold livery that meant Blue Temple guardsmen.

Outside, a large quantity of smoke hung in the air, and Amintor could see that the house he had just got out of, though built mostly of bricks and stone, was trying to burn down.

The other buildings nearby were largely intact, but still there were signs of war down every street. Nearby, the Corgo flowed stained with blood, and rich with debris, including bodies. The whole city of Tashigang was reeling under the combined assaults of human armies and of gods.

While Amintor was still inside the house, the thought had briefly crossed his mind that he might try out his newly acquired weapon in the melee there, against one side or the other. But the Baron had rejected that notion as soon as it occurred to him. None of the humans in that house were likely to be his friends, whether he helped them now or not; and a god's gratitude for any kind of help was certain to be chancy at best. He did pause, now that he was outside, and look at his Sword's hilt, anxious to learn which weapon he had seized.

Farslayer itself! He almost dropped the weapon when he saw the small white target on the hilt. Instead he looked around him quickly to see if he was being pursued, and ran on when he saw that he was not. Right now, he thought, Sightblinder would have been a luckier acquisition, almost certain to mean a safe passage out of all this. He was uncertain of the exact limits on the powers of the Sword of Vengeance, and not at all anxious to have to try them out in open combat. As matters stood, the only playable move for him right now was a quick retreat, a maneuver which Amintor proceeded to carry out with as much dispatch as possible.

Fortunately for himself, the only folk he encountered directly in the streets of Tashigang were refugees, even more frightened and certainly more disorganized than he. They all gave a wide berth to the great bare blade that he was carrying, whether any of them recognized its magical potential or not.

At each intersection that he came to, the Baron paused, and he looked carefully down each street before he crossed it. He avoided anything that looked like the colors of any army, and anything that even suggested the live presence of organized troops.

Now and then the Baron would pause in his course to squint up at the sun. Frequently it was obscured by one column of smoke or another, but he could estimate the time. Many hours would have to pass before darkness came to help him make his way out of the city. It was now no later than midafternoon, and the dust and smoke of the city's suffering still hung over everything in an evil fog.

The walls that completely surrounded the city were everywhere too high, and the gates too few, to encourage casual passage at the best of times. These times were not the best. The Baron's first objective was the Hermes Gate, but when he came in sight of its inner doors he could see that they were still closed and defended.

Breaking his way into a tall building through a poorly barricaded rear window, he went up many stairs. Looking down from the high rooftop, he thought he could see soldiers of an assaulting army massing on the road just outside the gate, with reinforcements coming up. He was going to have to find another exit.

Back in the street again, Amintor chose a route that roughly followed the curving course of the great, ancient walls, that went uphill and down like the Great Worm Yilgarn. He was looking for a way out, but discovered none until he had come back to the river, the same broad stream that flowed beside the House of Courtenay.

Even after all he had already seen today, the Baron was astonished by what he now beheld. One of the huge watergates guarding the approaches to the city by river had been torn down. Very little was left of its gigantic frame of magically rust-proofed iron and steel. Later the Baron was to learn that the gate had been wrenched from its granite sockets by the hands of Vulcan himself, before the Sword of Force had had the chance to work its strange weakening doom upon him.

Amintor was on the point of committing himself to the river as a swimmer when he was presented with what he perceived as yet another opportunity to better his condition; he seized this one as quickly as he had the other two. This one appeared in the form of a tall, fat pilgrim wearing the white robes of Ardneh, who came wandering through the streets toward the docks and declaiming against the horrors of war around him.

With Farslayer's long blade in hand, Amintor had little trouble in getting the man's attention and urging him into an alley. There, away from any likely interference, the man was persuaded to divest himself of his fine white robes before they should become stained with blood; such stains would have detracted from the pilgrim image that Amintor wanted to present. As matters turned out, no bloodstains anywhere were necessary—once stripped of his dignity, the pilgrim sat down in a corner of the alley and wept quietly.

Trying on the white robes over his regular garments, the Baron confirmed to his satisfaction that they were long enough to let a man carry a long Sword under them almost inconspicuously.

Now, to the river again. After the earlier evacuation, and this much fighting, there were no boats available at any cost, in money or in blood. Wrapping up his newly acquired Sword in his newly acquired robes, Amintor floated the resulting bundle in front of him upon a sizable chunk of wood. In this mode he plunged in and went splashing strongly upstream through the open gateway and was not killed, though for some reason someone's soldiers who were now manning the flanking defensive towers decided to use his bobbing head for target practice with their slings. Fortunately for him, they were still out of practice when he was out of range.

The Baron did not pull himself out of the river until he had made a long kilometer upstream. Luckily the river was almost free of traffic, military or otherwise, upon this martial afternoon. When he did get out of the water he took shelter in the garden of someone's abandoned suburban villa, from which vantage point he was able to observe developments around the city itself. He gathered more information by intercepting and questioning a lone refugee or two who passed the villa.

Amintor found some food that others had overlooked, and remained in his suburban garden until the following morning. By then he had seen and heard enough to feel sure of who was going to win, or had won, the battle, and therefore the war that so heavily depended on it.

As soon as he was sure that his side had lost, the Baron, thinking it would be a long time, if ever, before he laid claim to that title again, melted away into the countryside, as did a thousand others who had found themselves in more or less the same predicament.

During the next few days, foraging for survival as best he could, he saw a great many of those thousand others. Many of them were his own former comrades in arms, from the army of the Silver Queen. His new white robes saw little use. Amintor's appearance, his reputation, and his ability to assert leadership, even without the great Sword now at his side, would have let him recruit as many of these people as he wanted to follow him. But he was very selective in his recruiting. Right now he did not want an army of followers, all of them hungry and poorly organized. He foresaw the scouring of the countryside for such bands that was sure to come as soon as the victorious armies had enjoyed a breathing spell in which to care for their wounded, bury their dead, and put out the fires that were still threatening the city.

That scouring, that hunt for escaping and reorganizing enemies, came just as the Baron had foreseen it would. But by the time it came, he and the handful of new followers he had recruited were well away.

"It is a very remarkable tale," said she who had once been Queen Yambu. "But no more than I would have expected from you. And a long time has passed between that day and this; I should like to hear more of what you have done."

But Amintor got lightly to his feet and bestowed another bow upon the lady. He caught himself as he was about to offer thanks for her hospitality; the servants had never appeared, and he had never been given the wine he might have taken. He said: "Your Majesty is kind. I only wish I could stay long enough to tell you the rest."

"No more of that, no titles. So, you have gained the weapon that you came here to get."

"If the Sword of Mercy can really be called a weapon."

"Hm. You'll find a way to make it one. I could think of one or two methods myself if I were any longer interested in weapons . . . what will you do with it now?"

He gestured lightly. "The great game goes on, my lady, even if the gods themselves no longer play. I for one have not finished my turn."

"All right, don't tell me, then. I still wish you well. You are a great rogue, Amintor, but I still wish you well."

8

IN the gathering dusk, the dark, winged shape that sat on the shad-owed ledge of rock above Zoltan was all but invisible, except for its eyes. They were almost like human eyes, he thought, except that he could feel as well as see their gaze as they swept over him. One pair of eyes, and what looked like wings, and behind them movement in dark-ness, and that was all he could see of what or who was on the ledge.

Abruptly he discovered that he could not move. His booted feet felt as if they had taken root in the bottom of the stream. His arms were numb and hung down limply at his sides. Enchantment. Zoltan tried to cry out and could utter only a feeble croak. It might be magic that had disabled his voice too, or it might be fear.

As Zoltan stood paralyzed, ankle-deep in flowing water, another fig-ure came as if from nowhere into his field of vision, standing on the far bank of the stream. This new shape, visible in the unshadowed moon-light and the very last of the fading glow of day, appeared, in the circumstances, startlingly ordinary. It was that of a man of indetermi-nate age, dressed in a soft robe and slippers, as if for lounging in a palace.

The man stood in an arrogant pose facing the stream, and he ap-peared to be inspecting Zoltan. That was a trivial task and occupied him for only a moment. Then he turned away and his whole attitude changed abruptly. With the submissive air of someone approaching a superior, he made his way quickly along the bank until he stood just below the winged shape on its high rock. There he bowed deeply and addressed a few words to the being above him in some language that Zoltan was unable to understand.

Up on the rock there was a stir of movement in the depth of shadow.

Now it seemed to Zoltan that two forms were there, one the size of a riding-beast, the other of a man, and it seemed to him that both of them were winged—but even beyond that, there was something grievously wrong, unnatural, in the shape of both.

Now speech came from the man-sized shape, which was standing, or crouching, slightly in front of the other one. It was answering the man below and spoke in the same tongue that he had used, and Zoltan listening could still understand nothing at all.

He thought that the voice of the thing on the ledge did not sound fully human. There was something too whining and catlike about it. But even so it conveyed a royal firmness.

The man standing on the riverbank replied, bowing repeatedly as he did so. He was working harder and harder to acknowledge his inferiority with regard to the other.

The two of them in their incomprehensible conversation moved across the edge of Zoltan's consciousness like figures in some dim, cloudy dream. There was a roaring in his ears, and he had to struggle desperately to keep from fainting. All he could think about now was his own paralyzed body, his helpless situation.

Now that it was too late, Zoltan was able to understand clearly that for the past several days, from the time when he was inside the cave— *from the exact moment when he had looked out of the cave and seen the girl*—he had been under some form of evil and dangerous enchantment. The spell had not only compelled him to come alone on this mad expedition, but for days it had prevented him from seeking help from Karel or anyone else who might have helped him.

Zoltan did not faint. Perhaps fainting was not allowed.

Now the strange man on the riverbank and the even stranger being who sat above him were debating between them what was to be done with Zoltan. He could tell, because they were both looking his way now, and the man gestured in his direction.

Again Zoltan tried to cry out, but he could not.

And now he saw, with a sense of nightmare, that a third being had joined their conference. This newcomer was a dim figure, a human male in hat and robes. He stood on the same bank of the stream as the other two, and he faced Zoltan from a position between and somewhat beyond them.

Now this third presence became more distinct, and even after all that he had seen already, Zoltan blinked. In the moonlight the newcomer appeared like a caricature, a sketch based on the popular idea of what a wizard should look like, even to the conical, wide-brimmed hat and the robe speckled with strange symbols.

The figure on the high rock and the man standing on the riverbank below each glanced once in the direction of the new arrival when he first appeared. But after that, to Zoltan's surprise, they totally ignored him and went on with their mysterious dialogue as before. And the new arrival was content with silent observation.

Zoltan's capacity for surprise was pretty well exhausted. It scarcely seemed odd to him at all when he found himself suddenly capable of understanding what the creature on the rock and the man below were saying to each other.

". . . what I must have was lost," the Shadowed One above was saying to the obsequious man, "eight years ago. I am convinced now that you know nothing of that Sword's whereabouts. Nor do I think that it is near this place. But it is possible that you will learn something about it; and anything you learn of it must be communicated to me as soon as possible."

"I understand that, Master." Again the man below bowed deeply. He hesitated, then added: "You can trust me to do so. Such knowledge would only be a burden to me—he whom I formerly served, the Dark King, would be able to testify to the dangers of that weapon, were he still alive—and I am thankful that you stand ready to relieve me of it, if it should ever come into my possession." The man paused, then added blandly: "I am sure that you are aware of the dangers, and can deal with them."

"The Dark King?" said the shape perched on the ledge, managing in the three words to express a great deal of contempt. "Be assured that *I* can deal with it, or with any Sword, and still accomplish my own purposes while doing so. If indeed you are worried on that score, Burslem, you may set your mind at ease."

Burslem. Zoltan could not remember ever hearing the name before, and it meant nothing to him now.

"Then I think," said Burslem softly, making obeisance once again, "that you are more than human."

"Whether I am or not is a point of no particular importance, as far as you are concerned. Think of me either way you like." But Zoltan, listening, thought that the creature, whatever it was, was pleased by the suggestion.

The man below raised pleading hands. "Forgive my ignorance, Master—but are you then one of the gods?"

This time the thing that sat above him was not pleased. "The creatures that you called the gods," it whined in irritation, "were merely artifacts of the collective imagination of humanity."

And meanwhile the silent observer in the background continued to do nothing but watch, and listen. It was as if he, like Zoltan, were paralyzed.

"They were real, the gods," said the man on the riverbank. He was agitated, and again he made obeisance, as if trying to excuse the contradiction even as he uttered it. "Possessing a certain reality, surely. Consider the Swords—"

The smaller shape on the ledge above him waved something that emerged from the deepest darkness looking like a wingtip. "The gods could kill you, if that's what you mean. They could do horrible things to you—to most people—if they bothered to try. But remember that I am of a much higher order of reality than were those you call the gods, and I can do worse."

The man below went down upon one knee. "I shall not forget," he murmured rapidly, his voice quavering.

"Let us hope that you do not. Now, I see no reason not to approve of your plan of action as you have outlined it. This one you have caught"
—here again something like a wingtip came briefly out of shadow, gesturing in Zoltan's direction—"and can hold for ransom. But that will not be enough. You should take other hostages, or take some other action of equivalent force against the ruling house of Tasavalta. It is my wish—my command to you—that they be neutralized, lest they eventually interfere with my plans elsewhere. I am going to be occupied elsewhere for a long time. For months or years, perhaps."

"I hear and obey."

There was more to the conversation, but Zoltan heard very little of it. His understanding of the strange language was failing again, the words becoming gibberish in his mind once more. His mind was reeling, and the murmur of speech that sounded only partly human was like that of the stream that flowed around his ankles, going on and on and meaning nothing.

He was only vaguely aware when both of the shapes on the high rock departed, rising up together into the night sky. Together, the large and the small, they made a winged form of shadows that was much larger than a man, but still hard to see against the stars. Soon the composite shape was out of sight altogether.

Now, with that departure, it was as if some strain had been relieved, and Zoltan was free to become fully aware of his surroundings once again. He realized vaguely that at some point during the last few minutes the third figure, the silent onlooker, had disappeared.

He and the man named Burslem, who still stood on the riverbank, were alone.

Burslem was no longer bowing and scraping, but again standing arrogantly erect. Now he made a wizard's gesture at the starry sky, then turned toward Zoltan and stepped into the shallow water. He was coming to look his prisoner over at close range. Even as he approached, there was a splashing in the water some meters behind him, a pale, leaping shape. And now the dark-haired girl, her misshapen body half silver and half shadow in the moonlight, was sitting on the bank behind the approaching magician.

The man must have been aware of her arrival, but ignored her. He approached Zoltan closely and prodded his arms and ribs as if to see whether his paralysis had reached the proper stage. He looked into Zoltan's eyes and ears. Then he moved around Zoltan's immobile figure, his magician's fingers busy, weaving some additional spell into the air around his captive.

Then the wizard turned his head, suddenly taking notice of the girl on the far bank. He snapped his fingers at her, and she vanished, splashing into the water with a movement more fishlike than human.

And then the wizard himself was gone, without a splash, without a sound of any kind. Zoltan was alone.

He waited for one of the strange presences to return, but none of them did. It was as if they had all forgotten him. The moon looked down, the water gurgled endlessly around his ankles. He stood there like a statue and could not fall, but he could grow tired. His injured leg, with his weight steadily on it, hurt like a sore tooth. His ribs stabbed him with every shallow breath.

The moon was down, and dawn was approaching, and he had begun almost to hope that he had been forgotten, before the magician returned, as silently and inexplicably as he had gone.

Burslem stood again on the riverbank, looking more ordinary now in the light of the new day, but not less terrible. Now for the first time the magician's face was clearly visible to Zoltan, and it was startlingly human, only the face of a man.

Zoltan tried to say something, but he could not speak. Now he thought it was magic that sealed his tongue, though by all the gods his fear was great enough.

The other smiled at him. "Well. So, you must be kept in storage, somewhere, somehow. For some undetermined time. How shall it be done?"

Still Zoltan could not answer. At some moment soon, surely, he would wake up. Suddenly tears were running down his cheeks.

The wizard paid no attention to any of this, but stood back, making controlled, decisive gestures. Zoltan's legs, abruptly moving again, though still under alien control, turned him around and marched him through the water to the high bank that ran along the other side of the river. Able to look at that bank for the first time in twelve hours, the boy could see that there was a deep hollow there, really a cave. The entrance to the recess was curtained naturally by a growth of vines that hung over it from above, and screened by tall reeds that grew from below.

His own muscles moving him like alien hands, Zoltan was turned around, then cast down inside the muddy, shallow cave like a discarded doll. Then his position was rearranged, once, from the unbearable to the merely uncomfortable.

"Might want those joints to work when I take you out again." The magician's voice was genial. "Of course, on the other hand, I might never take you out."

There was a silent arpeggio of magic. Mercifully Zoltan was allowed to sleep.

Zoltan awoke, suddenly, to a realization of his physical surroundings, which were apparently unchanged.

It was late at night. The moon was high, and there was something strange about it. Eventually he understood that it had waned for several days from full. He stared at the gibbous shape for a while, trying to comprehend the implications. But in a moment the moonlight falling on the earth outside his cave showed Zoltan something that distracted him from other thoughts.

The same figure he had seen before as a silent listener, that of a little old man, a caricature of a wizard, was standing on the far side of the stream. But this time, after the first moment of confrontation, the witness was far from silent.

Speech burst from the little old man, a torrent of childish abuse that seemed in a way the maddest thing that Zoltan had experienced yet. "What are you doing in there, you stupid? You shouldn't be there at all. Come out!" The tone was one of anger and relief combined.

The man came closer, and as he neared the stream his aged, dried-apple face was plainly visible in the moonlight. Zoltan could not recognize it, but for a moment he thought that he should.

"Come out of there! Out of there, out of there! Ooooh! Why are you in there at all? There, now you can talk, answer me!" The voice was gravelly and phlegmy most of the time, but on some words it squealed and squawked. In general it was hard to understand.

"I want to come out," croaked Zoltan, suddenly discovering that he was able to talk again. His own voice, after a week of silence, sounded not much better than the old man's. "I can't move, though. Help!"

"Help? Help? I've been trying to come back here and help. You think it's easy?" the aged wizard-figure shrieked like a madman. The body in the strange robe bent and twisted, gesturing. Now he seemed to have hold of the landscape, and twitched and tugged at it, heaving until the land, stream and all, was shaking like a rug. Water rose up in a thin, foaming wall, and for a moment Zoltan feared that he was going to be drowned.

Not only the mundane landscape was affected. Invisible walls went shattering, impalpable bonds were torn apart. It was a painful, fumbling process, but Zoltan at last popped out of his cave, like a bug shaken from a carpet, to splash into the stream again. The water was a cold shock that assured him he was at least fully awake. Moving again, he felt amazingly better than he had feared he would. His arms and legs were full of pins and needles, but they were functioning. And his ribs were only lightly sore, as if the long enforced rest had healed them.

The world was quiet after its purging. The new wizard stood on the riverbank, bent over with hands on knees, peering at him.

Zoltan cleared his throat and demanded, almost prayerfully: "Who are you?"

The other straightened up and answered in a rapid voice that sounded stranger and stranger the more it chattered: "Names are magic. Names are magic. That one who flies would like to grab my name and bonk me, but he can't. He knows your name already, but not mine. Couldn't even see me when I was here before, so there, ha ha!" And the old man laughed. It was a mad and disconnected sound that wandered up and down the scale of human voice-tones.

With something of a chill, Zoltan realized that he could see moonlight through the edges of the figure, as if it were not really, solidly, there at all.

But after everything else that had happened, he wasn't going to quibble about that. "I still need help, sir. Can you help me get home?"

The wizened wizard shook his head. "No, no, no! You are supposed to be out adventuring, Zoltan. You're big, you're all grown up, and you can't go home yet."

That was a shock. "Why can't I?" He wiped his eyes, his face. He was almost sniveling.

"Why? Don't you know? I turned the words around so you could understand them, when those two were talking. Your—your uncle Mark needs help." The wizard stood with fists on hips and glared.

"Oh." Zoltan, feeling shamed, squelched his way out of the water and sat down on the bank. "How can I help him? What can I do?" Then, without waiting for an answer, he jumped up again. "Uncle Mark or whatever, I've got to get out of here before they come back—and how did you do that, just now? Get me loose, I mean?"

"I know tricks. I found out some pretty good tricks, to get things loose. Good old Karel, he put together some great elementals." The wizard chuckled and slapped his bony thigh. Mere image or not, the impact sounded solidly.

"Are you a friend of his, sir?"

There was a pause. "We've met a few times." And the old man, mouth slightly open on his snaggled teeth, squinted sharply at Zoltan, as if to see whether Zoltan had got the joke.

Zoltan, who could see no joke, once more asked for help.

"You've got to go and help your uncle first," his rescuer repeated relentlessly.

"If—if Uncle Mark really needs me, I'll do what I can." Zoltan swallowed. "I'll help. But you've got to tell me where to go, and what to do, and—and how to do it."

The other stood with his fists on his hips, nodding his head sharply. But his speech, just at first, did not sound all that confident. "I don't know if I can tell you all that. But I think I know what I can do—I think. Oh, fuddle-duddle, I can do it. Tell you what, Zoltan. Right now you look very tired, so why don't you go to sleep?"

That was alarming. "I've been asleep. Don't make me go back again. I thought you were going to help me."

"You are tired. Good sleep this time. Go back to sleep."

And Zoltan did.

When he awakened again he had no idea of how much time had passed, but he could see that it was still night—or maybe it was night again. This time he could not find the moon.

At least he had not been stuffed back into the cave. He was in motion —somehow. He was in a sitting position, and his legs were resting, floating, with his knees bent and raised to the level of his chin. He was sitting on something—or in something—but he was moving.

He was really moving. That brought him fully awake. He was in the stream, submerged in water with only his head and shoulders and knees above the surface, but he was not cold or wet.

When he looked down to see what was carrying him, Zoltan discovered that, as far as he could tell, he was being borne up and along by the river itself. Bits of small driftwood ringed him around almost like a gentle fist, urged by some invisible power to offer him support, but it wasn't the wood that kept him floating. It had to be some invisible power because there wasn't enough wood. In this stream there should hardly be enough water.

And when he looked ahead he saw that the land itself was making way for him, trees nodding and swaying as if they walked, rocks bending out of his path where the rapids ordinarily ran swift.

He was borne upstream, through the rapids, easily and safely.

Then came a long stretch of almost level flow. He felt no fear. He was beyond fear now.

A giant fish came to splash beside him, and leap, and splash again. The reality of the night supported him, and once more he slept.

9

MARK kept a log of distance traveled every day, and after several weeks of the journey he began to watch for certain landmarks, hills of a peculiar configuration that had been described to him in Sarykam. The borders between Tasavalta and the land of Sibi were as a rule not defended, or even sharply defined, but at length he was satisfied that he had crossed them. The clothing of the few people who came into sight was different from that of Tasavaltan villagers, and the only dwellings now in sight were of inferior construction.

When the landmark hills at last came into sight, the Prince felt sure that he was near the Temple that he sought, and he sent a human scout ahead as a routine precaution. His beastmaster of course had birds in the air already—they made faster scouts than human riders, particularly where the terrain was difficult, and often brought back vital information. But there were relative subtleties in things observed, sometimes even things as important as the color of uniforms, which remained beyond the capabilities of the birds to perceive and describe.

The scout received his orders and cantered off, soon leaving behind the main Tasavaltan body that continued to travel at a more modest pace.

Within an hour after he had disappeared the lone rider was in sight again, coming back at a gallop.

Barking orders, the Prince had his small force ready for action well before the scout had come close enough to shout his news, whatever it might be. The ranks had closed around the litter—in which Prince Adrian was now spending almost all his time—and the Master of the Beasts had sent all but one of his flying creatures into the air, where they circled, keeping a high lookout.

The rider, clattering up at last to the head of the column, delivered his message out of breath.

"I found the Temple, and there's been some kind of trouble there, Your Highness. They've scraped up some kind of extra barricade at the front gate, and there's what looks like a triple funeral in progress. There were three coffins. If three people have died suddenly in a Temple that holds Woundhealer, well, I thought something strange must be happening. I didn't go in, just took a look and came right back."

"A wise decision. Any signs of fighting?"

"No sir. Nothing I could see. But I thought you'd best know as soon as possible what's going on."

Mark nodded, and considered. "All right. We'll go on to the Temple. But with double outriders, on alert."

With the scout leading the way, the column proceeded at the same pace as before. Within the hour the Prince had come near enough to the Temple, which lay in a small flat valley, to see the signs of trouble for himself. The funeral was over now, but the black bands that meant White Temple mourning were still in evidence, stretched across buildings and strung between them. And there, as the scout had described it, was the extra barricade built from the piled-up timbers and sandbags and even furniture, and looking more a sign of panic than of determination. The space inside the Temple's outer wall was thick with people, standing or sitting or milling about, but there was no sign of military activity.

The Prince motioned his own people forward. Within a few more minutes, the column had reached the outer barricade, traversed the passage through it, and arrived at the gate proper. There the single White Guard on duty, his teeth chattering, was brave enough to ask them what they wanted.

Mark, who had already halted his column, now raised his right hand in a sign of peace. "We mean no harm. We have come only to seek a healing from the Sword of Mercy."

The man on guard appeared to be in a chronic state of shock. He looked back at the Prince as if he could not understand what Mark was talking about. Then at last he replied: "It's g-gone."

"Gone? Where? You mean Woundhealer has been stolen?"

"Yes sir."

Mark looked past the guard, into the compound. Now he understood the mournful look of the swarm of invalids who occupied most of the courtyard inside the gate. A White Temple was generally a hospital as well as a place of worship, but this one appeared grievously overcrowded with patients. And a faint moaning in many voices, as of some general sorrow, went up into the pleasant sky. A few nurses and physicians were going slowly and tiredly about their traditional job of trying to alleviate the sufferings of the sick and injured. The air of defeat hanging over the Temple was almost palpable.

Mark turned to Ben. "Set up our camp here, outside the walls. Post guards as usual. We will remain here for a little while at least."

Now priests were approaching from inside the compound, looking as tremulous as their guard had been at first. When they observed that the guard was still alive and armed, they drew courage from the fact and approached the gate more boldly, crying out their grief that the Sword of Mercy had been stolen from them.

Quickly Mark began to question the white-robes, probing for solid information. "Who was it that took the Sword from you? When? How many were there? Which way did they go?"

He was provided, willingly enough, with times and descriptions. Witnesses' accounts differed somewhat, but were alike enough for the Prince to feel that he was getting a fair idea of the truth. Once the priests were sure of Mark's identity, their faces brightened and they began to look at him hopefully.

One of the older white-robes said encouragingly: "They were in no hurry to get away, Your Highness. Only bandits. If you are quick you ought to be able to overtake them."

Mark shook his head. "You say they are many hours ahead of us. My people and my animals alike need rest before we can undertake a long pursuit. And I hope that you can spare us some provisions."

"We can. We can. We will do everything we can to help you, if you can bring us back our Sword."

Mark dismounted, then turned back to the priests with another question. "Why do you say that the bandits were in no hurry?"

"Because, Your Highness, their leader dawdled here. He delayed and spoke for a long time with one of our long-term guests—she who was once Queen Yambu."

Standing just outside the leafy doorway, looking into the bower's cool interior, the Prince said: "I thought perhaps that you had vanished with the Emperor."

"No," replied the dim figure seated at a table inside, and let her answer go at that. When Mark appeared at her doorway she had raised to him a face so changed by time and events that for a moment he did not recognize her at all.

After a moment, she who had once been the Queen got to her feet and asked the Prince to enter. When he was inside she began at once to speak of trivial matters, the weather and the timidity of her servants. She felt a great reluctance to talk about the Emperor, who, on that last battlefield, had asked her for the second time to marry him. For the second time she had refused. Only he, the Emperor, would have made such an offer to a defeated enemy. And only she, perhaps, would have rejected him as she did.

What had kept her from accepting was the fierce need to assert her independence, a need that had been with Yambu all her life. It still ruled her behavior.

With an effort she brought her attention back to the man who was now standing in front of her.

Mark was saying: "I think that some of the white-robes out there are already angry with me, as if it were my fault that their Sword was stolen. They expect me to gallop after it at once and bring it back."

Yambu roused herself to be hospitable.

When her guest was seated and some refreshment had been brought for both of them, she said: "Well, servants of Ardneh or not, there are idiots and worse in the White Temple, just as there are in the other Temples. Or anywhere else. I've lived here long enough now to know that."

Mark sipped from the mug that had been placed in front of him, then took a deeper draught. "You have chosen, then, to live eight years among idiots?"

"Oh, they have their good qualities too. They tend to be peaceful idiots, and for the most part it is soothing to live among them. When I came here I wanted nothing but to be soothed—I made them a large donation—a very large donation—and I expect to get my money's worth in return. But never mind them. Have you now come at last to kill me? Or arrest me?" She sounded more interested in the answer than afraid of what it might be.

"I have no particular wish to do either. Who stole the Sword of Mercy?"

"Ah, of course. It is the Sword that brings you here, too; I should have known that at once. Well, I can tell you without hesitation that it was Amintor who took it—you'd find out soon enough anyway. He sat where you are sitting now, and took some time to pay his respects to me, in token of the times when we were together. And then he recited to me something of his own history during the past eight years."

Mark's mouth moved in a faint smile. "An exciting tale, that must have been. Perhaps some of it was even true. What hints did he drop, or seem to drop, about his plans, now that he has Woundhealer?"

Yambu thought back. "Why, he said nothing at all about his plans. I didn't ask him about that."

"Not that you'd want to tell me if he did."

"On the contrary, Prince. I think I might well tell you. I suppose I like the two of you about equally well, though you were once my enemy, and he was once my officer—and more. I'll answer any questions you may have, if they are decently put, and if I can find the answers— why not?"

Mark looked at her, and she could see him taking note again of the extreme changes in her since he had seen her last, and thinking about what must have produced them.

Then he asked: "Where is Soulcutter now?"

Her aged eyes searched him in turn, as if she were disappointed in him. She asked: "Why d'you want that? Can't you see what it's done to me?"

He shook his head. "It's not that I want it particularly. But I'll use it if I can. If I have nothing else to use. I'm ready to use anything."

"Then give thanks to all the surviving gods you haven't got it." The former Queen sat back in her chair.

"You don't know where the Sword of Despair is now? Or you won't tell me?"

"Even Amintor didn't ask me about that one. Why should you?"

"Maybe Amintor is not as desperate as I am. Where is it?"

The lady shrugged. It was a gesture that conveyed sadness and weariness more exquisitely, Mark thought, than any extravagance of behavior could have done.

Then she said: "I really don't know. My belief is that the Emperor took it with him, when he . . . withdrew."

"Withdrew?"

"From politics. From war. From the affairs of humanity in general."

"And where is he now?"

Again the lady shrugged, even more delicately than before. "I don't know. But I don't suppose you're going to find him and Amintor in the same place."

Mark talked with the lady once more, on the following morning, just before he and his people departed on Amintor's trail. But he learned nothing useful from her.

Among the people in Mark's small force were a couple of trackers of some skill. But as matters turned out, their skill was not really needed. Amintor, and the score or so of riders he evidently had with him, had left a trail that would have presented no real problems even to the most inexpert eye, even though it twice forded streams and in several places crossed long stretches of hard ground.

The bandits' trail at the start led straight west from the Temple, or as near to that direction as the local difficulties of terrain allowed. The land here verged on wasteland, harshly configured but in its own way beautiful. There were signs that grazing was sometimes practiced upon the scanty vegetation. But once the precincts of the Temple were left behind, along with the roads that approached the complex from north and south and east, all signs of human habitation soon dropped from sight.

Mark was not minded to contemplate nature, or beauty of any kind. He had undertaken the pursuit of Amintor because he saw no real alternative, but he was gloomy about the chances of success. To begin with, his riding-beasts and loadbeasts were still tired from the long journey they had already made. But to bivouac any longer in front of the White Temple would give the Baron too great a start.

Secondly, Mark knew that he could expect no help. The few scattered inhabitants of the territory through which he was now passing obviously were not going to provide any; and nowhere did the White Temple have any respectable armed force of its own. They had only the White Guards, best suited for keeping order in a waiting line of invalids, and with some effort usually able to repel the sneak thieves and vandals that might pester any Temple. As an army in the field, or a bandit-hunting posse, the White Guards were nonexistent.

But Mark's greatest difficulty now was that he was compelled to bring his son with him on the chase. It would have been unthinkable to leave Adrian at the Temple, where he would be prey to kidnap or murder by the next set of desperadoes who happened along. Mark had the idea that there would almost certainly be more of them. Word of the Sword's presence there had gone out far across the world, and many would be scheming to try to profit from it. Nor would the Prince have been able to leave any substantial number of guards at the Temple to protect his son—the band he was pursuing was comparable to his own in size.

But the presence of an invalid child inevitably slowed down the pursuit. Even under the best of conditions, Adrian was unable to ride swiftly, and the best of conditions seldom obtained. Nor could the litter, slung between two beasts or strapped to one, make anything like the speed that might be necessary in war. The boy could be carried in front of someone's saddle for a time, but that was awkward and in combat it might prove fatal to child and rider alike.

Still, Mark did not consider the pursuit hopeless. Amintor's people were only bandits. And by delaying to chat with his former Queen, the Baron had shown himself to be in no breakneck hurry. Furthermore, the Baron would have no reason to expect any close and determined pursuit; he ought to have no cause to believe that Mark was on his trail.

During the first days of the chase, Mark had scouts, both winged and mounted, out continually during the daylight hours. Camps were dry and dark, and were broken before dawn, as soon as the light was good enough to allow the following of an obvious trail.

The young Master of Beasts who accompanied the column—his name was Doblin, and he was an intense youth, though he tended to be plump—got little rest by day or night. The birds in his care were sent out on one mission after another mission with a minimum of rest. Two of the messenger-scouts were of a nocturnal, owllike species, friends of humanity since time immemorial.

On the third day of the pursuit, one of the birds that flew by day came back with multiple wounds, as if from an encounter with a leather-wings—one of the more savage types of flying reptiles, which the Dark King and his old allies had frequently used as their human enemies used birds. The wounded bird was in no shape to be sent out again, and the beastmaster kept it in its cage and practiced upon it what healing arts he knew and then enlisted the help of the accompanying physicians. The creature rested on a confined perch as best it could, jouncing along upon a loadbeast's back. It could not or would not communicate the nature of the attack that had disabled it.

Meanwhile the night-flying birds brought back strange reports of something large and terrifying that passed them in the sky and from which they had fled in terror, escaping only with great difficulty. The Master of Beasts was not sure how much of this story to believe. Certainly his creatures had encountered something out of the ordinary, probably some kind of winged dragon; in any case, there was little that he or anyone else could do about it.

Meanwhile, Adrian's condition remained essentially unchanged. Mark observed with mixed feelings the stoic indifference—or so it seemed to him—with which his son bore the increasing discomfort of the long journey. The father feared that it was not courage that sustained the child, but only an ever-deeper withdrawal from the world around him.

Somehow, father and son were exchanging even fewer words than usual these days.

Adrian would—sometimes—eat food when it was put into his hands. He would drink water when someone held a cup or a canteen to his lips. He would let himself be led to the latrine pit and back; but sometimes at night he still wet his bed. He would sit when asked, stand when told to stand, usually hold himself in a saddle for a time when he was placed astride a mount. Eventually, after being put somewhere, he would change his position, and if he was in a saddle when that happened he would very probably start to fall out of it. So far someone had always been at hand to catch him safely when he toppled.

For a day now Mark had given up altogether trying to put his son into the saddle because all signs agreed that the enemy was now not far ahead. There were the wounded birds, and the trail was obviously fresher. The column had to be constantly ready for action at a moment's notice. If Adrian was bothered by being confined to his litter almost constantly, and separated from his mother and the other people of the Palace, he gave little sign of it. He put up with everything, with a cheerfulness admired by those who did not know him as well as his father did. To Mark it seemed like sheer infantile indifference to the world.

10

A LL hope vanished that Amintor might not know that he was being followed. The Tasavaltans' only surviving nocturnal scout came in exhausted at dawn to report that some of the human enemy were hiding themselves in a place of ambush ahead, overlooking the trail on which their pursuers could be expected to pass. Meanwhile the main body of the Baron's force, perhaps about fifteen riders—birds were notoriously poor at counting—pressed on. This morning the bird had nothing further to report of the leather-wings, or whatever the mysterious aerial nighttime presence had been that had earlier attacked and disabled its mate.

Mark considered what he knew of the lay of the land ahead, taking into account his scouts' reports in addition to what he could see for himself. To avoid the area of the reported ambush completely would take a discouragingly long time. Besides, the fact that Amintor had divided his force opened opportunities that he was reluctant to pass up.

Ben was evidently thinking along the same lines. "If the Baron knew that we have Shieldbreaker with us he might not be so eager to risk a fight."

The Prince shook his head. "Or, on the other hand, he might know. He might be ready to take the risk. He probably knows how to fight against my Sword if he can get close enough to me. Well, we'll give him what he's looking for. We appear to have some advantage of numbers."

The morning was chill, with a sky that soon developed a good crop of low, scudding clouds. Driven by gusty autumn winds, the rack reduced the chances of successful aerial reconnaissance, though two birds went up to try. Mark wondered if the turn in the weather might have been brought about at least in part by magical interference. His own magicians could not be sure on that point, but offered to attempt counter-spells. He wished silently that Karel himself were here. But wishing was pointless. The people he actually had with him were skilled, or Karel would not have sent them on this journey. Smiling at his magicians as if he really had the highest confidence in them, Mark told them to con-serve their powers until later. There was no way to be sure what quality of opposition they might be facing.

As matters stood, the weather continued to make scouting difficult for anything that flew. Since Mark knew of the ambush already, he decided that this situation was more likely than not to be favorable to him, and preferred to act before it changed.

He turned command of the column over to Ben.

Then the Prince selected half a dozen of his best riders and fighters, people he judged outstanding even among the already elite group who had been chosen for this march. With this handful of troops at his back, he set out to surprise the ambushers.

Meanwhile the remainder of the little Tasavaltan column proceeded as before, with the litter protected at its center, following the broad trail left by the Baron and his people. Ben had saddled the six spare mounts and brought them from the rear up into the regular formation of riders. Lances and bedrolls tied to the saddles of the riderless beasts might, Ben hoped, deceive any flying reptiles or birds that might be able to get through the weather on scouting missions for the enemy.

Mark and his half dozen shock troops moved away from the trail that the main group continued to follow. The seven plunged into a thicket of scrubby trees on a fast and difficult ride.

If the birds had been accurate in their description of the topography and the enemy dispositions, all should now be well. If not, the Prince and the people riding with him would have to take what came.

As Mark drew near the place where the birds had located the am-bush, he slowed the pace of his advance. Very slowly he climbed what ought to be the last hill. When he was almost at its crest, he dismounted and crept up the last few meters on foot. Wind howled, and rain spat-tered him from the clouds close above his head.

Peering over, he allowed himself a small sigh of satisfaction. As seemed to happen so rarely in war, things were as he had hoped and expected them to be. There, half a kilometer away now, beyond and below the place where the enemy should be, wound the broad, faint trail along which moved the blue-green uniforms of his own party. Among them he could pick out Ben's imitation riders; once the bandits who were waiting in ambush saw those, they would be likely to understand the reason for them, and anticipate a counterattack.

After this hasty glance at his own column, Mark fastened his gaze on the place, much closer, where the ambushers had to be, if the birds were right. It was a cluster of eight or ten trees, with surrounding lesser growth. The enemy were well concealed, if they were really there, and Mark could not see them yet. They would have their animals hidden in the small grove with them, but if the scouting report was correct the enemy were too few to mount a cavalry charge against the Tasavaltan force. Rather, they would be planning to loose a volley of stones and arrows and then beat a quick retreat, after having inflicted what casualties they could upon the column as it passed beneath them.

Mark had seen enough. He turned and scrambled down to where a soldier was holding his riding-beast for him. In a few words he outlined the situation to his companions. Then, remounting, he drew Shieldbreaker and with one swift silent gesture commanded a charge.

From the moment he aimed the Sword forward he could feel the magic of it thudding softly in his hand and wrist. As yet the noise that always accompanied its magic was not loud, as if the Sword could understand that its possessor now wanted silence.

The seven Tasavaltan cavalry mounts, smelling war and eager for it, thundered down one short slope and up another. The enemy among the trees a few score meters distant had not much time in which to be aware that the charge was coming, yet they were not taken totally by surprise. Slung stones sang out, passing Mark with invisible speed, and he had one momentary impression that the air around him was full of arrows.

With the first appearance of enemy weapons, Shieldbreaker's voice became a heavy pounding. The Sword was controlling itself now, moving into action with a force and speed that must certainly have pulled it from the Prince's grip had not an equal force appeared to weld it to his hand. Its rhythm went tripping into syncopation. A slung stone, which Mark never had the chance to see, was shattered in midair upon that blade. He heard the fragments whine. Arrows—one, two, three of them, faster than he could count—were wiped aside by the Sword of Force before he could well comprehend that the first shaft had been about to hit him.

Mark's picked troops were keeping up with him so far. He himself, in the center of the charging line, had been the chief target for the enemy. But he had come through the hail of missiles unharmed.

The moments had already passed in which the enemy—they were indeed dressed as mere bandits, Mark saw now—might have decided to retreat, and managed to escape. Some of them did want to flee at the last moment, when, perhaps, they had already recognized the Sword. But by then it was too late.

A few of the people who had been hidden in the little grove were now trying to mount their riding-beasts to meet the Tasavaltan charge. Others dodged on foot among the trees, ready to strike at the Prince and his riders as they passed.

By now Mark's powerful mount had moved him a few strides ahead of the others in his party. For a long moment he fought alone, almost surrounded amid the enemy. The Sword of Force went flashing right and left, pounding like a pulse in some great climax of exertion. The blade dissected enemy armor, flesh, and weapons, all with razor-sharp indifference. Clamped in its user's hand, it twisted the Prince and his riding-beast from side to side together, meeting one threat and then the next, or two simultaneously. Whether by sheer speed, or perhaps sheer magic, Mark thought he saw his own right arm, with the Sword in it, on both sides of him at once.

That first shock of combat ended in the space of a few heartbeats. Only now did Mark have time to realize that there were more bandits here among the trees than he had expected, perhaps ten or a dozen of them in all. Without Shieldbreaker, this counterattack of his might well have proven a disastrous mistake. As it was, no more than half of the enemy had survived their closing with him. And the survivors, those who had so far stayed out of the Sword's reach, were now simply trying to get away.

The Prince and his comrades-in-arms gave chase. His powerful mount, a truly royal animal, was gradually overtaking the fastest of the fleeing mounted bandits. At the last moment the fellow twisted in his saddle to fight, aiming his long-handled battle-ax at Mark in a despairing two-handed swing. Shieldbreaker had fallen silent, but now it thudded again, twice, as fast as the sun might flicker from its blade. Mark's own mount pounded on, slowing as he reined in gently and steadily. Behind him on the ground there lay a broken ax, a fallen and dismembered rider, a wounded riding-beast struggling to get up.

Mark turned his own animal and rode it slowly back. The fight was over; only two of the enemy had not been killed, and they were prisoners. The Sword was quiet now, and he was able to let it go. He wiped it —in an instant, as always, it was perfectly clean—and put it back into its sheath. Then he flexed the numbed cords of his right hand and wrist. His whole right arm felt strange, as if it might begin to swell at any moment. But it was functioning; and, all things considered, the Prince was not going to complain.

The action away from the Sword of Force had been savage also, and the Prince saw that two of his own people were down with wounds, though it appeared that both of them would survive, and, almost as important, be able to ride if not to fight. Matters were under control.

He rode back to the hill from whose top he could easily be seen from the old trail below and waved his blue-green column on, giving them the agreed-upon signal for a victory. He heard a thin cheer go up, and the column started. Ben had halted it, just outside the effective range of missiles from the ambushers' original position.

The Prince added another signal, summoning one of the physicians to hurry ahead; then he rode quickly back to where the two enemy survivors were now being held.

Leaving Shieldbreaker in its sheath, he dismounted and approached the captive men. Here were two who had been ready to rain stones and arrows from ambush upon his son. Without stopping to think about it, Mark drew his dagger as he came.

"Mercy, Lord Prince," said one of them, a haggard, scrawny fellow. "You are known as a good and merciful man."

He looked at them intently, one after the other. He knew that they served Amintor, so there was no point in questioning them about that, except perhaps to see if they were inclined to tell the truth or not.

Mark dug the tip of his dagger into the nearest man's throat, just hard enough to draw a little blood. No matter how many times he drove a weapon into flesh, it was always something of a surprise to him how little pressure was required.

"Who is your master?" he demanded. "Speak!"

"Uh. The Baron, we call him. Uh."

"Good, you've told me the truth once." Mark maintained the dagger pressure, though his right hand still felt strange and was still quivering from the grip of magic that other blade had fastened on it. "Now try again: What is the Baron's destination, now that he has his new Sword?"

"He never told us that. Oh, ah." The man died almost silently; the point of the dagger in Mark's hand had dipped down to the level of the victim's heart before it plunged in through his shirt.

Even with this example to contemplate, the second man was no more informative before he died. His passing was almost as quick as that of his fellow had been. There was no possible way of bringing prisoners along on a cavalry chase; and no way in which these prisoners could be released. Mark considered that the world now held two less poisonous reptiles, who had been all too ready to strike at Adrian, and at himself.

There was no time to waste; now it was certain that Amintor knew they were after him. The weather was still too bad to allow the aerial scouts to bring word of the Baron's current position, and perhaps allow a shortcut. In minutes the pursuit was going on as before, following the trail.

That evening the Baron's own flying reptiles did manage to get into the air for a while, and back to him in his camp, bringing him news of the failed ambush.

At least, he thought, listening to the reports as his beastmaster translated them, at least some ground had been gained on the pursuers. But that gain was certainly overshadowed by the fact that more than a third of his own total force had now been wiped out.

When he had gleaned all the information that he could from the animals through their human trainer, a process that involved many questions and several patient rehearsings, the Baron's face was grave. He had never believed that a leader ought to hide his feelings at all times from his subordinates. A commander in his situation would be thought a madman, or an absolute idiot, if he appeared to be unaffected by the loss of so many people. There was no getting around it. The attempted ambush had wasted nearly a third of his entire force. And the efficiency with which the ambush had been detected and crushed boded ill for the survival of the rest.

Amintor was strongly minded to do an ill turn to whoever was responsible.

There was one ray of hope: his pursuers, whoever they were, did not appear to be able to travel very fast. The reptiles reported that the Baron and his surviving people had been able to gain ground on them since the chase had resumed.

From the scanty description that the winged scouts had been able to provide, he strongly suspected that his pursuer was Prince Mark of Tasavalta. Amintor knew Mark of old, and considered him an enemy, but would have much preferred him as an unsuspecting rather than an active one. And from what the reptiles had been able to communicate about the fight, the Baron had little doubt that the Sword in the Prince's hand was Shieldbreaker, which he was known to possess.

None of this would be good news to Amintor's remaining people, and Amintor had not yet informed them of his conclusions.

He would have to get a look at those who were chasing him to make sure who they were. Much would depend on making sure of that.

Glancing around at the brighter people among his subordinates, the Baron decided that they were probably capable of making the same deductions he had made regarding the opposition they now faced. It would be a mistake to carry honesty too far—one could very easily do that. With an effort he brightened up, told his people what he thought was going on, and began the job of convincing them that they were still going to be able to survive—not only that, but win.

"Well, it can't be any overwhelming army that's coming after us; the flyers couldn't be that far wrong about numbers. And whoever it is, for some reason, is not coming very fast. Very determined, because they broke the ambush—so if they're not moving fast, it's because they absolutely can't."

He looked around him. The faces of his followers still looked grim. Sometimes he wished he could be rid of them all. He added decisively: "We turn east tomorrow. I want to get a look at just what is coming after us, and how many of them."

Amintor's next step was to go into a close conference with his beastmaster and his enchantress to discuss just where the best place might be for this doubling back and observation. The two aides bickered with each other, as usual; neither of them was particularly competent.

The Baron had already rejected the idea of splitting his force into two or three parts, or even scattering it into single trails hoping to reunite at some distant rendezvous. He suspected that if he tried that, the Prince might have some way of singling out and following his—the Baron's—trail. Still, Amintor might try splitting his people up, if everything else failed—but everything else had not failed yet.

His enchantress, having somehow driven the beastmaster away, told Amintor: "The Prince pursues us because we have Woundhealer."

"Likely enough. Likely enough, but we can't be sure of even that as yet. Unless you have some proof in magic of what you tell me . . . ? I thought not. Tomorrow, as I say, we must get a look at him."

And next day, Amintor, tired from a hard ride, refusing to allow his tiredness to show, did manage to get a look. Lying on his belly on the grass atop a gentle hill, he scanned the hunters' formation as they moved along his trail. They were less than a kilometer distant in a direct line, though if they continued simply plodding along his trail they were still many kilometers behind.

The first thing that leaped to the Baron's attention as he inspected the Tasavaltans was the blue-green uniforms, confirming that Prince Mark was indeed his adversary. The second thing was the presence of the litter. Just the kind of all-important clue that the damned idiot reptiles could be expected to ignore.

"Not your usual equipment for a difficult pursuit," he commented to the enchantress, who had crawled up to be at his side. "Considering it in conjunction with the fact that he's trying to get Woundhealer, what is your conclusion?"

The woman said promptly: "That he was coming to the White Temple. That he has come a long way from Tasavalta, bringing with him someone in need of healing. That this person is unable to ride, or at least unable to ride well. That when the Prince reached the Temple, the Sword was already gone. And—"

"Enough, enough. And now I would like to know whether you can confirm something I have heard about the ruling family of Tasavalta, which seems to me quite pertinent to our present situation?"

Magic would not likely be required to answer that. The private affairs of the mighty were a constant topic of discussion among the high and low of all nations.

The enchantress said: "That the Prince's eldest son has been a cripple since birth."

Amintor nodded. He was smiling.

11

ALTERNATELY waking and sleeping all through the night, never quite sure at any given moment whether or not he was dreaming, Zoltan was carried steadily upstream at the pace of a modest walk. He was still sitting in the water and could feel the movement of it around his body, but he had no sensations of wetness or cold. This bizarre mode of transportation was soft and effortless, and whether he was borne up falls or rapids, or along stretches of the river that were almost level, the speed of it was unvarying.

During one of Zoltan's wakeful periods he was clearminded enough to realize that the stream had been maintaining an almost level course for an inexplicable distance. This made him wonder if he was still in the Sanzu, which he remembered as an almost endless string of falls and rapids. This stream might well be one of that river's small tributaries— or, for all he knew, he had been translated entirely to some realm of magic where all things, including rivers, were new and strange.

Zoltan was now wakeful enough to take increasing interest in his mode of travel. The stream itself, he saw from close observation, was continuing to flow normally downhill. Only a small localized swirl or eddy, centered on Zoltan's body and perpetually bearing him along with it, moved in a direction contrary to nature. He supposed it was a weakened water elemental; the strange-looking wizard had hinted at something along that line. There were no other signs of enchantment. The trees and rocks and land along the shores were ordinary-looking objects, even though the total landscape that they made was unfamiliar.

Eventually, as the eastern sky began to gray with morning, the forces that were impelling Zoltan upstream appeared to weaken. First his feet began to drag in mud, and then his bottom thumped against a rock.

Shortly after that first jolt his upstream progress slowed noticeably. Then it stopped altogether and he sank to the bottom.

Enchantment had now vanished totally. He was sitting in the cold water, little more than ankle-deep, of some stream he still could not recognize in the brightening daylight. He was certainly far from home, and lost. But he was free.

Numbly, Zoltan judged that Karel's river-elemental, which must have been propelling him along, had now died, or dissipated, or whatever such powers did when they reached the end of their existence.

But who had that scrawny, crazy, gibbering wizard been? Like someone out of a dream—but it was no dream that here he, Zoltan, was, set free. Was the rescuing wizard some aide or ally of Karel's? That was hard to believe, from the way the peculiar man had talked. Karel himself, in disguise? That was impossible.

Whoever the strange little magician was, Zoltan understood that he owed him his life.

Sitting in the shallow stream, he became suddenly aware of a great thirst and turned himself over on all fours and drank. Then with a sigh of repletion he got stiffly to his feet and looked about him in the light of early morning. Still, nothing about the landscape looked familiar.

All of Zoltan's limbs were tingling now as if he had hardly moved them for a week—which he supposed might be the actual explanation. But his legs were still able to support him. He waded out onto the southern shore of the small stream and started walking, his face toward the morning, assuming vaguely that his home must be somewhere in that direction. He looked ahead of him for the familiar hills but could not see them yet. At least the country was open, and progress easy.

The girl came suddenly into his mind—not that she had ever completely left it. He was freed now of the enchantment that had made her an obsession, but he had not forgotten her. He seemed to remember having seen her change into a fish, and back again.

Probably she wasn't human at all, but only a creation of her human master, the man who had bound Zoltan with spells and thrown him into the cave. Or possibly she owed her existence to that harder-to-define and even more frightening presence that had worn small, arm-sized wings and ridden much larger wings up into the night sky. . . . Zoltan shuddered and looked round him warily in the clear morning. It was hard to believe, here and now, that that had been anything but an evil nightmare.

His imprisonment in the mud-cave had been more than a nightmare. His stomach certainly felt as if he hadn't eaten for a week.

Presently he roused himself from speculation to find that the morning's new sun had somehow come around to his left, and he was walking south.

He corrected his course, but in a few minutes, to his renewed surprise, the sun was on his left again.

This time he stopped and stood thoughtfully for a moment. But there was nothing to do but try to go on.

Again he corrected his course, and this time proceeded carefully, paying attention to his directions at every stride. Soon he realized that he was being guided by a gentle tilting of the ground. Even when the way to the east lay on a gentle downhill slope, the angle of the earth somehow reversed itself where he actually stepped on it. East became a perpetual climb, and south, the easy downhill course. This experience of the tilting earth was similar in a way to what he had felt when he was in the cave; yet in another way this was different, somehow purposeful. South was now always invitingly downhill, though when he walked south he never descended any lower than the surrounding plain. But east was forever uphill, and the slope under his feet became steeper and steeper the longer he tried to persevere in maintaining that direction.

Home lay to the east. If he could be sure of anything he could be sure of that. Zoltan gritted his teeth and persevered. If this enchanted slope got any steeper he was going to have to climb it on all fours. His wet boots were drying now, and his feet had begun to hurt in them, but he plowed on anyway, climbing and climbing. All right, then, he *would* climb on all fours . . .

He had just let his body lurch forward and gripped the earth with his two hands to crawl when a recognizable pair of boots, elongated toes comically turned up, came into view a few meters in front of his nose.

Zoltan looked up to see a familiar figure in storybook wizard's conical hat and figured robe. The wizened face was angrily looking down, the gravelly voice shouted abuse at him.

"Do you want the bad people to have you again, Zoltan? You're a dummy! Don't you ever want to get home to your mother?"

Zoltan stopped, abashed. Slowly he stood up. Still facing east, he had to lean forward to keep his balance. He hadn't realized that this trick was his benefactor's doing also. "Sorry, sir. I'm only *trying* to get home. And my home is to the east of here."

The magician's face paled; no, it wasn't that, it was his whole figure, becoming faintly transparent. Yes, Zoltan could definitely see through the old man's image, out around the edges. But it shouted at him as loudly and vigorously as ever: "Zoltan, you dum-dum, Zoltan! I'm trying to help you! I brought you as far as I could through the water, but now you have to walk. You can't go right home. There's something else you have to do first. Didn't I say that? Didn't I say?"

None of this sounded at all to Zoltan like the sort of thing that any respectable wizard, or any elderly person, ought to shout. But Zoltan, above all, did not want to meet the bad people again.

"Yes sir," he said. And with slumping shoulders he turned and walked on, in the way that he was being guided. It was easy walking that way—it was all downhill. When he looked around with another question, the figure of the wizard was gone again.

Much of the morning had passed. Zoltan's boots—after he had paused to take them off, drain them thoroughly, and dry them as well as possible—were becoming wearable again. Walking south continued to be easy. He thought, from time to time, about trying to turn east again, but so far he hadn't quite dared. So he hiked on through an open but inhospitable landscape, going he didn't know where, and he was getting very hungry. The provisions he had stuffed in his pockets on leaving home had long ago been reduced to watery garbage.

The pins and needles and the stiffness had worked out of his arms and legs by now. But now all of Zoltan's limbs, his whole body, were beginning to grow weak with hunger.

He looked about him hopefully for fruit on the strange low bushes, or for any of the kinds of plants whose roots he knew were edible in a pinch. He had not yet reached the starving stage, where he would be willing to go grubbing after insects, but he wasn't sure that stage was far away. Nothing more appetizing than insects had appeared. And already his thirst was coming back. The land around him did not promise anything in the way of water.

Except—yes. He was coming over a low rise of ground now, and straight ahead of him, perhaps a kilometer away, a short, straight line of fresh trees were just coming into view, like the boundary of an oasis.

Maybe this was why the wizard had insisted that he go south. Keeping the trees in view, Zoltan held a steady pace.

Presently, having crossed what seemed like several extra kilometers of barren landscape, he began to approach the supposed oasis closely. When Zoltan actually came within a stone's throw of the line of trees, he found them low and thick, making up a formidable thorny hedgerow a straight half kilometer or so in length. Their sturdy freshness certainly indicated a nearby source of water.

Zoltan turned at a right angle and walked beside this tall hedge until he came to a small gap, where he cautiously pushed his way through. The barrier was not as thick or difficult as he had expected, and he discovered that he had just crossed the boundary of a surprisingly well-kept farm. The border hedgerow was much more pleasant to look at from inside. From this angle it was a flowering hedge, thick enough to keep livestock from straying, but he could catch glimpses of the desert outside. The barrier did not appear to be at all difficult for a human to push through, once you made up your mind that you really wanted to do it.

Within the outer boundary of trees, the land was divided into fields and plots by shorter, thinner hedges. The entire farm, Zoltan saw, peering around him, extended over at least a square kilometer; it included pastures, orchards, cultivated fields planted in several kinds of crops, and, in the distance, a cluster of farm buildings. There were enough trees near the buildings to partially obscure them.

Zoltan started walking in the general direction of the buildings, along a path that wound gently between the bordered fields. Meat-cattle grazed contentedly in a lush pasture. Then the lane that Zoltan was following broadened, leading him between more short hedges toward the small house and the farmyard. Even more surprising than the cattle and the pasture were the bountiful crops in the well-cultivated fields. Here and there he could see small irrigation ditches, which explained some of the difference between the land of the farm and that outside its boundaries.

At a little distance he beheld a single human figure moving, hoe in hand, working its way methodically down a double row of some kind of vegetables, just where a plot of garden bordered on an orchard.

Zoltan hesitated briefly, then turned aside from the cowpath and entered the field where the lonely worker labored. Treading carefully between the rows of vegetables—noticing in passing how healthy they all looked—he approached the man cautiously and saw nothing in him to be alarmed about. He was a bent figure, somewhat gnarled, with calloused hands and a sunburnt neck. Whether he was landowner, serf, or hired hand was not obvious at first sight; the man was dressed in rough clothing, but Zoltan had plenty of experience with powerful people who were disinclined to wear finery.

The man, intent on his labor, did not notice Zoltan's approach. His back to Zoltan, he kept at his hoeing, the implement in his rugged hands attacking weeds, churning the rich black soil with a regular chuffing sound.

Remembering his manners, Zoltan kicked a clod of earth when he was still a few meters from the man, making a slight noise. Then he cleared his throat and waited.

The man looked round at him with only minor surprise. "Well! What be you doing here, then?" he asked mildly enough. His words came in what was certainly a country dialect, though Zoltan could not place its locality.

"Trying to get home, sir." The *sir* was something of an afterthought; but the man's tone had certainly not sounded like that of a serf or slave.

"Home," said the man, leaning on his hoe. "Ah, home!" he cried, as if now he suddenly understood everything. Then with an air of profundity, he said "Ah!" again and turned away and shot up a long arm. Pulling down a waterskin, obviously his own supply, from where it hung on the stub of a treelimb in the shade, he offered it to Zoltan with a quick gesture. "You've come a far way, then. What's your name?"

"My name is Zoltan. Thank you," he said, wiping his mouth with the back of his hand after the most delicious and invigorating drink he'd ever had in his life. For a moment he'd wondered if it was something more than water.

"Zoltan—good old Tasavaltan name." The man nodded judiciously. "I am called Still, young sir. Just plain Still is quite good enough for me, though it's Father Still that some folk call me. Appears that old age is starting to creep up. But I keep busy and I hardly notice, most days." The old man laughed heartily—Zoltan decided that he must really be an old man after all, despite the vigor of his gardening. "But you'll be wanting food, too—and I've already finished off the last of my lunch. Go on to the house, go on to the house, and she'll take care of you." He accompanied this advice with violent gestures, as if he thought that Zoltan might after all not be able to understand his words.

Zoltan obediently turned and started for the house, then paused uncertainly to look back. He was reassured when the farmer, already hoeing away industriously, waved him on with a motion of his hand and went on working. There was apparently no time to waste.

Back on the cowpath, Zoltan realized that the house was farther off than it had appeared at first—indeed, the whole place now looked even larger than it had at first glance.

As he moved on toward the house Zoltan kept looking for other laborers. He looked to right and left, in one field after another of beautiful crops, but he could see no one. Probably, he thought, most of the hands were still taking their noontime rest under one of these rows of trees. Certainly there had to be a large force of people at work to keep the place in the magnificent condition that it was.

Tall, multicolored flowers of a kind that Zoltan had never seen before surrounded the perfectly kept patch of short lawn right at the front door of the house. Bees were busy here; and the perfume of the flowers was as different as could be from that of the pale blooms along the river. The front of the house was flanked by two shade trees, their foliage starting to turn orange and yellow with the onset of fall. The door was wood, solidly built and painted white, and it stood ajar just slightly, in a hospitable way. Somewhere out of sight, toward the rear of the house, dogs were starting to bark to signal Zoltan's arrival—it sounded more a mindless welcome than a challenge.

There was no bell or knocker on the farmhouse door. Zoltan rapped firmly on the white frame, and immediately the white door, perhaps jarred slightly by his knocking, swung open farther as if in welcome. A sunlit parlor was revealed, furnished with enough chairs and tables for a large family, though at the moment it was unoccupied. Then footsteps, soft but brisk, were coming down a hall.

The woman who emerged from the interior of the house was silver-haired and generously built, garbed in a flower-patterned dress of many bright colors, which was half-hidden by an apron. She looked at Zoltan with an expectant smile, as if she might have been anticipating some messenger who bore good news. Zoltan could not guess whether she was the mistress of this house or only a servant, and for the moment at least it hardly seemed to matter.

He said to her: "The man out there in the field—Still, he said his name was—sent me here. I need—"

He never did get the chance to spell out what he needed. Perhaps his needs were all too obvious. The woman, talking much faster than Zoltan in his present state could follow, swept him in with great gestures of the straw broom in her hand. He followed her to the kitchen, where in a moment the broom had vanished, to be replaced by a plate of small cakes, and then another of sliced melon. Next thing he knew, he was seated in a sturdy wooden chair at a broad wooden table, with plates in front of him. The kitchen was a huge room—the house, he realized, must be a little larger than it had looked from outside. A small fire crackled in the huge cooking hearth, and the air was full of magical vapors, of a kind that the visitor had sometimes experienced in the kitchen at High Manor. Here—he had never been so hungry—the aromas were of doubly concentrated magic.

Mother Still was a large woman, much bulkier than her good man out in the field. But like him she was hard to place in terms of age. Now she was bustling everywhere. For a moment Zoltan thought that she was in two places at once. "Call me Goodwife Still, or Mother Still—it's all one to me, my laddie. Have some cheese; it goes well with that melon."

Zoltan, his mouth full, discovered that it did indeed. Experienced people had told him that if you were really starved it was a mistake to stuff your belly to its limit as soon as you had the chance. But, by all the gods, this was a special case. Maybe starvation that occurred under enchantment wasn't the same as the more dreary, ordinary kinds of the affliction, and required special treatment.

Meanwhile he observed that his hostess was starting—what else?—to cook dinner. The carcass of some small four-legged animal, pale and plump, was being adroitly skewered on a spit.

That Zoltan—he got the impression that it would be the same for anyone else in her presence, or in her house—might have the bad luck to be attacked by hunger appeared to strike the goodwife as a personal affront. The boy, with arrays of dishes growing on the table before him, was bombarded with offers of cold milk to drink—drawn up in a stone crock from some deep well—and a clean fork appeared on the table in front of him, and yet another plate, this one holding a slab of fruit pie that Zoltan, after the first bite, was prepared to swear was the most delicious thing that he had ever tasted.

"A little something to keep you going until dinner's ready." For all the incomprehensible amount of work that she was somehow getting done, Mother Still never seemed to hurry. Now she had joined Zoltan sitting at the table, a mug of tea in her large, roughened hand; and now finally she allowed the talk to shift away from things that he might like to eat or drink. "Is someone chasing you, child? How do you come to be here in this condition?" She was still indignant that the world had treated him so poorly.

Zoltan, who had not realized that his condition was quite so obviously bad, told her the story as best he could, beginning with the strange experience he had shared with the younger children in the cave. Mother Still made appropriate sounds of sympathy as she heard about that and about the magical events that had afflicted Zoltan later on, but he wasn't sure that she really believed him—given the nature of the story he had to tell, he was prepared to understand anyone's not doing so.

But Mother Still asked questions as if she might believe him. When he mentioned the name of Burslem, she frowned and shook her head. The two of them sat there in the kitchen talking for some time, and they were still sitting there when from outside there came the lowing of cattle, a sound that in Zoltan's experience usually accompanied the animals' being driven back to the barn.

He got to his feet, loosened his belt a notch, did his best to suppress a belch, and offered to help bring the cattle in.

Mother Still smiled at him approvingly. "The old man'll be glad of help. Just trot out, then."

He went out the back door and pitched in to help. Still, unsurprised, welcomed the assistance and sent Zoltan out to another field where there were more milk cows that needed prodding. All the animals were fat and healthy; by now Zoltan would have been surprised to find otherwise.

There was a well just outside the kitchen—a cool, stone-lined shaft complete with windlass and bucket—and when the cattle had been brought into the barn Zoltan hauled up two pails of water and carried them into the kitchen and set them beside the big stone sink. It was the kind of thing he hated doing when at home, but he'd plenty of experience of it for all that. There weren't always a lot of servants ready to wait on you at High Manor.

Presently dinner was announced, and Zoltan, after a thorough washup, reached the table right on the heels of Still. He was hungry again—it was as if all the food that he'd eaten since his arrival had already packed itself away into his bones and blood and muscles, leaving his stomach ready for more.

Dinner was roast meat, with delicious accompaniments—bread, vegetables, pickles, more pie—and conversation.

"Just the two of us here now. Children all grown and gone."

Zoltan had seen enough farms to recognize that this place was a gem, and he said so several times. It was obvious to him that there had to be more workers around somewhere, a bunch of them, but somehow he didn't want to come right out and ask where they all were. He just wanted to get through the rest of this day without any further complications.

An oil-lamp was lighted, making the parlor almost as cheery as it had been during the day, and Mother Still—somehow, incredibly, she had managed to clean all those dirty dishes already—sat down with her knitting.

Meanwhile Still had reached up to a high shelf above the mantel and brought down some kind of a board game with pegs; he challenged Zoltan to a game and started to explain the rules even as he set up the board for play. Zoltan, trying to make sense of it, could hardly manage to stifle his yawns.

"Better sleep in late tomorrow, young one. Then, soon as you're able to get up and about, we'll set you some chores."

"I'll do chores. I'll do them"—yawn—"for you tomorrow. But I don't see how I can stay here any longer than that."

No one reacted to that statement. It was as if they might not have heard it. Mother Still suddenly uttered a wish that she were back on what she called the big farm; "but then we have to do as best we can."

Struggling to stay awake, Zoltan indulged his curiosity. "Where's the big farm?"

A hearty laugh from Still. "It's way out in the country, laddie. That's the best place for them. But, it's a little harder to get to than this one. And we thought there might be visitors."

His wife shook her head, as if her husband had made an objectionable joke. Or, more like it, as if he had repeated an old one once too often. Then she smiled at Zoltan and changed the subject. "So, your uncle Mark is Prince of Tasavalta now."

"Yes, ma'am. He has been for the last eight years," Zoltan acknowledged, wondering. "Do you know him?" Zoltan thought that would not be strange. His own father had died as a low-ranking soldier, and he could remember something very like poverty in his early childhood. Uncle Mark had not always moved in royal circles, and to his nephew

those earlier years of his uncle's life had always seemed the most interesting.

"Must be the same Mark that Andrew knew," the old man commented abstractedly while taking another of Zoltan's painted game pegs
off the board.

"Well, of course, Father!" Mother Still sounded patiently and mildly
exasperated. "I do wish you would try to keep up, where there's family
connections and all."

Family connections? Zoltan thought. But he was too sleepy to think
about it much.

"I keep up, Mother," Still grumbled. "I keep up pretty well. Andrew's the one that Yoldi married. Rest her soul."

Andrew, in Zoltan's experience, was a fairly common name. Yoldi
was not, though. In fairly recent family history—things that had happened after Zoltan was born, but when he was still too young to remember them now—there had been Dame Yoldi, the almost legendary sor-
ceress and companion of Kind Sir Andrew. Could these two simple old
farm people be talking about that Yoldi and that Andrew? Zoltan didn't
really believe they could, and anyway he was too tired and too confused
to ask.

But now, incredibly, Mother Still was talking about her late sister,
who, it seemed, had unfortunately got mixed up in being an enchantress, and all that kind of thing. And it sounded as if her sister were
Yoldi. Zoltan couldn't credit it. He was half sleep and knew he was
getting into some kind of hopeless muddle.

"And in the end it killed her." Mother Still shook her gray head,
knitting furiously. She looked at Zoltan as if he was the one arguing
with her. "No, laddie, that kind of a life is not for me. I'm too plain for
that."

Father Still, squinting into the yellow lamplight that fell across the
gaming table, nodded patient agreement.

Then he put out a gnarled hand and deftly cleaned the last of Zoltan's
pieces off the board.

There was a steep stair and a small, upstairs room at the top of it;
Zoltan was sure before he saw the room and bed that they would be
clean and warm and comfortable. In the moment before sleep came, he
had just time to ponder whether he would be better off starting for
home right after chores in the morning, or resting here another day.
And eating one or two more meals of Goodwife Still's cooking . . .

* * *

In the morning, Zoltan slept comparatively late. On awaking, in the broad daylight of a fully-risen sun, he jumped up, feeling somewhat guilty for having stayed so long in bed, and hurried downstairs. Mother Still was in the kitchen, and he asked to be given chores.

"That's fine, laddie. There're still eggs to be picked up in the henhouse." Mother Still added that her good man was already out in the fields.

After bringing in the eggs and polishing off a gargantuan breakfast, Zoltan got directions from Mother Still as to where to find her husband and went out to join him at his labors. Zoltan felt he could hardly refuse at least one full day's work to these people who had saved his life.

This morning, as it turned out, the job was harvesting gourds and pumpkins, which grew intermingled in the same field. A small, phlegmatic loadbeast pulled a cart along while Still and Zoltan cut the fruit from vines and lifted it into the cart. As before, there were no other human workers to be seen. Zoltan felt his scalp creep faintly. All right, some kind of magic was at work here. He should have realized it yesterday; he would have realized it if he hadn't been exhausted and half-starved when he arrived.

The great wizard Karel had told him that it was easy to tell good magic from bad, provided you could get a good look at all of the results. The results here, as far as Zoltan could see, were anything but bad.

It didn't seem right to simply ignore the situation. Straightening up to stretch his back, Zoltan remarked: "Seems to me awfully unlikely that two people could manage to run a farm this big without any help."

The man grunted, lifting a big pumpkin into the cart. "Can always use some help."

"But you don't really *need* any?"

Still appeared to be faintly amused. "Laddie, I live in the real world, and I expect to work. Long as there's work here, I expect to get it done. My share of it, anyway." He rapped the loadbeast on the rump, getting it to move along.

Zoltan didn't push the subject any further. Maybe there were kinds of beneficial magic that were spoiled if you talked about them.

As he and Still were returning to the house for their noontime meal they were both surprised to see a traveling wagon, with two riding-beasts in harness, parked on the grass immediately in front of the house. The animals were lean and worn, as if they had been hard-driven. Two people, a middle-aged couple in clothing that had once been expensive but was now worn and stained as if from a long journey, were standing beside the wagon, talking to Mother Still. The goodwife had evidently just come out of the house because a kitchen towel was still in her hand.

She turned her head and called out cheerfully: "Father, Zoltan, we have more visitors!"

The newly-arrived man and woman looked around. Zoltan saw that the man was holding an elaborate leather swordbelt and scabbard out in front of him, supporting it awkwardly in both arms, as if he did not quite know what to do with it and was ready and eager to give it away. A large black hilt projected from the scabbard.

Now the man, still holding out the black-hilted weapon and its harness, approached Zoltan and the farmer. When he came closer Zoltan could see that he looked as worn as the team that drew his wagon.

"Your good wife here," the visitor said hoarsely, "doesn't understand. We have been commanded to bring this weapon here. So here it is. It's your problem now." And he thrust the weapon toward Still with a commanding gesture.

Still, however, was in no hurry to accept the present, but stood with arms folded as if he did not yet understand what this was all about.

Zoltan was now close enough to the black hilt to get a very good look at it, and he could feel his scalp creep. He had been allowed, once or twice, to enter the royal treasury in the Palace at Sarykam, and he had seen Swords before. The white symbol on the hilt of this one was a small, winged dragon.

"You've got to take it." The man from the wagon sounded agonized. He shook the swordbelt at the farmer so that the massive buckle jingled faintly. "We've put up with all we can. You people must be wizards, warriors, something. You'll know what to do with this. I've been assured that you won't hurt us. I'm only a trader, myself. My wife is only my wife."

"Why do you bring us this weapon?" Still asked, sounding suddenly not so much like a farmer. "Wasn't just by chance you came here, was it?"

"No. No. Because of him. He drove us to it." The visitor looked around, as if hopeful of being able to see the person he referred to, but not really surprised when he could not. "I mean the little old man. A little old wizard. In peculiar clothing, as if he were made up for some part on the stage. He's been driving us crazy, hounding us for days and days. He wouldn't accept the Sword himself when I wanted to hand it over to him. Oh, no, wasn't able to carry anything himself, he said. I wasn't about to argue with him, not after the way he picked up the road under our wagon and shook it like a clothesline. So he told us where to find the Sword and made us dig it up and bring it here. And now it's yours, because I'm giving it to you whether you want it or not." And the man glared at Still and Zoltan with a courage obviously born of desperation.

"Little old wizard, hey?" Still grimaced as if he found that description distasteful. And very puzzling. "Did this feller tell you *why* we were supposed to get a Sword?"

The man's arms, holding out the swordbelt, sagged with exhaustion. "He said we had to bring it here because Prince Mark needed it. I suppose he means Prince Mark of Tasavalta, that's the only one I ever heard of . . . and someone here would take the Sword on to him."

Still continued to take thought. He stroked his chin, almost like a rustic considering an offer for his pumpkins. Almost.

"It's taken us weeks to get here!" the man holding the Sword agonized.

"Prince Mark needs it?" Zoltan asked.

The visitor, with new hope, switched his attention to Zoltan. "Yes! That's what the wizard tells me!"

"Then I will take it to him." And Zoltan reached out for the Sword. He had handled weapons before, but still somehow the weight surprised him; no wonder the man's arms were tired.

The man babbled with gratitude; his wife, in the wagon, urged him to get in and drive. "Let's get out of here!"

But they were not to be allowed to leave that quickly. Goodwife Still had them in charge now. They could, and did, protest that they wanted to depart at once, but protesting got them nowhere. Visitors to this farm could not be allowed to go away hungry—that was some kind of a law. And besides—this was undeniable—their team needed attention. "See to the poor animals, Father!"

Mother Still led the couple, who were still muttering objections, into her house.

Zoltan stood holding the Sword in its belt while Still, who had already started to unharness the team, paused to watch him.

Zoltan's right hand smothered the white dragon. The sheath, wherever it had come from, was beautiful. But then its beauty, that of merely human work, was eclipsed as the bright blade came slowly out of it.

Seeing the Swords in the Tasavaltan treasury was one thing, but drawing and holding one was something else.

After a few moments Still asked him: "You'll be taking that to your uncle, then?"

Zoltan nodded.

"Reckon you're grown-up enough to do your duty, if you be grown-up enough to see what it is."

12

MARK raised his right hand abruptly, and the dusty, weary column behind him reined in, some of the animals stumbling as they came to a halt.

The single, small shape in the late morning sky, approaching from dead ahead, was not one of their own Tasavaltan scouts returning. Already it was possible to see that the set of the wings was wrong for that.

It was one of the reptilian enemy scouts. But this one was not content to circle high overhead and observe.

The creature flew straight for Mark, and from an altitude of about fifty meters—so close that stones and arrows were on the verge of being loosed at it—it dropped something, a small packet that came plummeting down almost at the feet of the Prince's riding-beast. In the next moment the messenger was spiraling upward to a safe altitude, where it drew wide circles in the sky, as if waiting to see how the communication it had brought might be received.

"Why do the bastards always use reptiles?" Ben asked of no one in particular.

"Because," said the chief magician, "reptiles have a certain affinity for demons." He gestured to an assistant.

" 'Ware poison, Highness! Let me look at that present first!" The aide cried out and in an instant had swung down from his mount and carefully taken charge of the object that had been dropped. It was a small leather packet, not big enough to hold much more than a folded sheet of paper.

When all due magical precautions had been taken and the packet was opened, the contents proved to be exactly that. And when the folded paper was opened, it revealed a neatly lettered message.

> Salutations to Prince Mark, from an old acquaintance:
> I am prepared to trade Swords with you. Yours for mine, Woundhealer for Shieldbreaker, even up, fair and square. Consider that it is impossible for you to overtake me now, and that we should both benefit from such a trade.
> There has been fair dealing in the past between the two of us personally, and there is no reason why that cannot continue now.
> Look atop the next cliff to which my trail brings you. Someone will be there to talk about a truce and a conference.
>
> Amintor

Mark read the message through once more and then read it yet once again. As he read he knew a sinking feeling located somewhere near his stomach because he recognized that he was seriously tempted by the offer. Whatever the worth of Shieldbreaker might be, it was never going to heal his son.

By this time Ben had ridden up beside him and was openly reading the message over Mark's shoulder. Others had crowded around, and the Prince let them have the paper to pass around among them and read. Already Ben was profaning gods and demons, and a murmur of derision was beginning among the others present at the idea of Amintor's even proposing such a trade.

But Ben perhaps realized the true state of affairs. He was not smiling, and he was watching Mark closely.

Mark said: "It won't hurt us to look atop the next cliff, as the note suggests."

An old soldier was openly surprised. "It won't?"

At once a lively discussion sprang up among Mark's aides as to what kind of treacherous ambush the former Baron was likely to be preparing for them now.

The beastmaster advised: "The best you could possibly say for this note is that it's an effort to delay us."

Mark thought that as such it would be unnecessary. If Amintor was already somewhere beyond the next cliff, as he must be, then he had gained high ground; and if he was not actually as far ahead as Mark had feared, he certainly had the advantage of terrain. There was no way the

Prince was going to catch him now—not unless Mark were willing to leave his son's litter behind and set out with picked riders at full speed. Then it might be possible.

He nodded, listening to the ongoing outrage of his friends at the suggested trade. Then he said to them: "And yet—I can remember times in the past when the Baron *did* deal fairly."

"When he thought it was in his interest to do so!"

"Of course." The Prince looked at the trail ahead, squinting into the bright sky. "But I think that I will talk to him anyway. We'll be on guard against another ambush. And a few words cannot hurt."

One of the magicians muttered some words of doubt about that. But it was not a reasoned objection, even in terms of magic, and Mark ignored it.

The column advanced again. Presently, as the designated cliff grew near, a lone figure did appear on its low crest. The man was well above the advancing Tasavaltans and so out of their likely range of success with bow or sling; yet he was not too far away to conduct a shouted conversation.

Mark might not have been able to recognize that figure at first glance had he not been expecting it. Baron Amintor, never thin, had bulked fatter in the past eight years.

The figure waved, and called in a powerful, familiar voice. "Halloo! Do you have my message?"

The Prince rode a little closer before he shouted back. "Why should I trade anything with you? How do I even know what you're carrying in that scabbard?"

And even as he uttered the words he realized that the man before him was wearing two swords, one on each side.

The Baron, right-handed and therefore a little awkward with the motion, drew the blade at his right side and held it up. The hilt remained all but invisible, smothered in his grip; but the sun caught on the blade, and even at that distance his claim to have one of the Twelve Swords became quite convincing.

Again his voice came firmly to Mark across the gulf between. "As to why we ought to trade, Prince, I think I can leave that up to you to answer. Surely you can think of at least one good reason. Why is your elder son not riding at your side today?"

Just behind Mark, Ben's voice, sounding like a rumble of distant thunder, began to swear.

Amintor had paused for a shouted reply that did not come. Now he called: "If you are worried about what I plan to do with the Sword of Force when it comes into my possession, be assured that I have no ambitions ever to be anything more than a minor brigand. Not at my time of life. I will do nothing that might inconvenience in any way the royal family of Tasavalta—or their armies—that is the farthest thing from my intentions. Still, the Sword I hold is mine now, and I do not propose to give it up for nothing."

"How much gold do you want for it?" Mark heard himself calling back.

"No, Prince. Not gold. I don't think you can be carrying enough of that in your little train there. No, I have told you what I want, and I do not intend to bargain."

"If Your Highness is minded to do business with that man," said the disapproving voice of one of Mark's magicians, "then let him come into our camp alone, with the Sword, under a flag of truce. And let him loan us its power, for as long as it will take to treat Prince Adrian. You might ask him what price he will accept for that."

Mark, shouting, put the proposition to the Baron.

"Why I might do that," the answer came booming back. "I might. I should warn you, though, that my price for such a loan will be exactly the same as for the Sword itself. And if I am there in your camp, alone, how is our trade to be carried out?"

"How is it to be carried out in any case?"

"I have some ideas on that subject," yelled Amintor, "that I believe you will find satisfactory. And let me repeat, after the trade is made, I have no plans to do anything that will disturb you in any way. My modest ambitions will take me in another direction entirely."

Mark and his aides now fell into a low-voiced conference. There was of course no reason to think that the rogue wouldn't lie, and the Prince's advisers were unanimous in rejecting the idea of trying to conclude such a trade as the Baron proposed. At the same time, they had to admit there was a certain plausibility in what Amintor said.

The vision of Adrian was in Mark's mind when he turned back to face Amintor; but he could feel at his back the uneasiness of those who could not see that vision with the eyes of a father. He knew they were wondering why he didn't reject out of hand the idea that such a trade might be possible.

Yet still the Prince hung back from complete acceptance. At last he shouted back: "I must think about it!"

The Baron's distant figure nodded, a generous gesture visible at long range.

"Think wisely, and well," his return shout counseled, "but do not think too long. My business, such as it is, requires that I depart these regions as soon as possible. Let your shadow lengthen by only a hand, and I'll expect an answer. Shout again when you are ready."

With that, the figure on the clifftop turned round nimbly and disappeared. Mark supposed that a riding-beast might be waiting just over the crest.

The first move the Prince made was to redeploy his own troops so they should not be where Amintor had just seen them. Then Mark set out a double guard and again called all of his chosen advisers into a council. He was disregarding the deadline of a hand's change in his shadow's length; shadows were starting to disappear altogether as clouds gathered for what might well be another afternoon of rain and difficult aerial scouting. Anyway, Amintor was the one who had suggested a truce and proposed a trade. That meant the Baron was truly interested in such a deal and was not going to ride away while a chance of it still existed.

The people with Mark were still unanimous in their opposition to the idea.

His magicians, having now investigated the matter in their own way, advised him that the Sword the Baron offered was indeed Woundhealer —the conclusion made matters no easier for Mark in making up his mind.

The cavalry officer pressed him: "With neither side trusting the other, Highness, how could it be arranged, assuming you were willing to go through with it?"

"There's probably some way to manage that."

"You will pardon me if I speak frankly, sir."

"Go ahead."

"I think you cannot be serious about wanting to give away such an advantage in war."

Ben had perhaps the most powerful argument. "It may be true that our friend over there is only a brigand now. Probably he is. But if he had Shieldbreaker at his side, to go with his smooth tongue, who can say what he might become? I don't believe for a moment all that about his 'time of life.' "

A magician chimed in. "And, once he has the Sword of Force, he might be able to trade or sell it to someone else. Someone who does have an army, and ambitions."

"What was that other sword that he was wearing, I wonder? An ordinary blade, maybe, or—?"

"You are the magicians, not I. Discover the answer if you can, and tell me. If you cannot, I must make up my mind without knowing."

Mark had answered firmly, but he felt a chill. Complications, unpleasant possibilities, were piling up. Things he hadn't thought of before, in his absorption with the problem of his son. Still, he remained stubbornly unwilling to give up the idea of the trade.

He could think of at least one argument to put in on the other side. "We know how to fight against Shieldbreaker."

Ben scowled. "Aye, and so must many others. Including Amintor himself, even if he hasn't yet shared the secret with his followers. Are you trying to say the Sword of Force is of little value? Consider how well it served you yesterday."

There was no arguing with that. But Mark would not let himself be argued out of trying to make the trade. He said: "It's vital to the whole realm that Adrian should be healed. It's not just that he's my son."

The others were silent. But he could see in their faces the grudging admission that the point was valid.

Ben was not through arguing. "Is there any reason to think that Amintor does not know how to fight against the Sword as well as we do?"

"Those troops he left to ambush us—"

"When he set up the ambush I'll bet he didn't yet know who was following him, and he didn't have any idea that he was up against the Sword of Force. You'll find he deploys his people differently the next time he tries it. There'll be two men, at least, unarmed so the Sword can't hurt them, ready to jump on you and drag you from your mount. Others, well-armed, close around those two, to protect them from your armed friends."

Mark forced himself to smile. "You make it sound easy."

Ben shook his head stubbornly. "Not easy, but it would be possible. If Vulcan could be overcome that way, you're not too tough."

The Prince and his old adviser argued on while the rest of the council, though agreeing still with Ben, sat by in stubborn silence. The more the arguments went on, the more Mark favored trying to make the trade. None of those who objected to it were able to suggest another way in which he might obtain the Sword of Healing for his son.

Ben got up angrily at last, turned his back on the Prince, and walked away.

Mark glared after him in black anger. But he did nothing about the snub. Instead he mounted and rode back to the approach to the cliff where he had last communicated with Amintor. Reining in his mount, he called out in a great voice.

There was no answer. He called again, roaring in a voice even louder than before.

Stung by a sudden apprehension, he rallied his people to him and spurred up onto another rise of land nearby.

There, in the distance, through oncoming mist and rain, he could see a group of riders that must be Amintor's band, traveling at good speed along a road.

Even as Mark was getting his column slowly into motion again, a flying scout came in to report that the enemy were making good time into the distance and gave no sign of wanting any more conferences.

"After them!"

But within the hour it became apparent that as long as Mark's troops were hampered by the litter, he had no hope at all of overtaking the other party.

13

NEAR midnight in a high tower of the Palace at Sarykam, Karel, the chief wizard of the house of Tasavalta, dreamed.

Karel's dreams were often very much stronger and stranger than those of other men, and the visions he endured this night were no exception.

He saw the small Prince Adrian lying as still and pale as death in his small bed inside a tent. He saw Prince Mark riding into battle, surrounded by a furiously spinning profusion of Swords, all the Swords there were in the universe and more. And in his dreams the wizard Karel heard the roaring of an unseen river in flood and saw young Prince Zoltan struggling against strange monsters.

Then came darkness and silence. Not the cessation of the dream, but an interval of empty night contained within it. And then, presently, as if he were emerging from deep shadow, the powerful wizard Karel beheld huge trees, of a kind that even his waking eyes had never seen; and now he could see the river that had roared in flood, and the serpent Yilgarn that lay in wait for everyone at the end of the world to swallow gods and men together. The serpent in the dream was trying to swallow the mightiest river in the world, and in turn the river tried to strangle the serpent and kept on running always to the sea.

That scene faded. Karel twitched in his bed, in his high lonely chamber in the royal Palace of Tasavalta; and the benevolent guardians that never left him by day or by night, the invisible powers that he, like other wizards good and evil, relied upon against his enemies, tried to keep the worst of his dreams from gaining too much hold over him. But there were limits on how much his powers could do.

The wizard, as helpless in his own sleep as ordinary men might be in theirs, dreamt on. Against a sky aglow with fantastic stars and comets, he saw the griffin that flew by midnight, and he saw who rode upon the griffin's back.

Karel woke up when his dream showed him that. His body jolted upright in a moment, and he was screaming like an abandoned child.

For a long moment he did not know who he was or where he was. Fear had dissolved everything. He sat there in his narrow bed, trying to control his sobbing breath and listening to the night wind that howled around the high stone corners of the Palace tower that held his room.

It had been only a dream. Only a dream. But the wizard was still afraid, still terrified, because he knew what the dream meant.

Once upon a time it had been possible to confine the worst things in the world in a dungeon under the world. But no one, not even an Emperor's son, could do that now.

Princess Kristin, too, was wakeful on this night. There were no dreams for her unless they came in the mere sound of the wind as it moaned around the carven stones. To keep her thoughts from being snatched away by the wind she listened to the surging surf of autumn crashing remotely in the darkness. As a child she had loved falling asleep to the sound of that autumnal surf.

But tonight sleep was far away. She got out of bed, went to look in on little Stephen, and found him sleeping peacefully, as ever untroubled by what the night side of the world could do. On her way back to her own chamber the Princess paused to glance at another small bed, this one empty. The scrolled-up storybook that everyone had forgotten to pack for Adrian lay on the bedside table. His mother, gazing at the bed and book, was mortally certain that Adrian, wherever he and his father might be at the moment, was having a seizure. And she was not there to hold and comfort him.

That was a foolish thought. How could she be there?

She had just returned to her own room and was about to get back into bed when a familiar tap came at the door. One of her maids was there to tell the Princess that her uncle Karel was at the door of the royal suite saying it was vital that he see her now.

Suppressing her fears, Kristin quickly put on a robe over her night-dress and went to greet her uncle in a sitting room, where the servant had already brought out an Old-World lamp.

By that mellow and steady light, a signal that the world could somehow be controlled, the old man first hastened to reassure her that the things she must fear most had not happened—it was not irredeemable disaster to her husband or her oldest son that brought him to her door at such an hour.

The old man sighed. "Still, certain things have happened. I have had visions, and I decided that the telling of them had better not wait until morning."

"Then tell them to me. I am ready to hear them."

He sat opposite her, on the other side of a small table, with the lamp turned to a subtle glow, almost between them. "Kristin. I am going to say some names. Tell me if any of them mean anything to you."

"Say on."

"Deathwings. The Master. The Ancient One."

She considered each name carefully, as seemed to be her duty, then signed that they were strange to her.

"He has gone by other names as well." Karel rubbed his sleep-tousled hair. "He has at least one other name, very powerful, that is very much older—and I would give much to know it. But I know now that he is still alive, and actively our enemy."

"The Dark King?"

Her uncle shook his head. "Would that it were only he."

"Only? Who is it, then? Tell me! What is the danger?"

Karel seemed almost at a loss to explain. "The danger is himself, and that he must be our enemy," he said at length. "I am talking about an incredibly ancient and evil—and powerful—magician. I had thought that he was dead, many centuries ago. Everyone thought so, as far as I am aware. But he has somehow—I do not know how—managed to survive into the present. It would take me all night to tell you all I know and suspect about him, and the telling would help you very little."

"I see," she said, and wondered if she did.

"I am afraid you don't see," her mentor told her sharply. "You cannot. Perhaps it was foolish of me to wake you in this way. I can see only a little, and . . . you think I mean that he is merely old. That would not disturb me so. There are others who have achieved centuries."

Something prickled down the back of Kristin's neck and then went on down her spine. "What do you mean, then?"

"If the Beastlord Draffut is still alive," said Karel above the howling wind outside, "he will be able to identify this man—if the one of whom

I speak can still be called a man. Probably no other being on the planet except the Great Worm Yilgarn has survived so long."

"So, what are we to do?" the Princess asked.

"What we can. Get your husband back here, to begin with. We must contend now with greater problems than a healing."

She said: "I had word upon retiring—I was going to tell you tomorrow—Zoltan's riding-beast has been found, unharmed. It was grazing along the Sanzu, not twenty kilometers from the cave." There could be no doubt of which cave the Princess meant. "The saddle was still on it."

"But no clue to where the boy himself might be?"

"Nothing."

"I will want to look at that riding-beast tomorrow," said Karel abstractedly. Suddenly the Princess noticed that he looked very old. "About the Ancient One of whom I spoke—I am sorry that I woke you tonight; there is nothing we can do immediately."

"It doesn't matter. I couldn't sleep."

"I must warn you, though. He is truly abroad in the world again, and there is no way that I can match him. Nor can any other magician who lives today. Only the Swords themselves, perhaps, will stand above his power. My hope is that the Ancient One will busy himself with other matters and not turn against us directly yet. That he will attack us only through his surrogates, Burslem and others."

"As you say," said Kristin, "we will do what we must and what we can. Beyond that it is all in the hands of Ardneh."

"I would," said Karel, "that Ardneh were still alive."

He arose from his chair, slowly and heavily, and turned as if to depart. Then he faced her again. "Tell me about Rostov. What is the General planning to do tomorrow?"

"Working on ways to use the army more efficiently in hunting for Zoltan, and patrolling the frontiers. Our army is not very large these days, as you know. I'm considering the idea of sending reinforcements after Mark. The news his birds have brought in has not been reassuring."

The wizard nodded. "Let me talk with you again in the morning before you issue orders. I am going to sleep no more tonight."

"Nor I, I think. Good night."

In the morning there was more news by flying messenger, none of it particularly good. Certain other units of the army were still being deployed into the area beyond High Manor and the surrounding hills, where Swordface had been found. A renewed and expanded search was being pressed in that area.

And then a message came in from Mark, informing his wife that the Sword he had sought was stolen from the Temple—and he was taking their son with him and going after it.

The Princess passed on the news to her advisers. And then she tried to pray to Ardneh.

14

ON the evening of the day on which his hand first drew the Sword of Heroes from its sheath, Zoltan told his hosts that he intended to leave the farm in the morning, taking the Sword with him. "My uncle needs it, if what we have been told is true. As I must believe it is. I don't know where to find him, but I must try."

He was half expecting the old people to try to argue him out of that course of action—to tell him that the news about Uncle Mark, like the Sword itself, had come to him in a strange way and ought to be distrusted. Zoltan had his own argument ready: he couldn't take that chance. But the Stills did not argue. They only promised him, calmly, such help as they could manage.

Early in the morning Mother Still called Zoltan into her pantry, where from a shelf devoted to remedies she took down several small jars and packages for him to carry with him on his journey. These medicines she labeled carefully and packed into a bundle. Meanwhile Father Still was making preparations of a different kind. He said he thought he knew where there was a saddle in the barn, and he expected he could spare one loadbeast from the harvest.

Saddlebags and a roll of blankets appeared from somewhere. And in the kitchen, Zoltan was loaded down with food until he had to cry a halt, fearing that his loadbeast would be staggered with the burden.

Approaching that animal for the first time, Zoltan thought he could see why Father Still had been so sure it could be spared from the farm. It was an aged and bony beast, with a considerable amount of gray in its brown coat, and the farmer had to expend much tugging and swearing just to get it out of the barn. Under ordinary conditions the appearance of this mount would have been enough to discourage Zoltan from starting even the simplest journey. Even the finest farm animal was not the kind of beast you could ride out on thinking seriously of adventure, and this creature was not the finest. Once he was mounted, the thick shaggy hide and hard rib cage under him felt as if they might be impervious to beatings, if and when he should have resort to that method of obtaining greater speed. And the saddle, now that he got a good look at it, was an old one and a poor one, with the additional drawback that it had doubtless been designed for a riding-beast. It seemed in some danger of sliding from the animal's back at every jarring step.

But Zoltan accepted as courteously as he could the gifts that were meant to help him, and at last all was ready for his departure. With his new Sword hung from his waist upon its fancy belt and Farmer Still walking ahead to show him the way, Zoltan rode to the gate, ready to push on.

The farm, Zoltan discovered, had one real gate to the outside world. He had never seen that gate until now because it was on the opposite side of the farm from where he'd come in.

Mother Still, too, had ungrudgingly taken time out from her work to come as far as the gate with Zoltan and bid him farewell.

Father Still, on parting, gave Zoltan directions and advice. His uncle Mark ought to be somewhere between here and Tasavalta—especially if, as seemed likely, Mark was out in that area searching for his missing nephew. And, if Mark truly was in need of Dragonslicer, it stood to reason that he was, or was about to be, in some kind of trouble with a dragon. Large dragons, the rare few that survived to grow into the landwalker stage, were the only kind that meant real trouble, and one thing large dragons always needed was plenty of water. The only way to get plenty of water in this country was from one of the relatively few streams that crossed it. Anyone who had trouble with a dragon would have it near a stream.

"Simple enough? Hey?" The farmer grinned at his own logic.

Zoltan had to admit there was a certain sense to it.

Now Zoltan's route, according to this scheme, was also simple. Once outside the gate, he had only to follow the boundary hedge of the farm around its perimeter until he came to running water, the stream that was here partially diverted for irrigation purposes. Then, if he followed that tumbling creek downstream, he'd find that it flowed into the Sanzu. Following that river upstream, in turn, would bring him back at last to

Tasavalta. If Zoltan went that way and still failed to encounter his uncle Mark, he would have done the best he could, and he ought at least to be able to find his way home again with the Sword-treasure that he'd been given.

The main gate of the farm, pulled easily open now by man and wife, was a high and sturdy construction of wood and twisted iron with decorations of what looked to Zoltan like ivory and horn. Vines with shiny green leaves grew over all. Only when the portal was opened to let Zoltan out did the road on the outside become visible. The couple who had brought the Sword to Zoltan, once more greatly impatient to leave, had this morning followed him to the gate in their wagon. Their team, after one night of rest and food, looked ready to go again.

The road outside the gate led straight away from the farm, and the man in the wagon whipped up his team and sped that way at once, without looking back.

Zoltan's path immediately diverged from the road. The gate closed promptly behind him, at which time his loadbeast decided to stop so suddenly that it nearly pitched him over its head. He kicked the animal in the ribs and got it to amble forward.

The Sword at his side swung as he rode, banging awkwardly against his leg and the animal's flank. Zoltan could wish he had been required to carry Wayfinder or Coinspinner instead. From what he had heard of the powers of those two, either would be able to guide him in short order to Uncle Mark. But Dragonslicer told him nothing as to which way he should be going or what he should be trying to do. Its powers were very specialized.

He wondered what sort of dragon Uncle Mark was going to have to fight. Until now Zoltan had never even seen a dragon at all, except for contemptible small-fry, the almost froglike early stages. And even those he had glimpsed but rarely.

There was no problem in finding the stream he was to follow. Leaping down from one small tumbling rapids to another, it looped close to the farm's hedge-fence and then away again. From the quiet intermediate pool at the exact boundary, a ditch, barred from the outside world by its own grating—a simple barrier to keep cattle from wandering out —drank from the stream and led some of its water away inside the hedge. The volume of the little river did not appear to be much diminished by this drain and remained considerably larger than the Sanzu was near its source. Why, Zoltan wondered, couldn't the river-elemental have delivered him here?

But there was no point in wondering about that. He kicked his loadbeast in the ribs again and journeyed on, now following the river downstream.

Twice before nightfall he stopped to eat, using up some of his excess baggage of provisions. During his second rest stop he scanned the sky and realized that he was now under the surveillance of an aerial scout. The creature was too far away when Zoltan first saw it for him to be able to tell whether it was a friend or an enemy. Its presence was not accidental, for it kept him in sight, but did not come any closer.

When darkness overtook Zoltan he continued riding for a while, hoping to shake off the hostile observer. Progress was difficult, and he lost sight of the flyer in the night sky. After an hour Zoltan gave up and pitched camp, letting his loadbeast drink from the stream and then tethering it to a bush. He unrolled his blankets nearby and forbore to make a fire.

Suddenly he felt very much alone. He wished for Uncle Mark and the search party. Failing that, he wished that the crazy magician would reappear, even if it was only to favor him with another lecture.

The voice of the tumbling stream provided a kind of company. The stars had turned through several hours above him when a more purposeful splashing woke Zoltan up.

He knew somehow what he was going to see even before he turned his head. He could just perceive the fish-girl, or rather part of her. One eye, some hair, part of a bare, white shoulder in the light of moon and stars.

She was about ten meters from Zoltan, and this time he could see with certainty that she was sitting right on the bank of the stream. It was plain, too, that she was swishing not feet but a fishtail in the water. Her dark hair, already drying, fell down over her very human breasts.

The girl only sat there, looking directly at him, but saying nothing.

Go away. He formed the words but could not say them. With vast relief he made sure that he no longer felt a hopeless compulsion to jump up and pursue her, as he had before. He felt a fear of her, contending with his curiosity, but so far the fear was manageable.

Nothing happened. Her eyes still regarded him. He could not read the expression on her face.

Zoltan rose slowly to his feet. "What do you want? Who are you? I'm not going to chase after you anymore."

At last the girl spoke. "You don't have to chase me anymore. And I am glad. I didn't want to make you do that, but I had no choice. I was enslaved to the Ancient One. But now I have been set free."

"The Ancient One?"

"A wizard. A very bad man. You must have seen him, on the night of that day when you first saw me. But he can't use me any longer. Someone helped me to get free."

"Someone?"

She moved one white arm in a graceful, puzzled gesture. "A strange little man. I think he helped you, too."

"Yes. The one who helped me is strange, all right." Zoltan shifted his position. "Who are you, then?" he repeated.

"I don't know who I am." The voice of the mermaid, suddenly pitiful and ghostly, shifted into a strange, unfamiliar accent. It brought a small shiver along Zoltan's spine. It was as if only now had the girl in front of him become completely real.

"But are you . . ." He couldn't quite bring himself to say it.

"Am I what?" It was a tragic whisper.

"Are you a human being or not?" he whispered back.

There was a pause. "I don't know that either," the girl answered finally. "I don't know what I am now. Certainly I was human once—I think."

A few minutes later Zoltan was sitting closer, almost close enough to touch the girl, and she was explaining that although she was no longer subject to the commands of the evil wizard, she still experienced sudden changes of form, from being entirely a fish to this half-human state, and that she had almost no control over them.

"I am no magician. I cannot help you."

"Perhaps no one can." The girl went on to recount something of her earliest memories, of a village beside a much larger river than this one. Something terrible had happened to her there to end that phase of her childhood.

She related also how she had seen Zoltan being set free from the riverbank cave by the same peculiar old wizard who had rescued her— or partially rescued her—from the evil enchantment that had enslaved her.

There was enough moonlight to let Zoltan see plainly the long fish-shape of her lower body, and what ought to have been her legs. The marvel was certainly genuine enough. Starting at a little below her navel, human skin shaded into bright scales. In the back of his mind, the suspicion that this might be only some renewed trick of his enemies persisted, but it was fading steadily.

She was a girl—at least the top half of her was. More than that, she was lovely—at least certain things about her were. Before long Zoltan was quietly moving closer to her again, and soon he moved a little closer still.

As he was reaching out, about to touch her hair, she looked at him with alarm. There was a white streak of movement, a splash, and she was gone.

He returned to his blankets and wrapped himself in them again for sleep. Slowly, half-unwillingly, he drifted into slumber.

When he woke again the sun was up. Zoltan ate some breakfast from his ample stores—catching fish would have taken time, and besides, hooking any fish just now would have given him a very peculiar feeling. Then he resaddled and mounted his loadbeast and went on following the little river downstream.

Looking up at frequent intervals to see if the flying scout of yesterday had returned, he at last received something of a shock when he saw not one winged presence in the sky but a squadron, thin black shapes against bright blue.

As the creatures drew closer, Zoltan could tell from the shapes of their wings that they were reptilian and therefore almost certainly his enemies. Certainly they would not be his friends.

Until now, with one or two doubtful exceptions—yesterday and high in the sky above High Manor—Zoltan had never actually seen an unfriendly aerial scout. But he knew that the enemies of Tasavalta had used such creatures in the past.

The creatures in this current flight were much bigger than he had realized at first. Their true size became apparent as they came closer, landing to rest on logs or rocks that Zoltan had already passed as if they were cautiously sniffing at his trail. And they were certainly reptiles. Some strain of dragon, he thought, of which many more subspecies existed than were usually seen in the vicinity of Tasavalta.

His heart was beating faster, more with exhilaration than with fear. Here was evidence that the crazy-looking little wizard knew what he was doing after all. Dragonslicer appeared to be the very Sword that Zoltan was going to need today. He rested his hand on the black hilt but, somewhat to his surprise, could feel nothing there but its solidity. So far, the Sword of Heroes was quiet in its sheath.

Now the reptiles had started diving at the stream, fifty meters or so ahead of where Zoltan was. Something large and white was under the surface there, something that splashed violently, trying to escape the onslaught from above. A silvery fish that looked too big for this small stream.

Zoltan suddenly tried to kick his loadbeast into greater speed. When that effort failed, he jumped down from the saddle and ran at the reptiles, yelling, challenging them to fight. He had drawn his Sword now, and with each stride that brought him closer to the enemy he expected that the power in it would be activated. But nothing of the kind occurred.

The creatures, not at all unwilling to fight someone who wanted to interfere with their own hunt, turned on Zoltan. The flashing blade in his hands did not appear to impress them in the least.

The Sword of Heroes remained silent and lifeless in Zoltan's grip as he lifted it on high. The enemy came at him in a black swarm.

15

E ARLY on the morning following his parley with Mark, the Baron received a disquieting report from one of his flying scouts. As interpreted by its trainer, the animal reported that their pursuers were now gaining ground on them again, despite the fact that Amintor was now driving his own people and animals at a faster pace.

Amintor scowled, and demanded: "How can they be gaining ground while they have that litter in their train?"

The beastmaster tried, with little success, to put that question to his charges. As before, the animals were unable to tell, or at least unable to say, whether the pursuing force still included a litter or not. All the beasts were sure about was that the enemy were getting closer.

While his aides, knowing it was time to keep silent, watched him closely, Amintor thought the situation over. He could, of course, send back a human scout to see what was really happening. But unless the Baron slowed down his own retreat after that, a rider might have a hard time catching up with him again to deliver his report. Whereas the flyers, as long as the weather was tolerably good, brought back their news within an hour.

Breaking camp, getting ready to move out again, he pondered on Mark's motives. "Still really interested in my Sword, is he? Maybe I should have tried to make the trade with him after all. Maybe he was really ready to go through with it."

Amintor's enchantress, riding beside him now, complained that she did not know what plan he really had in mind, and it was hard for her to work with him under such conditions.

The Baron, who had been listening to her snore for most of the night, ignored her now. He summoned his beastmaster to him again and briefed the man carefully on what he wanted to find out.

An hour or so later the new report came in from the flying reptiles: Yes, there were now two groups of mounted people in pursuit. One of these formations progressed quite slowly and was thus falling ever farther and farther behind. But the other group, as previously reported, was gaining ground, and therefore seemed more important to the scouts; it was the only one that they had mentioned in their previous report. Humans had long tried to impress upon them the need to report the nearest and the swiftest-moving of the enemy.

The Baron recalled to mind the configuration of the last few kilometers of land that he and his people had passed over. Then he acted swiftly.

He picked out a dozen or more of his best troops, grimly aware that he was undoubtedly going through a very similar process to the one that the Prince must have followed on being forewarned of Amintor's attempted ambush. With this assault force set aside, the Baron ordered the remainder of his people, with all of the spare mounts and the meager baggage of his train, to continue their retreat in the same direction as before. Sniffing the wind and scanning the sky, he could hope that the Prince's aerial scouts would not report his splitting his force and doubling back with part of it. Clouds and wind were both increasing now, rapidly enough to give the Baron hopes of that.

Then, with his dozen picked men following him, the Baron rode in a wide loop, heading for the place where he thought the litter ought to be now if it had advanced steadily since last reported. At the moment there did not seem to be any of the Tasavaltan birds aloft. He could hope that they would not observe his maneuver, but he could not rely on their failure to do so.

In a matter of minutes, Amintor and the fast riders with him were thundering down an arroyo, heading in a direction exactly opposite to the one in which they had been industriously retreating only a few minutes earlier. He felt reasonably confident that he had now outflanked the rapidly advancing forces of the Prince.

Presently, mounting a hill, he came in view of a small plateau, ahead of him and a trifle lower; the far side of this tableland fell away precipitously. Amintor could see the small Tasavaltan baggage train progressing across the top of the plateau, the litter in the middle surrounded by half a dozen guards. Also beside the litter there rode one white-robed figure, doubtless a physician. That was all. The Baron's striking force had the Tasavaltan Guard detachment seriously outnumbered.

Wasting no time, the Baron maneuvered his people closer, up to the near edge of the plateau where the slope was gradual, then led them breaking into view and charged.

The guards around the litter hesitated when they saw the bandits coming, but then realized they were badly outnumbered, and retreated, galloping to save their lives. The physician, abandoning his patient, fled with the rest.

Now the loadbeasts of the Tasavaltan baggage train, including the one that bore the litter, finally decided that it was time for panic. They started off at the best lumbering run that they could manage, in the general direction of the cliff.

Amintor shouted, kicked his heels into his mount's ribs, and led the chase. In a matter of moments the litter was overtaken. One of the Baron's people grabbed the loadbeast's harness and brought the stampeding animal to a halt. Meanwhile Amintor himself had ridden up beside the litter, ripped open the canvas shade covering one side, and looked in to see—an empty pallet.

Understanding came to him even before he heard the shouts behind him. From nearby woods, along another edge of the tableland where the slope was gentle, there now burst out a wave of Tasavaltan uniforms, a cavalry charge with leveled weapons. In the center of the line rode the Prince himself, with Shieldbreaker brandished high. Meanwhile, the guards who had pretended flight were turning as one rider and coming back at a gallop toward the baggage train.

Amintor's people were now outnumbered and caught between two forces. They had already scattered, beginning their pursuit of the various baggage animals, and the Baron made no attempt to rally them. Not against a disciplined force of superior strength. And most especially not against the Sword of Force. Never that without most careful preparations, none of which had been made. Instead, the Baron instantly abandoned his own comrades-in-arms, even as they were scrambling to abandon him. He fled for his life.

The blue-green uniforms were closing in on three sides of him. A sword—not Shieldbreaker—came swinging at his head. He parried it in a ringing crash with Farslayer, whose own magic still slept. It would be useless to evoke that particular power in the face of a dozen enemies. Amintor rode on, bent low over his mount's neck. His riding-beast was swift but not the equal of the one the Prince was riding, he was sure. The lack of speed would doom him if the cliff ahead did not; but there was still one chance.

The Baron's people were all out of action. His foes in dozens were thundering after him, behind him and on each flank, all closing in. Yet, in midgallop, he managed to replace Farslayer in its scabbard at his left side, and then, awkwardly, he worked the Sword of Mercy out of its sheath at his right. Behind him closer than ever he could hear the Prince's voice, calling thunderously for him to surrender, shouting to him that he was trapped. Ahead the tableland ended abruptly, at the edge of what must be a considerable cliff. Well, Mark was a good fellow and all that, but Amintor was not minded to become Mark's prisoner— not right now. Not just after being tricked into trying to take the Prince's darling son a hostage.

Slung stones and arrows sang past the Baron's head. He tried to dodge them, bending his neck beside the long neck of his steed. The animal stumbled, it was wounded, but it did not go down.

The edge of the cliff ahead was rushing closer. There was no doubt that the gulf beyond was one of deadly depth.

If this desperate attempt should fail, thought Amintor, then still it has been a good life, all in all. Would he want to live it all over again, making the same choices? One thing he did know, he wouldn't trade the life he'd had for one, or two, or three of the ordinary kind. He thought: I have led an army, an army of people who were eager to follow me; and I have bedded a beautiful queen; and I have stolen from a god.

His riding-beast was superbly trained and had never yet refused to do anything that the Baron asked of it in combat. Nor did the animal now betray his confidence; running at full gallop it went high and nobly off the cliff. Only when he was falling did Amintor allow himself to look down, to glimpse the flat hard rock and rocky soil some fifty meters below.

He felt the animal's muscles tense convulsively beneath him in midair and saw its limbs begin to windmill. It tried to turn its neck back, halfway through the long fall, to look a question at its master.

Clutching Woundhealer to his chest with all his force, Amintor felt the galvanic pang of the silvery blade entering his very heart. Force poured from that enchanted steel, a power that, far from killing him, would have altered him into someone else if he had let it do so. Fiercely he resisted that godlike force, clinging to himself, to being what he was, what he chose to be.

Still in midair, somewhere past the middle of the long fall, he separated himself deliberately from the animal that had been carrying him. Now it was as if he still had an infinitely long time to consider what was happening, to think of things that he might do. With both hands he held the Sword of Mercy by its hilt, keeping the blade inside his body, transfixing his own heart. He saw his stallion moving away from him a little as it fell, its four legs still working, trying to gain purchase on the air.

He did not look down again, never saw the last rush of the ground coming at him. He only felt, beyond pain, his body shatter with the impact at the bottom of the fall, the bones in his legs go splintering away as he came down feet first. Now at last he let himself look down, to see a flash of terrible white sticks, their jagged ends protruding through his leggings.

But his flesh was boiling with the awful power of Woundhealer, an energy that expunged shock and pain. As if he were cutting himself into pieces, Amintor drew the blade of the Sword of Healing, still plunged as it was into his chest, down through his torso to his crotch, then, still not withdrawing it completely from his body, into one leg after the other. The steel knit bones together as it passed through them, restored his flesh, renewed his nerves, set right the hopeless-looking havoc of the fall. Even his skin closed seamlessly behind the bright blade as it passed.

In moments the white of bone was gone. His legs were straight again. Inside Amintor's leggings, which were soaked with his red blood and still torn where his jagged bones had pierced them, he could feel that his bones and muscles already were whole and strong once more.

He sprang up on his feet and carried the Sword quickly to where his riding-beast lay broken, not even trying to get up. The animal was breathing with a hideous noise and endeavoring to raise its head. He pierced the heaving torso with the blade, making sure first of the heart and lungs. Then he sliced at the strangely angled limbs, beholding the miracle, feeling the smooth flow of power in his hands. He kept on using Woundhealer until the animal was standing, quivering and whinnying as he stroked it with his hand, its body whole and ready to run again.

Then Amintor turned at last and looked up at the clifftop above him. There was the silent line of his enemies, some of them dismountd now;

all of them balked at that last jump. They were looking down at him with their weapons—even Shieldbreaker—hanging useless in their hands.

And now the Baron could see how the Prince was holding the small form of his son before him, just in front of his saddle. The cloak that had earlier concealed the child had now fallen back.

One good trick deserves another; the Baron saluted them all with the Sword of Healing.

"Now," he shouted up to them, "are you ready to talk about a trade?"

Already, while they watched him heal himself and then his riding-beast, they had had a little time to think the situation over. Almost at once Prince Mark shouted back: "Suppose that I were minded to trade, Baron—how would we manage the exchange?"

"Why, easily enough. You climb down here—make sure you come alone. I'll stand well back, never fear, and give you plenty of room."

The Baron went on to describe how he thought the trade could be managed from that point.

Thinking over the proposed conditions, the Prince turned in his saddle and handed his son over to the senior physician in his train. It was obvious that the hard ride and the combat had been a bad experience for Adrian, and the boy was now in the earliest stages of what looked like a severe seizure. His face was paler than usual, and there were tremors in all his limbs.

Ben drew the Prince aside. "Are you really going on with this mad scheme of trading Swords?"

"I am. Unless you can think of some more certain way to get Woundhealer into my hands."

Ben scowled at him ferociously. The effect would have intimidated almost anyone. "I could hardly think of a more certain path to trouble —but have it your way."

"Thank you."

"You'll have it your way anyhow. And at least let us do something to help you. I'll take one or two people over that way, along the cliff to where those trees hide part of the slope, and come down to the bottom on a long rope. He won't be able to see us."

Mark looked around, wondering if Amintor had any similar trickery in mind. But it was pretty plain that there was no point in worrying any longer about any part of Amintor's force except the man himself. Those who had survived the skirmish around the litter had scattered in flight, and Mark was morally certain that they were fleeing still.

He said to Ben: "All right. I thank you. But once you and the two others are at the bottom, don't do anything unless I signal you. His riding-beast is healed and ready to go, and he'll be off like an arrow if he suspects there's anything wrong."

Ben nodded and moved away. He took the precaution of posting a few of the best archers along the edge of the cliff, though Amintor had already withdrawn to a distance that would make their best shots very chancy. True to his word, the Baron gave Mark plenty of room when the Prince, Shieldbreaker at his side, began to clamber down the cliff.

Since the baggage train, when reassembled, contained enough rope for two long lines, Mark used one to have himself lowered. The descent would have been possible without the security of a rope, but using one increased both speed and safety. Ben had Mark's line secured at the top and took care to keep his own conspicuous figure in sight, in order that Amintor might not wonder what had become of him. Ben had had second thoughts about going down the other rope himself and had delegated that job to several lighter and more agile folk.

Partly through luck and partly by design, Amintor had now placed himself in an excellent position. There was an easy escape route at his rear, and his enemies were all in front of him, in such a position that it was going to be very difficult for them to get at him. From where the Baron was standing now, stroking the riding-beast beside him, it should be possible for him to see Tasavaltans approaching him from any direction when they were still a bowshot away. He would be able to jump on his mount and be gone before anyone coming down the cliff at any point could begin to get near him on foot.

Mark's descent on the cliff, as he was lowered on the rope, could have been quite swift. But he deliberately created minor delays, fussing over knots and loops, wanting to give the people who were using the other, hidden rope plenty of time to get down. Still, he did not want to protract his delays to a suspicious length, and soon he was on the bottom, standing ankle-deep in a small stream that flowed there along the foot of the precipice.

He disengaged himself from the rope and at once turned and began to walk toward the Baron, who stood waiting almost a hundred meters distant. Mark continued to advance until Amintor raised a hand.

Then the Prince halted. He was now about fifty meters from Amintor and approximately the same distance from the foot of the cliff he had just descended.

The voice of his enemy floated toward him. "Let me see if the sword you have brought me is indeed the Sword I want, Prince. If you don't mind—ah." Even at the distance, there was no mistaking what kind of blade it was that caught the light as Mark held it up.

As had been agreed, Mark, having resheathed the Sword of Force, now unbuckled the belt that held it, and cast belt, Sword and all on the ground in front of him.

Amintor in the same manner was unfastening one of the Swords he wore and putting it down on the ground. Mark was sure it was the one he wanted—his magician had already advised him that the other Sword carried by the Baron was Farslayer. If Amintor were to be given a choice between keeping the power of healing and that of vengeance, Mark had no doubt of which one the Baron would elect to keep.

Now, as had been agreed, both men began to walk. Amintor was leading his riding-beast close beside him as he moved. They walked two clockwise arcs of a great circle, keeping diametrically opposite each other. Each could see that another Sword was waiting for him, where his adversary had put it down.

Mark did not look back at the cliff, or at his friends on top of it. But he calculated that the people who were to have come down secretly must be at its foot by now, if all had gone well, and ought to be watching for his signal.

Amintor, as if he might suspect some such trickery, had chosen to walk his circle in the direction that took him farther from any possible ambushers, not closer, and kept them in front of him. If anyone were to try to rush out at the Baron from concealment near the foot of the cliff, the greater speed of his riding-beast would let him scoop up one Sword or the other from the ground and be gone before he could be touched.

But so far no one was rushing out. Mark's people were well-disciplined, waiting for his signal. The situation balanced on a knife-edge. Mark felt the time of the slow walk being counted out in heartbeats. His adversary was almost too far away for the expression on his face to be visible at all, but the Prince thought that the man was smiling.

Now each man was approaching the Sword that his adversary had put down. And now each quickened his pace just a little. Mark came within a stride of the Sword in front of him and bent to pick it up without lowering his gaze more than momentarily from the Baron, who was simultaneously bending to take up Shieldbreaker. Mark observed that Amintor, doubtless mindful of the possibility of treacherous arrows or stones, had put his mount between himself and the clifftop. But once Shieldbreaker was in his hand, he stepped out boldly from behind the animal.

We might, thought Mark now, have shot at the animal and disabled it. Then we might have rushed him . . . but there was no use now thinking about possibilities that had not been foreseen, pondering plans that had never been made.

Amintor now had the Sword of Force in hand.

But Mark had Woundhealer. The hilt of the Sword of Mercy had come into his hand, bringing with it a flow of gentle power; this Sword was one of those he had held before, and the touch of it was unmistakable. It brought back, with a rush of memory, the days when he had first come to know Kristin, when for a time the two of them had been alone against the world, and princely power was far away.

Triumph shone in the face of Amintor as his right hand closed upon the hilt of the Sword of Force. But the Baron did not delay for even a moment to savor triumph. Nor did he deviate in the least from the behavior that had been agreed upon.

Mark had anticipated the possibility of treachery by the other at this point. But the Prince knew how to fight against Shieldbreaker and was ready to disarm himself before Amintor could gallop across the space that intervened between them. And the other would have to consider that Mark might not disarm himself, but might instead wield the Sword of Mercy; what Woundhealer might do in direct opposition to the Sword of Force had never been tested.

But that test was not to happen now. Amintor was keeping to the letter of his agreement regarding the exchange. Now astride his mount, the Baron saluted Prince Mark with his new possession, and now the triumph in Amintor's face was unmistakable. In another moment he was off, cantering briskly toward the line of trees that marked the course of the small stream after it meandered away from the foot of the line of cliffs.

Mark looked down at the black hilt in his own fist and at the small, white, open hand that marked it as a symbol. A moment later he had turned his back on the retreating Baron and had in fact almost forgotten him. The Prince moved quickly to meet the friends who ran toward him.

Adrian's eyes were open when Mark stepped into the tent. The boy was lying on his back but sat bolt upright on his pallet as soon as his father approached with the Sword in hand. Both of the Princeling's small hands came up, eagerly groping, to touch the blade of Woundhealer as his father held it out toward him. The small fingers played freely over the invisible keenness of those edges and came away from them undamaged.

But Mark could feel that no real power had yet gone forth from Woundhealer. The sightless gaze of his son still wandered as before, and Adrian's small voice was silent.

Now Mark, with his friends crowding unheeded into the tent behind him, knelt down beside the pallet of his son and thrust the Sword forward again. It touched the head of Adrian, and that keen point passed across his eyes and through them. But still those eyes saw nothing, and still Mark could feel nothing in the hilt.

"Light," the child said suddenly. "Father, light!"

"Yes!"

But then Mark's son lay back in his bed, his hands still groping in the familiar gestures. His eyes refused to follow the physician's hand when it passed back and forth in front of them. It was obvious that his blindness was no better than before.

Another hour had passed before Mark emerged from the tent at last. He stumbled into the sunlight as if he too were now blind. Ben was at his side, trying to think of words to say to him. But the Prince had the look of a man who could not hear, almost the look of a man who is ready to die.

Woundhealer had done absolutely nothing for his son.

16

THE mermaid was struggling fiercely if not very effectively against the reptiles that swooped at her from the air. Her broad, flat tail thrashed up sheets of water, her small fists struck out at jaws and wings that came within their reach. She screamed at them in her human voice, using the wizards' language that Zoltan did not know, and for the first few seconds the sound of the words seemed to upset their attack.

But in a moment they came screaming and clawing back at her, renewing the assault.

The beasts were larger than eagles, with teeth and talons big enough to kill. All that saved the fish-girl from immediate and serious injury was the water. She had luckily found an unusually deep pool, though even here she was almost too big to submerge entirely in her half-human form. The water could not protect her completely from the diving, reaching talons. The flying creatures, though reptilian, were not amphibious. But they could evidently tolerate brief plunges.

Next time the mermaid came up, she was armed with rocks in both hands and hurled them at the leather-wings. They ignored the missiles and dove at her again.

But by now Zoltan was standing on the bank beside the mermaid's pool. Dragonslicer was a bigger and heavier sword than any he had used in practice, but it was not too big for him to swing. And never, in practice or anywhere else, had he handled a weapon as keen and deadly as this one. Though no magical power had yet manifested itself as it ought to have done against true dragons, neither were the creatures he was fighting protected by the incredibly tough armor of a dragon's scales. In Zoltan's capable two-handed grip the weighty steel drove razor-sharp through leathery skin, sinew, and bone. Any of the attackers that he managed to hit solidly fell dead or crippled from the air at once.

The human voice of the mermaid gasped and sobbed for breath whenever she had to bring her head above the surface of the water. Apparently she was forced to come up for air like a human. In the hasty glances he could spare to look at her, Zoltan could see that she was wounded and bleeding about the arms and shoulders. But she defended herself as best she could with rocks and fists, and showed no sign of disabling injury as yet.

Abruptly the enemy broke off the attack, leaving three of their number dead or wounded on the ground. Dragonslicer had taken off the head of one of them completely, and two more were crippled. Some of the reptiles still airborne were flying as if they had been wounded too, nicked or scraped by the Sword that had not been quite quick enough to take their lives.

Zoltan, panting, standing ankle-deep now in the water of the stream, rested his weight on the Sword of Heroes, feeling the sharpness of the point cleave its way slowly into the bottom of the stream between rocks. He was still uninjured, and he knew a savage pride. He was fighting off these dangerous and determined creatures without the help of any magic, under his own power.

The girl's head broke the surface of the water in the pool beside him, and Zoltan looked at her. She was floating on her back, gasping and bleeding in a very human way.

"Can you get away," he asked, "while they are gone? Swim downstream? Is there a deeper pool within your reach that way?"

She watched the circling creatures in the sky. "No. Not close enough. They would have me before I reached it." She floated on her back, resting, tail stirring the surface weakly. *"He* has sent them after me," she added. "I am not worth a greater effort on his part, I suppose."

And then the enemy, whose black swarm had briefly receded, were coming back again.

Once more the mad confusion of the fight descended upon Zoltan and his companion. Fighting, he had no time to think or feel or be afraid, no time to do anything but swing the Sword and duck and dodge to try to make the clawing, biting enemy miss him, and straighten up swinging the Sword again.

Two of the beasts came at him at once. He felt a claw fasten in his scalp, his flesh tearing with appalling pain. He screamed, and twirled the Sword above his head, and felt an impact as the blade bit leathery hide and bone. The talon in his scalp pulled free.

Again the enemy broke off the attack.

And yet once more, before Zoltan had time to rest or breathe, the onslaught was renewed. Blood was flowing from his torn scalp, but fortunately it ran around his ear, not into his eyes. He hacked yet another reptile out of the air.

At last, the four leather-wings who could still fly, dripping their own blood and hissing half-intelligible imprecations, flapped off, making unsteady headway into the northwest.

Zoltan, gasping, leaned on his Sword again and watched them until he was sure it was a genuine retreat. Then he looked around. The nymph, mermaid, whatever the right word for her was, had completely disappeared again. Turned back completely into a fish again, he supposed, and diminished in size, or he'd be able to see her somewhere in the water nearby. He wondered how much control she had, if any, over her changes of form. She might have saved herself some harm by doing the fish-change sooner. Or maybe the smaller body of the fish would have been hooked out of the river on a talon and torn apart.

Moving unsteadily, on shaking legs, he went to one after another of the wounded reptiles on the ground and finished them off with economical thrusts and chops of Dragonslicer while they screamed curses at him. One closed its eyes before the Sword came down. It was the closest Zoltan had ever come to killing a human being.

Now he had achieved a silence that would let him rest.

Zoltan wiped his Sword clean on grass, then knelt down and drank from the stream. Next he tried to stanch the bleeding of his scalp. Tied on his belt was the small medical kit that Mother Still had given him. Inside it he found a small jar labeled FOR BLEEDING. Using the Sword itself, far keener than any other blade he'd ever handled, he hacked awkwardly and blindly at his curly hair until he thought the wound was as exposed as he could safely get it. Then he loaded a finger with the unpleasant-smelling salve and pressed it directly into the flow of blood. Immediately the bleeding diminished, and in a matter of moments the flow was stanched completely.

Only then did Zoltan remember to look for his mount. He was suddenly afraid of what the reptiles might have done to it while he defended the mermaid; but the loadbeast was unharmed. Perhaps the leather-wings had been under orders to concentrate on the escaping mermaid. She had said something about their being sent after her by some enemy.

Zoltan remounted and pushed on. He continued downstream, paralleling the river.

Hardly was he well out of sight of the place where he had fought the reptiles when a familiar figure reappeared. It was the crazy-looking little wizard again, standing directly in Zoltan's path.

This time Zoltan was treated to praise and concern. "You're a brave boy, yes. Oh my, that was fine. But your head is hurt. Oh, oh, oh, oh." And the wizard, his dried-apple countenance pinched up as if he felt the pain as much as Zoltan, did a little hop-dance of helpless sympathy, meanwhile waving his arms ineffectively.

Zoltan felt called upon to be patient. "It'll be all right. The bleeding's stopped already. Mother Still gave me a medicine that worked beautifully."

"Are you sure? I don't know her. Oh, oh."

All Zoltan could think was that this wizard, despite the power that he had demonstrated, did not inspire much confidence. Raising a hand, he gingerly explored the area of clotted blood where his hair was now cut short. "Yes, I'm sure."

"That's good. That's good. Then you should go on."

"I mean to do so."

"That's good, Zoltan. You're a brave boy."

"Thank you, sir. Who are you?"

"I don't think I ought to tell you that. Because if I tell anyone, *he* might find out somehow, and—and anyway, whoever I am you still have to go on and find—and find your uncle. No matter what."

"Where is Uncle Mark?"

The wizard gestured nervously again. "I think you should look for the trail of a dragon."

"Oh. If I follow a dragon's trail, it'll lead me to him?"

"Something like that. Yes, I think that would be the best thing for you to do."

"All right. But wait, what does a dragon's trail look like? I've never seen one."

The figure of the wizard hopped from one foot to the other, speaking faster and faster in its gravelly voice. "You'll know. Oh, you'll know it when you come to it, won't you? Go on, hurry, hurry! I can't stay here arguing all day."

And, almost as soon as he had uttered those words, the strange wizard disappeared again.

Zoltan forged on, still heading downstream. He assumed that was still the proper direction, not having been given any instructions to the contrary. If finding his uncle Mark meant trailing a dragon, well, he would never be any better equipped for that than he was right now. Pride was growing in him as he realized how successfully he had fought off the attacking leather-wings. Not that a dozen of them were the equivalent of a real dragon, of course—but he felt ready to fight the dragon himself if it came after him.

At least, almost ready. That was a chilling thought. Well, possibly the creature wasn't very large. The smaller landwalkers, he had heard, were no bigger than loadbeasts.

Zoltan had expected soldiering and adventuring to be painful and sometimes frightening. But now he wondered if such activities were always as confused and filled with uncertainty as this. Somehow this wasn't quite the way he had imagined things would be.

He pushed doggedly on, along the stream.

That night he camped on the riverbank again, and lay awake, watching the surface of the water ripple in the moonlight, and waiting. Before he could fall asleep the girl came back, a splash and then a silvery outline, a dreamlike presence in the moonlight.

Zoltan wasn't sure if he was relieved or worried at her presence, but he moved to sit beside her and talk to her again. He offered his medicine kit but she declined; he could see that her wounds were superficial and were already partially healed, showing rough scabs and crustings on her skin.

The air was colder tonight, and Zoltan brought his visitor one of his blankets as she sat on the rock. She thanked him politely. They congratulated each other on surviving, and she thanked him for his aid against the reptiles.

He told the girl his name and explained to her that he was taking the Sword of Heroes to his uncle, who was going to have to fight a dragon. She said that she had heard of the Swords of Power, and sounded as if she had some idea of what they were.

"But how are you going to locate your uncle?" the girl asked.

"Our friend, the strange-looking little wizard, tells me that I have to look for the dragon's trail first. Then my uncle will be nearby somewhere."

"What is our rescuer's name, I wonder? And why are you so sure you must do what he tells you? If he tried to give me orders, I should be very doubtful about following them."

"So far I don't believe he's lied to me. But I don't know his name." Zoltan went on to tell the girl more of his story than he had told her previously. Then he got around to asking her if she had yet managed to recall her name.

"No. It may be that my name is gone forever. Along with half of my humanity." She flicked her tail, sending up spray.

"I asked the strange little magician for *his* name, but he wouldn't tell me."

"That is not so strange, for a wizard. Names are things of great power in their lives."

"I'm no wizard. My name is Zoltan—I told you that before. I wish you could remember yours."

The girl shrugged, a delicate motion. "There are certain names of power that I remember—ones the Master used to call me by. But I am afraid that if I uttered one of those, I should be completely enslaved to him again. And the other man, the lesser wizard to whom he gave me, sometimes used those names—but I will never say or hear them again if I can help it. You should call me whatever pleases you. I think that I have never had a name I truly liked."

Zoltan's mind was a buzzing blank. "I'll try to think of something." And he went on to tell her something more of his own story.

The mermaid assured him that she believed his story; it was, after all, perhaps not so unbelievable as her own.

Not that she could remember very much. She had been somehow kidnapped from a fishing village—she seemed to remember it as a fishing village, along a river very much bigger than this one—at a very early age, and conscripted into the evil Master's service—she was very vague about the details of how all that had happened.

She hesitated suddenly, in midspeech, staring past Zoltan as if she saw something there that frightened her. Before he could turn, the transformation, which until now he had not witnessed directly, happened before his eyes. There was a large puff and cloud of something like steam in the moonlight, close enough for him to feel it; and he caught one clear glimpse of a large, leaping fish before it splashed into the water.

Late next morning, Zoltan, still following the stream downhill, came upon a trail—he didn't know how to describe it except as a trail—that was unlike anything that he had ever seen before. A vast, shallow gouge in the hard, dry earth, wide as a wagon road, knee-deep in the center and shallowing toward both sides. Desert bushes and other small plants had been uprooted and rocks torn out of the earth and dragged. At least it was easy to see which way the trail led. It looked to Zoltan as if some cylindrical weight the size of a substantial house had been dragged in a gently curving path across the land.

The track went right across the river and away from it again on the other side. Zoltan was still sitting on the bank, around midday, frowning at it, when the mermaid emerged partially from the water to talk with him again.

This time she sat in the sandy shallows instead of climbing out. She frowned at the strange scar that wound across the earth, and announced at once: "It is the track of a great worm."

Zoltan stared at her for a long time before he spoke. "Oh" was all he said when he did answer. Deep inside him, somewhere between his stomach and his heart, a lump of ice had suddenly congealed.

Almost everyone had heard at some time of great worms, though neither he nor the mermaid had ever actually seen one of the creatures. Very few people in this part of the world had ever done so. They were the final phase in the life cycle of the dragon and a thousand times rarer even than the landwalkers.

Immediately after the first shock of fear that Zoltan experienced, doubts began to arise. Certainly this was not what Zoltan had had in mind as the spoor of the dragon. He had been intent on finding gigantic footprints of some unknown shape—but in some vague way, reptilian-looking—showing the marks of great unretracted claws. But this—this looked, he thought, as if an army had passed by, dragging all their baggage on sledges, obliterating by this means all of their own footprints and hoofprints. Such an effort might have wiped out even the tracks of dragons, landwalkers, Zoltan supposed, had there been any.

"Are you sure?" he asked the girl.

"Oh, yes. I am afraid so. I am afraid that this can scarcely be anything else."

He was silent, thinking. Was it possible that any army would march with a dragon, or several, in its train? Zoltan had been reading and listening to martial stories since he was old enough to read, and he had never heard of the creatures being used as war-animals. The beasts were said to be too stupid and uncontrollable for anyone to try to use them— though, now that he thought about it, Uncle Mark and Ben told tales of a dragon, constrained by magic, that had once been set to guard the treasure of the Blue Temple.

Suppose, Zoltan thought, someone could harness a landwalker, a big one, and make it pull a sledge. Maybe, conceivably, it would produce a trail something like this . . . or maybe a gouge like this one would need a squadron of landwalkers. Now, following the trail slowly as it curved away from the stream—there was no doubt of which way it led —he had come to a spot where even small trees were bent and broken. One of the treetrunks was almost as thick as a man's body.

Wide as a wagon road, yet without ruts, the broad concavity went curving gently across the rugged countryside.

If this was indeed the dragon's path, then Zoltan's duty was to follow it. To do so, he was going to have to leave the stream, perhaps for good, and with it abandon his alternate plan of getting back to Tasavalta that way. Also he would miss his sometime companion, but there didn't seem to be any choice. Of course, the wizard's actual instructions had been to stick to the river. But having found something this unusual, it was hard not to assume it was the trail he had been told to look for.

He returned to the place where the trail crossed the river, and knelt to fill his leather water-bottle. The mermaid gazed at him sadly, and Zoltan tried to explain his difficulty to her. "I don't know if this is really a dragon's trail or not. But I suppose I have to follow it."

She was silent. Then he saw with vague but deep alarm that she was starting to weep.

"It is the trail of a dragon, as I have said," she told him presently. "But I wish that you would not follow it. I think that you are now my only friend, in all the world. And it will kill you."

The lump of ice was back, bigger than before. Other sensations, less definable but equally uncomfortable, accompanied it. Zoltan muttered something incoherent, and for some reason he could feel himself blushing.

As if with an effort of will, the mermaid ceased to weep. Brushing hair and tears out of her eyes, she predicted that the trail would loop back to the river again within a few kilometers because of the dragon's great need for water. "Unless of course it should be going to another river. Or some lake or pond."

"I do not think that there are any lakes or ponds near here."

But she was crying again and could not answer.

Zoltan finished refilling the waterskin that Mother Still had given him, and struck out away from the river, following the awestruck track, whatever it was, across country.

He came presently to a place where there were blurred hoofprints that he took to be those of several wild cattle, small convergent trails which terminated at the edge of the purported dragon's track. Here on the barren earth was a spurt of what might be dried blood, and here, nearby, was a fragment of a wild bull's leg, complete with hoof, some hide, and lower bones. But otherwise there were no bones or other debris to be seen in the area.

Zoltan pushed on. Presently he came to a place where there were droppings—what looked like a mound of dung, several days old and high as a man. Sharp fragments of large bones protruded from the mass. There were scales, too, and other products of digestion less identifiable.

He dismounted and poked at the mass with Dragonslicer, and swallowed. He had just felt, for the first time in his life, a stirring of power in a Sword.

Despite the mermaid's warnings, that gave him a shock. Of course there might be tiny, mouse-sized dragons burrowing in that compost heap. He knew it wasn't likely. That small, he thought, they should be living in a stream. Or . . .

The trouble was that a single creature that could make a trail like this and leave a pile like this—that was an alternative that hardly bore thinking about. Zoltan didn't want to believe that something like that could really exist, that he might really have to face it.

He moved on.

Looking back at the titanic spoor, just before he rode out of sight of it, he still couldn't make himself believe that it was really what it looked like. Someone must have gathered together all the droppings of the animals of the whole army, and . . . but why should anyone do anything like that?

No. No one creature could be that big. There wasn't any possibility of such a thing. Besides, how could such a monstrous creature catch anything to eat? Certainly not by stealth. It could of course consume vegetation, he supposed, whole thickets and trees. But there wasn't a lot of vegetation in this country. And in the pile back there, the bones, the evidences of carnivorism, had been plain.

Zoltan felt a little better when he saw that the trail was indeed leading him back to another loop of the river, about a kilometer away. He hurried ahead and found the mermaid already waiting for him there.

"I think you may have been right," he told her, and explained.

"Oh yes, I am right. It is the track of a great worm, Zoltan." She sounded sad, but resigned now, not tearful. "It is very much like an enormous snake. A great worm can move very fast for short distances. It can knock down anything you could put in its way. And I do not see how your uncle can fight it, even if the Sword that you are bringing him is magic as you say. How do you know where, in all that length, to find the heart?"

"How do you know so much about them?" The ice was still in his gut, and now his lips were going dry.

"That is something else that I cannot remember. Perhaps I saw a great worm once, when I was—when the evil people had power over me. Perhaps I saw—" Then the girl was silent, a pause that stretched on and on.

"Tell me more," Zoltan urged.

Her human lungs drew in a deep breath. "There is only one way I can think of by which it might be killed. A creature like this must seek some kind of shade, under trees, and lie still through most of the day. Otherwise the heat of the sun will kill it—it cannot find enough water here to lie in. Or it may be that the Master has given it the protection of his magic, too. Then even the magic of your Sword will do you no good at all. And if that is not enough, there is one more danger. The worm can hypnotize large animals and even sometimes people, and force them to march right into its jaws."

"But I must follow it." He could do that much. That was all he had to think about now, following it. If and when he actually came in sight of it—then he would decide what had to be done next.

Pushing on again, following the trail, Zoltan came to more droppings, and more bones. He found himself thanking Ardneh that the trail was still old. He estimated several days old, from the condition of the uprooted plants.

A thing this size could even gobble a landwalker. Especially if one came along that was not too large.

How do you know where, in all that length, to find the heart?

17

AGAIN the moon was almost full. Baron Amintor, riding alone, observed the off-round shape of it just beginning to materialize in the eastern sky at dusk as he began to jockey his riding-beast uphill around a minor waterfall, which occupied most of the width of a small canyon. The Baron, after a month of lonely travel, was still wearing his two Swords, one at each side.

He had been traveling almost steadily since trading Swords with Prince Mark, and he had come a long way on a winding route. The Baron's goal, a prearranged meeting place, was very near now. It lay just upstream along the river he had now reached. Amintor had never seen this river, the Sanzu, before, but he knew that its headquarters were somewhere deep in the rocky hills of Tasavalta, a good many kilometers to the east and north of here.

It was not the Baron's habit to hurry unnecessarily, but now he was peering somewhat anxiously ahead of him through the dusk, and when his riding-beast began to demonstrate an increasing reluctance to go forward, he kicked it in the ribs to urge it on. Amintor did not want to risk being late for the impending meeting. The appointment he was trying to keep had cost him a great deal of time and energy to set up, and it was of inestimable importance to his future.

The past month had not been unpleasant. As a rule he actually preferred traveling alone. No member of that band who had been with him before he'd taken the Sword of Mercy would have been a suitable companion for the grander enterprise upon which he was now entering; and by now the Baron felt almost grateful to Prince Mark for helping him to be rid of them all. Under the new conditions they might well have proved something of an embarrassment.

Amintor had expected, when he sent messengers to propose this meeting, that he'd be coming to it with Farslayer and Woundhealer at his belt—but as matters now actually stood, he thought he was in a substantially stronger position even than that.

Here, as on the even higher reaches of the Sanzu, none of the individual falls and rapids were very high, but there were a great many of them, which made progress difficult for anyone on foot or mounted who sought to follow the stream closely. When he had attained the next level spot where there was room, the Baron paused to let his mount breathe while he gazed up at the next splashing fall above and muttered to himself—it was a habit that had begun to grow on him during the past few weeks of solitude.

"No sign as yet he's here at all. And I'll not find him at all should he not want to be found. But I'm still convinced he's here and wants to talk to me."

Impatiently he cut short the pause for rest and pressed on. And, rounding the next rugged bend in the stream, the Baron had good evidence that his conviction was correct. Not that he saw the eminent wizard he had come here to meet; but what he did see awaiting him in the dusk appeared to be something even more unusual.

It lay like a fallen log across the earth and made a gently sagging bridge across the stream. And it was a roughly cylindrical, horizontal shape. But it was too thick and far too long—even had it not been disposed across the canyon in great snakelike curves—to be any fallen log that Amintor had ever seen.

At first glance he thought it might be some peculiar earthen bank, showing where the river had once followed a slightly different course. But here in the canyon that would be impossible, and anyway the configuration of the object was all wrong for that. Here and there it rose above the earth.

And then, even as the Baron studied it, the thing, the formation, whatever it was, moved. Shuddering longitudinally in a majestic, large-scale ripple, it shook off the fallen leaves that had begun to drift upon its top, and started up small animals which had been huddling next to it. The thought crossed Amintor's mind that the thing must have been lying immobile for quite some time if small animals had started to regard it as part of the landscape.

But his main, overwhelming impression was of sheer awesome size. Now another part of the vast length, thirty or forty meters from where Amintor sat his mount, rose up from the earth. Something that had to be a head, though it looked to Amintor as big as a small chariot, reared up at that distance, topping the small trees. Yes, those two bright plates in the dusk were *eyes.* Impossibly huge, round and green as fishbowls, with such a span of shadow in between them that the Baron found he had some difficulty in drawing his next breath.

He looked to right and left along the rugged canyon floor, trying to see where the curves of the titanic body ended. What with the trees, and the shadows of the oncoming night, he couldn't tell. One thing was certain: there appeared to be no way for him to get around the creature, not in the confines of this gorge. Yet his instructions had been plain in the answer his messenger had brought back; this was certainly the way he had to pass if he was going to follow those instructions. And he was sure that this obstruction was not accidental.

The Baron's mount, faithful enough to jump off a cliff upon command, was growing restive in the presence of this monstrous creature, and he had to struggle for control to keep the riding-beast from bolting. He knew what to call the thing that blocked his way—a great worm— though in all his travels he had never actually seen one until now.

It was the terminal phase in the life cycle of the dragon; and not one in a million of those beasts ever reached it.

His two Swords in their metal sheaths clattered with the motion of the terrified riding-beast under him. Neither Farslayer nor Shield-breaker was of the least good to him now. The one Sword that might possibly be able to help a man against such a creature was one Amintor did not have.

As he struggled with his mount, wondering meanwhile what to do next, a man's voice called to him from beyond the dragon. "Come on, then! Climb over!"

It was an authoritative voice, and though it was completely unfamiliar to the Baron, he had no doubt of who its owner was. Very well, then, he would climb over the waiting dragon.

If he was going to do so, there was no choice for him but to dismount and leave his mount where it was; to his relief the riding-beast quieted as soon as he got off its back—it grew peaceful with magical suddenness indeed, he thought wryly—and let itself be tethered.

Then he approached the scaly wall of the worm's side, trying to look as if this was something he did every day, or once a year at least. As he did so Amintor thought that there were smaller eyes, eyes on a human scale, regarding him from a high ledge of rock beyond the beast. But he ignored that gaze for the time being.

The thickness of the creature's enormous, snaky body was approximately equal to Amintor's height. He gained a small advantage from stepping on a handy stone on the near side, stepped once more upon a roughly projecting scale—the beast took no more notice of his weight than would a castle wall—and vaulted to the top and over, dropping down nimbly enough on the other side.

"Up here, Amintor."

On a ledge of rock beside the next small cataract—a shelf of stone overgrown with vegetation and several meters above the worm—a figure waited. It was that of one who could only be the wizard Burslem.

Amintor had never seen the magician before, but one who gave orders here could hardly be anyone else. The Baron chose a route and clambered up to where the other man sat regally awaiting his arrival. The other arose from the fine chair he had been sitting in, as if belatedly deciding to offer that much courtesy; and the two men stood in the moonlight sizing each other up.

Burslem was quite a young man in appearance, though Amintor did not allow himself to be deceived by that. Indeed, the magician had the look of a somewhat bookish youth, wearing a soft robe that like his chair would have looked more appropriate in a library than on this desolate hillside surrounded by splintered rocks, grotesquely growing trees, and rushing water.

But the strangest things in the immediate environment were not those, perhaps not even the great worm. Amintor could sense living things whirring and rustling in the dusky air above the wizard's head, but they were almost impossible to see, and Burslem never looked up at them at all. The limb of a tall, dead tree projected through that space, and above the tree, a higher ledge. And, perched on that ledge, where the shadows of several taller trees congealed together, was a solid form, that of something that might have been a reptile—unless it was some kind of creature even less savory. Something in the Baron recoiled from that presence. He did not know what it was, and quickly decided that he did not want to know.

The wizard's youthful face was solemn as it regarded him. Had someone been watching at this moment who had also known the evil emperor John Ominor, of thousands of years in the past, the observer would have been struck by a certain resemblance between the two.

There was, perhaps, also a likeness to that ancient ruler in the brusque way that this man talked.

"What is the purpose of this meeting, Amintor? I am a busy man." The voice was nondescript.

"Indeed, we are both busy men." Calmly the Baron refused to be rushed or rattled by the impressive reception the other had provided for him. "So I will come at once to the point. My thought is that each of us has certain skills—powers—that the other lacks. Therefore we might do very well to form a partnership."

The other, hands clasped behind his back, looked at him in silence for what seemed to Amintor a very long time. It was as if the magician were reassessing an earlier impression.

"Your recent acquisition of Shieldbreaker," Burslem admitted at last, "has increased your status in my eyes, to a considerable extent. I should like to hear the story of how that was accomplished."

"Gladly."

And the Baron retold the story, in its broad outline, as succinctly and truthfully as he could, not omitting his own mistakes along the way. He then returned, without pause, to his theme. "Separately we are both of us strong, but together we will be stronger still. I am a dependable military leader and have a knack for finding the right way to talk people into doing things—not a skill to be sneered at in matters of diplomacy and war. The fact is that I see no practical limits to what we might be able to accomplish in a partnership."

Burslem at least did not immediately refuse the proposal, or laugh it to scorn. Instead he gestured with his left hand, and what had been a rock became—or seemed to become—another comfortable chair beside his own. There on the small ledge above the little waterfall the two men sat and talked well into the night, with the great worm coiled—or at least looped—below them, right athwart the space that any other physical being would have had to cross in order to approach them from below.

Only the gods and demons, thought Amintor—and my friend here— know what may be blocking the way into this canyon from above. He also found himself wondering, in the occasional pauses of the conversation, how fast the creature below him might be able to move if and when it decided there was a need for speed. He could not imagine anything that a great worm would feel the need to run away from, but it must require enough food for an army, and catching that might well require some quickness sometimes. And, how long had it taken to travel here, from whatever strange place it had been summoned?

"A most formidable guardian," he remarked at one point, indicating the limbless dragon with a gesture.

"I have lost," Burslem muttered, "some of my faith in demons." It was as if the wizard were speaking more to himself than anyone else.

The Baron was not sure that he saw any relevant connection between demons and dragons, but he did not choose to pursue the matter.

The magician turned slightly in his chair to face him. "Let us speak plainly."

"By all means."

"You invite me into a partnership. Between partners, there is always one senior to the other."

Amintor spread both hands, a gesture that caused the Swords at his sides, in their metal-bound sheaths, to chink faintly against rock. The wizard had totally ignored the priceless weapons so far, and continued to do so now.

The Baron said: "I would certainly not claim seniority over one who was the chief of security and intelligence for King Vilkata."

Burslem grunted. "If he had listened to me, he would be alive today. Not only alive. He would have won the war."

In those days Amintor himself, of course, had been at the right hand of the Silver Queen. But he made no claim now to having given advice that, if taken, would have altered the outcome of the war. Instead the Baron said only: "When one of these Swords finds itself in a ruler's hand, there is a tendency for it to dominate his thinking." Vilkata had held the Mindsword, then. "Or her thinking, as the case may be."

Burslem laughed. It was a hissing sound, unpleasant and somewhat labored, quite out of keeping with his ordinary appearance. Amintor found himself thinking he would not be surprised if a serpent stuck its head up out of the man's throat. The great worm had long since lowered its head again, become a silent wall that curved through deepening night. But the eyes of the other thing on the ledge above, whatever it might be, were still there watching.

"Well," the wizard said, "we may hope that the Sword of Love now dominates the thinking of Prince Mark. Maybe it will lead him into trying to do good unto his enemies."

"May it be so indeed," agreed the Baron heartily. "He has done a fair amount of troublesome things to me, though in the end I had what I wanted from him."

"Is it possible that you will want more from him in the future?"

"I should say it is quite possible. By the way, Burslem, I have here a small flask of wine of a certain rare vintage. Would you share a drink with me? A toast, to the future prosperity of both of us?" The Baron stopped short of proposing that they drink to a partnership that had not yet been finally agreed upon.

"Why not?" Burslem reached over with a well-kept, ordinary-looking hand to take the flask. At that moment Amintor was conscious of the faintest throb of power inside the length of Shieldbreaker as it lay along his thigh. Weapons of magic arrayed in opposition meant no more to the Sword of Force than did those of steel. *None stands to Shieldbreaker.* But the Sword's reaction was nothing serious as yet; a preliminary stirring, he supposed, a response to some magical precaution activated by his host when Burslem took the drink into his hand.

Now the wizard was holding up the small flask of wine in both hands and gazing at it, as if he were somehow able to study the fluid inside the leather skin. Amintor, expecting to be able to perceive something of testing at this moment, could just detect, with his mind more than with his senses, the passage of something in the air immediately over his own head. He looked up. He had a sense that it had been of considerably more than human size, but already it was gone. The small green eyes that he had seen, of something perched upon the higher ledge, were now gone too.

As soon as the airborne presence had passed, the wizard heaved a great and human-sounding sigh. Then he opened up the flask and drank, without any hesitation but with little evidence of enjoyment either. Even as the magician swallowed, the Baron felt a mild glow inside his own belly, as if it were there that the wine had landed.

Burslem passed back the flask and wiped his mouth. As the Baron drank in turn, the great worm again raised its head upon the column of its neckless body, just enough so it could turn its gaze at him. The huge eyes still glowed with the faint reflected light of the night sky. The Baron made a little gesture in the worm's direction with the flask, a kind of to-your-health, and sipped again. The Sword at his side was quiet; was the great worm a weapon? Probably not within the logic of Shieldbreaker's protective magic. The dragon could come and kill him and the Sword of Force would be a sword in his hand and nothing more, as useless against such an attacker as against an earthquake.

He understood that at the moment he might well be relatively vulnerable to the wizard's power; but he also thought that for the moment he had nothing to fear from that.

Burslem, as if his mind were running in the same track, suddenly remarked: "You realize that I could take those two Swords from you at any moment."

Amintor, who had dealt with Swords before, realized nothing of the kind. Except for the controlled presence of the dragon, he would have been tempted to laugh at the idea. Even for the dragon to reach him would take time, and he and Shieldbreaker would not be idle in that time.

But the Baron was not going to try to dispute the point just now. "Thereby depriving me," he answered calmly, "of the pleasure of putting them willingly at the service of my senior partner—or am I to take it that our agreement is not yet formally concluded?"

The other laughed again. "Yes, perhaps I do need your skills at negotiation, Amintor. Very well, the agreement is concluded. Keep both your Swords, for now. They are likely to be of the greatest use upon a battlefield, and you are much more likely to find yourself on such a field than I am."

The talk between the two men resumed, now in something of a new key. It soon turned to practical planning.

The magician said: "One of your first duties will be, of course, to raise an army, substantially larger than the mere guard force—about three hundred soldiers—I have at my disposal now. There are times when nothing but a real army will do, if one is to be taken seriously enough in the world."

"Indeed."

"Yes. The worm below us, for example, is capable of taking a city, or defeating an army in the field. But no matter how cleverly it is given orders, it cannot very well collect taxes, or guard an entire frontier."

"Certainly."

"We shall have to discuss the question of what exact size and composition of the force will be most practical. The recruitment, organization, and training will then be left almost entirely in your hands."

"If such matters are to be done properly, they inevitably take a great deal of time."

"Yes, time and patience. But until the army is ready, our greatest plans, as I see them, must be held in abeyance."

Amintor was silent.

"You disagree?" Burslem asked sharply.

"I only venture to suggest that there are some great plans that by their nature do not require an army."

Shortly after that remark was made, and before it could be amplified in discussion, the first conference between the partners was adjourned. There were matters, Burslem said, for which he had to prepare, and the preparations were of such a nature that they had to be accomplished without human company. So far he still had not taken up Amintor's hint about great plans.

The talk between the two men resumed on the following afternoon, in a pleasant camp above the canyon rim. Amintor had led his riding-beast up out of the canyon, and it now cropped grass under a tree nearby the camp. There were a handful of servants in attendance, all of them apparently quite human, who quietly and efficiently saw to their masters' needs. The worm was gone—somewhere. Amintor had not tried to see where its great swath of a trail led.

Shortly after this newest session of talk began, Burslem abruptly asked to see Shieldbreaker. Amintor at once drew the Sword of Force and held it up. He was gritting his teeth, preparing arguments for a refusal to hand it over, but the wizard made no such demand on him, being instead content to gaze upon the blade from the other side of his comfortable pavilion.

"It still remains a mystery to me," the magician commented at last, "how Vulcan lost it."

The Baron, who had been actually on the scene—or very nearly so— when that loss took place, had also been for a long time unable to come up with any reasonable explanation. At last his meditations on the subject had convinced him of what the explanation was; but he offered no answers. He only related what he had seen while his new partner listened to the account with keen interest.

Amintor concluded: "And the giant figure with the Sword in its hand —I am sure now that it could have been no one but Vulcan—was still knocking and slashing about with the blade, in a fair way to knock the very building down, when I got out. But the more I think about what I saw, the more certain I am that, with very few exceptions, the men and women who struggled against him were not hurt by that Sword. Not even though it struck and pierced their bodies again and again."

"We are partners now," said Burslem solemnly, "and you may very well carry Shieldbreaker into combat in our common cause. Therefore I must tell you what I have discovered about it."

"Which is—?" inquired Amintor with all the innocent eagerness that he could muster. He felt quite sure that the disclosure would tell him no more than he had managed to deduce for himself some time ago.

"That he who strives *without weapons* against the Sword of Force," Burslem proclaimed, "cannot be hurt by it."

"Ah." The Baron blinked three times. "That may well be so. That would account for the exceptions."

"I tell you that it is so. Think back on what you saw that day, and tell me if I am not right."

Amintor did his best to look as if he were thinking back with great concentration. "You are right," he said at last.

The other nodded. "Also, the wielder of the Sword of Force is well-nigh powerless to resist, by any other means, such an unarmed attack as you say these people were carrying out against Vulcan. Because the Sword, so long as he holds it, draws most of his strength into itself; nor will it allow him to let it go, as long as his enemies still confront him."

That was an idea that Amintor had never worked out explicitly for himself. Yet now that he heard it stated clearly, he thought that it must be so; otherwise, how could that gaggle of struggling humans ever have overcome even a weakened god?

"A strange imperfection, that, for the ultimate weapon to have," the Baron meditated aloud.

"Ah, yes. But do not forget that it *is* the ultimate weapon, when it is set in opposition to any other." And the wizard was looking at him sternly now, as if he might be thinking: *I see I shall have to do more of the mental work in this partnership than I had hoped.*

In fact those identical words were running through Amintor's mind. Well, great skill in magic did not necessarily mean great wisdom, or even an efficient practical intelligence.

The Baron said: "I will not forget it." Then, not wanting to overplay his effort to appear somewhat inferior in intellect, he added: "That is one reason why I never tried to use Farslayer, even as a threat, against the ruling house of Tasavalta, though I consider them my chief enemies.

You know, a little old-fashioned blackmail. Dear Princess Kristin, send me ten thousand gold pieces right away, or you'll wake up one morning to find your husband, as he lies beside you in your snug bed, is wearing a new ornament above his heart. Like a half a meter of god-forged blade."

"You were probably right not to make the attempt." Burslem nodded. "Farslayer would very possibly have failed to work against a man with Shieldbreaker in his possession. And, by the way, what was your other reason? You implied that there were two at least."

This time Amintor allowed himself to display an intelligent smile. "I am not a dolt, Burslem. It didn't take me long to realize that Farslayer is not the blackmailer's weapon of choice against any well-loved man who spends most of his time surrounded by his friends. The threat in that case is unlikely to be credible. Of course, for a blackmailer with Shieldbreaker in his possession, matters may be somewhat different—then he can expect any return stroke to be warded off."

The wizard returned the smile. "You might have tried it against someone else, who had not so many friends around him."

The Baron laughed heartily. "I'll certainly never try it against a wizard of your caliber, either. Though I have turned that idea over in my mind, in reference to a magician or two other than yourself."

"Indeed? Just who are these other wizards, of my caliber?" It was very hard to tell from Burslem's voice whether he was ready to admit the possibility of the existence of such folk or not.

Amintor shrugged. "To a blade of grass, like myself, all trees look about equally tall."

The other grunted and gave him a long, considering look over the rim of a golden goblet of light, bubbly wine. Then Burslem said: "Now you have both Farslayer and Shieldbreaker in your hands. Are you ready now to attempt to blackmail the house of Tasavalta?"

"I also have a partner now. I must find out what you think of the scheme first."

"That is a good answer," said Burslem, leaning forward, setting down his wine. "And there remains Woundhealer to be considered. And other things . . . Let me tell you of my own most recent contact with the house of Tasavalta. I, too, thought that I had a kidnapping arranged, a number of most valuable hostages in my grasp. And my plans, too, were unexpectedly upset."

"Tell me," said Amintor with genuine surprise.

18

FOR several days now the Tasavaltan party had remained camped in the same spot. Mark was struggling with himself, unable to bring himself to give the order to begin the long march back to Tasavalta.

As he saw it, his only other choice besides starting for home at once was to pursue Amintor again. But neither could he bring himself to order his people to fight against the Sword of Force. Especially not after he, the Prince, had traded it away.

An alternative would be for him to pursue Amintor alone, leaving it to Ben and the rest of the escort to see Prince Adrian safely home. It would be easy for Mark, in a way, to run off after Amintor and postpone the full acceptance of responsibility for what he had done.

But two things held Mark back from any pursuit of the Baron. The first was uncertainty. Was the Sword's failure to heal Adrian somehow a result of something Amintor had done, deliberately or not? The Prince could not be sure of that. The second difficulty was that Mark knew he was needed at home—the birds had brought him word that Zoltan was missing, and there would be other problems demanding his attention.

The Prince could not make up his mind. Never before had he known the power of any Sword to fail when called upon under the appropriate conditions. There were moments when he was convinced that the Baron had somehow cheated him deliberately, had done something to the Sword that rendered it powerless to help Adrian—or else had created some magical imitation of the Sword and traded that to Mark. The Prince had seen a similar trick performed once in the past.

But all of the magicians in Mark's party had examined the Sword in his possession, and all of them had testified that it was genuine.

Most convincing of all, the Sword with the white hand on its hilt could work its healing magic as powerfully as ever upon the wounded in his camp. Except for its failure to help his son, there was no reason to doubt that it was genuine.

But Mark could not fathom the meaning of that one exception.

Anyway, Amintor was no magician, nor was a bandit leader likely to have a great enchanter in his employ. And why, supposing the Baron had the power to do so, should he have directed such an effort against Adrian? As far as Mark knew, the pointless infliction of pain had never been one of the Baron's traits. He had no objection to the happiness of other people—as long as they did not dare to deny him anything he wanted.

The fact was undeniable: the Sword of Mercy could cure the hurts of everyone except Adrian.

Why?

Could its magic be somehow blocked by the only equally powerful force Mark knew of, that of another Sword? He could not see how.

Or might there be some other source of power that was even stronger than the Swords?

Whatever the answer, he could not sit here indefinitely in the middle of nowhere, bemoaning his fate. Mark at last, reluctantly, gave the order to start for home.

But scarcely had the march begun when a group of riders came in sight, approaching from dead ahead. There were three white-robed figures in the group, and when they had come closer Mark could be sure that they were priests of Ardneh. At least one of them was of high rank, to judge from the way the others deferred to him. These were accompanied by half a dozen armed servants and attendants.

Mark called a halt and exchanged greetings with the priests of Ardneh. A conference began, and all of the White Temple people were overjoyed to learn that the Prince had indeed been able to retrieve Woundhealer.

"We will erect a statue and a shrine in your honor, great Prince, above the new repository where we keep the Sword."

Mark gave the speaker back a black look in return. "You may erect my statue if you like. But there will be no such repository."

The others gazed at him mystified.

"I mean I am not going to return the Sword into your care. I am taking it home with me to Sarykam."

The ones in white robes were aghast. "It is ours, Prince; it was stolen from us. What can we do to persuade you to give it back?"

"You can heal my son."

"The Sword cannot heal him?"

"Can you? With the Sword or without it?"

The priests looked at one another. "We will do what we can," the leader announced.

Ordering their servants to establish camp, they set up a tent and brought the patient into it. After a lengthy examination, the white-robes declared that they could do nothing for him. They were as mystified as Mark by the Sword's failure.

One of the priests offered the opinion that Adrian's condition might be the result of some punishment inflicted by Ardneh himself.

It was not a wise thing to say. The Prince was enraged.

"And you want me to return the Sword to you? What for? So that the next bandit gang that comes along can take it away from you again and sell it to the highest bidder? Then you can all weep and wail some more and accuse me of not being there to defend you. And accuse this child of having offended the kind gods . . . I want to hear no more of gods, or of you, either. Get yourselves out of my sight."

"But, our Sword . . ."

"It belongs to me now, if it belongs to anyone. And it can cure just as many folk in Tasavalta as it can in your oasis in the middle of nowhere. More, for we'll retain it."

The priests of the White Temple were accustomed to courtesy, if not respect, from almost everyone whom they encountered. This outburst surprised and offended them. But, observing the black expression of the Prince, they withdrew with no further protests.

Hardly had the Tasavaltans resumed their progress toward home when a handful of lame and diseased folk, having materialized seemingly from nowhere out of the barren landscape, appeared in the path of the column. These approached the Prince, crowding around his riding-beast, pleading to be allowed to benefit from Woundhealer's power. Somehow they had already learned that it was in his hands.

Mark called a halt again and gave orders to the physicians that they should use the Sword to help the sufferers. And all indeed were healed.

Ben, observing the process, commented: "If we stay in one place very long, Prince, we're going to find ourselves surrounded by an army of 'em."

"And if we move, I expect we may find more waiting wherever we arrive. Well, we'll do the best we can. I'll not deny Woundhealer's help to anyone who asks for it."

For several days the Tasavaltans' march toward home continued without further incident.

The fundamental question about the Sword's failure would not cease tormenting Mark.

"Why, Ben? Why?"

Neither Ben nor anyone else could answer that.

Ben mumbled and scowled and was glad when he could find some excuse to turn away. The Master of the Beasts turned his head also and scanned the skies, as if suddenly hopeful that one of his missing scouts might yet return. The magicians and the doctors scowled when Mark questioned them yet again, and said as little as they could.

Once, one of the magicians answered: "Perhaps Karel can tell us the answer, Highness, when we are home again."

And through all the puzzling and the questioning, Adrian lay for the most part wrapped in his own dreams, enfolded in his own blind world. He spoke sometimes to his father, who in turn said nothing to his son of Swords or illness or danger, but tried to tell him that they were going home and cheer him with thoughts of friends and toys and good food waiting there. The condition of the young Prince was apparently no different than it had been before the Sword of Mercy was brought to him. No seizures had assaulted him since then, but often in the past, periods of many days had passed without an attack.

Meanwhile, Shieldbreaker continued to be much in his father's thoughts. Once Mark said to Ben: "Gods and demons, why didn't you bind and gag me before you let me give that Sword away? I think that, after all, the scoundrel's swindled me somehow."

And Ben could give no answer.

Mark had ridden out a little in advance of the small column, scouting the way ahead. He was gazing into the distance when, quite near, a strange figure appeared to him. It was that of a wizard, a caricature that gabbled a strange childish warning, cautioning him that he ought not to return home yet. He was able to see the figure only indistinctly and could understand only a word or two of what it said.

The Prince was suspicious of this warning and hesitantly decided not to heed it. He reported it to Ben and his own magicians when the others rejoined him, but they could make nothing of it.

"Had you seen this figure anywhere before, sir?"

"I . . . I was about to say no. But yet . . . there was something familiar."

On the next day, a certain man appeared among a group of other feeble travelers intercepting the column. This man was young and would have been robust and active except that he suffered with an infected wound in one arm, which came near to driving him mad with pain. He was also terrified that any ordinary surgeon who treated him was certainly going to amputate his arm.

The fear was well-founded, thought Mark, looking at the injury. But when Woundhealer had rested on the limb for a few moments, the smell of gangrene was gone. A few moments more and the man sat up, flexing his biceps and proclaiming himself ready to draw a sword.

He drew no blade, however, but rather, in the relief of being healed, made a confession.

"I must tell you, Prince—I was one of the bandit band of Amintor who fought against you. I was wounded in the fight on the day that he attempted to kidnap your son."

Mark stared at him, feeling a sullen hatred, knowing that its indulgence would bring him no peace. "Well," he said at last. "That is over. Here you are, and here I am. And my son is as well as he has ever been. Go your way."

"First, Highness, I would pay my debt to you—and also to him, who deserted me on the battlefield and saved himself." And the man spat on the ground.

He went on to relate his knowledge of Amintor's plans, including the time and place for meeting Burslem. This man claimed to have dispatched the flying messengers that carried word between Burslem and the Baron as they planned their meeting.

Mark had learned enough to bring him to the point of a new decision. Ben and the others who had listened to the story agreed that the man was probably telling the truth.

"So, Amintor is taking Shieldbreaker on to Burslem, trying to form a partnership—I'm sure of it now, Ben. The answer to our problem with Woundhealer lies somehow with the Baron . . . that smooth smiling devil has swindled me somehow. I gave him the Sword I promised.

Now there's nothing to keep me from taking it away from him again. He has no more than three days' start, on a long journey. With my mount I can catch him before he meets Burslem, since I know now where he's headed."

Someone, one of the mounted troopers spoiling for another fight, let out a whoop of triumph.

But Ben waited soberly for what was coming next.

Mark strode to the tent in which his son was sleeping, put back the flap, and looked inside. "Take him home for me, Ben. I leave you in charge of magicians, doctors, soldiers, everything. Much good have they done me, or Adrian. Take them all, and see that my son gets home to his mother safely."

"Yes, Your Highness. Immediately, sire. And where in all the hells of the Blue Temple did you say that you were going? I don't think I could have heard it properly."

"After Amintor."

"You're going alone? As he goes to meet the great magician?"

"I was alone in giving my Sword away, was I not? If what our informant told us is true, I should be able to overtake the Baron while he is still alone as well." Mark went into the tent to speak to his son.

"And what if our informant, as you call him, lied after all?" Ben's question outside the tent went unanswered.

Inside, the Prince bent over the small pallet. "We'll win out, son. Or we'll lose. But we'll not lose by staying home and waiting for the sky to fall on us. Are you with me? I have the feeling that you're with me." And Mark gently squeezed the painfully thin hand and arm that lay within his grip. "Not that you can ride with me. Not yet. Ben will see you safely home. I'll be home when I have Shieldbreaker back."

19

MARK, once he had gripped Ben's hand and had formally left him in command of the Tasavaltan force, did not look back, but completed his hasty preparations and rode out in pursuit of Amintor.

He was barely out of sight of his own column when again he heard a strange, crabbed voice calling him: "Prince! Prince!" But the next words, though conveying a sense of urgency, were garbled.

Mark turned quickly in his saddle and caught a glimpse of the strange little figure, as of a caricature of a wizard. But, as before, he could not get a clear look at it. And in a moment, both voice and image were gone.

Ben, left in command of the Tasavaltan column, angrily issued orders to continue the march home. He disapproved of what Mark was doing now, even as he had disapproved of trading off the Sword of Force in the first place. Of course, he was not the sprout's father, nor was he Prince.

With the column in motion again, he rode along at the head of it, grumping steadily. The other people in the train left him alone as much as possible. It was unusual to see Ben of Purkinje in a foul temper, and it was all the more ominous for that.

He thought he heard a faint cry behind him. Ben turned his mount to ride briefly beside the litter. Pulling aside the canvas cover, he saw that the Princeling's eyes were closed. The small body turned stiffly under a light cover. To Ben, who would have admitted he was no expert, it looked more like restless sleep than a real seizure.

A physician looking over Ben's shoulder sighed. "Should we call a halt, sir?"

Ben frowned at him. "To what purpose? This doesn't look like a fit to me. And what if it were? The child is always having them anyway, isn't he?"

"Frequently, sir."

"And they never kill him. My orders are to get him home. If you think he needs treatment, do what you can for him while we keep moving. Unless you think it essential that we stop?"

"No sir." The man sounded defeated, almost indifferent. Ben would have discharged him in an instant if he'd thought there was a better replacement available. "I have no reason to believe that it's essential."

Without further speech Ben urged his mount to a faster pace, leading the column on.

The next few hours of the journey passed uneventfully. The crying from the litter was not repeated. Then a keen-eyed soldier reported flying creatures in view, approaching from almost directly ahead. The column was alerted; but as the winged forms drew near, it was plain that they were friendly birds. A faint cheer went up from some of the human travelers.

Three of the birds landed at once, perching wearily on the backs of the loadbeasts that now bore the empty protective cages. One of the arrivals was an owl, flying now in daylight with hooded eyes, relying on the guidance of its diurnal escort. Meanwhile the remaining flyers continued to circle powerfully above. Ben, squinting upward, could make them out more clearly now. He had heard the beastmaster back in Sarykam talking about them, but none had been available yet when the column left the city. They were hybrid creatures, bred of owl and hawk and magic. Grown to a size and ferocity beyond those of any other bird, they were intended by the Master of the Beasts in Sarykam to serve as escorts through dangerous air for the smaller though more intelligent messengers. The new hybrid aerial fighters unfortunately did not tolerate burdens well, even the smallest message capsules. Their brains were not well suited for making observations, or at least for relaying them in ways understandable to humans. Nor were their marginal powers of speech good enough to repeat messages accurately.

The packets that the messenger-birds had brought were quickly opened.

The three message packets—all holding the same information, in deliberate redundancy—came from the Princess herself and were addressed to Mark, but under the circumstances Ben made no scruple about opening them.

He skimmed impatiently through the first short paragraph of personal communication. Kristin missed her husband but refrained from actually urging him to hurry home before completing the mission that he had undertaken. All was well at the Palace except that Zoltan was still missing, though his riding-beast had now been found unhurt. The boy's mother was naturally taking it very hard, as was his sister Elinor. The efforts of the search parties continued and were now being directed more to the southwest. It was quite possible that Mark and his escort on their way home might encounter some of the patrols.

That was about it. Ben, seeing no reason not to do so, passed on the messages for others in his party to read. He ordered the resumption of the march while trying to compose in his mind a reply to send the Princess.

Back in the Palace at Sarykam, Princess Kristin was having a difficult interview with General Rostov.

He could report no further success by the parties searching for Zoltan. Except for one detail—the discovery, many kilometers to the southwest of the place where Swordface had been discovered, of the trail of what had to be a great worm. Such a trail was certainly a remarkable phenomenon in itself, in this part of the world particularly, but it was hard to connect directly with any of the strange and tragic events that had prompted the search.

It had to be assumed that Prince Zoltan had somehow come to grief. The one ray of hope was that as yet no ransom demand had been received, from the villain Burslem or anyone else.

Kristin, when her turn came, had some bad news to report to Rostov also.

A few hours ago a messenger-bird had straggled in, bearing word from her husband. The note it carried identified it as the last bird he had available, and she had sent out additional replacements. That was not the bad news.

The bad news in the message was that Shieldbreaker was now in the hands of the former Baron Amintor. And that Woundhealer, though obtained at such a great price, was doing nothing to help Prince Adrian.

Prince Adrian was not foremost in Rostov's thoughts. On hearing of the loss of the Sword of Force, he raged, though out of respect for the Princess he almost managed to keep his anger silent.

Almost. As he stalked off, announcing that he could not delay a minute in starting to adjust the defenses of the realm to take into account this new catastrophe, he muttered something.

The Princess wondered if she could possibly have heard it right. She summoned Rostov back to repeat what he had just said.

Standing before her again, the General burst out that the Sword of Force, upon which so much depended, had now been simply thrown away.

"You said something more than that, General. I thought I heard the words *high treason*. Is that true?"

"I am sorry, Princess," he muttered hoarsely.

Color flamed in her cheeks. "If it were anyone but you, Rostov . . . understand, once and for all, that I will allow no such muttering in my presence. Especially when my husband is the object of it. If you have anything to say on the subject of treason, it is your duty to say it to me loudly and clearly. Now, have you?"

"No, Madam." He was almost whispering. "I am very sorry that I said what I did."

"You should be. Now off about your duties." She waved a hand in a gesture of unusual violence.

The General was gone in a moment.

She had no more than a few moments to herself before she was informed that the chief wizard Karel wanted to see her. As soon as she was alone with her uncle, he announced his latest discovery: that Burslem and Amintor had now hooked up in an evil partnership.

What made matters even worse, their partnership was somehow related to a third party, the Ancient One, whose presence Karel had warned Kristin about earlier.

Karel was making preparations to dash off to the southwest, in an effort to forestall the enemy's plans against Mark and Adrian—the wizard thought he could now see those plans taking shape.

Kristin's uncle was still with her when the captain of the Palace Guard came to her with a report that a strange reptile had just dropped a note on a high roof of the Palace. The unwelcome beast was now perched arrogantly upon an even higher steeple, as if awaiting a reply.

The Master of the Beasts seemed to consider this invasion a personal affront.

"Shall we have the damned leather-wings down at once, Your Highness?" he asked angrily. "My owls will rend it as soon as night falls. Or I could call upon the captain of the Guard for archers." He did not seem to find this last alternative so pleasing. The hybrid birds that could have destroyed the formidable intruder by daylight were not yet returned from their escort mission to Prince Mark.

"Wait." The Princess, despite her own jumping heart and nerves, managed to be soothing. "If the intruder brought a message, let us first find out what the message says. It is not impossible that there may be some reply." In her own mind she was certain that a ransom demand for Zoltan had arrived at last.

Karel dispatched an assistant to the roof and presently had the message packet in his own hands. After taking all due magical precautions he opened it, and without reading the unfolded paper passed it directly on to the Princess.

Kristin took it, and read:

> Ask your husband, dear lady, what has happened to the Sword Shieldbreaker that was once given into his care.
>
> If he no longer has with him the Sword of Force, then he must begin to 'ware Farslayer's bite.
>
> I will be glad to send you another message, confirming the continued good health of the noble Prince Mark, but such assurances are expensive and difficult to obtain.
>
> Pray enclose with your reply to this two of the finest pearls for which the treasury of the house of Tasavalta is so justly famous. Such a present will ensure that your written answer is accorded the close attention that it will undoubtedly deserve.
>
> Amintor

Kristin read the message through twice. She made no comment, but passed it back to Karel, whose eyebrows went up as he scanned the neatly lettered lines. Otherwise he betrayed no surprise.

The Princess's heart rose. All she could think was: *Then they have captured no one yet. No one. All they can do is threaten us with Farslayer.*

To her wizard she said: "Catch up with Rostov, who was just here, and have him read this too. He must know all the problems that we are facing."

Then she turned her gaze to the Master of the Beasts. "Meanwhile, spare the leather-wings. Give it some water—it is only a messenger. I am going to compose an answer for it to carry back, and I do not want my reply to go astray." She hesitated. "You may read the message too. There is nothing in it I want to keep secret."

The two men bowed as the Princess left the room. Then Karel hastily sent a messenger, on two legs, after Rostov.

Alone in her own suite, Kristin sat at her desk and closed her eyes for a long moment. Then she took up a pen and a sheet of her personal notepaper, and wrote:

> Amintor—I have learned that you are now in partnership with one who is, if possible, more depraved than yourself. It seems to me that only one of you at a time will be able to possess the Sword of Force and benefit from any protective powers that it may possess. Therefore, I think that you and your notorious partner should both beware of sending me, my husband, or any of my friends, the gift of Farslayer, under any circumstances that might cause us to feel unkindly toward either of you.
>
> Kristin, Princess Regnant of Tasavalta

As soon as the ink had dried she carried her reply back into the other room, where the two men were still waiting, and handed it to Karel to read. He scanned it quickly, smiled at Kristin as if he had expected nothing else, and then folded the paper and sealed it with something on his ring. Then he passed it on to the Master of the Beasts to see to its swift dispatch.

Having done all that, Kristin's uncle bowed before her and remained in that somewhat awkward position until she told him brusquely not to be a fool but to stand up and get busy.

The Master of the Beasts, on his way out of the room, paused in the doorway. He was a trustworthy man, but incurably curious.

"My lady," he asked, "is there to be any enclosure with this? Shall I pass the word that you would like the mistress of the treasury to attend you?"

"Don't be absurd," the Princess said, and waved him out.

As soon as the men were all gone, a maid came in and stood waiting for orders. The Princess was standing alone in the middle of the floor and trying to think. She did not want to bother to go to a roof, or a window, just to see the leathery wings climbing like the shadow of death above her Palace.

Instead, announcing that she was tired, she dismissed her maid and went alone to her bedroom, leaving orders that she was not to be disturbed save for the most serious emergency.

Once alone, the Princess cast herself down on her fine bed and wept. It seemed to her that a faint odor of her husband's body still clung to the bedclothes, though they had all been changed several times since his departure. This made her weep the more.

A little later small Stephen, after being put to bed in his own room by a nurse, found his way in, to his mother's side, and tried to comfort her.

Meanwhile Karel was not idle. He confirmed that his messenger had caught up with Rostov. Then he started toward his own rooms in his own high tower, where many tasks awaited him.

Entering the marble-lined, semiprivate corridor that ran the length of the Palace's uppermost full floor, Karel muttered an imprecation under his breath. Someone was waiting to intercept him.

It was Barbara, the diminutive, dark-haired wife of Ben of Purkinje. She was dressed in fine fabrics and jeweled a little beyond the limits of good taste. The wizard groaned silently when he made sure, from her bright, anticipatory gaze, that he was her objective; he simply had too much to do to be bothered with this woman now.

"There you are, sir wizard," she said briskly, putting herself directly in his way. Small she might be, but Barbara was not easily impressed by wizards, or, indeed, by much of anything else. Karel had heard she had been a great hand at twirling a sling in combat when she was younger. Behind her, looking helpless, was a young officer of the Palace Guard charged with keeping these upper corridors clear of those who were not supposed to be here.

Karel nodded sympathetically at the officer, who no doubt lived somewhat in fear of the lady's husband. The wizard prepared to handle this himself.

He cleared his throat impressively, but that was as far as he got. Barbara was not in the least shy about coming out with her problem or the difficulties she had encountered for several days now in trying to see

Karel. His underlings always reported that he was too busy, and what was one to do in that case but come in here after him?

"Whatever your problem is, Madam—"

"My little girl. She's afflicted."

"The Palace physicians, Madam, must be available to you. And they—"

"I've tried them. It doesn't seem to fall into their sphere, and besides, I don't think they know the first thing about dealing with children. Despite all the experience they must have had. They listened and looked and threw up their hands. One of them did show a glimmer of intelligence in telling me I ought to consider consulting you. Especially since it seems that you are in some way involved already."

Karel did not rise to that bait. Instead he made a mental note to find out which physician had said that, and arrange some kind of minor revenge as soon as the opportunity arose.

For the present, he gave up. "Very well, then, what is it? As briefly as possible."

Fortunately for his nerves, long-windedness was not really one of Barbara's faults. "My little girl, Beth. She's ten. She was with the other children that day when they were all caught in the cave—"

"Yes, of course. What about her?" Karel could remember the child. He had talked with her, briefly, as he had talked with all the others who had come through that ordeal, not really expecting that he would learn much from them. His expectations in that regard were confirmed. The truth was that Karel did not particularly like children, though on occasion he felt somewhat guilty about his attitude and extended himself to put on a show for them.

"She's been having nightmares ever since that day in the cave. Not just ordinary nightmares."

"Madam, as I'm sure the physicians must have told you, after an experience like that it must be perfectly normal to—"

"Don't waste my time, sir. I'm not here to waste yours. I've been taking care of that child for ten years, and I know what ordinary bad dreams are like. And I know when something out of the ordinary is happening."

The wizard had already started trying to edge his way past the little woman. "I can't spend my time on—"

She maneuvered herself boldly to keep in front of him. "It's the one dream in particular. About a strange-looking little wizard and the commands he seems to be trying to give her. He orders her to tell you about someone riding on a griffin."

"—on children's dreams. If you—" Karel had taken one more ponderous step before his progress slowed to a stop. "On a griffin? What wizard is this?"

"The one who keeps talking to my daughter in her dreams is strange-looking, as I said. She describes him as looking like the painting on the nursery wall, here in the Palace. The one who rides the griffin is more frightening. She can't see him at all well."

Beth's mother, with confidence equal to her determination, had brought her along to the Palace. Zoltan's young sister Elinor had come along too, whether to offer support or receive it. She and her mother were staying at the Palace now, that they might be the first to hear any news of Zoltan that might come in. In a very few minutes, Karel was escorting all three females up into his tower.

Once, on the winding stone stair, Karel stopped so suddenly that he startled all three of his visitors. Confronting the girl Elinor with a fierce glare, he demanded suddenly:

"On the day that you hid in the cave—"

"Yes sir?"

"*Why* did you pick that particular cave in which to hide? I mean, did you think of it, or Zoltan, or what?"

"No sir, it wasn't either of us, really," Elinor decided after a thoughtful pause. "Adrian just kept tugging us along. Not as if he could see, but like there was somewhere he really wanted to go."

"I see," said Karel after a moment. He turned and once more led them up the stairs.

There, a minute or two later, Barbara and Elinor were firmly lodged in an outer room while Beth was privileged to enter a certain chamber that few other human eyes had ever seen. Not that she was aware of the honor; Karel saw to it that there was little or nothing odd in the appearance of the place just now.

He seated her courteously, as if she were an adult visitor, and sat down across from her. "Now then, Beth. Tell me all about the strange dreams that have been bothering you."

Despite Karel's precautions, the sturdy ten-year-old was just a little awed by this place. Certain vibrations could not be quenched. But soon she was talking volubly about the dreams.

"And, you know, he's a funny-looking little old man, and he seems to know me. And he keeps telling me to do things, like tell you about the griffin."

"What about the griffin, exactly?"

"Like someone is riding on it—I don't know, I get scared every time the dream gets that far. This stupid little old man keeps shouting at me, and I don't know what to do." Beth drew a deep breath. It was obviously making her feel better just to have this chance to talk about her problem.

"Do you know what a griffin looks like?"

"I've seen pictures."

"And what does this little old man look like? How do you know that he's a wizard?"

"Well—he just *looks* like one. And I saw him once when I wasn't dreaming." She looked up at Karel with a strange expression. "I thought it was you, sort of. I was really sure that it was you."

"Aha. Why were you sure that it was me?"

"Because you did it for us once before, at Midwinter Festival. You made the funny wizard. It was years ago."

"Ah," said Karel, and closed his eyes. Then he opened them with determination. "Tell me about the day you hid in the cave. What did the funny wizard do then?"

"Oh. The other kids were in the cave already, and Stephen and I were trying to find them—you know, playing hide-and-seek."

"I know the game. I myself was a child once, believe it or not—go on."

"Well, I didn't think we were ever going to find the other kids; there were just too many places to hide. Then this funny-looking little old man popped up, like right out of the rocks on the hillside. He said: 'Go on that way, Beth, Stephen, hurry, hurry.' And it was like he was all excited. And he said: 'Don't tell anybody I told you, I'm not supposed to do this,' or something like that."

"And why didn't you tell me all this before now? That same day, when I was questioning all the children about what had happened?"

"I—I guess I thought then that it was you. Someone said that you were helping us that day. Later, when things got real dangerous. So I thought it was you, earlier. If it wasn't you making the image of the funny wizard, who was it?"

"We will come to that later," said Karel softly. "When I have made

sure of a few more things—so, you and Stephen ran on to the cave—
very fortunately for you, as matters turned out."

"Yep."

"And you found the cave, with the other children already in it, just
where the funny-looking old wizard had indicated that you should go."

"Yes sir."

Karel sighed. "I think I ought to talk to Stephen, too."

The conversation was interrupted at this point while Stephen was
located, summoned, and reassured.

By now the Princess herself had got wind somehow of what was
going on and appeared in Karel's tower, insisting on sitting in on the
next round of questioning.

Stephen confirmed Beth's statement, in its essentials.

"Why didn't you tell me, darling?" the Princess cried.

"I thought the funny wizard winked at me, like to keep a secret. I
thought it was part of the magic, not to tell. I thought I couldn't." For
once the five-year-old looked alarmed.

"It's all right," Karel assured him. "All right. But now, now is the
time for all of you children to tell us everything else you can remember.
I can make it come out all right—I think I can—if you tell me all about
it now."

Beth's ten-year-old brow was creased in a thoughtful frown. "I
thought I knew the wizard," she said, "because I had seen him before."

"Where?"

"There's a book, I think," she said at last.

The scrolled-up storybook lay on the little bedside table in Adrian's
quiet room. Karel held the book up in his two hands and felt of it and
looked at it, not only with his two eyes. It had been much used and read
and even chewed on, but the linen was strong and durable, and some of
his own arts had been invested in the paints. The colors in the painted
pictures were still quite strong and clear.

"This is the book?"

"Yes sir."

"Show me the picture."

They found it immediately. The friendly, funny wizard, with some
storybook name, helped the children in the story through the jolly adventures that befell them. Beth had read this book when she was

smaller, and Stephen read it sometimes now, and Adrian had liked very much to be read to out of it.

The Princess was staring at the worn scroll. "I thought Adrian took that with him. I thought that the maid packed it. But it was probably here, in the bed or somewhere, and didn't show up until they'd left."

She took the book from her uncle's hand and frowned at the pictured wizard. "I've seen that costume before, somewhere. I know, the Winter Festival." And now she stared at Karel.

"That's what I said!" chimed in Beth.

Karel gazed at the picture too. Yes, he remembered now. Years had passed since he'd done anything for the children at the Festival, and this imitation wizard hadn't been a big part of it, even then.

He said: "I'm surprised that you remember that, child. I confess that I'd forgotten all about it myself."

And now Karel was on the verge of beginning to understand.

20

A MINTOR was standing in a tent, trying on his new uniform in front of a mirror. The tent was real enough—or at least he thought it was—but the mirror was certainly not glass, and perhaps it wasn't there at all. Still, he could see himself as if it were. And the splendid new uniform had magic in it too, for it kept changing colors on him, slowly and subtly. Burslem, it seemed, had not yet made up his mind on the proper livery for his army. Right now the Baron was decked out in a plum-colored turban, trousers and boots of ebon black, and a jacket that kept shimmering between crimson and silver.

The uniform looked all right, Amintor supposed, allowing for the chromatic inconsistency, but right now he hardly saw it. His mind was too much absorbed in other matters. The Baron had been forced to put aside, for the time being, the planning and problems involved in attempting to create an army practically from scratch. Burslem was insisting on an immediate advance, and attack in some form, against Tasavalta. They were to march at once, with whatever forces were immediately available.

The wizard had promised to explain his change in plans en route. For the time being, Burslem's three hundred or so armed guards—backed up, of course, by the power of the great worm—were going to have to suffice as an army. It was necessary to move against Tasavalta at once, and Amintor would be told why in good time.

The man who had commanded the three hundred guards until Amintor's arrival, a baby-faced scoundrel named Imamura, was naturally resentful of the Baron, who had appeared as if from nowhere to take over his command. Amintor understood this reaction perfectly, though Imamura did his best to mask it. Accordingly the Baron had done his best to placate his displaced colleague by promising him that he would soon have more people to order about than he had ever dreamt of—and, of course, all the wealth, rank, and privilege that went with such a powerful position as chief of staff of a large army.

But now even that problem was going to have to wait. Somehow, for some reason, they were going to have to move against Tasavalta, leaving at once and doing all their planning en route.

The urgency of Burslem's decision had apparently been increased by an unpleasant discovery he had just made and had related tersely to Amintor: A hostage that the wizard had thought he was holding securely, one of the minor Princes of the Tasavaltan house, had somehow escaped or been set free. That in itself did not seem to the Baron a reasonable cause for panic. Obviously more was going on here than he had been told about, a state of affairs that he intended to rectify as soon as possible.

Amintor had already put forward the suggestion that if for some reason it was really essential to move at once against the Tasavaltans, the wisest idea would be to try to kidnap Prince Mark and his heir, rather than recapturing the hostage who had somehow got away. (And the mere fact of that reported escape preyed upon the Baron's mind as well—had he somehow overestimated the quality of the magical power with which he was making such an effort to ally himself?) It was almost certain that Prince Mark, traveling as he was with an escort including a caravan of baggage, had not yet reached home; though probably the invalid child, having benefited from treatment with the Sword of Mercy, was now riding as robustly as anyone else.

If both Mark and his offspring could be taken and held for ransom, there would probably be little need to do anything else to bring the proud Tasavaltans into the position of a subject state. It was even possible, thought Amintor, that then, with a little face-saving diplomacy, even the Tasavaltan army might become available for certain tasks.

The Baron had already suggested that possibility to Burslem, and it had been moderately well received by the wizard; but in truth Amintor himself had grave doubts about it. He had just received Princess Kristin's answer to his demand for pearls, and that answer had not been at all encouraging. Possibly the lady was even tougher than the Baron had suspected—or maybe she really wanted to get rid of her husband.

He still thought the blackmail scheme had been a worthwhile gamble, but there had been several drawbacks to it from the start, not the least being, as in all extortion, that you had to reveal yourself as an active enemy before you really struck at your victim. And as for the weapon employed, the last line of its verse in the old Song of Swords certainly signaled caution:

> *Farslayer howls across the world*
> *For thy heart, for thy heart*
> *Who hast wronged me!*
> *Vengeance is his who casts the blade*
> *Yet he will in the end no triumph see.*

Other verses of the old song had turned out to have truth in them, all too often for Amintor to feel that the warning in this one could be disregarded. He meant to be very cautious when it came to actually using Farslayer; but he had hoped to profit from the threat.

And then, in these matters there was always the nice question of exactly how much to demand from the victim. Amintor, an experienced hand, was convinced that it was at this stage that many blackmailers went wrong. They asked too much, so that the victim elected a desperate defiance rather than cooperation. And he ought not to have underestimated the Princess Kristin. He had carefully calculated—or miscalculated, as it now appeared—his demand for two pearls. Maybe, he could not help thinking now, if he had asked for only one . . .

Behind the Baron, the flap of his tent was rudely, without warning, jerked open from outside. An image of Burslem's head, swathed in a purple turban, appeared in the magic mirror. "Come!" summoned the wizard's voice imperiously. "We can delay no longer!"

Amintor had thought that he was waiting for Burslem, but he made no argument.

"Very well," he replied, and gave his collar a last tug as if it were indeed his uniform that had been engaging his attention. As he turned away from the mirror he saw from the corner of his eye how it went out, like a blown candle-flame.

Squaring his shoulders, he marched out of the tent after Burslem, to where servants ought to be holding their riding-beasts for them. He—

He stopped and stared.

Forty meters or so ahead of Amintor, the great worm lay quiescent, its mouth closed, eyes half-lidded, enormous chin resting on the ground. A dozen humans, clambering on and around the vast hulk of its body, were attaching what looked like a howdah—a roofed basket big enough to hold five or six people—on the back of what would have been the creature's neck if it had had a real neck. The howdah was ornamented with rich side hangings, now furled out of the way, and it appeared to be stuffed with pillows. Standing on the ground in front of the legless dragon's enormous nose, several minor magicians chanted and spun things before its glassy eyes.

Two more assistants held a ladder and beckoned to the leaders. Burslem was the first to climb into the basket, an honor that the Baron had no intention of disputing.

The worm, carrying the two partners in the howdah on its back, led the procession toward Tasavalta, with the army of three hundred following, and after that a baggage train. As soon as the march got under way, some of Amintor's apprehensions about the worm—though not the worst of them—were confirmed. This despite the fact that, in its regular mode of forward travel, the head and what corresponded to the neck were preserved from the most violent of the side-to-side undulations that propelled the legless body forward.

The howdah, just behind the head, balanced aloof from almost all the lateral vibration. The mass of the body just beneath it poised nearly motionless, armored belly a meter or two off the ground, for a period of several seconds, long enough for a human to draw a breath; then, accelerating fast enough to jerk a rider's head back, it shot straight ahead, more or less, for twenty or thirty meters. After the shudderingly sudden stop, there again ensued a nearly motionless balancing as the twisting body behind caught up. The cycle repeated endlessly.

The motion, and the sense of the earthshaking power latent in the enormous body underneath him, began to make Amintor giddy almost at once. He could easily picture the walls of castles going down before this battering ram beneath him. As always, Shieldbreaker and Farslayer were both riding at his sides. The chance to use both of them, he was sure, would come in time.

Dizziness became transformed into a kind of giddy exaltation. In the silence of his own mind, the Baron cried out: *With wizard, worm, and weapons of the gods, all to do my bidding, who shall stop me?*

Exalting, in a way, the motion of the worm might be, but in practical terms such lurching back and forward made it all but impossible for the passengers to conduct any rational discourse. Accordingly, after a quarter of an hour, the partners called a halt and by mutual consent switched to more conventional transport. Climbing down from the basket, attempting to appear nonchalant, Amintor had the distinct sensation that his guts and possibly his brains as well had been churned into a homogeneous jelly.

Soon the whole column was under way again, the two leaders now mounted on riding-beasts. The monstrous, legless dragon, still of course under Burslem's magical control, propelled itself along in the same direction, on a parallel course some hundred meters distant from the mounted humans. The sound made by the dragon's passage was a continuous, hoarse crashing, a pronounced, slithering roar of displaced rocks and dirt and vegetation.

All human attendants were also keeping themselves at a distance from the leaders. Now at last Burslem could broach the subject he had been unable to discuss coherently in the howdah.

"It comes down to this, Amintor: we are both of us being tested."

"Ah? How so?"

"The failure of your extortionary scheme and the escape of my hostage render it all the more imperative that we succeed in this, our greater effort. It will not be well for us if we do not succeed."

"I eagerly await the details."

"Even as you applied to me for a partnership, so I too applied to one whose power stands above my own." Burslem was on the verge of adding something to that, but refrained. His manner was uncharacteristically defensive, even worried; their double failure had affected him even more than Amintor had realized until now. The wizard wiped his forehead nervously. Now it seemed that he had said all that he intended to say.

"What do you mean?" the Baron asked with what he considered heroic patience. "You have applied to someone as a partner?"

"I mean just what I say." And the magician looked around again, as if he thought they might be followed by someone or something other than his own small army.

This news of another and even more senior partner was startling to the Baron at first. But when he began to think about it, certain matters that previously had puzzled him started to make sense.

"At our first meeting . . ." he began.

"Yes!" Burslem examined the sky carefully.

"When I first observed the presence on the high rock, I thought that it was merely one of your—familiars—"

"No!" Burslem swiveled his head back, glaring. "That was *he*, sitting on the ledge above our heads."

"I had thought that—whatever it was up there—was some kind of beast. I thought I saw it fly away."

"Hush!"

"I only mean—"

"You did see wings, large wings, take to the sky. But let us have no discussion about shapes."

Amintor remained silent for a few moments, listening to the methodical hoofbeats of the riding-beasts and the serpentine roaring of the dragon's progress at a little distance, scales scouring the land. But it would be too stupid to remain indefinitely in the dark on this subject. There were things he simply had to know.

"I meant no offense," he resumed presently in an apologetic voice, "to whatever—whoever—was up there. But I had the distinct impression that it flew away. I mean, it looked to me just as if—"

"Yes, yes. The—ah—personal configuration of the Master's body has —ah—become unusual. But what you saw—at least *part* of what you saw—was a griffin."

"A griffin."

"Yes. The Master frequently rides on one."

Again the Baron remained silent for a time. The Master, hey? And he had thought that griffins were purely mythological.

Now Burslem peered at him closely, as if aware of his doubts and reading his thoughts. "It would not be wise," the wizard counseled, "for you to inquire too closely into the Master's nature, shape, or other attributes. It is enough for you to know that he exists and that he has triumphed at last over his ancient enemies—even over Ardneh himself. And that we, in partnership with him, may conquer the world."

"Indeed."

"Indeed. And that, if he should decide we are inadequate, he has but to lift his hand to replace us with other partners. In that case, it would be better for us if we had never been born." Burslem choked just a little on that last word, but he got it out with an air of finality. Then he turned his gaze back to the sky.

"I see," said the Baron, and rode through another interval of quiet thought. But when he spoke again it was as firmly as before. "You may believe," he said, "that you have now told me all you want to tell me. But it seems to me that it is not enough."

"No?" Burslem, incredulous, frightened, and ready to bluster, glared at him again.

"No." Amintor did his best to sound firm and soothing at the same time. "Look here, if I am to cooperate intelligently, there is more I need to know. Just what is the nature of this person, or power, that we are serving? Just what does he, or it, expect from us? And what can we expect in the way of help in return?" Amintor's earlier mood of exaltation was rapidly dissolving in the radiance of Burslem's fear. And, even as the Baron spoke, he could feel his resentment continuing to grow, that he had been led into such a relationship with some unknown being, without the consequences of his bargain being explained to him beforehand.

But now Burslem too was growing angry. "It was you, was it not, who approached me and pressed me for a partnership? You did not demand of me then to know who else might be my ally, nor that all the possible consequences be explained to you ahead of time. Indeed, I would have thought you a madman if you had done so."

And the Baron, though he scowled darkly as he thought this over, eventually had to admit that it was true enough.

Now again both rode on for a little way in silence. Then Amintor asked: "But tell me this—is this power you call the Master overseeing us now, this very moment? Is he somehow listening to our every word?"

"To the best of my knowledge, no, there is no such program of surveillance. The Master has many other matters to occupy his time."

"Such as what? Or is that too impertinent a question?"

Burslem was dourly silent.

"All right, then, I withdraw it. I am a reasonable man and do not pry unnecessarily. But, if I am to cooperate intelligently with the Master's plans, and yours, I must have a better notion than I do now of what is going on. To begin with, where is our Master now, and what is his chief strategic objective?"

The wizard heaved a sigh. "I believe that he is somewhere far to the southwest of here. Even, perhaps, at the far edge of the continent, ten thousand kilometers away."

"Ten thousand!"

"But one who rides on a griffin can be here and there in a matter of only hours."

"Really," said Amintor. "What does he—" Suddenly he frowned and nodded past his companion. "And where is the great worm going now?" The gigantic creature had suddenly taken a diverging course, bearing more to the south.

Burslem looked too, and altered his own course accordingly, waving a signal to his army to do likewise. "We must keep close to the worm now. It possesses certain senses that will be of great help in locating our objective."

Then he turned in his saddle to glare at Amintor again. "As to what the Master requires of us, all I know with any certainty is what you have already heard: we are to proceed against Tasavalta. The method is up to us, so long as our efforts are forceful enough to distract the rulers of that land, keep them from undertaking any adventures elsewhere. Bringing the house of Tasavalta into complete submission would be ideal, but it is not essential. For some reason it is of great importance to the Master that someone or something connected with that land be neutralized, prevented from interfering with his own plans elsewhere. Also, there is one of the Swords that he particularly desires to have."

"Not one of mine, I take it." If that were the case, the Baron assumed that an effort would have been made to get it from him already.

"No, nor one of Prince Mark's either. The Master is especially interested in the Mindsword, of which both you and I, I think, have had some experience in the past. I take it you have no clue as to its present location?"

"No, none," Amintor murmured abstractedly.

"You and I, to be sure," said Burslem, "play a secondary role in the Master's designs. But if we do well, greater things will be entrusted to us."

"I see," said the Baron again.

"As to what help we can expect from the Master against Tasavalta, I should say that, for the moment at least, the answer is: very little."

"Hah."

The wizard looked at Amintor severely. "I know more than I have told you, but at the moment I am not at liberty to share my knowledge. I would remind you, however, that as between the two of us, I am the senior partner. Let it suffice for you that I am satisfied."

"You are the senior partner," agreed Amintor meekly. "And if you are satisfied with our arrangements with this one who is called the Master, I should be foolish to proclaim myself discontented."

"Exactly." Burslem, grimly satisfied at having made his point, sat back in his saddle. In his mind's eye he could see himself hauling Shieldbreaker out of its scabbard and riding away, letting those who wanted to stop him try it, washing his hands of the whole business. But he wasn't sure what such a move would accomplish for him, except that it would certainly make enemies of two very accomplished wizards.

And, there was the worm. How fast could it move? If Burslem sent it after him, perhaps it would catch him and gobble him up, along with his two Swords and his riding-beast to add a little body to the snack.

Amintor rode on in silence. Since his first meeting with Burslem, he had been confident of his ability to manage the magician. But the mysterious Master added new dimensions. An ancient foe of Ardneh, still alive? Amintor did not believe all that he had just been told.

But the complications were growing. He was getting in deeper, but this wasn't the time to break away. It would have to be sometime when the worm was distant, if he decided to break away at all.

Under the edge of his new turban he could feel his forehead sweating.

21

ZOLTAN sat his loadbeast, looking down on something totally unexpected, in the shape of a mighty cruciform scarring of the earth.
He had come to a place where the trail of the great worm intersected
itself.

There was no other way to read the sign, no doubt that that was what
had happened. It was plain also that the new segment of the trail was
much fresher than the old one; the loop that the worm had traveled
before returning to this spot must have been a lengthy one. Nor was
there any difficulty in telling in which direction the new trail led.

He moved first to scout out the area surrounding the intersection.
Running parallel with the new trail, at a distance of about a hundred
meters from it, was another broad obvious track, this one instantly
recognizable if still surprising. It had been left by what Zoltan took to
be an entire army—certainly many more riders than were in the
Tasavaltan patrols whose signs he had observed much earlier. Nor was
the army Tasavaltan. Here and there a clear hoofprint, showing the
form of an iron shoe, indicated that very clearly. And a few bits of
equipment, worn or broken and cast aside, offered confirmation of this
conclusion.

They were headed in the same direction as the great worm in its most
recent passage, and certain signs indicated they had passed through
here at about the same time. Were they hunting the creature? Or might
it have been hunting them? Zoltan's imagination, when he beheld that
scoured-out track, could create the image of a monster whose proper
prey was armies.

He shuddered a little, despite himself, and regardless of the fact that
Dragonslicer hung at his side.

All he could do was continue what he had started, the job of following the monster's trail; if there was an enemy army ahead of him as well, he would just have to do his best to avoid it. He moved now with a new urgency and a new alertness, for neither monstrous creature nor enemy army could now be much more than a day ahead of him, and might be considerably less. The signs in both cases were unmistakable.

And both army and worm were headed east, in the general direction of Tasavalta.

Praying for some kind of guidance, Zoltan forged on.

Ben and the small column of the command that had been entrusted to him were moving on the same direction, toward Sarykam and home. Ben was not praying for guidance, but muttering oaths under his breath as he listened uncomfortably to the blind Princeling's babble from inside the nearby litter. Today the mad crooning and muttering was almost continuous. At least the child did not sound as if he were suffering. Crazy, maybe, but not in pain.

Partly with the goal of avoiding that sound of a time, partly out of general impatience, Ben spoke a word to the cavalry officer, who was now his second in command, and then cantered on ahead of the column, taking a turn at scouting.

A few minutes later, while trying to discover the best way through a large outcropping of rocks, he was distracted by a sudden jumping of the land beneath his feet. It felt to him like an earthquake, or the sudden manifestation of an elemental.

In another moment Ben was confronted by the bizarre figure of a small wizard wearing a strange robe covered with symbols of obscure meaning.

This apparition, crouched among the jumbled rocks, waved to Ben and shouted at him: "Go and find Prince Mark! Hurry! Prince Mark is in trouble and he needs your help."

Ben turned his mount around. The image he was looking at was obviously just that and not an ordinary human being. He judged that the only way to deal intelligently with it was to get magical assistance.

As soon as he had turned his mount, the ground beneath the hooves of the riding-beast shifted back again, so he was left facing the same way as before.

The strange magician-figure, in front of him again, cried out: "Don't run away, Ben! Listen to me!"

"I have my orders," Ben managed to get out, and tried once more to turn his steed.

But he had to listen to more shouted pleadings before he was allowed to leave.

When Zoltan saw that the fresh trail he was now following was bringing him back to the river—or *some* river—once again, his spirits rose as before. He was looking forward to possibly encountering the mermaid again.

The trail was going upstream now, along what looked like the same river he had followed downstream only a few days earlier. He wondered if something out of the ordinary could be happening to the geography of the land through which he traveled.

At least it did make sense that the dragon should need the river, as the maid had told him. Here was another indication, a place where the beast had obviously tried to submerge itself, to wallow in the stream, though the channel here must actually be smaller than the diameter of its own body. Both banks and the vegetation on them were spattered and coated with dried mud for many meters, and a small pool had been scraped and scoured into a pond.

The thrown-out mud looked dry. But when Zoltan probed at a thick clot of it with his fingers, the center was still moist. Certainly not very many hours could have gone by since the creature passed here.

The Sword at Zoltan's side remained quiet as he crumbled the dried mud between his fingers.

He had no more idea now than when he had left the farm, of where his uncle Mark might be. The idea was beginning to grow on Zoltan that he might be the one who had to wield the Sword of Heroes when the time came. He could neither accept the idea nor reject it. It was just there, like a boulder in his mind.

Doggedly he stayed with the trail until nightfall, doing his best to overtake the thing that had made it.

A few hours before sunset he came to a place where at last the parallel trail of the human riders diverged from that of the dragon. And here the mounted force had split into two unequal groups, which had then ridden off in different directions.

Now there were three diverging trails. Zoltan stayed with that of the great worm.

After dark he once more made his fireless camp beside the stream.

And once more, to his joy, the maid appeared, popping up briskly out of the water shortly after he had wrapped himself in his blankets and lain down.

"I was afraid to show myself during the day," she began calmly. "The leather-wings might have seen me again."

"I have seen none of them," said Zoltan.

"That is good. You know, don't you, that the dragon is not far away now? Under water I can hear him burbling and splashing. I think he is resting right in the river somewhere."

Zoltan swallowed, with difficulty. "Does it ever more around at night?"

"Oh yes. Sometimes . . . listen! It may be that you will be able to hear it moving now."

He concentrated, listening intently. There was the sound of the river itself, and he could not be sure of anything else.

The maid asked him: "Where is your uncle?"

Zoltan shook his head. "I still don't know. I have no more idea than I did before."

"What are you going to do, then?"

"I don't know that, either. Except that I must keep on following the dragon. Once I get within sight of it, keep it in sight. And, when Uncle Mark shows up, give him the Sword."

"You will not try to use the Sword yourself?"

"Not if I can help it," said Zoltan after a pause. "He's—he's much better at it than I am. He's done it before."

"I will weep for you," the maid breathed, "if you are killed."

He didn't know what to say to that.

In the morning Zoltan started before dawn; there was no need for a great deal of light to follow a trail like this one. He came in sight of the dragon's tail as it was heading out of a huge thicket.

In the growing daylight he recognized the farm ahead, its distinctive boundary of trees no more than a kilometer away. And he saw that the dragon was now heading directly for it.

22

BURSLEM, after much heavy conjuring in the firelight of their nightly camp, announced to Amintor that the time had come for them to split up their forces.

"Is it permitted to ask why?"

"Prince Mark and his child are both within our reach, but they have separated. The Prince himself is now coming toward us again, either alone or with a very small escort; while the child is being taken on toward Tasavalta. If you, with a small squad of cavalry, can intercept and capture Prince Mark, I, with the remainder of my army, will overtake the force escorting Adrian."

"Where is the Sword of Mercy now?"

"Mark does not have it."

"Ah. And why this particular division of labor?"

"Because, my friend, you are the one equipped with Swords and should not need an army to protect you against one man—and I feel more comfortable with most of my army where I can see it. Would you like to exchange assignments?"

Amintor thought it over. "No," he said presently. "No, if matters are as you say, I can take him prisoner. What of the worm?"

Burslem demonstrated anger. "Some kind of magical interference has come up. It's interfered with my control."

"Karel, perhaps, is striking at us?"

"I suppose so. At any rate, we can't count on the worm just now. Neither can the enemy properly control it, of course; and I expect it'll give them something to think about besides us as it goes ravaging their countryside."

"You've lost control of it?"

"I've said that, haven't I?"

The Baron stared at him. "What if the demon-damned beast had got away from you while we were riding it?"

Burslem glared back. "I had it more directly in my grip then—anyway, nothing happened. You have your orders. Carry them out."

Zoltan, meanwhile, was doing the best he could to get himself and Dragonslicer in front of the great worm and to keep the creature from getting at the farm. There was no mistake; it was the same farm; he could recognize the gate and certain trees of the boundary, even at this distance. But even as he tried to get his loadbeast to gallop, he was confused by the fact that the farm did not seem to be at all in the same place, geographically, where he remembered it as being. He had ridden for days away from it, and here he was already back again. He had not, he was sure, been traveling in a great circle ever since he left. That would have been too elementary an error. Yet there they were, the boundary hedge and gate, just as before . . .

But now, they lay directly in the dragon's path.

The monster, fortunately for Zoltan's plans, was in no great hurry. If it was yet aware of him and his loadbeast, it was so far willing to ignore their presence. It let him get himself and his beast in front of it.

Once having reached the position he wanted, he dismounted and paused to let his loadbeast rest and to await the thing's advance. Zoltan could still nurse a hope that the dragon might, after all, decide to go off somewhere else, avoiding the farm altogether.

Meanwhile, the monster was moving only intermittently, and he had a little time available. Enough to open the medical kit that was still tied to his belt and extract from it a certain glass bottle that he had noticed earlier. This one was labeled AGAINST THE HARM OF FIRE AND ACID. Dragons, according to everything that Zoltan had ever been told about them, had plenty of both those powers with which to assail their opponents.

He smeared himself—face, hands, then as much of his skin inside his clothing as he could cover—with the vile-smelling stuff of the bottle, using the entire contents. Only then did he wonder if he ought to have saved some to give to his uncle. Well, it was too late now.

The dragon had been moving again, and now it reared its head over the small rise just in front of Zoltan, not fifty meters from him. There was no doubt that it saw him now.

The immediate effect was that the loadbeast panicked and threw Zoltan off just as he was trying to leap back into the saddle and before he really had time to panic, himself. Furious anger rose up in him and for the moment drove out fear. Dragonslicer was humming in his hands now, the full undeniable power of a Sword at last manifesting itself for him.

The monstrous head confronting him raised itself, eyes staring intently—then lurched away, angling to one side at the speed of a runaway racer. It was as if the demonstration of power in the Sword had been enough to warn the creature off.

The dragon changed its course slightly again. It was still headed for the farm, but it was going to detour around Zoltan to get there.

Zoltan stood frozen for another moment, watching—then he looked for his mount. But the treacherous loadbeast had run away.

He chased it and was able to catch it—the animal would exert itself fully, it appeared, only when the dragon was coming directly at it.

Back in the saddle, he rode desperately. His mount shied at the last, and he couldn't get close enough to the worm to strike. Quickly he leaped from the saddle and ran forward desperately.

The monster was almost past him now—but he managed to reach one flank of it, back near the tail, and there he hacked into it boldly with his humming Sword.

Amintor had been provided by Burslem with good directions as to exactly where to find Prince Mark. Now the Baron, with Shieldbreaker and Farslayer as usual at his side, and what he trusted were a dozen good cavalrymen at his back, was very near the calculated point of interception. Given the force at Amintor's disposal, it seemed to him very unlikely that he could fail to take the Prince, most probably alive rather than dead; but he was wary of Mark's ability, and of the unfathomed powers of the Sword of Mercy as well, if the Prince should have that weapon with him.

When Zoltan hewed into the dragon's flank, the blade in his hands parting the armored scales like so many tender leaves, the beast's reaction came fiercely, though somewhat delayed. The vast scaly body looped up over his head and came smashing down, making the earth sound like a drum and knocking Zoltan off his feet with the violence of the shock that shook the ground beneath them. The dragon did not turn or pause to see whether he was dead or not. The spur of Dragonslicer had been enough to send it into flight.

Its first flight was not straight toward the farm, which gave Zoltan time to recover and catch his loadbeast again.

Mounted again, he was once more able to get between the indirectly advancing dragon and the farm. The loadbeast was not unwilling to be ridden in the dragon's general direction, or at least no more unwilling to carry him that way than any other. Only when Zoltan tried to get it to go within what it considered actual striking distance did it rebel.

The dragon now had reached yet another of the river's pools, and halted there. Zoltan could hear it drinking and saw it twisting the forward portion of its snakelike body in an apparent effort to splash cooling water on its sun-heated upper scales.

Zoltan urged his mount as best he could to get in front of the dragon. It was here or nowhere that he must stop the beast; he was now almost within a stone's throw of the farm at his back.

He jumped from the saddle, Sword in hand.

Now he saw that, whether by accident or design, a bight of the huge scaly body had been thrown across the stream, making a crude dam. A deeper pool than before was rapidly forming upstream from this obstruction, and now the dragon's head was lowering toward the pool to drink.

I will kill it now, thought Zoltan, or I will never kill it.

Raising the humming Sword above his head, he ran silently toward the drinking beast.

> *Dragonslicer, Dragonslicer, how d'you slay?*
> *Reaching for the heart in behind the scales.*
> *Dragonslicer, Dragonslicer, where do you stay?*
> *In the belly of the giant that my blade impales.*

23

THE Baron was belly-down in the desert, watching from concealment Prince Mark's slow mounted approach. The Prince, as Burslem had predicted, was quite alone. Behind Amintor, the dozen troopers who had been detailed to go with him were presumably making their
own preparations to carry out the ambush. The riding-beasts of
Amintor and his party were in concealment too, being well-trained cavalry mounts that would lie down and jump up on command.

The Baron turned his head partway in the direction of his men, and
whispered softly: "Let him ride right into us, if he will . . . save us the
trouble of a chase. That's a powerful mount he rides."

Then Amintor, his attention caught by some sound or perhaps un-
wonted silence among his men, turned to observe them more carefully.
He saw them all in the act of divesting themselves of their weapons.

In the blink of an eye he was on his feet, with a Sword out in each
hand. He had thought ahead of time about the possibility of some such
move as this. Prince Mark could wait.

Shieldbreaker, because it could be relied upon to manage itself in a
fight, was in the Baron's left hand. And Farslayer, in his right fist, was
ready to exert its magic too—if any such magic should become necessary beyond that of sharp steel and skill.

The lieutenant gave terse orders, and a few of the troopers, some
brandishing weapons and some not, tried to close in on Amintor. The
Sword of Force, hammering loudly, picked out their weapons as they
came against it, and disposed of them, along with a limb or two. And
Farslayer, working superbly if in mundane fashion, took care of those
who tried to attack Amintor unarmed.

Half a minute after it had started, the fight had reached a bloody standoff. Three men were down, dead or bleeding to death rapidly. Amintor could not chase down all his enemies, nor did he dare relax his vigilance. But there appeared to be no way for the surviving troopers to overcome him.

The officer changed his tactics and tried negotiation. He called to the Baron: "Our master Burslem says if you give up the Swords, we are to let you go."

"Yes, of course. To be sure. And what has he promised you and your men?"

No one answered.

"Whatever it is, I can give you more. And I will do so if you, or any of you, will switch your allegiance to me."

Refusal was plain in the officer's face. Mixed emotions, with fear and doubt predominating, ruled in the faces of the other men.

The Baron looked them all over as well as he could. Then he picked out one of them and locked his gaze on the man's eyes. "Sergeant? What about you, ready to join me? Or are you determined to collect one of these god-forged blades of mine in your guts?" The Baron paused, then once more addressed them all. "I repeat, those who are loyal to me are well rewarded. Not like these three on the ground. If any of you know anyone who served in my army under Queen Yambu, you know I speak the truth."

He got no immediate response, but now the officer was worried. The situation, balanced.

When the break came, Amintor was almost as much surprised as the lieutenant was. The sergeant approached the officer as if for a private conference—and then struck at him without warning. The officer managed to parry most of the force of the swordcut, sustaining only a light wound, and in the next instant striking back. In the next instant a bloody melee had broken out, the troopers in two opposing factions hacking and slashing at each other energetically.

In a matter of only moments, the lieutenant and a few who remained with him retreated. First one group and then another reached the riding-beasts, and in a few moments more the fight, now a small cavalry skirmish, had swirled over the next dune.

Discipline, thought Amintor, could never have been good in Burslem's little army—and now, doubtless, it was never going to be.

"After them! Finish them!" he shouted orders after his new allies.

Now the thudding noise in Shieldbreaker quieted and Amintor was able to sheathe the Sword again. His whole left arm felt strange from holding it, but he was confident that the sensation would soon pass.

And now, with distractions out of the way momentarily, for the Prince. Quickly Amintor looked back in the other direction. There was Mark, a hundred meters or more away, evidently out of earshot of the noise of fighting. Mark was upwind, which would have muffled the noises somewhat. The Prince had dismounted, as if he meant to camp for the night, though nightfall was still hours away. No, now he was tugging at one of the legs of his mount. It looked like there was some trouble with his riding-beast's hooves or shoes.

Amintor, studying the figure of the Prince as well as he could at the distance, frowned as he observed that Mark was apparently unarmed. Oh, there might be a knife at his belt. Doubtless there would be a weapon or two somewhere, but . . .

Burslem had said that Woundhealer was now with the caravan escorting Adrian, and doubtless that was the case.

Now, the Baron judged, was the time for him to act boldly, before his own treacherous escort, or any part of it, could reappear. He rose partially from concealment and hurried forward, alternately trotting and crawling. For the moment he preferred to leave his own mount behind, so he could get closer without being seen.

When he was about fifteen meters away from the Prince, he stood up straight and called out in a loud voice for Mark to surrender.

Mark jumped to his feet, giving little sign of surprise. Apparently unarmed, he stood silently facing Amintor.

Shieldbreaker was thudding faintly again, and the Sword's hilt stung the Baron's wrist as his arm swung past the scabbard; he feared that the weapon was going to leap out into his hand. Let him once grasp the hilt of the Sword of Force now, and he would be unable to cast it down whatever Mark might do. And Shieldbreaker would never be effective against an unarmed man. To be safe, Amintor unbuckled the belt that held the Sword of Force at his side, and let belt and all fall to the sand.

Next the Baron drew Farslayer—obedient, controllable Farslayer— and smiled. He advanced upon his foe.

Mark waited until Amintor was quite near him. Then the Prince bent swiftly, plunging his arms into the sand at his feet. When his hands emerged, they were holding the hilt of a bright Sword.

Amintor assumed the weapon was Woundhealer, though there was no way he could be absolutely sure. Damn Burslem for an incompetent wizard!

"I suppose there is some logic in your behavior," he remarked, doing his best to conceal his rage.

"As much as in yours, I suppose. The next time you try to set an ambush, you should bring quieter companions."

The Baron glanced back over one shoulder, directing a contemptuous look in the direction of his vanished patrol. "Your advice is good, Highness—had you no trustworthy friends either, that you come seeking me alone? Or is it some other object that brings you here like this? I cannot think why you would want to encounter me again."

"Can you not?"

"No."

"Then tell me, bandit chieftain, how you worked your trick." Mark's own quiet rage could be heard in his voice.

"Bandit chieftain!" The Baron genuinely felt offended. "Come, Prince, you should know by now that I have advanced a step or two beyond that status."

"Really? You have acquired fine new clothing since I saw you last, I see that much."

Amintor frowned. He still did not understand Mark's presence here, and it bothered him that he did not. "Which trick do you mean?" he called to Mark. "It must have been a good one if it has brought you here seeking me with such determination."

The Prince, his face quite unreadable, stared back at him for a long, silent moment. At last Mark said: "The Sword of Healing will not heal my son."

"Ahh." Amintor let out a long, soft breath. Then he added, more to himself than to Mark: "Then it may be, after all, that there are powers in the world that can overmatch the Swords." It was not a reassuring thought for one who was relying upon Shieldbreaker against tremendous wizards.

"I have no explanation," the Baron continued aloud, after a moment's thought. "But then, I gave you no guarantees when I traded you that Sword. No, Prince, I worked no trick upon you in that way. There would have been no point in my doing so. I was content to see you go your way in peace—of course, now that you are here—"

The Baron had weighed the probabilities as best he could. Now he raised Farslayer and rushed in to strike. His object was not to kill but to disable, and he had little fear that Woundhealer would be able to do him any direct harm. Anything was possible, but a man had to be ready to take some risks.

But Mark, younger and more agile, evaded the rush. Then, running to get past his opponent, he dashed toward the spot where Amintor had cast Shieldbreaker down.

The Baron had not been careless, and had not let himself be drawn too far from where he had dropped that most effective Sword. In fact he had even begun to count, in a way, on Mark's trying to get to it. Still, it was a near thing. Amintor, hurrying back to defend his treasure, had to lunge desperately with Farslayer at the last moment to keep Mark from getting his hands on the Sword of Force. Mark nearly lost a hand in reaching to grab it up but managed to pull his arm out of the way of the slash in time, and danced away unhurt.

Still, Amintor did not want to pick up Shieldbreaker and bind himself to it indissolubly for the duration of the combat. Farslayer would do just as well for now. Holding the Sword of Vengeance ready, he slowly advanced once more.

Mark held his ground, waving Woundhealer gently before him in a two-handed grip.

The imponderables brought into the situation by the Sword of Mercy slowed the Baron's feet and stayed his hand. If he were to throw Farslayer against it, what might happen?

Then, behind him, he heard the unmistakable sounds of several riding-beasts approaching, at a slow pace.

He backed away from Mark until he felt he could risk a turn-and-look. Then he allowed himself to relax slightly; it was the sergeant and three of the men who had been with him. One of them at least was wounded, pale and swaying in the saddle.

The sergeant, after pausing to take in the situation, spoke. "The lieutenant"—he paused to spit—"and those who followed him are dead, Sir Baron."

"Good," said Amintor, breathing heavily. "Now we have another problem here."

"Indeed we have, sir. Though perhaps it is not the one you think."

Careful to keep Mark in one corner of his field of vision, the Baron turned again and regarded the sergeant silently.

"Colonel Chou, at your service," said the mounted man with stripes on his sleeve. "I am, I may say, a trusted friend and adviser of the

Magister Burslem. At the moment I am charged with collecting all the Swords for him—the late lieutenant was to undertake the same task for our former commander, Imamura, but he, as you can see, has failed. I shall not fail. Both of you, put down your Swords, please. The Sword that would help you now is at the moment out of reach of either of you, I see."

Amintor, with his eye on the speaker's midsection some thirty meters away, began to swing Farslayer in an arc. It was a certain killer, having the serious disadvantage that with one use of its power it was gone. Once the erstwhile sergeant was dead he would have to deal with the other people somehow—

Only too late did the Baron see the practiced motion of the slinger's arm on the mount beside the newly self-proclaimed colonel. With a shock of mind-splitting pain the smooth stone struck the Baron on his left leg, near the knee. He went down before the impact, as if the leg had been taken off completely. The world was a mosaic of red and black before him. Yet he would not, could not, give up. Farslayer was gone, out of reach somewhere, fallen from his grasp before it could be launched. He crawled forward, dragging himself by his hand toward Shieldbreaker—

But at the same time the former sergeant was galloping forward like a trick rider, reaching down from his saddle to grab up the Sword—

The shaft of a small arrow sprouted from the rider's turban, and he fell from his saddle, rolling inertly toward the prize. His riderless animal swerved away.

Amintor groaned, heaving with his arms to drag himself forward toward the treasure. But now he could not move. His broken leg was caught, snared in some trivial trap of desert vegetation. When he tried to move, he blacked out momentarily with the pain. He drew breath, then let out a piercing whistle, calling his war mount. In the background he could see Mark raising Woundhealer, sparring with one of the mounted troopers. The trooper was hesitating to close against the unknown Sword, but still he managed to block Mark's path toward the greater prize.

And, beyond that, on the crest of a small rise, was a huge mounted figure Amintor could recognize as that of Ben of Purkinje. A figure now cocking a crossbow, with a single simple motion of arms so thick that they made the weapon look like a child's toy.

And Amintor still could not move forward—

He looked back, then centimetered himself backward on hands and belly and the one leg that worked. Farslayer's dark hilt came again within his grip.

He saw Ben shoot a second trooper from the saddle, then duck under the swing of a battle-ax, aimed at him by a third.

Amintor's own specially trained war mount came near enough to brandish its shod hooves defensively above its fallen master— By all the gods, a bit of luck at last! The beast crouched down when Amintor gasped another order at it. It got down low enough for him to hoist himself somehow aboard it, into the saddle.

Mark and Ben between them had now finished off their last opponent. Mark dashed past the Baron and grabbed up Shieldbreaker.

Baron Amintor, sweating and grimacing with the agony of his broken leg, of broken plans and broken life, hauled out Farslayer—he had had to sheathe it to get himself mounted—and began to twirl the Sword over his head.

He had known, for a long time, the proper recitation, and he began it now.

"For thy heart, for thy heart—"

Mark now had Shieldbreaker in hand. Quickly he tossed Woundhealer to Ben, who held it before him like a shield.

"Who hast wronged me—"

The Sword of Vengeance, howling, left Amintor's hands in a streak of rainbow light.

Burslem, consulting certain indications, saw that now, as he had hoped and expected, his magic had completely overwhelmed the small Tasavaltan escort force that had been protecting the Princeling Adrian on his way back to Sarykam.

On separating from Amintor, the wizard had led the bulk of his miniature army to the place where, his magic assured him, Adrian was to be found.

Leaving his troops waiting on a small rise of land nearby, Burslem advanced alone toward the camp of the paralyzed Tasavaltans. His magic was in full control here, and he felt more than adequately protected by it.

Some of the riding-beasts and loadbeasts were on their feet, others lying as if dead or drugged. None of the humans were standing. Some sat on the ground, staring ahead of them with empty eyes as if they were drugged or dead. Others lay at full length, or curled up, eyes closed as if they were only asleep. Some people had been starting to put up a tent when they were overcome, and canvas, attached to a couple of erected poles, flapped idly in a small breeze.

In all that small section of landscape, as Burslem had intended, only one figure moved. He had withheld the full power of his magic from the Princeling himself. Valuable goods should not be damaged unnecessarily.

The child himself, small and golden-haired, had gone a little apart from all the rest to sit right beside the stream. Appearing unperturbed by what had happened to the members of his escort, the boy was dipping a hand into the current and pulling it out, over and over again, letting the water run out of the cup made by his frail fingers. With each trial he watched the result carefully, as if the way in which the drops fell sparkling in the sun might be the most important thing in all creation.

The child turned as Burslem approached, looking up at the wizard with pale blue eyes. At first those eyes stared almost blankly, but then they widened with growing fear.

Burslem, as he took the last few steps, was not even watching the child closely. Instead his thoughts were on Amintor—ought he to have trusted the newly-promoted Colonel Chou to be able to get the Swords from him? Burslem had, or thought he had, a magical hold on Chou that would make rebellion on the colonel's part all but unthinkable—but one could never be perfectly sure of anyone or anything.

But Burslem had been too much afraid of Amintor, and of the Swords, to make the attempt himself. Prince Mark had Woundhealer with him. Let Amintor and him fight it out. Burslem would be ready to face Swords again when he had his great worm back under control.

And where was the great worm now? Would his inexplicable loss of control over it bring on the Master's serious displeasure? Burslem was in fact looking up and around at the sky again, even as he bent to snatch up the small body of his hostage from the riverbank.

His reaching arms passed through empty air. The ground he walked on had changed beneath him in midstride so that he overbalanced in his movement and nearly fell.

Where was the child?

The sky above Burslem, calm a moment ago, was going mad, as was the land around him. Discolored clouds swirled about the zenith, and the ground heaved underfoot.

Only a moment ago those hills on the horizon had been arranged in a configuration drastically different from the one that they presented now. The land was stretching and recoiling, like fabric stretched upon the earth's tremendous loom, with titans' shuttles plying to and fro beneath.

The boy was gone. The stream at the wizard's feet was boiling coldly, like water in a churn, with clouds like chunks of darkness coming up from it. Chaos, like gas, appeared to be escaping from the tormented surface in great bubbles.

Something stung Burslem in the back; he skipped away from the attack and turned to see how the altered plants of the riverbank were lashing at him with new arms and claws.

Only now, belatedly, did the wizard realize that his own protective powers had been scattered like blown leaves before this change. The soldiers of his army, too, had scattered—he could hear them howling their terror and could see some of them in panic flight, going over the next hill in the altered land, and then the hill after that. This, then, was the vengeance of the Master, Burslem's punishment for some known or unknown sin. It was useless to resist, he knew, but still he had to try, to fight for his survival.

His intended victim had disappeared completely, no doubt preempted in some way by the Ancient One himself. Burslem was standing all alone under a darkling sky, his feet rooted in the middle of an enormous and forbidding plain. The clouds were quiet now, and the river had vanished completely from this odd space that centered itself upon him. Even the distant mountains now seemed to have been ironed away.

The colors and shapes of everything that he could see were changing.

Even if he had somehow displeased his Master, why should punishment be visited upon him only now, when he had at last achieved a measure of success? The wizard could not understand it.

And now, gratefully but incomprehensibly, his scattered powers were coming back to him. Was there hope in resistance, after all? Or had the Master relented?

No. This was not the Master's doing after all. Burslem could achieve no sense that the Ancient One was here at all, or acting here. And the overwhelming magic that had so wrenched out of shape the world around him had no real feeling of art to it at all. It felt like nothing but raw power. Like something born of rage and fear compounded . . .

On only a few occasions in his seven years of life had Prince Adrian sensed the presence of people who truly wished him harm. The presence of other human beings was usually a matter of indifference to him, though there were a few—his parents, a small handful of others—who were almost always welcome.

One instance of terrifying hatred, accompanied by direct violence, stood out sharply in his experience. It had taken place on the day when he and the other children had gone to play in and around the caves. On that day Adrian had been a witness to the slaughter of the soldiers who had been detailed to protect them.

Not that the little Prince had been physically present at that scene of horror, or that he had seen it with his sightless eyes. Rather he had observed and experienced it in the same way that he saw the rest of the world around him: with the inborn vision of a true, natural magician. And even that vision had been blinded for a time by the horror of the killing of the guards. For Adrian that experience had been shattering.

From that moment a profound transformation had begun in Adrian. The first manifestation of it had been his mind's instinctive defense of the cave against the magical, demonic powers assaulting it from outside. After that had come an even deeper withdrawal from the world.

Then the defense of himself and his friends had been resumed in a conscious though indirect way.

Adrian had also been steadily aware that his parents and the other humans with whom he had close contact had also been alarmed and horrified by the ambush, and that they were in some way doing what they could to meet the threat that it represented.

From Adrian's infancy he, like other infants, had been able to sense the feelings of those around him as well as hear their speech. Now, after the shock, he paid more and more attention to their words. Not that they often spoke in his hearing about things of real importance. But more and more the constant threat of physical danger, remote though it was, had turned Adrian away from his lifelong absorption with the magical aspects of the world, had made him reach out beyond the suddenly inadequate perceptions of the world that he could achieve with magic.

The little Prince knew when his father rode off from the train alone, though he did not fully understand the reasons. He missed his father and could follow him, most of the time, with his nonphysical perceptions. In the same way Adrian had a fair grasp of the locations of many other people whom he knew as individuals. And he had already begun to do more than keep track of their whereabouts.

If no one would listen when he tried to tell them things directly, perhaps they would listen to a wizard.

And the elementals, the ones originally aroused by Karel on the day of the children's entrapment in the cave, had not been allowed to meld their energies back into those of the earth itself. Instead, Adrian had discovered how to keep them alive. He had played with them like toys, sending them here and there, augmenting their power and then allowing it to diminish while he tried to decide what else he might be able to do with them. It appeared that they might possibly be a useful means of defense.

And then, at the moment when he belatedly become aware of the presence of Burslem, almost upon him, Adrian had called the elementals back to full life and had concentrated them all close around himself. It was almost a purely instinctive reaction, the only thing that he could think of to do at the moment. Another small child might have hidden his head in his arms, or jumped into the river to get away.

From the day of the alarm at the cave, Adrian had spoken directly to no one else about what he feared, or what he was trying to do. The experience of his life to date was that no one else was really able to communicate with him. His parents tried to do so only through speech, and then almost always spoke only of the simplest things. It was as if they were totally unable to see the world of magic that lay all about them. The physicians who attended Adrian were hopeless, being concerned, as far back as he could remember, with nothing but getting answers to their questions about his body: Had he eaten? Had he slept? Had his bowels moved properly? Did anything hurt him, here, or here, or here? And the magicians, if anything, were even worse. They looked around him, never exactly at him, with their arts; like the physicians, the wizards peered and probed and examined, going about their own preconceived plans as best they could with their limited perceptions.

It was the way the world was.

Adrian had experienced something of a shock when he realized, at a very early age, that the workers in magic, like everyone else he knew, were at least half blind. They seemed almost totally incapable of any real communication with him, even when he sought their aid. And magic, Adrian was beginning to realize now, was not a very good tool of communication anyway. It was much more effective as a means of concealment and manipulation.

The friendly workers in magic who sometimes attended Adrian were often more clever in their manipulations than he had yet learned to be. But in many ways they were also weaker and less able. And Adrian was beginning to realize that often they could not see as well as he could what was happening around them.

The notion of using his physical powers of speech to try to warn them had scarcely crossed Adrian's mind. One difficulty was that few people ever listened to him anyway; another was that most of the people with whom he was suddenly anxious to communicate were now scattered well out of the sound of his voice.

Among the several new needs that he was beginning to feel strongly was a better way to see. He had to establish stronger contact with the perilous world around him in order to find new ways to control it.

Entrancing discoveries rewarded his first real efforts to use his eyes. The new sense could not be quickly perfected, but now, day by day, and even hour by hour, he was making progress in its use.

A time came when Adrian realized that magic from some threatening source had ensorcelled everyone in the caravan around him. The threat was definite, though not yet immediate. He was disturbed enough to get up from his bed and leave his tent. His vision was developing strongly, and for almost the first time in his life he went wandering through the physical world unguided.

He ought to help his friends who had been struck down. But he did not yet see how. Looking, thinking, he allowed himself to be distracted by the glory of the physical, visual world surrounding him. His eyes were focusing properly at last, and his brain had learned to use the signals from them. For almost the first time he was able to see the world in full color and crisp detail. The sound of the stream drew him, and he approached it cautiously. Then the familiar feel of water became attached to the sparkling, never-before-seen dance of droplets in the air.

The magician Burslem had been able to approach very near to Adrian before the young Prince sensed his presence. The perception came in the form of an image of evil magic and threatening physical size, compounded into one.

Shocked into panic, Adrian did what he could to remove himself from the evil presence and to erect barriers between himself and it. He saw with all his senses that the effort had created a perilous turmoil in his immediate surroundings, an upheaval through which he himself was forced to struggle, as through a dream.

And suddenly he was aware of a place, not very far away, where he should go.

Burslem's own powers had recovered in time to protect their master from the shock of this local alteration of the world. The alteration could be undone, and they could undo it for him; only a little time was necessary for the task.

He was just beginning to be able to establish some mastery over his environment when a new sound distracted him. His powers were massing on one side of him, laboring there to build the most impenetrable wall of magic that they could create.

The impenetrable wall burst open at its center. Burslem had no time at all in which to hear the howl and only a moment of life remaining in which to see the streak of rainbow color coming straight at him.

24

A S Zoltan ran toward the great worm and the pool that the creature had created, the head of the monster turned toward him. Then it rose and swung away, avoiding the shrilling Sword that Zoltan held before him as he ran.

Recklessly he ran in under it and hewed again into the gray-green wall of the creature's flank at the first spot he could reach.

Scales the size of flagstones flew left and right. Again the Sword emitted its piercing sound and carved into the worm's integument as if those armored plates were so much butter.

This time Zoltan was closer to the heart and brain, and the reaction of the beast was swifter than before. A vast wounded loop, spraying dark blood, went coiling up, high as a house, to come smashing down again almost on Zoltan's head, with a noise like a falling castle wall. The carvable plates of the scales were suddenly impervious armor once again, so long as they avoided Dragonslicer's gleam. The descending mass crushed into splinters the riverside trees that happened to be beneath it. It shattered sandstone into sand and dust.

Once more, Zoltan narrowly escaped being caught under the falling bulk and flattened.

The upper limbs of one of the flattened trees caught him in the whiplash of its fall and sent him rolling, bouncing across the ground. He was bruised, scraped, and dazed.

He stumbled to his feet. The Sword had been knocked from his hand. Now it was gone.

There it was, only a few meters away. In a moment he had the hilt of the Sword of Heroes in his grip again.

But by now the dragon was a hundred meters away and receding swiftly to an even greater distance. It was still thrashing like a hooked fishworm and hissing like a windstorm with the pain of what he'd done to it. But it was not about to come back and try to get revenge against the Sword.

Zoltan realized that it was still making headway toward the farm.

He ran to get ahead of the monster again, with Dragonslicer howling in his two-handed grip. The Sword seemed to leap in his fists, as if to urge him on and drag him with it faster.

Momentarily the beast stopped its retreat to turn and raise its wagon-sized head and stare at Zoltan with its enormous eyes. Vague memories of childhood dragon-stories had started to come back to him; now there stirred one of such a story in which these beasts sometimes developed hypnotic powers, feeding themselves by bidding herds march down their throats. The nameless mermaid had mentioned something of the kind.

He felt no compulsion to let the dragon eat him. But now it was moving toward the farm once more, and he wasn't going to be able to catch up with the thing on foot.

Zoltan turned and ran after his loadbeast. It allowed him to catch it once again.

The animal allowed him to mount and ride, and willingly carried him ahead of the monster. He had lost count now of how many times he had overtaken it.

And now, for a second or third time, the dragon got around him. As long as he stayed mounted, his mount panicked at the crucial moment and fled; if he was afoot, he could not go fast enough to keep the thing blocked from its goal. If the dragon had had wit enough to keep moving quickly, it might have easily got around him to the far side of the farm and entered there to begin its devastation before he could catch up with it again. But it had no more wit than an earthworm, as far as Zoltan could tell.

And once it made a short detour, pausing to scoop up the carrion carcass of a feral cow or bull into its mouth.

Taking advantage of the delay, Zoltan was once more able to get directly between the giant creature and the farm. Then he jumped off his mount for the last time, drew Dragonslicer, and quickly cut the loadbeast's throat with the keen blade.

Working feverishly, he opened the loadbeast's belly with the same sharp tool and pulled out the entrails still pulsating and steaming lightly in the chill air.

Then Zoltan worked himself into the dead beast's body cavity, where he lay in gory warmth and darkness, gripping the hilt of Dragonslicer with both hands.

Trying to control his own breathing, he could hear the breathing of the dragon as it approached, perhaps lured on by the odor of fresh blood. Next Zoltan could feel it, feel the earth quivering with the movement of the approaching mass.

His plan had been to jump out at the last instant, when the head was lowering over him, mouth about to open. But it was impossible to time things that exactly. The creature was very near, and for an instant the noises stopped. Zoltan was suddenly afraid that it had sensed the presence of the humming Sword. But his next fear was of something else altogether. In another instant, darkness and swift motion had engulfed the dead loadbeast. It was being swallowed.

The boy could feel the carcass that enclosed him being crunched and ingested by the great worm. The process was tumultuous, almost deafening, the noise a compound of gaspings, crunchings, hissing, and the throbbing of the gigantic internal organs. Accompanying this came a wave of incredible stench, so that Zoltan found it almost impossible to breathe.

The great teeth, actually small for the size of the creature that they fed, hooked the loadbeast's carcass no more than twice as they sent it along into the dragon's gut.

Zoltan struggled to draw breath. Utter darkness had closed around him, and air had been almost entirely cut off. The physical pressure was such that he could hardly straighten his arms or move his elbows. Though Dragonslicer shrilled loudly, he was almost helpless. With wrists and forearms he wielded the blade, and then, with a desperate, surging effort, succeeded in straightening his arms so that the Sword of Heroes thrust out blindly.

The blood of the dragon jetted over him from some deep reservoir. The fumes of blood burned at Zoltan's lungs next time he managed to draw a little breath.

By now he had worked his arms and shoulders free of the loadbeast's carcass and was carving a space clear around his head. There came a whistling roar and a blast of air as he cut into the windpipe. Blood was threatening to drown him anyway. And now Zoltan thought that the blade in his hands was trying to pull him with it in one direction, as if it would lead him toward the heart.

Meanwhile, the titanic body around him was convulsing with redoubled violence. Only the tight, soft cushioning that gripped Zoltan's body on all sides saved him from severe injury.

With his last conscious energy, he strove to hack a way out through his enemy's ribs. In utter darkness he could feel how massive bones were separating before Dragonslicer's magic. He carved and carved again. At last light struck his almost blinded eyes, and again fresh air hit Zoltan, like a rush of icy water. Simultaneously the great worm's body convulsed in a spasm more frenzied than any that had gone before. Still inside the thrashing body, Zoltan could see that the opening he had cut was sometimes toward the sky and sometimes toward the earth.

Mark and Ben found themselves in possession of two Swords, Shieldbreaker and Woundhealer, and of the field of battle.

Amintor, having hurled Farslayer, creating a streak of light that dwindled rapidly toward the horizon to the east, had at once urged his mount to speed and was now rapidly disappearing in the opposite direction.

Neither Mark nor Ben were ready to pursue the Baron at once. Ben had been wounded in the skirmish just concluded, and the use of Woundhealer was the next order of business.

"Why are you here?" Mark demanded. "Where is my son?"

"I'm here to save your neck. Acceptable?"

"Sorry." The Prince drew a deep breath. "But what's happened to Adrian?"

"Happened to him? Nothing. All was well when I left the escort. He's well on his way home, many kilometers from—"

"Then what is *that?*"

Ben turned to look. Then the two men stood together, looking with awe at the bizarre effects that appeared to be transforming a portion of the world before their eyes. It was the same area into which the Sword of Vengeance had vanished when it left the Baron's hands. And on the fringe of it the Tasavaltan camp was visible. At the distance a few people, moving about slowly and lethargically, could be seen within it.

"That cannot be," said Ben. "I left the encampment days ago, to try to follow you."

Mark said, at last: "Reminds me of the time we looted the Blue Temple."

Ben nodded. "We seem to have entered a land of magic again—and this time without a wizard."

"I don't know about that."

"What do you mean?"

The Prince looked up at the sky and at the dead enemies on the earth around them. "I'd say that someone's been trying to take care of us. I was thinking that Karel must be responsible for some of this at least."

Some of the magical distortion of the landscape was clearing away, but something else, also out of the ordinary, had appeared.

"What in all the hells of Orcus can *that* be?"

"It looks like a farm. A well-kept, irrigated farm, here in the midst of nowhere. In the midst of a cauldron of magic."

"I," said Mark presently, "must go to that encampment and see about my son." The Prince turned his head and pointed. "You scout that way. Take a look at that farm, if that's indeed what it is. We can hope it's something Karel's sent us; we could all use fresh food and rest. But good or bad, we must know."

And the two men separated.

Karel was still kilometers to the east of the epicenter of the magical turmoil, though he was riding as fast as he could toward it. Even from a distance, he got the distinct impression that the local geography had been pretty well jumbled, and he was impressed. It was a long time since he had seen anything of the kind. At least there was no doubt of where he ought to go. You didn't need to be a wizard to see the signs.

Elementals had created most of the turmoil before him. As he approached, the wizard watched with awe the elephant dance that they were still performing.

"What have I done?" he asked himself. "How did I ever manage to accomplish it? Ardneh himself could hardly . . . but wait."

Karel assumed the elementals were the same ones he had created many days ago, now revivified and stalking the plain before him and the nearby hills, diverting the little river from its proper channel. But if these were indeed the same elementals, someone had really been working on them, had salvaged and reenergized them from the entities that Karel had left dying, like so many smoldering fires buried in the earth.

They were now bigger, more powerful, more sharply defined, and closer to sentience than any that Karel had ever managed to raise before.

He rode a little closer to the turmoil, until his steed began to grow restive at the mumbling and the rumbling in the earth. Then he stopped and looked matters over again. Now he could be certain that this was not the work of the one who called himself the Master. He hadn't really thought it was, but—

But now he could let out a long, faint, quivering breath of relief.

And now someone—the figure of a wizened little old man, clad in a peculiar stage-wizard costume—was standing a few meters to Karel's right and waving at him.

Karel had been looking forward to this encounter. He turned, nodding to himself. Beth and Stephen had done a good job of describing the apparition. The image was really very good, though slightly transparent along the edges.

The lips of the figure moved. "Karel, Karel!" it rasped at him in its old man's voice. "You must help me!"

"Yes, I will help." The magician who was seated on the riding-beast shook his head and pulled at his gray beard. "Do you know, some of this is my fault . . . I know who you are, by the way, though it is not easy to believe."

"I know who you are, too, Karel. Who cares about that?" Now the voice sounded angry, and frightened, too. "Go back home if you can't help me. Can't you help?"

"I will help. I see that things are starting to get away from you here. But be calm, you have done marvelously well, considering everything. These elementals have doubtless saved your life, and others' lives as well. But now they're turning dangerous to you. Dangerous even to your—"

"Help me, then! Help me!"

And Karel did.

25

IT took the experienced wizard even a little longer than he had anticipated to soothe and quell the elementals down into quietude, for their
rebellious power had grown great. But eventually even their gargantuan
energies had been tamped and dampened back within the earth. The
local clockwork of the world was ticking on reliably once more. The
image of the ancient-looking wizard in the unintentionally comic dress
had disappeared, and Karel did not expect ever to encounter it again.

Once the job of settling the elementals was done, Karel remounted
his riding-beast—the animal, relatively experienced though it was in
these matters, required some soothing first—and proceeded on his way.

The unruly portion of the world had quieted—if it had not exactly
gone back to its original conformation—and the local geography was
once again almost completely stable. Almost, because Karel could see
the farm still there ahead of him, and he knew from past experience that
the farm had a way of its own with geography. He was not really
surprised to see it right before him now, though the last time he had
seen it (under quite different circumstances) it had been many kilometers from here.

When he reached the tall gate, with its green wreaths of vine and its
decorations of horn and ivory, he found it unlocked. That was no more
than Karel had expected. He rode on in, remembering to close the high
gate carefully behind him lest any of Still's livestock wander out. Here
on the farm you always had to keep such practical matters firmly in
mind.

As Karel approached the house he saw that he was expected, which
by now came to him as no surprise. Outside the front door, two people
were standing waiting for him. The first of these, to Karel's great relief,

was young Zoltan. The boy looked older than when Karel had seen him last, and a bit banged about and bruised, but essentially unharmed. Zoltan was dressed in clean farmer's garb, and his half-curly hair was damp as if he might just have had a bath. He was holding a piece of pie in his fist, and his mouth was full.

Bulking beside Zoltan was Ben of Purkinje, still grimy and smeared with dried blood as if he had just come from a war. Ben was looking somewhat confused—Karel, remembering his own first visit to the farm, could sympathize. Ben welcomed the appearance of Karel as that of a familiar face in a strange land.

As Karel dismounted he smiled reassuringly at Ben. When the first round of greetings was over, he told the huge man: "There is magic, Ben, and then there is magic. Not all of it is accomplished with a chant and a waving of the arms. Not all of it turns parts of the world upside down."

And then the Stills themselves were coming out of the house, and Karel spent some time in the joyful task of greeting his old friends in the way that they deserved. He showed them great respect, and also some of the envy that he could never help feeling when he visited here.

The Stills were prompt to assure him that Prince Mark himself was safely on his way to join them and would be arriving at the farm presently.

And now one more figure, a small one, had appeared in the open doorway of the house. Prince Adrian stood erect, looking at Karel with clear blue eyes; and then he somewhat shyly held out a hand in greeting. Karel was much moved. He half genuflected as he grasped the child's hand and muttered something.

A minute later the gathering had adjourned to the kitchen—something that always seemed inevitable in this household—and everyone but Mother Still was seated at the table while she bustled around it, dealing out heavy plates and cups. A feast was rapidly taking shape before them.

Ben, who had stopped at the sink first to wash the stains of combat from his arms and face, was marveling at the seeming ease with which these preparations were being accomplished. Karel caught his eye, and said to him in an aside: "Whatever the task on this farm, working or fighting, it will be done well and quickly if someone works at it. That is the secret magic that these people have."

Ben smiled vaguely, wanting to be reassured, not really understanding as yet. It took most people several visits, Karel had observed.

Adrian had been listening. "And it works for reaching the farm, too," the child said. "Don't forget that. My father is going to find it, because I'm here, and he's really working at finding me."

It seemed to Karel that the preparations had hardly started, the last clean plate dealt out on the table, before Mother Still was announcing that the feast was ready and taking her own chair at the table. At that point conversation was abandoned for a time except for the terse courtesies that were required to maintain a flow of serving dishes from hand to hand around the table.

Everyone took part in the cleaning-up that followed, and again it was all done almost before the visitors were sure that it had started. Each of them felt faintly disappointed that there had not been time for him to contribute more.

And then the party were all seating themselves in the parlor, and Farmer Still was lighting the lamps there against the first lowering of the shadows outside.

When Mother Still had established herself comfortably in her rocking chair with her knitting, she turned at once to Karel across the table and asked him: "Tell me, are you blood kin to the Princess Kristin? Or are you this child's relative by marriage only?"

"Indeed I am blood kin. The mother of the Princess was my sister."

"That explains it, then." Nodding with satisfaction, the goodwife rocked her chair and shooed away the calico cat that was menacing her supply of yarn. "I thought as much," she added. "Then the child has a powerful inheritance of magic on both sides of his family."

Adrian, sitting close beside Father Still at the moment, was listening intently.

"How's that, Mother?" The farmer squinted at his wife. Meanwhile his large, gnarled hand had paused over the lamplit table, where he was starting to show Adrian the game of pegs.

"Father, I do wish you would try to keep up with family affairs." The goodwife's needles clicked. Her chair creaked, sawing at the floorboards, back and forth.

"Haven't heard much from that part of the family," he grumbled mildly. "All busy over there wearing crowns and being royalty and such."

"Never mind," his spouse chided him. "It's still family, and they have a lot of things to worry about." The cat (who was really quite ordinary in appearance) now sprang right up into her lap. Rocking industriously, Mother Still added: "His grandfather on his father's side is the Emperor himself, you know."

"This lad? Oh yes, I know." Not appearing overly impressed, Still was now jiggling the Princeling on his knee.

"When," Adrian asked them all in a clear firm voice, "is Daddy going to get here? I want to see him. I know he's on his way, but when?"

Ben had turned his head and was looking at the child again with profound amazement. The huge man had eaten well at dinner—it was hardly possible to do otherwise in this household—but had had little to say, before the meal or after. Continuing to wear his battle-harness, and still showing some of the marks of war, Ben sat in a chair and marveled silently.

"The Emperor himself," Goodwife Still repeated with quiet emphasis.

"Yes, of course," her husband agreed. Either he had remembered all along about the Emperor, or he was trying to sound as if he had. Now he went back to teaching Adrian the game.

No one had yet answered the Princeling's question. "Your father," Karel said to him, "is really safe, and he is really on his way here. The people who were trying to harm him are either dead now, or far away."

"I know," said Adrian.

"Good. Well, then, about your father. People, or certain people anyway, can find this farm whenever they really start to look for it. At least they can if it's anywhere near them at all when they start. And you're here, and I'm sure your father is really looking for you. So he's going to be here very soon. If you're impatient, you could look for him yourself."

"I've walked so much today that my legs are tired," the small boy said. And in truth he looked and sounded physically exhausted. "And I don't want to do any looking with magic. I don't want to do any magic at all for a while."

"A wise decision," Karel nodded.

"Then play the game with me," Still encouraged the child. "It'll help you keep awake until your daddy gets here." Then, having caught yet another pointed glance from his wife, he protested: "I *did* remember about the Emperor."

"And I, for a time," said Karel, rubbing his eyes, "forgot about him, and that Adrian is his descendant. To my own peril, and that of others, I forgot."

"Will someone tell me one thing, clearly?" Ben of Purkinje boomed out at last, startling everyone else. "Why couldn't Woundhealer help the lad? And what've you done for him now that's worked this cure?"

"The Sword of Healing could not restore his sight," said Karel, "because he was never blind."

Ben only looked at him. Ben's mouth was working as if he were getting ready to shout again.

Karel sighed. "I did not express that well. Let me say it this way: Adrian's eyes, and the nerves and brain behind his eyes, had nothing wrong with them. He simply had not learned to use them yet."

Mother Still, busy with her knitting, smiled and nodded. The farmer frowned at his pegboard game. Adrian was looking from one of the adults to another, and his expression said that he was too tired to talk just now unless it became necessary, and at the moment they were doing well enough without his help.

Ben muttered exotic swearwords under his breath. "Then why, by all the gods and demons—?"

"He began to use his eyes to see with," Karel went on, "as soon as a real need arose for him to do so. He was ready by then to use his eyes. When that time came, he turned away from the world of magic, for almost the first time in his short life, and he entered the world that is shared by all humanity."

Ben was still staring—now, the wizard thought, with the first glimmerings of comprehension.

Karel pressed on. "Take Woundhealer's blade and draw it through the legs of a day-old infant—the babe will not jump up and begin to walk. Its legs have not been healed, because they were not crippled to begin with. The child is simply not ready to walk yet."

"Talk about children!" burst out Mother Still. Her fingers continued their tasks with yarn and needles, but she gave the impression of someone who was unable to keep silent when a favorite subject had come up. "If you've ever had little ones about and watched 'em closely, you'll have noticed that they generally work at learning one thing at a time. The important things, I mean, like walking and talking."

"And seeing?" Ben was trying to grasp it.

"There are different ways of seeing," Karel continued. "To Adrian—

who has, I think, the greatest natural gift for magic that I have ever encountered—the most natural way to see is not with the eyes at all."

Mother Still impulsively threw her needlework aside and held out her arms. Adrian, faced with this silent summons, jumped down from her husband's lap and came to her on tired legs.

She lifted the boy into her own lap and passed a hand across his forehead. "These little eyes are learning to see now. But for a long time there was no need—or so it seemed to the little mind behind them. Because there were so many other things for that mind to do. So much to be learned, to deal with the other kind of vision that he has. Things that vision brought him might have hurt him badly if he had not learned how to deal with them."

"To my shame," said Karel, "I never really looked at him until today." Turning to Ben, the wizard added: "Until now, Adrian has seen every person and every object in the world almost exclusively by the auras of magical power and potential that they present. It took me decades to learn such seeing, and I have never learned to do it as well as he can now. It is of course a fascinating way in which to perceive the world—but for a human being it should never be the only way. And for a child of seven there are certainly dangers—you remember the seizures he was subject to."

Ben said: "He's not been troubled with those, I think, since the Sword touched him."

"Nor will they bother him again, I trust. Now he should—I think he must—put away all the things of magic for a time. Let him look at the world by sunlight and moonlight and firelight. Let him see the faces of the people in it. Let the struggle that has separated him from them be at an end."

"For a time," said Adrian suddenly, and they all looked at him.

"For a time only," the wizard confirmed, "let magic be put away." He looked around at the other adults. "It is a shame," he said again, "that I did not understand the problem. None of us understood it—but I might have. Only I did not take the trouble. When I considered the child at all, I wasted my time, looking into the air and space around him for evil influences, spells and demons that were not there."

"Come along, boy," said Father Still, getting up from his chair suddenly and holding out his hand. "Someone's at our door."

Adrian stared at him for a moment, then jumped up.

At the front door of the house the two of them, with the others crowding close behind, met Mark just as he was lifting a hand to knock.

Adrian stared for the first time at his father's face. Then with a cry he jumped into his arms.

Dusk had deepened into moonlit night when Zoltan wandered out of the house, closing the door behind him on the firelight and laughter within. He paused, content for the moment to breathe the fresher, colder air outside. Then an impulse led him along the short wagon road, not the one leading to the gate but another track, which terminated at the edge of the cultivated land, just where a ditch fenced with a grill-work barrier let in water from the stream flowing just outside the farm.

Zoltan, standing just inside the fence and clinging to it, looked for a long time at the undiminished stream outside as it rushed down a hill-side. At length he turned away, starting back to the house.

There was a splash behind him, and he turned back just in time to see a small log bob to the surface at the foot of the miniature waterfall. Then the piece of wood went dipping over the next brink down, moving along briskly on its journey to the distant sea.

THE SECOND BOOK OF LOST SWORDS:
SIGHTBLINDER'S STORY

1

THE sun was up at last, somewhere beyond the cliffs that stood above the far end of the lake. While the bright disk itself remained invisible, it projected a diffuse radiance through morning mist and lake-born fog, making a pearl-gray world of land and air and water. It was a world in which no shape or color was able to remain quite what it ought to be. Small waves of soft pearl nibbled at the slaty rocks of the uneven shoreline. On the steep slopes rising just inland, pine trees with twisted trunks and branches grew thickly, their gray-green needles gathering pearls and diamonds of moisture out of the leaden shadows that surrounded them. Land and lake alike seemed to be giving birth to the billows of almost colorless vapor that moved softly over earth and water. Fog and light together worked a brief natural enchantment.

A man was standing alone on the very edge of the lake, leaning out into the mist. With one of his huge hands he gripped the twisted trunk of a stunted tree, while the other hand held a black wooden staff in a position that allowed him to brace part of his weight on its support. He was very nearly motionless, but still the attitude of his whole body showed the intensity of the effort he was making, trying to see something out over the water. He had a large, round, ugly, stupid-looking face, his forehead creased now with the effort of trying to see through the pearl-gray air. His mouth was muttering oaths, so softly as to leave them totally inaudible. Gray marked his dark hair and beard, and his age appeared to be closer to forty than to thirty.

Somewhere, only a matter of meters to the man's right as he looked out over the water, a lake bird called, sounding a single, mocking, raucous note. Despite its nearness, the impertinent bird was quite invisible in mist. The watcher paid it no attention.

He was thinking that a clear midnight, even with no moon, would have made for better seeing than this hazed near-nothingness imbued with sunlight. At least at midnight you would not expect to be able to see anything. As matters stood now, the man could only suppose that there were still islands out there in the middle of the chill lake, the islands he had seen there yesterday, no more than a couple of kilometers away. He supposed he could take it for granted too that there was still a castle on one of those islands, the castle he had seen there yesterday. And maybe he could even be sure that—

Nearby sounds, the scramble of feet in heavy gravel, the impact of a blow on flesh, jolted the watcher away from suppositions. The sources of these sounds were as invisible as the noisy bird, but he was sure they were no more than a stone's throw away, along the shoreline to his right. After a momentary pause there followed more energetic scrambling and another blow, and then a cry for help in a familiar voice.

The watcher had already launched himself in the direction of the sounds, moving with surprising speed for someone of his great bulk, well past his early youth. And as he ran along the jagged shoreline, avoiding boulders and trampling bushes, new sounds came from behind him, those of another pair of running feet. Those pursuing feet sounded lighter and more agile than his own, but so far they had been unable to overtake him. He paid them no attention.

The big man's wooden staff, a thick tool of black hardened wood somewhat longer than he was tall, was raised now in his right hand, balanced and ready to do the service of either spear or club.

And now, after only a couple of dozen strides, the younger feet behind him had begun to gain. But still the big man did not turn his head. The sounds of struggle ahead continued.

Both runners saw that, despite their quickness, they were too late.

Rounding a spur of the rugged shoreline, one after the other in rapid succession, they came in sight of the noisy struggle, in which three men had surrounded one. The three men, though wearing soldiers' uniforms in gray trimmed with red, were all unarmed. The man surrounded had showing at his belt the black hilt of a great Sword, but he was not trying to draw the weapon. And now, an instant later, even if he had wanted to draw it, it was too late, because his arms were pinioned. He was a tall and powerful man, and still conscious, but he had lost the fight.

The huge man roared a challenge and ran on, doing his best to reach the fighters. But he and the runner who followed him were still too far away to have any influence upon the outcome. The three who had the one surrounded were now lifting him up between them, as if they meant to make of him an offering to some strange gods of mist or lake.

And now indeed, coming down out of the low, tree-grazing clouds, a winged shape appeared. Those descending wings surpassed in span and thickness those of almost any bird, reptile, or flying dragon that either of the would-be rescuers had ever seen before. But still those wings appeared inadequate to support this creature's body, which was as big and solid as a riding-beast's. The head and forelimbs of the quadruped were those of a giant eagle, covered with white feathers shading into gray. But the body and the rear legs resembled those of a lion, clad in short, tawny fur and thick with muscle. The thing appeared too bulky for its wings, despite their size, to get off the ground. And yet it flew with graceful power.

Whatever the nightmare creature was, it had already fastened the taloned grip of its forelimbs on the heavy body of the man who was being held up for them. Up he went again, right out of the hands of his human captors, the undrawn Sword still at his belt.

And now at last the huge man running came within reach of the victorious three, and sent them scattering with a swing of his black staff. They did not run far. Instead they were quick to seize up weapons of their own, swords and knives that had been lying concealed among the low bushes and the rocks.

The big man and his companion, who had arrived right at his heels, met their three opponents. The length of black wood, held now like a quarterstaff, knocked a long knife from one man's hand, and then with a straight thrust doubled up the man who'd lost the blade.

"Ben!"

Thus warned, the big man spun around quite gracefully, in time to catch a hurled rock on his left arm, which by now he had adroitly shielded in his rolled-up cloak. He advanced on the thrower. Off to his right he could hear, and see from the corner of his eye, young Zoltan and the third opponent sparring, a clash of swordblades and then another clash, with gasping pauses in between.

Mist still flowed in from the lake and purled around the fighters, in billows sometimes so thick that one pair of them could not see the other. The man who had thrown the rock now sought to win against the staff by dancing in and out, waving his battle-hatchet. But he could make no headway against the tough wood of that long shaft, and the arm that held it. A few hard-breathing moments later, the staff came crashing against his skull, ending plans and trickery for good, driving out all thoughts and fears alike.

Ben quickly turned again. The third opponent, seeing the fight going against his side, risked all on a deceptive thrust. Young Zoltan, well-taught, sidestepped as was necessary, and the enemy impaled himself on Zoltan's blade. He staggered back, uttered a strange sound, and fell. The fight was over.

But yet, once more, feet scrambled in the gravel. The man Ben had knocked down at the beginning of the skirmish had now got his brain working and his legs under him again, and was rapidly vanishing inland amid the mist and dripping trees.

"After him!" Ben roared. "We need to find out—" He saved his breath for running. Young Zoltan was well ahead of him, already sprinting in pursuit.

Running uphill as best they could, the two allies separated slightly, chasing the sound of their quarry's receding footsteps inland. Trees grew thickly on these slopes, and their branches of soggy needles slapped, as if with a malignant will, at every rushing movement. Having been through a run and a fight already, Ben's lungs were laboring. Whenever he paused to listen, his own blood and his own breath were all that he could hear. The mist rolled round him, blinding him effectively. The chill sun seemed to make no headway in the sky.

Then there came Zoltan's voice, calling him from somewhere ahead. Ben ran again, stopped to listen once more, and once more resumed the chase, or tried to.

When he had labored onward forty meters or so he paused again and choked out breathless curses. The sounds of running feet were fainter now, and they were all behind him. The surviving enemy must have doubled back toward the lake.

Panting more heavily than ever, Ben caught up with young Zoltan at last, though only on the very shoreline. Side by side they stood, their sandaled feet in the small waves, watching as a small boat, its single occupant furiously working the oars, vanished into the mist, heading directly out from shore.

"What do we do now?" Zoltan gasped at last. "The Prince is gone.

Whoever they are, they have the Prince—and Shieldbreaker with him. What do we do?"

Ben leaned against a tree. "Seek help," he got out at last, and paused for a wheezing breath. "And pray"—he drew another desperate breath —"we find it."

2

THE mirror was made of real glass, smooth and relatively unblemished, so clear that it almost certainly had a silver backing. Even the wood carving of the frame fastened so carefully to the wall was not entirely inept. All in all, it was a finer thing than you would expect to find out here in the hinterlands, in the only inn of a small town that was very little more than a fishing village. Certainly it was the best mirror that the lady who now occupied the little room had seen in a long time. And during the tedious days of waiting for the boat that was to carry her on down the Tungri, she had been taking full advantage of the opportunity offered by the glass for a new self-appraisal.

The face that the mirror showed her had never been ethereally beautiful—it had too much of a nose for that. But a dozen years ago—no, say only ten—it had possessed considerable attraction. Or at least a number of men had found the lady who wore this face desirable as recently as that. Even now it was still a good face, its owner thought, comely in its own earthy way. Or it would be a comely face, and even relatively youthful, if you thought of it as belonging to a woman of sixty.

The trouble with that qualification was that she was scarcely more than forty, even now.

The woman who had been waiting for days in the small, cheap, temporary room, she who had once been Queen Yambu, dropped her grayish gown—it was almost a pilgrim's garment—from her shoulders, and stood before the mirror unclothed in the light of midday. She was still trying to give herself a more complete and objective appraisal.

Her silvery hair went well with the gray eyes, but stood in discordance with her full breasts and her upright bearing. Her body looked much younger than her face, and now the overall effect was nearer her true age.

Women—and men too—who had the skills of magic, or the resources to hire those skills, frequently turned to magic to fight back advancing age, or at least its visible effects. But Lady Yambu had no great aptitude of her own for working spells, and as for buying the appearance of youth, she had never seriously considered that course of action, and did not do so now.

Had she been truly dissatisfied with her appearance, a first step, simpler than magic and less risky, would have been to dye her hair back to its own youthful raven black. That might have made her look younger —would certainly have done so until the beholder looked upon her face.

Yes, the problem, if it was a problem, was in her face.

She had one of the Swords to thank for that.

"Hold Soulcutter in *your* hands throughout a battle," she had once said to a man she knew almost as well as she knew anyone, "and see what *you* look like at the end of it."

The good mirror on the rough wall was giving her a harsh truth, but truth was what she wanted, now more than ever, and she did not find it devastating. Really, the glass only confirmed what she had been telling herself of late: that youth no longer really mattered to her, just as for a long time now neither power nor the thrill of competition had been subjects of concern. More and more, with time's accelerating passage, the only thing that she found of any importance at all was truth.

Pulling on her gown again, the lady turned from the mirror and took the three steps necessary to approach the open window of her second-floor room, through which a chill breeze entered.

Like the mirror, the single window presented a vision that seemed worthy of a finer setting than this poor room in a rude settlement. The sun, now approaching noon, had long since burned away the morning's mystery of mists from the glassy surface of Lake Alkmaar. Much of the twisting, irregular length of that body of water was visible from the lady's window.

Fifteen or twenty kilometers from where she stood, beyond the distant eastern end of the lake, rose the high scarp of land walling off the eastern tip of the continent. Above and beyond those cliffs lay Yambu's former life, her former kingdom, the other lands she had once fought to conquer—and much else.

But the truth she wanted did not lie there. Not her truth, the truth that still mattered to her. Not any longer. Where it was she did not know exactly, but certain clues had pointed her downriver, far to the south and west.

Halfway between her window and the far end of the long, comparatively narrow lake, a couple of dozen small islands were clustered irregularly near the center of the kilometers of water. Even at this distance, in the clear sunshine, Yambu could descry the gray bulk of a castle upon the largest of those bits of land.

If she had ever suspected that any portion of the truth she sought might lie out there upon those islands, the events of the last few days and the stories spreading among the townsfolk and the travelers at the inn had effectively changed her mind. The good wizard Honan-Fu had been conquered, overthrown. That was not his castle any longer.

She raised her eyes yet once more to that even more remote scarp of land, blue with distance, that represented her past. Then she turned from the window. She was not going to retrace the steps of the journey she had begun. There was nothing for her back there now.

Approaching the most shadowy corner of her little room, the lady was greeted by a peculiar noise, a kind of heavy chirp. It came from her toy dragon, which was perching with great patience upon her washstand. This dragon was a peculiar, winged beast, no bigger than a barnyard fowl but of a quite different shape—the joint product of the breeder's and the magician's art.

Going to stand beside the creature, whispering into its gray curling ear with soft strange words, Lady Yambu fed it the living morsel of a mouse, which she took with firm fingers from a cage beside the stand. Delicacies were almost gone now, for the lady and her pet alike. She still had a substantial sum of money left, and a few jewels, but she meant to save her modest wealth against some future need; her journey downriver might be very long. Tonight, she thought, the dragon might have to be released from the window of this room to forage for itself. She hoped that the creature would come back to her from such a foray, and she thought it would; she trusted the one who had given her the pet almost as much as she had ever trusted anyone.

Restlessly Lady Yambu moved back to the window again. Down at the shabby docks, some of which were visible from this vantage point, there was still no sign of the long-awaited riverboat that was to carry her out of the lake and down the Tungri as far as the next cataract. The *Maid of Lakes and Rivers,* she had heard that the riverboat was called.

The *Maid* was days overdue already, and she supposed more days were likely to pass before it arrived.

If it ever did. She had heard also that traffic on the lower river was at best far from safe.

This was her eleventh day of waiting in this inn. It was good that the earlier years of her life had schooled her thoroughly in patience and self-sufficiency, because—

Making a brisk decision, the lady suddenly scooped up a few small essential items that she did not want to leave unguarded in the room while she was out of it, and moved in two strides to the door. Locking the door behind her, she strode along the short and narrow upstairs hall of the inn, and down a narrow stair. This stair, like most of the rest of the building, was constructed in rustic style, of logs with much of the bark still on them.

As the lady descended, the common dining room, now empty, was to her left, and the small lobby, with three or four pilgrims and locals in it, was to her right.

She had almost reached the foot of the stairs when she saw, through the open front door of the inn, to her right, the figure of a man who moved along the middle of the unpaved street outside, advancing toward the waterfront with a steady, implacable-looking tread. No doubt it was the size of the man, which was remarkable, that first attracted her attention—his form was mountainous, not very tall but very bulky, and not so much fat as shapeless. Lady Yambu could see little of this man but his broad back, but still his appearance jogged her memory. It was not even a memory of someone she had seen before, but of someone she ought to know, ought to be able to recognize. . . .

Moving quickly through the lobby and out the front door, she stood on the log steps of the inn above the muddy and moderately busy street, gazing after him. A second man, much younger and much smaller, was walking with the one who had caught her attention, and already both of them were well past the inn, heading down the sloping street in the direction of the docks. The big man carried a staff, and the smaller wore a sword, which was common enough here as in most towns. Both were dressed in rough, plain clothing.

The lady, on the verge of running after the two, but not choosing to brave the mud and the loss of dignity involved, cast her eyes about. Then with a quick gesture she beckoned an alert-looking urchin who was loitering nearby, and gave him a trifling coin and a short verbal message. In a moment his small figure was speeding after the two men.

"Alas," the lady was saying to the huge man a quarter of an hour later, "I doubt that there is any messenger, winged or otherwise, to be found in this village who could reach Tasavalta sooner than you could yourself."

She was back in her room at the inn, sitting on one end of the small couch that also served as a bed, while the two men she had invited in from the street stood leaning against the outer wall, one on each side of the window. They had now been in the lady's company long enough to tell her their story about the kidnapping of Prince Mark at dawn, only a few hours ago. She had heard them with considerable interest; the Prince of Tasavalta had been a person of some importance in her old life.

The lady asked her informants now: "And he still had Shieldbreaker with him when he was taken?"

The smaller, younger man nodded. He was called Zoltan, and had been a total stranger to Yambu until today. He said: "But my uncle did not draw it. As you must know, lady, that would have been a mistake in a fight against unarmed attackers—doubtless they knew he was carrying a Sword, and which one of the Twelve it was. And they knew the only way to fight against it. Or they would not have attacked him without weapons of their own in hand, or at least at their belts."

"So Shieldbreaker has presumably gone to the master of those men now, whoever he may be. And he commands a griffin. That is not good. I have never even seen a griffin," said the lady, and sighed, reminding herself that the time was long past when she had to concern herself with such things as the balance of power. "And of course now you are in a desperate hurry to send word to Tasavalta, and get help from Princess Kristin and the others, or at least let them know what has happened. But I have no messenger to lend you."

In response, the huge man, Ben of Purkinje, looked pointedly at the lady's pet winged dragon, which was still perched on the washstand.

Yambu nodded. "Yes, that creature could serve as a messenger, of sorts. But I fear my pet could not be made to carry any word back to Tasavalta for you. Still I would like to do something to help Prince Mark, provided he is not, as you fear, already beyond help. Though we were enemies, I suppose he is now as close to being my friend as anyone who walks the face of the earth today." She paused. "And you, Ben of Purkinje, though I think we have never seen each other before today— you have been much in my mind for the past several months."

That surprised the big man, distracting him if only briefly from his deep concern over his Prince. "Me? Why me?"

"Because between us, you and me, there is a connection of a sort—I mean apart from our having been enemies across the battlefield. You knew my daughter."

"Ah," said Ben, distracted even more, against his will. "Yes. I knew Ariane."

"That is her name. I have no other daughter. And you were with her, eleven years ago or thereabouts, in the vaults of the Blue Temple."

The impression made by her words on Ben was deepening. Eventually he said in a dull voice: "She died there, in my arms." And Zoltan, so young he was, perhaps not even fully grown as yet, looked at the older man with sympathetic wonder.

Yambu said: "And you had been with Ariane for a long time before that."

Ben gazed back at her in silence. His face was grim, but beyond that hard to read.

She who had once been the Silver Queen went on: "As you know, I have been living for years in a White Temple, withdrawn from the world. Almost, I have ceased to have either friends or enemies at all. Now I am only an old woman, making my way out into the world again to try to wring some answers from it. I am sure you can provide me with some of the answers that I want—a portion of the truth about my daughter. In return I will be willing to do whatever I can for you, and for your Prince. Perhaps there will be nothing I can do; but I am still not entirely without resources."

For a little time Ben prolonged his thoughtful silence. Then he said: "As I suppose you know, lady, Ariane suffered a head wound when we were fighting down there in the Blue Temple's vaults. For a time after she received the injury—for many minutes, perhaps an hour—she was able to speak and move about. Then suddenly she collapsed. I was standing beside her, and I caught her as she fell. A few minutes later she was dead."

"The two of you were lovers?"

The huge man turned away to look out of the window momentarily, and then turned back. His ugly face was full of pain. "We had known each other for a matter of a few days—no more. From the day that Mark and I and the others broke into a Red Temple and brought her out, until the day she died in that damned hole."

"I want to know," said Yambu, royally persistent, "whether Ariane was still a virgin when she died."

"How can that matter now?"

"And I want to know much more than that." The silver-haired woman was still capable of ignoring questions in the manner of a queen. "I would like you to tell me everything, any detail you can remember, about those days the two of you spent together. Whether the truth is harsh or tender, I would know it. Lately the fate of my only child has come to be of tremendous importance to me."

"I have no objection," Ben replied, "to telling you the whole story. Someday when I have time. If both of us live long enough. Right now, as I have explained, Zoltan and I are both extremely busy. We are in danger, and we need help."

"I understand; we have a bargain, then, and I will do what I can to help you. Tell me, why was the Prince here, so far from home, and with so few attendants?"

Ben hesitated; then he nodded and took the plunge. "The largest of the islands in this lake is, or was, the home of a friendly wizard of great power, allied to the White Temple. His public name is Honan-Fu. In his academy a few select apprentices—"

"I know something about Honan-Fu," Yambu rapped out impatiently. "Go on."

"The Prince wanted to learn something about Honan-Fu's establishment. He thought that by coming here incognito—"

"You need not be so cautious with me, big man. By now everyone knows about Mark's eldest son. Adrian's still only a child—he'd be nine years old now? No more than ten—but blessed with great magic. Or would 'cursed' be a better word for his condition?"

"All right, then. Mark wanted to see the place at first hand, before he sent his nine-year-old heir to be apprenticed."

Yambu was nodding. "That should be interesting—one day to see a true magician-king upon the throne of Tasavalta."

Ben grunted. "As for the Prince being unattended on this trip, well, you see his entire escort before you. Zoltan and I came with Mark down the Sanzu, then down the cliffs beside the Upper Cataract to reach this lake. That part of the route you must have taken yourself.

"We brought no magician with us—a grievous mistake, perhaps. Still, we thought we were headed for a friendly reception in the castle of an enchanter stronger than any we could have brought with us. But from the moment when we arrived on the shore of Lake Alkmaar two days ago, we could tell that there was something wrong out there on the magician's islands. We knew that Honan-Fu had been expecting us in a general way at least, and anyway I suppose a wizard of his stature ought to have known that we were here. But he did not know. At least no boat came for us, and no messages.

"We were suspicious, and hesitated even to go into any of the villages. At last we talked to a few of the fisherfolk who live in isolated huts along the shore. They were reluctant to speak to strangers, but certainly something else besides our presence was bothering them.

"And then this morning, at last, we had our greeting from the island." Ben gestured savagely toward the lake.

The lady moved to stand beside the huge man at the window, and rested one hand lightly on his shoulder, as if to seal a bargain. She said: "I have dealt for many years with magicians—most of whom were far indeed from any alliance with the White Temple. And so I think I know that other kind, know them well enough to smell them when the air is as thick as it is here and now with their effluvium. Sometime during the past ten days, Honan-Fu has been supplanted on his island. How, and by whom, I know not, though the town is full of rumors, and suddenly invading soldiers in gray and red are everywhere. They have little to say about the one they serve. But obviously the new ruler is a wizard of tremendous power, who is no friend of the Prince."

Then with a decisive motion she turned from the window, toward the odd little dragon that still perched preening itself upon its stand. She said: "It will be best, I think, if we dispatch a messenger."

"You said that creature was no messenger."

"I said that it would take no word to Tasavalta for you. But as for bringing help here for the Prince—it may just possibly be able to do that. And the sooner it is dispatched the better, I think, if Mark is not already beyond help."

Moving beside the washstand, the lady whispered a few words into the beast's small curving ear.

With this the backbone of the dragon stiffened, and its demeanor changed abruptly. It drank noisily from a jar of water beside it on the stand, then hopped onto the lady's wrist. Ben could see semitransparent membranes on its eyes, which he had not realized were there, slide back to leave the orbs a shiny black. The creature had turned its head toward the window, and stared out into the sunlight.

Lady Yambu carried it to the sill and sent it out with a sharp tossing motion. The wings of the small dragon beat rapidly and it rose with surprising speed into the sky.

"What message did you give it?" Zoltan asked. "Where is it going?"

"There is only one message that it will carry. Trust me. I have a reason for not offering you a better explanation now."

Ben, squinting up into the bright sky, presently rumbled an oath. There were a few patchy low clouds above the lake, and out of one of them a set of leathery wings far larger than those of the small dragon had appeared. This creature was not nearly as big as the griffin that a few hours ago had carried off the Prince, but still large enough to be a formidable hunter of game no bigger than the messenger.

Now Zoltan muttered too; a second and then a third of the predatory flyers had come into sight out of the cloud. Their grotesque shapes sped in pursuit of the small dragon.

The issue of the chase was lost in yet another cloud.

3

A LITTLE before sunset of that same day, all three of the predatory flying creatures Ben had watched returned, gliding, to their new base on the island that had so lately been the domain of Honan-Fu. On their return to the magician's castle all three flyers selected flight paths that would tend to shelter them from observation, and each came down as softly and as unobtrusively as possible upon a different high place. For their final descent they chose a moment when almost all the human eyes within the castle walls were focused elsewhere.

And, having landed, they avoided reporting to the Master of the Beasts, or any of their other human masters, who were the recent conquerors of this island and the domain around the lake. Instead of delivering information on potential enemies, on resources discovered, or perhaps news of some prey that had escaped them—and thereby risking punishment—the creatures brooded on their perches, waiting silently to be fed, and dropping dung down the once-spotless walls of the stolen castle.

Very few of the humans inside the castle walls were at all aware of the flyers' return. None of the people who might have seen them were paying the hybrid creatures any real attention at the moment.

Perhaps the human breeders of the hybrid flyers had made them a touch too intelligent for their intended purposes.

The beasts looked down upon a crowd of several hundred people, mostly soldiers in gray and red, who were gathered in the castle's largest open courtyard. Only days ago this court had been a fair place, bright with flower gardens and musical with fountains. The flowers had all been trampled into mud since the castle's new master had taken charge, and half of the fountains had ceased to run. The pipes were broken in several of the fountains, including the largest, in the center of the court, which had been smashed, the sculpture on its top destroyed. In place of the statue of some otherwise forgotten woodland god, erected there by Honan-Fu because he liked the art and craft that had gone into it, a flat-topped altar had been hastily and crudely constructed, out of beams and slabs of wood laid horizontally on piles of rock and broken statuary.

The slabs that formed the center of the high table were now already dark with drying blood, the human blood of Honan-Fu's apprentices and servants, required for sacrifice to the powers of dark magic.

Upon a balcony overlooking this altar, an improvised throne had been set up. The occupant of the throne sat with his back close to a wall of the keep, and it would have been hard for anyone to approach or even see him from that direction. Nor was it easy for the people in the courtyard below the balcony to right or left to see him because of the tall screens that had been placed at each side of his chair.

Only from directly in front of the man on the throne, where the high altar stood, was anyone able to view him at all clearly. From there it could be seen that the shape of his body was only partially that of a man.

The right hand of the one who sat upon the throne was more plainly visible than the rest of his figure. That hand was extended at shoulder height, and clutched the black hilt of a Sword. The gleaming blade of this weapon, a full meter long, was dug lightly, point-first, into the floor of the balcony at the base of the makeshift throne.

Anyone standing close enough to get a good look at the fist that held the Sword could see that it was gray and taloned, almost as much like a bird's or a dragon's claw as it was like a human hand. Its owner's survival over the millennia had not been easily accomplished, and it had involved him in several compromises, of which the one involving alterations in his physical shape had been only the most noticeable.

The courtyard was nearly quiet now, a deepening pool of shadow as daylight began fading from the sky. Torches were being lighted, and once a long flame snapped like a banner in a gust of wind. But here, inside the castle's outer walls, the wind did not persist.

Only recently, within the past hour, had this quiet been achieved. Some of Honan-Fu's apprentices had fought back against their conquerors even as they were being dragged to the altar, or even after reaching it; and some of those apprentices had been, by any ordinary standard, magicians of considerable strength. But against the powers that had seized this castle from their master, their best efforts had been infantile, completely useless. All of their powers were scattered before the sacrifice, and in the process of the sacrifice itself their bodies were burned and minced, their minds dispatched to meet whatever fate the minds of magicians encountered after death.

The resistance of their master, Honan-Fu, had been more prolonged, but in the end no more effective. He had been overcome in magic, but he had not been burnt in sacrifice. His vanquisher considered that he had better use for him than that.

The still-living body of Honan-Fu was bound now between a pair of tall stakes standing before the altar, and certain human servants of the conqueror were dousing the defeated magician with pails of cold water filled at the pulsing spray of a broken fountain. Magic, the magic of his conqueror, against which Honan-Fu was no longer capable of fighting, was going on him with the water, and his sparse frame and wrinkled face were being rapidly covered with a mail-coat of ice. The crystalline white coat was still thin, and it cracked with his uncontrollable shivering almost as fast as it was formed; but with every pail of water thrown upon him it inexorably grew thicker.

"There will still be room inside your icicle for you to shiver, if not to breathe," called down the one who sat upon the throne; his was a human voice, harsh but not extraordinary. "You will find yourself able to dispense with breathing for a while, at least as long as you are under water. As most of your future existence lies in that environment, I thought it best to arrange something of the kind."

If Honan-Fu had any response to make, it must have been a silent one. He was a small man with wispy gray hair and epicanthic eyes, who had said very little to any of his conquerors since their first onslaught took him by surprise. And perhaps he was silent because by now his ice-encrusted lips had already grown too cold and stiff to talk.

"You will be brought out of the lake from time to time," called down the man—or being—on the throne, "to talk to me. You and I have much to talk about. But I am somewhat pressed for time just now, and our talk will have to wait. Unless there is something you feel you must say to me before you go. Any defiance you feel compelled to offer? Any bargainings you'd like to try? Now is the time, or they will have to wait indefinitely. . . ."

Still, the shivering little wizard had nothing to say in reply. Instead he had one more counterattack to try—magical, of course—and it was more subtle and ingenious than any he had previously essayed. The man on the throne, despite his own ancient powers, had no inkling that the attack was coming until he was informed of it by a thrum of power in the Sword he held. Only half a heartbeat later did the conqueror's more conventional defenses, his personal spells and demons, come into play; they would have protected him adequately, he was almost sure, but even before they were activated the counterspell of Honan-Fu had been rendered harmless by the Sword of Force.

The man on the throne was surprised and delighted to observe the effectiveness of his latest acquisition.

"Shieldbreaker, hey?" He held the Sword up at arm's length and admired it. It and its eleven fellows were of divine workmanship, he had been told; he had discounted that theory until now. But now, he realized, he was going to have to trace down the truth of their provenance.

"I could feel that power," he said, more to himself than to anyone else. "I like it. This toy is going to remain at my side for some time to come, though as a rule I have a dislike for carrying edged weapons of any kind."

He wondered now, in passing, how effective this Sword might have been in an earlier era of his life, if it were set in opposition to the titanic powers of Orcus or of Ardneh—but those were tests, thank all the gods and demons, that he would never have to face again. The magician on the throne, who had been no more than human in that era, had somehow managed to survive both of those superpowers.

And, from what he had seen of this future world during two years of tentative exploration since his arrival in it, he expected to be able to reign supreme.

Honan-Fu was by now completely encased in ice if still not exactly frozen solid. At a signal from the throne, burly attendants now untied the defeated magician from the tall wooden stakes, and dragged him away to be lowered into the lake. The spot selected was in its own little courtyard, really a grotto, a deeply arched recess in the wall of the keep itself. Behind its gate was a deep permanent well of fresh water, maintained by a direct connection to the lake outside the castle walls. Originally this well, or pool, had been intended to provide easy access to drinking water even during a hard-pressed siege. The grotto holding the well was accessible from the large courtyard through a small gate.

As the former master of the castle was carried through the small gate and out of sight, the man on the throne heaved a sigh, like one who has disposed of yet another dull duty in a busy day. He toyed with his newly acquired Sword, spinning it briefly like an auger, so that light of torches flickered from its brightness, and the keen point bored a very little deeper into the stone floor of the balcony.

And then his whole being appeared to change. Where he had been grotesque, only marginally human, he now appeared as a muscular young man, golden-haired, blue-eyed, and of surpassing beauty.

"Now," he called in an unchanged voice to his chief subordinate, an aging, bulky man in military uniform who stood below. "Bring out this Prince who owned this lovely implement before me. I'd like to have a word with him before he's put away."

"I know him, sire," the man below responded. "And I think he will repay more than a few minutes of Your Lordship's attention."

The officer turned away and made an economical gesture of command. Presently the captured Prince Mark, battered and still somewhat bloody about the face from the morning's fistfight, was brought out of a dark doorway in the lower castle wall, and bound up in the place just vacated by Honan-Fu, between the altar's stakes. The men who bound him, as soon as they were finished, began to fill their pails with water again.

At first Mark, having endured some hours of utter darkness in a dungeon, had to squint even in the faint light of the sunset sky and torches. Looking around him, he could see no sign that either of his Tasavaltan friends were also being held captive. That was faint consolation, but it was all he had.

There was only one face in the hostile throng that Mark could recognize, and he saw it without surprise, though with a sinking in his heart toward despair.

"Amintor," he said through dry lips that were still caked with his own blood.

The military officer, obviously here in a position of considerable importance, returned the Prince a salute, gravely but silently. Mark noted that the aging, portly baron, once a fearsome warrior himself, was limping heavily on his left leg. Mark had no doubt that the limp was a result of their last encounter, two years earlier.

But there was an even worse sight than the face of his old enemy for the Prince to see. Despairingly, Mark identified the hilt of Shield-breaker, visible in the well-formed fist of his still-unknown chief enemy.

The occupant of the throne now leaned toward him slightly. His harsh voice was completely strange to Mark. "You are another man, Prince, to whom I intend to speak at some length. I believe that we have several matters of some importance to discuss. But alas, conversation must wait. Unless you have something you urgently wish to tell me now."

The first bucket of water splashed on Mark. He shivered involuntarily, though at first the wet chill felt good on his cracked lips and swollen face.

"An indefinite time of discomfort awaits you, Prince. But at least the ice will not be eternal; sooner or later your time in the cold lake will be interrupted. Draw comfort from that fact if you can. But remember that how long you are allowed to spend out of your bath will depend upon how entertaining and informative I find your conversation."

The second pail of water splashed over Mark, and he felt the intense, magical cold of it, deeper even than the chill of ice, and fear and understanding began to grow. Meanwhile the handsome—nay, beautiful—man on the throne was studying him carefully. As if he wanted to watch the details of the freezing process, or perhaps as if Mark reminded him of someone that he had known long ago.

Mark did not utter another word. His captors did not insist. The Ancient One exchanged a few words with Amintor. And soon the two of them were watching Mark, pale and with his teeth chattering, being lowered inside his own maturing icicle to a place in the deep lake beside the wizard Honan-Fu.

4

WITHIN a few minutes after Lady Yambu had released her dragon from the window of the inn, she and her visitors brought their conference to an end. It was mutually agreed among the three of them that the less they were seen together, the better.

Leaving the inn by the back door, Zoltan and Ben at once turned their steps uphill and inland, climbing the gullied, unpaved alley behind the inn toward the edge of the settlement, which was hardly more than a stone's throw away.

Their chosen alley led them to an almost deserted street, and the street in turn, still climbing uphill, passed out of town and in a short distance had become little more than a narrow footpath. Turning to look back as they passed the town's last scattered buildings, they found themselves well above most of the settlement they had just quitted. There, standing out among lower and shabbier roofs, was the inn, one of the few two-story buildings. On the upper veranda that ran along its inland side, easy to see from here, was the place where Yambu was to leave a visible signal whenever she wanted another conference with them.

As the two men continued hiking uphill along the path, they debated whether they were going to be able to trust her or not. Zoltan, who knew comparatively little about Yambu, voiced his suspicions. Ben shared these doubts to some extent, but he was more optimistic. He could remember more about the lady than her public reputation of years past.

"She was your enemy then, and Uncle Mark's," Zoltan objected. "Why should we trust her now?"

"Aye, I know she was. But there are enemies and then there are enemies. And whether it was wise or not, we've already made the decision now and it's a case of trying to work with her. We've no other choice that makes any sense at all."

Zoltan had to agree, however reluctantly. The alternative to staying on the shores of Lake Alkmaar and trying to help Mark would be to leave at once for home. Tasavalta was months away, by riverboat until the cliffs were reached, and above them by foot or riding-beast. Doubtless more months would pass before they would be able to return with help. A slightly better choice than that might be for one of them to head back alone—Zoltan would probably be the swifter traveler—while the other one waited here by the lake, keeping an eye on developments as well as possible.

Of course when the Princess in Tasavalta failed to receive a winged courier from Honan-Fu bearing word of her husband's safe arrival, the Tasavaltans would begin to be alarmed and would take action anyway. Their first efforts at probing the situation, by winged scouts and by long-distance magic, would be under way long before either Zoltan or Ben, hurry as they might, could bring home word that help was needed.

Sending a message from Triplicane directly by a flying beast would speed up the Tasavaltan mobilization enormously. Ben had hoped to find some such creatures available at the docks, but Lady Yambu had assured him there were none.

Zoltan asked now: "What was that business of hers with the little dragon?"

"I don't know."

"A dragon's not something our people in Tasavalta would be likely to use, or our allies either. More likely our enemies would use one—have you any hope that anything will come of it?"

Ben trudged on. Eventually he said: "I don't know that either. If you decide to trust someone, then trust them. Or don't. Half measures only do harm."

Scouting yesterday among these hills with Prince Mark, trying to find some native willing and able to tell them what had happened on the wizard's island, Ben and Zoltan had observed an abandoned hut or two, with tattered nets of thin string still stretched outside, suggesting that the dwellings had once been inhabited by fowlers. These huts were now the objective of the two men, on the off chance that there might possibly be someone still living in the area with a flying messenger that could be bought or hired—or stolen—and might make it all the way to Tasavalta in a matter of a few days.

As he went up the hill behind Ben, Zoltan was thinking gloomily that the odds of his uncle still being alive were not good, and they were worsening by the hour. He was also wondering if he, being somewhat faster, ought to suggest that he run on ahead of Ben and search. The trouble with that idea was that neither of them were quite sure where they were going. The supposed fowlers' huts had been on this long and uneven hillside *somewhere.* . . .

Ben, who was still trudging a little in advance, stopped so suddenly that Zoltan almost ran into him.

"What—" Zoltan began, and then fell silent, staring past Ben's shoulder.

An easy bowshot up the hill, Prince Mark, dressed just as they had seen him last, was standing looking down at them.

Mark was poised alertly just off the nearly overgrown path where it ran between two pine trees. Even at the distance, Zoltan could see the marks of the morning's fight on the Prince's face, but he gave no sign of having been seriously hurt. As his nephew and his old friend stared up the slope at him, momentarily too shocked for speech, Mark raised a hand in a gesture that was more a signal of caution than a wave.

Ben started uphill again, almost at a run. And was stopped after only two or three strides by a sudden pushing gesture of Mark's palm.

The Prince, his voice calm, called down to them: "Wait. Not now. Wait for me to come to you."

And then he stepped off the trail and disappeared into the nearby trees.

Ben and Zoltan turned stunned faces to each other. Then, facing uphill again, they stood waiting, still speechless with surprise.

Hardly had they begun to recover from their shock when they caught sight of the Prince again, as Mark became briefly visible through the trees a little way up the slope. He was still moving away from the path and following a course that angled down the hill. He shot a glance downhill and saw Ben and Zoltan watching him. Again Mark paused, just long enough to send them a reassuring wave. He was considerably closer now, and Zoltan could see the marks of the morning's fight more clearly.

And again, as soon as Zoltan and Ben started toward the Prince, he called out sharply to them. "Wait, I told you! Have patience, and I'll be with you shortly." Again his tall form moved out of sight, still on his angled downhill course.

Groaning with a delayed sensation of relief, Ben began to mumble curses. In a moment he had slumped down to rest on a small rock outcropping. But a moment after that he was on his feet again, gazing with impatient curiosity toward the place where Mark had most recently vanished. There was no one to be seen there now.

The two men waited. They looked uphill and down. Heartbeats of time stretched out into minutes, but Mark did not reappear.

Nor was any sign of him to be found when his nephew and his old friend, stirred into activity again, reached the place where they had seen him last. Except that Zoltan found a small mark, badly blurred but very fresh, in a patch of wet earth exposed on the slope. The footprint, if it really was such, was too vague and incomplete to offer any hope of identification.

Time ticked away. Now Zoltan and Ben began to gaze at each other in fresh bewilderment. Zoltan once stood up and drew in breath as if to shout Mark's name, but Ben, suddenly scowling in suspicion, jabbed at him with a hand, almost knocking him off his feet, to keep him silent.

Zoltan was now trying to recall the exact words Prince Mark had shouted to them. What he could remember was not at all encouraging. Mark's declarations had been vaguely reassuring, but not at all informative.

An effort to find more fresh tracks along the course the Prince had been following downhill soon came to nothing. There were a few old footprints blurred by rain, and the marks of little animals, but nothing useful.

Ben was scowling fiercely. "Had he Shieldbreaker still with him just now? It seems to me I saw a swordhilt at his waist."

"No. No, I am sure that he did not."

Each held to his opinion on that point; though otherwise, they agreed, the Prince had been dressed just as they had seen him last.

"And he told us to wait here. Didn't he? Isn't that what he called to us twice?"

"All right. Yes, he did tell us that. Where did he go, though? Just to run off like that again without a word . . . this is madness."

"He might have got past us and be heading down to the settlement."

"That's just what he did. But why should he do that? Without stopping to give us a word of explanation?"

The two men repeated to each other the exact words they remembered the Prince uttering just a few minutes ago. The differences in their two versions were insignificant. He had really assured them that they did not have to worry about him. And he had ordered them to stay where they were.

Therefore they settled in, howbeit grimly and impatiently, to wait.

Shortly after her two visitors departed, Lady Yambu had gone out of her room, down the upstairs hall, and out onto the upper veranda. She had no particular goal in mind; such little walks had become her habit during the dreary days of her stay at the inn.

Standing on the narrow rustic veranda, looking up toward the hills in the direction that she supposed her new allies must have taken when they departed, she observed a single figure moving, angling down along the partially wooded slope. Somehow, even at the distance, it did not appear to be one of the local people. It was certainly not the bulky form of Ben of Purkinje, and what she could make out of the clothing indicated that it wasn't young Zoltan either. Unless for some reason the youth had changed his garments in the few minutes since she'd seen him last. . . . The distance, a couple of hundred meters, was too great for her to see much more of the figure than the movements of its arms and legs, but there was something about it, some tinge of familiarity, that tugged at her memory. Vaguely uneasy, she remained on the veranda, watching.

Less than a minute later the same figure came into her view again, much closer now. With movements that impressed her as furtive, it emerged from behind some trees and entered the highest street of the town proper. It was a man, she was sure of that now, and he was near enough for some details of his appearance to be observable. Yambu was able to focus on the figure for only a moment before it vanished again, this time behind a building.

That moment had been quite long enough. A wave of faintness came over the lady watching. She, who had once been a queen, was not accustomed to such a reaction in herself, or minded to tolerate it, and she fought against the weakness fiercely.

That she should have a strong reaction was understandable. She had just seen the Emperor, the father of her only child. He had been cloaked in gray and masked in a black domino, as she had so often seen him in the past.

Yambu hurried back to her room. Her hands were shaking as she put on her pilgrim's rugged footgear and her traveling outfit of trousers and cloak. Leaving her room again, she hastened back to the upper veranda, where she set out the prearranged signal, a simple bright-colored rag snagged on a rugged railing, which would indicate to her new allies that she wanted to meet with them at once.

Having done that, Yambu left the building and went out into the muddy street. She climbed through the town to the place where she had seen the gray-cloaked figure pass, on the highest of the town's three streets that ran parallel to the waterfront.

So, the Emperor was here. But what did his presence signify? Years had passed since she had seen him last, and that had been on the night before a battle.

Peering up and down each street as she came to it, she saw only a few of the townsfolk going about their business, and a few of the new garrison of soldiers in gray and red. There was no sign of the Emperor, or any other person or thing of interest. After hesitating briefly at the edge of town, Yambu continued on the path that went uphill, to the appointed place of meeting with Zoltan and Ben. This was well away from the settlement, beside a small stream on the rocky hillside.

Only a few minutes after she arrived there the two men joined her. When they did, they found her pale but composed.

"We saw your signal—" Ben of Purkinje began.

The lady cut him off with an imperious hand. "Ben."

"Yes, ma'am?"

"You told me that after the stone struck Ariane in the head—down there in the treasure vaults of the Blue Temple—she was still able to move about. For some time."

This was obviously not what Ben had been expecting as an opening to this hastily summoned meeting, and he frowned. But after looking closely at the former queen, he did not protest the apparent wild irrelevance. "That's right," he said.

"And then, some minutes or an hour after being hit, she suddenly collapsed."

"Yes."

"And died."

"And died."

"But are you quite certain that she was dead?"

He looked around at the wet woods and back at her. No, he hadn't been expecting this at all. "Of course I am. She died within a minute or two of losing consciousness—but why do you ask about that now?"

"Because," said the former queen, "I have just seen my daughter." She ignored their brief clamor of questions and pressed on. "On the hillside not far below us here. As if she were just coming up out of the town. I would have gone to her, but she waved me away. And she was smiling. As soon as I recovered from my shock I went to the place where I had seen her, but she was gone."

Zoltan muttered words of astonishment. But Ben had been hit too hard even for that. The color had faded suddenly under the weathered surface of his skin.

Lady Yambu went on. "I should tell you that despite the depth of my surprise her appearance was not totally unexpected to me. Because I met her father once, years after she was supposed to have died. And on that occasion he assured me solemnly that Ariane was still alive."

Using both arms, the lady made a gesture expressive of both frustration and determination. She went on: "He has, as everyone knows, a reputation for insane jokes; I, who have borne one of his children, can tell you that the reputation is well deserved. But I can tell you also that he was not joking when he told me Ariane was living. To have told me such a thing at such a time could not have been a joke, not even an insane one. No, he was very sober and convincing." She paused. "Still, at the time I did not believe him."

"Why not?" asked Zoltan.

The lady, as he had more than half expected, ignored his question totally. She said: "Also, I thought that I saw him, my daughter's father, walking here upon this hillside only a few minutes before I saw her."

Ben said hoarsely: "Her father was—is—the Emperor."

"So you know that. And presumably you also know something about him—? Good. I shall not have to try to explain that he is not the figure of simpleminded fun that common folktales paint him." Yambu heaved a sigh. "Not that I really could explain that man. Yes, her father assured me that she was still alive, despite what had happened to her down in the treasure vaults. He told me that she had been living with him for several years."

"Living with him." Ben's voice was a hoarse mutter. "Gods and demons. Where?"

"The gods only know that. Or perhaps the demons know. Wherever he chose to live, I suppose."

Long moments went by in which all three of them were silent. Ben was staring intently at the lady. Then at last he said in a choked voice: "You lie. Or he lied to you. I tell you I saw her die."

Yambu appeared to think the accusation too ridiculous to deserve her anger; she only sniffed at him imperiously. "Why in the world should I lie to you? And as for the Emperor lying to me on such a matter—no, I think not. Not on that occasion anyway."

Zoltan spoke up again, after a hesitation but firmly enough when the words came. "Lady, you have told us you did not believe him."

"True, I did not believe him when he told me, or for years afterward. But recently I have been giving the matter much thought. And I know who I saw today."

Ben was staring at her as if there were some truth that he too had to have and by staring he could force it somehow into visibility. He appeared to be unable to find anything to say.

At last Yambu repeated her earlier question to him: "Was Ariane still a virgin when you saw her die?"

Ben was slow to answer, and his voice was low. "We loved each other, she and I. She was very young and very beautiful, and the daughter of a queen, and when you look at me I know it sounds ridiculous to say she loved me. But so it was."

Yambu measured him with her eyes. "I have not said it was ridiculous."

Zoltan, meanwhile, was staring silently at the huge man, as if he had never seen him before. It was quite plain that Mark's nephew had never heard this story before, or suspected anything like it.

Ben, gazing into the past now, went on. "We had only a few days to try to know each other. And not so much as a quarter of an hour, in any of those days, to be alone together. So if it is of any importance to you, yes, your daughter remained a virgin until she died. At the time, the point was of considerable magical importance to the wizards. And so I know that it is true, even though she had been in the Red Temple." Ben jumped up from the rock he had been sitting on. "And if I thought —if I could believe for a moment—that Ariane was still alive, I would leave all that I possess to go to her."

Yambu asked him harshly: "Would you leave even your Prince?"

Ben's enormous shoulders slumped. He said: "That decision does not have to be made. My Prince, alive or dead, is here, and here I stay until I have done all that I can do for him. And your daughter is dead. I tell you that I saw her die."

Abruptly the three people fell silent; they were all aware that someone, a single person, was passing on one of the hillside paths not far away. From behind intervening evergreen shrubs they observed the passerby with great interest. But it was only some local peasant, bearing a small load of firewood, and they turned away.

The place where they had met and had been talking until now was relatively public, and by common consent they moved to continue their conference at a place farther from any trail. The new site, also on the hillside, had the advantage of better concealment, of allowing them to overlook much of the town, while being themselves screened from any likely observation by a growth of low evergreen bushes. Zoltan, looking down, thought that the bunched needles made the town beyond them look like a drawing half-obliterated by the mad scrawling lines of some determined vandal.

Their discussion was just getting under way again when it was once more interrupted. All three of the people on the hillside saw, at a distance of a hundred meters or so, a peculiar figure walking in the nearest street of the settlement below.

What drew their attention to the figure was first the darting, scrambling way it moved. Second was the fact that the other people in the street turned to gaze after it as it darted from between buildings on one side into an alley on the other. After it had passed, some of the townsfolk appeared to exchange looks, and perhaps words, with one another before going on about their business.

The three on the hillside studied the figure itself as well as they could at the distance; then they also exchanged glances among themselves. If they had marveled before, they were dumbfounded now.

Ben said: "It was your daughter, walking in the street. And I am going down to her."

"It was she," Yambu agreed in a stunned voice. "I will go with you."

"Wait!" cried Zoltan. His voice was not very loud, but something in it stopped the other two.

The young man looked at them, one after the other. He said: "Lady, I have never seen your daughter Ariane. What does she look like?"

It was Ben who answered. "You could not have missed her just now, among those shabby commoners. Tall, and as strong as most men, but there's no doubt from her shape that she's a woman, and still young. And her red hair, like a long flame down her back. She moved across the street quite near the intersection, jumping over the worst of a puddle. . . ." Ben stopped. Yambu was nodding her agreement.

But Zoltan's face was contorted, his eyes squeezed shut as if he were in pain.

"I did not see her," he announced.

"What do you mean?" Yambu demanded.

"I saw *someone,* a single person, cross the street near the intersection, just as you did, and jump the mud puddle while the townspeople moved away. But it was certainly not a young woman, with red hair or without. It was Prince Mark again, my uncle, whom I know well."

There was a brief silence while the others digested this.

"That red hair!" Ben ripped the words out like an oath. "There can't be any mistake!"

"What red hair? I tell you the one I saw just now was a man, brown-haired and bearded!"

They all three looked at one another, all of them trying to master their emotions, all trying to think. Yambu said: "Then what we have seen is magic—"

The three of them uttered the word almost in unison: "Sightblinder!"

"Or some spell equally powerful. Yes, that must be it."

They were sitting down again, in the same place, and Ben said those words, and the other two heard them, without conviction. All three of the people on the hillside had handled some of the Twelve Swords at one time or another—it was hard for any of them to believe in the existence of any such equally powerful spell.

"We must investigate," decreed the lady after a long silence, sighing as she spoke.

"Whoever is carrying Sightblinder came down the hillside alone a little while ago," said Zoltan. "And perhaps he or she will soon be going up again."

"If not," Ben decided in a heavy voice, "we must go down into the town and search for him, or her. Though for Zoltan and me it would be wise, as we all agreed earlier, to appear there as seldom as possible."

The three decided to wait where they were for a while longer before trying to search the town.

Before an hour had passed they saw a lone figure ascending the path again. And for each, as each whispered to the others, it was someone they loved or feared. This time for Ben it was his wife, who was at home in Tasavalta and in logic could not be here at all.

Firmly disregarding the evidence of their senses, the three moved out of their ambush and closed in, as upon a dangerous armed enemy. Zoltan and Ben held weapons ready. Their quarry, whoever it really was, saw them coming and displayed alarm, and cried out warnings to them, words that reached the ears of each of them in the tone of some voice that had long been loved or feared. It cost each of the three an effort of will to ignore those pleading warnings and close in.

At last, in a brushy hillside ravine well off any of the regular footpaths, they managed to corner their quarry, who by now was moving slowly and erratically, as if nearly exhausted.

Ben saw Barbara, his own diminutive, dark-haired wife, looking at him piteously. Making a great effort, he called to her: "Throw down that damned magic blade, whoever you are—I know you have it there!"

Yambu, this time, saw the Emperor again, turning at bay to face her, and wondered if it was her love for him or fear of him that the Sword played on to cast his image. She too moved forward implacably, though she was unarmed.

Zoltan moved forward against an image of the Prince, his uncle, who now appeared to him with a Sword that might have been Shieldbreaker raised in a two-handed grip.

"Stay back, all of you! I warn you!" called out the one voice that was heard as three quite different voices.

But the three came on.

The wielder of the Sword of Stealth raised it, making a halfhearted and inexpert defense.

Still, it took courage for Ben to swing his staff against a Sword that suddenly looked like Shieldbreaker, gripped in the hands of Mark—Ben had not blundered, there was only a clang, as of hardwood on ordinary steel, and the Sword-holder, mishandling the weapon awkwardly, staggered back. Zoltan sprang forward to grapple with him, or her.

Zoltan in the next moment found himself seizing his own mother's arm and twisting it painfully—somehow the experience was even worse than he would have imagined such a thing would be. It wasn't only that he saw his mother. He felt her tender flesh, heard her soft breath, he *knew*—though no longer quite with certainty—that it was her. But he gritted his teeth and persisted while his mother struggled wildly against him, screaming. Then Ben's hands clamped upon the foe, and the struggle was over.

There was a clanging thud, as of an arm's length of steel falling to the rocky ground.

Pinned upright by Ben's grip upon his arms was a shabby, hungry-looking figure, lean and ill-favored, a mere boy, younger than Zoltan and not as big or strongly built. The youth was sobbing now, as with relief.

On the earth at his feet, which were clad in worn country shoes, lay a black-hilted Sword. But only after Zoltan's hand had touched the black hilt could he clearly see the small white symbol of a human eye upon it.

> *The Sword of Stealth is given to*
> *One lowly and despised*
> *Sightblinder's gifts: his eyes are keen*
> *His nature is disguised.*

"Who are you?" Ben was shouting at the boy. "What's your name?"
The answer came between great gasping sobs. "Arnfinn."

5

A RNFINN'S blubbering was not entirely the result of fear. A part
of the cause was sheer relief, relief that the strain of the last few
days was over. The responsibility of what to do with the terrible weapon
he had been carrying had now been lifted from his shoulders. Whatever
happened next, at least he was not going to have to support that oppressive weight any longer.

He was sitting where he had been pushed down on the rocky earth of
the hillside, collapsed in defeat and futility, while close around him
stood the three people who had thrown him down and taken the Sword
away from him. And even now, in the depth of his fear, he was struck
by what an oddly assorted trio they made. One was the biggest, stron-
gest-looking man Arnfinn had ever seen; the second was an elderly lady
dressed in pilgrim's gray; and the third was a young man only a little
older than Arnfinn, of sturdy build and rather ordinary appearance.

Or, more exactly, the young man's appearance had been rather ordinary, until he had started to handle the Sword.

As soon as the young man picked up that magical blade, Arnfinn saw
him changed into a rapid succession of other people. First came
Arnfinn's own father. Then a bully from the village of Lunghai, who
more than once had made Arnfinn's existence miserable; and after that
a certain lady, really only a girl, the beauty of whose image, however
false, could still make Arnfinn catch his breath. One figure followed
another, each evoking either love or fear, or sometimes both. The se-
quence returned at last to Arnfinn's father, who had been dead for
years, and Arnfinn buried his face in his hands and wept again.

Meanwhile the giant and the old woman were paying little attention
to whatever transformations the Sword might have been causing their

companion to undergo in their eyes. Their attention remained thoughtfully fixed on Arnfinn.

When Arnfinn heard rather than saw the young man put down the Sword again, he dared to raise his face once more. These people had not killed him yet, and maybe they were going to let him live.

It was the gray-robed woman, her voice imperious, her accent aristocratic, who shot the first question at him: "What were you doing with this blade?"

"Nothing," Arnfinn responded automatically, defensively, without thinking. That answer was almost the truth, but obviously it was not going to be satisfactory, though so far they were letting him take his time and think about it.

Using his sleeve, he wiped his face of tears and sweat, achieving with the rough cleansing a kind of fatalistic calm. "I brought it here to town to try to sell it."

"Brought it from where?" the young man demanded.

"From my home village. It's a place called Lunghai. About three days walk to the west of here."

"And how came this Sword into your hands?" This was the giant, anger still rumbling dangerously in his voice.

Arnfinn continued the slow process of getting himself under control. "Some children of our village found this weapon—they said they found it under a bush, I suppose they were telling the truth but I don't know how it got there—and they were playing with it. Frightening everybody, and—"

"And so you took it away from them."

"Yes. For their own good. The gods know what trouble they might have caused with it." Arnfinn looked up, appealing to the three grim faces. "I intend—I intended to share the money with them, and with their parents, when I had sold the Sword. Their parents were very much afraid. They just wanted to be rid of it."

Anger still threatened in the huge man's voice. "Who did you think you were going to sell it to?"

Arnfinn gestured toward the water. "I had heard there were good wizards living on the islands in Lake Alkmaar—that's what all the people in my village believed, though our people seldom came here to Triplicane. I didn't mean to do any harm."

"What harm do you think you've done?" This was from the young man. Despite his youth he somehow sounded more like a leader than either of the others did.

Arnfinn shifted his position on the rough ground. He drew in a deep breath and heaved it out again. "I don't know," he said. "I don't know."

There was a pause. Then the woman asked him: "How long have you been here, then?" And the young man at the same time: "What kept you from going through with the sale?"

Now words poured out of Arnfinn in a rush. "I've been here for days. I've lost count how many. When I got here—well, I was carrying the Sword, and so naturally everyone in the town acted strange every time they saw me. The gods only know who or what they saw, or thought they saw, when they looked at me. If there's any way to turn the power of this weapon off, I don't know what it is. And of course I didn't dare to leave the thing anywhere, for fear of losing it. I hardly dared to set it down. So—I haven't had much actual contact with the people here. I've been sleeping out, up there on the hill."

"And you're saying," the lady asked him, "that you never actually tried to sell the Sword to anyone?"

"That's right. I never showed it to anyone, or talked about it."

"Why not?"

"I was afraid to try, ma'am. As soon as I arrived in town, I began to hear that there were strange things going on out on the islands. I could see that there were quite a few soldiers in the town and they had taken over the docks. And there were strange rumors about Honan-Fu and what might have happened to him. The people I talked to were all worried."

"What did these strange rumors say, exactly?"

Arnfinn managed a shrug. "That there were new rulers out there on the island, and they were evil. One man had heard a story about huge flying shapes, reptiles, demons, the gods know what, dropping out of the sky at night over Honan-Fu's castle. And there were stories of how the new rulers had done bad things—even kidnapped a few people from villages along the mainland shore. I didn't want to sell the Sword to anyone like that."

The giant said: "Fortunate for you, you didn't try, I'd say. Well, you won't have to worry any longer about selling the Sword. It's in good hands now."

Arnfinn nodded hastily.

Zoltan looked at his two companions, then back at Arnfinn. He said with authority: "You'll be compensated for it someday. You and the children of your village who found it for you. If your story about how it came into your possession turns out to be true."

"I've told you the truth." At least he had told them a lot of it. What he had held back, he thought, would probably not be of any importance to them; and it was not something he was going to tell to anyone, whatever happened.

Arnfinn wiped his face with his sleeve again. "Now, can I go?" When nothing intimidating happened to him in response to this question, he dared to get back to his feet.

That move, too, was accepted. At least nobody knocked him down again. Instead, the big man pointed a huge finger at the ground, and grumbled a warning at him, that he should stay right where he was; and then the three moved to a little distance, where they could confer without their victim hearing them. Obviously the subject of their conference was what to do about him.

Watching them, Arnfinn could imagine them coming to one of at least three possible decisions. One, they could determine to kill him after all, in which case he ought to be bounding down the hillside right now, running for his life. He wasn't doing that, so it followed that he didn't really believe that he was going to be killed, not after their having talked to him so reasonably. Two, they could try to enlist him in their cause, whatever that might be. Three, they could send him home. In Arnfinn's current mental state he wasn't sure which alternative would be worse.

The three did not take long to reach a decision. In only moments they were coming back, surrounding him again.

The gray-robed woman had pulled out her purse and was counting out some coins. Arnfinn felt a little dizzy; at least they were not going to finish him right now.

"What will you do," the young man asked, "if we tell you you are free to go?"

"I'll go home," said Arnfinn promptly. "I'll leave here this instant, and never come back."

The big man added his endorsement of that plan, emphasizing it with a brutally graphic statement of what would happen to Arnfinn if he did come back.

"I won't."

"See that you don't."

The lady extended the coins to him in her hand, and Arnfinn muttered thanks and took them—he put them into his pocket without counting, but still it looked like more money than anyone in Lunghai except the lord of its manor had seen for a long time.

He turned away. The moment he started downhill toward the town, three voices challenged and warned him.

He stopped and turned again, explaining that his road home led in that direction. "But I'll not stop in the town. I don't know anyone there, and none of them know me." Which was true enough, for none of the folk of Triplicane had ever seen him without the Sword.

The three let him go on, evidently convinced by his fright, which was certainly real enough.

Even though Arnfinn knew no one in the town, and no one in the town knew him, still there was one stop he had to make, someone in the neighborhood he had to try to see. He knew it was mad foolishness, but still he had to try to see her once more, even if he knew it could be no more than one look from a distance. Even if the three came after him and killed him for it.

He kept on going straight through the town, a stranger insignificant and unnoticed, until he came out on its other side. There he presently found himself standing in front of Triplicane's most substantial dwelling. It was a low, sprawling manor house, which was invisible from the road behind high walls and trees. It was obvious that wealth and power dwelt here.

Arnfinn had entered the grounds of this manor before, but now he knew that he would never be able to enter them again. Now, without the Sword of Stealth, the best he would ever be able to do was to wait outside, loitering in the road. If he did that it might be possible for him to see her just once more—perhaps catch a brief glimpse through the strong bars of the gate. It was not much of a chance, but it appeared to be all that he now had left.

The realization was sinking in on him that in losing the Sword he had lost whatever chance might have remained of repairing the ruin he had managed to make of his life during the few days when he'd had the Sword in hand.

Arnfinn began to weep again. This time his sobs were quieter, slower, and more bitter. Looking back, it was hard for him to see how he might have been able to do things differently.

6

HIS journey to sell the Sword hadn't started out in hopelessness. Far from it; in the innocence of its very beginning it had been something of a lark.

The presence of the Sword of Stealth in the village of Lunghai had been kept a secret from the great majority of the villagers, at least up to the time of Arnfinn's departure. The very few people who knew what he was up to, a small group of immediate family and close friends, had seen him off with quiet rejoicing. At the last moment a couple of his relatives had suggested that it would really be better after all if someone accompanied him. But that point had already been discussed, and really settled. Everyone else in the little group of people who knew about the Sword had work to do in the village, work it would be impractical for them to leave. Arnfinn would have little work to do until the harvest started, and he swore he would be back before then. And if Arnfinn went alone, taking the Sword with him, it was possible no one else in the village would know about the real purpose of his trip until he was back with the money he had realized from its sale.

The day of his departure was fine and promising, in the lull of work before the harvest began in earnest. Arnfinn, riding a borrowed loadbeast, took pleasure in the sheer novelty of the journey. And not long after he had left his own village behind him, he began to appreciate the possibilities of fun in the miraculous power of the weapon he was carrying.

A pair of poor farmers, one of whom Arnfinn recognized when he chanced to meet them on the road, suddenly put on unintentionally comical expressions and cleared themselves hastily out of his way. This pleased him disproportionately, and he tried in vain to imagine who, or what, the Sword had made them see. At the next tiny hamlet that Arnfinn came to, shortly after his encounter with the farmers, the peasant women who saw him pass ran from their huts to grab up small children and bring them inside.

Arnfinn, grinning as he tried to guess in what image, terrible or awesome, the Sword had presented him to the women, rode past all of them on his phlegmatic borrowed loadbeast and said nothing. Whenever he cast his eyes down at his own body, even if he did so at the very moment when people were retreating from him in fear, he saw only the same poor clothes as always, covering the same scrawny and unimpressive frame. Only within the past year, after his sixteenth birthday, had he begun to admit to himself the possibility that he was never going to grow much bigger than he was, never going to be huge and powerful.

Even earlier in life he had been forced to concede in his own mind that he was never going to be handsome. His face had never actually frightened anyone—not until the magic of the Sword of Stealth had begun to alter it in the sight of others. But with his nose and Adam's apple standing out like brackets above and below the bony projection of his chin, his was a countenance that had provoked more than a few jokes.

After passing through that first hamlet Arnfinn came to a long stretch of road where there were no more villages. Nor, for the time being, were there any other travelers for him to meet. In solitude the loadbeast kept plodding methodically forward. The sun turned through a sky hazed lightly with the onset of autumn.

And, he kept thinking to himself, he hadn't even *drawn* the Sword to frighten any of those people. Sightblinder—that was what it had to be—was just hanging there in its fancy scabbard, from the fancy belt that had been with it when the children found it. Belt and scabbard alike were skillfully sewn of fine sturdy leather, and both were mounted with what Arnfinn assumed were real jewels; he suspected that those decorations might be treasure enough in themselves to enrich the village of Lunghai considerably.

Or, perhaps, more than enough to get the whole village into trouble. Even in Lunghai people had heard of the Twelve Swords, magical weapons forged by the gods themselves more than thirty years ago. If Arnfinn and his people hadn't known of the good wizards on their island, he wouldn't have any idea of where to go to try to sell this marvelous blade. But Honan-Fu the wizard was known to be a good man, kindly to the poor, and trustworthy in all his dealings; not that Arnfinn himself had ever met him, but all the common folk who had met him said so. The good wizard would advise Arnfinn on what to do, and not cheat him out of the village treasure that had been entrusted to him.

The next village that Arnfinn came to was totally new territory to him. He had never in his life before traveled so far in this direction. And this village saw the end of the lightheartedness with which he had begun his journey.

The road passed directly through the small village square, a plot of brown grass and a few trees. A woman who was seated on a bench at one side of the square stared at Arnfinn as he approached. Her face grew pale, very pale. And then, jumping to her feet and giving a cry suitable for a death or a birth, she appeared to go mad.

Arnfinn, already alarmed, panicked now and kicked his loadbeast to make it go faster. But the woman overtook the trotting animal and then ran beside it, clinging to Arnfinn's knee, entreating him to stop. She kept calling him over and over by some name he could not understand, one that he had never heard before. The woman's cries resounded, bringing people out of the little houses around the square. She was not young. Her graying hair fell in disheveled curls beside her weathered cheeks. Her eyes, enormous with emotion, never left Arnfinn's face.

Arnfinn, in his embarrassment and growing fright, was unable to imagine what might happen if he did stop and try to talk to this screaming madwoman. How could he explain? That would mean giving up the treasure of the Sword, if only for a moment, trying to demonstrate its magic. And to give it up was something that he dared not do.

Obviously the woman thought that he was someone she had deeply loved, someone she had not seen for many years—perhaps someone who was dead. Unable to remain silent in the face of her clamoring entreaties, he made abortive attempts to reassure her, to explain, to somehow shut her up. But despite his stumbling efforts, all she could see and hear was her loved one, inexplicably riding on, refusing to stop for her. Some of the other people of the village, this woman's neighbors and perhaps her relatives, were looking on aghast, though they made no move to interfere. Eventually, Arnfinn thought, even as he struggled to get away, they will be able to help her. Because each of them will have seen me as a different person, and sooner or later they will all realize that what has ridden through their village was an enchantment. Then soon they will all get over this.

And how could Arnfinn stop? What could he have said to her, what could he have done for her if he did stop?

At last he clamped his own lips shut and kicked the loadbeast into a run. This too, at first, only seemed to make matters worse. The woman's grip on the loadbeast's saddle was brutally broken when the animal began to run. But she still tottered down the road after Arnfinn. For a long time she kept up the hopeless pursuit, begging him to come back to her. It seemed to him that he had to ride for an hour, sweating in the chill air, trying to shut his ears, before the sound of her cries had faded entirely away.

When night came he slept in the open. And for a day or two after that incident he avoided villages altogether, making a long detour whenever a settlement of any kind came into sight ahead.

He could not avoid encountering other travelers now and then. Inevitably they displayed either one of two basic reactions, and Arnfinn wasn't sure which one was worse: the fear or the strange, puzzled love. Puzzled, he supposed, because the loved one was behaving so strangely, offering no recognition.

But Arnfinn no longer found anything enjoyable in either reaction. And so he ceased to wear the Sword. Taking off the belt and scabbard, he wrapped them in his only spare shirt, making an undistinguished-looking bundle, and then contrived to tie the bundle onto the loadbeast's rump along with the rest of his meager baggage.

On the following day he was traversing a particularly lonely stretch of road when two men suddenly appeared out of the scrubby forest no more than an arrow's flight ahead of him.

More to reassure himself that his treasure was safe than to seek its protection, Arnfinn reached behind him and felt inside the bundle for the hard hilt of the Sword. And the moment he touched it, his perception of the two men changed.

In Lunghai, robbers were very rare indeed. But stories about them were common enough, and many of the village men were reluctant to undertake even necessary journeys on these roads, except in groups. Arnfinn, listening to the stories, had mentally allied himself with the braver village men, and had tended to dismiss such fears as a sign of timidity. Now, however, matters suddenly wore a somewhat different aspect.

There was no obvious reason to assume that these two men were robbers. But Arnfinn, from the moment he touched Sightblinder, was certain that they were. When they looked toward him, and then started in his direction, he stopped his mount, then turned it off the road at an angle, urging it to its greatest speed. It was a young animal, and healthy enough, but the healthiest loadbeast was not a riding-beast, and certainly not a racer.

Behind him now the men's voices were hailing him, in friendly tones, but Arnfinn ignored the call. He steered his animal among trees, and forced it through a thicket, trying to get himself well out of their sight.

Halfway into the thicket his mount rebelled against this strange procedure, and came to a stubborn halt. He saw, through a thin screen of dead leaves, the two men on their swift riding-beasts go cantering by on the road he had just left. They were a savage-looking pair now in their anger, muttering curses as they rode, and Arnfinn noted with a feeling of faintness that they both had drawn long knives from somewhere. Robbers, no doubt about it. Murderers. He twisted in his saddle as soon as they had passed, and with shaking hands he started to undo the bundle that held the Sword.

His fumbling fingers let the burden go, and with a noisy crash it fell from the animal's rump into the dry twigs of the thicket. At once one of the robbers' voices sounded, startlingly near; they must have already turned, they were already coming back to kill him.

Jumping, almost falling, from his saddle after the Sword, Arnfinn, praying to all the gods whose names he had ever heard, scrambled after Sightblinder on the ground. At last he reached it. Unable to get the bundle open quickly, he thrust his right hand inside and grasped the Sword's hilt, and felt the full power of it flow into his hand. That flow was not of warmth, nor cold, it was of something he could not have described, but it passed through the skin as cold or heat would pass.

He was still in that same position, crouched awkwardly on all fours almost underneath his puzzled animal, when the two men on riding-beasts came crashing into the thicket after him.

As soon as they saw Arnfinn both of them reined in their mounts so suddenly that one of the riding-beasts tripped and almost fell; and the alteration in the two men's faces was immediate and remarkable. Arnfinn was reminded of the first two farmers he had encountered on the road.

One of the bandits looked down at his own drawn blade as if he were surprised beyond measure to find it in his hand; then, favoring Arnfinn with a sheepish effort at a smile, he sheathed the weapon and turned, and rode away even more quickly than he had approached. His companion meanwhile had been trying to find words, words that sounded like a terrified effort at an apology. Then he too put his knife away—he had to thrust with it three times before he found the opening in the unobtrusive sheath—and turned and fled.

Slowly Arnfinn regained his feet. He stood there beside his loadbeast, listening to the crashing sounds of the enemy's retreat. It sounded to him as if they were afraid he might be coming after them. Soon the hoofbeats sounded more solidly on the road, and soon after that they dwindled into silence.

Arnfinn stood there in the middle of the thicket a while longer, his eyes closed now, his right hand still gripping Sightblinder's hilt. His shivering fear, even before the tremors of it died out in his arms and legs, had almost entirely transformed itself into something else. Before his eyes opened, he had begun to smile.

He had never seen Lake Alkmaar before, but when first he came in sight of the broad, shimmering water there was no doubt in his mind that he had found it. He stopped and dismounted, letting the beast rest after the long, slow climb up the landward side of the hills. Arnfinn remained standing on the tortuous road for some time, petting his mount absently and looking down.

Well below him, and still at some little distance, lay the biggest settlement Arnfinn had ever seen, which had to be the town of Triplicane. Even now, in the middle of the day, the smoke from more than a dozen chimneys faintly marked the air. At the lakeside docks in this town, his advisers in the village had assured him, he would be able to find a boat that would take him out to the castle.

He raised his gaze slightly. There, on an island out near the middle of the lake, was the castle, looking appropriately magical, just as it had been described to him. The home of the benign wizard Honan-Fu himself.

The wizard, Arnfinn had been told, was a little old man with a wispy beard and a kindly manner. He tried now to imagine what it might be like to talk to such a powerful man, and what the good wizard might be likely to offer Arnfinn for such a Sword.

But now, for the first time, Arnfinn felt a stirring of reluctance to give

Sightblinder up, even at a price that would have made the people of Lunghai very happy.

Frowning slightly, he remounted his loadbeast and started down the road to town.

As he passed to and fro along the windings of the descending way, the landscape below him changed. The far end of the town came briefly into sight, bringing with it his first glimpse of the roofs and grounds of an extensive lakeside manor.

Arnfinn had scarcely given that house a single conscious thought during his journey, but even before he had started he had known of its existence. And he knew the name of the person who was said to live there, who must be grown-up enough by now to have her own establishment apart from her father's. Only now, when he was actually in sight of the place, did the idea suggest itself to him that maybe, on his way to sell the Sword, he might just dare . . .

To do what? He wasn't sure exactly. But what harm could it do to simply go out of his way a little bit, enough to ride past that manor house on the road that ran directly in front of it. If he were to do that, then maybe, just possibly, *she* would see him from a window. See him not in his scrawny, ugly, ordinary body, but transformed, if only for a moment, into what he would wish to be in the eyes of such a lady. Even if he became something that frightened her, for just a moment . . .

Twice already in his young life, Arnfinn had seen Lady Ninazu. The first time had been five years ago, when he was only twelve and she apparently no older. At that time she, already well on the way to becoming a great lady, had happened to pass through Lunghai, escorted by a troop of the constabulary who served her father, Honan-Fu. Important-looking men, though the wizard himself was not among them, had surrounded the half-grown girl on every side. The appearance even of her escort in their uniforms of gold and green had been fine almost beyond belief in the eyes of poor country folk like Arnfinn and his neighbors. And as for the young lady herself . . .

Until that moment the boy Arnfinn had never dreamed such beauty could exist. He remained staring after her helplessly, until people began to make jokes and poke him to rouse him from his trance.

* * *

She was, his fellow villagers told him in response to his questions, the only daughter of Honan-Fu himself, and she lived with her father in his island castle.

The insistent routines of village life soon occupied Arnfinn's attention again, but he did not forget the young lady and what he considered her transcendent beauty.

He did not start to dream about her, though, until he had seen her again.

That had happened only a little more than a year before Arnfinn undertook his trip with the Sword. The place was a larger village than Lunghai, where folk from all the district round were gathered to see a traveling carnival in one of its irregular local passages. Again Arnfinn caught only a brief glimpse of the daughter of Honan-Fu. She had grown and changed, of course, though not as he had changed, for she had only become more beautiful. Her beauty was now less childlike and unworldly, more womanly. This time he asked no more questions about her; he could see very well that there was no point in asking.

Now, when he was about to ride into Triplicane for the first time with Sightblinder at his side, Arnfinn hesitated at the last moment whether to wear the Sword into town, regardless of the sensation that might produce, or bundle it up again behind his saddle. After some hesitation he decided to continue to wear it. If lonely roads were likely places to encounter robbers, big cities, at least in all the stories that he had heard, were notoriously worse. Arnfinn supposed that Triplicane was not really a big city. But to him it looked more than big and strange, and impressive enough to make him wary.

There were so many streets in this town that he could not immediately see how many there were, enough to make the passage through it somewhat confusing. Though Arnfinn kept as much as he could to the less traveled streets, still everywhere he looked there were more people about than he was used to seeing in one place.

To his surprise, many of those who passed him in the street did not appear to notice him at all, even though he was wearing the Sword. He was sure its power was still working, because many did stop and stare at him. But then, most of those who stopped soon went on again about their business, as if perhaps they thought they had been mistaken at first in what they had seen.

The modest stock of food Arnfinn had brought with him from home was running out, and with his few coins in hand he went into a store. He hoped also to be able to learn something about transportation to the castle on its island.

He dared not leave Sightblinder on his loadbeast tethered outside, and so he carried it into the store with him. He could only hope that a storekeeper in a city like this one might be ready to ply his trade in spite of marvels, as capable of indifference as some of the passersby appeared to be.

But that was not what happened when he entered the dim shop that smelled of leather like a harness shop, and of food like a pantry. Instead, the young woman behind the counter turned pale with her first look at Arnfinn. "You've come back!" she breathed.

"I only want some food," he answered, having come in stubbornly determined to stick to business no matter what.

She looked quickly toward the curtain that closed off the back of the store. "My husband—" she began.

At that point a burly, bald man appeared from behind the curtain, as if on cue, or as if perhaps he had been waiting there, listening suspiciously, from the moment Arnfinn entered. At the sight of Arnfinn, fear and hatred filled the shopkeeper's face, even as a more mysterious excitement had filled that of his wife. But then the balding man was quick to mask his feelings. He stood with folded arms, waiting silently for what Arnfinn might say or do.

Silently Arnfinn played the role of customer, picking out bread, sausage, and cheese. The woman served him, gathering his choices on the small counter.

Suddenly she burst out with a question, as if she could contain it no longer: "Does Honan-Fu still survive?"

Arnfinn was sure that he had heard her question clearly, and yet it made no sense to him at all. "Why should he not survive?" he countered, trying to sound confident.

At that the goodwife relaxed somewhat, and even the man's tension seemed to ease a trifle. "I was sure," she said to Arnfinn, "that you must be with them. The new masters out there. Do you suppose you could put in a good word for us? We have no finery for sale here, and their soldiers wear their uniforms, but still they'll want to buy something, won't they? And they'll all be having to eat like anyone else."

"I'll do my best," said Arnfinn. At that the man actually made himself smile, though he was sweating with the struggle he had to make against his fear. And even in his presence his wife looked at Arnfinn with open invitation in her eyes.

Speaking together, man and wife refused his coins when he would have paid them for the food.

Arnfinn did not insist. He feared that he might need the money. Slowly he moved out into the street again, where he stood munching bread and sausage as he watched the endless parade of passing strangers. He puzzled over what the people in the shop had said to him. Why should not Honan-Fu survive? He was going to have to find out.

The most direct route from his present location to Lady Ninazu's manor, as Arnfinn calculated it, lay through a busy-looking part of the town. But he felt that he was beginning to grow accustomed to his situation with the Sword. And he wanted to talk to someone. Someone would have to tell him what had befallen the good wizard.

Passing through what he thought was probably the busiest street, Arnfinn was suddenly accosted by a young girl who bore a baby in her arms. It was obvious from the girl's first words to him that she saw Arnfinn as her former lover, the baby's father, and demanded some acknowledgment of responsibility from him.

Then she fell back a little, as if amazed at her own temerity in accosting him thus. He remained silent, trying to think of what he ought to say. Meanwhile the girl's baby, looking at Arnfinn, displayed the greatest curiosity and delight.

Then suddenly the infant, still looking at him, screamed in terror.

Taking advantage of the distraction, he broke away from the girl, and moved on at a fast walk, leading his loadbeast, the sheathed Sword banging against his leg. People scattered at his approach.

The girl followed him a little way, then gave up, screaming some despairing insult. When he was sure that she had abandoned the chase, Arnfinn paused for breath. To a small boy who stood staring at him he spoke, asking directions to the docks. And was promptly hailed by an old man who, with tears in his blind, staring eyes, groped his way with trembling arms to Arnfinn, and seized him in a hug.

"Come home with me now, Will! Your mother's there. She'll be so glad to see you're safe after all—"

Arnfinn, his control deserting him, broke free from the old man's grasp and ran again. He rushed like a madman through the remainder of the town, looking neither to left nor right. When from behind him he heard yet another cry, as of despair, he did not stop to see whether it was directed at him or not.

Dusk was coming on when at last he found himself standing at the edge of open country, in front of the manor house where he was certain *she* must live.

Arnfinn stared at the closed heavy grillwork of the tall front gate leading to the grounds. He was physically very tired after his day's journey, and also worn by the strain of all that had happened since his arrival in the town. But now he found that he could not rest until he had managed to learn something more about *her*. Could she be safe, if there was doubt as to whether the powerful wizard, her father, was still alive?

Not even with the powers of the Sword in hand did he dare to simply present himself at the gate of the manor and ask—or demand—to be admitted. There would be guards and attendants there, and the gods only knew who they would think he was. They would let him in, by reason of love or fear; of that much Arnfinn felt certain. But what then? What would he say to the people he encountered inside?

What could he say to *her* if she appeared?

Trying to make up his mind as to what to do next, he circled the manor at a little distance, staring at the high stone wall that ringed it in. He was at some distance from the road, in an empty field that sloped down to the shoreline of the lake, when he heard the music of a lute, coming from somewhere beyond the wall. A moment later he heard the voice of a woman singing, and he imagined that that sweet voice must be hers.

There was another, smaller gate in the wall back here, and this one was standing open slightly. Looking through it, Arnfinn could see that it led to stables. There was a soldier slouching against the wall just outside the gate—Arnfinn knew little enough about soldiers, and could not have identified the red and gray uniform worn by this one even if it had occurred to him to try.

But the soldier was looking in his direction now, and he was going to have to do something. He walked forward, wondering what he was going to say.

The soldier snapped silently to attention, saluted, and drew the gate wide open. Arnfinn walked through, leading his loadbeast with him— the music of lute and voice seemed to draw him like a spell.

Just inside the gate he handed his animal's reins over to one who reached for them with quiet efficiency. Then he walked on, unopposed, into the grounds. There were scattered trees, neat hedges, and broad lawns, now turning brown with autumn. And in the middle of one of those grassy spaces an arbor that must have been a pleasant shady place in summer, overgrown as it was with vines. But the leaves on the vines were dead now, and the oncoming night was already turning chill.

But she, the young lady Ninazu, was there anyway, sitting in the arbor, dressed as gloriously as he remembered, though in different garments. At her first glimpse of Arnfinn, even in the failing light, she jumped to her feet, letting her lute fall with an unmusical thud to the wooden floor of the summerhouse.

"By all the gods," she said to him, and her voice had in it such soft intensity that his own voice, despite all that he could do, almost broke out, stuttering a protest. "By all the gods," she breathed, "it's you, and you have not forgotten me. My crystal foretold that I would see you soon."

And for once the emotions written by Sightblinder upon a human countenance were too complex for Arnfinn to interpret.

But the girl had jumped up from her seat and was running toward him. And in the next moment he was being passionately embraced and kissed.

7

"**A** PIECE of good luck for us at last," said Ben, looking at the Sword, complete with belt and sheath, where Zoltan had dropped it on the ground at their feet. The three had brought Sightblinder back with them to their hillside observation post, which lay behind a screen of low evergreens through which it was possible to watch much of what went on in the town below. The youth from whom they had taken the Sword of Stealth had already completed his hasty descent into the town, had appeared briefly in those streets below, and then passed out of their sight. Already Ben, at least, had almost forgotten him.

Zoltan now put out his hand and stroked the hilt of Sightblinder again. As he did so, he momentarily became Prince Mark in the eyes of his two companions. Then Zoltan drew back his hand and squatted, gazing silently at the Sword of Stealth.

Ben went on: "But even the best luck is no good until it's used, and we must find the right way to use it."

"We must also keep in mind," said Lady Yambu, "that Shieldbreaker is almost certainly on the island now, in the hands of the one who sent the griffin to carry away your Prince. And the person who carries it will doubtless be the most dangerous enemy with whom we shall have to deal. Whoever has the Sword of Force in hand will be immune to the powers of Sightblinder or any other weapon."

"And so far we have no idea who he is. Or she," Zoltan put in. He got to his feet and stood staring toward the islands.

"I have been here in Triplicane eleven days," said Yambu, "listening to the rumors that pass among the townsfolk. And I can give you an answer to that question. The new ruler of that castle in the lake is called the Ancient One, or sometimes Ancient Lord. He . . ." She fell silent, observing Zoltan's reaction.

"If that's his name I have seen him once before," said Zoltan. "And I was lucky to survive."

Ben, looking at him, nodded slowly. "Two years ago, or thereabouts, that was. Well we remember it, in Tasavalta. But we still know little of this Ancient Lord. Our ignorance about the enemies we face here is certainly enormous." The big man turned to the lady. "I wonder what Sightblinder would show the new ruler of the magician's island if one of us appeared carrying it, and if its power were not blocked by Shieldbreaker?"

"An interesting question," Yambu acknowledged, "even if not immediately pertinent. What, or whom, does this Ancient Master of evil fear above all else? It is probably pointless to try to imagine anyone whom he might love."

Ben nodded. "But as you say, those questions will have to wait. Now we face others that must be answered. Two or three people cannot share the powers of this Sword. One of us must take it to the island, and use it to look for Mark. Now, which of us carries it? And what do the other two do to help?"

"The question of who takes the Sword must lie between you two, I think," said Lady Yambu. "Because I ought to be perfectly able to visit the mysterious islanders without its help." Reading the question in her companions' faces, she explained: "Why should not I, as a former queen, pay a courtesy call upon whatever power now rules those rocks?"

Ben ruminated on that idea. "We certainly don't have to tell you how great the risks might be. Are you really willing to accept that danger, to help a former enemy?"

The former queen spoke sharply in reply. "You certainly do not have to tell me about the risks, especially now that you have already managed to do so. We have made an agreement, you and I, and I intend to abide by it. And remember that in my day I have faced the Dark King himself; so I feel no uncontrollable trembling at the prospect of encountering this usurper; let him be as ancient as he likes."

Zoltan was nodding. And Ben, after a little more thought, nodded his approval too. "All right, my lady. Make your visit to the island as you wish, if you are able to arrange for one. Meanwhile the Prince's nephew and I will somehow settle between us the use of the Sword. But I have one more question for you, my lady, before we wrestle with that decision."

She returned him a look of cool inquiry.

He asked: "About that little dragon you dispatched. What result may we expect from it, assuming that the creature was not devoured in midair?"

"If I were you," the lady answered, "I should expect nothing. We must do what we can on our own." Then she softened a trifle. "I have good reason for keeping silent, I assure you."

The men exchanged a look but said no more on the subject.

"You have a means of transport to the island?" Zoltan asked the lady.

"I have said I do not expect much trouble in arranging that."

Ben shrugged, and said: "It is agreed, then. We will make our separate ways out to the castle on the island, and meet and communicate with each other as best we can when we are there." He paused, considering. "A mad-sounding plan, if it can even be called a plan at all. But we lack the knowledge to make plans with any greater intelligence, and I for one cannot simply sit here and wait."

"Nor I," Zoltan put in quickly.

"Then it is agreed, as you say," Yambu answered firmly. "And now, gentlemen, I bid you good-bye for the time being. And good luck."

A few minutes later, Ben and Zoltan were making their way along the shoreline of the lake, heading east, in the direction away from the town. Zoltan carried Sightblinder, balancing in one hand the belt, the jeweled sheath, and the blade that it contained.

Their tentative plan, which they were trying to put into a more solid shape as they walked, was to commandeer a small boat somewhere along the shore—given the Sword's powers, there should be no great difficulty about that. Once in possession of a boat, they would make their way out to the islands. Whether there would be any advantage in waiting for darkness before they set out across the water was something they had not yet decided.

"I should be the one to carry Sightblinder when we go," said Barbara, Ben's diminutive, dark-haired wife, walking now beside Ben where a moment ago Prince Mark had been striding blithely along. Then Barbara turned her face toward Ben, grew in stature to his own height or a trifle more, and suddenly possessed blue eyes and long hair of a flaming red. He had to look away.

"You'll be my prisoner," his companion went on, now speaking to Ben in a voice Ben had never forgotten, that of Yambu's daughter, Ariane. "No one will try to stop us on the way to the island dungeons—every castle has a dungeon, doesn't it?—and that's where we'll find Uncle Mark. There should be no problem unless we run directly into whoever now has Shieldbreaker—what's the matter?" The speaker's voice abruptly deepened at the end.

Ben dared to turn his head for another look, and saw Prince Mark walking beside him again, engaged in plotting his own rescue.

"Therefore," said Ben, "we must take care not to run into him." He nodded grudgingly. "The plan you propose has some merit. Not much, but perhaps more than any other we are likely to be able to devise in the small time we have to work with."

Striding around the shoreline of a cove, they passed a small wooden dock, on the verge of total abandonment if not already past it. The only vessel at the dock, a small rowboat, now rested half-sunken in the shallows, where, if moss and discoloration were any evidence, it had been resting for a long time. A couple of meters inland stood an upright post, which had probably once supported a partial roof over the facility. Stuck lightly to this post, and stirring in the breeze as if to call attention to itself, was a torn and shabby paper poster. Ben, driven by a vague though desperate yearning for any kind of information, paused to peel the loosened paper from the wood—it was an advertisement for what sounded like a traveling carnival, described in large, crude printing as the Magnificent Traveling Show of Ensor.

Still clutching this piece of paper absently in his hand, Ben walked on. Zoltan, now wearing the aspect of Ben's young daughter Beth, walked at his side. Ben looked down at the sturdy, half-grown girl taking her short steps, and said to Zoltan: "Did your uncle Mark ever tell you how he once played a role in a small traveling show? I was in it too. Probably this one is much like that one."

"He's mentioned something about it," Prince Mark said, taller than Ben again and taking long strides, longer than Ben's, beside him. "You were the strongman, of course?"

"No," the huge man answered vaguely. Again becoming aware of the paper still in his hand, he looked at it. " 'The next performance in Triplicane,' " he quoted, " 'will be at the time of the Harvest Festival.' Which must be rapidly approaching in these parts, I suppose, though there can't be much growing on these rocky slopes for anyone to harvest."

"Unless they're counting the lake's fish as the main crop. And I thought I saw some indication of vineyards on the high slopes there, farther on." It was Ariane who gestured at the hills.

Half an hour later Ben and his variable companion were still walking along the shore, having had no success in finding a suitable boat, when with little warning a small cloud of fierce flying creatures fell upon them from the clouded sky.

Ben fought back with his staff, and Zoltan raised the keen-edged Sword. But in a matter of moments they realized that they were not under attack at all. The strange hybrid flyers were not coming to tear them apart, but to offer service. They circled nearby, then landed on the ground, wrapping themselves in leathery wings; they recoiled from the blows of Ben's staff, not as attackers would dodge back but cringingly, jaws closed and ears laid back in submission, like beasts trying to avoid punishment.

"What dolts we are!" said Ben. "It is the Sword, of course. They take you for someone else, some human lord that they are bound to serve." He spoke openly, having no fear that beasts like these would be able to understand more than the simplest words of human speech.

"Of course," said his wife, Barbara, and lowered Sightblinder's keen steel. "What do we do now?"

Before Ben could decide upon an answer, a new factor had entered the situation. A griffin descended from the upper air to circle majestically, looking the scene over. Presumably it was the same creature that had carried off Prince Mark—even in the stories there was never more than one griffin at a time—but it was now equipped with a saddle, saddlebags, and stirrups.

After circling round the two men several times at low altitude, making the smaller flyers scatter in excitement, the griffin landed near Zoltan, who recoiled somewhat in spite of himself. The creature crouched there with its great wings folded, its eagle's eyes staring at him over one feathered shoulder. When he did not move, it backed toward him a short distance and crouched lower.

Ben edged away a little. The griffin ignored him totally.

"Ben?" Zoltan's voice quavered slightly. "I think it expects me to get on and ride it."

Somehow the dignity of the beast's gaze made it look more intelligent as well as larger than any of the more ordinary flyers—not a difficult standard to surpass.

"Ben? Magicians do ride them, don't they?"

Ben opened his mouth and closed it. He didn't know what to advise.

The griffin was looking at Zoltan as an intelligent riding-beast might have looked, waiting patiently for its master to climb into the saddle.

"I'm going to do it," Zoltan decided.

"Maybe I should be the one to ride it," the big man muttered, but even as he spoke he was edging away from the griffin a little more, and he was unable to muster any great enthusiasm behind the words.

"You obviously can't—you weigh a ton and a half, to begin with."

"I doubt that would matter much to a griffin. From all I've heard, they fly more by magic than by muscle."

But Zoltan, though showing signs of trepidation, was already climbing aboard the half-feathered and half-furred creature's back. In a moment his feet were in the stirrups and he was as firmly in the saddle as a man could be. Now it was apparent that there were no reins to grip.

All was not well, however. The great beast clamored and snarled, and breathed out other noises less definable. It moved on its feet and stretched its wings, but it did not take off. Instead, with Zoltan helplessly on its back, it stood up on its two mismatched pairs of legs and turned toward Ben. Awkwardly it walked closer to him, still making unearthly noises. When its beak opened, there were no teeth to be seen, but the beak itself looked as dangerous as a scimitar.

"I think," Ben said, gripping his staff, "it doesn't like me."

"Maybe it recognizes you somehow as an enemy. Might the problem be that it doesn't want me to leave you here unguarded?"

"That's an idea, but I don't know what we can do about it. Chop my head off before you go."

Meanwhile the squadron of lesser flyers, apparently taking a cue from the griffin, had reformed itself in the air and was fluttering around Ben, cawing and snarling menacingly. The moving circle of the creatures tightened on him. His repeated gestures of submission had no effect, nor did Zoltan's tentative efforts to take command.

Neither man had any idea of how to go about giving these creatures orders, beyond shouting human speech at them, and making crude gestures. Zoltan tried these methods now, to no avail.

"Wait, I have an idea," Zoltan announced. He shouted at the beasts until their clamoring had stilled to some degree. Then he spoke to Ben. "See that shed over there?"

Ben turned to look. There was some fisherman's outbuilding, big as a small house, dilapidated and by all appearances long-deserted, but intact in basic structure.

Zoltan went on: "I'll lock you up in that. What do you think? Close the door on you anyway. At worst it shouldn't take you a minute to kick your way out again, once we're, uh, out of sight."

Ben got the idea, and walked ahead when Zoltan, once more dismounted, urged him along with an imperious gesture. In a few moments they were at the shed. When Ben pulled open the ill-fitting door, the interior proved to have two rooms. The floors in both rooms were of earth, and both contained piles of crates and other fisherman's gear, looking long disused. And a good part of the back wall of the building was actually missing; there were holes in it through which a man would be able to crawl out any time.

Such niceties were evidently beyond the understanding of the small flyers who were circling the building now. These happily abated their clamor as soon as Ben had gone inside the shack and passed out of their sight. Meanwhile the griffin, maintaining its dignity, remained in front.

With a sigh of relief Ben moved through the first room, on into the room that was farther from the door. There, a narrow space between the rough planks of the wall facing the beach offered a chance for him to observe what happened next.

He could hear Zoltan stumbling around somewhere in the first room, behind him; there was a slight delay before the young man appeared in the doorway to the second. There he stood, regarding Ben with a rather odd expression.

Ben demanded: "What's the trouble? If you don't want to trust yourself to that thing in flight, well, I don't blame you. But I'll give it a try if you don't."

"Never mind," Zoltan answered after staring at him a moment longer. "Here I go." He turned and left the room.

And a moment later Ben, looking out through the crack between the planks, saw Prince Mark stride out to greet the waiting flyers, and Barbara vaulted again onto the griffin's back. In a moment the whole flock was airborne once again. And only moments after that they were well out over the water, fading rapidly into the dusky sky.

* * *

Yambu, after bidding her new allies a farewell on the hillside above the town, had returned directly to the inn. There she quickly hired a man to transport her modest luggage down to the docks—she might easily have carried the few things herself, but now it was time to consider the matter of status once again. As she was paying her bill at the inn the proprietor told her that the *Maid of Lakes and Rivers* had arrived at last. She took the news as a good omen.

In another few minutes she was at the docks. There the captain of the newly-arrived riverboat made an effort to intercept the determined-looking lady before she could step onto his deck. He told her that if she was the passenger he had heard about, the pilgrim lady who wished to go far downriver, she would have to wait. He had already been summoned out to the island, with his boat and entire crew.

That was news to Yambu, but she would not admit it. "But of course, my man, I want to go to the island. You may cast off as soon as my luggage is on board."

A moment later, Yambu was standing on the deck. And the captain was at least half-convinced that her wish to visit the island was the real reason he had been ordered to take his boat there.

The dirty deck and modest deckhouse offered no spot suitable for a lady to sit down, and so she stood, with dignity. Her attire of course was far from queenly; but then it was the dress of a pilgrim, and even a queen, once she put on the gray of pilgrimage, might become hard to distinguish from a commoner.

Yambu was still waiting on deck for the short voyage to begin, gazing unseeingly at the remnants of a white poster of some kind affixed to a nearby bollard, when a high, wild, inhuman cry, faint with distance, made her look up into the darkening sky.

The moon, near full, was newly risen; and as she watched a dark shape passed across its disk, as of a flying creature that bore a human being on its back.

8

EMERGING cautiously from the shed into the rapidly thickening dusk, Ben looked out over the lake. The islands now were no more than ghostly little clouds, almost invisible in the last light of the sun and the rising glow of the newly risen moon.

He wished Zoltan well.

He began moving carefully eastward along the shore, still determined to gain possession of a boat if it was humanly possible to do so. With the Sword gone to where it was more urgently needed, he might need to use craft or violence to achieve his purpose. But he was determined that somehow, before the dawn—

He had proceeded for no more than about twenty paces along the shore when a sound behind him made him whirl. Out of the ruined shed a figure staggered, then turned through the dusk toward Ben. It was holding one hand to the top of its head.

Ben raised his staff to guard position and moved to meet the apparition. In a moment he dropped his weapon, recognizing Zoltan.

"Gods and demons! Why aren't you—?" Helplessly Ben shifted his gaze out over the darkening lake; the griffin and its passenger had long since passed out of sight. He turned back to the swaying form before him.

Zoltan sat down with a crunch in the rough, damp shingle that made up the shoreline here. "I'm not out there, if that's what you're asking, because I'm still here. I was just on my way into the shed for a last word with you. . . . Someone must have hit me over the head. I'm getting a lump the size of an egg."

"Hit you? Hit *you*? Then who in all the hells was *that,* astride that flying thing?"

"It was whoever hit me, I suppose. How the hell should I know? I couldn't see him."

Ben closed his eyes. In memory he could see how Zoltan had come from one room of the ruined shed into the other. And he, Ben, had seen Zoltan as Zoltan, not as Mark or Barbara. "I should have known," the big man muttered to himself, and opened his eyes again.

His fears were quickly confirmed. There was no longer any swordbelt at Zoltan's waist. No jeweled scabbard, and, of course, no Sword.

Again Ben turned his gaze out over the darkening lake, then back to Zoltan. He said: "Whoever it was, it seems he has taken Sightblinder with him."

Zoltan nodded, then paused for a few breaths to deal with whatever was going on inside his skull. Then he asked dazedly: "What do we do now?"

Ben swore a few more oaths. Then, in a quiet voice, he said: "As soon as you're able to walk a straight line agian, you can help me find a boat. What else?"

The wind from the south side of the lake was picking up, distant thunder also rumbling from that direction, and the surface of the water was growing choppy when the *Maid of Lakes and Rivers* under light sail eased up to the small docks at the foot of the castle. The small stone docks seemed pinned down by the frowning mass of those high, gray walls.

Basket torches, hanging from those high walls, and mounted in several places on the docks themselves, made the immediate surroundings very nearly as bright as day. Lady Yambu, still intent on reestablishing her rights as a person of importance, froze the captain and some crew members with a single glance, and was allowed to be the first to disembark once lines had been secured. The captain even bowed his head in her direction as she stepped ashore. She felt inclined to pardon his earlier lapses in matters of protocol, as doubtless he had other matters on his mind that he considered much more important. Yambu had heard him talking to his mate during the brief crossing, both men were worried that their boat was going to be seized by the new masters of the lake and islands, and what would happen to them and to their crew in that event they did not know. Still, they had not dared to refuse the summons to come here.

Quite possibly, thought Lady Yambu, they were too much afraid of demons to do that.

She herself, during her years of power, had had too much experience of those inhuman entities to fail to sense their spoor now. It was not an immediate presence, but still the subtle sickness of them hung about this castle like a polluted mist.

Behind the lady, as she stood on the dock waiting to be noticed by someone in authority, the riverboat's crew had begun a hasty unloading of her cargo, apparently in obedience to orders already received somehow from within the walls. Whatever part of the lading the new masters of the castle might find valuable would doubtless go no farther.

She took note that several beautiful sailing craft, as well as vessels of a more utilitarian nature, were already tied up at these docks.

On the mast of one of the sturdy cargo boats nearby was stuck a poster; in the torchlight Lady Yambu could read its largest print, advertising the forthcoming return of the Magnificent Show of Ensor, whatever that might be.

And now her presence had indeed been noticed by someone in authority. And the first decision regarding her had already been taken. A man in a uniform she took to be that of a junior military officer appeared at an open gate, and with a few words and a deferential gesture indicated that he was ready to conduct her within the walls.

They passed in through a postern gate that was doubly guarded, and after, a brief passage between tall stone walls, beneath a narrow strip of clouded sky. Then they entered another door. This led them to a dark chamber furnished with several benches, worthy to be the anteroom of a prison. Lady Yambu was invited to take a seat, then left to wait alone.

Again she chose to remain standing. Her wait had lasted only a few minutes when another official, this one obviously of higher rank, appeared. This man, bowing low, announced that the Ancient Master was willing to see the great Queen Yambu at once.

"Queen no longer," she declared.

But the elegantly dressed courtier, holding the door open for her now, might not have heard her objection. He led her from the anteroom and along a different passageway. Soldiers in uniforms of gray trimmed with red, a livery she had seen in the town but still did not recognize, opened door after door for her, offering salutes. Torchlight showed the way, indoors and out, but the castle as a whole was now too deeply bound in darkness for her to form any estimate of how strongly it might be defended—making such assessments was a habit that had stayed with her, it seemed.

At one point she passed a descending stair, ill-lighted, that looked to her like a way down to a dungeon. Yambu made a mental note, as well as she was able, of the stair's location.

She was making swift progress, she believed, toward the Ancient Master, whoever that might be. Evidently no games of power and rank were going to be played in the nature of keep-the-old-lady-waiting. Probably the new lord of the castle was something of a stranger to this part of the world, and he expected, or at least hoped, that she might be able to provide him with some useful information. Well, perhaps she could.

It was good that she was not going to be kept waiting. Still, she could almost have wished for a few hours' delay, to give her two allies time to get to the island.

It seemed oddly reasonable and natural to Yambu that she should be here, inside a castle again, with men of rank bowing deferentially before her, and events of great moment to be decided. Suddenly she found herself wondering how far she really would be willing to go to help her old enemy, Prince Mark. And what had happened to her search for truth? Only hours ago she had been serenely convinced that finding some abstract truth was all that mattered to her any longer.

But that, of course, had been before another Sword had touched her hand.

She had just finished congratulating herself on her swift progress toward her meeting with the Ancient One when she was made to wait once more, this time in a more comfortable place. Hardly had she settled herself to inspect the artwork on the walls—left over, she supposed, from the days of Honan-Fu—when a door opened and a man entered, dressed in rich garments and wearing a jeweled collar. He was a large man, aging, scarred, and somewhat overweight, and he limped heavily on his left leg.

"Amintor," she said, surprised—but then on second thought she was not really all that surprised. This man had served her as a general, years ago. And more than once during those distant-seeming years he had also shared her bed.

Amintor bowed. "The last time we met, my lady, you were certain that you had withdrawn from the world."

"I have discovered no other world but this one in which to live." She looked him up and down. "You seem to be prospering, Baron."

"Indeed, fate has been kind to me of late."

They chatted for a few moments, of old times, mostly of inconsequential things. Presently Amintor turned her over to the guidance of another officer, who led her out into the corridors of the castle again.

Following her new guide, she climbed steep stairs.

They emerged from these stairs onto a balcony overlooking a central courtyard of the castle, an enclosure much disfigured by what must have been quite recent vandalism. A crude new construction, looking like a sacrificial altar, occupied the center of the space. But she had little time to look at this, or the rest of the setting—the figure that awaited her on the balcony demanded her attention.

This figure was manlike—with some surprising qualifications—and as the former queen drew near, it rose from its throne as if to greet an equal.

The torchlight here was adequate, and her first good look at the Ancient One, his vestigial wings and certain reptilian attributes, afforded Her Ladyship something of a shock. But Queen Yambu had seen strange things before, and she was not going to show that she was shocked unless she chose to do so.

The formalities of greeting were got through routinely, despite the no more than half-human aspect of her host. In a minute Yambu found herself seated near the throne, on a chair almost as tall as it was, and of fine workmanship compared to the crudity of the throne itself. No ordinary throne would have done for this particular ruler, Yambu realized; there was the problem of accommodating his tail.

But she had to pay attention. Her host, in his harsh and somewhat absentminded voice, was declaring that the fame of Queen Yambu, great as it doubtless was in these regions of the world, had somehow escaped his ears until very recently. The implication seemed to be that until very recently he had been far away, in some other part of the world altogether. But he did not say where he had been.

She asked: "And where, my lord, are these remote areas, in which I am unknown?"

He chuckled. "It is not a matter of *where,* so much, dear lady, as of *when.* But that doesn't matter now." He paused. "My leading counselors inform me that you are an old and bitter enemy of Prince Mark of Tasavalta."

"Indeed, sir, until now my relationship with the Prince has been conducted almost entirely across battlefields."

"And I am given to understand that you are also an old acquaintance of Baron Amintor, my military commander?"

"I am more than an old acquaintance, I should say. He is a skillful officer, and served me well."

"Ah, my lady, I could wish that I had met you sooner—I wonder how many more of your former associates I am likely to encounter in these parts?"

Already Lady Yambu was morally certain that this man knew something of her meeting in the inn with Mark's two companions. She said: "I myself have seen one other, during the past two days. And with him was one who was presented to me as a nephew of the Prince—but I cannot vouch for the truth of that relationship."

"Ah." The beast-man did not sound surprised. "And your old friend was—?"

"Hardly a friend of mine. An interesting fellow, though—Ben of Purkinje is his name. Which way he and the princeling nephew went after I had terminated our meeting, I have no idea."

"And in what way—if I ask—is this man interesting?"

"You may ask of me whatever you like, dear Ancient Master—is that title an appropriate one for me to use to you?"

"It will do, Your Ladyship, it certainly will do."

"Good . . . an interesting man, then, and I do not mean only in physical terms—I suppose you will have heard about his remarkable strength. He was presuming rather desperately on his status as an old enemy, to ask my help."

"An intriguing thought." The tailed creature shifted on its throne; for just a moment Lady Yambu had the impression that it, or he, was flirting with a change of shape into a much more fully human aspect. "And what did you tell him, dear lady, if you do not mind sharing your discussion with me?"

"I do not mind. The idea of helping an old enemy—at least some old enemies—might have its interest. But I have other interests now. Ben was disappointed when he learned that my status as a pilgrim is quite genuine."

"Your status, then, is *still* quite genuine? Your pardon, Queen Yambu, I did not mean to question your sincerity. But I thought that you might now be in the process of returning from some spiritual quest, and therefore ready to replace your gray robe with something more—well, more regal."

"Alas, no. My pilgrimage, though it is several months old, can hardly be said to have begun as yet."

"I see. A difficult venture, then. I thank you for interrupting it to visit me. And what god or goddess is its object, estimable lady?"

"The goddess Truth, Your Ancient Lordship."

The figure on the throne threw back its head and gave vent to an honest laugh, which gave the impression, if not the look, of greater humanity. "I do not know that goddess yet. But then I have been absent from the world's affairs for a long time."

"I do not know her either," Yambu admitted readily enough. "Oh, once or twice in my life I think that I have seen her, passing through the air above a battlefield; but never did she linger there for long." And now the tone of Lady Yambu's voice changed suddenly; a certain dreaminess appeared in it, as if in anticipation of a pleasure. "And now, sir, I have a question of my own. I would like to know what you have done with Prince Mark."

"I have done that which ought to please any old enemy of his." Having said that, the Ancient One paused for a moment as if in thought. "He is another interesting man, this Mark. They tell me he is a child of the Emperor, though I am not sure in what sense that description is to be taken. The expression is new to me, a part of this new world in which I find myself. Proverbially, it would mean anyone subject to great misfortune, would it not?"

"Something like that, sir. But in Mark's case I think it is meant in a literal sense. There really is an Emperor, you know."

"There were those who claimed that title in the world from which I came. Perhaps they had earned the right to it. But I understand that this Emperor is something different." The Ancient Lord's eyes, purely reptilian for the moment, probed at Yambu. "They tell me further, Your Majesty, that when you were only a girl yourself you bore the Emperor's girl-child. At that time, apparently, he was still considered a person of some importance."

"He was so considered by many people. Yes." There was much more that Yambu might have said on the subject, but she saw no reason to enter into such a lengthy discussion now.

"Interesting. But not a matter of vital concern, I think. Rather an example, it sounds to me, of a potentially important power whose day has already come and gone." The grotesquely misshapen man stroked his chin—more precisely, his lower jaw—and said to her: "Of much greater interest to me in this new world are the Swords—all the more since I have seen what one of them is capable of doing."

And with a flourish the figure on the throne leaned forward slightly, into fuller torchlight. The Ancient One's right hand brought forward, where Yambu could see it, a black-hilted weapon that she was sure must be Shieldbreaker, though just now whatever symbol might be on the hilt was covered by a clawlike hand.

The man who was holding the Sword said to her: "I have heard that the adoptive father of Prince Mark was the smith who actually worked at the forge to make these twelve fascinating toys."

She shook her head. "Look at the workmanship, dear Ancient Lord. If that is even an adequate word for it. I think it transcends workmanship; it almost transcends art. Can you believe that it is merely human? Even Old-World human? No, it was Vulcan, the god, who forged these blades. But I believe there is some truth in the story, that the man called Jord was also there, pressed into providing some kind of assistance—and Mark was born to Jord's bride less than a year thereafter."

She had made sure to register restrained surprise when first the Sword was shown to her. And now she let herself react again, when her host suddenly leaned the cruciform hilt a little closer to her, and moved his claws to let her see the small white hammer-symbol on the black.

Yambu said: "I have, at one time or another, held others of the Twelve in my own hands. But never this one."

As if he suspected that she yearned to hold it now, its present owner drew it back. He asked: "You would agree that this is the most powerful Sword of all?"

The lady smiled at him faintly. "All twelve have great magic. And also little tricks. The most powerful Sword of all is that one whose powers happen to be required at the moment."

"Well answered, Queen Yambu!"

"Queen no longer, as I have already told your people."

"But queen again, perhaps, one day."

She wondered suddenly if this man might really be anxious to recruit her to his cause. If all this part of the world was truly new to him, it might really be hard for him to find trustworthy and capable subordinates—that was hard enough to do at any time.

She said: "I think not, Lord of the Lake—but that sounds too small a title for a man of your obvious accomplishments."

"Oh, it is, Your Ladyship, far too small. I mean to be Lord of the World one day—one day not too far distant." He sounded calmly confident.

He drank wine then, and suddenly arose from his throne. A rich cape, which had been draped behind the chair, now fell about his body, covering most of the deformity from the shoulders down. Standing, the Ancient Lord was taller than Yambu, somehow considerably taller than she had expected.

Around his upper back his cape bulged out, a symmetrical enlargement quite unlike the deformity of a hump. And as Yambu watched, the bulge stirred lightly, giving her the sudden idea that rudimentary wings might be enfolded there. Wings on a man, she thought, would make no sense at all; but they would not be the first thing about this one that did not make sense.

He said: "Come with me, lady, and I will show you what has happened to Prince Mark."

They descended the interior stairway from the balcony, and this time turned out onto the courtyard and across it. On its far side a postern gate let them out through a comparatively thin interior wall. The place they entered was more a grotto than a courtyard, a narrow space surrounded by high walls, in which a narrow rim of paving surrounded a well or inlet of dark, chill water. On the far side of the well a low arch of stone covered the entrance to a watery tunnel under the castle, which was defended by a heavy steel grillwork against any commerce with the lake outside.

Standing on the narrow stone rim of the pond, Lady Yambu watched as attendants took hold of a heavily secured rope and hoisted an ice-encrusted form, in human shape, out of the water in which it had been shallowly submerged. Lake water, she thought, oughtn't to be quite *that* cold, not at this time of year anyway. Magic, of course.

Two of the soldiers who had done the hoisting held the bound form up between them, while another leaned forward and struck it where the face ought to be. The blow seemed impersonal, as if he were trying to get a good look at a frozen fish. The soldier's fist shattered the white integument sufficiently for Yambu to be able to recognize the features of Prince Mark. The Prince's battered face was blue and gray with cold, and there was bright blood around his mouth, as if he might have bitten his tongue with the violence of his shivering, perhaps, or in some effort not to cry out. But Mark's eyes were open, and alive, and when they rested on Yambu she thought they recognized her.

A moment later she had taken a step forward, and swung her own arm. It was more like a warrior's blow than an old woman's slap, and the Prince's helpless head bobbed sideways with the impact.

Yambu stepped back with a sigh. "I have long dreamed of doing that," she assured her host. And in the privacy of her own thoughts she marveled at this strong new evidence of how suddenly and completely her dedication to the abstract truth seemed to have evaporated. Evidently some things, after all, were more important.

"Is there anything else that you would like to do?" her host inquired. When she turned to face him she saw that his reptilian aspect was entirely gone, and the wings too; in place of the grotesque creature she had been talking to now stood a fully human man, young and strong and of surpassing beauty. The rich cape hung now in different, straighter folds. Golden curls fell to the young man's muscular shoulders; his clear blue eyes regarded her.

"Not at the moment, Your Lordship," she replied, and bowed her appreciation of his magic.

At a nod from the lord of the castle, the Prince was allowed to splash back into the lake. He sank like a stone, his rope tugged taut again.

Then Yambu gestured toward the second rope nearby, which presumably led to another submerged form. "And who is our dear Prince's companion, Ancient One?"

"None other than this castle's former owner, my dear queen. Another acquaintance of yours, perhaps—? No? Well, no one can know everyone of importance in the world. I should like to try to do so, though."

Interruption in the form of a flying messenger spiraling softly down between the grotto's walls came at that point to cut their conversation short. The Ancient Lord, having heard the message that the beast had come to hiss into his ear, announced as much, with what seemed genuine regret.

"But we have much more to say to each other, dear Yambu. I insist that you remain here as my honored guest for some time before you resume your pilgrimage."

She would not have dreamt of trying to decline.

9

ARNFINN awoke, on that unreal morning after his first arrival at Lady Ninazu's manor, into what seemed at first a gloriously prolonged dream. He was lying naked amid the marvelous white softness of her bed, and he thought the place was still warm where she had lain beside him. Even after he had experimentally cracked his eyelids open, it was perfectly easy to believe that he was still dreaming. This world in which he found himself this morning seemed to bear but small resemblance to the ordinary waking universe in which he had spent his life before encountering the Sword of Stealth.

It was in fact the nearby voice of the young lady herself, raised in shrill and ugly tones as she berated one of her servants, that convinced Arnfinn of reality.

Turning his body halfway over amid the bed's incredible luxury, he lifted himself up on one elbow and surveyed the room in which he had awakened. Lady Ninazu's voice sounded from beyond rich draperies concealing a door, and for the moment Arnfinn was alone. His own clothes, the few poor garments he had worn upon his journey, made a crude and grimy scattering across the floor's thick bright rugs and colored tiles. But the Sword of Stealth, with sheath and belt and all, was with him in the bed. Even at the peak of last night's excitement he had remembered to make sure of that. If the lady had been at all aware of Sightblinder's presence between her sheets, she had been diplomatic enough to say nothing about it.

She had said several things, though, that were already, despite the considerable distractions he now faced, coming back to Arnfinn's thoughts this morning.

For example, at one time last night she had said: "I am surprised, lord, that you have come to me alone and unattended." Only to amend that a moment later with: "But then I suppose a wizard with powers like yours is never really unattended anywhere."

Last night Arnfinn's attention had been consumed by other matters. But this morning that last statement struck him as important. He could not help thinking that it could be of great importance indeed to know exactly which wizard Lady Ninazu thought he was.

It appeared that he was going to have a few moments longer for reflection; Lady Ninazu was still out of sight behind closed and brocaded draperies, tongue-lashing her servants in the next room over some female triviality of hairdressing or clothing. He shifted again in the bed, marveling anew at its whiteness and softness. He had never really imagined that anyone lived like this.

And now another memory of last night came back: Her Ladyship, unbelievably naked, incredibly lying in bed with him, sleepily clasping Arnfinn's workworn, underfed arms and shoulders in her hands, and murmuring, without the least trace of mockery in her voice, about how marvelously muscular he was.

And again she had declared, in a voice soft with passion, "I sometimes wonder, lover, whether I fear you or I love you more."

And again: "It is now, as you must well remember, two years since we first met—a little more than two years. And yet sometimes I feel I don't know you at all."

And yet again, in what now seemed to Arnfinn her most mysterious utterance of all: "I have heard from others that there are times in which the appearance of your body changes. I hope that is only a lie, spread by your enemies."

"Changes?" Arnfinn had dared to ask. She wasn't, at least he hoped she couldn't be, talking about the changes wrought by the Sword of Stealth—but if not that, what?

And that was the only moment during the night in which the lady had apparently come close to being disconcerted. With lowered, fluttering lashes she had murmured: "I meant no offense, my dread lord."

"It does not matter," her supposed dread lord had responded awkwardly, not knowing what else to say, having no idea of how a real lord might have phrased the thought. And the lady had looked blank for a moment, as if something in her bed-partner's speech or manner puzzled her. But still the power of the Sword prevailed; whatever else the victim of its deception might suspect, the identity of the person who held

Sightblinder was usually the last thing that the victim could be made to doubt.

After that exchange of words Lady Ninazu had busied herself again with dedication to Arnfinn's pleasure, and he had forgotten her words until now.

And now he forgot them again, for the draperies opened. The lady, wrapped in a loose garment of white fur, stood in the doorway smiling down at him for a long moment before she closed the curtains behind her again and came over to the bed. On her way toward it she paused to wrinkle her pretty little nose at some of the disgusting peasants' clothing on the floor, and kick it out of her way. "Where can *that* have come from?" she murmured crossly to herself.

But she was smiling again by the time she reached the bed. "I am very pleased," she said, "that my lord, who for a thousand years, or perhaps ten thousand, has had his choice of women, continues to be pleased with me."

Arnfinn, who had had exactly two women in his lifetime previously, without the idea of choice having really entered into it on either occasion, swallowed. "How could I not be pleased?" he responded.

The lady curtsied, a small movement that flirted with mockery while still managing to give an impression of humility; but at the same time he, even Arnfinn the innocent, could see the calculation in her eyes, and the fierce pride.

She whispered: "And will I continue to please you?"

Despite the enchantment of her beauty, there was something . . . Arnfinn could feel a wariness developing in him. What would a real great lord have said in response to her question? "You will always please me. But there are many demands upon my time."

"I am sure that there are more than I can possibly imagine. But now you have at least established firm control of my father's stronghold. Tell me—that bothersome man—my father—I take it he is no longer in a position to bother anyone?"

Moment by moment the dream was developing imperfections. There was something in the way this girl spoke of her father that began to curdle both lust and satisfaction.

"No," Arnfinn answered, going along with what she evidently wanted, again not knowing what else to say. "He is not." This, then, he was thinking, was a daughter of Honan-Fu. And a daughter who rejoiced in her father's downfall. Once again Arnfinn knew the beginning of fear. Without really understanding why, he could feel a disagreeable knot beginning to form in the pit of his stomach.

Approaching the bed, the lady sat down close beside him. Then, as if it were a gesture requiring boldness, she reached out to put her hand on her dread lord's arm.

"And"—her voice dropped; something of great importance was about to be said—"my twin brother. How is he?" Lady Ninazu seemed to be holding her breath as she awaited her wizard lord's answer to that. Her eyes were enormous.

The lady was hanging on Arnfinn's response so raptly that it almost seemed that she had ceased to breathe. The rise and fall of her breast was almost suspended. Arnfinn could feel the knot in his own gut grow tighter in the presence of this intensity of will and of emotion, neither one of which he understood.

What to say?

"He is as well as can be expected," Arnfinn replied at last. "Under the circumstances."

"Ahh!" It was more an animal's unthinking snarl than it was a word. Her eyes blazed at him fiercely, though what the passion was that made them blaze he could not tell. "What does that mean?"

A moment ago this girl had been all fluttering subservience, and now she was almost threatening. The fear induced in her by Sightblinder had been and continued to be genuine, though she was keeping it under control; what could bring her to raise such a challenge despite her fear?

Arnfinn's own fear awoke again, as if in sympathy with hers. He knew that if he once allowed himself to give in to his own timidity in this situation, terror could overwhelm him. Instead he forced himself to sit up straight on the edge of the bed—making sure that he was still touching the swordbelt with one hand—and to stare at the woman with as much regal authority as he could try to mimic.

She quailed at once; before he had to say a word, her eyes fell before his gaze.

"Oh, well," she murmured. "If you will not answer." Then, to Arnfinn's amazement, a tear appeared in the corner of Lady Ninazu's eye. She folded her arms in the sleeves of her white fur robe and rocked back and forth in the immemorial way of women grieving. Her voice dropped so low that he could barely hear it. "It has been more than two years since my brother and I have been allowed to see each other. Since that day on which we served you so well, master, he has not even been allowed to see the light of day. And year after year, day after day, my father has treated him so cruelly. He was still like a child two years ago; and anyway what we did was right—Kunderu and I opened the way for you to come into this world, didn't we? Isn't it wrong, isn't it monstrous, that his punishment should have gone on so long?"

"Your twin brother," Arnfinn muttered to himself, gaping at the lady, trying to understand. It was the first time he had ever heard of the existence of any such person.

"My dread lord, do not toy with me!" The words burst from the lady's lips, though a moment later she would have bitten them back. Arnfinn had never seen anyone so gripped by emotion—not even the madwoman in the village, though she had been much noisier.

In the next moment Lady Ninazu had fallen on her knees before him. "My brother, Kunderu. Why cannot you let me see him now? Even though he is a great wizard himself as you well know, all power is in your hands now. Can you not at least allow me to see him? If I could see my brother again, if I could know that he is free, and happy—for two years now I've lived for nothing but that. Oh, great lord, oh, great lord, help me!"

The world was beginning to turn gray in front of Arnfinn. Shame and love and guilt and fear swept over him together. He had all that he could do to keep himself from leaping up and running from the room, even as he had run from the poor people on the roads and in the town, the deluded fools who had thought that he was the most important person in their lives.

"I will be your loyal slave forever," she implored him. "What does it matter to you now that he once angered our father? Unless—unless, oh, gods, unless you have some agreement now with Honan-Fu—?"

It was like that woman in the first village all over again, only a hundred times worse. Like the girl with the baby in the town square, only a thousand times more terrible.

"I will do what I can!" Arnfinn barked at last, almost shouting. At the same time he jumped to his feet, and even as he jumped his left hand went out and grabbed the jeweled belt, dragging the Sword with him. It came with him as inexorably as some prisoner's chain. With muscles energized by desperation, he pushed the lady violently away from him.

Ninazu cried out in pain as her body crumpled to the floor on a soft rug.

Arnfinn stood momentarily paralyzed. Now, on top of everything else, he had hurt her, bruised her physically. He stood in the middle of the room, eyes shut, hands clenching his head, one arm looped through the swordbelt, holding it to him, in agony lest in his own fear and torment he should commit some greater violence that would hurt her yet again.

But Lady Ninazu was not much hurt. She scrambled to her feet, and in a moment was at Arnfinn's side again, murmuring in his ear, soothing him when she saw that he appeared to be stricken. It seemed that she had made an amazingly swift recovery from her grief and pain. Now she moved lightly about Arnfinn, talking, almost as though a moment ago she had not been on the verge of hysterics.

And Lady Ninazu must have given some signal to her servants, for now some of them were entering the chamber, pushing before them a cart that rolled on large silver wheels and was topped with a golden tray. The metal part of the cart looked liked solid gold to Arnfinn, and it was laden with food on golden plates. He could recognize none of the dishes, but the aromas reminded Arnfinn, even in his distress, that he had not eaten for many hours.

Despite his ravenous hunger, he had to get away. He could no longer face the lady, knowing how he had deceived and cheated her. Her every worshipful glance accused him. Her beauty and her tears had become more than he could stand.

He kissed her once more, hopelessly and chastely this time. To her look of astonishment he muttered half-incoherent promises of return and promises of help. Meanwhile he was busy pulling on his clothes, going through contortions in the process so that the Sword of Deception should remain always close at his side.

Then he fled, at the last moment grabbing up some food from the cart to eat on the way. When Lady Ninazu called after him, Arnfinn only roared at her and rushed on, as he had run from one woman in the small village, and from another in the streets of Triplicane.

He was out in the grounds of the manor, heading for the rear gate where he had come in, when he encountered one of the stable's supervisors, who dared to speak to him.

The man bowed nervously. "It's about the, uh, the griffin, my lord."

"The griffin."

"Sire, the steed on which you arrived last night. If it needs care, feeding . . . I confess that none of us this morning are able to see it as anything but an ordinary loadbeast." And the man smiled, shaking his head in humble awe at the power of the lord's magic.

"Then care for it as you would a loadbeast. I will return for it later." And Arnfinn stalked on.

He wasn't going to need the loadbeast now because he wasn't going home. He couldn't go home now. . . .

On foot he wandered despairingly back toward the town. He was hopelessly, cruelly, insanely, suicidally, in love with Lady Ninazu. And in trying to love her, taking advantage of her, possessing her so falsely, he had wronged her terribly. If she were ever to find out how he had tricked her with the Sword . . .

But worse than her revenge, infinitely worse, would be the fact that then she would know him as he really was. The contemptible, vile, ugly, scrawny, cowardly, deceitful wretch he was—

Arnfinn sobbed as he walked, almost staggering with the burden of his guilt and his remorse. Not knowing, hardly caring, where he was going at the moment.

It seemed to him inevitable that he would be found out. And when he was, the lady, or the powerful wizard who must be her real lover, would have him cut up into small pieces, and the pieces burned. But no, before it ever came to that, he would kill himself out of sheer shame. It was impossible that he could ever find a way to make amends for what he had done to her—

If I could see my brother again, if I could know that he is free, and happy . . . I live for that.

Arnfinn could feel the terrible weight of the Sword dragging at his side. With such a weapon even a coward might be able to accomplish almost anything.

Between the lifeless trees of autumn he could see part of the lake, and the castle on its island.

Kunderu, she had said the man's name was. Her twin brother, held prisoner out there for—how long, two years?—in punishment by their father, the oh-so-kindly Honan-Fu. In punishment for what? Arnfinn wondered briefly. She had said, implied, something about how she and her brother had helped the wizard she now called her dread lord. . . .

But then that thought was pushed aside by another. Everyone ought to have known better, thought Arnfinn, than to believe that such a powerful old man as Honan-Fu could really be as benevolent as the stories painted him.

Arnfinn found a quiet place on a hillside, a little off the road, where he could sit down with his Sword and stare out at the castle. He had decided that he was ready to lay down his life, if need be, for the lady he had so cruelly wronged. He would find her twin brother, if the man called Kunderu was still alive, and he would release him.

The trouble was that Arnfinn had no idea of how to begin to go about performing such a feat. Except that he would have to take Sightblinder to the island, and somehow use its powers to achieve his end.

He would have to go out there to the castle ruled by the commander of the soldiers in red and gray, who had all the folk of Triplicane terrified. Out there into the den of the murderers and torturers. He, a country yokel—he knew what he was—would have to stand alone among them. Even if he did have one magic Sword, a weapon whose powers he scarcely understood—

Arnfinn was trying to picture himself where he had never been, in a world that he had never seen and could not very well imagine. In his imagination the parts of that world that he could not see clearly quickly filled up with terrible shadows.

Suppose, just suppose, that he were standing there now, in the great hall of that castle, making demands of one who sat there upon a throne —of one who was in all likelihood the real and jealous lover of Lady Ninazu. In a great hall with columns taller than the trees of the forest, and filled with people, crafty and deadly people, devious magicians and brutal warriors who did not know what it meant to be afraid, men and women whose business had been plotting and uncovering plots almost from the day that they were born.

If he, Arnfinn, who now feared to cross the town square because of the strangers who might accost him, were in that castle, what would he be able to do there?

Assuming that the magicians on the island were as subject to Sightblinder's powers as the peasants along the road—but how could he even assume that?—then what would happen? What image would those wizards and clever warriors see when they looked at Arnfinn? When no two of them, perhaps, saw him as the same person, how long would it take them to understand what was happening?

For an hour he sat brooding on the hillside, the drawn steel of Sightblinder in his hands, digging little holes in the earth with the god-

forged point of it and cutting up twigs with the almost invisible keenness of its edge.

Fear receded gradually. His breathing grew easier, his heartbeat
slowed and steadied, and the knot in his stomach began to untie itself.
Because he wasn't going to start for the island this moment. No, he saw
now that he couldn't do that. This was going to require some planning.

Later in the day, wandering hesitantly among the hills at the far end
of town from the manor, unable to make up his mind on any decisive
course of action, Arnfinn came upon a deserted hut. The shack stood at
some distance from any of the regularly used paths and roads that
crossed the landscape. The hut provided him with partial shelter, and
that night and on succeeding nights he slept uneasily in it, with an
intermittent drizzle penetrating the overhanging branches and the
ruined roof. At least he felt secure that no one was going to bother him
here.

Each night, after a day of aimless wandering and scrounging food, he
dozed off in the hut, hoping that no one would find him—and hoping
even more fervently that no wild beast was going to come along, indifferent to the personal identities of its human victims as long as they had
flesh and blood to eat. But in his cooler moments, Arnfinn supposed it
unlikely that any such large predator would lurk so close to a large
town.

He was still living in that hut three days later, scrounging food in and
near the town as best he could, avoiding human contact as much as
possible, and trying to nerve himself for the attempt to do what Lady
Ninazu wanted done, when the three ill-assorted strangers waylaid him
and took his magic Sword away from him.

And an hour after he had lost the Sword, rousing himself from his
hopeless vigil across the road from the gates of Lady Ninazu's manor,
he moved and thought with a fatalistic calm. There was nowhere in the
world for him to go, nothing else that he could do, until he had retrieved the Sword—somehow—and used it as he knew he must, to try
to make amends to the lady he had so cruelly wronged.

When, later, Arnfinn saw the huge man and the shifting form of one
who must hold the Sword, walking together along the shore of the lake,
he stalked them.

10

A GAINST this terror, the Sword of Stealth was as useless as a pin. Riding the griffin high above the lake, Arnfinn gritted his teeth to keep himself from screaming in dread of the sheer drop below him. In the distance, the last tinges of the sunset were reflected in the water, but directly underneath him there was nothing but an incredible gulf of air with black water at the bottom of it.

In the next moment he had to close his eyes as well. But even with his eyes closed he could still feel in his stomach that he was aboard a flying creature, with only a vast emptiness beneath. Even the escort of small creatures with which he had left the shore had now been left behind.

He remembered once, when he was a small boy, seeing a small flying predator struggling terribly to lift a half-grown rabbit, and in his guts he could not really believe that this beast beneath him could go on from one moment to the next supporting his weight.

Arnfinn's right hand was entwined in a deathgrip in the long hair of the griffin's leonine mane, while his left hand, close beside the right, was having trouble finding a solid grip. It grabbed at one tuft after another of what felt like eagle feathers, which pulled loose every time his fingers clamped upon them. He opened his eyes long enough to shift his grip, getting a firm hold with both fists on the hairy mane.

If this had been a riding-beast or a loadbeast Arnfinn would have felt reasonably confident of being able to control it, even without reins or saddle. But he was totally ignorant of the proper way to give this creature orders. He wondered if it was interpreting his efforts to cling to its back as some kind of commands.

That possibility was unsettling enough to force Arnfinn's eyelids open again. This latest terrified glimpse suggested to him that he had now reached an altitude almost equal to that of the surrounding distant hills. On the positive side, he made the reassuring discovery that if he did not look straight down, he could keep his eyes open.

Presently he was sure that the griffin was now descending gradually, in almost a straight path toward the approximate center of the watery plain ahead, where from an island there arose the shadowed shape of the dark castle, marked here and there with sparks of torchlight.

Arnfinn had not appreciated how swift the griffin was, until, unbelievably, the castle was already very close beneath him. And then the creature was down, achieving a soft and springy landing. In a moment Arnfinn slid from its back and once more had solid rock beneath his feet, though he was still high above the surface of the surrounding lake.

Here, atop the highest tower of the castle, was an aerie the size of a small house, a place set aside to serve the arrivals and departures of aerial spies and messengers, and to provide the beasts with living space as well. Right now most of the roosts and cages stood empty. Whatever birds had once been kept there by Honan-Fu were dead now or departed, and evidently most of the reptilian and avian creatures serving the new masters of the castle were out on patrol.

The newly landed griffin, bulking larger than a riding-beast when it spread its wings, dominated the space. The few smaller creatures present were sent flapping and fluttering out of its way, making noisy cries of protest.

Arnfinn, once he had slipped gratefully from the creature's back, lost no time in getting clear of it altogether. At the moment he scarcely cared where his feet were taking him, as long as they were firmly on solid ground again.

But even as the griffin moved away, walking somewhat awkwardly on its two mismatched pairs of legs, Arnfinn realized that a pair of human observers had witnessed his arrival. One of these men was standing by with a broom in hand, while the other held a small measure of grain. They were obviously low-ranking beastmasters, handlers and caretakers of the creatures here.

It was equally obvious that the two unquestioningly accepted Arnfinn as a person of overwhelming importance, for they bowed themselves immediately out of his way, one of them spilling the grain from his measure in his haste to do so. Behind them as they moved, Arnfinn observed the upper end of a ladder. When he had scrambled down it he saw the head of a descending stair.

Flames in wall sconces of twisted metal burned at intervals on the way down, set close enough together to let him see the footing. After two turns of the spiral, when Arnfinn had reached a place where he was for the moment sheltered from all human sight, he paused. Leaning his back against the wall he took a few deep breaths. Clutching the talisman of his Sword with one hand, Arnfinn used the tattered sleeve of his free arm to wipe sweat from his face, despite the chill draft blowing down the stair.

He had done it now. He was really here.

The next question was, where would an important prisoner like Kunderu, a wizard and a wizard's son, be likely to be hidden? Though Arnfinn had never been inside a castle before, he like everyone else knew that they were supposed to have dungeons underneath them. But he had also heard an old story or two in which prisoners of high rank and deemed especially important, or for some other reason deserving of special treatment, were kept locked up in high towers instead.

Anyway, since he had arrived atop the castle's highest tower, he might as well begin his search efforts at the top.

There was another problem, which only now occurred to Arnfinn: once he had located Kunderu, and somehow secured his release, how were the two of them going to return to the mainland? Briefly he toyed with the idea of persuading the magically powerful griffin to carry two passengers at once. The flight had been a hideous experience, and he had no wish to repeat it, but it had the one blessed advantage of being quick; either he and Kunderu would promptly effect their escape, or else they would be promptly killed. The alternative to using the griffin would be to commandeer a boat. . . . Arnfinn decided he wasn't going to make his choice just yet.

At the next landing down the tower stair, about twenty steps down from his first rest stop, he came to a narrow window through which he was able to survey the deepening night outside. Light enough remained for him to see that his griffin-mount, along with an escort of smaller flyers, had just taken off again, evidently heading out once more on patrol.

One question settled. He and Ninazu's brother were going to have to get away by boat, and that in a way was a relief. He would not have to fly again.

Arnfinn moved on down.

Presently, now only moderately high in the castle's architecture, he came out on a small terrace. This would be a good spot, he thought, from which to try to see what might be going on below, where parts of several open courtyards were visible. There were several lighted windows, as well, at his own level or a little higher, which he thought might repay investigation. He stood there beginning a survey.

Some time ago, Lady Yambu had given up listening at the door of the apartment to which she had been conducted as a guest. It was a comfortable enough place, even somewhat luxurious; but she was quite sure that if she left, or tried to leave, there would be a confrontation. She was effectively a prisoner. It was no more than she had expected.

Is this how I search for truth? she thought. But if I were not here, if I had determined to persevere very strictly in my pilgrimage, where would I be? Back at that damned room at the inn, probably, still waiting for another boat that might or might not be willing to take me down the Tungri.

Looking out from one of her gracefully thin windows—these quarters were certainly quite a change from her room at the inn—she saw, on a balcony at a slightly lower level, the figure of the Emperor. He was wearing his gray cape and a clown's mask, and looking tentatively about him. In that first moment of recognition, despite her experience only hours ago, she had no doubt that it was really the Emperor she saw.

Only when she saw him inexplicably turn into the hideously pallid figure of the Dark King, dead now these many years, did Yambu suddenly realize that this must be Zoltan or Ben. One of them at least must have managed to reach the island with the Sword of Stealth.

Lady Yambu brought a candle over to the window, and began some cautious signaling.

Arnfinn's attention was drawn to one window by the tiny movement of the flame inside it. The window was not many meters away, and despite the poor light, he at once recognized the gray-haired lady as one member of the infamous trio who had assaulted him and taken away the Sword. He was more than a little surprised to see her here. What she and her companions had said when they took his Sword away had made him think that they were not connected with the new lords of the lake and islands.

But, who was she seeing when she looked at him? Obviously not someone she greatly feared.

Arnfinn waved back, a slight, cautious gesture, and then began to work his way nearer her apartment, a task made considerably more difficult by his complete ignorance of the interior layout of the castle. Traveling through corridors that were almost completely dark, he found his vision somehow enhanced, he thought, by Sightblinder. What little was shown him by stray glints of light was easier to interpret in terms of real surfaces and distances.

He came out on another untenanted small balcony, from which he hoped to be able to see the window, and found to his satisfaction that he was closer to it. Taking a shortcut that involved some risky climbing—by this time risks were assuming a different proportion—he soon found himself standing on yet another balcony, near enough to the lady's window to allow them to conduct a quiet conversation.

"Who is it?" she whispered out to him, the imperious tone that he remembered still lingering in her voice. "Zoltan or Ben?"

Arnfinn, trying to understand that question, wondered if the lady could be speaking of a pair of twins, so that she did not know which one she thought she saw. Or, were Ben and Zoltan two different people, and had she seen him as first one and then the other as he approached?

"What does it matter?" he whispered back. Then, bluntly: "I must know. Where are the important prisoners being held?"

He could see her shake her head impatiently and blink. "Prisoners? I know where the one of most importance is, at least. If you can get me out of this comfortable cell, I'll take you directly to him."

11

A S soon as Zoltan felt steady enough on his feet to travel, he continued with Ben along the shoreline in the direction away from Triplicane. They met no one as they walked. From time to time Ben cast a glowering look out over the lake, but the griffin, along with its unknown rider, and their flying escort of lesser creatures, had all disappeared into the distances of the darkening lacustrine sky.

Still Ben and Zoltan moved on. As the dusk deepened around them they stumbled around and over two more deserted docks, but except for one half-sunken hulk there were no boats of any kind to be discovered.

By this time both men were almost staggering with weariness. Abandoning their efforts for the time being, they sought shelter in a small hillside grove of evergreens, only a stone's throw from the water. There, on ground softly carpeted with needles, they slept until it was almost dawn.

Zoltan, who was the first to come fully awake, immediately set about scrounging up some breakfast. Seldom had he ever undertaken a journey of any length without bringing along a fisherman's line and a few hooks, and this trek to Alkmaar had been no exception. He could hear the downhill rush of a small stream that ran nearby, screened by trees. The underside of a log yielded a few juicy grubs for bait. Meanwhile Ben, groaning himself awake at last, came up with the flint and steel necessary to get a fire started.

Zoltan's skill, aided by moderate good luck, soon provided a few fish. As the two men breakfasted, discussing their problems and peering out over the lake, a pair of large rowboats came into sight through the usual sunrise mist and the accompanying strange optical effects. The boats, filled with soldiers uniformed in gray and red, were following the shoreline from the direction of the town.

Ben cast a quick glance upward, making sure that his small fire was producing no visible smoke. But the soldiers in the boats were not scanning for evidence of campfires. A little farther along the shore, in the direction they were going, stood a small fisherman's house, dark and deserted-looking in the dawn. But the house proved not to be deserted. When the big rowboats grounded in front of it and the troops poured ashore and into the building, screams and cries for mercy followed quickly.

Soon the soldiers were dragging a woman out of the house, while screams in a man's hoarse voice went on inside. And now they were bringing children out.

Zoltan, young as he was, had seen bad things before, but still he could not watch this. Instead he moved to a little slope facing away from the house, where he sat with his fingers in his ears.

Ben, his ugly face looking as if it were carved from stone, the breeze from the lake ruffling his graying hair, sat watching through it all. He wanted to know all that he could about the enemy. Even at the distance he tried to pick out individuals among them, for possible future reference.

The officer in charge of the troops, a red-haired man with a penetrating voice, looked on indulgently during the rape and killing. When that had been concluded, he ordered a few of his men aboard the single small fishing boat tied at the dock beside the house. The little craft appeared to be leaky—Ben could see the prize crew bailing industriously before they put their oars into the locks. Soon all three boats were rowing back in the direction of the town.

Ben swore gloomy oaths. He said to Zoltan, who by now had rejoined him: "One of the things the bastards are doing, then, is rounding up all the available boats. No wonder we couldn't find one to borrow last night."

"If we'd just kept going a little longer we might have had that one," Zoltan grumbled, watching it disappear. He was still pale from listening to the screams, and now and then he touched the place on the back of his head where he had been hit.

"And it's small wonder, too," Ben went on, "that we have seen practically no people on the shore. The fisherfolk all around the lake, or this end of it anyway, must be abandoning everything and moving out."

"So what do we do now?"

"I don't know."

Zoltan turned his head. "Sounds like someone coming. Uphill, that way."

There was a path in that direction, not very far away, but pretty effectively screened by evergreens. And now there was a lone man, in drab civilian clothing, walking on the path.

"Shall we keep quiet, or say hello to him?"

"Let's ask him how the weather's been."

When they appeared suddenly on the path, one in front of the man and one behind him, he collapsed at once in a terrified heap, signing that his pockets were empty and he had nothing to give them. But he was quickly convinced that they were not robbers and meant him no harm. Then he became willing to talk; indeed it was almost impossible to stop him for long enough to get a question in.

He was a wiry man of middle size, with bushy black eyebrows starting to turn gray. His name, he said, was Haakon, and he was, or had been, a part-time weaver of fishing nets, as well as a former member of the constabulary serving Honan-Fu. It had not been a very energetic or well-disciplined outfit, according to Haakon, and now he, like the other members that he knew about, was lying low and had even burned his old uniform.

Haakon went on to relate how, at the time of the takeover a few days ago, he had seen a small army of the invaders come down one of the small rivers that emptied into the lake, and approach the castle. He estimated now that there had been about two hundred soldiers, in ten or twelve boats.

"You and your constabulary made no resistance?"

"We weren't even called to duty before it was all over, the castle lost, and Honan-Fu dropped out of sight. Anyway, it would have taken us days to mobilize effectively."

Ben fixed his eyes on the man in a steady gaze. "I think it's time you got together now. Going by what you say yourself, there's no huge army occupying the castle—not yet anyway. It could be retaken, if you didn't advertise that you were coming."

Haakon appeared to consider that. "Well—there could have been other troops arrive that I didn't see. And I'm not one of the constabulary officers."

"Then find your officers, man. Or choose new ones. Did you see what just happened to that family of fisherfolk down there? Where is the rest of this constabulary now?"

"I don't know. Scattered about." Haakon obviously was beginning to regret that he had spoken so openly to these strangers on the subject. No, he had no idea as to where any boats could possibly be found now. The invaders had been gathering them all up.

"And where," asked Zoltan, "can we find you if we should want to talk to you again?"

The man looked from one of them to the other. "They know me at Stow's shop in Triplicane," he said at last. The information was given out so reluctantly that Ben and Zoltan, exchanging glances, both believed it was the truth.

Presently, after making their informant a present of the single fish left over from their breakfast—a gift he accepted gratefully—and wishing him good luck, Ben and Zoltan walked on.

When the two were sure they were alone again, Zoltan asked: "We are going to keep on looking for a boat? Despite the evidence that there aren't any available?"

"Unless you have a better idea."

"We could have a try ourselves at raising this constabulary that our friend talked about."

Ben shook his head. "If they can't raise themselves under these circumstances, we wouldn't have much chance. We're outsiders, strangers. They'd never be willing to trust us in time to do Mark any good."

Zoltan trudged on another score of paces before he spoke again. "We could remain in hiding until night falls again, and then swim out to the castle on a couple of logs."

"That's crazy. But all right, we're going to have to do something. And what we're doing now is getting us nowhere."

"Look out."

The soldier who had just appeared on the slope ahead spotted them an instant after Zoltan had seen him. His bold command to halt was directed at their fleeing backs.

A moment later a whole squad of voices had joined in the clamor. There would certainly be pursuit. The two who fled had not much of a start, and each glance back showed soldiers coming on in energetic fashion. And now, to make matters worse, a couple of enemy flying scouts had ceased their observant high circling out over the water and joined in the chase across the land.

When these creatures, emboldened by their gathering numbers, dared to dive within range, Ben beat at them with his long staff and drove them off. After that the flyers stayed at a safe altitude, circling and cawing raucously to guide the soldiers in the right direction.

The chase went on, with the enemy gaining slightly. Their gasping quarry climbed a difficult rock slope, and clambered down another, getting a little farther ahead again.

Zoltan, when he had time and breath to spare, threw rocks and curses at the flyers, and prayed to all the gods and demons for a sling. But he had no sling, and none appeared.

The moments in which the two fugitives dared to pause for rest were rare. And now, slowly, they were being forced back in the direction of the town.

One of the flyers suddenly broke away from the circling flock above and flew in that direction.

"The people chasing us have signaled it to call for reinforcements," Ben grunted. "They'll try to pen us in between the patrol that's following us and troops come out from the town."

But no reinforcements appeared, and still the two Tasavaltans were not caught. The chase continued in zigzag course; the day wore on until the sun had turned past its high point. Here and there a rill of water, tumbling from broken rock, offered the fugitives a chance to get a drink. As for eating, they had no time.

Either the flyer had had trouble in locating a responsive officer in town, or the enemy were beset by other difficulties and had none readily available. All day long the hiding and chasing continued inconclusively. The sky turned gray, and a fine, misting rain began to fall.

At last Zoltan, crouched wearily in a dripping thicket, could say to Ben: "Another hour and it'll be dark."

And then somehow, at last, it was dark, and they were still alive and free. Now the chance existed for the two of them to slip away, get through the hills and on the road back to Tasavalta.

"Not that they mightn't catch us tomorrow," Zoltan qualified in a weary voice.

But Ben had a different idea. "I think that we ought to go into town instead."

Zoltan raised an eyebrow, considering. "Well, they won't be expecting us to do that."

"No, they won't. And there'll be boats there, we can be certain of that much. Guarded, no doubt. But hanging around out here in the hills, we have small chance of staying alive, and no chance of accomplishing anything useful. I say it's either go into town or head for home."

"If we were going to run for home," said Zoltan, "we would have done it long ago."

At least the rain had stopped again, and their pursuers had apparently given up for the night. After an hour's sorely needed rest, Ben and Zoltan ate such scraps of food as they still had with them, and then made their way slowly and cautiously toward Triplicane and into its streets.

But hardly had they got well in among the streets and houses when there sounded a renewed outcry and pursuit.

They ran again. A dark alley offered a moment's respite, but there were all too few dark alleys in a town this size. Ben grunted. "We must split up, it's our only chance."

"And meet where?"

"At the castle on the island," Ben answered grimly. "When we can. Or in the next world if there is one."

Zoltan looked at Ben as if he would have said some kind of a farewell. But then he only nodded, and, with lots of running still in him, went dashing swiftly away.

Ah, youth, thought Ben with heartfelt envy. He slumped down quietly where he was in the shadows, and just sat there for a few moments regaining some breath and energy while he listened to see if Zoltan should make good at least a temporary escape.

Before distance had entirely swallowed the sound of the young man's running steps, they broke off in an indeterminate scramble. Ben strained his ears, but he could hear nothing more. There were no cries of triumph, or other indication that Zoltan had been killed or taken.

He could, of course, proceed himself in the same direction and try to investigate. But, no, whatever had happened, the two of them had split up. One of them at least had to get out to Mark, on the island. The damned island; it was beginning to seem half a continent away.

When Ben moved again it was in the opposite direction from the one Zoltan had taken.

He went down the remaining length of the original dark alley, and then was pleasantly surprised to see the mouth of another one just across the street. After that alley there came another. When he had progressed for some distance in this fashion, he dared to cross a space of open moonlight. He was heading as best he could toward the water, where surely there would be boats, even if they were guarded.

Then again there were torches behind Ben, and voices, and he thought he heard a warbeast snarling, or perhaps it was only a dog. A good tracking dog would be bad enough. That was all he needed on his trail. He had to have the water now, and no question about it.

A street went by him, an alley, and then another street. And presently, now on the very edge of town, he found his way blocked by a high stone wall. As far as Ben could tell in the darkness, it extended for a long way in both directions.

Ben was much better at climbing walls than his bulky shape suggested. The mass of his huge body was very largely muscle, and now his great strength served him well, letting him support himself wedged in an angle of the wall, where enough little chips of stone were missing to give fingers and toes a purchase. Tall as the wall was, he got himself to the top of it and over.

It was almost a four-meter drop into complete darkness on the other side, but fortunately his landing was in soft grass.

He crouched there, listening for news beyond the weary thudding of his own heart, trying to tell whether or not his arrival had been noticed. So far there was no indication that it had. Silence prevailed, except for the usual night insects, and darkness extended almost everywhere. It was broken only by the concentrated glow of a couple of ornate lanterns that shone on latticework and barren vines a modest arrow-shot away.

Getting to his feet, Ben stole as softly as he could toward the lights. He saw now that the vines, leafless with autumn, wreathed and bound a summerhouse of latticework, built larger than a peasant's cottage. The lanterns glowed inside.

Ben circled close to the arbor, meaning to go around it. He did not see the young lady in almost royal dress who was seated within, against all likelihood in the chill night, until she had raised her own eyes and looked directly at him.

"I see you," she announced in a firm voice. "Come here and identify yourself."

12

WHEN the soldiers sprang upon Zoltan in the streets of Triplicane they kept their weapons sheathed and were obviously determined to take him alive. His arms were pinned, and before he had the chance to draw his own weapons they were taken from him. He struggled fiercely as long as he thought he had the slightest chance of breaking away, but when he found himself in a completely hopeless position, he let his body go limp and saved his strength.

His captors, working with quiet efficiency, bound him firmly, while at the same time they took care to cause no serious injury. They had nothing to say to him beyond a few passing comments on his ancestry, but Zoltan gathered from the few words they spoke among themselves that they considered him a catch of some importance.

Bound hand and foot, and aching from the blows he had received during the struggle, he was carried through the streets and conveyed quickly to the docks. There a command post had been set up, and he heard a couple of officers exulting over his capture before one of them ordered him placed immediately in a small boat. From what Zoltan could hear of the officers' conversation it was certain that they knew he was Prince Mark's nephew.

The only consolation Zoltan could find was that Ben was not in the boat with him, and that the soldiers, from what he could overhear, were still pressing an urgent search for someone.

Whatever might have happened to Ben, it now appeared that he, Zoltan, was going to get to the island after all.

As soon as he had been tossed into the boat, Zoltan wriggled and turned until he was lying on his back near the prow, his head and shoulders sufficiently elevated to let him see out over the gunwales. He was facing the backs of six soldiers, who now bent to their oars, and the sergeant on the rear seat was facing Zoltan along the length of the boat.

At a word from the sergeant the backs of the rowers bent in unison, and oars squeaked in their locks. The lights of the docks and the town began to move away. Staring out over the darkening face of the lake, marked here and there by a few lonely sparks of fires upon its distant shores, Zoltan pondered a temporarily attractive scheme of trying to roll himself out of the craft once it was well out into deep water. If he could manage to drown himself, tied up as he was, he would at least have succeeded in avoiding interrogation.

The moon was coming up now, its light beginning to make things ghostly.

For two thirds of the distance to the castle, the boat made uneventful progress, the sergeant only now and then growling a command, the men rowing steadily and in near silence.

But at that point in the journey, just as the craft was about to pass between two of the smaller islands, Zoltan observed something strange. It was as if a piece of one of those islets, which was some forty meters or so distant, had detached itself from the main body—detached itself, and was now drifting silently through the gloom toward the boat. A tiny, moving islet, whitish in the darkness and the peculiar moonlight. His imagination suggested something out of a story of the far northern seas, a drifting floe of ice, which might perhaps be big enough to let a desperate man use it for a raft. Zoltan watched it as if hypnotized . . .

Because the appearance of the thing gradually convinced him that it was neither a drifting island nor a chunk of ice. It possessed too much mobility, and it changed shape. It was alive.

Zoltan had once seen a living dragon that was bigger than this mysterious object. But this was no dragon, though it had eyes. Eyes the size of plates, reflecting impossible colors from the night. And fur, a pale silvery mat that became visible for what it was, roaring a cascade of water back into the lake as the thing began to rise out of the shallowing water with the nearness of its approach.

For long seconds now every soldier in the boat had been aware of this bizarre apparition. One after another the men had ceased to row; and now, as if a signal had been given, they all started shouting at the same moment.

Their shouts had no effect. The furry mass was wet and dully glistening, and the moonlight seemed to play strange tricks of light within its surface as it rose higher and higher, the top of it now three meters above the lake. Atop the silvery form Zoltan could now distinguish an almost human head, manlike but gigantically magnified, supported upon almost human shoulders.

And now there were two arms. Limbs quite unbelievable in size, but there they were. And now one of those arms was reaching with its great hand for the boat.

Long moments had passed since the soldiers had ceased to row. Uttering cries and oaths, they had begun to scramble for their weapons. Now one of them, the sergeant, swung with an oar against that reaching hand; the wooden blow landed on a knuckle, with a sound of great solidity, and had not the least observable effect.

The huge, five-fingered hand was thickly covered with the same strange fur as the rest of the creature's body. The hand was big enough to enfold a man's whole body in its grasp, bigger probably, but still it was very human in its shape. And now it had clamped a hard grip on the nearest gunwale, and Zoltan could hear the planks of the boat's side grind and groan and crunch together.

The boat was tipping now, the side held by the great hand rising, about to spill its contents into the lake on the side away from the silver monster.

By now most of the soldiers had their swords in hand. But they were too late to use them—if indeed such puny weapons could have done them any good. Everyone aboard the boat, Zoltan included, shouted aloud as it went over.

Zoltan had just time to close his mouth before the splash and grip of icy water claimed him. His bound feet touched bottom, less than two meters down, and he twisted his body in the water in an effort to stand erect, or at least float with his head up, so he could breathe. But he need not have made the effort. A hand as big as the one that had tipped the boat closed gently around his body, and he was lifted from the lake almost before its chill had had time to penetrate his clothing. He was able to catch one glimpse of the crew of military rowers, all floundering to swim or stand or cling to their capsized boat, the men in neck-deep water just starting to get their feet under them, before he was borne away.

He was being carried by the being who had overturned the boat, and who was now wading away from it through water no deeper than his thighs, though already quite deep enough to drown a man. The giant's two columnar legs sent up their roaring wakes in alternation, making speed away from boat and islands into water that was deeper still; the bottom dropped off sharply here.

Meanwhile, one of the giant's hands still cradled Zoltan, while the fingers of the other plucked with surprising delicacy at the cords that bound him. One after another, like withes of grass, those strings popped loose.

In the next moment Zoltan, his arms and legs now free, had been lifted up to ride like a child sitting on the giant's furry shoulders, astride his neck. Meanwhile his savior, almost chest-deep in the lake now and rapidly getting deeper, continued to make impressive speed away from the shouted outrage of the soldiers surrounding their tipped boat.

By using both hands to cling to silvery fur, Zoltan managed to keep his seat. He delayed trying to speak; the noise made by the great body beneath him in its splashing passage would have drowned out any merely human shout. But presently the splashing quieted almost completely as the giant began to swim. Zoltan's small additional weight upon his neck apparently made little difference to him in this effort.

At last, in the lee of another of the smaller islands, Zoltan was set down upon a sandy shore. The tipped boat was hundreds of meters distant now, and the castle even farther away, beyond the boat.

As soon as he had solid land under his feet again, the young man made a low bow to his rescuer. He said: "My lifelong gratitude, Lord Draffut."

"You know me, then." The giant still stood erect, surveying more distant events from his six-meter height; the voice from that great throat was manlike, except that it was deep as any dragon's roar. Then he looked down. "But I do not recognize you."

"We have not met before, my lord. I am Zoltan, nephew of Prince Mark of Tasavalta."

"Ah." Draffut now squatted in the shallows, bringing his head down closer to the level of the man's. "And where is the Prince himself tonight?"

Zoltan turned briefly and raised a hand toward the torch-sparked castle and its reflection in the lake. "In there, somewhere, I am afraid. If he is still alive."

"Ah. And was it he who sent the little flying dragon to find me, bearing the only message that it could, that my help was needed?"

"Lady Yambu did that," said Zoltan, feeling suddenly guilty for his past suspicions. Then he hesitated. "Did she know, when she sent the dragon, that it would bring you?"

"Doubtless she at least hoped that it would. Fortunately I was already traveling this way when the message reached me, on my way to Tasavalta from the far south. I bear grim news, and the Prince is one of the people that I meant to see—but that can wait. How strongly is the castle defended?"

"I have heard an eyewitness account of the arrival of about two hundred troops." And Zoltan explained what little he and Ben had been able to learn on the subject.

Draffut was just about to respond to this information when he suddenly raised his head, gazing up into the night sky. Zoltan, looking up also, saw that one of the small flying scouts from the castle had discovered them in the moonlight and was circling overhead.

As soon as the flyer began to clamor its discovery, Draffut emitted a startlingly shrill cry from his own huge throat. It sounded like the flyer's own primitive form of speech, and it had an immediate effect.

Draffut had called the creature, and it came spiraling down to him— and he caught it gently as it came down, much as a man whose hands were quick enough might have snatched a small bird on the wing.

Then for several minutes the Beastlord held conversation with the little flyer, while it remained perched on one of his fingers. Draffut managed to match the sounds of its voice so perfectly that Zoltan, looking on in awe, was often unable to tell which shrill tone proceeded from which throat.

Then suddenly the conversation was over, and Draffut tossed the flyer lightly back into the air. The small winged thing silently flew up and away, headed now for the dark shoreline in the opposite direction from the castle.

"Now it will no longer serve our enemies," said Draffut. He went on to explain that since his arrival in the vicinity of the lake he had already persuaded a number of nonhuman creatures to abandon their service to the new ruler of Honan-Fu's domain. He had convinced them that they would be better off to desert that unnatural cause, allied with demons as it was, and adopt a way of life more in keeping with their own true natures.

Then he shook his huge head, as if at some unpleasant memory. "I regret to say that some of them would not listen to me."

"What happened then?"

"I wrung their necks—that, you understand, is an option I do not have with humans who are determined to persist in evil. My own nature forbids that I should harm any human."

Zoltan looked back toward the tipped boat. Other craft, with torches, had come from the castle and were now approaching the scene of the disaster to find out what had happened and rescue those still in the water.

Draffut was smiling. "I wanted to ask questions of a soldier. Or better yet, ask them of the soldiers' prisoner, once I saw that they had such a person in their boat. But before I tipped the boat I had first to make sure that the water there was shallow enough for the men aboard to stand in. Some of them might have been poor swimmers."

The young man shook his head impatiently. "I was beginning to hope that you could even force your way into the castle, and its dungeons. My uncle Mark is there."

Draffut shook his head in turn. He drew back his lips in what might have been a smile, displaying carnivorous-looking fangs that would have served a dragon. "If there are human defenders on the walls, as I am sure there must be, I cannot attack them. Nor could I do much damage to the demons who would be called up to help those men, though in the case of demons it would not be for want of trying."

"Ben and I are both determined to get into the castle." Zoltan thought of trying to explain his own reason. But then he just left it at that. He gestured toward the town. "I don't know if Ben's still living either."

The Lord of Beasts gazed at him in silence for a moment. Then Draffut said: "I can probably create enough of a distraction for you to get into that castle, if that is what you really want. But before you do, you ought to know what kind of an enemy you are going to face there."

"I'm sure he's formidable. And whatever he is, he now also has Shieldbreaker in his hand—but still I must go."

"I understand that men are sometimes willing to go to almost certain death, and that Ben of Purkinje would feel so. The Prince has saved his life more than once."

"And my uncle has saved mine also."

"Very well. But even if the one who rules in the castle now did not have Shieldbreaker—you should know something of his nature before you go to face him."

"Is he called the Ancient One? If so, I have seen him once before."
And Zoltan shivered. The night was wearing on and growing colder.

"That is the name by which he is called now," said Draffut quietly.
He drew a deep breath into the cavern of his chest and let it out again.
"Thousands of years ago, when Ardneh was alive upon the earth, this
same man walked the earth as a servant of the evil emperor John Ominor. He was named Wood, then—that at least was his public name—
and his body was more fully human then than it is now. You said that
you have seen him?"

"Yes. About two years ago." And Zoltan shivered again.

"Then there is much that I need not try to explain. In olden times his
mind and soul were more fully human too, though nonetheless evil, I
suppose. For about two years now he has been here, active in our world.
How he can have survived until now I do not know, except that he must
have made a pact with some unknown evil that allowed him to traverse
the ages swiftly, or lie dormant through them. And the pact has
changed him for the worse. . . . I was certain that Orcus, the grandfather of all demons, had slain him, even before Ardneh died."

All this was beside the point as far as Zoltan could see. He quickly
brought the discussion back to present problems.

"Lord Draffut, what can you do to help Prince Mark? And our companion, Ben of Purkinje. It would be a great help to me to know
whether he's still alive or not."

"I am going to do what I can to help the Prince. First we must be
absolutely sure that you are still determined to get into the castle where
he is."

"I am determined," said Zoltan.

And he thought that with those words he had spoken his own doom.

13

THE young lady who confronted Ben under the glowing lanterns of the autumnal summerhouse was of slender build and considerable beauty. The soft appearance of her hands, the length of her well-cared-for fingernails, the royal elegance of her clothing, all indicated that she had led a sheltered and wealthy life. But despite the sophistication of her manner and her clothing, Ben judged that she was really no older than Zoltan.

There was a certain natural alarm in her eyes—along with other things less easy to read—as she gazed at this giant and uncouth intruder. But there was less alarm than Ben would have expected; certainly there appeared to be very little chance that this particular lady was going to scream or run away in panic.

Still Ben moved very slowly, doing his best not to alarm her any further. Shuffling a step or two closer to the pavilion, nodding and smiling subserviently as he moved, he allowed her to see him plainly in the lantern light.

He topped the performance with a little touch of his forelock. "Begging your pardon, ma'am, I don't mean any harm, I'm sure. They were after me with dogs and such out there—don't know why, I'm sure." And he went through the humble little routine of bowing and nodding and smiling again.

The girl, still seated but now holding herself very erect, was swiftly becoming even more judgmental and less alarmed. "Who are you?" she demanded. The question was deeply suspicious, and she was looking down at him like a magistrate from the slight elevation of her chair on the raised floor of the arbor.

"Name's Maxim, ma'am." Inspiration had come seemingly from nowhere. Some of the best ideas, Ben had noticed, arrived in such a way. "They call me Maxim the Strong. I'm with the show, ma'am. Magnificent Show of Ensor. We'll be coming to Triplicane again soon for a performance, and they just sent me on ahead. To put up a few posters, like, ma'am, and just kind of look things over in the town."

"Ah!" the lady exclaimed, as if his answer had enlightened her on some subject of great importance. "The *show!*" And it was as if the mention of the Show of Ensor had given her, or at least suggested to her, some profound idea.

"Yes'm, that's it. The show." Ben bowed again.

She relaxed a little, leaning back in her cushioned chair. He still had not been able to think of any good reason for this attractive young girl to be sitting alone in this chill place in the middle of the night. Unless it had something to do with magic.

Meanwhile she went on: "And you have come to Triplicane to put up posters—tell me, Maxim the Strong, have you been to visit the castle yet? Out on the island?"

"Oh, I know where the castle is, ma'am. But, no, ma'am, I haven't been out there yet. Not this trip."

"But you are going out there." It was an eager assumption.

Ben took the cue. "Yes, my lady, I expect so. We've always been welcome at the castle in the past."

"True. True. My father"—and here the young lady's eyes blazed for an instant with some inward fire—"always enjoyed your *shows.*" This time the last word held unveiled contempt. One of her small hands, resting on the table before her, clenched itself into a white fist.

"Very true, my lady." Ben decided to risk dropping some of the peasant speech and mannerisms. They had been natural to him at one time early in his life, but he was no longer sure he could maintain them steadily.

At the same time, after hearing that "My father" he was wondering if this could be the reclusive daughter of Honan-Fu. The evidence of wealth tended to confirm the suspicion. If so, he supposed she might be expected to welcome and help any enemy of the new regime. But Ben prudently withheld any announcements along that line until he could be sure.

The lady gave no sign of noticing any alteration in his speech. "So you do intend to go out to the castle? How?"

"I—don't know, precisely, ma'am. I was noticing that boats do seem hard to come by in the town."

"A boat can be arranged." Again she leaned forward, and this time lowered her voice. "But you must take me with you. And we should go now. Tonight. At once."

Ben opened his mouth, then closed it again.

His grand hostess, who Ben now thought must be even younger than Zoltan, stood up with a graceful and decisive movement. "There is someone out there whom I must see. And—they don't call you Maxim the Strong for nothing, do they? How are you at fighting, Maxim?"

"Fighting, ma'am? Can't say I care for it at all. But I can do it when I must."

"Yes, you look like you can. There might be one or two people here at the dock who wouldn't want us to take a boat. But you can deal with them, can't you? Especially if I can bring them to you one at a time, and unsuspecting." Her gaze ran appraisingly over Ben's shoulders and down his arms.

Ben was thinking furiously—or at least he was furiously trying to think, despite a feeling that his tired brain was getting nowhere in the attempt. "I—I—I'll do the best I can, my lady, of course. But—"

"Excellent!" The young lady's eyes flashed again, appraising him. "Maxim the Strong—yes, excellent. Yes, I am guarded, Maxim. But I'll have a gold piece for you if you can row me out to the island at once. The boats are just outside that gate back there." And with a motion of her head she indicated a direction in the darkness.

In a moment she had left the arbor and the lantern light and was walking with deliberate, regal speed in that direction. Ben hastened to follow, keeping a couple of paces behind her in the darkness, his feet moving through well-kept grass that was wet with the recent rain. Apparently the young lady had eyes like a cat. Ben couldn't see much of anything for forty paces or so, but then a high stone surface loomed ahead of them again, and presently they stood facing a small closed wooden gate that pierced the outer wall of the manor grounds.

The lady wasted no time. With word and gesture, she made Ben flatten himself against the wall, where he would be within reach of the gate, yet almost out of sight to anyone looking in. Then she rapped sharply on the wooden portal, using the massive rings on her soft hand, and called in an imperious voice.

Presently a small grating high in the gate, something like the spyhole in a prison cell, slid open, and a man's voice outside mumbled something.

"What do you think I want?" the lady shrilled. "I want you to open up this gate, you fool! I cannot speak to you like this."

There was another mumble, sounding disgruntled. But a moment later there was a rattling sound, as of bars being taken down. The gate opened and a guard, wearing the gray and red of the castle soldiers, stuck his head in.

"I want a boat," the mistress of the manor demanded sharply of the sentry. "I want it now."

"Oh, yeah? Really?" The man, with an insolence that Ben found utterly surprising, started to look around. "Is that all you made me open the gate for, to start that again? Because if—"

Ben had not lied about his dislike of fighting, but he had long ago trained himself not to be in the least squeamish when violence became essential. In a brief flash of his mind's eye, even as his hands reached out for the man's neck, he saw a poor fisherman's house, dark and quiet in the early dawn.

"Very good, Maxim!" the lady exulted almost silently, but with high good humor like a schoolgirl on some lark. "Oh, you are marvelously quick and efficient!" At her feet the uniformed body twitched once more and then was still, and Ben thought for a moment she was about to give it an exuberant kick.

But instead she went to peer cautiously out through the opened gate. Ben could see now that it had been strongly barred on the outside, as if to prevent a determined effort at escape, with less concern for entry. She said: "Evidently there was only one on guard tonight, I see no one else around. They've been so busy—come along, now we can get a boat."

Then she turned back, gazing down at the dead man. "Bring him out, Maxim. We'll stuff a rock into his jerkin; that'll make him sink."

That sounded like a practical idea to Ben; and he had known too many ladies, young and old, of high rank, to be surprised that one of them should demonstrate ruthlessness and efficiency. He scooped the body up.

The small docks that served the manor directly were just outside the gate. In the distance the castle on its island was speckled gaily with flecks of torchlight. The lady moved with Ben, guiding him through the darkness toward the little boathouse. Her clothing, a long, delicate-looking dress and frivolous shoes, wasn't what he would have recommended for a night row across the lake, but this girl, whoever she was, was apparently as ready to ruin her finery as she was to kill, and Ben wasn't going to be the one to bring the subject up.

The dead guard, duly weighted, went off the dock into what was probably reasonably deep water with only a small splash. They might think, when they found him, that he had broken his neck accidentally. Ben supposed they would have to be pretty stupid to think that, but the possibility couldn't be ruled out.

There were two small rowboats waiting at the docks. Ben found a pair of oars just where his guide said they would be, inside the little boathouse, and started to put them into one of the boats.

His hostess meanwhile stood idle, waiting like a true lady to be helped into the boat when the time came. But before Ben could get to that, there were voices coming through the night across the water, and the sound of more than one pair of oars in locks.

She was as fiercely alert as he. "They're coming right from the castle. Quick, Maxim, back inside!"

Muttering powerful but silent curses, Ben got back through the gate with his new young mistress, and pulled it shut and latched it on the inside. The real bar, the one that had been on the outside, of course could not be replaced. The implications of that were not too good. In a minute or two, boats, more than just a couple of them by the sound of it, began to arrive out there. So far there were no sounds of alarm, and Ben could begin to hope that he and the lady had not been seen out on the dock. Quite possibly the boathouse had screened them from the approaching craft while they were disposing of the sentry.

But that the men outside would not even notice the absence of their sentry was too much to expect. Soon there came a hearty pounding on the gate, and soldiers' voices murmuring questions to each other. Ben waited, looking to his hostess; it was up to her now to come up with some cleverness. But she continued silent and passive; then she turned her head back toward the manor house, and there were small sparks as of torches reflected in her eyes.

A man, by the look of him a steward or something of the kind, was hurrying out from the house. He was being lighted on his way by torches in the hands of a couple of lesser servants.

When the steward came close enough to get a look at Ben he stared at the big man uncomprehendingly, even fearfully; but he asked no question and made no comment. It was as if he feared to question any presence that the lady obviously accepted. A moment later he had shifted his hopeless gaze toward the gate, where the soldiers' knocking continued with grim patience.

"Never mind that noise," the lady snapped at him. "What have you come out here for?"

"There has been—an arrival at the front gate, my lady."

"What sort of an arrival? Speak up!"

The man gestured helplessly. "First, a number of wagons, Lady Ninazu. Half a dozen of them at least. It is the Show of Ensor. And then a—a crowd of soldiers."

"Ah!" she cried with delight, and looked at Ben. "Come with me!"

For a moment Ben considered trying to vanish into the orchard, but the lady's imperious eye caught him and dragged him along. He consigned himself to the fates, and followed with a sigh. His only hope was probably her protection anyway, he thought.

Maintaining a respectful interval, he followed her into the house and through its splendors. This was a very long, wide structure, all or very nearly all of it built upon a single level. When they had passed outside again through the front door Ben could see the front gate of the grounds standing open some thirty meters ahead of him. Beyond the open gate more soldiers were milling around.

Lady Ninazu hurried eagerly toward the gate, but he hung back.

Then he saw something that made him advance until he was able to see a little more. Outside the gate, soldiers were indeed arriving, and nonmilitary wagons too, a poor-looking little train of them with crude signs blazoned on their canvas sides. The Magnificent Show of Ensor.

The lady turned and beckoned Ben impatiently, signaling him to join her outside the gate. Slowly he complied. Amid a sudden new prodigality of torches, which were rapidly being lighted at the orders of the lady of the manor, Ben moved outside the gate, where he gazed with dull wonder at the five or six poor wagons, being pulled by tired-looking loadbeasts into camp position.

"Ho, there!" One of the officers in red and gray, who appeared to be in charge of the milling troops, bellowed impatiently toward the wagons. "Who's the boss of that flea circus?"

At once the driver of one of the wagons waved back energetically. He reined his animals to a halt and jumped down from his high seat. Ben, staring at him, felt something in his heart almost stop; and then his blood was pumping steadily again, a little faster than before.

Meanwhile the officer had turned away, to deal with some evidently more urgent problem just brought to him by a noncom. The proprietor of the show had changed course and was now coming straight for Ben.

Ben waited. It seemed that there was nothing else that he could do.

The proprietor of the show was a middle-sized, sturdy-looking man clad in nondescript gray, with a short cloak to match. Dark hair, showing no sign of gray, curled crisply. The only remarkable feature of his attire was a magnificently painted clown's mask that covered his own face completely.

He approached Ben with the familiar manner of an old friend—or perhaps an old military commander. He said, in a pleasant though undistinguished voice: "Maxim! I'm glad to see that you have found the right place."

"Uh, yessir."

"Between us, Maxim, no formalities are necessary." And the masked man reached out with one hand to clasp Ben familiarly by the arm.

No one else, for the moment, was paying the least attention to their conversation. Ben licked dry lips. He said: "We have met before—I think. You are the Emperor."

The other nodded. "Of course. And we *have* met—but you had no way of knowing me then. I sat on a hillside overlooking the sea, and greeted you as you climbed past me. You answered, but you were not minded to stay and talk to me that day."

Ben swallowed and nodded. Since that day years ago he had learned a great deal, about the nature of the world and the powers that moved in it, and now he felt relief almost as at the arrival of a friendly army. And yet at the same time he felt newly uneasy, even somewhat fearful, in this man's presence.

"Will you join us for the evening?" the other went on in his mild voice, gesturing toward his wagons. "Or for longer, if you like."

"I . . . for this evening, certainly, if you wish it."

"I think it would be a good idea. Each member of my little troupe here must be ready to play his or her assigned part. Tonight I have the urge to be a clown. Often I have that urge, and give way to it. A little joke or two, here and there, hey, to lighten up the world?"

Ben nodded again. "Your son," he said, choking a little, "Prince Mark, is out there on the island. I mean, I don't know if he's—"

"Oh, he's alive," the Emperor assured Ben quickly. "Not as fully and pleasantly alive as he has been, or ought to be, but . . . it is not easy to kill one of my children." The eyes behind the clown's mask glittered out at Ben. "My daughter Ariane lives also. You may see her again, one day, when both of you will have to make great decisions."

Ben could not speak.

The smaller man clapped him reassuringly on the arm again. "Come, strongman. Did you see which wagon I was driving? Hop up into it, and put your costume on. You'll find it there. Then be ready to use your strength to help your Prince."

Feeling somewhat dazed, Ben walked out among the wagons. Momentarily he felt now as if he had returned to the days of his youth. He had spent years then in the carnival with Barbara, the dragon-hunter Nestor, and later with Mark himself, long before there had been any suspicion in Mark's mind that he might one day occupy a princely throne.

Glancing in under the canvas of the other wagons as he passed them, Ben saw in one a small mermaid coming out of a bathtub-tank. She looked like one of the creatures that Zoltan had described to him, who could be found rarely in the rivers hereabouts, and somewhat more commonly farther south. This one was certainly not an animal captive, but another member of the small troupe, chatting with a woman in pink tights who was now handing her a towel.

Outside the next wagon were a couple of young men in the tight costumes of jugglers or acrobats, looking enough alike to be a team of brothers. And there, a pair of short-skirted dancing girls who resembled each other even more, enough to be twins.

He came to the indicated wagon, found a step, and hopped right aboard, pulling back the canvas flap. His weight made the light frame tilt strongly on the wooden springs. Someone's cramped living quarters, perhaps those of the Emperor himself. No one else was in it now. Hanging on a prominent peg was a large garment of some leathery animal skin, with spots of fur still on it, and on the floor below it waited a pair of buskins sized for large feet.

Ben changed quickly into the costume, which fit him well. Meanwhile he wondered how in all the hells the Emperor had known to greet him as Maxim. Ben had made up that name on the spur of the moment —or he thought he had.

Might he have seen it or heard it somewhere else? He couldn't recall doing so. But that problem, like some others, would have to wait.

A couple of minutes later, when he rejoined the Emperor and the other members of the troupe in the field outside the front gate of the manor, the process of setting the show up for a performance was already well under way. Little had to be done, beyond arranging some scanty decorations to mark out a portion of the field in front of the manor as a circus ring, and moving a couple of wagons to provide wings behind which it might be possible to organize something approaching a theatrical entrance.

Already the audience too was more or less in place. It was bigger than Ben had expected, certainly over a hundred people. Most of them were soldiers, with servants from the manor and a random scattering of other civilians attracted by the assembly. There were of course no seats, and the soldiers in particular were not settled in to watch. Whatever they had originally come here for, they were only pausing as their officers had paused, to see what might be interesting about this motley group of fools who had come to put on a show.

It was not the kind of audience Ben would have chosen, but he had already decided to obey orders. "What am I supposed to do?" he demanded loudly of anyone who would listen to him. He could see no weights, no strongman paraphernalia anywhere. And even as he spoke, the clown passed right by him, apparently ignoring his question completely. No one else paid him any particular attention.

Next, the clown, having reached the approximate center of the open field, assumed the role of ringmaster. He made a short speech, punctuated by exaggerated bows and obeisances, which earned him a faint titter of laughter from the civilians in the crowd—only a few hoots and muttered curses from the soldiers. Giving a very good imitation of terror, he scampered back behind one of the wagons.

A moment later, to the music of simple drum and flute, the two dancing girls came prancing out from behind the other wagon. It was a simple dance, more comic than erotic. But the assembled soldiers greeted it with a roar of serious lust.

The girls had barely reached the center of the ring when the first of the soldiers rushed from the sidelines to grab at them. One performer was whirled around in a helpless parody of a dance; the other, pawed by a dozen hands, already had part of her costume torn off.

The two victims were able to escape only because fighting broke out almost immediately among the soldiers. As an officer shouted into the confusion, the dancers made good a quick retreat, their faces pale, holding their ripped costumes about them as they ran.

Naturally the dancers were frightened. No, thought Ben as they passed him, it would be more accurate to say that they looked as if they had been frightened, even terrified, a moment ago. But now already they felt safe. They had managed to escape from the small arena, and with monumental trust they were ready to leave their problems in the hands of the clown.

Ben had already moved a step forward. But against a hundred soldiers his interference on the dancers' behalf would have been hopeless; and now it appeared that it might not be necessary.

The clown, enacting a parody of bold defiance, had sprung forward from somewhere to confront the armed mass of the soldiers.

The masked figure had drawn from somewhere a rusty, toy-sized sword, and he waved this weapon wildly as in a thin, hopeless, angry voice he challenged the whole garrison of the town to come against him.

The soldiers laughed. At the beginning it was almost a good-humored sound.

One of them, not bothering to draw a weapon, came at the clown with fist uplifted, ready to knock this preposterous obstacle out of his way with one half-drunken swing. But he couldn't do it, couldn't hold himself together long enough.

Helpless with laughter, the soldier staggered around the clown, who continued to challenge him, and halfway across the ring toward the waiting girls. But before he reached them he had to give up and sit down, abandoning himself completely to hilarity.

The laughter had spread quickly through the military audience, and it was growing steadily louder, though the clown was doing nothing to enlarge his simple routine. The officers, their next reaction anger, the instinct to maintain discipline, were soon as badly infected as the men.

Men and officers alike, they roared, they bellowed, they guffawed. They shrieked and screamed and howled. The noise they made was rising to an unnatural level. Officers abandoned their dignity entirely. Choking helplessly on their own mirth, they rolled on the ground.

The lady of the manor had come to stand beside Ben, watching, waiting.

Turning, looking until he caught Ben's eye, the clown made a sign, a gentle push as of dismissal. It was an expressive gesture, and Ben knew it meant that he and Lady Ninazu were now free to be on their way.

14

ONCE again Draffut hoisted Zoltan to his shoulders. Then, swimming and wading, the giant carried the young man with him through the lake, back in the direction of the castle.

When they reached the area of shallower water that surrounded some of the smaller islands, the Beastlord enjoined silence, then set his passenger down again on a dark beach. Some of the victims of Draffut's attack had evidently reached a different island, where they were waiting in hope of rescue; their mournful voices carried through the night.

Draffut crouched beside Zoltan and together they awaited the approach of the next boat.

"What if there's no more traffic on the lake tonight?" Zoltan whispered.

"I think there will be. Even before I tipped that boat, something was stirring the soldiers to activity, in the castle and in the town."

Looking in the direction of the castle on its island, Zoltan found something dreamlike in the appearance of the structure, with the multitude of tiny flames that were trying to light it all reflected in the water. Even more lights had appeared in the stronghold in the few minutes since he had taken his last deliberate look at it. And the docks at the foot of those high walls displayed increased activity. Miniature human figures could be seen swarming over them, though at the distance it was impossible to see just what they were about.

Draffut, who had been peering in the other direction, toward the town, now hissed softly, signaling for renewed silence. Crouching lower, the Beastlord whispered: "Another boatload of soldiers is coming in our direction—no, I think there are two boats this time." Draffut's whisper was a peculiar sound, like the rushing of an almost silent breeze across the night.

Very soon Zoltan, peering over the low, dry elevation of the barren islet, was also able to hear the oars. And shortly after that he believed he could tell that there were at least two boats approaching.

Tugging childlike at the half-luminous fur of the crouching giant beside him, he whispered very softly: "Ben might be on one of those."

The Beastlord nodded his great head once. "When we approach these boats, I'll signal with a roar if I see that they carry no prisoners. Then you can go on to the castle, as you are determined to do, if fortune grants you the chance. But if I am silent, then there are prisoners, or at least one, and you should probably wait to confer with them first."

"I agree."

Presently Zoltan was able to see the dark shapes of the slow-moving boats intermittently silhouetted against the twinkling lights of the distant town.

Moving his lips closer to Zoltan's ear, Draffut whispered a last question: "Are you a good swimmer? Good enough to reach the castle from here, in water as cold as this?"

"Good enough."

"Then do what you must do. And the help of all true gods go with you."

With that Draffut slid away, moving in eerie silence, and, almost without causing a ripple, submerged himself to his neck. In this position he began to swim very quietly toward the two approaching boats. Zoltan, still fully clothed, moved after him.

In only a few moments the Lord of Beasts had reached the boats, and once more the night erupted in clamor and confusion. Once more the giant reared his full height out of the water, and closed his grip upon a wooden gunwale. And in rapid succession these craft too were tipped and emptied of their screaming rowers. Again the men in the boats had scrambled to grab up their weapons and use them against this incredible apparition—only to find themselves in the water, struggling just to breathe and find their footing, before they could even attempt to fight.

Draffut was roaring now, giving the signal agreed upon that there were no prisoners here for him to rescue; and Zoltan reacted accordingly. He, unlike Draffut, was under no compulsion to avoid harming the enemy. Swimming methodically into the tumult of bobbing heads and thrashing limbs, Zoltan picked out his target quickly. Close ahead of him the faint glint of moonlight on partial armor showed him a foe who was ill-equipped for watery combat.

Approaching this man from behind, Zoltan struck silently, taking his victim around the neck and thrusting him under the surface. The bubbles of the man's last breath came up unnoticed by any of his struggling comrades.

A few moments later Zoltan was fumbling under water to lift the helmet from the lifeless head, and pull the drowned man's short cape free at the neck and shoulders. The remaining armor, he thought, ought to be enough to weight the body down.

With the helmet now jammed uncomfortably on his own head, and the waterlogged cape trailing behind him, he waited his chance to seize one of the drifting oars. Once he had this minimum of support in hand, he struck out through the cold water for the castle, paddling with his free hand and kicking briskly.

In the water around him, on every side, others were making progress in similar ways. None of the soldiers were now close enough to Zoltan to get a good look at him, or exchange conversation. He did his best to maintain this situation, preserving a certain distance.

The cold was numbing, but his steady efforts gradually brought the castle nearer. Looking up at those stone walls and towers from the very level of the lake, Zoltan saw them grow more and more intimidating. But it was too late now for second thoughts about his plan; he doubted that he would be able to reach the distant mainland from here by swimming, and there was no telling where Draffut might have got to now.

By now he was close enough to the castle docks to get a good look at the soldiers there. But their activities were not that much easier to comprehend. People appeared to be getting into boats and out of them again. Perhaps some large exchange, as of entire companies, between the castle and the town's garrison had been in progress when Draffut began to disrupt traffic.

Whatever orderly process had been going on had been disrupted, and small wonder, with all the screams and havoc out on the darkened lake, and now with half-drowned, half-frozen refugees swimming in. By now the officers on the dock must have communicated with their superiors, and there would be a discussion going on of what had happened, and whether it was necessary to involve the next higher layer of authority. There were more torches now than ever on the docks, and by their light men were trotting to and fro, into the castle and out of it again.

Zoltan, swimming now within a few meters of the dock—and really sure for the first time that he was going to be able to reach it—took note of what was happening as one man and then another climbed out of the water ahead of him. He rejoiced to see that these arrivals were going almost unnoticed. And now a further distraction for the officers on the dock—out of the darkness behind Zoltan another burst of distant oaths and splashing. Draffut, in timely fashion, had evidently found yet another boat to capsize.

No one on the docks paid more than momentary attention to Zoltan as he, in his turn, scrambled up out of the water, shivering and gasping, to crawl across the stones. No one came forward to help him, any more than they had helped any of the half-dead stragglers who lay wheezing and quaking on the paving blocks around him. Those men who were able to stand up immediately after their swim were being ordered on into the castle through the small connecting gate that now stood open. A sergeant who stood beside the gate was bawling something about a formation in a courtyard. Deeper inside the castle, bugles were sounding, and drums beating; it was evident that at least a partial alert had been declared.

Trying to jam his ill-fitting helmet more securely on his head, Zoltan got quickly to his feet and hurried in through the gate. Here there were fewer torches, and he paused to try to wring some of the water from his cape, meanwhile looking about him. So far, in the semidarkness and confusion, no one had noticed that his clothing under the cape was not a uniform.

Water splattered from the cape as he squeezed and twisted its rough fabric. Not far ahead of him, framed by another gateway, Zoltan could see a large courtyard aswarm with military preparations. It was from there that the drums and bugles sounded, and it was there that he particularly did not wish to go.

On his right, a darkened stairway offered the most obvious opportunity to turn aside; Zoltan seized that opportunity, and went trotting lightly and silently up.

On the first dim landing he paused briefly to listen and look back, trying to make sure that no one below had noticed him slipping away. Then, deciding that he had already attained a level comfortably above most of the lights and activity, he started out to explore.

Exploring in darkness, through totally unfamiliar territory, was slow and difficult work at best. Presently, seeking to find an area in which he could at least see where he was going, Zoltan took another stair upward. This ascent was a narrow and winding one, and proved longer than he had expected. When at last he came to a window he was able to see, on the tower levels of the castle that were higher still, more lights and several sentries. These guards were standing at attention or pacing slowly, and appeared calmly unaffected by the turmoil among their comrades at ground level.

Zoltan stepped back from the window, drawing a deep breath. Slowly an unwelcome fact was impressing itself upon him: now that he was here, he had no plan of what to do next. It had been easy enough to say, at a distance: find Prince Mark. But if Mark was here, and still alive, where was he being held?

Doing his best to think constructively upon that point, Zoltan decided that any prisoner so eminent and important would more likely be locked up in one of these towers than in a dungeon. He had of course no real evidence to support that point of view; but now it crossed his mind that Lady Yambu, assuming she had been able to reach the castle and was still here, would probably also be housed in one of these towers. He could not really picture her being thrown into a dungeon whatever happened. And if Zoltan could reach her, she might be able to help him, or at least provide him with some information about Mark.

After another pause, to squeeze more water out of his uniform cape and other clothing, Zoltan began trying to work his way toward the base of one of the towers that he considered promising. Since he was totally unfamiliar with the layout of the rooms and corridors here, and having at times to grope his way through almost total darkness, a number of false starts and detours were inevitable. At one point, alerted by approaching torchlight, he took shelter in a darkened niche as a youth he took to be a messenger went trotting by.

Pausing in yet another darkened passage, trying yet again to press more water from his garments, the shivering Zoltan wondered whether he ought now to dispose of helmet and cape, and try to pass himself off as a servant or some other civilian worker. He had seen a few such, at a distance, since entering the castle. But he supposed that if he did that his wetness would draw more attention. His clothes were not going to dry quickly on this chill, damp night. Until he could manage a total change of clothing, he had better stay as much as possible in darkness.

He moved on slowly, looking for an opportunity to change his garments. Here was a row of doors, and some of them opened willingly enough when he pushed on them—these were small storerooms, but either empty or filled with moldering, useless junk. It seemed that Honan-Fu, or someone in his household, had been unwilling to throw anything away.

It appeared that nothing so convenient as a clothing store was going to present itself to Zoltan's need. When he had moved past the last of the storerooms, more windows showed him another tower, a good part of it lighted. In one of those high rooms, he thought with a shudder, his archenemy himself might well be quartered. He who called himself the Ancient One might even be peering out of one of those high windows at this moment, while receiving reports from his officers on the disturbances in the lake below. Zoltan shuddered once again, remembering his one contact with that man—if indeed he could be called a man— some two years ago.

Zoltan moved on from the windows. At last, in a disused closet, he found some garments hanging on a row of pegs along a wall. There was a dry, shapeless, almost sizeless smock, which hid most of his own clothing when he put it on. Concealing the helmet and the still-dripping cape behind some junk in a dark corner of the closet, he at last felt ready to try to pass among the enemy.

He would have to be one of the lower class of servants now; no one else would wear a garment so disreputable as this smock. Acting on an inspiration, Zoltan grabbed up a pot sitting on the closet floor. The vessel looked as if it might once have been used to carry water, or grain; he would take it with him. Looking as if you were already busy was the best protection against the curiosity of authority.

Now he could postpone the real search for his uncle no longer. Ready or not, he was going to have to let himself be seen.

He made his way, with some difficulty, from the area of the storerooms and closets into the base of one of the lighted towers. Zoltan could curse himself for not having foreseen the complexity of this place; but he had not, and the only thing to do now was try to get on with the job. Still, it was beginning to seem to him that the job of finding his uncle must be a hopeless one.

Then he urged himself to get a grip on his nerves. Surely it would not be necessary for him to search everywhere inside the castle. The number of apartments in this particular tower was certainly quite limited, and when he had somehow eliminated all of them he would move on to the next—

Rounding a sharp corner, Zoltan unexpectedly found himself confronting two figures in the corridor just ahead of him. The taller was a being with reptilian attributes: short, leathery wings, and a face no more than halfway human. In an instant he knew that he was facing, for the second time in his life, the terrible wizard known now as the Ancient One.

Zoltan recoiled, his hand going to his side in search of a weapon that was no longer there, that had been taken from him when he was captured. A weapon that would have been useless in any case, because—because—

The horror in front of him was standing still, looking at him, saying nothing. But over its bestially deformed shoulder there appeared another face, calm and recognizable, that of Lady Yambu.

She said: "Zoltan, you need not be afraid. This is not who you think."

Zoltan sagged against a wall. "Ben?" he asked softly.

The horror shook its head. "I am not Ben," it informed him.

15

THE fastest and most direct route from the front of Lady Ninazu's manor back to the docks lay through the grounds rather than around the outer wall. Ben, half-urging the lady, half-towing her with him, was moving from the arena where the performance had taken place back toward the main gate. He was about to reenter that gate and then cut through the grounds to reach the boats when he was accosted by two men wearing rough civilian garb.

He might have pushed them aside, but at the last moment he recognized the younger one as Haakon of the bushy eyebrows, who had once introduced himself as a member of Honan-Fu's constabulary.

Ben stopped. Haakon and Ben gazed at each other for a moment in silence. Both of the local men ignored Lady Ninazu completely. On the field in front of the manor, meanwhile, the laughter was becoming louder, more certainly hysterical.

Raising his voice to make himself heard above the noise, the man who was accompanying Haakon said to Ben: "Haakon tells me you are no friend of those rats who have moved in on the island. Well? Quickly, we have no time to waste."

"Well then, Haakon is telling you the truth. What of it? I'm in a hurry too."

Lady Ninazu did not appear to be offended by the fact that the men were ignoring her. She stood waiting patiently for the moment, looking from one to another of the three men as if trying to gauge the truth about them.

"Nor are we friends of this invader who calls himself the Ancient One," said the speaker to Ben. He was tall, with brown skin, white hair, and a grave manner. "I am Cheng Ho, and I was once a captain in the

Triplicane constabulary." He jerked his head toward the Emperor, who was still cavorting down at the far end of the field while waves of noise, noise that could no longer be called merriment, surrounded him. "Who is this man in the clown mask? We have served Honan-Fu for years, and have seen the magicians who visited him, and their contests; and yet we have never seen wizardry like this."

Suddenly Lady Ninazu seemed to awaken. She was impatient to be gone, and not about to allow Maxim the Strong to waste any more of his time with this riffraff.

Ben didn't want to lose her, or offend her either, and so he had to be quick. He said to the two local men: "All I can tell you in a few words about the one in the mask yonder is that you should trust him, if you are no friends of the invading soldiers. That is what I am doing now, trusting his advice. As far as I know, he is a magician without equal— and certainly he can have no love for those who now occupy the castle on the island."

Haakon and Cheng Ho had both taken notice of the lady now, and it seemed to Ben that they were about to speak to her—or to him about her. But her brief interval of patience was evidently exhausted. She would brook no further delays, and Ben allowed himself to be towed and ordered after her.

The uproar made by the soldiers in the field behind them went on without pause as Ben and the lady passed through the unguarded gate and reentered the manor grounds. Taking a last look back Ben could see that the great majority of the civilian audience had already departed. A few of the soldiers were still on their feet, and appeared to be running aimlessly about. But the ground was covered with bodies in gray and red, kicking and convulsing.

The sounds made by the Emperor's enemies followed Ben and Lady Ninazu all across the darkened grounds. Again she led him at a fast walk, as if her vision was indeed keener in the dark than that of any ordinary girl or woman. Or perhaps it was only that she had spent so much time in these grounds that she knew the location of each tree. Presently they were moving past the arbor in which Ben had first encountered her, its lanterns now burning low; and now they were once more approaching the gate that led out to the boathouse and the docks.

Together they listened carefully at the portal before Ben opened it. All was quiet outside, and when Ben swung back the gate there was no one there. Probably, he thought, all the soldiers had gone round to the front of the manor, attracted by sounds the like of which they had never heard before.

Those sounds, not much diminished by the modest distance and the intervening walls, were still a great deal louder than he would have preferred.

The oars that Ben had begun to put in place were still where he had dropped them, in the bottom of the little boat. There was no one to stop him now as he handed the lady down into the boat, and saw her seated in the stern, wearing an attitude of somewhat precocious dignity.

"You are a worthy servant, Maxim." She gave the pronouncement a judicious sound.

"Thank you, ma'am," Ben returned. *And I may at last prove myself a worthy friend,* he thought, *if I can still get out to that demon-damned island in time to do the Prince some good.* And he told himself, for perhaps the thousandth time since Mark had been taken, that whoever had taken him was not likely to have killed him as quickly as this, or even to have harmed him very much as yet. They would be hoping to learn too much from him to do that. Hoping to learn too much, and also to collect a royal ransom.

Ben cast loose the boat, and then settled himself on the middle thwart, and with steady, powerful strokes of the oars he began to propel himself and Lady Ninazu toward the glittering, magical-looking castle on its distant island.

He rowed and rowed, but for a long time the terrible laughter of the stricken soldiers, like the dancing reflection of the manor's lights, continued to follow them over the water. Plainly all of the townspeople of Triplicane, from one end of the settlement to the other, would be able to hear that sound. Those who had been present would spread the story. All who heard the sound or the story would marvel, and some of them would be brave enough to investigate to find out what was happening. Before morning the great bulk of the local population would be aware that the invaders had been dealt a serious blow. Ben had not stayed long enough to be sure exactly what was happening to the garrison, but he suspected that a good portion of their fighting force was being effectively wiped out.

If the lady, seated on her cushions in the stern of the rowboat, had any thoughts at all about the horrible laughter and what might be happening to those who laughed, she kept those thoughts to herself. It was rather as if she was almost entirely caught up in the anticipation of reaching some long-desired goal, and that goal involved her getting to the castle. Holding herself elegantly erect, she leaned forward slightly on her seat, staring into the night past Ben. Evidently she was feasting her eyes upon the torchlit structure ahead of them as his efforts slowly but surely brought it nearer. From time to time, in crisp impatience, she uttered a sharp word or two, urging Ben to greater efforts at the oars.

He responded with eager nods and smiles to these commands, and continued to set his own pace, which was already about as brisk as he felt capable of keeping up across the distance without exhaustion. He expected that he might well need some reserves of strength and wind when he arrived.

Facing the stern of the boat as he rowed, Ben observed how the dark bulk of the manor and its surrounding walls and trees still hid the continuing performance of the Show of Ensor from his sight; a concealment for which he continued to feel grateful. Even with his own immediate fate to be concerned about, along with Mark's and Zoltan's, he still found even the sounds of that performance to be unpleasantly distracting. There were stretches of time as Ben rowed, sometimes periods of several minutes, in which the cacophony of that murderous laughter seemed to be abating not at all with the increasing distance.

Only in Ben's imagination could he now see what might be happening in the arena of the performance; and that uncertain vision showed him the Emperor still playing his own kind of joke, still cavorting in the guise of humility and humor even while the ground around him was littered thickly with his victims, who one after another expired in purple-visaged chokings.

There was no wind tonight to blow those sounds away, and sound as always traveled far over water. At least what slight current there might be in the lake appeared to Ben to be favorable, bearing the rowboat on toward its goal.

Ben rowed, and in the midst of his rowing there came a noisy but more natural-sounding disturbance from some distance in the darkness to his left. He looked in that direction, but the faint glow of moonlight on the broad expanse of water showed him nothing helpful. Now the noise came again, of men's voices shouting raggedly, followed by a heavy splashing as if a boat might have been somehow overturned. Ben altered his course a trifle, intending to give a wide berth to the trouble, whatever it might be.

"What are you doing, Maxim? You are turning off course."

"Beggin' your pardon, ma'am, but it sounded like some trouble off that way. Drunken soldiers or whatever. We don't want to be stopped now, we want to get on to the castle without any interference."

"You have a point there, Maxim. Very well, you may deviate. But not too widely."

Again the lady sat gazing at the faerie structure ahead, all faint moonlight and mysterious shadows punctuated by sparks of flame. "That is my home, Maxim. And now at last, after many years, I am going there again." Suddenly she fixed Ben with a sharp look. "You have never seen my twin brother, have you? The young Lord Kunderu?"

"No, ma'am. I haven't had that privilege."

"You are right to put it in those terms. He is, you know, more like a god than like a man, more beautiful even than . . . and when I think of what our father has done to him—I do not see why the new lord of the castle refuses to set him free."

Ben had no ideas on that subject, and in fact he judged it best to keep as silent as possible on all matters political and familial. He grunted and wheezed a little, to demonstrate that he was going to need all his breath just to keep up the pace at which he continued to row. And in truth he was in a hurry. Looking at the stars and estimating the remaining distance to the castle dock, he judged that they would do well to complete the trip within an hour.

Briefly he considered whether he might do better to pull all the way around the island, and try to come ashore on the side opposite the castle docks. But there might well be no way to get into the castle on that side. And besides, the lady's growing tension as they approached the island convinced him that she would stand for no further detours without a very vigorous protest. There would be screaming, at the least.

So far the wench had said no more about her father. Even stranger than that, perhaps, was the fact that her father seemed to have had her under long-term house arrest, in her own house—and still more curious, the new regime had evidently continued the confinement.

What would be the reaction of the soldiers on the docks when they saw that the daughter of Honan-Fu had been rowed out to them? Surely she had at least some arguable right to visit the castle, and so a simple, bold approach would be the best. As for Ben himself, particularly in his strongman's costume of animal skin, with arms and legs left bare, he was probably not the most convincing personal attendant for a lady of high rank. But he was committed now to playing the role—and the Emperor had seemed to think he was capable of succeeding in it.

By now, at last, those horrible sounds from the mainland had faded to the point where they could only intermittently be heard at all. Chances were that the people in the castle would not have heard them, and very likely they would not know that anything untoward had happened to their garrison ashore.

Such was the continuing confusion on the docks as the little boat approached that its arrival was scarcely noticed. One large rowboat appeared to be loading with soldiers, at the direction of a shouting sergeant, while another one unloaded. And all the time occasional swimmers came straggling in, some supporting themselves on oars or bits of driftwood, others relying upon no more than their limbs and lungs. Some of these attempted to cling to the boat that Ben was rowing as he drew near the dock, but at a sharp command from the lady he beat them off with an oar. When he saw that they were castle soldiers he had no reluctance to do so.

As soon as they touched at the dock, Ben jumped out briskly and tied up. Then he turned to offer proper assistance to the lady. She accepted his arm, as impersonally as she might have gripped a ladder's rung, and stepped ashore to face the blank stares of a pair of officers in red and gray. By now these men had become aware that this arrival represented something unusual, even for this night, and they had suspended their argument over some other matter to see what the lady's presence might portend.

Confronting these officers with her best regal stare, Lady Ninazu demanded: "I am the daughter of Honan-Fu, and the twin sister of your prisoner Kunderu. You will take me to my brother at once!"

The officers exchanged wary glances with each other, then turned back to this demanding woman. Ben reflected that it was probably not strange that they should not recognize her—they were doubtless as much outlanders here as he was himself.

At last one of the men replied, with cautious courtesy: "I know of no such person in this castle, lady."

"Oh, do you not? Then I will see to it that you soon learn. Take me at once to your lord, the Ancient Master. He will teach you to speak to me with more respect!"

That set the pair of them back a little. After a brief whispered conference their next step, as Ben had already foreseen, was to summon a superior. Meanwhile Ben himself stood back as much as he could on the small dock, trying to be as unobtrusive as his size and costume would allow, a model slave or servant. If the superior when he arrived should happen to be one who happened to be able to identify the much-sought Ben of Purkinje at a glance . . .

But the fates were kind, and it was a total stranger. This man, bowing lightly to the lady, took charge of the situation skillfully. Treating her with soothing words, he got her to follow him, telling her that in a minute or two all would be arranged just as she wished.

Ben, feeling impossibly large and conspicuous to fit his chosen role of shadowy attendant, nevertheless fell in behind. He would seize the first chance that presented itself to let him slip away.

Before that chance came, he and the lady were led into a kind of waiting room, grimly furnished, and the door closed behind them. Lady Ninazu, trying to open the door again to shout some demand at the men, discovered that it had been not only closed but locked. Immediately she was outraged; but her shouts and her pounding on the wooden panels went unheeded.

16

ARNFINN, having as he did the powers of the Sword of Stealth at his command, had experienced no difficulty in obtaining Lady Yambu's release from her comfortable confinement. He had not even found it necessary to speak to the quards who flanked her door. The moment he appeared in the corridor before them they had bowed themselves out of his way.

Stepping forward, he reached for the handle on the door, found that it was unlocked, and went on in. The lady, wearing her pilgrim's gray, was standing in the middle of the room looking at him with an air of confident expectation. And there was something stranger than that in her expression. Arnfinn thought it was almost the same look she had worn at their first encounter, when she and her two friends had taken away his Sword.

Gripping Sightblinder's hilt tighter than ever, Arnfinn moved backward a step to stand against the door as he closed it behind him. He thought to himself: *If those other two are here now, and they try to do that again, I'll kill them. I'll hack them to bits.* Even his untrained hands could feel that, apart from magic, this weapon had just the edge and weight needed to do that kind of work. And no one was going to take it away from him again.

But no men came rushing at him from concealment among the draperies, or leaped up from behind the furniture in ambush. Instead there was only the old lady, who stood alone in the middle of the floor and faced him calmly. Still looking at Arnfinn rather oddly, as he thought, she repeated her earlier question: "Is it Zoltan, or Ben?"

By now, Arnfinn thought he could guess who Zoltan and Ben must be. He said: "I am neither one of them. They are not here to help you now."

For a moment the lady's calm wavered, and she almost stuttered: "If it is—if you are—"

"I am a friend of Lady Ninazu, and also of her imprisoned brother. Who are you?"

The lady seemed to find the question reassuring. Her face assumed a sort of friendly blankness, and for a short time she was busy with her thoughts. Then she said: "I am Lady Yambu. I do not know the lady you speak of, or her brother either. What is his name?"

"His name is Kunderu, and they are twins, the daughter and son of Honan-Fu the wizard. Tell me where Kunderu is being held, and nothing bad will happen to you." Gripping the great Sword with both hands, Arnfinn swung the blade a little, suggestively. But the old woman's eyes did not follow it; as like as not, he supposed, the image she saw of him would not be bearing a weapon.

If she was aware of the Sword in Arnfinn's hands she was managing to ignore it. All she said was: "I have not heard of either of them."

"I tell you Kunderu and Ninazu are the old wizard's children." Arnfinn could not escape the sudden feeling that this woman was making a fool of him again, or at least there was great likelihood of her doing so.

"That may well be," she replied calmly, "but I am only a sojourner in this country, a pilgrim, and their names mean nothing to me. Now tell me, who are you?"

With the sullen conviction that he was somehow losing all the advantage that the Sword ought to have given him, Arnfinn grumbled: "What image do you see when you look at me?"

The lady looked him up and down. "My eyes tell me that you are the magician who is called the Ancient One, who is now lord of this castle and of much else besides. And I hear your voice as his. But by your words and your behavior I am quite sure that you are someone else, and that you have with you the Sword of Stealth, although I cannot see it. Besides that, when you were out on the balcony a few moments ago I saw your image change before my eyes—that often happens when one is holding that Sword. Sightblinder is powerful, but like the rest of the Twelve it has its limitations."

"I suppose so," said Arnfinn, trying his best to sound like an expert in these matters. He hesitated, then took a plunge. "Lady Yambu, I mean you no harm. Have those guards been set outside your door to keep you in, or to keep others away?"

"To keep me in. The one whose image you now wear has so far treated me with courtesy, but . . ." With a small gesture, as if to appeal to fate, the lady left the sentence unfinished.

"Then I can set you free. But in return you must help me find Kunderu, and free him too. That is all I want."

"I accept your offer," the lady replied with very little hesitation. "With Sightblinder to help us we ought to be able to do that much if we use a little cleverness. I don't suppose you would be willing to let me carry it for a while—? No, I thought not. But still I believe an alliance between us will benefit us both. You see, I am interested in the welfare of another man who is a prisoner here."

"All right." Arnfinn slowly sheathed the heavy Sword. "You and I have an alliance, then. I would be willing to bet that you know more about castles than I do. What do we do first?"

"I think, Your Ancient Lordship, that we must begin by exploring and finding things out. If everyone here in the castle sees in you the same image that I do, which I suppose is quite likely, then that part should be easy enough. If not, we improvise. Out into the corridor, then I suggest turning right. I believe that will lead us into more interesting territory. You go first, I'll walk half a step behind, as would be appropriate if you were really the one you look like. You turn to me if we meet someone and you wish advice on any point. Or I'll whisper in your ear if and when I think it necessary."

Arnfinn was willing to accept this plan, and said as much. Opening the door, he led the way.

The two guards had returned to their posts beside the door, but again they backed away making obeisances as soon as he appeared.

Ignoring them, Arnfinn turned to the right and strode on. As soon as they had rounded the first corner, the lady whispered in his ear: "Above all, we must do our best to avoid the real master of this stronghold. And if we—but wait."

She laid her fingers on Arnfinn's arm. Just beyond the next turn of the short hallway, someone was approaching.

It was a young man, walking alone, who came into sight. Arnfinn, with some surprise, recognized him as the one he had struck down to regain the Sword. Now the youth was wearing a disreputable servant's smock, and he recoiled instantly as soon as he saw Arnfinn.

At once the lady, looking over Arnfinn's shoulder, said to the other: "Zoltan, you need not be afraid. This is not who you think."

The youth in the smock let himself sag against the wall. "Ben?" he inquired softly.

Arnfinn shook his head. "I am not Ben."

"Who are you, then?"

But again Arnfinn would answer that question only with stubborn silence.

The lady interceded. "Zoltan, we can discuss that matter later. Right now we are on our way to release a couple of prisoners—including the one in whom you and I are interested. And as soon as we've accomplished that, we can all start on our way back to the mainland. Our anonymous ally here should have no trouble in arranging passage for us all aboard a boat."

Zoltan brightened quickly at this news. "And just where are these prisoners to be found?"

"I know where to start, at least," the lady answered, somewhat to Arnfinn's surprise. "At ground level, just off a certain courtyard. Come along, both of you, I'll show you."

Under Lady Yambu's unobtrusive guidance, and with Zoltan following two steps behind in his role of humble servant, they proceeded down some stairs and out into the open night. Small gatherings of people, almost entirely male and military, were in the various courtyards, and parted silently to give the three room to pass. Arnfinn rejoiced; apparently there were times, as Lady Yambu had suggested, when all onlookers saw the one who carried the Sword as the same person. There were salutes and deep bows directed at Arnfinn, and a few heads turned to look after him and his two companions, as if in wonder as to where the Ancient Master was going with the lady and the wretched-looking servant; but no one asked a question. He acknowledged the salutes with a vague gesture, and did his best to look as if he knew where he was going.

As the three were crossing one of the wider open spaces, there came a faint sound from high above. Looking up in the direction of the tallest tower, Zoltan saw the griffin, small with height, and with the figure of a man astride its back. It went leaping out of the aerie into the night sky. The creature's wings worked powerfully, and in a moment it and its rider were out of sight among the stars.

Some of the onlookers in the courtyard dropped their gaze from the

starry sky to Arnfinn, then looked back up into the night again, as if
they could not believe their eyes. But if their suspicions were aroused,
they were not expressed, at least not within hearing of their great lord
who apparently stood before them.

Lady Yambu was again holding Arnfinn by the arm, as any lady
might hold that of her escort. This allowed her to exert a slight pressure
by which she guided him in the direction she wished to go. In this way
they crossed the central courtyard with its grim high altar, charred and
empty now, and reached a small closed gate. Here, too, guards stepped
aside. Arnfinn himself pushed the gate open.

When some of the guards would have followed the three into the
dark, grottolike space behind the gate, Lady Yambu whispered in the
ear of her lordly escort. And at his gesture the intruding men fell back,
one of them first handing him a torch.

And now at the last moment before they passed into the darkness
beyond the gate there was another delay. An officer came hurrying
across the wide courtyard, approached Arnfinn, and whispered to him
so quietly that not even Lady Yambu could hear. The message was that
one who claimed to be Lady Ninazu had reached the island in a small
boat and insisted on seeing the lord of the castle.

Arnfinn's heart leaped in his chest. He was ready to order that he be
taken to Ninazu at once, or she be brought to him. But her presence
would add another complication to the rescue of Kunderu, and besides
he was still ashamed to face her. His duty lay here, trying to free her
brother as rapidly as possible.

"Have her wait," he replied to the officer, who murmured his acknowledgment of the order and faded away.

But still the delays were not over. There was a fresh outcry on the far
side of the court.

Lady Ninazu, on finding herself locked into the dank waiting room,
had wasted no time in futile shouts and protests. Instead, she gave up
rattling at the door after only a couple of ineffective shakes, turned to
Ben, pointed dramatically at the lock, and ordered: "Break it open!"

Ben liked the locked door much less than she did, but he had a
tactical suggestion. "Your pardon, my lady, but there's likely to be
someone in the corridor outside who would take notice if we did that. It
might be wiser to take a look at the windows first." Their place of
detention was on the ground floor, and a quick glance through the

windows showed a darkened areaway outside that offered some prospect of escape.

The lady thought for a moment, then nodded her agreement. Ben found that the inward shutters opened easily. Then to his disappointment, but hardly to his surprise, he discovered an iron grillwork on the outside of the windows that effectively prevented any passage. The bars looked no more than ornamental, not really the kind of barriers you would find in a dungeon, but they were discouragingly thick and his first trial of barehanded strength against them achieved nothing.

There were voices in the corridor outside the door; that way still did not look attractive. Ben concentrated his attention on one of the windows while the lady looked on with approval. She would have liked, Ben was sure, to urge him to greater efforts, but she evidently realized that nagging at him now was only likely to slow things down, and with a major effort was managing to restrain herself.

As Ben cast about for something to serve him as a wrecking bar, his eyes fell on a wooden bench that made up a large part of the plain furnishings of the room. A brace that ran along the bench's back was long and stout enough to serve as an effective lever, he thought. Ben picked up the bench and with a few swift movements knocked off its ends and legs against the stone wall. A moment after that he had violently separated the back and seat from the component that he wanted. The whole process had made only a moderate amount of noise.

Now Ben had his sizable chunk of timber, long as a man's body and thick as his arm. With this inserted between the bars, Ben was able to pry at them and start them moving. But he was able to bend the ironwork only a small distance before his timber lever was balked by coming against the heavy masonry at the side of the window.

But now the tenure of the metalwork in its sockets had been much weakened. Ben dropped the lever. Taking his time, he tried out several grips, getting his hands into the most effective positions that he could find. Then he exerted all the strength that he could summon up.

He could feel the veins in his forehead standing out, and what might have been the tearing of muscle fibers in his quivering arms.

Gasping, he let go and slumped against the stonework. The bars were not going to yield. Not yet, anyway. He had to rest for a few moments.

While he was resting, panting and leaning against the wall, the lady came closer, bright-eyed, to watch him. But still, thankfully, she had no advice to offer or orders to declare.

He looked at her, and nodded his appreciation for her noninterference. Then he bent to his task again.

It just came down to this. That he was going to have to bend these bars. He could not afford to remain locked up here, helpless, until someone came along who recognized him.

With a small explosion, one end of one bar came free of its mortared socket in the wall. The break sent small fragments of stone and brick spraying almost silently out into the night.

Once more Ben rested, gasping. A gap had been created now, but it was probably not wide enough for even a slender lady to slide through. Probably, he thought, two more bars were going to have to go.

Still, he could use only his bare hands. But now he could shift his grip and obtain a great advantage in leverage. In only a moment the next bar had assumed a U-shape, looking as if it might now fit the hoof of some giant riding-beast.

Again he paused, just long enough for a few gasping breaths. His hands were callused from a lifetime of hard use, and when he looked at them he saw that the skin was still intact. Good. He was going to need all his blood and energy.

The lady, her patience wearing out, began to nag at Ben in a whisper, sounding like the angry child she was. If only, she was saying, she could get to speak to the Ancient One himself, all would be well. She would have these incompetent officers who had delayed her boiled in oil. And then, when at last she reached her brother and made sure of his release, she would have Ben rewarded—

Ben ceased to pay attention. He forbore to ask her just why this Ancient One, if he was truly her great friend as she claimed, still insisted on keeping her brother locked up. Instead he gently hoisted the lady through the window, then forced his own great shoulders out. He had to bend the second bar yet a little more before he was quite able to fit through. Then he and Lady Ninazu were standing side by side on the dark pavement, with nothing between them and the stars.

Ben whispered: "Now, where are the prisoners kept? Have you any idea, ma'am?"

She raised her eyes. "My brother will be found high in that central tower. If we were on the other side of it I could point out to you the very windows of his room. But—before we go to him, I think I ought to talk to the Ancient Master." She paused, looking around her uncertainly.

"Are you sure that would be a good idea, my lady?"

"Of course it would. Who are you to question my decisions on such a matter?"

"I am no one, my lady." He wondered if the time would come when it would be good policy to strangle her.

"Of course you are not." She looked round her and appeared to get her bearings. There were several exits from the areaway in which they stood. Ben prepared to follow, at the most cautious distance she would tolerate. At the earliest opportunity he meant to separate himself from her and start in earnest to look for Mark—or try to make contact with Lady Yambu, if the opportunity offered. He felt reasonably confident that she was here somewhere.

Boldly the young lady started walking straight toward the central tower, the one she had indicated earlier. Ben followed, out of the areaway and into a relatively well-lighted court. But before he had moved more than a score of paces, there was an outcry behind him.

What seemed like a whole company of soldiers were running after them; the uniforms seemed to come pouring out of every passageway and crevice in the stones. There was no way to avoid them. Before Ben could quite decide that the time had come to fight to the death, the odds were hopeless, and he and the lady were both closely surrounded.

"My lady," an officer shouted, "you were told to wait!" There was no great courtesy in his tone.

Lady Ninazu flared back with angry words, which seemed to make little impression on the officer. Ben had just resigned himself to the probable necessity of making a hopeless fight after all when a shout from somewhere in the middle distance made him wait again. "What— ho? What have you there?" The voice, unfamiliar to Ben, was harsh and masculine.

Ben, turning slowly and carefully, beheld a tall, ghastly, half-reptilian figure. From the fervent descriptions often given him by Zoltan, he had no difficulty in recognizing one who had to be the Ancient One himself.

The call had interrupted Lady Ninazu's heartfelt and outraged protests; she too had fallen silent for the moment. Like Ben she had turned to look across the courtyard to where the tall, malignant figure stood waving at their captors.

A moment later Ben, experiencing a sensation of dislocation, realized that the small, pale face looking toward him over one of the figure's shoulders was that of Lady Yambu. And that the face of Zoltan, looking not at all like that of a defeated victim, was peering at him past the other. Even at the distance Ben thought that Zoltan looked as if he would have liked to wink but did not quite dare.

Ben let out his breath, making a sound somewhere between a chuckle and a sob.

The guards who had surrounded Lady Ninazu and himself were saluting the monster across the courtyard, and they were not slow or slovenly about it. In response to gestures and shouted orders from that commanding figure, they put up their weapons and withdrew.

Ben, moving on shaky legs, led the way across the courtyard. Lady Ninazu, for all the demands that she had made to be taken to the new master of this castle, was not so eager now, and hung back slightly. A moment later Ben and the two ladies, along with Zoltan and whoever had the Sword, were shut inside the little grottolike enclosure surrounding the deep, black pool.

When at last Arnfinn, Zoltan, and Lady Yambu were inside the grotto, Zoltan pulled the gate closed after them again. Then he and Arnfinn looked around them uncertainly. It was a narrow place, open to the sky but closely confined between high walls into which fantastic niches and decorations had been carved and built out of the dark stone. The grotto was only a small place, but still the single torch, in the hand of the Sword-bearer, seemed inadequate to light it.

Almost all of the ground space was taken up by the surface of the black, deep-looking pool, with only a rim of pavement around its edge. Ben looked in puzzlement at the surrounding walls, and the two ropes that went down into the still water. On the far side of the pool, a dim mouth blocked by heavy metal bars was open in the stone, the beginning of a watery tunnel that led out of the pool to some unknown destination.

But Lady Yambu paid no attention to this setting. She went directly to the edge of the well, where the two secured ropes went down into cold, dark, quiet water. She knelt down there, close by the great iron ring to which the ropes were fastened, and rested her fingers on the ropes, one hand to each.

Closing her eyes, she said: "The two of them are still alive down there —I have just enough of the art myself to be able to feel that. Still alive now, but I fear that hauling them back up into the air is likely to kill them."

"The Prince is down there? Under water?" Zoltan was outraged.

"Down there?" echoed Ben.

The lady ignored the mild outburst. "Before we haul them up, we should have a counterspell prepared, and someone with skill enough to make it work."

As if involuntarily, she and Zoltan both raised their eyes to the impressive image of the great wizard that stood beside them.

During the last few minutes Arnfinn had been making a firm resolution to strive for suavity and dignity befitting a master magician in all he said. But he forgot his resolution now. "I haven't got," he protested, "magic enough to chase a flea."

Meanwhile Lady Ninazu had been very quiet, almost ignoring the others. She had backed up slowly, moving from the others, and away from the pool as far as the confined space would allow, until her back was leaning against one of the enclosing walls. She had been staring down at the black water and its secrets as if she could guess what those secrets were, and found them frightening.

Now, suddenly, in a tight voice she announced: "Kunderu is not down there. I don't see how he can be."

"If you are the daughter of Honan-Fu," the older lady told her, "then your father is down there. Along with someone you do not know."

The girl appeared to find that relatively acceptable, but still it frightened her. "My father," she repeated thoughtfully.

"So I have been told. Quickly, are you enchantress enough to save these men's lives if we pull them up at once?"

Ninazu nodded abstractedly. "I am a very good enchantress. I could do more than that."

"That will be sufficient for the moment," said Yambu in her queen's voice, and gave a signal. Swiftly Ben and Zoltan stooped over the ropes. Seizing one at random, they began to haul.

As they were working, Lady Yambu straightened up and whispered to the one who had the Sword. He nodded, and in a moment had opened the gate again and was calling out to the soldiers in the court, telling them to bring plenty of food and hot drink, blankets and dry clothing for two men.

Within moments Ben and Zoltan had pulled a human figure out of the water. Lying on the stone pavement with steam forming in the air around it, it appeared to be little more than a whitish blob of ice. The clothing and all the details of its shape were so rimed in pale needles and granules as to render the figure quite unrecognizable beyond the fact of its humanity. It was quite large enough to be the Prince. Only an occasional twitching of the limbs, and a slight, fitful turning back and forth of that ice-encrusted head showed that any life at all remained.

Lady Ninazu, meanwhile, remained drawn back as far as possible from the rescue operation. She had fallen silent again, and the fear she had displayed before was now intensified, and focused on the frozen man.

Suddenly she raised her head, with a motion so sharp and sudden that others turned to look in the same direction. There was only the square darkness of the central tower rising against the stars, punctuated at a few points with the narrow sparks of lighted windows.

"He's not down here," she announced positively. "He's up there." And she raised an arm and pointed with assurance.

"Are you going to help these men?" Yambu demanded in a threatening voice. "You must do it now."

The younger lady might not have heard. She continued staring at the tower.

Yambu went to her and shook her. When that rough treatment had no apparent effect, she slapped Ninazu in the face. The swing was more like a man's blow than a woman's, and it brought forth a little shriek of sheer astonishment.

The slap took Arnfinn by surprise. He shouted at Lady Yambu and took a step toward her. But she ignored him and did not shift her attention from Ninazu.

The older woman pointed with a bony finger to the form stretched on the pavement. "Help this man!" she barked.

And Ninazu, yielding to the other's will, moved closer to the icy figure. Murmuring softly, she began to work a spell.

With a sudden gasp the man on the pavement began to breathe again. The sound of his breathing, hoarse and deep, came as a new presence within these dark stone walls.

Meanwhile the hands of others had been gently picking and brushing the frost away from the Prince's gray-blue face. Already much of the frost was falling and melting away from his body.

After that first deep breath, Mark's body was racked with convulsive shivering. But his breathing continued, gradually steadying into an almost normal rhythm.

And now Zoltan and Ben were drawing the second body up out of the dark water.

And again Ninazu was retreating, shrinking back against the stones of the confining wall. She murmured: "That can't be him, I tell you. He's up in the tower."

Once more Yambu had to bully her. "As I have told you, this man is your father. And you will help him, now, if you want us to help you any further."

The younger woman's eyes turned to Arnfinn. She raised her hand in a gesture of appeal, with wondering eyes, as if she was amazed that he would allow her to be so insulted.

He was silent for a few moments, looking from her to Yambu, and back. Then he said to Ninazu: "My lady, help him. If you please."

Ninazu nodded, with acknowledgment of his command if not belief. Her look was one of dazed incomprehension.

But she turned back toward the pool and repeated the spell that she had used before.

Both victims were now undoubtedly alive and breathing, but neither of them was fully conscious, and it was obvious that both were going to need further help.

There was a rapping on the gate, and Ben opened it to admit soldiers who had come delivering food, hot drinks, the clothing and the blankets that had been ordered, a whole mound of them. Arnfinn went to help Ben take delivery.

Zoltan, attending to the two semiconscious men, muttered: "If we could only get them out to Draffut now—we need a boat for that."

"There is—" Ninazu began, and then stopped as if she thought she had better say no more.

"There is what?" Arnfinn asked. "What, my beautiful one?" he coaxed.

"There is a small boat here," Ninazu went on reluctantly. "The workers who maintain the pool use it to get back into the channel that leads from the lake into the well."

By bending over and peering back into the tunnel's mouth, it was just possible to see the boat where it was tied up. Reaching it would require opening a metal grillwork that blocked the tunnel entrance.

The grillwork could be opened only from inside the grotto, and

Ninazu demonstrated how. In a moment Zoltan was splashing through the water, pulling in the little boat.

Meanwhile Ben and Yambu were frantically busy getting the two victims into dry clothes and trying to feed them broth and brandy. Then they put them into the boat.

"We must get them to Draffut," Ben decided. This was a tactical decision, and Ben was in command.

Zoltan, at Ben's orders, got in and started paddling. The boat was a tiny thing, unseaworthy, really meant for only one occupant. To take it out on the lake with three people was chancy, and to put any more in it would be suicidal.

Now Lady Ninazu approached Arnfinn. "I insist," she dared to say, "that you take me to my brother at once."

17

At about an hour past midnight, the man who called himself the Ancient One had jumped astride his griffin and launched himself confidently into the night air from atop the highest tower of his captured castle.

His main objective was to find out what was happening on the mainland, in particular what had happened to his garrison at Triplicane. The last winged messenger to reach the castle from there had croaked out an almost indecipherable tale of calamity, a disturbing though incoherent report of what sounded like mass slaughter confused with entertainment, the performance of some show. To the Ancient Master it at first sounded like diabolically clever treachery by some member of that garrison.

As soon as the creature had delivered this message, it had simply flown off again into the night, in direct disobedience to orders. That had been more than an hour ago, and the flyer had not returned. Nor had any of the others.

It was also the powerful magician's intention to discover what had suddenly gone wrong with his winged scouts. When he had climbed to the high aerie where his griffin rested, he had found the place empty except for the griffin, the cages and roosts used by the lesser beasts deserted. The two humans who were supposed to be in attendance on the beasts had looked on helplessly, fearful of their master's wrath; the Ancient Master had only glowered at them, a look that promised much, before he hurried on.

Ordinarily he would allow no one but himself to ride the griffin, and unless he gave the griffin special instructions it would refuse to carry anyone but him.

Besides the difficulties on the mainland and the trouble with the scouts, there was another problem also requiring the wizard's attention tonight. Something bizarre was reportedly moving around out in the lake, tipping boats and terrifying troops. All in all, the Ancient Lord had already become sufficiently concerned to take the first preliminary steps toward calling up a certain squadron of demons he had been keeping in reserve, a group that could be mobilized with relative ease. And the calling of demons was not a step that this wizard took lightly; he knew from bitter personal experience how great could be the dangers in trying to use such creatures as servants or allies.

Once he was well airborne, soaring high over the lake, he was able to see that a great many more lights were burning in and around Tripli-cane than was usual at this hour of the night.

From this altitude he could also see that the lakeside manor occupied by young Lady Ninazu was illuminated even more prodigally than the rest of the town. He decided that he would probably look in at the manor before returning to the castle, whether or not the garbled report of disaster proved to be a false alarm. There was no doubt that Ninazu could be an entertaining wench. There were several things about her that the wizard found especially intriguing, and if he had not been so busy trying to consolidate the gains he had won from Honan-Fu, he would have spent more time with her, or perhaps brought her to the castle—

The griffin was rapidly bearing the magician closer to the town and manor. Now he observed that the open field close before the manor was also encircled by torches, some of which had burned out, though a number were still guttering. They shed enough light upon that field to let him see that it was littered with what appeared to be the bodies of many soldiers, in uniforms of gray and red. The sight banished all thoughts of pleasure for the time being. The wizard who rode the mid-night air commanded his griffin to descend. He needed no magical sub-tleties now to be sure that the report of disaster had not been false.

He was unable to count the bodies quickly enough to have the total before he landed, but certainly there were more than a hundred of them. More than half, at least, of the entire garrison.

What had caused the officers to gather their men here? And what had struck the troops down, once they were assembled?

The wizard landed and at once leaped from his steed's back, drawing Shieldbreaker as he did so. The griffin, as accustomed as any beast

could be to even stranger sights than this grim field, sat down as a dog
or a lion might, with its forequarters high and its avian forelegs straight.
In this position it waited quietly.

The Ancient One, Sword ready in his right hand, looked about him.
Shieldbreaker was quiet, indicating that no enemies were lurking in the
immediate area now. All across the field the bodies lay in a kind of
random distribution; here a pile of several together, there a scattered
few, there again an open space. And everywhere the ground could be
seen it was lightly trampled, as if by hundreds of human feet.

There was something odd here, something beyond the fact of the
slaughter in itself. It took the wizard another moment to realize what it
was: many of the signs of a conventional battle were missing, including
the inevitable broken weapons, the bits and pieces of equipment cast
aside. He could hear no moaning wounded. And in fact, he realized
after another moment, there was no blood at all to be seen. The men of
his army had fallen in scores, perhaps in hundreds, but not one of them
appeared to have drawn his weapon or tried to defend himself.

The light of the moon, now close to setting, combined with the orange glow shed by the guttering flames of the remaining torches,
showed him a great, silent mystery.

The magician was not really surprised that no one had yet appeared
from the manor or elsewhere to mourn the dead or begin the rituals of
burial. The only real surprise, he thought, was that no robbers had yet
appeared either. None of the bodies looked as if they had been rifled.
Pouches that would hold personal belongings were still intact, here and
there rings still showed on fingers.

It was only now that the Ancient Master noticed what appeared to be
wagon tracks, running here and there across the short grass and the
barren earth. He paced the field eagerly, muttering a short spell that
served to enhance his eyesight temporarily. Yes, perhaps half a dozen
four-wheeled vehicles, pulled by loadbeasts, had been here briefly, had
circled, had unloaded at least part of their cargo and then had loaded
up once more and moved out. It appeared that the wagons had departed
in the general direction of the southern end of Lake Alkmaar, where it
was drained by the outflow of the Tungri. The magician knew from
scouting reports that the last road running in that direction ended at a
dock, a few kilometers out of town. And at that dock was the beginning
of the downriver water-route leading to the lands of the south and west.

There must be some connection, the magician thought, between the wagons and the massacre. But what that connection might be was not immediately apparent.

He intended to find out.

For a time now the Ancient One, raging silently at his bad fortune in being thus victimized, walked back and forth among his dead.

And only after he had walked upon this field of corpses for a time, his thoughts busy with other matters than the physical reality around him, did he realize that not all of the fallen men around him were as yet completely dead.

It was a sound that told him, a soft and intermittent little noise that came and went like breath, and yet did not much resemble any other sound that he had ever heard from human lips. He located the source of the sound, and approached it, and saw one of the fallen bodies moving slightly, shaking lightly on the ground.

Only then did it occur to the wizard that the sound he was hearing might possibly have some relationship to human laughter.

He bent down, and with his strong hands seized this man who unlike his fellows was still breathing, and hoisted him to his feet in an effort to compel him to tell what had happened. But despite his magic the only reply that the magician could elicit was a continuation of the ghastly rhythmic croaking, forced out between swollen lips. The victim's eyes were puffed shut as if with weeping, his whole face was swollen and discolored, and he appeared to be in the last stages of exhaustion.

The wizard now called upon deeper powers, making a renewed effort at enchantment. But still the man died, standing on his feet and trying to laugh, before he could be forced to speak more coherently.

The wizard withdrew his magic, letting the body fall.

Well, if one man had survived, so might another. The magician prowled, striding swiftly, until he found another of the fallen figures stirring, this one a little more vigorously than the first.

In response to a spell directed at him by the magician, this man even managed to get to his feet.

And now he came shambling toward the wizard, a quivering, blank-faced survivor, his uniform begrimed, his weapons still unused at his belt. He stumbled to a halt within a long stride of the Ancient Master.

Commanded to speak, the man rasped out: "The wagons . . . Show of Ensor . . ." The words trailed off.

"Go on! Speak! Speak, I command you!"

". . . dancing girls came out. Men in the front row grabbed 'em. I was thinking, why couldn't I have been standing there, get a chance at a good feel at least. . . . Then . . ." The man's voice died again.

"Then what?"

"Then . . . we all . . . the laughing started."

"The laughing? Speak up clearly!"

"Yessir. Laughing. Like—hee, hee—first there was this big man, in a strongman's costume. He stood behind the girls. And then—*ho, ho*—there was this little clown—"

The soldier swayed on his feet. Sounds, almost recognizable as a kind of laughter, bubbled from his lips again, the last laugh turning into a bright red bubble of blood.

The second man fell dead. The Ancient One bent over him, gesturing. But all the powers of magic that the wizard could bring to bear were ineffective now.

The magician stood back and sent forth a calling spell above the fallen. But there was no spark of life left in their ranks to respond to the power he emanated.

The Ancient Master turned abruptly until he was facing toward the manor's torchlit gate, which was standing closed. That gate had been deserted by those who were supposed to guard Lady Ninazu, and by every other human presence as well.

The wizard had already heard enough about the mysterious figure called the Emperor to think that he could recognize him in this strange new "little clown."

"And now the damned villain has taken flight—got away somewhere —before I could come to grips with him. But no matter. I'll get my hands on him eventually."

He who called himself the Ancient Master remained standing in the middle of the field, his mind and soul engaged now with the next step in the process of summoning up his demons. His eyes, more reptilian than human now, stared at nothing. As he stood there, all but oblivious to his physical surroundings, the stars turned indifferently in their high smooth paths above him. An hour of the night slid by, and then another.

Then suddenly the Ancient Master moved again. Signaling his griffin to follow him, and with the Sword of Force gripped firmly in his right hand, he strode on toward the manor's front gate. Surely someone in there would be able to give him a better report than either of those he'd heard so far.

There were still no attendants in sight as the Ancient One approached the closed grillwork of the gate, but a single shout was enough to bring them out of hiding. Figures in servants' garb scrambled about, and the gate was quickly opened for him from inside.

"What has happened here?" He swept an arm behind him, indicating the field of fallen men. "Why was I not informed of this?"

The steward, summoned by lesser servants, had already appeared and was struggling to find answers. "The flying messengers have all disappeared, dread lord."

"I know that. Someone could have brought word in a boat of what had happened here. Did you see what happened?"

"Not I, sire. But there was nothing that we could do to help your men—"

"Yes, yes. I'll hear about your problems later. Where is Lady Ninazu? She, if no one else, ought to have been aware of what was happening out here. Don't tell me she slept through it all."

"Sire—" The steward was more devastated than ever. "Sire, the lady has disappeared."

"What?"

The servants, though none of them would admit being eyewitness to anything important, took turns in trying to tell the story of the night's events—or rather in trying to avoid personal responsibility for its telling. But eventually it came out in a fashion. After the destruction of the garrison, they had discovered first the lady's absence, and then that a boat was missing. Then a drowned sentry had been found in the water near the docks. And then—

It was at approximately this point that the magician observed one of the stablehands staring at the griffin, as if he had never seen anything like such a beast before, which his Lord knew was not the case.

"What ails you?" the Ancient One demanded sharply.

The man stumbled and stuttered. "Sire, it is only that I had thought that there was only one of them. I mean the one that's still in the stables. The loadbeast one."

"What in all the lands of the demons are you raving about?"

The man stuttered and staggered his way through an explanation of sorts. A trip to the stables to view what he said was really a griffin revealed a very ordinary loadbeast, with no detectable tinge of magic about it at all.

"And you say that *I* came riding on this peasant's animal, and left it here?"

"It must be that I am wrong, sire. Very wrong."

"Either that or you are very mad. Or else someone has been playing jokes." The magician issued terse orders for the man to be locked up until he could return to question him some more, or have him brought to the island for that purpose. But there was no time to investigate this matter now. Indeed, the whole trip to the mainland had taken the Ancient One longer than he had expected. By the time he remounted his griffin and urged it into the air again, the sky in the east was beginning to turn pale with the first faint hints of dawn.

The affair of the slaughtered garrison represented a setback, of course, and he had not made much progress toward solving it. Still, the wizard remained basically confident of his position. With Shieldbreaker at his side, and his demonic reinforcements on their way, he could not see that he had anything seriously to fear.

By now the water of the lake, stretching in a flat plain far to left and right beneath his griffin's wings, was no longer black with night. Now it was glowing very faintly with the reflection of the first beginnings of daylight in the sky.

Something, some moving presence in the lake, drew a slow dark line across that faint metallic glow. Some object tall as a tree, in its majestic passage through the water, was leaving a long triangular wake. The object was a towering, almost man-shaped figure that waded on two legs between two of Lake Alkmaar's little islands—

The Ancient Master uttered a soft exclamation, followed by several magical incantations. Then he murmured a command in his griffin's ear, and the creature turned aside from its direct course to the castle. Down they went.

The wizard had been worried when his subordinates told him of what was happening out on the lake at night, that some strange presence there was wreaking havoc on his boats. And he had become all the more worried, as paradoxical as that seemed to his subordinates, when it became clear that this strange new enemy was not actually killing any of his men. He feared that he could recognize a certain signature in that reluctance—and now in the first tentative light of day that recognition had been confirmed.

The Ancient One commanded his steed to circle Draffut at low altitude, and at a respectful distance. The wader stopped, and his great head turned, following the flight of griffin and wizard without apparent surprise.

At last the shadowy giant, half-enveloped in a rising billow of morning mist, called out: "I am here, little man. Bring here your Sword and try to kill me, if you will."

But the man who rode the griffin knew better than to attack any unarmed opponent, let alone this one, with the Sword of Force. Instead he turned his mount without replying, and sped on to his castle, landing at the high aerie. Soon he would have demons on hand to do his fighting for him.

18

THE faint splash of Zoltan's paddle could still be heard receding down the tunnel when Lady Ninazu moved away from the others and came around the edge of the grotto pool to Arnfinn, who had already drawn a little apart. He saw her eyes gleaming with the reflection of distant starlight as she drew near him, and he heard her say: "I am ready now, my Ancient Lord, for you to lead me to my brother."

Arnfinn dreaded the thought of having to lie to her any longer. "And if I were to tell you, my lady, that I do not know where he is?"

Her gaze flickered away and back to him. Her chin lifted in conviction. "Then I would think that you were pleased to jest with me, great lord. You are the master of this castle, and must know what is within it. And, even if you did not, I know where Kunderu is."

"Where?"

In solemn silence Ninazu turned slightly away from him, and raised one slender arm to point. Her small, pale hand extended one finger toward the top of the castle's central tower.

Arnfinn said: "If you can lead me to your brother, Lady Ninazu, then I will set him free."

Her marvelous eyes searched him. "You promise that?"

"I swear it."

The solemnity of her regard lasted for only a moment longer. Then it melted in the ghost of a smile. She said: "We can start from here, in the grotto, and go along a secret way. Kunderu and I used it often when we were children."

She turned away from Arnfinn, and to his surprise began to climb along the wall, stepping on an irregular series of carved and built-in decorations that made a kind of fanciful stairway. Arnfinn raised the torch he was still holding and looked at the wall. The narrow, uneven steps that Ninazu was climbing gave the impression of not being a real stair chiefly because they went nowhere at all, ending in the middle of the wall where there were three shallow decorative niches. Beyond that point the inner wall of the grotto stretched up flat and unclimbable. Lady Yambu and Ben were watching her with curiosity as she went up.

When she was very nearly at the topmost step, Ninazu turned, and beckoned to Arnfinn with one finger.

He followed her. It was only when his climbing feet had attained a man's height above the surface of the pool that he was able to see that the stair went somewhere after all. What had looked from below like a blind decorative niche, set between two more shallow niches just like it, turned out when seen from this angle to be the genuine entrance to a passageway.

Ninazu's smile became more impish, or perhaps simply more child-like, when she saw Arnfinn's surprise—or rather the surprise of the person whose image he was wearing in her eyes. She said to him: "My father delighted in building such tricks as this. And when Kunderu and I were children, we found new uses for them." She giggled.

The passage into which she now led Arnfinn was narrow, barely wide enough for one person, and windowless. Chill air blew through it gently from somewhere up ahead. And as they went it soon became so dark that Arnfinn, following the lady, had to put one hand in front of him and touch her back to make sure she was there. He had the Sword sheathed now, and his left hand rested on its pommel.

The passage climbed, on little steps. He knew that they must now be threading their way upward through the enormous thickness of the outer wall of the keep itself. After some minutes of silent ascent they emerged, to Arnfinn's surprise, in the prosaic environment of a lofty storeroom. Obviously the place, with dust and cobwebs everywhere, had not been much used of late.

Now he could see Ninazu again, by the faint moonlight coming in through a tall, narrow window. Still smiling, she led him through the cavernous storeroom and opened a creaking door. Together they peered into the corridor outside, which was lighted only by remote torches, and locally deserted. Motioning for Arnfinn to follow, the lady moved out into the hall and turned to the right, where the corridor soon ended in a peculiar little balcony, open to the night.

The balcony, when they had gone out onto it, seemed to come to a dead end. But when they walked around a decorative column, they came to another narrow, unsuspected opening in the wall.

Before he followed Ninazu into this dark doorway, Arnfinn looked around to get his bearings. They were already at a considerable height above the dark lake, and about to enter the base of the castle's central tower.

The wall through which this second hidden passage ascended was not as massive as that of the lower keep, but still it was a good three meters or more in thickness, allowing plenty of room inside it for the narrow, hollow way.

They had barely started up through this second passage when Ninazu turned her head to gibe at Arnfinn like a little girl. "Admit it! You, the high lord of the castle, didn't even know that these tunnels were here!"

"I have already admitted it."

They moved on, with impervious darkness closing in on them again.

Into the darkness Arnfinn said: "These secret passages must not extend all the way to your brother's prison room, or else Kunderu would have used them to get out."

The lady ahead of him stopped suddenly, and he could hear her suddenly indrawn breath.

Then she moved on, climbing more stairs, but only for a short distance. Before Arnfinn was expecting the climb to end they came to a window that looked out over the darkened lake, under the starry sky. A few lights, small fires, speckled the distant shore. Here Lady Ninazu stopped. Arnfinn could faintly distinguish her profile against the stars as she stood looking out.

After some time had passed in which she said nothing and gave no sign of moving on, he prodded: "Well? Aren't we going on?"

"I don't know," she said after a time. And it seemed to Arnfinn that her voice was strangely altered.

"You don't know?"

She didn't answer.

Arnfinn persisted. "I thought you were so anxious to see that your brother was set free."

Still Ninazu had nothing to say to him.

He squeezed past her where she was standing at the window, and then sat down just above her on the narrow stairs. He did not know why, but he was rapidly developing a sense that doom was closing in on him.

Presuming on his supposed authority, he spoke to Ninazu more sternly: "Answer me! Are you afraid of what we're going to see when we find him? Are you afraid that he's no longer alive?"

"I know that he's alive," she answered instantly, as if disgusted that such a question could even be raised.

"What, then?"

In answer she sank down on the narrow stair, sitting just below him and leaning on his knees. "Great lord," she murmured. "Hold me. Help me."

"I will! I will!"

"Have you any magic that can heal the heart and mind?"

"Ah, gods, Ninazu! Whatever magic I have to offer you is yours!"

And after that she would say no more, but clung to Arnfinn's legs and wept. She would not move, nor respond to his questions, nor answer his entreaties. They sat there through the long hours of the night.

Ben, wearied with a day and a night of struggle and flight, had fallen asleep more or less wedged into a stony niche at the base of the grotto wall, near the steps that did not look like steps. Roused now by faint sounds, he awoke to find the head of another old campaigner, Lady Yambu, pillowed on his ample stomach. Ben shook her lightly, and in a moment she was wide awake, head up and listening in the earliest light of dawn.

The sound that had awakened Ben came again, softly. It was the faint splashing made by a paddle in the tunnel.

"Zoltan's back," Ben whispered, and moved to crouch beside the pool, straining his eyes into the darkness of the tunnel's mouth across the narrow reach of water. The grillwork gate, unlocked last night, was still swung back.

Ben and Yambu were both on their feet and watching when the boat appeared. There was only one occupant—a tall man in his early thirties, now looking very much like his old self. When Mark stood up and stepped ashore, Ben seized him in a fierce, silent embrace, then held him at arm's length. "You're well?"

"Well enough." Mark sounded like himself. "Zoltan got us out to Draffut; and he, all the gods be thanked, was able to restore us. Then Zoltan stayed there with Honan-Fu, to explain to the constabulary about Draffut, and the Swords."

"The constabulary? I talked with Haakon, and some officer, Cheng Ho. They're planning to move against the castle?"

Mark nodded. "With Draffut's help. Lady Yambu, a thousand thanks for your efforts on my behalf. Zoltan has told me of them."

The lady smiled remotely. "They were efforts well invested, I should say."

Ben sighed, feeling the relief of being able to hand over responsibility as well as that of seeing the Prince alive and well. "What do we do now?" he asked his leader.

Mark looked around at the confining walls, and up toward the cleverly constructed niche where Ninazu and the Sword-bearer had disappeared. He said: "We can't take the boat out into the lake now. It's too light, and they'd kill us from the walls when we came out. So we find a place, somewhat less inconspicuous than this one, in which to spend the day. Honan-Fu was able to give me a hint or two."

As the first light of morning began to creep into the narrow passage where Ninazu and Arnfinn had spent much of the night, the lady stirred, then jumped to her feet to look out of the window. Arnfinn, straightening his stiffened limbs to stand beside her, was in time to see the Ancient Master returning from the mainland on his griffin. The winged creature landed a hundred meters away, atop the one tower of the castle that was even taller than the one from which they watched.

Ninazu stared at this aerial apparition in amazement. When it had vanished into the aerie she turned to look at Arnfinn, and some of her sudden tension left her again.

"I understand," she said. "That was a deception, of course. A magical counterfeit of yourself, a phantom launched so that others would believe that you had left the castle, while all the time you really were with me." And she took him trustingly by the arm.

Arnfinn drew in a deep breath. "Of course," he said. Then something made him turn his head. There was no danger to be seen in the half-light of earliest dawn. There was nothing alarming to be heard. But something was certainly wrong.

"What is it?" he muttered. "I feel sick."

The lady looked pale, and her eyes were closed. "It is only demons," she murmured. "As my lord knows very well."

"Demons." Arnfinn swallowed. "Where?"

Ninazu did not answer. She was leaning on the stone sill of the narrow window again, gazing out. The sky was now as clear and innocent as it could be at dawn.

Fiercely Arnfinn determined that, no matter what, he was not going to be incapacitated by these queasy sensations that seemed to come from nowhere. Nor was he going to waste any more time if he could help it. Looking about him, he took note that the passage going on above them was no longer a well of total darkness. Light, very faint and indirect daylight, was coming into it from somewhere higher up. Now Arnfinn could see that after a few more steps the passage turned inward in a sharp bend. These walls were not thick enough to accommodate much turning. A room of some kind, with windows, must be just ahead.

Arnfinn drew a deep breath. "Of course," he repeated. "I am the lord of this castle. Now I am going on, into that room above us. Are you going to follow me?"

Before the morning's sun had risen entirely above the cliffs that served as distant guardians of Lake Alkmaar's eastern shores, the demonic presences summoned by the Ancient One had begun to manifest themselves more strongly in his vicinity.

As yet the demons had not become physically visible, but they were making their presences known in their own way. A vague, inward sickness was spreading throughout the local human population, a malaise, a foreboding that descended on people with the power of physical illness. Only a few magicians, already inured to such evil, were immune to the effect.

The demons here, like all their brethren scattered about the world, were very old, within a few years of the age of Draffut himself, as old as the changing of the world itself from Old to New. Not since that great changing of the world—or so said the magicians who claimed to know about such things—had any new demons been created. But despite the demons' antiquity, some of them still had very little experience in the world of human affairs.

On this morning the first physical manifestation of their presence took the form of a clouding of the atmosphere before the eyes of the Ancient One, who was standing atop the highest tower to watch their arrival. Soon, other human watchers in and near the castle were able to see something of them too.

Then the leader of this demon-pack, whose name was Akbal, appeared more distinctly to the human who had summoned him, in the form of a smoky column that hung in the air close in front of the high tower.

"Hail, Master Wood," said a voice that issued from the faint, dark column. "I am surprised to see you in this time and place." It was not a human voice, nor was it loud. The only man who could hear it was reminded, as he usually was on these occasions, of dead leaves being blown through loosely piled bones.

"All times and places are mine now, Akbal," the man replied. "How many others have come with you?"

"There are five others, Master Wood."

The man sighed. If any other human beings had been with him atop the tower, close enough to hear that sound, they might have found it surprising that such evidence of commonplace humanity could issue from those lips, which had now resumed their reptilian form again. "It is a long time," he said, "since any have called me by that name. A very long time indeed."

"Then by what title shall I know you, master? I know that Wood is not your true and secret name—"

"It is quite good enough. Yes, it will do. Now, Akbal, to business. Are you strong?"

"Indeed, Master Wood. I do not mean to boast, but I have grown considerably in strength since either you, or that accursed one I now see wading in the lake, has seen me last. I take it that he, the Accursed One, is the reason for this summoning."

"You gauge my purpose correctly, demon. Now attend me carefully, Akbal, and you others, also."

While the shadowy forms of five other demons hovered in the air nearby, their leader, Akbal, was given his instructions by their human master.

The briefing did not occupy much time. When it was over, the demon professed to be pleased that he had been chosen to lead an attack on Draffut.

Then Akbal and his cohort, drifting lower over the lake, moved out to several hundred meters' distance from the castle, and the same distance from Draffut, whom they began to engage in a dialogue.

The humans who were able to observe this confrontation from the islands, or from the mainland, could not hear most of what was said. Only the magician who had called up the demons was able to hear most of their talk, by means of magic.

But all of the humans who watched could see how one of the lesser demons, perhaps stung by some taunt from Draffut, suddenly took on physical form—that of a giant, sharklike fish—and in this shape went plunging from the air into the water.

Before the water of the tremendous splash had fallen back, the great fish had darted to attack Draffut.

Grabbing one of its jaws in each hand, Draffut lifted the hideous creature thrashing from the lake. The demon emitted a terrible and most unfishlike scream as its jaws, white shark-teeth showing, were stretched to the point of dislocation and beyond.

The body of the fish steamed and seemed to dissolve in air as the demon shed as rapidly as possible the physical form that it had so recently assumed.

Honan-Fu and Zoltan, cowering together on the sandy shore of an islet near where Draffut was standing in the water, were doing what they could to shelter themselves from demonic observation. In Zoltan's case this consisted of little more than keeping his eyes shut and attempting now and then to heap sand over his own body. Honan-Fu presumably had rather greater powers at his disposal, but judging from the urgency of his muttering he was little more sanguine about the results.

The two, before the demons' arrival, had already held brief conversation with some members of Honan-Fu's old constabulary. The officer Cheng Ho, after talking briefly and privately with the Emperor, had dared to row himself out here during the night to talk to Draffut, and had been delighted to welcome his old lord Honan-Fu back to the land of the living. But Cheng Ho had been prudent enough to row away again before these demonic fireworks had started.

Draffut now turned his head to the two men remaining with him, and observed their concern. The giant said calmly: "I should perhaps explain that my compulsion against hurting people does not extend to demons—indeed I would like nothing better than to destroy them completely. But the death of any demon is practically impossible to accomplish, unless one has access to its hidden life."

"Which, in this case," gritted Zoltan between clenched teeth, "you do not have."

"Alas, that is true. Still, I am not helpless, and can defend myself effectively, as well as any companions who are careful to stay close to me." Draffut turned away to survey the situation once again.

By now the demon whose jaw had been nearly torn from its joints had melted back into insubstantiality. And it was still fleeing, deep now in aerial distance, and still howling with persistent pain.

At the moment there appeared to be no other challengers ready to take its place.

"Most of them," Draffut confided quietly to his two human companions, "respect my powers too much. If they were willing to make a concerted effort they might destroy me, but they would be hurt in the process. Probably they would all be badly hurt. Courage is a virtue, as you know, my friends, and therefore demons have it not."

Meanwhile the wizard Wood, high on his battlement, was thinking that the six demons as a group ought to be powerful enough to destroy the Lord of Beasts utterly—and yet they hung back, cowardly as usual, and would not accept the pain that would be necessary for them to accomplish his will.

He vowed their punishment if they did not obey his orders; and they understood that it was no idle vow.

So now Akbal, leader of the pack, drifted toward Draffut once more. Akbal alone of this group of demons had skirmished with Draffut in the past—in the far past, those old days when the New World was truly new. In those days the powers of Orcus and of Ardneh had moved across the earth. And now Akbal was minded to taunt the Lord of Beasts with his defeat in those days by the demon-lord called Zapranoth. Akbal hoped by this means to encourage his fellows, so that they would be persuaded to rush in a group to the attack whether he went with them or not.

"And remember, dog-god," the boaster concluded, "that we here around you now are stronger than our brother Zapranoth ever was!"

"Around me? You do not stand around me. I see you all clustering together, as if for mutual protection. And I have no doubt that you are stronger liars than Zapranoth was, and that is saying a great deal. But do not forget, while you are boasting of your strength, that I am still here, while Zapranoth the Liar is long dead."

At that reply the insubstantial forms that danced above the water all hissed and steamed and rumbled in their rage. Akbal screamed: "But you are unable to touch *our* lives, o dog of gods and god of dogs! For we have them all hidden safely. And this time there will be no little human being coming with a spell to save you!"

"Here I am, if you care to attack me. As for human beings, little or great, perhaps you have something to learn of them as well."

This reply so incited the anger of Akbal that, forgetting his caution and his clever plans alike, he too dared to take on solid form alone and try the strength of Draffut. Plunging into the water, the demon strode against him in the shape of an armored man as tall as Draffut was. Chest-deep he waded toward the Lord of Beasts, amid the billows of the morning mist now rising from the lake.

The two grappled. But still the ancient power that had made Draffut what he was endured in him, the power of that other lake, the Lake of Life, older by far even than Wood and his magic, as old perhaps as the Great Worm Yilgarn. And the demon Akbal, rage and struggle as he might, was unable to withstand him.

With a last desperate effort the demon managed to twist away. He lunged into a retreat, half-drowning himself before he could completely shed the material body he had adopted for the trial.

The Beastlord roared with laughter at the sight. "And you call yourself stronger than Zapranoth? Only in lies and malice, it may be."

And now the entire squadron of angry demons gathered in conference, each trying to convince the others that they ought to hurl themselves in a group against Draffut and overwhelm him. But each demon's fear of him was too strong; and it was with relief that they heard the voice of their human master, summoning them back to the castle. Rather would they face Wood's punishment than Draffut now.

Prince Mark, who with Ben and Lady Yambu had been peering over the top of the low wall that separated the grotto from the adjoining courtyard, watching the demons, suddenly sprang to the top of the wall as the demons again clouded the air almost directly overhead. "In the Emperor's name," Mark shouted to the demons, "I send you far!"

Ben, who knew the Prince and his powers, had been more than half anticipating some such action. But Yambu cried out in surprise. Her cry was echoed by a whistle from above, deafeningly shrill, which stirred the clouded air above the castle. And then another whistle sounded, like the first but slightly different in its pitch; and then another and another. Louder and louder rose the chorus, at last becoming a mad shriek that seemed to split the sky before it was transformed into a lower, polyphonic howling. This last sound was as filled with fear and rage as any human outcry might have been.

And then in turn the howling faded. And with its fading there diminished also the cloudiness of the morning air, and the sense of sickness that had afflicted almost everyone. The sound of the demonic voices faded rapidly at first, and then more slowly, and more slowly still, so that no human being who heard it was ever quite sure that it had really come to an end.

But whether or not the sound of their departure had ever ended finally, the whole collection of demonic presences that had befouled the air above the castle were now indubitably gone.

Wood, who was still standing with Shieldbreaker in hand upon his highest battlement, had never expected anything like this. He did not see Mark jump up to give the order—the courtyard and grotto were out of his direct line of sight—but he heard the man's voice raised in the shouted command that sent the demons scattering.

He had heard almost nothing of the Prince's voice before, and he did not recognize it now. But again there leaped into his mind the stories his advisers, Amintor in particular, had told him about Mark. Never had Wood really believed that Prince Mark possessed such power over demons, but he would certainly have raised the subject in his planned interrogations of the prisoner.

Wood for the moment could only wonder whether Mark was in fact his prisoner still.

And if conceivably Mark was free, what then of Honan-Fu?

The Ancient One determined to investigate, and quickly. But now, with the morning mist beginning to blow away, and the sun coming into its full powers, Wood saw that Draffut was deliberately approaching the castle. Coming closer in full sunlight, the shaggy head and shoulders of the wading giant loomed above the last tendrils of the fading mist. An impressive figure, certainly, but small seen from this height. In fact it seemed to Wood that the God of Beasts was somewhat diminished from the creature he had been thousands of years ago.

Using a touch of magic to amplify his voice, Wood shouted out a taunt to that effect.

Draffut heard him, and paused to look up toward him. The Lord of Beasts needed no magic to amplify his voice when he chose to use it at something like full power.

"Whatever the centuries may have done to me, small man, I think they have done worse to you. For you are sadly changed."

"Changed? Yes, you animal, changed indeed! But stronger now, I assure you, than ever I was then!"

19

STARTING the long climb down from the griffin's aerie where he had been standing as he watched his demons routed, the Ancient Master took note again of the absence of small flyers, and reminded himself grimly that for the time being at least he was going to have to rely upon human eyes and ears, stationed in these high towers and elsewhere, to gather intelligence about what was happening on the lake and along its shores. He would of course use magical methods of observation when they seemed appropriate. And if a desperate need arose he could always mount his griffin again and ride out to see for himself.

But for the time being the problems of gathering intelligence outside the castle could wait. There was another question for which he had to find the answer as soon as possible: What had happened to his demons? Who, what power, had been able to sweep them out of the sky like so many drifting cobwebs?

Having descended the ladder that led immediately down from the tower's top, he started down the stairs, meanwhile casting about him with his own magical powers for an answer. But Wood was unable to confirm anything about the event he had just witnessed except that the demons were definitely gone. Whatever force had banished them had left no trace of itself behind.

As soon as he reached a level of the tower where there were soldiers within easy call, Wood summoned several, then hurriedly sent them scurrying on ahead of him, bearing his orders in different directions.

First of all he wanted to make sure that his important prisoners were secure. Particularly the one named Mark—Prince of Tasavalta, said to be the adopted son of a blacksmith named Jord. And the natural son—

if the stories Wood had heard were true—of the enigmatic magician now called the Emperor.

Could it really be true that this child of the Emperor, or anyone else, innately possessed such powers? Wood doubted that, but so far he had been unable to discover any other clue to an explanation for his demons' disappearance.

Mark had shown no sign of magical ability during his first brief confrontation with the Ancient Master. But if Mark was now shouting demons out of the sky, it could be assumed with a fair degree of certainty that he was no longer bound under the water by Wood's enchantment.

Reaching the lower levels of the castle, Wood now passed from the base of the aerie tower into the central keep. In a moment he had reached the room that he ordinarily used as his headquarters. On entering this chamber, his first act was to call for General Amintor.

Before the general had arrived, a messenger came running to the wizard with information on the prisoners. The two men who last night had been sunken in the well were missing this morning. Not only that, but Lady Yambu was gone from what had seemed a secure cell in a tower.

There was additional unlikely news. Lady Ninazu, who had arrived in a small boat last night and had been put into a waiting room to await her lord's pleasure, had also disappeared along with her strange attendant. The bars on a window had been forced—

"She came out here, to the castle, last night?" It was on the tip of the wizard's tongue to demand to know why he had not been told last night of her arrival; but he, of course, had spent much of the night over on the mainland.

A subordinate said nervously: "Your Lordship, if you will allow me to remind you, I informed you of the lady's presence shortly after she arrived."

"You informed me? When was this? Where?"

The officer quailed. "In the central courtyard, last night, sire. It was about an hour after midnight."

The man who made this statement now to Wood had not, in the past, impressed the magician as being more than ordinarily stupid. And he appeared to be currently in full possession of his faculties.

Wood looked at him steadily. "Are you completely sure of this?" he asked.

"It was last night, Your Lordship. Just as Your Lordship was entering the grotto with Lady Yambu. When I—"

"Wait. Wait. Start over. Tell me all the circumstances of this supposed encounter between us."

The soldier he was questioning grew increasingly nervous, but Wood was patient. As the story came out it forced all of his other problems temporarily out of his mind. Someone, as recently as last night, had been successfully impersonating him within the castle. So successfully, indeed, that the idea of an impostor had never entered the minds of even his close associates.

General Amintor had entered the room during the course of this questioning, had quickly grasped the situation, and now had a suggestion to make.

"Sire, this strongly suggests one thing to me—that the Sword of Stealth has been introduced into your castle by one of your enemies. In fact I know of no other way such an impersonation could be accomplished."

Wood could think of at least two other possibilities in the realm of advanced magic for achieving such an effect. Using one of these himself, he was accustomed to being able to alter his own appearance between two modes, more or less at will. But he had to admit that Amintor was very likely right about the Sword.

The Ancient One's next step was to order a full alert of all his troops, and then a thorough search of the castle, and the fringe of island surrounding it, for the escapees.

Then Wood informed his chief subordinates of where he himself intended to be during the next few hours while the search was in progress. If they believed that they saw him anywhere else during that time, they would be looking at an impostor. In that event they were to keep the masquerader under surveillance and bring word to their real master at once.

Having issued these and a few other orders, Wood turned his attention to the castle's garrison and the other components of its defenses. In what other way might they have been undermined without his knowledge?

But here, at least, the reports he got were reassuring. Just under four hundred troops were present, well armed and ready for duty, within the castle walls. The morale of the men had reportedly been somewhat shaken by the events of the past few hours, and the Ancient One decided that his next step ought to be to address that problem.

He commanded a general muster of all the troops except a few sentries who were to continue manning the walls. He intended to speak to his soldiers and reassure them.

Certainly, he thought, the garrison ought to be more than adequate to defend these formidable walls against the strongest attack that the ragged followers of Honan-Fu could mount—assuming the old wizard had any followers left, and assuming he had indeed managed to make good his escape to the mainland. Now that a search for the prisoners had started, reports were coming in to Wood of the chance discovery of secret passages within the castle, and that kind of an escape no longer appeared such a remote possibility.

Particularly with Draffut roaming the surrounding lake . . .

Mustering almost all his men in a formation to hear their commander speak meant necessarily delaying the search for the escapees, but Wood determined to take that risk.

From what the officers and the sergeants could tell him, it was not the doubtful capabilities of Honan-Fu that worried his troops. It was the mysterious fate of their mainland garrison, and, even more than that, it was Draffut.

Wood could understand that last apprehension, because in a way he shared it. But he was not going to allow any kind of fear to demoralize his men.

He strode out onto a high balcony, overlooking the assembled troops, hundreds of faces squinting up into the noon sun.

"Hear me!" he roared in his amplified voice. "I know what bothers you, and in a way I cannot blame you, because in your ignorance you cannot help yourselves. Let me instead enlighten you.

"To begin with, you have all heard rumors about what happened to the garrison at Triplicane. The truth is that they relaxed their vigilance when I was not there to protect them, and a powerful magician struck them down. He fled the field afterward, not daring to face me directly. I am here, and as long as I am your leader he is not going to come back. Enough on that subject.

"The next most popular subject of rumors is yonder monster out in the lake. He's fierce enough against boats, and, I grant you, against demons too, as some of you have been able to see for yourselves this morning.

"But, as those of you who had to swim last night can testify, he is too tenderhearted to so much as scratch the skin of any human being. Did we lose a single man to him last night, for all his pranks and bellowing?"

There had indeed been, as Wood well knew, at least one man reported drowned among the occupants of the capsized boats. But one man, among the dozens who had been tipped into the lake, might well have been sheer accident. At least no one was brave enough to raise the subject of that one man now.

"No, we did not!" Into the uncertain silence Wood shouted his own answer to his own question. "And we'll lose none to the great dog, today or ever!"

For some time he continued in this vein, and when at last he paused to consider the temper of his audience, he thought that they had been considerably encouraged.

In a somewhat lower voice their master went on: "No, we can hold these walls against him. One sword or one pike or one arrow may not be able to do him much damage—but let him stand within our reach, and we can hew the flesh from his bones eventually, so he'll have to back away or die. The walls here are at least twice as tall as he is, and he cannot climb them as long as we are alert and ready to discourage him in the attempt. And, let me say it again, he cannot, I repeat he cannot, ever do any one of us the least harm!"

It was as rousing a climax for his speech as any Wood was able to conceive at the moment, and he let it end there. The troops, at a signal from their officers, managed to produce a cheer that had some energy and some flavor of spontaneity about it. Marching rank by rank out of the courtyard, they seemed to their Ancient Master to be moving with new determination.

When he came in from the balcony, officers were waiting for him with more good news for the defense. There was plenty of stored food on hand, provisions prudently stockpiled by the castle's previous owner, against the possibility of a siege that had never come. And there would of course be no difficulty about fresh water, even supposing that Honan-Fu and his allies could really manage to mount and maintain a siege.

All in all, Wood foresaw no real problems in his defense of this castle, unless an attack should be made with sudden, overwhelming force. And there was no reason to anticipate anything of the kind.

He had business outside these walls that he was anxious to get on with. But that business would require that he travel a considerable distance, and he did not want to leave the castle while there was a possibility of a successful impostor still lurking within.

Once more Wood summoned General Amintor, and when the limping old soldier had arrived, discussed with him the friendly reinforcements that were supposedly on their way. Some of Amintor's lieutenants ought now to be leading those troops—perhaps five thousand men in all—here from the west. This force was to form the nucleus of a large army that in time would move into the north, challenging Tasavalta and the other powers of that region for supremacy.

Wood announced his intention of sending Amintor out now, riding the griffin. The general was to meet this army of reinforcements, which was still probably a two-week march away, and survey its size, condition, and rate of advance. Then Amintor was to report back to Wood, within twenty-four hours.

Amintor, experienced warrior that he was, could not entirely conceal his dismay when he heard about the means of transportation that he was to use. Wood had noticed in the past that the general preferred not to get too close to the griffin.

"The griffin," Wood assured him, "is very fast and reliable. It should be able to manage the distance in that time without any trouble. Well, what do you say?"

The general thought briefly, then asked: "Will the creature obey my orders, sire?"

"It will obey all the orders that you may need to give it. However, it will come back to me here tomorrow, whatever you may say to it in the meantime. See that you are on it when it begins its return flight."

Amintor bowed. If the thought of flying on a griffin terrified him, he was at least not trying to shirk the duty, and that was all that Wood could ask of him.

The two men climbed to the aerie—Amintor getting up stairs and ladders slowly on his bad leg—and Wood gave the necessary magical commands. A moment later, squinting into the afternoon sun, he had seen the griffin and its somewhat reluctant rider off.

Naturally Wood had remembered to inform the officers conducting the search of the fact that he was leaving his headquarters room, and of his destination. One of these officers met him on his way down from the high tower, with word that the impostor had been spotted. Someone looking exactly like Wood himself—in which of the two modes of his appearance the informant did not say—had been glimpsed by several people, looking out of one of the higher windows in the little-used central tower of the castle. As yet no attempt had been made to close in on the offender.

"That is good. I myself will lead the way." Resting his hand on the hilt of Shieldbreaker, Wood smiled grimly and set out to deal with the impostor.

20

ZOLTAN too had managed to get some rest and nourishment. After rowing Mark and Honan-Fu out to Draffut, he had waited in the small boat until the Lord of Healing had healed the damage done by the Ancient Master's magic, had restored the two men by holding them in his hands, and set them on an island. By that time some people from shore, members of the constabulary, were beginning to come out to Draffut, emboldened by whatever conversation the Emperor had held with them. Eventually Zoltan had gone back with some of these people to the docks at Triplicane.

Meanwhile Mark, as soon as he was healed and had rested enough to feel nearly recovered, insisted on returning to the castle, where Ben and Yambu were still in peril. But Honan-Fu declined to go with him, deciding instead to stay for the time being on the small island where he had been placed by Draffut. This afforded the old wizard an advanced position from which he would be able to command the amphibious assault he was already planning in order to retake the castle.

The town of Triplicane, like the rest of the territory surrounding Lake Alkmaar, was now free land once more. The only effective troops in the area still loyal to the Ancient One were now confined within the castle walls. The people who welcomed Zoltan ashore were rejoicing over this state of affairs, but by this time he was almost too tired to care. He talked briefly with some of the leaders of the constabulary in town, enjoyed a good meal, and then stretched out on a borrowed bedroll inside a shed.

Zoltan did not awake until midafternoon. When he came out of the shed, he discovered that preparations for an amphibious counterattack against the castle were farther advanced than he supposed, and the attack was to be launched during the coming night.

Already a surprising number of boats had been gathered from around the lake. Some of these were craft that had been successfully concealed from the invaders; and some were the very boats that the soldiers of the Ancient One had used in their invasion. These craft had been seized at the town docks after the destruction of the garrison, and were now to be turned against the enemy. Also included in the invasion fleet were two large rowboats that Draffut had overturned during the night, then righted and emptied so they could be easily rowed ashore.

Transport for several hundred men was thus available. Nor had there been any difficulty in gathering sufficient arms. Besides the weapons that had been successfully hidden away during the brief occupation, enough more had been picked up from the field in front of the manor to arm at least a hundred men.

Zoltan had heard that there were a few military survivors of that massacre, and he had even talked to one of them, a young private soldier in a dirty uniform of red and gray, who was now confined under guard in a shed next to the one in which Zoltan had been sleeping.

The youth appeared somewhat fearful of what was going to happen to him next, but the main impression that he conveyed was of sheer gladness in being still alive.

"Why are you still alive, do you suppose?" Zoltan asked him curiously after the prisoner had told him a brief version of the disaster.

The other young man shook his head, as if at some wonder he could not understand no matter how he tried. "I don't know. I just don't know. When that show started, everyone around me, almost, started laughing. . . . Were you there?"

"No. But I've talked to someone else who was."

The former enemy shook his head again. "I just don't know why I'm still here. Everyone was laughing, but I just didn't see nothing to laugh at. Them girls having their clothes ripped off, that wasn't funny. Nobody had ought to do that. And the little fella in the clown suit, he acted like he was trying to protect 'em, even if he got himself killed. I wouldn't have had the guts to do that, but I didn't think it was funny either."

"No," said Zoltan. "No, I wouldn't have laughed at that."

"And all the rest of my company are dead, they tell me, and here I am still alive. It's strange. I'm just lucky, I guess."

Zoltan left him in the shed. The young man was still marveling at his own survival, and ready to tell the story again, if someone else would listen.

It was well after dark when the assault force finally pushed off, some two hundred men and a few women in more than twenty boats. Zoltan, having eaten heartily again, and armed from the common stock of weapons, was aboard one of them.

At sunrise, as soon as the brief sickness brought on by demons had suddenly abated, Arnfinn had gone on alone into the hidden rooms of the central tower. By that time he had temporarily given up trying to persuade Lady Ninazu to come with him. He didn't know what was wrong with her—as near as he could tell, she was afraid that her brother would not be here after all. Or else she was afraid he would.

As Arnfinn soon discovered, there were four rooms in this hidden suite, two on the level entered from the tunnel and two more just above, on the highest interior level of the tower. He spent an hour alone in these rooms, searching them carefully, making sure in his own mind that Ninazu's brother was not here. No one was, except himself. Nor was there any sign that anyone had lived here very recently, nor was there anything about the rooms to make Arnfinn think they might have been used as a prison.

The four rooms, two on one level and two on the next, connected by a single narrow interior stairway, occupied the top two stories of the central tower. The tower narrowed slightly here, toward its top, and none of the rooms were very large. All of them were furnished, and they did contain plenty of potential hiding places: there were beds with spaces beneath, disused cabinets and wardrobes, and closets stuffed with junk, much of it children's toys. Arnfinn had done as thorough a job as he possibly could of searching through all these nooks and crannies, making sure that neither Kunderu nor anyone else was lying in concealment.

Each room was lighted and aired by two narrow windows, built out in a slight bulge of wall and equipped with interior shutters, most of which were standing open. Arnfinn supposed a slender person might have been able to squeeze his way in or out through one of these windows, or at least could do so if there were anything but the sheer face of the wall outside. There were no other visible entrances or exits to the apartment, except the tunnel through which Arnfinn and Ninazu had come up.

As Arnfinn went through these rooms he received a strong impression that no one could have occupied them for a long time, perhaps for years. A thin film of dust covered all horizontal surfaces, and there was unmistakable evidence that some of the waterfowl so plentiful around the lake had taken advantage of the open windows to come in from time to time.

Several times during the hour that he spent alone in these rooms Arnfinn had interrupted his examination of the place to look out into the dim passageway again and speak softly to Ninazu, trying to persuade her to join him. He had almost given up on being able to do this, when he looked up from the examination of a cabinet and saw her standing in the doorway of the passage, looking in at him.

For a moment neither of them spoke. Then Arnfinn said gently: "Your brother isn't here after all."

She looked back at him helplessly, saying nothing. Her elaborate long dress, not made for boat rides and climbing through dark passages, was smudged and slightly torn in a couple of places, and her hair hung round her face in disarray. She was absolutely the most beautiful thing that Arnfinn had ever seen.

Arnfinn, now feeling as helpless as the lady looked, cast his gaze around the room in which they were standing. It was on the lower level of the apartment, and roughly semicircular in shape. There were chairs and dusty tables in the middle of this room, as if for some kind of bookish work, and shelves of books around the curving walls. Arnfinn had learned to read, better at least than most of the people in his village. But he had never seen as many books as this, and many of the titles were in languages he did not know. Even those in his own language were hard to understand. At least some of them, he was sure, must have something to do with magic.

He said: "I suppose you and Kunderu must have lived in these rooms. There are beds in the two rooms upstairs."

"Yes, my brother and I lived here much of the time." Ninazu came closer to him, walking slowly into the center of the room. It was as if she had forgotten again that there was something here of which she was afraid. "We were always together when we were children. We made up our own games, Kunderu and I. Even when we were very young we knew we were both going to be magicians."

"Like your father."

"Oh, father, yes. Father pretty much let us do whatever we wanted." The lady shrugged. "He was usually busy with his own work."

Arnfinn felt a tremendous relief that she was at least talking to him rationally again. "What about your mother?" he asked. "You've never told me anything about her."

Ninazu drew symbols with one finger in the faint dust on a workbench. She said: "I don't know much about her. She died when Kunderu and I were very young."

"That must have been very sad for you."

"I don't remember." Ninazu's voice was remote. She turned away from Arnfinn and went to a set of cabinets, tall and ornately carved, that stood against the flat interior wall beside the doorway to the adjoining room, and below more shelves of books. She pulled open the doors of one of the tall cabinets, and then stood looking at the diverse objects arrayed on the shelves inside as if she had expected to see something rather different. Many of the things on the shelves were hard for Arnfinn to recognize. There were bones and a stuffed bird, and little piles of what looked to him like rather ordinary rocks.

The lady was pointing at one of the small piles of rocks now. She said thoughtfully: "Kunderu was trying to evoke a demon once, when he was only twelve. He was using these. Father found out before he got very far and made him stop."

Arnfinn was aghast. "Fortunately!" was the only comment he could find to make.

Lady Ninazu looked at him with almost open rebellion in her eyes. "My brother could have controlled a demon, with my help."

"But—Ninazu, a *demon!* You felt the ones outside just now. How could you have wanted—that? How could your brother want it?"

Ninazu's gaze had become almost demure. *"You* have never dealt with demons, lord?"

"That—that's beside the point."

She shrugged boldly. "We didn't know quite what it was going to be like. But we could have managed, we could have stayed in control, Kunderu and I together." Then the growing, visible anger of his wizard-image crushed her opposition, and she shrank back timidly. "Oh, great lord, we were very young."

"Yes. You were. You must have been. Demons are tremendously dangerous, and I am glad that you did not succeed." Arnfinn spoke with great conviction, as if he really were a wizard and knew what he was talking about. Maybe, after this morning's brief whiff of demons in the tunnel, he knew enough.

Ninazu looked at Arnfinn strangely now. "I have told you, my lord, my lover, that you were our first success."

"I?"

"Yes, lord. I see that you are pleased to have another jest at my expense."

"How, in what way, was I a success for you? When? I want you to tell me."

Ninazu stood with downcast eyes, almost in the attitude of a child fearing punishment. Still her tone dared to be reproachful. "It was two years ago, lord. A little more than two years now . . . but you know all this as well as I do, lord. You know it better."

"Tell me, I say. I want you to tell me what you are talking about, what happened, just as you remember it."

"Yes, lord. I am talking about the help we gave you, Kunderu's help and mine, that enabled you to find your way here across the ages."

"Across the what?"

Ninazu ignored the question. "We were looking for something that would—irritate our father, show him what we could do, that we could be magicians too."

"The help you gave *me?*" Arnfinn was struggling to understand, but at the same time not at all sure that he wanted to understand.

"You and I have talked about all this before, my lord and lover." Ninazu sighed. "Many times we have laughed about it in our bed."

Arnfinn was very tired. He sat down on a stool before one of the tables. "Never mind that. I would hear it all again."

The lady leaned against the other table, her arms folded. She recited: "Kunderu and I were very angry at our father for being so oppressive all the time. We had been experimenting with ways to get back at him. We worked and worked, until finally our efforts—brought us in touch with Your Lordship, across the gulf of years."

Arnfinn couldn't understand what she meant by the gulf of years. "You were trying to evoke a demon, I suppose. And you got me instead."

"Have I displeased you, great lord, with my poor telling? Did it really happen in some other way?"

"I don't suppose so, Ninazu. No, you must know what happened. I am sure it must have happened as you say." Arnfinn rested his chin on his fist and tried to think.

Ninazu was musing aloud, as if she too were grappling with some kind of puzzle. "You could have found someone else in this time to help you, I suppose. But Kunderu and I were the ones you chose." Suddenly grief and fear overwhelmed her again. Raising her head, she cried out: "Kunderu, where are you?"

A gull-winged lake bird had been just about to land on the sill of one of the open windows behind her, and her sudden outcry frightened it off. The bird veered away from the tower, letting out a loud, harsh cry.

Ninazu screamed, and spun around in terror.

Arnfinn experienced a sudden insight. "It was only a bird, Ninazu. Are you really so afraid of your brother as all that?"

"You are wicked to say that!" Then, aghast at her own boldness, she brought her hands up to her mouth.

"You were afraid to come into these rooms when you thought he might still be here."

"I love my brother, and I will save him!"

"Are you sure that he is really a prisoner? How are you so sure? These rooms are not a prison," Arnfinn pointed out. "We got into them easily enough, without passing any locked doors or guards. Kunderu, if he was here, ought to have been able to get out the same way. Besides, it doesn't look to me like anyone has lived here for a long time."

"He was here!" Ninazu whispered the words with tremendous conviction.

"He's not here now. Maybe he's somewhere else in the castle. Or maybe somewhere else altogether."

Lady Ninazu's eyes had closed, as if she were in agony. "Kunderu is here somewhere," she breathed, softly but with great intensity. "My brother is here, and I am going to save him."

"All right, if you say so. But I don't see or hear anyone in these rooms but us. He's not here now."

"Great lord," she breathed more softly and hopelessly still, "I had thought that you were going to help me."

And with that Ninazu slumped down into one of the dusty chairs and abandoned herself to the saddest, most hopeless weeping that Arnfinn had ever heard.

In a moment Arnfinn was at her side, all his efforts to be firm and practical crumbling into dust. "I will help you. I will help you, whatever you say. Whatever I must do." And he held her fiercely, in bewildered helplessness.

Mark, with Ben and Lady Yambu nearby, had been standing atop one of the lower parts of the grotto wall when he shouted at the demons to disperse.

"The same shout that sent them off," Ben commented, "will draw some people here. People of a kind I fear we'll like no better than the demons." He gestured at the wall with the hidden exit. "Let's move on up."

"Yes, it would seem to be time for that."

With Mark in the lead, the three of them climbed to the niche where Ninazu and the latest Sword-bearer, whoever he was, had disappeared. They entered the dark tunnel that they found there, and advanced cautiously. As they climbed farther they began to speculate in low voices on the possible identity of the person who was now carrying the Sword of Stealth.

Yambu, ascending between the two men, said that she now felt reasonably sure it was the youth Arnfinn they were following.

Ben, who was bringing up the rear, was more than a little skeptical of that suggestion. "That scrawny peasant? I find it difficult to believe he would have had the guts to come after Zoltan and me, and hit Zoltan over the head in that shed. And then, to get aboard a griffin, and ride it out here—"

Here in the dark tunnel where no one could see her, Yambu allowed herself to smile broadly. "What you tell me you went through to get here, my friend, was hardly less fantastic."

Ben grunted something, then swore softly when he stumbled in the darkness. Mark, alertly in the lead, was silent.

The three of them went on up.

Their general plan now was to reach one of the hiding places high in the structure of the castle recommended by Honan-Fu; also Mark and Ben in particular nursed some hopes of being able to get back the Sword of Stealth from Arnfinn, if it was really he who was carrying it again.

Their whispered planning session had not made much headway, nor had they gained much distance upward along their gloomy escape route, when Ben hissed for silence. His two companions halted with him, holding their breath. In a moment they were all able to hear the soldiers arriving in the grotto they had just left. It sounded like one had come over the wall to open the locked gate for the others. In another moment there was a whole squad of them in the grotto, beginning a clamorous search.

Mark, Yambu, and Ben crept on, as silently as possible. Almost at once cries of surprise sounded from below and behind them, indicating that the soldiers had found the two ropes severed and the prisoners gone.

Mark methodically continued upward. The two others followed. Either the soldiers would quickly locate the hidden exit from the grotto, or they would not. After a minute Ben muttered: "I could wish for Wayfinder in a place like this. Or Coinspinner at least."

"Go ahead," Mark whispered over his shoulder. "But you won't have either one of them in hand after you've wished. So let's get on with what we have."

Which was not, Mark added silently to himself, much in the way of weapons. Ben had left his staff behind him long ago, and Lady Yambu was an unarmed pilgrim. Mark himself had brought one dagger back with him from his trip out into the lake, a gift from the officer Cheng Ho passed on to Mark by Draffut.

At least all three of them had eaten heartily last night, and all had been granted an interval for rest. These benefits, along with Draffut's healing treatment of Mark, had restored them all to something approaching normal strength and energy. Before they left the grotto Ben had refilled a couple of last night's drink containers at the well, and slung them on his belt; if they could find a hiding place, they ought not to die of thirst for a day or two at least.

Presently the three came to the end of the first hidden passage, to find themselves in what looked like an ordinary if almost unused storeroom. Mark paused in the entrance to the storeroom, frowning. This was really not what any of them had been expecting. Honan-Fu's directions for finding a hiding place had been hurried and perhaps unclear. The three paused for a brief whispered conference.

There were two doors to the storeroom, besides the one by which they had entered, and the three people had no means of telling which way Ninazu and her Sword-bearer might have taken from this point.

Before the three had chosen a way to go, they could hear movement outside one of the doors.

Quickly and efficiently, making plans with no more than a swift exchange of gestures, they had arranged themselves in ambush, with the men against the wall behind the door.

The door swung in. There was only one soldier, and he had come alone here to look for someone or something, not expecting trouble. He saw Yambu, standing alone in the middle of the dingy storeroom, and he took a step toward her and started to ask a puzzled question.

He never got the question out. A moment later, Ben was able to unbuckle the swordbelt from the soldier's body; he needed to pick up the soldier's dagger, too, and use the fine point to bore another hole in the belt before he could buckle that belt around his own waist over the strongman costume. While he was thus engaged, Mark dragged the lifeless body out of sight.

Yambu signed for silence, then made another gesture, pointing back over her shoulder. There were faint sounds, as of cautious footsteps, in the tunnel through which they had come up. Evidently the enemy had found the hidden entrance to the tunnel and were already following them up from the grotto.

The three went warily out into the corridor from which the lone soldier had entered. Mark shrugged over the choice of directions, and turned left. Moving in that direction, they quickly reached an ascending stairway, which took them steeply up again. Going higher within the architecture of any castle was very likely to bring you to a more defensible position. The structures were, after all, designed with defense in mind.

This stair went up a little way without a break, or any other exit, and then emerged onto the cylindrical outer surface of the tower. At this point it became almost uncomfortably narrow, with only a sheer drop on the left side, and continued up around the outside of the tower in a spiral.

The stair did not quite reach the top, but came to an abrupt end some three or four meters below a gap in the parapet encircling the roof. From the top of the stair a removable wooden ladder extended the rest of the way to the top. The three went up this ladder and found themselves on the tower's flat, circular stone-paved roof, some ten paces in diameter.

There was a small roof cistern here, which had some water in it; Ben's jugs were probably not going to be necessary after all. Most of the tower's rooftop was open to the sky, but at the side of the roof opposite the cistern a small, half-open shed had been constructed, to serve as shelter for a lookout and perhaps for a small signal fire. Some wood was stacked for this contingency. In another place a pile of head-sized stones had been neatly pyramided, a routine provision of armament for any last-ditch defenders who wished to discourage their enemies from following them up the stairs.

The wooden ladder was obviously another means to that end, and Ben had already taken advantage of it, pulling the ladder up briskly after them. None too soon, perhaps. The ladder had only just been removed when Yambu took a quick glance back and down upon the exterior stair and saw red and gray uniforms coming up.

"Hush!" she warned her companions softly.

Listening, all three of them were able to hear a dogged, soft, dull thudding noise.

"Shieldbreaker," Mark breathed unhappily.

The other two nodded. They had all heard before the sound made by that Sword as it was carried into combat range of its bearer's enemies, whoever they might be.

Whoever now had the Sword of Force in hand was coming along their trail, up the exterior stairway. But whoever he was, he could not get at them, at least for the moment.

"But listen again," Ben whispered, frowning. "I could swear that there are two of them. Two Swords."

Straining his ears, Mark found that he could indeed make out an extra, doubled thudding.

"There cannot be two," Yambu objected softly but angrily, as if she were quietly outraged that the rules of the Sword-game might have been changed without her being told.

"Wait," whispered Mark. "I wonder. Yes, that must be it. Sightblinder."

The others frowned at him, then Ben's face brightened suddenly with understanding. "Yes, we've been following Sightblinder, or trying to. If that peasant, or whoever he is, is in some room of this tower just below us . . . and his Sword is doing an imitation of Shieldbreaker—yes, that would do it."

"Ho, on the roof!" The voice was powerful, and so loud that some manner of magic, or Old-World technology perhaps, must be in use to augment it.

"Do you suppose we ought to answer?" Yambu whispered very softly.

Mark and Ben exchanged frowns, giving the question silent consideration.

"Ho, there! This is the master of the castle speaking! Let your ladder down for us at once! You are trapped, and I will show you mercy if you come down now!"

After exchanging looks with her companions, Yambu made answer with a rock, which she handled over to the edge of the roof with wiry strength, and dropped just over the head of the stair below. Prudently she refrained from looking over the edge to observe the exact result. There was an explosive crash, and small rock-fragments sang through the air in all directions.

There were no more shouted demands after that. Listening carefully, the three on the roof could hear the people on the stairs quietly retreating.

Things settled down for the time being into a waiting mode.

The only place from which anyone could see the top of this tower was the top of the only higher tower, where the aerie was, at least a hundred meters distant. And if the three retreated under the lookout's shelter they would be invisible even from there, and probably immune from any speculative stones or arrows launched from that high place.

The afternoon was wearing on. As was perhaps inevitable, the talk among the three people on the roof turned to the Swords and their various powers. Long before the day was over, Mark had time to reminisce about the occasion upon which he had carried Sightblinder into the camp of the Dark King himself.

"And the Sword of Stealth has another power that is more subtle than the one of which we are always aware. The verse tells it: 'his eyes are keen . . .' I scarcely understood it at the time, but when I looked at the Dark King and his magicians, I could *see* their evil."

21

WOOD, ascending the exterior stair that curved around the tower, with the great Sword Shieldbreaker thudding softly in his right hand and a squad of picked troops at his back, knew that he had reached the top of the stair no more than a few minutes behind his quarry. Quite possibly it had been a nearer miss than that. He did not actually see the wooden ladder being pulled up out of his reach, but he saw the supports where it had rested, and he surmised its very recent removal. And Shieldbreaker was now signaling the near presence of his enemies. Wood could not see or hear them on the roof above, but he knew that they were there.

He smiled lightly to himself. He could hear a duplicated thudding, keeping time like a faint echo with the sound of his own Sword, and in the first moment after the Ancient Master heard that echo he realized where it must be coming from. It was coming from the Sword of Stealth, in the impostor's possession; and that Sword now had to be somewhere very near at hand.

Before calling on his prey to surrender, Wood took a moment in which to survey the general situation. Whoever was on the roof might well be trapped there, though for the moment in a snugly defensible position. Plainly there was no way but this stair to reach the tower's roof from the outside, short of using chains and grappling irons slung over the parapets—matters might eventually come to that—or by flying. The wizard took a moment in which to curse the decision that had made him send his griffin away with Amintor. But there was no help now for mistakes already made.

The outside stair on which he stood was undefended by any roof or even a railing. It curved three quarters of the way around the central tower, and at several points well above its curve, too high to be reached, were windows, indicating the presence of interior rooms. But there were no windows below the stair, or otherwise readily accessible from it. And not only were the windows high, but they were narrow, not much more than archers' slits; perhaps a child or a very thin adult might have been able to squeeze through one of them. And not only were the windows high and narrow, but they were slightly overhanging the stair, each pair of them built out in a small projecting bartizan.

It was quite possible, of course, that some kind of trapdoor gave access to the roof from inside the tower. The impostor, who had been seen looking out of one of these tower windows, could have gone up to the roof from the inside and then pulled the outside ladder up. Wood could wish now that he had personally taken a more thorough inventory of the castle and its architecture during his brief peaceful tenure.

Only minutes ago, before starting up this outside stairway, he had detailed men to search the interior of the tower for a way to reach the roof, or at least the upper floors, whose existence was indicated by the windows. Those men were to report to Wood before they closed in on their quarry, but so far they had not reported any success in finding an interior way up.

He was being foiled for the moment, it seemed, by some more of the architectural whimsy of Honan-Fu.

Now the Ancient Master, with his Sword ready—truth to tell, he had never been much of a swordsman—and speaking in his most terrible amplified voice, called upon those who were above him to surrender. "Ho, on the roof! Ho, there! This is the master of the castle speaking! Let the ladder down for us at once! You are trapped, and I will show you mercy if you come down now!"

There was only silence up above. His answer came in the form of a heavy, head-sized rock, dropped over the edge of the parapet by anonymous hands, hands that worked blindly but still managed to choose their aiming point with what would have been deadly accuracy had it not been for the Sword of Force. Shieldbreaker altered the rhythm of its monotonous thudding voice just slightly, putting mild emphasis upon a single syllable. The blade moved as if with its own volition, pulling Wood's hand after it in a single economical movement. Shieldbreaker flashed in the sun, arcing above the wizard's head. The rock, precisely intercepted in midair, shattered into a hundred screaming fragments, none of which touched Wood. The soldier who was just behind him on the stair muttered a low oath; one of those stone fragments had left a bloody track across his face.

The Sword of Force, the keenness of its edges undented by that blow, again was almost quiet, chanting its low rhythmic song of rage and barely suppressed violence as if it were singing to itself alone. And still the gentle echo of its counterfeit persisted, coming from somewhere nearby.

With a silent, emphatic gesture Wood ordered his squad back down the stair; even though his Sword would protect him personally against rocks or any other weapons, his escort was vulnerable here, and there was no point in wasting useful men.

The sound made by Shieldbreaker subsided as the Ancient Master carried it back down the stairs, and the echo of its imitation faded from his hearing also.

Once he had reentered the tower again, the wizard detailed a few of his men to make another ladder, or else bring one of the proper size over from another tower if that would be quicker. Of course, even if another ladder could be set in place atop that exposed stair and somehow kept there, the top of the central tower would still be very easy to defend. Undoubtedly there were more rocks up on the roof, and even when rocks were exhausted, still only one man would be able to come up a ladder at a time. And anyone standing on that last stone step, where it would be necessary to stand to set the ladder into place, would be an extremely vulnerable target to more stones dropped from above. A man carrying Shieldbreaker might win through, of course—depending on how much the defenders knew about the Sword. Wood did not intend to take unnecessary personal risks to get at them, nor did he mean to hand over the Sword of Force to any of his subordinates.

Remaining inside the tower himself, he led a quick exploration of the accessible levels, and confirmed what his people were telling him, that these ended one or two floors below the top. So it was possible, he supposed, that the only way to get into those upper levels without tearing part of the tower down might be from the roof. But yet Wood could not be absolutely sure of that—and suppose the impostor was able to get out some other way, and do more damage?

Still, every course of action had its risks. The Ancient Master decided to temporarily abandon his search for another way into the upper rooms, and started toward the highest tower of the castle, from whose top it ought to be possible to see the top of the central tower, and who was on it. Before he had even reached the base of that tower, a report was brought to him. A small flyer, carrying some object, had been seen to land on the roof of the central tower. One witness said that the thing the flyer carried had been a water bottle.

Wood swore oaths of great intensity. He yearned for his griffin, to be able to go and pluck the renegade water-carrying beast out of the sky. Draffut had somehow perverted Wood's corps of winged scouts, or some of them at least, to the cause of his enemies.

But in a way the news about the water bottle was reassuring—if water was being sent by that means to the people on the rooftop, that suggested they were pretty effectively prevented from getting it any other way.

On the roof of the central tower, Mark, Ben, and Yambu rejoiced to receive the written note that the flyer had brought out to them from Triplicane, along with the unnecessary leather bottle of water.

The handwriting of the note was recognizably Zoltan's. In it he assured them that Honan-Fu's counterattack was going to be launched tonight.

From her small pouch of personal belongings, Lady Yambu got out a little metal mirror, and began an effort at heliographic signaling to some of the boats in the lake, and then to the people in green and gold uniforms who were now gathering on several of the small islands. There were a number of boats near those islands now, and enough constabulary troops in gold and green on boats and islands to make it unlikely that Wood would want to send out his own amphibious force, risking his own remaining fleet of lake-going craft, to challenge their possession. But her signaling drew no response.

When the three on the roof strained their eyes in the direction of distant Triplicane they thought they could discern another gathering of boats along the dockside there.

Their talk came back to their enemy, and the Sword he carried. The sound of Shieldbreaker had faded away very quickly after Yambu dropped that discouraging rock. And with Shieldbreaker withdrawn, its voice muted, the echo-sound presumably made by Sightblinder had faded too.

"Where is Sightblinder then?" Ben asked, scowling.

Yambu had a logical answer ready. "Well, if it was not on the stairs when we heard it, then it must have been in one of the rooms just below us."

When the people on the rooftop at last peered cautiously over the parapet, they were just able to catch a glimpse of someone passing inside one of the projecting windows below them.

"Should we call out to them?" Mark asked his companions.

Before they could decide that question, a deadly distraction came from the direction of the castle's highest tower, in the form of a desultory bombardment with rocks and arrows. Their tower was too far away from the other, more than a hundred meters distant, for this attack to be effective, and it was not pursued. But the three on the roof tended now to stay within the shelter of the lookout's roofed shed.

Continuing to take a cautious inventory, they discovered a trapdoor in the approximate center of the roof. On the upper side of the trap there was no sign of any lock.

Mark asked: "What do we want to do about this? Open it and see what's under us, or block it up?"

Ben offered: "We've more or less come to the conclusion that the Sword-bearer is probably down there. What do you say, do we go after his Sword again?"

They debated it a little, and Ben's tentative effort to lift the trap discovered it to be locked somehow from below. Mark eventually decided it would be better to block the trap, for the time being.

It was not hard to find the proper materials for the job of blocking the trapdoor. The pyramidal pile of defensive rocks, in the busy hands of Mark and Ben, was soon being transferred right on top of it.

"There," Mark grunted some time later, setting the last rock in place atop the reconstructed pile, and pausing to wipe sweat from his face. *"You* might be able to push that trap open from below now, but I doubt there's another man anywhere who could manage it."

Ben squinted at the pyramid of stones and shook his head. "I wouldn't care to try."

The three on the roof got through the day, taking turns napping in the shade of the lookout's shelter. As old soldiers, they were all accustomed to not thinking about food for long intervals, and otherwise they were comfortable enough for the time being.

The patience of experience saw them through the day.

* * *

The night began with the three people on the roof taking turns at watchful listening and rest. It was about two hours before dawn when the enemy made an almost silent attempt to put a new ladder into place upon the upper end of the external stair. Lady Yambu happened to be on watch at the time. Listening attentively and timing her moves carefully, she put another rock neatly over the edge. This time the Sword of Force was evidently not on hand to fend it off. The missile fell for almost the full height of two men before it struck something. There was a muffled impact, followed by a fading, wailing cry, as of a man departing under the full acceleration of gravity. There followed the faint but rapid sounds of scurrying feet going back down the stairs. Then silence reigned again.

Early in the night there had been a discussion among the leaders of Honan-Fu's assault force as to whether they should try to recruit Draffut to pull some of their boats into position for the final attack. In the end it was decided that they should all row themselves into position, leaving Draffut to do whatever he thought best to help them in his own way. The Lord of Beasts had indicated that he would do something, but perhaps because he did not trust their human councils he had kept his exact intentions to himself until the flotilla of constabulary boats were ready to put out into the lake.

Zoltan watched from a distance as the Lord of Beasts left the lake and moved up into the hills, his head overtopping half the trees he passed. Draffut passed out of Zoltan's sight for a while, and when he returned he was carrying the stripped trunk of a pine tree that had been twice taller than himself. When he came down among the people again they could smell the aromatic sap oozing from the torn bark.

Draffut announced to Zoltan and those near him that this was going to be his scaling ladder.

The boats did not begin to move into their final positions for the assault until about midnight. Honan-Fu's planning allowed several hours for them all to get into position. The idea was to put men ashore simultaneously on all sides of the island, getting ready to assail every part of the castle's perimeter at once.

Knowing just where Draffut planned to land, Zoltan could see the Beastlord wade ashore, for the moment undiscovered by the castle's lookouts. The towering figure emerged from the water on the spit of sand that extended from the island's northern end, and before the enemy had spotted him, he was running toward the castle. When he was within reach of the wall that towered over him, the Lord of Beasts wedged the base of his treetrunk into the sand, and leaned the upper end against the castle wall, which it slightly overtopped.

At this point shouts of warning, cries that trembled on the verge of being screams of terror, went up from Wood's human lookouts. Draffut responded to them at once, with the most bloodcurdling bellow he could produce. In the next moment he was swarming up his improvised ladder, and a moment after that he was crouched apelike atop the thickness of the wall.

The sentries who had been manning that portion of the wall were there no longer, having delayed not a second in getting out of Draffut's way. There were a few more, now standing paralyzed with terror at a little distance, and Draffut waved his arms at them and bellowed again, effectively frightening them away.

Now he could get down to work. Wrapped around his body under his thick fur Draffut was wearing a couple of rope ladders, fabricated by the women of Triplicane in twenty-four hours of intensive work. In a moment the Beastlord had looped an end of one of these ladders over a merlon on the nearest parapet, then tossed the rest of the ladder out over the wall, so that the other end, if its length had been correctly calculated, would now be trailing on the ground.

He trusted that the people in the boats were already responding to his noise, and that by now the first troops of the landing were no more than moments from the beach.

Moving rapidly along the top of the wall, edging past a slender watchtower already abandoned by its defenders, Draffut disposed of his second rope ladder in the same manner as the first, and at a distance of some thirty meters from it.

As he was engaged in this operation, an arrow flew at him from somewhere, and stuck in a fringe of his heavy fur, almost between his eyes. It would be too much to expect that he could frighten all of the enemy away, and now some of them were waking up, regaining at least a minimum of courage. It was time for him to see what he might be able to accomplish at ground level, before his advantage of surprise and shock was entirely dissipated.

He let himself over the inner surface of the castle's thick outer wall, hung briefly by his hands, and then dropped into a courtyard. The shock of his huge weight dropping on the bones of his legs and feet was tremendous, but he was almost immune to internal injury of any kind. The powers that enabled him to heal others worked almost automatically within his own body.

From the courtyard where he had landed, a small postern gate opened through the outer wall. It was defended by some guards, and Draffut, three times as tall as a man, moved boldly toward them. He was able to frighten away this gate's defenders with another bellow and a blow of his fist against the wall near them, making the stones quiver. Then he sprawled on his belly to get a good look at the gate. There was an inner gate, a simple affair of wood reinforced with iron bars, and easy enough to pull open. When this was done he lay there groping with one hand beyond the inner gate, into the deep penetration of the wall, until he reached an outer gate and could punch it open too. Now he had provided yet another means of entrance for the attackers.

Meanwhile more arrows were sinking into his fur. And a javelin, hurled by some unseen hand, flew near Draffut as he rolled over and got to his feet again. He looked about him. There were no more gates here to be broken open, but there, at about the second floor level, a stony bartizan pierced with archers' slits looked out over what would otherwise have been a blind expanse of exterior wall. If those openings were enlarged sufficiently, they would provide another means of ingress once the people outside could get a ladder of modest length into position.

Thrusting a finger into one after another of the archers' slits, Draffut willed power into his hand. The stones softened, and one by one the openings dilated until he could pass his whole hand through each of them. The ancient power of the Lake of Life was working in the Beastlord still, and it was capable of temporarily animating even the very stones of a castle wall.

A small swarm of arrows stung his back. Turning round, he was unable to spot his assailants, who were keeping under cover as much as possible, but he did behold a much more welcome sight. The troops of Honan-Fu, in green and gold, were already in small numbers atop the wall where Draffut had just strung up the ladders. More were coming up the ladders all the time, but the attackers were not maintaining their foothold unopposed; already the defenders in red and gray were coming out in comparable numbers to meet them, and the fight was beginning briskly.

Draffut could take no direct part in the fighting, much as he might sympathize with those who were fighting to regain possession of the castle. And now another movement caught his eye—leaning over the parapet that guarded the flat top of the central tower of the castle, two or three human figures were gesturing to him. These were mere signals of encouragement, it seemed. One of the figures he thought was Prince Mark, but he had no time to make sure now, and in any case their identity was not of the first importance.

More wounds, from both javelins and arrows, were accumulating on the tough hide of the Lord of Beasts. The overall effect was increasing pain, though each hurt in itself was scarcely more than a pinprick to him. He paused now to brush from his body some of the hanging weapons whose points had snagged under his skin. At the same moment he saw by torchlight another javelin coming at him, and he blew his breath upon the weapon in midflight. In midair the spear was turned into a giant dragonfly. The creature veered away from Draffut and went darting innocently over the castle wall, going out above the lake. Before it had got so far as the shore, he thought, it would probably revert to inert matter and plunge into the water.

"I must get on with the job," the Beastlord muttered to himself, tearing a moderate accumulation of barbs out of his hide, and wincing with the pain. Yet even as he removed the weapons, more darts assailed him.

Now he went scrambling over one of the comparatively low interior walls of the castle, reaching another coutryard. At the base of a wall there was another gate leading to the outside, this one the main entrance by the docks.

With one wave of his fist Draffut frightened away the knot of soldiers who were gathered just inside this gate. In another moment he had knelt in front of it and knocked it open.

He stopped, staring helplessly at what lay before him, just at the edge of the docks, beneath the fragments of the shattered gate. And suddenly it was as if the world had ended for him, the world in which he had been doing what he could, for many thousands of years, to serve humanity.

What is that I see? What is it? And yet the Lord of Beasts knew only too well what it was. It was just that for a moment he could retain the comfort of being able to refuse belief.

But only for a moment. The God of Healing stood up unsteadily, like a man dead on his feet, so horrified that for the moment he was unaware of what he was doing. More darts, unnoticed, pierced his skin.

There had been a human being, a soldier, standing just on the other side of the last gate when it went down, and the momentum of the bursting gate had spent itself upon him.

Draffut could do nothing but stand motionless, his eyes riveted upon that crumpled, mangled body in its uniform of red and gray. He had just killed a human being. That he had not suspected the presence of the man, had not intended to commit the slaughter, meant nothing to him now.

Then his paralysis broke and he lunged forward, reaching through the gate to seize the lifeless thing and bring it to him with urgent tenderness. Meanwhile a terrible whining howl escaped his lips.

He held the body up with both hands. With all his energy he willed his healing power into it. Meanwhile more arrows, unnoticed, struck him on his flanks and back.

Draffut willed to achieve healing, but this time his powers could not heal. The damage to the small body was too great, death was a finality.

He, Draffut, had killed a human being.

He let the limp and bloody body fall. Then, shrieking out one horrible doglike growl after another, Draffut dragged himself somehow over the castle wall, and fled into the darkness of the lake.

22

ARNFINN was the first to hear the thudding sound.
About two hours had passed since he had entered the hidden rooms at the top of the tower, and an hour since Ninazu had joined him there. Full daylight had long since come outside. Their conversation had taken an increasingly tender turn, and they were in one of the upper rooms, making their way with many sweet pauses toward the bed, when the Sword Arnfinn was wearing began to make a muffled pounding noise. Listening carefully, he needed only a moment to determine that this sound was proceeding in sympathy with a similar pounding that seemed to be coming in through the high windows from outside.

Putting Ninazu gently aside, Arnfinn drew his weapon and stood looking at it in puzzlement. Ninazu's surprise as she gazed at the Sword was even greater. It was as if she had not known until now that her companion was carrying anything like it, but now she was ready to accept the weapon's presence as one more indication of his superlative wizardry.

Then suddenly a man's voice, unnaturally loud, came blasting in through the high windows. "Ho, on the roof!"

"On the roof?" Arnfinn whispered, looking up.

"Ho, there!" The voice blasted in at them again. "This is the master of the castle speaking! Let your ladder down for us at once! You are trapped, and I will show you mercy if you come down now!"

Arnfinn felt himself able to make at least a fair guess as to who those people on the roof were.

"But who is that shouting?" he whispered to Ninazu, perturbed. "Where is he?"

"There is a stair outside, going up the outside of the tower to the roof. But no one out there can see in here." Ninazu frowned. "It sounds like your voice, shouting."

What further comment she might have had on that point Arnfinn never learned. There was a violent explosion somewhere very close outside the windows, followed by a muted outcry. Hardly had Arnfinn's ears ceased ringing from that blast when he could hear whoever was on the stair quietly retreating.

He went on listening, in fear and total bewilderment, without any idea of what was happening now. He could only hope that his fear was not evident to this lady he wanted to help and protect.

This time it was Lady Ninazu who asked the question. "What was *that?*"

"An event of magic," said Arnfinn, swallowing. "Don't worry, I will protect you. Are you all right now?"

"Yes, great lord." She sounded confident in his protection.

"I have decided," he said, and had to pause to swallow again, "decided that it would be well for us to make contact with those people on the roof, whoever they may be."

"Do you think, lord, they will be ready to surrender to you now?"

"Actually it is not surrendering that I had in mind particularly. But I would like to talk to them at least."

Standing on the foot of one of the beds. Arnfinn located the trapdoor in the roof—there was a false panel concealing it, as Ninazu showed him. Arnfinn unlocked the trap, and tried to raise it.

He strained, pushing upward with all his force, but nothing happened. Some weight above was holding the door immobile.

At last, determined to make contact now, he called out. "This is Arnfinn here! I have the Sword of Stealth!" And he hammered on the trapdoor with the pommel of his Sword.

"Arnfinn?" Lady Ninazu questioned gently. "If that is one of your names of power, lord, it will be safe with me."

Arnfinn gave her a sickly smile, knowing that she doubtless saw the cowardly grimace as something else entirely.

Presently there were sounds from overhead as of heavy weights being moved.

At last, when he pushed on the trap again, it swung up.

Gray daylight flooded down into the bedroom. Arnfinn looking up at three people who were standing on the roof, found himself, with some relief, confronting huge Ben and gray Lady Yambu. Zoltan, who had been with them in the grotto, was gone; Arnfinn remembered he had seen him getting ready to row the boat away. But Arnfinn could not recognize the tall, brown-haired man who was now with the familiar pair. Certainly he did not see in this tall man one of the victims who had been pulled nearly dead out of the well some hours ago.

It was plain, from the way the lady and the huge man deferred to this newcomer, that they recognized him as their leader.

Arnfinn glanced back at Ninazu, who was scowling to see Lady Yambu again.

"We heard someone shouting on the stair," Arnfinn opened the conversation lamely.

"Your twin," Mark informed him. The Prince, even familiar as he was with Sightblinder's capabilities, was studying the shape that Arnfinn presented with fascination. "So, you are Arnfinn."

"I am. What of it?"

"Nothing. Never mind. I thank you for whatever contribution you made to helping Honan-Fu and me out of the well."

"That was you?"

Mark nodded. "Yes. I am glad you opened the trap . . . your twin upon the stair just now had Shieldbreaker with him. I suppose you heard what it did to the one weapon we tried against it."

"I heard the sound it made, whatever happened. And this Sword—"

"Performed an imitation, yes. We heard it. A word of advice, though, my friend. Don't use the Sword you have there against Shieldbreaker. Can I trust you not to do so?"

"It would be better," said the big man, "if one of us three had the Sword of Stealth instead."

"I agree," said Mark, his eyes not leaving Arnfinn. "But we should not be fighting this young man—we all have our real enemy to fight."

Mark was thinking back to his own boyhood, when he had run away from a small village, to find himself alone and far from home, with only the terror and beauty of a Sword to keep him company.

"Hard to get rid of, isn't it?" he went on, speaking to Arnfinn gently, indicating the Sword the other carried. "And hard to keep. I know something of how that goes."

"You?" The youth was obviously suspicious of him. "How would you know?"

"I'll tell you about it someday. So, if you refuse to give it up, then keep it. Perhaps you can do as much good with it as we three could. But mind what I have said about the Sword of Force. It'll mow you down like a blade of grass if you go armed against it, whatever weapon you may have in hand."

Ben grumbled privately, and would have tackled the youth again to reclaim Sightblinder, but Mark held his big friend back. The Prince was not going to have their two small groups fighting with deadly effect against each other; and it would be hard to fight against anyone who was using Sightblinder as a physical weapon because you would not be able to tell which way they were swinging or thrusting it.

"Lady Ninazu and I intend to remain in the apartment," Arnfinn called up to them.

"All right. Just as well. We three will keep to the roof for a time; they already know we're here and it lets us see what's going on." Mark hesitated, then called down. "What're you going to do if the real Ancient One finds that tunnel and comes up after you?"

Arnfinn had no ready answer for that. At last he said: "Even if he is proof against the magic of this Sword, the men with him will not be. Am I right?"

"Right."

"Then I will be able to confuse them at least."

Mark added: "Let me say it again. One thing you'd better do if he comes against you with Shieldbreaker, and that's disarm yourself. Your Sword won't help you against that one—he'll see you as you are anyway. But he won't dare attack you if you're disarmed."

Arnfinn nodded, though in his heart he still half suspected this advice might be a trick.

The trapdoor to the roof was closed again, but left unblocked and unlocked. Before this closing, Mark and Ben came down to look the apartment over, and to their satisfaction they found a warclub, hung up as a decoration, that would become an eminently practical weapon in Ben's hands. And before retiring to the roof again, they blockaded the tunnel entrance with a wardrobe. The barrier thus formed would hardly be proof against a determined assault, but would at least serve to give warning that the entrance to the apartment had been discovered.

Left to themselves again, Arnfinn and Ninazu got through the remainder of the day in the hidden rooms of the uppermost interior level of the tower. There was some dried food still in a cabinet, preserved with a touch of magic that left it reasonably flavorful; indeed, it was better than most of the food Arnfinn had eaten during his lifetime. And there was wine, of which he had but little experience, so that it went to his head and left him feeling giddy.

Now that she had come back to this apartment, Ninazu did not want to leave. And Arnfinn was in a way as subject to her enchantment as she was subject to the power of the Sword he carried. Whenever he looked at her, with Sightblinder held tightly in his own hand, he saw a mystery that seemed to him divine. This is, he thought, the mystery of courtly love that minstrels sing about. And I, though only a peasant . . .

When night fell, they quietly locked the trapdoor again, and then spent the night together in one of the beds in one of the highest rooms. Whether it had originally been Ninazu's bed, or Kunderu's, Arnfinn had no idea.

The two of them were roused roughly in the hours before dawn, when the racket of Draffut's invasion awakened the entire castle. Jumping out of bed, the lady and Arnfinn moved from window to window, trying to see what was going on outside, where the sounds of battle were unmistakable.

Then there was a pounding on the locked trapdoor above.

On the morning the battle had started, on a lower level of the castle, Wood rejoiced to see the at-first-mysterious rout of Draffut. This eucatastrophe was closely followed by another stroke of good fortune for the Ancient Master—his griffin had returned, and could now be seen circling in the clear morning sky above the aerie tower.

Wood's first elation at this sight was somewhat dampened by the fact that the beast was riderless.

Running out of his tower, across a first floor roof in the gray light of a clouded morning sky, Wood waved his arms in practiced gestures. The eagle-eyed creature saw him at once, and came gliding swiftly down to land on the low roof near him.

In a moment Wood had reached the griffin's side, and was rifling its saddlebags, in search of a written message from Amintor, or at least some clue as to what might have happened to the general. But there was nothing in the containers, not even the small amounts of food and other supplies that Amintor had had with him on his departure. The general might, of course, have fallen to some kind of enemy action. Or deserted.

Or he might have consumed his supplies, Wood supposed, and then fallen from the beast's saddle at high altitude. If so, that was that. Such an accident would not have been impossible, though decidedly unlikely; the griffin knew that it was supposed to return with the man who had ridden it away.

The griffin now turned its fierce impassive gaze upon its master, who glared back at it in frustration. The beast was possessed of many valuable powers, but those of speech or any other intelligent communication were not among them. The poorest of the small flyers could do better in that regard. For Wood to try to question this mount now would be about as profitable as grilling a riding-beast on what had happened to its human rider.

But the discovery of Amintor's fate, and even that of the expected army of reinforcements, would have to wait. Wood's main consideration at the moment was that he now had the griffin back for his own use. Smiling grimly, he vaulted into the saddle.

By the time Wood got back his griffin, Mark, Ben, and Yambu had changed places with Arnfinn and Ninazu. Mark and his people had gone down from the roof through the trapdoor, meaning to take a more active part in the fighting for the castle, at least to divert part of the defenders' strength.

Arnfinn, with Ninazu at his side, had gone out on the roof to see what was happening, with a vague plan of using the Sword to create a distraction of his own. He was ready to destroy Ninazu's real lover if he could.

There seemed to be fighting everywhere on the walls and in the courtyards below, and as near as Arnfinn could tell, the invaders in green and gold were winning. Before Arnfinn could decide on what false orders he ought to shout, to do his rival the most harm, there was a rushing in the air above him, as of giant wings, and he looked up. He was just in time to see Wood on his griffin come swooping down with intent to destroy the impostor and, if at all possible, capture another extremely useful Sword for himself in the process.

In a moment the griffin had landed on the rooftop. But no sooner had its master leaped from its back, than it flew away again, to circle the tower at a little distance, ignoring his commands to attack the man who stood armed across the diameter of the roof from him. The creature was as confused as any of the humans by the powers of the Sword of Stealth

—the beast did not know which of the two images of Wood it saw on the rooftop was the one it ought to obey. And as one of the two Woods it saw was ordering it to attack the other, it held back in confusion.

Meanwhile, the troops of Honan-Fu were adding to the griffin's difficulties by firing arrows and slinging rocks at it from below.

When Wood leaped off his griffin to the roof, Arnfinn saw facing him the hideous image of a reptilian warrior. The youth recognized the Sword of Force in the hand of this enemy, and heard the deadly thudding he had heard before through the high windows of Ninazu's bedchamber.

Ninazu, who had never seen Wood in his reptilian guise before, looked on this terrible arrival with profound loathing, and a fear that made her shrink closer to Arnfinn.

The half-human warrior ignored her. He looked Arnfinn over as if he could see him perfectly well, with growing, amazed contempt. Then the enemy strode toward him with easy confidence, raising Shieldbreaker casually, as if to strike against some unresisting target.

Arnfinn, with Sightblinder in hand, looked into the inward nature of this enemy, as he had scanned the two thieves on the road so many days ago, and had scrutinized the Prince, and Ninazu herself, a short time past. What he saw now revolted him.

Arnfinn dropped his own weapon as the Prince had told him. Now Sightblinder lay inert upon the stone paving of the roof, and its imitation of the other Sword immediately ceased.

Lady Ninazu had drawn her breath in sharply when Arnfinn cast Sightblinder down. But when Arnfinn turned to her in an agony of concern, he saw to his amazement that she was gazing at him as lovingly as ever, and nodding her approval. In a flash he understood. It was as if she were saying yet again: "A clever trick, my lord. This time you have made this hideous enemy see you as only a gawking peasant. I am sure it is all part of your invincible plan."

But now Wood, finding that he faced an unarmed opponent, retreated a step or two and cast down Shieldbreaker. He dropped the weapon close behind him on the rooftop, safe for the moment from any hands but his. He had heard too many warnings, and he knew better than to try to fight any unarmed man, even this woeful-looking peasant, with the Sword of Force in hand. The Sword would never harm an empty-handed foe, and, by drawing virtually all of Wood's physical strength into itself, would leave him helpless.

As soon as Wood threw down Shieldbreaker, Arnfinn grabbed up the Sword of Stealth again.

Now it was Wood, caught Swordless and unprotected, who for the first time experienced the full effects of Sightblinder's power. He saw the other man, who moved toward him, first as a roiling cloud of thicker demon-smoke than any Akbar or his surviving cohort were likely to produce. From this sight the wizard recoiled, sure for the moment that he once again confronted his ancient foe, the ultimate arch-demon Orcus. Wood stumbled back, and farther back, around the sharp curve made by the encircling parapet. Even as he shrank involuntarily from that image, it altered, the cloud turning pale and becoming laced with inner lightning. And now it seemed to Wood that he was confronted by an avatar of Ardneh himself.

And yet again the advancing image altered. It was that of a mere man now, deceptively ordinary in appearance, who walked on two legs and smiled at Wood and seemed about to give him orders, as he had commanded him of old, orders that the great wizard would be incapable of refusing. It was the image of John Ominor, an emperor of evil memory even to such as Wood.

"I tell you," the image of John Ominor commanded him, "to leave us alone."

Almost, Wood obeyed. Almost. But the sheer ferocity of his inner purpose saved him, kept him from yielding to that command through mindless terror. He stumbled backward.

Then he turned aside to regain Shieldbreaker, which was still lying where he had cast it down. The peasant, seeing this, disarmed himself by hurling Sightblinder at him from behind; the bright steel missed Wood, bounced on the hard roof before him, and skittered away to lie available for the taking. With a lunge Wood darted forward and grabbed up the Sword of Stealth. Magic aside, this one would be a tool with which even awkward hands could kill an unarmed man.

Ninazu, in the background, was calling out encouragement of some kind to her hero—but neither man was really aware of what the lady was now saying.

Then suddenly she had their attention. Now that Wood had Sightblinder in hand, she saw him as her brother Kunderu, and screamed, a scream that distracted both men for a moment.

* * *

Arnfinn now saw two Ninazus. One of them was standing in place and screaming, while the other smiled at him encouragingly as she approached, holding out her arms as if she wanted to give him comfort. Her small white hands were empty. Both Ninazus had the same smudges on face and gown, and the dress of each was torn in precisely the same way. The Sword of Stealth, meanwhile, had completely disappeared, as had Arnfinn's opponent.

The youth realized barely in time what this combination of appearances implied. Ninazu with her soft arms outstretched had almost reached him. He threw himself aside barely in time to dodge the invisible blow of Sightblinder, a blow that lodged the blade firmly in one of the wooden supports of the lookout's shelter.

And then Arnfinn's eye alighted on a Sword, another Sword, that was lying naked on the paving just across the roof's diameter. Running across the roof to grab up Shieldbreaker, Arnfinn looked back over his shoulder and saw his own father standing with his back to Arnfinn, wrenching at something connected with the shelter post, some object that was concealed behind him as he strove with all his might to tear it free—

Arnfinn grabbed up Shieldbreaker, and felt the gently thudding, remorseless power of it flow into his right hand. Now he could see with perfect clarity that it was his reptilian enemy who was struggling to pull loose a Sword, and who now turned to face Arnfinn with Sightblinder in hand.

Wood saw what Arnfinn had picked up, and hastily threw Sightblinder down, disarming himself again almost as soon as he had managed to get the weapon free.

And Arnfinn promptly cast down Shieldbreaker. He felt sure now that was the proper move to make, because he had seen his crafty enemy do it when their positions were reversed.

"I will help you, my love!" cried out Lady Ninazu suddenly, in a strong voice. And, before anyone could move to reach Shieldbreaker again, she had darted near the enemy and grabbed up Sightblinder.

There was an outburst of sound from somewhere below the tower, men's voices cheering, followed by calls for the Ancient One himself to surrender.

But no one on the roof heard that. For the moment it seemed that none of the three people there were capable of moving. Arnfinn was frozen looking at an image of his own father, who stared back at him in utter horror. Then he saw Ninazu as Wood in duplicate. And then Arnfinn saw her briefly as herself, and he could not understand why that should be, while she still held the Sword.

Her gaze swung round to Wood, who was now hesitating as to whether he dared try to make a rush for Shieldbreaker or not. The griffin, crying fiercely, was circling the tower swiftly, coming closer now in rapid orbit.

"You," the multiple, flickering image that was Ninazu said to the wizard. "Gods and demons, I see you clearly now. Clearly at last. How could I ever have—you make me want to puke!"

And then her gaze turned back to Arnfinn. Aided by Sightblinder's second and more subtle power, she was seeing him now, for the first time, for what he really was.

The changing image that was Ninazu shook its head. "Ahhh," was the sound that came from her throat, in a voice that was made up of many voices, and even if there were no words the tones of that sound spoke with great eloquence of utter denial and refusal.

She backed up farther, away from Arnfinn even as he took a step toward her, and farther still, even if it meant climbing up on the parapet behind her.

The Sword slipped from her grasp, and for a moment he saw her clearly. Her long dress tangled her feet and she started to go over.

Arnfinn was halfway across the roof toward the spot where she had disappeared when the claws of the griffin struck him down.

23

THE sun had moved well past noon before the last mopping-up operations had been concluded in the castle. But organized resistance had effectively collapsed much earlier when Wood was seen making good his own escape aboard his griffin, with Shieldbreaker in his hand. Besides the Ancient One himself, probably none of the intruders in red and gray had been able to get away.

Dead and wounded lay everywhere, indoors and outdoors, but none of the other fallen were near Arnfinn where he lay dead on the tower roof. Or near Ninazu, who now, still breathing, lay on a setback only a few stories down.

The victorious Honan-Fu had reached his daughter's side as soon as he was able to do so. Those who had been first to reach her had noted the twisted position in which her body lay, and no attempt had been made to move her.

Honan-Fu was squatting beside her broken body. Sadly, tenderly, fearfully, his hand was stroking his daughter's hair. He had already sent orders to his best physician to come at once and attend Ninazu. But that man was undoubtedly very busy elsewhere, and even if he heard the order and obeyed, it seemed unlikely that human medical care of any kind could make a difference.

The wizard had already helped her as best he could with his own magic. It appeared that in this, as in so much, his magic was not going to be enough.

As time passed, a few other people gathered around the father and daughter, to watch and listen. Ninazu's breathing was harsh and irregular, and her eyes were closed.

"If only," someone inevitably said, "we had Woundhealer here . . ." But of course the Sword of Mercy was nowhere near.

"If only the lord Draffut—" said someone else. And that line of wishing had to be allowed to die also. Draffut had not been seen or heard of since he had fled out into the lake at the height of the battle.

Ninazu's eyes remained closed, even when her father spoke to her. Her body had been covered with a blanket now, up to the chin, but the ominous lines and angles of her broken limbs and body showed through the covering.

Suddenly her father, in an awkward movement, sat back on the roof. He looked a totally exhausted old man, as if his physical energy and his magic had given out at the same time.

"Now my daughter is dying," he announced in a harsh voice. "And I am childless."

No one responded at first. Then Lady Yambu asked quietly: "What about Kunderu?"

Honan-Fu looked over at her as if he did not understand what she was talking about. Then comprehension seemed to dawn on him. He said: "Of course, you were with Ninazu, and listening to her. I suppose she talked about her brother Kunderu; she always did. But Kunderu died two years ago. It was at the same time that she—became ill."

Yambu appeared to understand now. But Zoltan did not. "Became ill?" the young man repeated.

"For the past two years," said the old man sitting on the roof, "her mind has been deranged."

Prince Mark was nearby, resting on one knee. He had carefully moved Sightblinder to a place just in front of him, where he could keep an eye on it. Now the Prince asked Honan-Fu: "She knew that her brother was dead?"

"She knew it, but she could never accept the fact. And at the same time she blamed me. It was more than I could bear, to hear her speak of him as if he were still alive—worse, as if I were holding Kunderu prisoner and punishing him. My son and I had our disagreements, even quarrels, but I never did that. I never could have done that. . . .

"And so, I had the manor on the mainland refurbished as her house. At first she seemed content to live there, or so it was reported to me, though she was always expecting Kunderu to come back to her.

"But it was someone else who came to her instead. The man who had been the real cause of her brother's death—though Ninazu would never believe that. The man who became—no, I cannot call him her lover. He was never that. He used her, that was all. Trying to get at me, to overthrow me. And I was too busy with the academy, and other matters, to discover what was going on. Always, even after Kunderu was dead, I was too busy . . ."

And now at last the eyes of the young woman opened. She did not try to speak, and perhaps she could not move. When she saw whose hand it was that stroked her hair, she turned her gaze away, as if she were looking for someone else.

When Ninazu had finally drawn her last breath, and enough time had passed for all of the survivors to rest as well as they were able, Honan-Fu publicly renewed his offer to take on Mark's son Adrian as an apprentice, when the academy was reopened. The student would of course be charged no fee, in gratitude for the help Prince Mark and his people had given Honan-Fu, and the sufferings they had undergone.

Mark had been expecting some such offer, and had had time in which to prepare a diplomatic answer. The truth was that he had already decided, in his own mind, against ever sending his child into the atmosphere of this place.

A few hours later Lady Yambu, thoughtfully walking in her pilgrim's garb upon the docks at Triplicane, was pondering silently upon the fact that she had been unable to catch even a brief glimpse of the Emperor during his short stay in this locality. She wondered that she felt such real disappointment as she did at the implication that her former lover did not want to see her again.

She was beginning to wonder whether the great downriver journey she had been contemplating had ever really been more than a search for him.

Prince Mark sought out Lady Yambu on the docks and expressed his thanks for her help more fully than he had yet done. Then he asked her: "And do you think, my lady, that you have found here any portion of the truth you sought?"

She considered carefully. "Perhaps I have been able to recognize a bit or two of it. But in any case I plan to go on, down the Tungri."

Mark nodded, unsurprised. "I have heard that the Show of Ensor was seen two days ago, loading itself aboard a couple of barges, to go down the river too. The man in the clown's mask still reportedly in charge."

"Indeed. And have the flying scouts brought any word of Amintor?"

"No word as yet."

Now Zoltan came to join his uncle and the lady on the docks. The young man said that Ben had told him about the mergirl in the Show of Ensor; and he, Zoltan, now asked permission of his Prince to accompany Lady Yambu upon her downstream pilgrimage, in the capacity of bodyguard, or any other way in which she would be pleased to have him. The lady herself, it appeared, had already indicated that he would be welcome.

After thinking the matter over briefly the Prince granted his permission. He said he hoped that Zoltan would return to Tasavalta within a year or two, and would bring with him some useful intelligence about what was going on in the southern regions of the continent. Draffut, before his abrupt departure, had dropped some disquieting hints about developments in that direction. As for Mark himself, though he felt now almost entirely restored to health, he was more than ready to hurry home for a rest in the company of his Princess and his children. He was going to take Sightblinder with him, and he was going to see that suitable compensation for it should be sent to the village of Lunghai.

Ben of Purkinje meanwhile was preparing to return to his own wife and child, in the Tasavaltan capital of Sarykam. But in the course of his preparations Ben paused, more than once, to think over what the Emperor had said to him about Ariane.

THE THIRD BOOK OF LOST SWORDS:
STONECUTTER'S STORY

1

TWO hours before dawn the dreams of Kasimir were disturbed by a soft noise at the tent wall no more than a sword's length from his head. The noise was the distinctive purring, gently snarling sound made by a sharp blade slitting the tough fabric.

Once this sound had been identified somewhere inside the unsleeping portion of Kasimir's brain, the remnants of his dream—a strange adventure involving the gods of the desert, and enormous distances of space and time—went flying off in tatters. Still, complete wakefulness did not come at once. With his eyes open to the partial darkness inside the tent, he saw by the filtering moonlight a figure moving silently. This figure had come in through the tent wall and gone out again by the same route before he who observed it was fully awake. But Kasimir had no doubt that he had seen it, a man's form, looking as slender and dangerous as a scorpion, clad in dark, tight-fitting clothes, face wrapped for concealment. Nor had he any doubt, when this apparition went gliding smoothly out through the wall of the tent again, that it was carrying a long bundle wrapped in rough cloth, held tightly under its right arm.

Kasimir sat up straight. He was alone in the tent now. No one else was sleeping in it tonight. Though it was quite large, much of the space inside was taken up by the more valuable portions of the caravan's cargo.

The intruder certainly hadn't been Prince al-Farabi, leader of the caravan. Nor was Kasimir able to identify that mysterious form as any of the Prince's followers who had been traveling with him across the desert. Then who—?

Almost fully awake at last, Kasimir leaped to his feet. Just at that moment an outcry of alarm was sounded at no great distance outside the tent. He dashed for the door but it was tied loosely shut, as was usual at night, and undoing the knots delayed him briefly.

Hardly had he got out into the open air before he collided with a figure running toward the tent.

"Thieves!" the other man shouted, right in Kasimir's face. "Robbers! Awake! Arouse and arm yourselves!"

Judging by the growing uproar, the other thirty or forty occupants of the camp were already doing just that. Other voices were shouting alarm from the perimeter. Men poured out of the half-dozen sleeping tents, and weapons flashed in the light of rising flames. Smoldering cookfires and watchfires were being quickly rekindled. Lieutenant Komi, second-in-command to the Prince during this journey, trotted past Kasimir, barking orders to his men. And now, in the middle of all this half-controlled turmoil, strode the Prince himself with his robes flying behind him. Al-Farabi was tall and dark and at the moment a menacing figure with scimitar in hand. He was demanding to know where the alarm had started.

Kasimir confronted him. "Prince, an intruder was in the cargo tent, where I was sleeping! He came through the wall. I—I wasn't in time to stop him—"

"What?" In a moment Prince al-Farabi had sprung to the side of the tent where the cloth had been slit. This was on the side opposite from the normal entrance, whose flap was now hanging open after Kasimir's exit. In the fabric of the tent's rear wall, Kasimir saw now, were two vertical slits, one right beside the other, only a couple of handspans apart. Of course, it must have been their cutting that had awakened him.

The Prince stepped into the tent through the largest of these rents, which was a full meter long.

Peering in through the same aperture, Kasimir saw, by the torchlight that glowed in through the walls, the tall man bending over the heap of baggage that occupied the center of the tent's interior. For a few moments the Prince tossed things about, obviously in search of something. Then al-Farabi straightened up to his full height, giving a great wordless cry as of bereavement.

Kasimir followed the Prince into the tent through its new entrance. "Sir, what's wrong?"

"It is gone." The face al-Farabi turned to the younger man was ghastly in the muted glow of firelight entering the tent from outside. The Prince appeared to be swaying on his feet. Almost shouting, he repeated: "It is gone!"

"I saw a man inside the tent with me when I woke up," Kasimir stammered, repeating the little information he could give. "He went out carrying a long bundle under one arm. I started to give the alarm but by then he was already gone."

Groaning unintelligibly, the Prince stumbled past Kasimir and out of the tent through its normal doorway. Again Kasimir followed.

Shouts coming from guards at the perimeter of the camp now reassured everyone that the animals were well and none of them had been stolen. But a moment later a new alarm was sounded. One of the guards, who had been posted nearest to the tent where Kasimir slept, had just been discovered lying motionless in the sand.

"Bring him here beside the fire!" Kasimir ordered sharply. "And one of you fetch my kit from the tent." It was the automatic reaction of a trained physician to a medical emergency. In a moment three men came carrying the fallen one, and laid him down on clean sand in the firelight.

The physician went to work. He found that the victim was certainly alive, and a preliminary examination disclosed no sign of serious injury. Kasimir hardly had a chance to begin a more detailed investigation when the man began to stir and grimace, moaning and rubbing the back of his head.

"Someone must have struck me down from behind," the young tribesman murmured weakly, trying to sit up.

"Sit still." Kasimir's exploring fingers found no blood, or even any noticeable lump. "All right, I suppose you'll live. Doubtless the hood of your robe saved you from worse damage."

Aware that the Prince had approached again and was standing beside him, Kasimir turned to repeat this favorable report. But then the young physician let the words die on his lips. The tall figure of al-Farabi, wild-eyed, stood gesturing with both arms in the burgeoning firelight. "The Sword is gone!" the Prince shouted in a despairing voice. It was as if the full enormity of his loss was still growing on him. "The treasure has disappeared!"

While others gathered around, Kasimir stood up from beside the fallen guard and moved still closer to the desert chieftain. In a voice that tried to be soothing he asked: "You mentioned a sword, sir. But how valuable was it? I had no idea that we were carrying any—"

"Of course you had no idea! Of course!" The tall man cast back his hood and pulled his hair. "The presence of Stonecutter was intended to be a secret."

"The presence of—"

"Of a Sword, the Sword of Siege itself! A priceless weapon! It was loaned to me by my trusting friend Prince Mark. And now it is gone. Argh! May all the gods and demons of the desert descend upon me and snuff out my worthless life!"

"The Sword of Siege," breathed Kasimir. "It is one of the Twelve, then." And suddenly the extreme dismay of the Prince was understandable.

Practically everyone in the world knew of the Twelve Swords, though comparatively few people had ever seen one of them. They were legendary weapons, for all that they were very real. They had been forged by the god Vulcan himself more than thirty years ago, in the days before the gods—or most of them at least—had disappeared.

Kasimir wanted to ask how the Sword of Siege had come to be traveling with them, in this rather ordinary little caravan—but that was not properly any of his business. Instead he asked: "Is it possible to overtake the thief?"

"Already I have sent some of my swiftest riders in pursuit," said al-Farabi, who was now standing with his face buried in his hands, while his own people gathered round him in dumb awe. "But to find and follow a trail at night . . . we will of course do all that we can, but I fear that the Sword is gone. Oh, woe is me!"

While Kasimir and others watched him helplessly, the desolation of the Prince became more intense and at the same time more theatrical. He tore at his hair and his garments, saying: "How will I ever be able to face Prince Mark again? What can I tell him? Even the worth of all my flocks and all my lands would scarcely afford him adequate compensation."

"Prince Mark?" Kasimir could think of nothing more intelligent to say at the moment; still, he felt that it was up to him to reply. All of the Prince's own people who were watching looked slightly embarrassed, and he had the impression that al-Farabi's outburst of grief was increasingly directed toward him.

The Prince had paused and was regaining a minimum of composure. In a milder voice he said: "Know then, my young friend, that my great friend Prince Mark of Tasavalta, despite many misgivings on his part, was generous enough to loan me secretly the Sword called Stonecutter. Why, you ask? I will tell you. In one far corner of my domain, hundreds of kilometers from here, there is a nest of robbers that has proven all but impossible to eradicate, because of the nature of the rocky fastness in which they hide. With the Sword of Siege in hand, to undermine a crag or two would be no great problem—but now the Sword is gone from out of my hands, and I am the most miserable of men!"

Kasimir felt moved to compassion. Ever since they had first encountered each other, a month ago, al-Farabi had been a most kindly and generous host, willing to provide an insignificant stranger with free passage across the desert.

"Is there anything that I can do to help you, Prince?" the physician asked. Though he had never visited Tasavalta, he knew it was a land far to the northeast, bordering on the Eastern Sea, and he had heard that its rulers were respected everywhere.

"I fear that there is nothing anyone can do to help me now. I fear that I will never see the Sword again." al-Farabi turned away, seemingly inconsolable.

Gradually the excitement in the camp quieted. With a double guard now posted, the fires were allowed to die down once more. An hour before dawn the riders who had been sent in pursuit of the thieves came back, reporting in Kasimir's hearing that they had had no success. When daylight came they would of course try again.

Kasimir, lying awake in his blankets in the cargo tent, hearing the extra guards—now that it was too late—milling around outside, thought that few members of the caravan were likely to get any more sleep during the last hour of the night. But at last, after vexing his drowsy mind with the apparently minor, pointless, and insoluble problem of why the tent wall had been slit twice—one gash was only a minor one, not really big enough for anyone to crawl through—he dozed off himself.

His renewed sleep was naturally of short duration, for at first light the camp began to stir around him once again. As soon as full dawn came, al-Farabi sent out a different pair of trackers. Then he ordered camp broken, and, with the remainder of his men, his passenger Kasimir, and the laden baggage animals, pushed on along the caravan's intended route toward the Abohar Oasis and, a day or two beyond that, the city of Eylau.

Choosing to ride side by side with the young physician, the Prince explained that his men as well as their animals needed to rest and replenish their supply of water at the oasis before undertaking what promised to be a lengthy pursuit into the wilderness. And al-Farabi himself appeared even more fatalistically certain than before that the Sword was permanently gone.

The conversation between the two men faded, and most of the day was spent in grim and silent journeying. The pace was steady and there were few pauses. In late afternoon tall palms came into view ahead, surrounded by a sprawling burst of lesser greenery. They had arrived at Abohar Oasis.

Several other groups of travelers, Kasimir observed, were here ahead of them; indeed he thought that there would probably be someone resting here almost continuously. He had already learned it was an unwritten rule that peace obtained in the oases, and that the rule was usually observed even when bitter enemies encountered one another. Water was shared, fighting rescheduled for some other time and place.

On this occasion, there was certainly shade and water in plenty for all, and no question of fighting. The Prince gave no sign that he observed any enemies of his Firozpur tribe among the people who were already resting at the oasis—and as for Kasimir, he was not aware of having an enemy anywhere in the world.

As soon as the caravan had halted the Prince directed his people, working for once in shade, as they busied themselves seeing to the animals, and laying out their campsite for tonight. Meanwhile Kasimir, wanting to enjoy a walk in the grateful shade himself, left them temporarily and went exploring.

He moved along cool, well-worn footpaths bordered by grass and shrubs, between inviting pools. Eventually, having chosen the largest and deepest pool of the oasis to quench his thirst, he noticed as he approached it that on the far side of the pool, upon a little knoll of grass, there stood a richly furnished tent. Though it was no bigger than a small room, such a pavilion obviously belonged to someone of considerable social stature if not of great wealth.

Kasimir threw himself down upon a little ledge of rock at the near edge of the pool to drink. As he finished and arose, wiping his lips, there arrived near him at poolside a woman from some tribe whose dress Kasimir was unable to identify. As she was filling her water jar, he questioned her as to whether any single traveler, or pair of them perhaps, had arrived at the oasis since last night.

She answered in a melodious voice. "No, I am sure, sir, that your party is the first to arrive today."

"How do you know?"

"My family has been keeping watch on every side, for some kinfolk who are to meet us here."

"I see. By the way, whose tent is that across the pond? Have you any idea?"

"Certainly." The woman seemed surprised at Kasimir's ignorance. "That is the tent of the Magistrate Wen Chang. He has been here for several days."

Kasimir blinked at her. *"The* Wen Chang?"

The young woman laughed again. "There is only one Wen Chang that I know of. Only one that anyone knows of. From what remote land have you come that you do not know him?"

"I know of him, certainly." Now the conviction was growing in Kasimir's mind that it was, or ought to be, somewhat below the dignity of a physician to stand here debating with a girl who had been sent to fetch water. He turned and started round the pool, ignoring a smothered giggle behind him.

The tent ahead of him was silent as he approached it, the entrance flap of silken fabric left half open. If this pavilion were really occupied by the legendary Wen Chang, then it appeared that the gods might be favoring Prince al-Farabi and his friends with a matchless opportunity.

The Magistrate Wen Chang was a renowned judge, whose fame had spread far from his homeland, which lay well to the south of the desert. In the more fanciful (as Kasimir supposed) stories, Wen Chang was credited with the ability to see into the secret hearts of men and women. It was said that he knew, as soon as he laid eyes on any group of people, which of them were innocent and which were guilty. It was even alleged —Kasimir had heard this variation once—that the Magistrate could tell, just by staring at the thief, where stolen treasure had been hidden. But Kasimir had never heard that the famed Wen Chang was wont to travel as far as this from his usual base of operations.

When Kasimir was still a score of strides from the tent's doorway, the flap opened fully and a tall, imposing man emerged from the dim interior. He was dressed for desert traveling in a gray robe, almost plain enough to be that of a pilgrim.

If this was indeed Wen Chang, he was a younger-looking man than Kasimir had expected, with black hair and a proud narrow mustache still quite innocent of gray; but there was that in his bearing that convinced Kasimir he was indeed confronting the famed Magistrate. From his elevation upon the little knoll the tall man squinted through narrowed eyes in Kasimir's direction; then he ignored the approaching youth and went unhurriedly to the edge of the pool, where he knelt down and with a silver cup scooped up a drink.

Meanwhile Kasimir had come to a stop about ten strides away, where he stood waiting in an attitude of respect.

Presently the tall man rinsed his cup, hurling water from it in a little silver spray, and rose unhurriedly to his full height. His eyes, turned again on Kasimir, were remarkably black. It seemed to the young man that those eyes glittered whenever they were not squinted almost shut.

Kasimir cleared his throat. "Have I the honor of addressing the Magistrate Wen Chang?"

"It is my name. And that was formerly my office." The voice was precise, and spoke the common tongue with a slight accent of a kind Kasimir had seldom heard before. "Whether you are honored by the mere fact of talking to me is something you must decide for yourself."

"Honored sir, I am honored. And I really think that the kindly fates have sent you here. Or they have sent me here to meet you. There is a matter in which your help is greatly needed."

"So?" The tall man eyed the youth intently for a moment. Then he said: "I believe this grassy bank provides a finer seat than any of the pillows in my pavilion. And out here the view is finer too. Let us make ourselves comfortable and I will hear your story. Mind you, I promise nothing more than a hearing."

"Of course, sir, of course." Kasimir let the older man choose a spot to sit down first, then cast himself down on the grass nearby. "Let me think—where to begin? Of course, forgive me, my name is Kasimir."

"And you are on your way to Eylau, to seek employment through the White Temple there."

"Yes, I—" Kasimir forgot his hope of making a good impression so far as to let his jaw drop open. "How could you possibly know that?"

The other made a gesture of dismissal. "My dear young man, I did not know it, but the probabilities were with me. The size and arrangement of the pouches you wear at your belt—the cloth container for drugs, the lizard-skin for items thought to have some potency in magic

—these identify you as a physician, or at least as one who has some pretensions of skill in the healing arts. Certain other details of your appearance indicate that you have already been more than a few days in the desert—therefore you are now traveling toward the city, which is only two days' march from here, and not away from it. And once an itinerant physician has arrived in Eylau, where would he most likely go, but to the White Temple of Ardneh, a clearinghouse for jobs in his profession?"

"Ah. Well, of course, sir, when you put it that way, your deduction seems only reasonable."

" 'Only,' did you say?" The Magistrate sighed. "But never mind. What is this most disturbing problem?"

Listening to the hastily outlined story to the theft, Wen Chang allowed his epicanthic eyes to close almost as if in sleep. Only slight changes of expression, tensions playing about the thin-lipped mouth, indicated to Kasimir that his auditor was still awake and indeed listening intently.

Kasimir in his relation of the events of the previous night had just reached the point where he had begun his examination of the stunned guard when the Magistrate's eyes opened, fixing themselves alertly at a point over Kasimir's left shoulder.

The young man turned to look behind him. Prince al-Farabi, walking alone, his eyes looking haunted and wary, was advancing toward them along the shaded path beside the pool.

Kasimir jumped to his feet and hastened to perform introductions. The two eminent men greeted each other with every indication of mutual interest and respect.

Then Kasimir announced: "I have taken it upon myself, Prince, to appeal to the Magistrate here for his help in recovering the missing Sword."

Once more al-Farabi demonstrated grief. "Alas! I fear the treasure has gone beyond even the power of Wen Chang to bring it back—but of course I would welcome any chance of help."

"Having just undertaken a long journey which came to naught," said Wen Chang, "and being in no particular hurry to return to my former place of service—there have been political changes there, which I find unwelcome—I have been waiting for two days at this oasis, in hopes of receiving some sign from the Fates to direct me. It appears to me that your problem may well be the sign I have been looking for. I have long been an admirer of Prince Mark of Tasavalta, though I have never met him; for that reason alone I would like to see that his property is recovered. Also, from what I have heard of this problem so far, there are certain aspects of it that are intrinsically interesting."

"Thank you, sir!" Kasimir cried.

"Almost," said al-Farabi, "you allow me to begin to hope again!" He wiped his forehead with the edge of his robe.

A few minutes later, the three men were seated more formally if no more comfortably inside the larger pavilion of the Prince, which by now had been erected in cool shade at the other side of the oasis from the pavilion of Wen Chang.

Here inside the Prince's tent, with a small cup of spiced wine in hand, Wen Chang began to ask questions, probing into one detail after another of the disappearance of the Sword.

"In what sort of container was the Sword carried? And why was it stored in that particular tent when the caravan stopped?"

"It was wrapped in blue silk, and that in turn in coarse gray woolen cloth, that it might seem an ordinary bundle and attract no special attention. And when we stopped for the night the Sword was always placed, in a pile with certain other pieces of baggage, in the same tent as my valued passenger here, who has been passing through my domain under my protection. I had no reason to believe that tent less safe than any other. Rather the contrary, as it was near the center of our small encampment."

"Nothing else was stolen last night? From that tent or any other?"

"Nothing."

"And was the pile of baggage in the tent disturbed?"

"It was very little disarranged, or perhaps not at all; until I began to search through it in hopes that the Sword might still be there. Alas!"

Wen Chang sat back in his nest of pillows. "Then it would appear that the thief, or thieves, knew just what they wanted, and where to lay hands upon it."

"So it would appear, yes." And al-Farabi once more raised his hands to hide his face.

Kasimir tried to reassure him. "They might have been—I suppose it is likely that they were—helped by powerful magic. Perhaps even the magic of one of the other Twelve Swords. Wayfinder, say, or Coinspinner. I have never seen those Swords but either of them, as I understand the tales, may be an infallible guide to locating some desired object."

"Then would that we had them both in hand today!" the Prince cried out.

Wen Chang was nodding thoughtfully. "That the thieves had either of those Swords is a possibility, I suppose. Or some lesser magic might well have been strong enough to let the robbers find what they wanted. Was any wizard traveling with you?"

"None, Magistrate." Al-Farabi shook his head. "I am a simple man of the desert, who lives more by the sword than the spell. With such trivial magical powers as I myself possess, I have of course already tried to get Stonecutter back. But as I say, I am no wizard. I suppose you will be able to bring to bear much stronger spells and incantations?"

"Probably not."

The Prince blinked at him. "Sir?"

"I prefer to rely upon a stronger tool even than magic."

"And what might that be, Magistrate?"

"Intelligence, my friend. Intelligence." The Magistrate drank spiced wine, and sighed, pleasurably. He moved a trifle on his pillows, like a man settling himself to play a round of some congenial game. "Now tell me. Who, before your caravan set out, knew that you were carrying Stonecutter with you?"

"Among my own people, only myself and Lieutenant Komi, the commander of the escort—and I would trust Komi as I trust myself. Our fathers were blood brothers, and I have known him all his life."

"*I* certainly had no inkling of the Sword's presence with the caravan," Kasimir put in.

Wen Chang nodded slightly at him, prolonged the look appraisingly for a moment, then returned his narrow-eyed gaze to the Prince. "And who, not among your people, would have known that you were carrying Stonecutter with you?"

Al-Farabi took time to give the question serious thought. "Well—the only people I can think of would be the Tasavaltans who delivered the Sword to me at the other edge of my domain. They were three, including Prince Mark himself, and one of his chief wizards, and the strong man called Ben of Purkinje. It was plain to see that the Prince trusted his companions as thoroughly as I trust Komi. And why would a man connive to steal his own Sword?"

The Magistrate was frowning. "There might be several answers to that question. If there is a good answer in this case, it is not immediately obvious. No doubt other people in Tasavalta might have known that the Sword was being loaned to you?"

"No doubt."

"Then, for the moment at least, this line of inquiry seems unproductive. Let us try another."

Al-Farabi, sitting with his head bowed again, said through his hands: "As soon as we have replenished our supplies and rested, we will return to the desert and try again to track the thief—or thieves. But I fear that the Sword of Siege is lost."

Wen Chang nodded. "And I fear that you may well be right. Still, the situation is not utterly hopeless, even if your pursuit through the desert should fail."

"It is not?"

"No. Not utterly. Consider—what will a thief do with such a treasure when it falls into his hands?"

"He'll most likely want to sell it, I suppose," Kasimir put in.

The narrowed eyes of the Magistrate turned on him again. "Almost certainly he will. And where would anyone go to sell an item of such value?"

Kasimir shrugged. "Why—he'll go to the metropolis, of course, to Eylau. There's no city of comparable size for a thousand kilometers in any direction."

"It would be more accurate to say for several thousand kilometers. Yes, I shall be surprised if our robber has not turned his steps toward Eylau already."

Al-Farabi was frowning. "But such traces of a trail as we were able to find by moonlight led out into the desert in the opposite direction from the city."

"That, I think, is hardly conclusive."

"I suppose not."

"Certainly not." Wen Chang drank spiced wine. He nodded. "If I am to continue my investigation I shall do so in Eylau."

"By all means—by all means." The Prince appeared to be doing his best to look politely hopeful. "Will you require money for expenses?—but yes, of course you will. And naturally I will provide it, in advance. And in addition a great reward, a thousand gold coins or the equivalent, if you are successful."

Wen Chang raised an eyebrow at the extravagant size of the reward. Then he bowed slightly in his seated position. "Both provisions will certainly be welcome. The expenses because I shall be proceeding as a private investigator, with no official status in this land, and the purchase of information—not to mention a bribe or two—may be essential. I presume that, although you will of course organize a pursuit, a part of your caravan will be going on into the city?"

"Yes. The remaining goods that my caravan is carrying must be delivered there, as well as our passenger. Meanwhile I, with some of my swifter riders, will endeavor to follow the thieves and overtake them— there is nothing else I can do."

"Of course not—how many men are you going to send into the city, then?"

Al-Farabi took thought. "Perhaps a dozen. That should be an adequate guard for my passenger and my cargo for the remainder of the journey."

"Good. When those dozen men have seen your remaining freight— and your passenger, of course—safely to their destination—by the way, I suppose there are no more Swords still with you? Or any comparable treasures?"

"No, nothing at all like that."

"I see. Then, when your dozen men who are going on to the city have seen to the safe disposal of your remaining goods, will you place those men at my disposal? Since I will be unable to call upon official forces in Eylau, it may be necessary at some stage to use a substitute."

"Of course—I shall place a dozen men, with Lieutenant Komi at their head, at your command." The Prince paused delicately. "You realize I cannot be sure of the attitude of the Hetman, who rules the city, toward such a private army. I do not know him."

"Nor do I. But a dozen men are hardly an unusually large bodyguard for a rich merchant, and many such must pass in and out of Eylau. And even if my true mission should become known to the Hetman, well, thieftakers are welcome in most cities."

"Then of course you may have the guard. And for your expenses, all the proceeds for the merchandise when it is delivered—may all the gods help you to recover and retain the Sword!"

2

SHORTLY after dawn on the following morning, Kasimir stood under tall palms beside the Magistrate, watching while al-Farabi and about two-thirds of his men finished packing up their tents, mounted their rested animals, and rode back out into the desert in the direction from which they had come yesterday.

Wen Chang's pavilion had already been struck, and his temporary servant dismissed. It only remained for him and Kasimir to mount their own riding-beasts and start out in the direction of Eylau, which was still two days' travel distant. Travelers going in that direction followed an obvious and well-traveled road that could hardly lead to anywhere but the great city. Lieutenant Komi, calling orders now and then to his comparatively small detachment of Firozpur troopers, rode a few meters behind Kasimir and Wen Chang. Eleven soldiers, looking fierce and capable, followed their officer today, with the pack animals bearing the caravan's cargo bringing up the rear. Among the cargo were a few latticework crates containing winged messengers, small birdlike creatures used as couriers. Al-Farabi had ordered his officer to let him know immediately of any and all developments affecting the search for his lost Sword in the great city.

Wen Chang opened the morning's conversation with his younger companion in a pleasant way, speculating on the nature of the city they were approaching, a metropolis neither of them had ever seen before. Soon Kasimir had been put thoroughly at ease. He found himself telling the older man more of his background, ending with the recent chain of more or less commonplace events which found him now on his way to the White Temple in Eylau, where the temple's usually efficient placement service would more than likely be able to help him find a good place in which to practice medicine.

Their conversation gradually faded, but the ensuing silence possessed a comfortable and companionable quality. Presently, when no words had been exchanged for some time, Wen Chang brought out a folded paper from somewhere in his traveler's robe; he unfolded this paper into a map, and squinted at it between glances at the ascending sun and the empty land around them.

"I suppose you are an experienced traveler, Magistrate."

"Not as experienced as I should like to be. To enter a strange land is to be presented with a vast and intricate puzzle."

By now they had been about two hours on their way. Wen Chang, map still in hand, muttered something and suddenly turned his mount aside from the well-traveled way. Making a detour to his right, he went riding for the top of a sizable hill that rose no more than a hundred meters from the road.

Kasimir turned his mount too, and followed, completely in the dark as to the purpose of this detour. Glancing back, he saw Lieutenant Komi, his expression stoic and incurious, bringing his men and the pack animals along.

At the top of the barren hill the leader halted, and then the whole group followed. From this vantage point there was nothing to be seen but more desert in every direction. Still Wen Chang sat his mount for what seemed to Kasimir a long time, his eyes narrowed to slits against the wind, and shaded under the folded gray hood of his desert robe. He was intently scanning the empty landscape on all sides.

Twice, as the silence lengthened, Kasimir almost broke into it with a curious question, but he forbore. He was for the third time just on the point of yielding to curiosity when Wen Chang spoke at last.

"The place where the Sword was stolen, according to the information given me by yourself and Prince al-Farabi, is a long way from the city. Too far, probably, for anyone to travel without stopping to renew his supply of water. And even if our thief's destination was not Eylau, he would still most likely need to obtain water somewhere in this region." The Magistrate paused. "But he did not come to Abohar Oasis for water while I was encamped there. The people there discussed each new arrival, whether by day or night. Therefore . . ."

"Yes sir?"

"Therefore he sought out another source of water, somewhere in this region."

"May I see the map, sir?" Gripping the paper tightly in the wind when the Magistrate handed it over, Kasimir pored over it for a few moments. Then he announced: "According to this there are no other oases or springs in the area we are considering."

"Exactly. Therefore . . ."

"Yes?"

There was no immediate answer from Wen Chang, who was still staring into the blue heat-shimmer that ruled the far horizon, but now had fixed the direction of his eyes. Following the aim of the Magistrate's gaze, Kasimir was at last able to make out what looked like traces of white smoke, or more likely dust, hanging in the distant air. He thought that if that dust indicated the presence of a body of people or animals, their movement must be very slow. The cloud, as far as he could tell, was remaining in the same place.

Wen Chang turned in his saddle. "Lieutenant Komi, have we reserves of water enough to safely take a side trip? An excursion as far as yon dust cloud?"

Komi, working his mount a little closer to them, squinted into the distance under the shade of a sunburnt hand. "Looks like that little cloud might be half a day's travel from here. But if Your Excellency wishes us to make such an excursion, water is no problem. Our supplies are ample." His tone was neutral, giving away no more than his expression did; it was impossible to tell what he thought of the advisability of taking such a side trip.

"Then we will do it." And Wen Chang immediately urged his mount down the side of the hill away from the road.

Midday gave way to afternoon as they traveled. Kasimir sipped sparingly at his canteen, and chewed on some dried meat and fruit. There was a stop to freshen the animals' mouths with water. In the hours since they had left the direct road to Eylau the country had changed, become more merciless, with smooth desert giving way to low crags and boulders and broken outcroppings of black rock. Here and there the landscape opened before the animals' hooves in a sudden crevice, compelling a detour. But gradually the wisps of white dust in the sky grew closer.

Komi's estimate of half a day for this side journey had been only a little too large. But eventually the source of the dust was near enough for them to identify it: a gang of laborers, several score of them, who toiled like well-disciplined ants in the hot sun, under the direction of whip-cracking overseers.

Before the investigators reached the work site, they came upon the recent product of the workers' labor. It was a road that did not show on the map, obviously newly made. It was a real road, suitable even for wheeled vehicles, as opposed to a mere trail through the landscape, and plainly its making had not been an easy or a pleasant task. As Wen Chang and his party began to follow the road, moving now at increased speed, Kasimir noted where minor crevices in the earth had been filled in, and a steep-sided arroyo bridged with rude stonework, leaving a passage under the bridge for rushing floodwaters when they came as occasionally they must.

The road's winding course among protruding rocks led Wen Chang and his followers inexorably toward the crew who still labored to extend it. But before the road drew very near the place where its creators were now toiling, it had to turn and run patiently along the side of a ridge. The ridge was a mass of sharp rock twice the height of a man, offering no soft spots to cut through, and no gentle slopes to offer a start for ramp-building. Then without warning the road turned again, almost at right angles, cutting straight and level through the obstacle.

Just as the Magistrate was approaching the smooth-sided cut driven through the rock, he stopped suddenly and held up a hand, halting his small cavalcade behind him. By now the workers on the far side of the ridge were so close that their metal tools, probably steel and magically hardened bronze, could be heard clinking against rock. A dozen or more of the laborers were chanting in surprisingly hearty voices as they worked.

So far there was no sign that anyone among the road-building crew had become aware of the approach of Wen Chang and his party.

A moment after Wen Chang reined in his riding-beast he had dismounted, and was closely inspecting the sides of the cut. Whatever he saw made him nod with satisfaction.

In an instant Kasimir had dismounted too, and was standing mystified beside the older man. But the young physician's puzzlement was only momentary.

"These are strange marks in the ridge," he breathed, with something like awe. "Long and smooth and easy, like those a knife or an ordinary sword might make in cheese or butter. I take these marks to mean that the Sword called Stonecutter has been used on this rock." And he gave Wen Chang a glance of open admiration.

"Exactly so." Wen Chang looked around, and it seemed to Kasimir for a moment that the Magistrate was almost purring with satisfaction. "Lieutenant," Wen Chang ordered, "send a few of your men secretly around to the other side of this work camp. If anyone should attempt to sneak out that way when we enter, detain them, whether they are carrying a Sword or not, and bring them to me."

The lieutenant had made no comment on the discovery of the Sword's marks in the cut rock, though Kasimir thought he could hardly have failed to be impressed. Now Komi saluted and turned back to his small column to deliver some low-voiced orders.

Presently Wen Chang remounted, and, with Kasimir beside him, and Lieutenant Komi, now attended by only seven troopers, supporting him in the rear, rode boldly forth, through the divided ridge, along the just-completed last hundred meters of the road in the direction of the laborers' camp. In a moment the first of the scores of workers had become aware of their approach, and the sounds of labor faltered. But almost at once the whips of several overseers cracked, and the chink of metal on stone picked up again.

From the square of shade produced by a square of faded cloth supported on rude poles, a foreman was now coming forward to receive his visitors. He was a corpulent man of modest height and middle age, wearing over his tunic a broad leather belt with an insignia of the Hetman's colors, gray and blue. He looked worried, not unreasonably, at the sight of all these armed men in the garb of desert warriors, who outnumbered his small staff of overseers. Still, he managed to put a bold tone into his salutation.

"Greetings, gentlemen! Our road, as you see, is not yet complete. But if you are willing to wait a few days, my brave men here and I will do our best to finish it for you."

Wen Chang squinted into the shimmering reach of emptiness extending to the horizon ahead of the road-builders, and allowed himself a smile. "My good man, if you continue to labor to such good effect as you did when cutting your way through this ridge behind me—why then I have no doubt that a few more days should see you at your destination, whatever it may be. What is it, by the way?"

The smile had congealed unhappily upon the foreman's beefy face. "I am given only a general direction, sir, in which we are to extend the road. Beyond that—" He shrugged.

"Of course, of course. It does not matter. My name is Wen Chang, and my companion here is Doctor Kasimir, a physician; and this is Lieutenant Komi, who with his soldiers serves Prince al-Farabi of the Firozpur. And your name is—?"

"I am honored indeed to meet all Your Excellencies! I am Lednik, foreman of this gang of the Hetman's road-builders, and holding the rank of supervisor both of the Hetman's prisons and his roads." Having bowed deeply, Lednik looked up suddenly and slapped both palms upon his leather belt. "Ho, there! Keep those fellows working! No one has told any of you to stop for a vacation!"

These last admonitions were directed at one of the supervisors, and a moment later a loud whipcrack detonated in the air above some workers' back; the sounds of work, that had once more slackened, hurriedly picked up. Kasimir, looking at the laborers, thought they looked a miserable lot—as who would not, wearing chains and doing heavy labor under the lash?—but still they were better off than some prisoners he had seen, at least well-enough fed and watered. Apparently the Hetman of Eylau and his supervisors were more interested in getting their roads built than they were in mere sadistic punishment.

He realized that Lednik the foreman was looking at him now. With a different kind of smile, and a small salute, the man asked: "Did I understand correctly, sir, that you are a physician? A surgeon too, perhaps?"

"I have a competence in both fields. Why?"

"Sir, a couple of my workers are injured. If it would not be too much trouble for you to look at them—? I appeal to you in charity."

"It would not be too much trouble." Kasimir, grateful for a break in the day's ride, got down from his riding-beast and began to unstrap the medical kit that rode behind his saddle.

"They will be thankful, sir, and so will I. Here, any man who cannot work is useless, and we can spare no food or water for those who remain useless for very long."

"I see. Well, show me where these injured workers are. I will do what I can for them."

Working under another simple shade-cloth that served here as the hospital, Kasimir put a splint and a padded bandage on one man's broken finger. After administering a painkiller he swiftly amputated that of another which looked beyond healing. According to their stories, simple clumsiness had wounded both. With bandaged hands and pain-killing salve, both men ought to be able to return soon to some kind of productive work, and indeed they both got to their feet at once, ready to make the effort.

From some muttered remarks among other prisoners who were getting a drink nearby, Kasimir understood that any injuries perceived as seriously and permanently disabling were treated on the spot with execution. There would be no malingering tolerated in this gang, and no benefit to be derived from self-inflicted wounds. Here, a crippling wound was a ticket to the next world, not back to a shaded prison cell in Eylau.

Meanwhile Wen Chang had accepted the hospitality of the foreman's own square of shade. Seated there in the foreman's own rude chair, sipping at a cup of cool water, he had also engaged the man in casual-sounding conversation.

"Unfortunately," Kasimir heard the Magistrate say when he was able to join him again, "we cannot wait for the completion of this road, however efficiently you may be able to accomplish it."

"Then what can I do for Your Excellency?" Lednik seemed to be doing an imitation of a certain kind of shopkeeper, all anxiety to please.

"You can," said the Magistrate in a soft voice, "tell me all about the man who brought the magic Sword here to your camp a few days ago."

"Sir?"

"I assure you, Lednik, that trying to look like a fish and pretending ignorance will not gain you anything." Wen Chang pointed with a firm gesture. "Those marks on the walls of the cut through the ridge back there testify far too loudly to the presence of a certain magic Sword in which I have an intense interest. I rather imagine that before the Sword showed up you were stymied for some days by that ridge—a piece of rock too long to get around, too steep to readily go over. And much too hard to dig straight through, in any reasonable amount of time—if you had been digging with ordinary tools, that is. So the arrival of the man with the magical Sword was very opportune, was it not? Tell me what agreement you reached with him, and where he has gone now. Come, Lednik, I bear you no ill-will, and if you tell me the truth you need not fear me."

Lednik was now sweating more intensely in the shade than he had been a few minutes ago out in the sun. "Magic Sword? Is that what you said just now, Excellency? Alas, I am only a poor man, and have never heard of such—"

"You will be a much happier poor man in the end, Foreman Lednik, if you do not try to treat me as an idiot. It is true that in this territory I have no official standing as an investigator. But I can go from this spot directly to the Hetman himself, and inform him of the suddenly improved technology of road-building in this portion of his domain. He will, I am sure, be interested to hear of it. And to hear the reasons why you, his trusted foreman Lednik, neglected to inform him of the presence in his domain of one of the Twelve Swords that—"

"I want no trouble, sir!" Lednik was beginning to turn pale under his tan and sweat and road dust.

"Then tell me, from the beginning, the truth about this visitor you had." Wen Chang turned his head to glance at Lieutenant Komi. The officer, Kasimir noticed, was moving closer to the others, to stand inside the square of shade, from which vantage point he was better able to follow the progress of the interrogation.

And now Lednik's story came out. Yes, a man, a complete stranger to Lednik, had indeed appeared at the work site only yesterday. And this man had worn at his side a black-hilted Sword of marvelous workmanship.

"Was there a device upon the hilt?" Wen Chang interrupted.

"A device?"

"A special marking."

"A device. Yes sir, there was such a thing. It was a little shape in white, the image of a wedge splitting a block. I did observe that much."

"Excellent. Continue."

Lednik continued in a halting voice with frequent hesitations, describing how the stranger had been willing to demonstrate the power that he claimed for the weapon, cutting away the rocky ridge as if he were digging in soft clay, or wood.

"No, not even like wood, sir. Like butter is more like it. Like melting butter, yes. And that thing, that tool, that must have come somehow from the gods, why it made a dull, heavy hammering noise all the time that it was working, even though it was just slicing along smoothly. My workers had to scramble to move the chunks of rock away as fast as he could cut them out. He demonstrated the power of his Sword beyond all argument, and then he took it away with him again. I did nothing to interfere with him. No, you may bet that I did not. Who am I to try to interfere with a wizard of such power?"

"His name?"

Lednik looked blank for a few seconds. "Why, he gave none. And I wasn't going to ask him."

"What did he look like?"

Lednik appeared genuinely at a loss. "His clothing was undistinguished. Such as everyone wears in the desert. He was thirty years of age, perhaps. Almost as dark as you are, sir. Middle height, spare of frame. I did not pay that much attention to his looks. I feared his power too much."

"No doubt. Well, be assured that my own powers are formidable too, Foreman Lednik. And they tell me that you have not yet revealed the whole truth. What was the nature of the bargain that you struck with this stranger?"

Eventually the full story, or what sounded to Kasimir like the full story, did come out. As payment for the stranger's help, Lednik had agred to release to him a certain one of his prisoners.

Wen Chang squinted suspiciously when he heard this answer. "And what were you going to say to your superiors when they asked you about the missing man?"

"It's unlikely that anyone would ever notice, sir, that one of them was missing. They are all minor criminals here, and no one cares. If someone should notice, it would be easy enough for me to say that the man died, and no one would question it. A good many do die in this work."

"And if someone should question it? And ask to see his grave?"

"Bless you, sir, we keep no record of the burials out here. No markers are put up. They go into the sand when they die, and the sand keeps them. How could we ever be expected to find one of them again?"

"I see." The Magistrate ruminated upon that answer, which had sounded reasonable enough to Kasimir. Then Wen Chang resumed the questioning. "And what was the name of the prisoner that you released, in return for getting your ridge cut through?"

The foreman gestured helplessly. "Sir, I do not know his name. They have only numbers when they come to me."

"I see. Well, had this man been with you long? What did he look like? Who were his workmates?"

"His number was nine-nine-six-seven-seven . . . I do remember that because I looked it up, wondering if it was an especially lucky number, which would be worth remembering next time I visited the House of Chance. But I don't see how that will be of any use to you. He had been here for several months, I think. Yes, he was young and strong, and might have endured a long time yet, so for that reason I was sorry to see him go. And as for workmates, he had no special ones. None of the men do, I see to that. It helps immeasurably, I assure you, sir, in cutting down on escape plots and other nonsense of that kind."

"Young and strong, you say. What else can you remember of his appearance?"

"I'm trying, sir, but there really isn't much I can tell you. Hundreds of prisoners come and go. I believe—yes, he tended to be fair instead of dark. Beyond that there isn't anything I can say. Oh, he and the man who rescued him were well acquainted with each other. They were real friends, I could see that from their greeting when they met."

"But, during the course of this joyous demonstration, neither of them ever called the other one by name?"

"That's right, sir, they were very careful."

"And presumably they left together yesterday, the stranger and his rescued friend?"

"Yes sir, exactly. They didn't want to hang around. Cutting through the ridge with that Sword took that strange wizard no more than an hour, while my workers scrambled to carry away the chunks of rock as fast as he could carve them free. He had brought a spare riding-beast with him, and he and his friend took three filled water-bottles from our supply. They headed out into the desert, sir, that way." Lednik gestured in the direction away from Eylau. "Have mercy upon me, Your Excellency, for I am only a poor man!"

3

IN response to Wen Chang's continued questioning, Foreman Lednik assured the travelers that the city of Eylau lay at less than two days' distance, back along the winding length of the completed portion of his road. To travel on to Eylau that way would be a shorter and easier journey than to go back to their original caravan route and approach the metropolis by that means.

Kasimir inquired: "And is there any water to be found on the way?"

"Not directly on the way, sir. The roadside wells are not yet dug. Of course you may happen to encounter one of our water-supply caravans outward bound, in fact it's quite likely, for one comes out almost every day. They will be happy to fill your canteens for you. Otherwise to get water it will be necessary to make a short detour to the stone quarry, where there is a natural supply. You will see the branching road about halfway to the city."

Presently Wen Chang and Kasimir were remounted and trotting back along the new road, with Lieutenant Komi and his full complement of men riding escort behind them as before.

When they had been riding for a few minutes, Kasimir asked, "How did you know, sir, that the thief had come this way with the Sword?"

Wen Chang roused himself from deep thought and glanced around him. "I only knew there must be water in this place, if men or animals could stay here raising dust so steadily into the sky. And I knew of course that the thief would almost certainly be seeking water. When I saw the marks left by Stonecutter in the rock, it was a pleasantly unexpected bit of confirmation—and also a sign that the thief had other things than water on his mind when he sought out the road-building crew."

"How's that?"

"Here in the desert, he who has water shares it freely. The thief would not have needed to make such a demonstration, endure such a delay, simply to refill his canteens."

"I see. You think, then, that Lednik told us the truth, after you frightened him?"

"I think so, yes." The Magistrate sighed. "But I suspect he had only a small portion of the real story to tell."

"What do you mean?"

"Whoever stole the Sword of Siege must have had a greater plan in mind than simply freeing a man from that road gang, though the fact that he brought an extra riding-beast along indicates that rescuing the prisoner had been some part of his plan from the beginning. A modest bribe in cash would have accomplished the rescue more simply and quietly. The foreman implied as much, and I believe him on that point . . . no, freeing the prisoner was only a part, though perhaps a very important part, of some greater plan. But the fact that the Sword-thief did it opens up a whole realm of fascinating speculation."

"I confess I am more bewildered than fascinated. If only we knew the identity of the freed prisoner!"

"Yes, who is number nine-nine-six-seven-seven? If Lednik gave us the correct number, we may eventually learn the prisoner's identity. Yes, I think that we are making progress. So far I am satisfied."

And the small party rode on. Kasimir glanced over his shoulder to see Lieutenant Komi riding not far behind, in a position where he might well have overheard at least part of the conversation. The officer's face still showed no real curiosity, but Kasimir thought that his stoic expression had acquired a thoughtful tinge.

That day they encountered no water-supply caravan coming out from the city, or indeed any other travelers at all, and that night made a dry roadside camp. Kasimir, stretching out upon his blanket to sleep, reflected that two days and two nights had now passed since the theft of the Sword. If it was not for the presence of the Magistrate, he would have considered the chances of its recovery zero. But Wen Chang inspired confidence.

Shortly after Wen Chang and his party resumed their march in the morning, they came to the first branching road that they had seen. There were no road signs, but Kasimir supposed this must be the way mentioned by Lednik as leading to a quarry.

Komi asked Wen Chang: "Are we detouring to replenish our water, sir?"

Wen Chang nodded. "I think that would be prudent. It is possible that the thief has visited this quarry too, and that we will be able to learn something to our advantage."

"And shall I send a few men around to the other side of the quarry, as we did at the road construction site?"

"You might as well do it again, Lieutenant, though I doubt the Sword will be here now."

The party proceeded according to this plan, and after they had ridden a few kilometers the quarry came into view; it was the rim of the great almost-square pit, seen from outside, that first defined itself out of the jumbled badlands. The road approached it from above.

At the point where the road began to switchback down a steep slope, to enter the quarry through its hidden mouth below, Wen Chang ordered a detour. While a small detachment under a sergeant moved around the quarry to take positions on the other side, the Magistrate led most of his escort toward a place on the upper rim of rock. From here it was possible to overlook the pit and its swarming laborers, with a good chance of remaining unseen from below. Looking down cautiously, Kasimir observed pools of water, looking clear and drinkable, in the bottom of the deepest excavation. Evidently it welled up naturally from the deeply opened earth.

The Magistrate's attention soon centered on that relatively small part of the great excavation in which the workers were now most active. Soon, in an effort to get a closer look at the area of fresh cutting, he moved over the rim and started climbing down. His goal was an area of huge rock faces, at the feet of which great blocks were lying, evidently having been recently split away.

Wen Chang reached one of the opened vertical faces, and began to examine it closely but had not been long at this inspection job before he was discovered by some workers. There was a shout, and one of the overseers who had seen the tall figure of a stranger moving among the rocks started forward, whip in hand—only to change his mind and withdraw quickly on catching a glimpse of the Magistrate's following escort.

When Kasimir came up to him, Wen Chang, smiling faintly, gestured slightly toward the vertical rock face just in front of them. Having seen similar evidence earlier on the road cut, Kasimir this time was certain of Stonecutter's signature at first glance—those long, smooth strokes were unmistakably recorded here too, their texture plainly shadowed by the glancing angle of the sun.

Now the Magistrate climbed the rest of the way down to the bottom of the quarry, in the process demonstrating a lanky agility, and a disregard of dignity that both pleased and surprised Kasimir. On the quarry's level floor, the two chief visitors, with their military bodyguard still filing downslope after them, confronted another foreman who wore the Hetman's gray and blue.

This man was smaller and younger than Lednik. He was also more openly nervous from the start on finding himself confronted by such a formidable caller as Wen Chang.

This foreman, whose leather belt of rank seemed to have been designed for and once worn by a bigger man, introduced himself as Umar. At first Umar, like Lednik, denied having had any visitors at all during the past few days. Nor had he any knowledge of a magic Sword. But when faced with the sort of pressure that had moved Lednik, Umar too caved in and admitted to a different version of the truth.

Yes, Excellency, two strange men had indeed arrived here the day before yesterday, almost at sunset, bringing with them a magic Sword of great power. They had been willing, even eager, to demonstrate what their tool could do, using it to split enormous stone blocks easily out of the living cliff.

"Yes sir, that Sword was a marvel! Just rest it on its point, under no more pressure than its own weight, and it could bury itself right up to the hilt in the solid stone. And its blade was a full meter long."

Wen Chang nodded encouragingly. "And what bargain did these two men make with you, in return for the work they did in cutting stone?"

"Bargain, sir?" Now little Umar's eyes were popping in apprehension. "No, I made no bargain. We gave them a little food and water, yes, but we would do as much for any honest travelers. What kind of a bargain would such wizards want to make with a simple man like me?"

"That was my question. Perhaps they sought the release of one of your prisoners?"

Umar appeared to find that a preposterous idea. "One of these scum? I would've given them one for nothing if they'd asked."

"So, they showed you what their Sword could do, purely for your entertainment it would seem, and then they simply went away again?"

"That's it, Excellency. That's just what happened." Umar nodded, glad to have the matter settled and understood at last.

Wen Chang, somewhat to Kasimir's surprise, abstained from pressing the line of questioning further, and apparently lapsed into thought.

Kasimir chose this moment to again identify himself as a physician and surgeon, and volunteered to tend whatever injured might be on hand. He had surmised correctly that here, as on the road job, there would always be at least a few men partially disabled.

The foreman, still smiling as if he now considered the matter of the Sword closed, immediately accepted the physician's offer. Kasimir was conducted into a shady angle of the quarry wall, and shown two patients lying there on pallets. These men had suffered, respectively, a head injury and a broken foot.

Kasimir opened his medical kit and went to work. The man with the head wound complained of continual pain and double vision. His speech came disconnectedly, at random intervals. Usually it was addressed to no one in particular and made little sense. He also had difficulty with his balance whenever he tried to stand. There was nothing, Kasimir thought, that any healer could do for him here, and there would be little enough even in a hospital.

The only attendant on duty in the rudimentary infirmary was a permanently lamed prisoner who handled other odd jobs as well for the foreman. This man stood by while Kasimir bandaged the second patient's freshly damaged foot.

This time Wen Chang had come along to watch the physician work. Leaning against the shadowed rock as if he had no other care in the world, the Magistrate observed to the lame man in a sympathetic voice: "There must be many accidents in a place like this."

The crippled attendant agreed in a low voice that there certainly were.

"And no doubt many of them are fatal."

"Very true, Excellency."

Wen Chang squinted toward the quarry's mouth. "And those who die in these sad accidents are of course buried in the sandy waste out there."

"Yes sir."

"And how long has it been now since the last fatal mishap?"

"Only two days, sir."

"Oh. Then it occurred upon the same day that the two strangers paid their visit?"

The attendant said no more. But under renewed questioning the little foreman Umar, who had also come along to the rude hospital, admitted that that was so.

"A very busy day that must have been for you." Then Wen Chang looked up at Lieutenant Komi, who was standing by alertly, and announced in a crisp voice: "I want to take a look at those bodies."

"Yes sir!" Komi turned away and started barking orders to several of his men.

Umar began a protest and then gave it up. He had more overseers under his command than the foreman of the road-building gang, and these were somewhat better armed. Still, they did not appear to be a match for the Firozpur occupying force.

Within a couple of minutes some of Komi's soldiers were making the sand fly with borrowed tools, at a spot out in the sandy waste about a hundred meters from the quarry's mouth.

They had encountered no difficulty in locating the two-day-old burial site—the grave had been shallowly dug, and from a distance flying scavengers were visible about the place. At closer range tracks in the sand were visible, showing that four-ledged beasts had been at the bodies too. Kasimir as he walked closer to the grave saw that a pair of human feet and legs had been partially unearthed by the scavengers and gnawed down to the bones. He opened the pouch at his belt containing things of magic, and began to prepare a minor spell to help disperse the odors of death and decay.

The first body unearthed by the soldiers was naturally the least deeply buried, the one with the gnawed feet, that proved to be clad only in a dirty loincloth. Undoubtedly, Kasimir thought as he began to brush the last dirt away from the inert form with a tuft of weeds, it was that of a quarry worker. In this dry heat, decay might be expected to move slowly; a few whip-scars, not all of them fully healed, were still perfectly visible on the skin of the back. The head had been badly injured, perhaps by falling rock, so that not even a close relative would have been able to recognize the face.

Kasimir was about to ask what else there was to look for when Wen Chang, who had squatted down beside him, grabbed the body by an arm and turned it over. A moment later the Magistrate nodded minimally and let out a tiny hiss of satisfaction.

It still took the physician a moment longer to take notice of the thin, dry-lipped blade wound entering between the ribs. If that wound had any depth to it at all, the edged weapon that made it must have found the heart, or come very close to it.

The physician nodded in acknowledgment.

The Magistrate stood up, and with an economical gesture ordered the first body dragged to one side. "Keep digging!" he commanded, and the soldiers did.

In only a few moments a second body, which had been buried right under the first, had come into view. Again the only garment was a loincloth. The back of this man had also been permanently marked with the lash, and his head too had been virtually destroyed, by some savage impact that had well-nigh obliterated his face.

This time Kasimir was the first to discover blade wounds; there were two of them in this corpse's back, and they might have been made by the same weapon as the wound in the first man's chest.

Wen Chang, showing little reaction to this discovery, stood with hands clasped behind his back, nodding to himself. "Keep digging, men," he ordered mildly.

The third corpse, found almost exactly under the second, was paler of skin than the first two, and showed no visible evidence of beatings. As if, thought Kasimir, this was not the body of a quarry laborer at all— though who else would be buried here? But the third body like the first two was clad only in a single dirty rag around the loins.

The face of the third man also had been obliterated, in a way that might be the result of the impact of heavy rocks. And there, under his left arm, was the entry wound of what might have been a sword.

Wen Chang lifted one of the limp arms, relaxed past rigor now, looked at the hand, and let the arm fall back. "A somewhat unusual accident," he commented dryly. "Three men killed in virtually the same way. I suppose that a number of very sharp objects, as well as heavy ones, fell upon them as they were laboring in the quarry?"

Umar had been hovering nervously near the resurrection party, alternately approaching and retreating, and Kasimir could not have said whether the foreman was aware of the discovery of the blade wounds or not.

However that might be, Umar chose not to understand the Magistrate's comment. "You see? These are just dead prisoners, we have them all the time. Who are you looking for? I will summon all my workers to stand inspection for you if you like. Maybe the man or men you want can be found among them."

"I will tell you presently who I am seeking." Wen Chang sighed, and shot a glance at Kasimir that seemed intended to convey some kind of warning. "But first, the two men with the magic Sword—which way did they go when they left here?"

"That way," said Umar immediately, pointing out into the desert, toward nowhere.

"I rather suspected as much. You may rebury these poor fellows now." He seemed about to add some further remark addressed to Lieutenant Komi, but then simply let the order stand.

Wen Chang, Kasimir, and Umar walked slowly back toward the foreman's shaded observation post, while the officer stayed behind to supervise the reinterment.

"I would offer you hospitality, Excellencies," Umar was beginning, "I would bring out refreshment for you, had I any worthy of the name to offer. But as matters stand—"

"You are wondering who I seek," Wen Chang broke in. "They are two men. The name of the leader, or the name I know him by, is Golovkin. I had information that he was foreman here. And that he was the man the Sword-bearing strangers came to visit."

Kasimir, who had never heard of any such person as Golovkin before, shot his mentor a curious glance. But the Magistrate ignored him and continued: "This Golovkin is about forty years of age, tall and powerful, black of skin and hair. Missing an eye. Unless I am badly mistaken, he is the man who wore, before he gave it to you, that foreman's belt that fits you so poorly. I intend to track him in the city of Eylau. Well? Have I described your predecessor in the office or have I not?"

Umar shook his head emphatically. "Not at all, sir, not at all. The man who wore this belt just before me was promoted two weeks ago, and transferred to the other end of the Hetman's domain. He is red of hair. His skin is not black, but freckled, and he had two good eyes when last I saw him. He couldn't possibly be this Golovkin or whatever his name is—you can ask anyone here!"

"His name?"

"His name is Kovil. Ask anyone here!"

Wen Chang blinked as if in disappointment. "Then it appears he cannot be the man I seek . . . when Kovil left, did not another man go with him? The second man I am looking for is some years younger than the first. Not red-haired, but light of skin, and jolly of face and manner, though not always so jolly upon further acquaintance. His—"

"No, no." Umar appeared to have taken renewed alarm. "Nothing like that. I mean no other man went with Kovil when he was transferred. Nor with the two strangers when they left. No, not at all."

The Magistrate tried again, in his best soothing manner; but Umar's latest fright was not going to be soothed away. Eventually Wen Chang expressed his regrets for having wasted the foreman's time, and signed to his companions that they were ready to leave.

In a matter of only a few more minutes, Wen Chang was leading his small party away from the quarry in the direction Umar had indicated, almost directly opposite from that where the city of Eylau lay.

Kasimir could hardly wait until they had got out of earshot of the quarry to begin his protest. "Why didn't you challenge the man, tell him we knew he was lying about those bodies? That they were all stabbed, and that one of them at least, the most deeply buried, was not that of a quarry worker!"

"I have my reasons for not challenging the man," Wen Chang assured him mildly.

Since they had left the quarry the Firozpur lieutenant had been riding close enough to Kasimir and Wen Chang to be able to join in their conversation. "That third body," Komi put in now, "could have been that of a newly arrived worker, one who had not been on the job long enough to acquire calluses on his hands, or even to be lashed."

"You are quite right," Wen Chang assented. "It could have been. But I am morally certain that it was not. For identification we must consider other evidence than the appearance of the body itself. Doctor Kasimir, how long would you say those men had been dead?"

"Two or three days would be about right, I'd say. Though it's hard to tell in this dry heat. Corruption and mummification fight it out and like as not the latter wins. They're slowly turning to stinking leather."

"He was wearing," said Lieutenant Komi stubbornly, "only a loincloth, like the other two. As for the stab wounds, perhaps the foreman —either the new one or the old one—grew angry, or went mad, and stabbed some of the workers. Perhaps one of the overseers went mad. Or perhaps there was a rebellion among the prisoners that had to be put down."

Wen Chang signed agreement. "Admittedly those are possibilities. But the cloth was not a new one—did you notice that? It was dirty, even more so than would result from the mere proximity of his decaying body. The fabric of it was creased and frayed, as if from long usage, while at the same time the skin of that third man's back was pale, not sunburnt as it would be if he'd worked even an hour here. The dirty loincloth was put on him only when he was buried, just in case there should someday be an investigation."

Komi fell silent, frowning. Kasimir asked the Magistrate: "All right, then, sir. If the third man in the grave was not a quarry worker, who was he?"

"I believe he was one of the two men who came to the quarry carrying the Sword. In fact, he was the thief, the man who three nights ago took Stonecutter from the tent where you were sleeping."

Kasimir sat back in his saddle, trying to digest it all. Looking at Komi, he saw with faint surprise that the lieutenant had been jarred out of his stoic calm at last.

Komi was shaking his head. But all he said was: "And then, the second body in the grave—?"

The Magistrate spoke gently. "Very probably it is that of the man who had just been rescued from the road-building gang—I hope he enjoyed his brief day of freedom. The third body, the last killed, the one buried on top, was most likely that of the man the other two were intending to set free from quarry labor.

"Using the Sword once, at the camp of the road gang, was a mistake on the part of our unfortunate thief, that might have been his downfall once I took up his trail. But he survived that blunder. Using the Sword again in the quarry proved fatal."

Kasimir thought aloud for a couple of sentences. "So, the thief and his newly released comrade came here from the road-building site. They demonstrated the Sword here as the thief had done there—and then they were both murdered?"

"We have just seen their bodies. Men have been killed for far less than a Sword. Of course the foreman here must have been their murderer—I mean the real foreman, the man his replacement was good enough to describe for me, and name as Kovil."

"You told Umar you were looking for two men."

"And so I am, now. Kovil, however self-confident he may be, would have preferred not to carry the Sword into the city alone to try to sell it.

He would have chosen someone as a companion, a bodyguard perhaps, if possible someone who knows Eylau and its ways . . . and possibly someone Umar fears even more than his old foreman. Umar was on the verge of describing that second man to us, but then he realized what he was doing and closed his mouth.

"I think we may rely, however, on his description of Kovil, the old foreman. Kovil has not been transferred peacefully away. Kovil is instead the chief instigator of the Sword-thief's murder. No one else in the small dictatorship of that quarry could very well have arranged it. It is easy to imagine. A few smiles, apparent agreement—then treachery. A surprise attack, a double killing—then the prisoner who had been the object of the rescue attempt slain also, for good measure."

"So, this man Kovil—and his companion if he indeed has one—they are now—?"

Wen Chang nodded in the direction of Eylau. "They left here two days ago. I presume that they are already in the city, doing their best to sell Stonecutter. Of course Kovil has also promised his assistant Umar a share in the profits. Probably the other overseers in the camp are also to get something for their silence."

"We can still arrest Umar."

The Magistrate shook his head. "Only on our own authority. The removal of the foreman from the quarry would very possibly create turmoil among the overseers and prisoners. This might result in escapes or even an uprising. We would very likely get ourselves into trouble with the Hetman—I do not know him, nor perhaps does he know me. And it is more than likely that at least one of the whip-carrying overseers still in the quarry is in on the plot also. And as soon as we were out of sight with our prisoner he would contrive to send a warning ahead to the man we really want, the one who took the Sword away. No, let them think that we are fooled. Come, we are out of sight of the quarry now. Let us turn back toward Eylau."

4

THERE was still half a day's light available for traveling, and Wen Chang set his party a good pace upon the road to Eylau. Calling Lieutenant Komi up to ride beside him, while Kasimir remained close on his other side, he took pains to rehearse both of his chief associates in what he wanted to do when they reached the city.

The Magistrate intended to appear there in the character of a wealthy merchant, one who was particularly interested in buying and selling antique weapons. It would be quite natural for such a merchant to travel with a large, heavily armed escort. That the members of his escort were men of the tribe of Firozpur ought not to arouse suspicion, for the people of al-Farabi's tribe had a reputation as reliable mercenaries, and hired out fairly often in that capacity.

Both men agreed that their leader's plan sounded like a good one, and the ride went on, largely in silence. Now there was a faint smell of water in the air from time to time. The fierce aspect of the landscape gradually moderated. Birds became plentiful, tree-covered hills could be seen in the distance, and irrigated fields began to appear at no great distance from the road. The Tungri could no longer be far away.

Now other roads intersected the main one. Gradually traffic increased, and there were other signs that a large city was near. It was near sunset when the party at last came close enough to see the stone-built walls of Eylau, topped with blue-gray banners, rise against the fading sky. Those walls were high, and extended for what seemed an unreasonable distance to both right and left. Even in the diminishing light they were impressive.

"It is said," the Magistrate mused, "that the walls of Tashigang are even higher than these. And in the south I have seen cities even larger than this one. But this is an imposing sight, nevertheless."

Wen Chang would not entrust the choice of an inn to anyone else, and so the whole party entered the city together as dusk approached. The busy gate through which they passed was manned by the city Watch, officers and men wearing the Hetman's livery. These guardians took note of those who entered—in this case the merchant Ching Hao and his party, fourteen men in all—and urged the peace of the city upon the wealthy trader's Firozpur bodyguard.

Once inside the walls the Magistrate's party split in two. While Komi and his troopers found their way to the warehouse where the caravan's cargo was to be delivered and the payment due thereon collected, Wen Chang led Kasimir expertly through the masses of would-be guides, beggars, and passersby of every description who clogged the streets in the vicinity of the great gate through which they had entered the city. The two men inspected, one after another, most of the inns which clustered in this area. After looking over several hostelries quickly but carefully, the Magistrate selected one whose sign in three languages—one of which Kasimir had never seen before—described it as the Inn of the Refreshed Travelers.

This inn was quite a large establishment, having as Kasimir estimated a hundred rooms or more. It was a fairly expensive one as well. When Komi rejoined them at the agreed-upon meeting place, and handed over the purse of his master's money, Wen Chang had to lighten that purse by a good many coins to make the required advance payment to the innkeeper.

Even before entering the city, the Magistrate had disguised himself in a subtle way, putting on some different clothes chosen from his own wardrobe, so that he even appeared a little shabbier than before, as would be expected of a wealthy merchant traveling through unknown and possibly dangerous territory. And he had adopted a slightly different speech and manner. He was still speaking the common tongue of the region, but now with a different accent.

As for Kasimir, he had been mostly quiet during the past few hours; he had been thinking deeply about his immediate future. It was now time for him to make a decision.

Wen Chang had evidently been aware that some such process of reassessment was under way. He had waited patiently for its conclusion, and realized that a moment of decision had now arrived.

He surveyed the younger man appraisingly. "So, Kasimir—is this the point at which we two part company?"

The physician shook his head. "I must admit that the White Temple holds no great attraction for me at the moment, and I am willing to delay going there indefinitely if you think I can be of the least help to you in your search for the Sword. I still feel . . . well, not exactly responsible for the loss of Stonecutter; but concerned in it. I wish I could do something to help Prince al-Farabi, who has treated me, a stranger to him when we met, with such great kindness."

"Then it is settled!" Wen Chang grabbed him by the right hand and shook it warmly. "You will share accommodation here at the inn with me. There is plenty of room in the quarters I have chosen. And I will be greatly obliged if you would undertake to assist me in one or two points regarding the investigation."

Kasimir knew a sudden sensation of freedom. "Thank you for the invitation, sir. That would suit me very well indeed, and I accept gladly."

The young physician when he inspected the chosen quarters agreed at once that they were adequate. The supposed merchant and his traveling assistant were to share a two-room suite on the third floor of the main building of the inn, while their military escort was quartered in a large room just below them. Their riding animals and loadbeasts were to be housed in a stable immediately under that. The suite on the third floor had a small balcony with a view, not too offensive, of nearby streets and the buildings that lined them. These were mainly other inns, taverns, and two-story houses with narrow fronts. A grillwork of wrought iron defended the balcony against at least the casual attentions of thieves and prowlers. The only regular entrance to the upper suite was by means of a stairway that came up through the room in which Komi and his troops were bivouacked.

Kasimir found that by putting his face almost against the grillwork on the third-floor balcony, and looking out over lower rooftops at a sharp angle, it was possible to see, in the distance, a conspicuous tall building faced with red stone. This, the innkeeper informed them, was the Red Temple of Eylau, now undergoing a remodeling. It was an imposing structure upon which a good deal of new, white stone-carving had recently been completed. More work of a similar nature was obviously in progress. Some larger-than-life-size statues had already been set in their places on the high cornice, and empty pedestals at several levels on the front of the building awaited others.

From his first sight of this temple, Wen Chang's attention was strongly engaged by it, so that Kasimir wondered briefly if his new associate was contemplating a serious debauch. But the Magistrate was content to remain in the inn, and nightfall soon blotted the details of the building from sight—the outline of the temple remained glowingly visible after dark, because of the torches and bonfires kept going at its corners. By such means a Red Temple commonly called attention to its existence, and sought to attract its devotees.

The process of their settling in at the inn was soon accomplished. Whatever money Wen Chang had brought with him, together with the expense money from al-Farabi, went into a small strongbox, and this box was put under Wen Chang's bed in the innermost of the two upper rooms. Kasimir kept his own modest funds with him on his person. A comfortable couch in the outer room offered him a softer rest than any he had had since setting out in al-Farabi's caravan many days ago, and with the door at the top of the stairway bolted his rest was undisturbed.

In the morning, breakfast was brought to the two professional men in their quarters by servants of the inn, while Komi and his troops were fed by turns in the ground-floor kitchen below. Over mugs of tea and plates of fruit and eggs and roasted strips of meat, with sunlight and cheerful street noises coming in the window, Wen Chang discussed his plans with Kasimir.

Discussion in the strict sense was short-lived. The Magistrate was ready to give orders. "The remodeling activity at the Red Temple leads me to believe that an excellent stone-carving tool, such as the one in which we are interested, might well find a ready purchaser in that establishment. I have never yet seen an impoverished Red Temple in any city, so it is quite possible that they would be able to pay enough for the Sword to obtain it from a thief.

"Your assignment, therefore, will be to present yourself at the House of Pleasure, and inquire whether they currently have any opening for a physician. It is highly possible that they will: Devotees who exalt the pleasures of the senses above all else frequently find themselves in need of medical attention."

Kasimir sipped hot breakfast tea. "Often, sir, a Red Temple will have an arrangement with the White Temple in the same city, by means of which the needs of medical care are met."

"I am aware that such arrangements are common. But it is not essential that you actually be given a job, only that you are able to spend enough time inside the Temple, away from the rooms usually frequented by customers, to conduct an investigation. That should not be too difficult; every large Red Temple has in it constantly a number of young men, particularly those from rural areas, applying for one kind of a job or another. I see no reason why you should be conspicuous among them."

"I am not from a rural area," Kasimir protested, somewhat stiffly.

His mentor smiled joyfully. "Splendid! Insist vociferously that you are not, employing just such an expression and tone. Thereby you will convince most of your hearers that you are. So you ought to be able to appear to dawdle aimlessly all day in those precincts without arousing any great suspicion. I say 'appear to dawdle.' Of course you are actually to use your time to good advantage, and obtain any scrap of evidence available bearing on the possibility that the chief sculptor there may have just acquired Stonecutter."

Kasimir frowned thoughtfully. "It is not obvious to me just what sort of evidence that would be, unless I should be able to catch sight of the Sword itself."

"That would be desirable, but I fear very unlikely. There are several other possibilities. Perhaps some workers in stone, no longer needed now that their work can be done faster without them, have just been told that their services no longer are required. Strike up an acquaintance with any employee you can, especially one who appears dissatisfied. Or perhaps you will be able to discover discarded scraps of stone bearing marks similiar to those we observed at the quarry and the road-construction site. It is really hard to think of every possibility in advance. At a minimum, you must learn who is in charge of doing the stonework for the temple; I feel sure it must be an artist of some stature."

Kasimir was still pondering the best way to go about this projected investigation of an unknown artist when Lieutenant Komi came up the stairs and looked in at the open door to ask about his orders for the day. Kasimir, while passing through the second-floor room last night before retiring, had observed that the officer had arranged a semiprivate sleeping chamber for himself by enclosing one end of the room with a couple of hanging blankets, while his men sprawled everywhere else upon the floor and furniture. Now Kasimir thought that the lieutenant, definitely an outdoor type, looked ill-at-ease here inside four walls, even such rough walls as these of the inn.

After routine morning greetings had been exchanged, Wen Chang first instructed the officer to follow Kasimir's orders at any time when he, Wen Chang, was absent. Next he urged him to keep his eleven men under sufficiently tight discipline, and to enforce moderation upon them in their patronage of the local taverns and brothels.

"You must also see to it that they speak and act always as if they were in fact mercenaries, in the service of a merchant who is in the market for fine weapons. Whether that tactic will bring us into contact with the current possessor of the Sword, I do not know. But we must try. That is all I require of you today. Stay—I suppose you will soon be making a report to your prince?"

Komi turned back from the stairs. "Yes sir, though I was hoping for something more to report beyond the fact that we have found lodgings. I have taken the cages with the flying messengers up to the roof of the inn, and one of my men is looking after them."

"Very good."

The officer, upon being dismissed, saluted and went downstairs, where Wen Chang and Kasimir could hear him speaking firmly to his men upon the subject of their behavior in the city.

Now it was time for Kasimir to make the few preparations he thought necessary for his own assigned mission. He would leave off his desert traveler's robe, and wear instead the street clothes of a professional man. He would carry with him only the small medical kit worn on his belt, not the large one that had occupied his saddlebags. And he would use his own name, as it seemed impossible that anyone in this city would yet have any reason to associate Kasimir, the obscure physician, with the famed investigator Wen Chang.

On stepping through the gate of the inn's courtyard into the street, the young physician began to walk with a certain sense of pleasure through the morning crowds. Around him thronged peddlers, shopkeepers, servants of the Hetman, beggars—no doubt there were thieves and pickpockets—busy people of every description. It had been a long time since he had traveled freely along the thoroughfares of a great city.

And there could be few cities in the world greater or more exciting than this one.

Kasimir spent the better part of an hour making his way gradually closer to the Red Temple. Frequently he lost sight of his goal in the maze of narrow streets that intervened, but he persevered, relying on a good sense of direction. At last he emerged from the maze on the western side of a great tree-lined square, whose eastern edge fronted directly on the temple he sought. Seen at this closer range the structure looked even larger than it had at a distance.

The Red Temple in Eylau was perhaps six stories high, somewhat broader than its height, and proportionately deep. The façade of the building, following the usual Red Temple style of architecture, was marked by columns, most of them frankly phallic in design, and some as much as two stories tall, going up the front of the building in tier above tier. Between the columns the statues Kasimir had seen last night as distant white specks, and had heard described by the innkeeper, were now visible in detail. They were finely and realistically carved, and larger than life. Distributed in archways and niches at all levels of the façade, they were almost exclusively of human bodies, generally nude. Most of the bodies portrayed were beautiful, with a few of calculated ugliness to provide comic variety.

The activities depicted among the statues were for the most part sexual, but involved as well the prodigious consumption of food and drink, and the amassing of wealth in games of chance. The ingestion of drugs also engaged the attention of certain of the figures, particularly in one frieze whose carven marble people appeared to float on marble clouds. Whoever had done that carving, thought Kasimir, was indeed an artist of more than ordinary talent.

Behind its new façade, the building must have been recently enlarged. New timber showed in several places, and the color of structural stone-work on the upper floors was slightly different from that on the lower. Again the job was not yet finished. Kasimir reflected again that this was indeed a very logical place to begin a search for the stoneworking Sword.

5

KASIMIR had just started across the square—a hectare and more of tesselated pavement studded here and there with fountains and obscure monuments—in the direction of the temple, when his attention was drawn by a noisy disturbance to his right, at the border of the paved expanse.

Some kind of official procession was making its way along that edge of the square. A modest crowd, quickly formed from the people in the busy square, lined the procession's route. Now mounted guards in the Hetman's colors of blue and gray were using cudgels and other blunt weapons to beat back a minority of the crowd who were trying to stage a chanting, arm-waving protest. The protesters, who were fewer in number than the troops and certainly not organized for resistance, promptly gave way. They had dispersed among the rest of the people on the plaza before Kasimir could get any idea of who they were or what they wanted.

His curiosity aroused, Kasimir moved toward the place where the demonstration had flared up. The procession itself, he saw as he drew near, was quite small. It consisted of an armed and mounted escort, twenty or so troopers, surrounding a single tall, lumbering vehicle. Loadbeasts pulled an open tumbrel, carrying a single figure bound upright—a man, presumably some object of the Hetman's wrath, who was thus placed on display for all the city to behold.

The progress of the cart was deliberately slow, and Kasimir had time to walk closer without hurrying. When the cart finally passed him, he was quite near enough to get a good look at the prisoner. The bound figure was dressed in baggy peasant blouse and trousers, both garments dirty and torn. He had an arresting face—people who didn't know a

man might elect him their leader on the strength of a face like that—
and he was paying no more attention to the modest crowds around him
than he was to those orgiastic statues looming across the square. His
eyes instead appeared to be fixed upon some unattainable object in the
distance.

A placard had been fastened to the front of the cart, but one corner of
the paper had been torn loose; it was sagging in a deep curl, and
Kasimir could not read it. Turning to a respectable-looking man who
stood nearby, he asked what was going on.

The sturdy citizen shook his head. The corners of his mouth were
turned down in disapproval. He said: "I have heard something of the
case. The man is called Benjamin of the Steppe, and they bring him out
of his cell every few days for a little parade like this. I believe he was
engaged in some treasonable activities in the far west, at the very edge
of the Hetman's territory. Something to do with organizing the small
farmers there over water rights and taxes."

"Organizing them?"

"To form local legislative councils. To vote, and govern themselves."
The citizen made a gesture expressing irritation. He obviously didn't
know, couldn't remember, exactly how those farmers had intended to
organize themselves, but it was an activity which he opposed in general.
"They're going to hang him on the first day of the Festival; it's traditional in Eylau, you know, to execute one prisoner then, and set another
free. It's hanging, drawing, and quartering, of course." The prospect of
that extremely gory spectacle didn't please the townsman either.

The cart had rumbled past; Kasimir cast one more glance after it.
Then he thanked his informant and turned away, reflecting that such
public executions were probably rather routine events in a city of this
size, even though, as far as he knew, the Hetman had no particular
reputation for ferocity. Kasimir supposed that very few rulers would be
willing to let people, even remote farmers, start governing themselves.
Once started, where would that end?

Still walking at a moderate pace, he now turned his steps again in the
direction of the main entrance of the Red Temple.

He approached the establishment with mixed feelings. In general
Kasimir considered the White Temple, devoted as it was to healing and
the worship of beneficent Ardneh, morally superior to any other, particularly to either the Blue or the Red. But in his opinion other forms of
religion, including both Red and Blue Temples, had their places in

society too. The Blue, at best, served the rest of the world as bankers, offering—for a price, of course—investments that were sometimes sound, and a secure depository. As for the Red—well, Kasimir liked to think that he enjoyed sex, food, and drink as much as the next man. Perhaps even a turn of the gambling wheel now and then. But he had grave doubts about the wisdom of worshipping the gods of those engrossing activities—or any other gods, for that matter. And as a physician he knew too much about the drugs that were so popular among Red Temple worshippers to feel any temptation along that line himself.

The main entrance archway of the temple was draped in red, with scarlet curtains hanging in long folds over the duller masonry. Through the gap between those curtains there came out of the dim interior a hint of crimson light, along with a taste in the air of some exotic incense. The pulsebeat of a drum was throbbing somewhere deep inside that doorway. As Kasimir delayed outside, making his last mental preparations, another man hurried past him and inside. And then a second customer. Business was not bad, even this early in the morning.

Having done his best to put on a businesslike mien, Kasimir followed. Just inside the curtains, as he had expected, a physically impressive attendant waited to exact a small fee from each person entering; a greater contribution would be required of each worshipper later, depending upon the form that his or her devotions might take today.

Today Kasimir managed to avoid paying the nominal entrance fee. In answer to his question, the attendant pointed to a small sign, so inconspicuous that Kasimir almost missed it even as he looked for it. This sign directed the business-minded visitor to the offices, which were up a narrow flight of stairs.

Ascending these stairs, and pushing his way through a double set of sound-deadening curtains at the top, Kasimir found himself in a moderately large room well lighted by several windows, and occupied by a minor episode of bedlam.

A clerk who looked as if he had been born to sit at a desk was on his feet and trying to stand taller than he was, while shouting instructions and vague warnings to a room full of men and women. Meanwhile all the people in this small throng, most of them young and physically attractive, were waiting restlessly, even anxiously—for what? So far Kasimir was unable to tell. While they waited they argued with one another, or waved their hands trying to get the clerk's attention.

Before Kasimir could decide how best to approach someone and ask for a job in a dignified and professional manner, a couple of assistant clerks entered the fray, just in time to keep their leader from entirely losing control of the crowd. Kasimir found himself taken by the arm by one of these assistants, and pushed into a line along with the rest of the job-seekers. He considered making an effort to establish his dignity as a physician, but then decided it would be wiser not to draw too much attention to himself. His first objective, after all, was not really to get a job but to spend as much time as possible within these walls. He relaxed, resolving to let himself be processed along with the rest.

"You," cried a clerk, pointing at someone in the line—randomly, as far as Kasimir could tell—and then pointing again and again. "And you! And you! Come with me now!"

The last jab of the clerk's finger had been aimed at Kasimir. With an unreasonable feeling of satisfaction at having been so promptly singled out—though he had no idea what the pointing clerk might have had in mind—he elbowed his way forward. Behind him, as he followed the red-clad fellow by whom he had been selected, the remainder of the line was quickly collapsing into a minor mob once more.

With the two who had been selected with him—both of them, Kasimir now realized, were sturdy, chunky young men of average height like himself—he was directed on up yet more stairs, and then still more, until he began to wonder whether they were going to come out on the roof.

But the termination of this stairway was not on the roof, but rather within a great open, well-lighted loft-space one or two stories below that ultimate level. It was a loft, or great room, whose high walls consisted mostly of draped canvas, like barriers meant to block off the sights and sounds of some process of construction. Indeed, other signs of new construction were all around, in the form of raw timbers and unfinished stonework.

Overhead was mostly more fabric, shades or awnings of translucent cloth now partially opened to the morning sky, which had turned gray. Kasimir supposed that treatment with oil, and perhaps magic, would serve to keep that cloth roof waterproof.

Ordered to stop where he was and wait without moving, Kasimir stood and looked about. A score or more of agitated people, including artisans, priests, and others less easily identifiable, were milling about the L-shaped loft, some of them shouting at each other in anger or excitement. In the middle of one of the long sides of the L, an open freight-elevator shaft yawned dangerously; above it a system of pulleys creaked in slow motion, and the taut chains and cables going down into the shaft vibrated. A man standing at the head of the shaft yelled something down into it, and presently an unhappy answering shout came back.

Half a dozen statues of gigantic nudes, most of them looking nearly finished, stood about the great room, surveying the scene with pallid marble gazes that passed above the people's heads. Some of these statues were still being worked on, and the rough boards underfoot were gritty with powdered stone. A background sound of chipping and hammering testified to the presence of more workers around the corner of the L, invisible from the place near the top of the stairs where Kasimir was standing.

Even amid all the confusion among the several dozen people present, there was no doubt, thought Kasimir, as to who was supposed to be in charge here. Or, rather, the number of candidates for that honor could be quickly reduced to two. Both of these were men, and one of them, garbed in glossy black richly trimmed in red, could hardly be anyone less than the Chief Priest of the temple. The second candidate for dominance was a man garbed in rougher clothing, as tall as Wen Chang, but unlike the Magistrate in having cold, pale eyes, and a blond beard trimmed with such fanatical neatness that it managed to look quite artificial.

This layman, who wore a sculptor's apron whitely powdered with ground stone, was moving about energetically, passing judgment upon a number of the other people present, who, as Kasimir now realized, were models or would-be models and had been brought up here for his consideration. The prospective models were being ordered to appear nude, two or three at a time, on low platforms or pedestals crudely built of packing crates.

The black-and-red-garbed priest, who kept following the sculptor tenaciously as the latter moved about, was in something of a temper. Evidently his anger had nothing to do with the prospective models, but a great deal to do with the sculptor himself, upon whom the priest's attention was unwaveringly fixed. Nor was the Chief Priest accustomed to being argued with. Especially not—so Kasimir gathered—by a mere artisan who earned his living by carving stone.

On the other hand, neither was the artist much impressed by ecclesiastical authority, at least not the one by which he was currently confronted. At one point the tall blond man interrupted his talent search to stalk over to a cluttered desk at one side of the huge workroom. There he rummaged in the litter of paperwork until he could come up with a sheaf of sheets that his shouts identified as a contract. This document he waved under the priest's nose as the two men resumed their peripatetic argument.

The burden of the argument, as Kasimir had by now determined, was twofold; first, whether or not the sculptor was going to meet his deadline for finishing his work in this room and clearing out of it so it could be returned to its original intended purpose of a gambling casino; and secondly, what was going to happen if he failed to meet the deadline. The deadline was the first day of the Festival—Kasimir had recently heard that mentioned in another connection—and for several reasons it was very important to the Red Temple that all the statues be finished and in place by then, and the gambling tables be opened.

The artist, while listening—or perhaps refusing to listen—to these arguments, went on in a coolly professional way about his business, inspecting one nude prospective model after another as they appeared upon their little sets of elevated stands, male on one side of the center of the room and female on the other. Most of the models were rejected as quickly and decisively as were the protests of the priest, with quick, curt gestures and a few well-chosen words.

And still the argument between the two men went on, the priest trying to convince the artist that it was all very well to be a perfectionist and have artistic scruples, but right here and now the important idea was to produce the contracted number and type of statues, so that the grand official reopening of the remodeled temple could go on as scheduled, in time with the Festival.

The blond man sneered over his shoulder. "You mean so that the passersby in the square will stop having doubts as to whether you're completely open for business, and will rush in to spend their money without hesitation."

It was not that at all, said the man in black and red, outraged at being thrown momentarily upon the defensive—it was important that the consciousness of all the people be awakened to their full sensuous potential!

Meanwhile, another model had just stepped up on a recently vacated stand, where she attracted Kasimir's attention. She was a graceful young woman, really only a girl he thought, not yet out of her teens.

Her face was unprepossessing and her hair, worn in awkward braids, the approximate color of used washwater. But her body was striking, tall and strong without being either fat or in the least unfeminine, and he found himself immediately distracted from trying to follow the argument, or even thinking about the Sword.

Kasimir's appreciative gaze was at once tempered with sympathy; even worse, he supposed, than having everyone in a roomful of people stare at you when you were undressed might be to have the same roomful ignore you almost completely. That was what was happening to the young woman now, and she did indeed look a little faint.

Kasimir was jolted out of his contemplation when one of the many clerks in this room grabbed him by the arm again and hustled him, along with the two men who had been chosen with him, across the floor of the great room and into a small antechamber lined with benches. Here and there on the benches were little piles of clothing.

The clerk snapped orders at them, in the tone of one who enjoyed being able to snap orders. "All three of you, get your clothes off, quick. What are you waiting for? Hurry, hurry!"

"But I'm applying for a job as—"

The clerk was already gone; and anyway, as Kasimir kept reminding himself, the purpose of his coming here was not to defend his dignity or even to get a proper job, but to discover as much as possible about this sculptor and his operations. So, in company with his two rivals, all three of them casting wary looks at one another, Kasimir removed his clothes and piled them on a bench.

In a moment the clerk—or another clerk who looked very much like the first one—was back, to shepherd the three sturdily built men, all now naked as infants, back into the great studio. Here each was urged to mount, like a trained circus beast, on his own small stand. Then they stood there waiting. From his new position of vantage on this modest pedestal Kasimir could get a better look than before into the far recesses of the vast room, and see a little farther into the other end of the shallow L. Over there, right under some windows where the light was particularly good, a number of workers were laboring industriously, chipping and sawing away at blocks that were not statues but doubtless would be part of the stonework out on the façade. Kasimir saw no indication that any of those workers were using magic tools.

Glancing back in the direction of the other set of little pedestals, he saw that the young woman who had attracted his attention was now gone, her place occupied by another, more voluptuous, more classically beautiful, but somehow less interesting.

And the argument was over, or at least in abeyance. The Chief Priest had retired, as if between rounds of a contest, into a far corner of the room, where he was now in conference with other red-clad figures. But his opponent was not resting. In another moment the domineering sculptor was standing directly in front of Kasimir, staring at his body with wildly urgent and yet abstracted eyes, as if Kasimir were a piece of stone that might or might not be of just the proper size and shape to meet some emergency need. It came to Kasimir suddenly that he had seen physicians who looked at their patients in a very similar way. He hoped he would never be one of them.

The sculptor, having examined Kasimir's physique from hair to toes, at last stared him straight in the eye.

"Who are you?" the artist demanded.

Kasimir gave his name, though not his profession. But to be snapped at in this discourteous way was very irritating. "Who are *you?*" he demanded right back.

One of the sculptor's assistants, hurrying after the great man with a scroll of notes and a pen, blanched when he heard that. But the artist himself accepted the question—as if it would take a lot more than an uppity model to upset him.

"I am Robert de Borron," he replied in a cold voice. "And this is my work you see all around you. I see no reason to believe that you are going to fit into it."

With a jerk of his head the artist signaled to his aides that Kasimir should be removed. In a moment the physician found himself making his way back to the dressing room, still naked amid a throng of indifferent people.

His clothing and his small medical kit lay on the bench just where he had left them, apparently untouched. He had begun to worry that his modest purse would be stolen, or perhaps some of the drugs taken from his kit. But apparently he need not have worried. Maybe the folk who worked in an artist's studio—or who wanted to work here—needed no other drug than the hectic conditions of their employment.

Kasimir dressed quickly. He supposed he could now return to the second-floor personnel office, and try to convince someone there that he was really applying for a physician's job. But he felt a need to regroup mentally, to get out of the temple for a while, before he tried again. Then in an hour or less he would come back.

Kasimir had just stepped out of the front entrance of the temple, under a sky whose gradually growing promise of rain was beginning to come true, when he caught sight again of the strongly built and graceful young lady with the faded braids. She was sitting on a bench not far from the front entrance, and she did not look well.

Perhaps she was poor and hungry—her blouse and trousers looked rather shabby—or perhaps the experience of posing in the nude had been too much for her. In a moment Kasimir had stopped beside her.

6

"IF I may intrude for a moment upon your thoughts? I am a physician, and you do not look well. Can I assist you in any way?"

"Oh." The young woman sitting on the bench turned up her face to Kasimir. Again he was struck by the plainness of her face. But her greenish eyes, seen at such close range, were unexpectedly impressive.

Her voice had an intriguing quality too, low and throaty. "It's a long story. But I expect I'll be all right." Then she frowned. "Didn't I just see you somewhere inside the temple?"

"No doubt you did, I was looking for a job. I noticed you in there too." Kasimir was about to add that it would have been difficult not to notice her in the circumstances, but he had approached her as a physician, and it was a little too soon to alter that.

The girl was still frowning up at him. "You were trying out as a model? I thought you said just now that you were a physician."

"I was. I am. There were a series of misunderstandings—originally I was supposed to be applying for a physician's job in the temple. Do you mind if I sit down?"

"No." She moved over slightly on the bench, adjusting her baggy peasant trousers. "Except that I have things to do, and I ought to get up and do them—did the sculptor hire you, then?"

Kasimir sat down. "No. It seems that something about my attitude displeased the great artist, Robert de Borron. Perhaps he didn't like my shape any better than my attitude. What about you?"

"Did you deliberately displease him?" Her frown vanished. "I'm glad, I would have liked to do that too—but I couldn't afford to. So he hired me. I'm to start modeling for him tomorrow."

"I'm pleased for you, if you are pleased. You don't sound exactly overjoyed about it."

"Oh, I am, though. Getting this job was absolutely essential for me." It was said in a tone of heartfelt seriousness.

"Then I can rejoice with you." At this point, inspiration came to Kasimir. "By the way, I missed my breakfast this morning—would you care to join me in an early lunch? We could at least get in out of this drizzling rain somewhere."

Her greenish eyes appraised him thoughtfully. She stood up from the bench. "That sounds like an excellent idea, thank you."

They went into a nearby wineshop, where sights and aromas provided an intriguing menu. Sausages were hung invitingly from the rafters, and cheese and fresh, crusty bread were displayed on a counter.

They sat at a table, and ordered wine and food. The young woman's name, she told Kasimir, was Natalia. As he had surmised, she was originally from a small village. But she had visited Eylau several times before moving here a few months ago. Economic conditions at home were poor. She ate hungrily—though not like one actually on the verge of starvation—of bread and cheese, but sipped sparingly at her wine. She also persisted in turning the conversation around to him.

"Have you been a physician long?"

"About five years. How long have you been a model?"

She smiled at him. "My experience in that line is very limited. I expect the hardest part will be just holding still for a long time. Well, the hardest part besides . . ."

"I understand."

Natalia tossed back her awkward braids. "I did study at a White Temple for a while. Not modeling, of course, but medicine."

"Really? Then we might have been colleagues."

"I never had the chance to finish."

"Sorry. Where did you study?"

She named a small city that Kasimir had barely heard of, hundreds of kilometers to the west.

Kasimir chewed a mouthful of his sandwich. "It's easy to tell that you're well educated."

"Thank you."

"But short of money just now."

Her green eyes questioned him. "I might have landed a different kind of job in the Red Temple, without too much trouble. But I'd like that even less than posing."

"Of course, of course. I sympathize."

During their lunch Kasimir, sounding out his companion as gradually and carefully as he could, at last admitted to her that he had had an ulterior motive in trying to get a job inside the Red Temple. Yes, he was really a physician—but his main occupation at this time was a partnership with the well-known dealer in antique and special weapons, Ching Hao.

Natalia blinked her green eyes, as if she had never heard of the famous Ching Hao—small wonder—but wasn't quite ready to admit the fact, because she realized she ought to be impressed.

Ching Hao, Kasimir went on to relate, was particularly interested just now in locating and buying a certain special sword, an ancient and very valuable weapon. There was reason to suppose that this sword might have come into the possession of the Red Temple, or perhaps even the hands of Robert de Borron, for whom Natalia would presently start modeling. It would be worth some money to Ching Hao and his partner—more money than a model was likely to get paid—if an insider at the temple could find some evidence that the sword was really there.

Natalia didn't respond at once, except to look at Kasimir thoughtfully.

He pressed on: "We wouldn't be asking you to take any risks. And it's not a matter of getting anyone in trouble. It would just be a matter of keeping your eyes open and reporting to me."

"How would I know this sword if I saw it?"

Kasimir drew in a deep breath. "It's an impressive-looking weapon, to begin with. The blade is a full meter long, of mottled steel. The hilt is plain black, with a simple white image on it, depicting a wedge splitting a block." He hesitated briefly. "Most importantly, the blade has the magical ability to cut stone, any stone, very easily."

The greenish eyes were wide, really impressed at last. "The magic must be very powerful, I suppose. Does this sword have a name?"

Probably out there in the remote lands to the west they weren't altogether caught up on what happened out in the great world. Evidently their ignorance extended even to the history of the Twelve Swords.

"Yes," said Kasimir. "Some people call it Stonecutter. Or the Sword of Siege."

Natalia, thinking the matter over as she finished her lunch, eventually agreed to act as Ching Hao's agent. She would receive a small advance now, an additional payment every time she reported to Kasimir, and a substantial reward if she could provide some useful information about Stonecutter. They made arrangements for their next contact, which would be in the White Temple.

When he left the wineshop, Kasimir, taking what he considered rather ingenious precautions against being followed, returned by a somewhat indirect route to the Inn of the Refreshed Travelers.

He felt reasonably well pleased with himself for what he had managed to get done today. He might, he thought, possess a hitherto undiscovered knack for this sort of thing. It hadn't taken him long to conclude an arrangement with a young man who was going to be one of Robert de Borron's models. Of course it would still be possible for him to go back to the temple and try again for the physician's job. But now it seemed to Kasimir that that would probably be unnecessary; with Natalia in place inside the temple he would be free to help Wen Chang in some other way.

Nor was that all he had accomplished today, Kasimir thought with satisfaction. He had discovered also that the sculptor, Robert de Borron, had a large reputation, and the ability to justify it. Also that de Borron was under intense pressure from the Red Temple authorities to complete his work; it seemed highly probable that he would suffer financial and other penalties if he failed to do so in time. When it came to business matters, Kasimir had observed, the Red Temple was likely to be as grasping and unyielding as the Blue. And sometimes, if the truth be told, the White could hold its own with either.

The day was getting on toward midafternoon when Kasimir returned to the inn. The place was busy, but as far as he could tell everything was peaceful. Lieutenant Komi and a few of his men were on guard in their second-floor room, seated around a table near the stairway where they played at some tribal card-game. A couple of the other troopers slept on cots. Three or four were absent, and Kasimir assumed that these were off duty, enjoying whatever they might be able to afford of the delights offered by the big city.

Komi looked up as Kasimir walked in. The officer appeared glad to see him, and tossed a casual salute without rising from the table.

"Ching Hao has not yet returned," Komi announced, giving the name of the supposed merchant a slight emphasis, as if he thought the physician might need to be reminded of the alias. "He left this note for you. Also there is a man waiting out in the courtyard now, who says he wants to see either the merchant or his assistant."

Kasimir accepted the casually folded square of paper but did not immediately open it. Close under the windows of the inn a street vendor screamed, hawking his dried fruit. "A man waiting? Who is he?"

"An elderly fellow who looks to me as if he might possibly have money. Beyond that I have no idea who he is—that is why I insisted he wait in the courtyard and not in any of our rooms. But he says that he is interested in possibly purchasing antique weapons from you."

"If he wishes to buy weapons then he can hardly be trying to sell Stonecutter." Kasimir spoke freely in front of the card-playing soldiers at the table; all the members of Komi's squad had been informed of the essentials of their mission. "Still, for the sake of appearances, I suppose I'd better see him."

"I'll point him out."

Looking out one of the small windows that opened on the inn's interior courtyard, Kasimir studied the figure the lieutenant indicated—a gray-haired man, garbed in the drab clothing of a desert traveler, sitting on the rim of one of the courtyard's two fountains, and talking to someone who might be another merchant. At this distance it was hard to get any very distinct impression.

Before descending to talk to the caller, Kasimir opened the note Komi had handed him. The message was recognizably in the writing of Wen Chang and seemed innocuous.

> Kasimir—if you have no urgent reason to go out again, remain at the inn until I return, which will probably be before dark.
>
> Ching Hao

Yes, it might very well be a communication from a merchant to his assistant. There was no hidden meaning that Kasimir could detect. He tossed the note carelessly on a table, almost hoping that some spy might find and read it—though he really doubted that any spy would be watching them at this stage of affairs.

In a moment he was going downstairs again.

When Kasimir came out into the courtyard, the man who waited by the fountain was alone, sitting patiently with folded arms. He got to his feet as Kasimir approached. Despite his gray hair and lined face, he was still erect and hale, of average height and build. The two men bowed, in the approved manner of polite strangers unsure of each other's exact status. Kasimir was wishing silently that he had been able to learn something about antique weapons before undertaking to play the role of a dealer in them.

"I am Kasimir, secretary to the merchant Ching Hao. Can I be of service to you?"

"It may be that you can, young man." The elder nodded in a benign way; he had a gravelly voice, and a vague accent that Kasimir had trouble trying to define. "I am Tadasu Hazara—few in these parts know me, but in my own region I have something of a reputation of a collector of fine weapons. Having heard that your master was here, I decided to find out if he might have any of the specialized kind of weapons upon which my collection is centered."

"And what kind of weapons are those, sir?"

"My chief interest lies in jeweled daggers of the Polemonic Epoch; also, if they are of the first quality, mail shirts of the bronze alloys made by the smiths of Aspinall." The hands of the elder gestured; they were gnarled but strong, those of a man who had at some time done a great deal of physical work.

Kasimir assured the other, in perfect truthfulness, that Ching Hao had nothing like that in stock just now.

"Ah, that is too bad." After considering for a moment, the gray-haired man announced that he was also unfortunately under the necessity of parting with one or two very old weapons that had once belonged to his father. Was the merchant thinking of purchasing anything just now?

"What sort of weapons are they?"

When it turned out that none of them was a sword, Kasimir, feeling that whatever more he did was likely to be a blunder, pronounced himself unable to make decisions on such matters. Tadasu would have to wait for the return of Ching Hao himself.

The visitor seemed annoyed at having spent his waiting time in the courtyard for nothing. After expressing his formal good wishes to Kasimir and his absent master he bowed again, more lightly this time, and walked on out of the courtyard, through the main entrance of the inn.

The rain had ended some time ago, the day was growing hot and muggy, and Kasimir would have returned to the comparative coolness of his upper room. But before he could leave the courtyard another prospective customer had appeared, forwarded to him by the helpful innkeeper. This latest potential customer was actually carrying with him a bundle in rough cloth that looked very much like a wrapped sword.

This man was much younger than the first, and appeared considerably more nervous. "You buy weapons?" he demanded tersely.

"That is our business."

"I have a sword here."

"Very good." Kasimir attempted to sound confident. "If I may see the merchandise?"

The other man's fingers hesitated on the wrappings. "If you like this weapon—it's really something special—then you can give me cash for it this moment?"

Kasimir had to suppress his excitement. He had never seen any of the Twelve Swords, but he had no doubt of being able to recognize one of them if it should come his way.

Carefully he said: "I do not carry large amounts of coin on me, but still cash is readily available. If your sword there should prove to be something that I really want, then you may have money in hand for it before you are an hour older."

After another few moments of cautious hesitancy, the potential customer unwrapped the sword he had brought with him. Kasimir knew bitter disappointment. When the weapon was at last shown it did not look spectacular—the hilt was not even black, nor had the steel of the blade the finely mottled look that everyone who had seen the genuine Swords remarked upon.

Then a thought struck the young physician. Having heard tales of magical alterations in the appearance of things, and having once, years ago, had actual experience of such a trick, he thought he had better apply one more test. Taking the cheap-looking weapon in hand, he made a trial of it against the stone edge of the fountain. The only result of this was an angry protest from the seller. What was Kasimir trying to do, ruin a fine blade?

By the time Kasimir had succeeded in soothing the angry man, and sending him on his way with his precious sword, sunset was near. Leaving the courtyard that was already deep in shadow, Kasimir looked in on the innkeeper and gave orders that a warm bath be brought to him in his upper room, with dinner to follow. Then he went plodding up the stairs. Over the past several hours, his earlier feeling that the investigation was making progress had gradually faded into a sense of impatience and futility.

The bathtub had been taken away again and he was just finishing his solitary dinner when the sound of feet ascending briskly on the stairs made him turn his head. But instead of the familiar countenance of Wen Chang or Komi, there appeared in the doorway, just at the top of the stairs, the visage of a scowling beggar.

Kasimir immediately reached for his dagger, and was about to bawl an oath downstairs at Komi for having allowed this stranger to get past him when the beggar called out a greeting in the voice of Wen Chang.

Kasimir's hand holding the dagger fell to his side. "You! But—is this magic?"

"Only a touch of magic, perhaps, here and there." The figure of the beggar doffed its ragged outer coat.

"Why such a marvelous disguise?"

"It is sometimes necessary to gather information on the streets," the Magistrate said, his voice a little muffled in the process of pulling off the shaggy gray facial hair that had concealed his own neat mustache along with most of his lower face.

"I never would have known you!"

"I trust not." With another muffled grunt the older man now tugged off a sticky something that had altered the shape of his nose and cheekbones, and tossed this flesh-colored object on the table along with his wig and beard. Now undeniably Wen Chang again, he straightened his back and stretched.

"Now," the Magistrate continued in a clear tone of satisfaction, "we must exchange information. My day has been a long and trying one. The beggars' spaces at the Great Gate are considered most desirable, but they are too jealously guarded and fought over for an outsider like myself to have any chance of forcing his way in. The same situation obtained in Swordsmiths' Lane, and again behind the Courts of Justice, where there was much rumormongering over the matter of the execution two days hence. But as it turned out, all those difficulties were undoubtedly for the best. When I finally found a place to put down my begging bowl, in the vicinity of the Blue Temple, I learned something that may prove useful to us indeed."

Kasimir could readily understand why there was no surplus of beggars near the Blue Temple, whose priests and worshippers alike were notoriously stingy. He asked: "And what was this most useful thing you learned?"

"Have you ever heard of the famous diamond, the Great Orb of Maecenas?"

"I admit that I have not."

"If you, Kasimir, were a lapidarist, or a jewel thief, or a priest in the Blue Temple, you would certainly give a different answer to that question. Know, then, that such a diamond exists, that it has recently been brought to the Blue Temple of Eylau in secret, and that it is there to be carved into several smaller stones in the hope of thereby increasing its total value. This is obviously a matter of concern to us, for it is certain that the Sword can be used in the precise cutting of small stones as well as great. But before we discuss that any further, tell me of your day. What did you discover at the Red Temple?"

As Kasimir began his tale with his arrival at the Red Temple in the morning, the feet of servants were heard on the stairs. Soon they entered once more bearing a tub and buckets of hot water. The physician delayed his story until the tub had been set up behind a screen and the servants had departed.

Faint splashing sounds issued from behind the screen as Kasimir detailed his adventures in the vicinity of the Red Temple, and Wen Chang listened. The young man's story of recruiting the girl model to act as a paid spy elicited only a momentary cessation of splashing.

Not until Kasimir described his leaving the temple area to return to the inn did Wen Chang comment aloud. "And you did not persist in your attempt to obtain employment there yourself?"

"No sir, I thought I had explained that. What I had managed to achieve at the temple seemed to me at least enough to deserve reporting —and of course when I reached the inn your note was waiting for me, asking me to remain here."

The Magistrate grunted. "And I suppose there have been no callers at the inn wishing to sell us Stonecutter?"

As Kasimir began to describe the first man who had come asking to buy weapons, there sounded a louder splash than before from behind the screen; a moment later the face of Wen Chang, staring narrow-eyed above the folds of an enormous towel, peered fiercely around the edge of the screen. "And you simply let him go?"

"But the man told us, both Komi and myself, at the start that he wanted to *buy* weapons—"

"Did it not occur to you that he may have begun that way simply as a precaution? That he wished to see if our merchant operation was a legitimate one before he approached us with his real treasure? What did he look like?"

Here, at least, Kasimir had not failed, and could supply a fairly complete delineation. But the description of the elderly would-be client did not tally with that of anyone Wen Chang was able to recognize.

Wrapped from shoulders to knees in his great towel, his bath for the moment forgotten, the Magistrate paced impatiently "Well, well, it is impossible for me to tell now whether he had any connection with our real business here or not. Did he give you the impression that he was coming back?"

"Frankly, he did not. Though I fear that also is impossible to know with any certainty."

"Then it is useless to speculate upon these matters any longer. Here comes my dinner up the stairs if I am not mistaken, and when I have eaten I intend to sleep. Tomorrow we must arise early. Unless there is some new development, we are going to interest ourselves in the gem-cutting project at the Blue Temple."

7

WEN Chang declined to discuss his plans for approaching the Blue Temple until morning. Even then he remained silent on the subject until, over breakfast in their rooms, Kasimir questioned him directly.

"How are we going to approach the authorities in the House of Wealth? If, as you say, this fabulous diamond is being kept there secretly, they are not likely to admit its presence, or that any special gem-cutting is about to take place."

"True, they will not admit such things to the merchant Ching Hao. But if they are approached directly by the famous Magistrate Wen Chang, their response might be more favorable—especially if I bring them information of a plot to steal the gem."

Kasimir paused with a tea mug halfway to his lips. "You said nothing to me last night of such a plot."

"Nor did I learn anything of one during my investigations yesterday. But today it strikes me as a very useful idea."

"I see. And who am I going to be today?"

"The very well-known Doctor Kasimir, or course. We shall both be surprised—raise our eyebrows politely, so—if any of them admits that he has never heard of you. You are my assistant—or my associate, if you prefer—and a specialist in forensic medicine."

Kasimir thought about that. "It is not a common specialty. In fact I have never heard of it. But I suppose the very fact that it is unknown makes it sound prestigious. Very well. And I think I do indeed prefer 'associate.'"

"So be it, then."

There was not a single shabby thread in any of the garments in which

Wen Chang arrayed himself this morning. Before starting for the Blue Temple with Kasimir, the Magistrate left orders with Lieutenant Komi to maintain the fiction of the merchant Ching Hao against any suggestion to the contrary, and to take careful note of any potential customers.

"In particular I am interested in the elderly man who was here yesterday and said he wanted to buy weapons. If he should return, send one of your men riding to the Blue Temple at once to let me know. And meanwhile detain this fellow merchant of ours, forcibly if necessary, until I return."

"It shall be done, sir." Komi saluted. His salutes meant for the Magistrate always looked more serious than the ones he gave Kasimir.

"Good. Have you been sending reports to the Prince?"

"I dispatched a flying messenger yesterday, sir, bringing him up to date. There has been no reply as yet."

Wen Chang had decided to go to the Blue Temple on foot; a riding-beast carried more prestige, but only if you were assured of a place to put it safely when you had reached your destination, and they had no assurance of being offered such hospitality. A good walk lay before the two men, for the Blue Temple was in a different quarter of the city. Wen Chang, who had observed it while in the guise of a beggar yesterday, reported that it, like the Red Temple, bordered upon its own vast square.

Their route took them close to the Hetman's palace, which like the great temples had its own plaza; in the case of the palace, the plaza surrounded the building completely. Wen Chang detoured slightly so that they should go right past the palace, crossing the surrouding open space. About all they were able to see of the great house itself were the formidable outer walls of gray stone, several stories high.

At one place on the pavement, no more than thirty meters or so from those walls, a few men and women in country garments were conducting a protest demonstration. Kasimir was reminded at once of the public exhibition he had seen as the tumbrel passed bearing the unfortunate Benjamin of the Steppe. Whether these were the exact same people or not he couldn't tell, but he supposed it likely. Here they were crouched, facing the high gray palace wall, which in this area was pierced by a few high, small, heavily grilled windows, appropriate for prison cells. All of the demonstrators were slowly and rhythmically pounding their heads—fortunately with no more than symbolic force—upon the plaza's paving stones.

Kasimir stopped, joining a few other passersby who had taken time out from their own affairs to stare at this bizarre behavior. Wen Chang paused too, to stand with his arms folded, observing. As moments passed, a few more gawkers gathered.

The crouching head-bangers were all dressed in loose peasant clothing. The loose braids of the women swung as their heads moved up and down. When one of the men, perhaps sensing that by now a sizable audience had gathered, raised his head and looked around, Wen Chang called to him, asking the reason for these actions.

Eager to tell his story, the man abandoned his symbolic head-banging and jumped to his feet. He spoke in an uncouth accent.

"Oh, master, the prisoner who is to be so unjustly and horribly executed on the first day of the Festival, Benjamin of the Steppe, is even now held captive in a cell inside this building!" Raising a quivering arm, the protester pointed at the palace. "All the people of Eylau should be here now, petitioning the Hetman for his release!"

The reaction of the small crowd was not generally sympathetic. Many jeered and made threatening gestures. Some looked over their shoulders and hurried away, lest they be seen by the Watch associating with these mad treasonous folk who seemed to criticize the government.

The Magistrate did not answer the speaker but turned away. Kasimir followed silently. They had other matters to discuss besides these hopeless protests, and were talking in low voices about the Sword again when at last their goal came into sight.

The Blue Temple of Eylau, like most of its kind elsewhere, was practically devoid of exterior decoration, and sported no statuary at all on walls or roof. To most of its clients as well as its managers, such ornaments would have indicated a tendency toward frivolous waste. Whenever Kasimir looked at the outside of a Blue Temple in any city he got the impression that an effect of shabbiness if not actually dirtiness, the grim opposite of frivolity, was what the proprietors were striving to achieve.

Nor was the style of architecture accidental either. This particular Blue Temple, true to type, was reminiscent of a fortress; even more, perhaps, of a miniature mountain, though the total bulk of this structure was somewhat less than that of the Red Temple across town, which looked less like a mountain than like a giant hive. Undoubtedly this fortress, the Blue Temple, would be an extremely good place in which to leave your money and keep your valuables on deposit. Nothing, not even an earthquake, was ever going to budge or threaten this building and its contents—that, at least, was the impression meant to be conveyed by the massive walls and foundations, and reinforced by the iron bars, each thick as a strong man's arm, that guarded all the windows.

Wen Chang confronted all this majesty of strength undaunted. He marched majestically forward, straight across the square in the direction of the main entrance of this formidable edifice. Kasimir, walking half a step behind him, observed that here as at the Red Temple the majority of worshippers entering were men.

There was no difficulty about entering, for men so respectably dressed. Once they were inside the lobby, all cool white and pale blue, the Magistrate did not delay to look around. As if he knew exactly where he was going, he made his way straight to one side of the marble counter where a massive and yet somehow discreet sign promised information. Already, here in the outer lobby, the impression of penuriousness was beginning to fade.

The imposing manner of Wen Chang's approach did not appear to make the least impression upon the well-dressed clerk behind the counter, who doubtless dealt every day with equally imposing folk.

Nor was the clerk shaken when the Magistrate fixed him with a narrow-eyed glare, and announced in a firm voice: "I wish to see the Director of Security."

The expression on the clerk's face remained perfectly neutral as he looked this grand visitor up and down. "And may I tell the Director who wishes to see him?"

The tall figure that stood in front of his marble counter became, if possible, even a little taller. "You may tell him that his callers are the Magistrate Wen Chang, and his associate Doctor Kasimir."

The expression on the clerk's face achieved something—not quite a real change, thought Kasimir, more like a greater intensity of neutrality. In a moment, speaking in a voice that now admitted a certain grudging courtesy, the man behind the counter invited: "Step this way, if you please, gentlemen."

Wen Chang, with Kasimir remaining more or less half a step behind him, followed the clerk through a curtained doorway behind the information counter. On the other side of the doorway, solid steps led up. As he climbed Kasimir observed, in the materials of walls and stairs themselves, that they were now definitely entering the plusher precincts of Blue Temple administration.

The information clerk conducted them up only one level, and into a small office where he left them standing in front of the desk of another functionary. This woman, upon hearing the Magistrate's identity, welcomed him and his associate with something approaching warmth. Then she promptly left her small office to escort the visitors on up to a higher level still.

This process repeated itself, with subtle variations, on several levels. In each new office Kasimir and Wen Chang encountered a pause in front of a new desk, new introductions, and a brief conference. All this was conducted in an atmosphere of cordiality tempered by suspicion, palpable though never openly voiced, that this imposing man might not really be who he claimed to be.

Early on in the game it became evident to Kasimir that the higher up you went in the Blue Temple, the closer you penetrated toward its center, the plusher, more luxurious, everything became. Inside this fortress it was no longer frivolity to display wealth. Instead it had become a duty to show it, or at least enough of it, to suggest how much more treasure must be available.

There was a great deal of affluence in sight already, and still he and Wen Chang had not penetrated to their goal. The Director of Security, Kasimir was thinking, must be a very important part indeed of this establishment.

But at last Wen Chang, with Kasimir at his elbow, was standing in the office of the Director himself, who came around from behind his enormous ebony desk to greet them with a moderate show of warmth, that somehow did not include revealing his name if he had one apart from his office. No great sensitivity was needed to detect a certain wariness in the Director's manner as he pressed his callers' hands, one after another. Inside this man's fine robes of blue and gold his body was very lean, as if perhaps the guardianship of such mind-boggling wealth as had been entrusted to his care left him with no time to eat.

The words of the Director's greeting, at least, sounded perfectly sincere.

"To what does our poor establishment owe the honor of this visit? Everyone has heard of the wise judge Wen Chang, whose eye is capable of penetrating with a glance to the very heart of wickedness. But I confess, Your Honor, that somehow I had pictured you as an older man."

Wen Chang bowed, lightly and courteously. "And I, even in lands far distant from this one, have heard of the Director of Security in the Blue Temple in the great city of Eylau. But we have not come here for an exchange of compliments however pleasant. Instead we are upon a matter of the most serious business."

"I am all ears. Please, be seated."

Wen Chang and Kasimir helped themselves to ivory chairs, while the Director resumed his place behind his desk of ebony. Then the Magistrate continued: "It was another matter entirely that brought myself and my associate, Doctor Kasimir, here to Eylau. But in the course of our investigations in this city there has come to our attention the existence of a plot to steal from this temple the jewel known as the Great Orb of Maecenas."

The Director blinked once, and then his face went totally blank. "What reason have you to believe that jewel is here?"

The Magistrate shook his head. "Come, come, sir, we are going out of our way to do you a favor. Do not waste my time or your own."

At this crucial moment there was a confused bustling and whispering at the door of the Director's office. In a moment a man entered, a fat and oily-looking man wearing a cape of almost pure gold, touched only with a little blue.

The two visitors got to their feet, and a fresh round of introductions began, this time with more ceremony than before. The new arrival was actually Theodore, Chief Priest of the Blue Temple in Eylau.

From the moment of his arrival in the room, the Chief Priest's manner indicated that he was at least somewhat mistrustful of everyone else, including his own Director of Security.

When all were seated again, Wen Chang repeated, for Chief Priest Theodore's benefit, his statement about the discovery of a plot to steal the jewel.

Theodore did not trouble to deny the presence of the Orb inside his establishment. Instead he asked Wen Chang bluntly: "How do you know this?"

"The circumstances in which I gained the information are closely connected to the original investigation upon which my associate and myself were engaged. More than that I cannot tell you at present. You will appreciate that I extend to all my clients the same confidentiality I would extend to you, were I retained by you personally, or by the Blue Temple."

This speech did not go down well with either of Wen Chang's priestly hearers, who exchanged grim looks. Then the Director still attempted to deny the presence of the Great Orb, and even disclaimed any knowledge of its whereabouts.

The Magistrate was growing impatient with them. "Come, come! I know that the gem we are speaking of is in this city, and I am almost certain that it is within the walls of this very building."

At this point the Chief Priest asked Wen Chang and Kasimir, politely enough, to step into another room while he had a private discussion with his Security Director.

Wen Chang signed agreement and got to his feet. "Of course, gentlemen. But I advise you not to take too long to make up your minds to listen to me. In this matter time is of great importance."

The Director glared at him. "It seems to me that we could all save time if you would condescend to tell us the source of your alleged information."

The Magistrate appeared to be maintaining his patience only with an effort. "Even if I was willing to break confidence with my client—which I am not—nothing I could tell you about the source would help you in the least to prevent the theft. By the way, I suppose you are perfectly sure that the stone is secure at this moment?"

This question threw the two high authorities into a state of considerable confusion, impossible to conceal. As an open argument began between them, Wen Chang and Kasimir were conducted away by an underling.

They were deposited in a comfortable anteroom and left alone with the door closed. They glanced at each other, but neither had anything to say. It was obvious to both of them that any conversation they held would almost certainly be overheard.

The duration of their wait dragged on, to a length that Kasimir, at least, had not expected. Wen Chang waited with newly imperturbable patience, hands clasped in his lap, his weathered face impassive as a mask. But Kasimir was bothered by mounting apprehension. Had they somehow unwittingly precipitated a real crisis in the local Blue Temple leadership? Had they—but such speculations were pointless.

Eventually a silent attendant brought them refreshment on a tray, tea and cakes in portions of hardly more than symbolic size. Both courteously declined. Following that they were again left alone for almost an hour, when a group of temple officials, including the High Priest and the Director of Security, suddenly entered the anteroom. They brought with them a newcomer, an outsider to the temple, a man attired in the uniform of an officer of the city Watch, in the Hetman's colors of gray and blue. This was a large grizzled veteran of about forty.

As soon as this man's eyes fell on Wen Chang, he stepped forward and opened his arms in greeting.

"Magistrate!" His voice was a bass roar. "They told me there was someone here I might recognize, but they never gave me a hint that it was you. It's years since we have worked together—how are you?"

Wen Chang, smiling, had arisen to return the greeting heartily. "I am healthy and busy as you see. And how are you, my friend Almagro? It is indeed too long a time since we have seen each other, but you do not appear to have changed much."

After Kasimir had been duly introduced to Captain Almagro, the two veterans spent a few moments more in private conversation, most of it reminiscing about a particularly filthy gang of bandits they had once succeeded in luring into an annihilating ambush. In this exchange of memories they must have removed from the minds of their priestly hearers any lingering doubts of the Magistrate's true identity.

The discussion turned away from the bandit gang. Almagro mentioned how, after several unlikely sounding adventures, he had come to be now in the employ of the Hetman.

"And a good thing I am here, too, for now I may be able to return the great favor that you, Magistrate, once did for me."

Wen Chang made a dismissive gesture and objected mildly. "It was a matter of no consequence."

"On the contrary, I consider my life to be a rather significant component of the universe. So tell me, what brings you and your friend to Eylau, Magistrate? A job of thieftaking?"

"I thank you for your generous offer of help, Captain, and it may be indeed that my associate and I will want to call upon you in the near future. As to the exact nature of our mission in Eylau, I must tell you that I am bound by an oath of secrecy. Just at the moment, however, our problem concerns the Orb of Maecenas. What can you tell us about its current safety?"

At this point in the conversation the Director of Security appeared to be trying to say something urgent, while at the same time wanting to avoid the disclosure of any information at all. He was rescued from this self-strangled state by the Captain of the Watch, who shook his head at him ruefully.

"I'm afraid the presence of the gem here in the temple is no longer a secret," Captain Almagro told the official almost apologetically. "One hears about it these days in the streets."

The Chief Priest, a vein outstanding in his forehead, was fixing a baleful glance upon his Director of Security.

"I am going," Theodore said, "directly from this room to the lapidary's workshop, there to see for myself whether the Orb is still in our hands or not at this moment." His eyes swept fiercely around the little group. "I want all of you to come with me!"

A moment later, with Chief Priest Theodore in the lead, the whole party was tramping through a series of elegant corridors, traversing one after another a series of doorways, each doubly guarded by warriors cloaked in blue and gold, the Blue Temple's own security force. At every doorway the guards saluted and stood aside at a gesture from the Chief Priest's chubby hand.

The party with Theodore at its head had not far to go before it reached its goal, a set of unmarked heavy doors. Here too guards stood aside. Then the doors were opened a crack from inside in response to an impatient tapping with the Chief Priest's heavy golden ring, and then they were thrown wide as soon as he was recognized.

The party of visitors filed into the room. It was a workshop, much smaller and cleaner, Kasimir noted, than the studio of Robert de Borron across town. This place was also much quieter than de Borron's studio, and it had not been at all crowded until their group arrived. Here, instead of noise and confusion, was a sense that great logic and precision ruled.

There were three people in the room already when Theodore entered with his entourage. The person in charge here was a short, intense, black-skinned woman of about thirty years of age, who was soon introduced to all who did not know her as Mistress Hedmark, the famed lapidary. It was one of those fields like forensic medicine, Kasimir supposed, in which one could be famous and at the same time almost totally unknown to the world at large.

The other two people already present were the famous woman's assistants. The Mistress, despite her lack of size, looked to Kasimir quite as hard and tough as the sculptor at the other temple. The physician got the impression that she would be quite capable of murder and robbery to get something that she really wanted.

Under a broad, heavily barred window, where the best light in the room obtained, an elaborate workbench had been set up. In response to a question from Wen Chang, Mistress Hedmark explained that she and her helpers had been busy practicing the techniques that they would use when the time came for the actual cutting of the priceless gem.

The surface of the workbench was largely covered with a framework of jigs and supports. Kasimir saw that there was a fine revolving grindstone along with other tools, some doubtless more magical than technological.

Having given a concise explanation of her work, the Mistress had a query of her own. "And now, gentlemen, I must insist on knowing what you want here. I don't like all these people in my workroom."

"Nor would I, ordinarily." Chief Priest Theodore shook his head. "But I want to see the Orb for myself, to make sure that it is still safe. And if it is I want to show it to them."

"Of course it is quite safe," said Mistress Hedmark automatically. Then she looked at Theodore for a moment, and then at his chief of security. Then she shrugged and drew a cord from around her neck and inside her clothing. It was a leather cord with a small key hanging at the end of it.

The Director of Security produced a similar key from somewhere. Meanwhile others in the party were making sure that the outer doors of the room were closed. Then Mistress Hedmark, together with the Director, went to a great metal box in one corner of the room. Kasimir had enough sense of magic to sense the immaterial barricades surrounding it, forces that subsided only when the Director whispered a secret word.

It was necessary for the custodians to use their two keys simultaneously. Then they were able to open the box and swing back the heavy lid.

Mistress Hedmark reached inside. The Orb of Maecenas was brought out and held up in her fingers for everyone to look at.

It was only the size of a small, faceted egg; somehow this came as a faint disappointment to Kasimir, who had unconsciously been expecting something the size of his fist. But then he had never found wealth in any of its manifestations overwhelmingly interesting.

"Are you satisfied, then?" Mistress Hedmark demanded of the delegation that had burst in on her.

"Yes, for the moment." Much of the tension was gone from Theodore's voice. His gaze had softened, resting on the gem, and he allowed himself a little sigh.

The lapidary asked in her sharp tones: "Has there actually been a plot to steal the Orb?"

The Magistrate spoke soothingly. "We have had an alarm. So far as I know there has been no more than that as yet. Has anything untoward happened here? Or to you or any of your assistants?"

The attention of the group focused on each of the aides in turn: No, none of them had anything like that to report. Kasimir found the denials credible.

Mistress Hedmark discoursed briefly to the others on the art of the diamond cutter, and the problems inherent in trying to cut so very hard a stone, the hardest substance known. The discussion sounded quite open and innocent to Kasimir.

He could see or hear nothing to indicate that this woman might already have the Sword of Siege in hand to help her with her work, or that it had ever entered her mind to try to get it.

8

BOTH the Chief Priest of the temple and his Director of Security were considerably relieved when they were able to verify with their own eyes that the almost priceless Orb was still in their possession. They were both ready now to consider what Wen Chang wanted to tell them.

The Magistrate, after a quick consultation with Captain Almagro, had several recommendations to make. The first was that arrangements should be made to station officers of the city Watch—not the Captain himself, he could not be spared—here in the lapidary's workshop as long as the gem was present. The Watch people would serve in shifts, so that at least one should be on duty around the clock.

The second recommendation made by Wen Chang was that an entire new squad of Blue Temple security people be brought in, to replace all those who were currently engaged in protecting the stone.

"I emphasize," Wen Chang continued, "that I have no reason to think any of the old crew are implicated in the plot to steal the diamond; no, I make this suggestion purely as a precaution."

Chief Priest Theodore exchanged glances with his chief subordinate in security matters. Then the chubby man shrugged. "Very well. A sensible precaution, I think. It shall be done as you say."

Mistress Hedmark was not happy, though. She complained that these changes would entail further disruption of the routine of technical practice and ritual in which she was engaged with her assistants. Peace and tranquility were necessary for her work.

The Chief Priest heard her out, then overruled her. "Now that the whole world knows the gem is here, we can take no chances."

Wen Chang tried to soothe the lapidary too. Then he said: "Now,

Doctor Kasimir and myself must be on our way. Captain Almagro, if you could withdraw with us? There is much we have to discuss with you in the matter of how potential jewel thieves should best be taken. And these gentlemen of the temple, and Mistress Hedmark, will also have much to discuss among themselves."

As the three of them were escorted out of the temple, Kasimir marveled to himself at the smoothness with which Wen Chang had been able to accomplish several objectives during their brief visit. First, they had determined with a fair degree of certainty that the Sword was not in the Blue Temple now. Next, to have an officer of the city Watch continuously present in the diamond-cutters' workshop ought to make it practically impossible for Mistress Hedmark and her crew to use the Sword secretly in their work, assuming they might have the chance to do so— and any efforts to get the Watch out of the way would signal that they were up to something clandestine. Finally, the priests of the Blue Temple were now convinced that Wen Chang was trying to help them.

There was little conversation among the three men as long as they were still inside the temple. When they had passed out through the front entrance, and were halfway across the fronting square, Captain Almagro muttered something that Kasimir did not entirely catch, but that made the physician think the Watch officer did not really care for the place they had just left.

Wen Chang's reply at least was clear: "Hot work in there, old friend, trying to get the moneybags to believe us. I think it might be time for us to ease our throats with a mug of something cool."

The Captain brightened immediately. "My idea exactly, Magistrate. And I know just the place, not far away."

"Lead on."

After making their way through several blocks of the activity that occupied the streets of the metropolis at midday, the three men were soon seated in the cool recesses of a tavern, a large, old building of half-timbered construction. The main room was filled with the delicious smells of cooking food, and occupied by a good number of appreciative customers.

One of the barmaids, who was evidently an old acquaintance of the Captain, served them swiftly. Wiping his mustache after his first gulp of ale, Almagro expressed his doubt that there was any real plot to steal the Orb at all—though he referred to the matter only indirectly. He bewailed the increasing tawdriness of crime in these newly degenerate days. Not only the times and the crimes, but the modern criminals themselves, suffered from degeneracy. By and large they were far from being the bold brave rascals that their predecessors of a decade or so ago had used to be.

"Hey, Magistrate? Am I right?"

"You are almost invariably right, old friend. And there is much truth in what you say now." Wen Chang groomed his own slim mustache with one finger.

"Damned right, very much truth. Want an example? Look at those people who're demonstrating in front of the Hetman's palace now, pounding their stupid heads on the pavement. If they choose to damage their own thick skulls, so what? What kind of a crime is that? And yet we've orders now to make them stop it."

The Magistrate made a gesture indicating resignation. "The subject of their protest—this Benjamin of the Steppe as he is called—he would not seem to me to be a very great offender either. To ask for a few local councils, voting on local matters, deciding such things for themselves. And yet it seems that he must pay with his life for his offense."

"Ah, that's politics. There's always that, and when it comes to politics the police must just do what they're told. If we had a different ruler, politics would go on just the same, only with different faces in the dungeons. Different feet climbing up the scaffold."

"I fear you are right."

"Damned right I'm right." The Captain belched, and drank again.

Wen Chang murmured something properly sympathetic, and Kasimir, taking his lead from his chief, did likewise.

"Not like the old days," Almagro summed up, and drank deep from his mug. "No, not at all."

"I wonder if you could do me a favor?" Wen Chang inquired.

"Glad to," was the automatic response. But then the Captain blinked in hesitation. "What is it?"

"I know the prisoner's number of a man who was sentenced, probably several months ago, to the road-building gang that is now working between here and the Abohar Oasis. I would like to discover as much as possible about the man himself—his name, his crime, whatever else you can find out."

"Is that all?" The Captain was relieved. "Sure, I can look that up. What's the number?"

"Nine-nine-six-seven-seven."

Almagro pulled out a scrap of paper and laboriously made a note to himself. "Nothing to it."

"But I suppose," said Wen Chang after a moment's silence, "that in this huge city, despite the degeneracy of these modern would-be criminals, and the futile protesters, there remain a small number of real thieves, and also some genuinely dangerous individuals."

"Ah yes, of course. If you say so, it's possible you're really onto something about a plot—to swipe the Orb." The Captain looked around him cautiously before uttering those last words. And now conversation was briefly suspended while the barmaid placed in front of each of them a bowl of steaming stew.

"Only place on the street where I'd order stew," Almagro muttered, taking up his spoon with energy. "But here it's good."

"Indeed, not bad," said Wen Chang, tasting appreciatively. Kasimir, who would have declined if he had been asked whether he wanted stew or not, tried the stuff in his own bowl and had to agree.

Half a bowl later, Wen Chang prodded the Captain: "You were saying, about the present elite of real criminals—?"

"Yes, of course. Well, in this city there are naturally lawbreakers beyond counting. But very few of this modern bunch would have the nerve, talent, or resources even to think of undertaking any job like the one you suspect is being planned at the Blue Temple."

"And I suppose that once such a gem was stolen, it would be difficult even in Eylau to arrange to sell it, or dispose of it in trade for lesser gems."

The Captain smacked his lips over the stew, and tore off a chunk of bread from the fresh loaf the barmaid had deposited in the middle of the table. "Difficult, yes. But in Eylau nothing is totally impossible. No matter how rare and unique an object of value may be, there'll be someone in this city who can buy it—paying only a small fraction of the real worth, maybe, but—"

"Naturally." Wen Chang nodded. "And it is part of your job to know who these folk are."

"I know most of them. And there are not many who'd want to handle something like the Orb—today there are even fewer, in fact, than there were just yesterday morning."

The Magistrate's hand paused, supporting a mug of ale halfway to his lips. "Oh? And what is responsible for this diminution in numbers?"

"I'd say it was the result of a disagreement between buyer and seller,

of just what property I don't know." The Captain went on to relate
how, only yesterday evening, one of the city's most rascally merchants
and most celebrated dealers in stolen valuables had been found dead, his
body drifting in a backwater of the Tungri, near the lower docks.

Wen Chang had set down his mug again without drinking. "And
have you turned up any clue, old friend, as to who killed this man or
why?"

"Interests you, does it, Magistrate? I should have realized it would.
No, I'm afraid that there's no such clue. Apart from the fact that whatever happened was a bit more than your ordinary little squabble. Two
other bodies were also found nearby, of men who must have been killed
at the same time, in the same fight. Don't know who they were."

"And there is no clue as to who killed them, either."

"Just so. Ah, we do our best, Magistrate. Whenever there's a com-
plaint of robbery or assault in the city we in the Watch will do what we
can to get the miscreants taken into custody, and hold them for trial
before the magistrates of this city."

"I am sure that you do your best."

"We do. But as you can well imagine, in a city of this size it would be
hopeless to expect to solve very many of the crimes."

Wen Chang drained his tankard. "It would interest me very much—
and I am sure it would interest Kasimir too—if we could see those
bodies, of the men killed yesterday."

"Ah? And maybe your interest is a little more than purely theoreti-
cal?" The Captain's eyes, suddenly shrewder than before, probed at
both of his companions from under shaggy brows. "Well, the gods know
I owe you a bigger favor than that, Magistrate. We'll see what we can
do, though the family of our late prominent merchant may not welcome
any more attentions by the Watch."

"It is the other bodies, the unidentified ones, that I find more particularly interesting."

"Oh? That's all right, then. Except that they may already have been
exposed on the northern walls. We'd best go right away and take a
look."

Kasimir and the Captain finished their drinks.

In Eylau, as Captain Almagro explained while they walked, the disposal of paupers' bodies, and any other unidentified or unclaimed dead,
was carried out atop a section of city wall, a tall spur of fortification

about a hundred meters long, which currently went nowhere and protected nothing. This section had become disconnected from the main walls of the city as a result of the destruction of some ancient war, and the subsequent rebuilding according to a different plan. Here, barely within the city's modern walls, and four or five stories above the ground, the remains were set out in the open air to be the prey of winged scavengers. Many of these creatures were reptilian; others, originally the product of experiments in magic and genetics, were hybrids of reptile and bird.

There were no human dwellings very near the isolated section of wall now called the Paupers' Palace, except for a few huts of the poor and almost homeless, who from their doorways could contemplate what their own final fate in this world was likely to be.

When the investigators arrived at the base of the mortuary wall, Captain Almagro sought out and spoke to a particular attendant. This man bowed and murmured his respect for the Captain, and passed the three visitors along to another man. This fellow conducted the three investigators up a stone stairway, dangerously worn and crumbling, to the wall's top.

Here, under the leaden sky, filling the broad strip of pavement between the parapets, was a scattered litter of more-or-less dried human bones, with here and there a more recent arrival. The older bones, pulverized and scattered, crunched underfoot; if you moved about at all there was no way to avoid stepping on some of them. Kasimir understood from a few words of explanation offered by the attendant that the bones finally rejected by the scavengers were gathered periodically and burned or buried somewhere.

By now it had begun to drizzle again in Eylau, and Kasimir had heard people talking about the fierce windstorms out over the desert. Up here atop the Paupers' Palace the drying-out of corpses was undoubtedly being set back by the wet weather. The smell here at the moment was rather worse than at the last opened grave, out in the quarry, and Kasimir once more pulled out an amulet from his pouch of magical equipment. Presently a scent of fresh mint began to dominate.

At a word from Almagro the attendant who had escorted them upstairs pointed out the two bodies that had been brought in with knife wounds yesterday afternoon.

Whatever the losers of that fight might have possessed in the way of clothing or valuables had of course been stripped from them already, either before or after they arrived at this last stop. By now, Kasimir noted, their eyes were missing as well, evidently the first gourmet morsels to be claimed by the scavengers. One of these reptilian beasts, the size of a large vulture but with iridescent scales, was in attendance now, and flew up heavily with a squeak of protest as the men approached.

But certain items of important evidence remained, and it might be possible to learn the essentials, thought Kasimir, even without making a very close examination of these bodies.

One of them was that of a red-haired, freckled man whose stocky build and thick limbs indicated that he had been strong, before someone's narrow blade had opened those thin fatal doorways in his chest.

"The treacherous foreman," Kasimir commented, almost at first glance. He chose to disregard the fact that his words could be heard by Almagro, who was standing back, watching intently to see what his old friend would be able to make of this evidence. There would be no keeping the Captain out of the matter now.

Wen Chang, kneeling by the first body, nodded abstractedly. In a moment he had concluded his own examination, and stood up, brushing off his hands.

"Treachery is a powerful medicine, and those who rely upon it are likely to die of an overdose. It is easy enough to imagine the scene yesterday. A meeting, somewhere near the river, between the murderous foreman Kovil, and the equally dishonest Eylau merchant, with each principal supported by at least one retainer. From the beginning, an enlightened distrust on both sides, who are strangers to each other. Then, the display of the stolen treasure—a vaster prize than even avarice had imagined—and then the sudden flare of treachery and violence."

In a moment he had turned his attention to the second body. It was that of a stranger to Kasimir, though it ought to have been identifiable, he thought, by anyone who had known the man in life. This fellow too had died of blade wounds, and these wounds were larger, as if made by a full-sized sword, perhaps Stonecutter itself. By all reports eleven of the Twelve—all except Woundhealer—were fine weapons apart from the magical powers they possessed.

"This one has been neither prisoner nor overseer at a quarry in the desert," Wen Chang muttered after a minute, standing up again. "His skin is everywhere too pale for that. I assume he is some minor criminal of the city." Then he turned to Almagro and asked: "I would like to see the place where the bodies were found."

"Of course."

They descended from the wall, and Kasimir was able to put away his magic scent. Next Almagro conducted them back into the center of Eylau. Standing on the bank of the river, he pointed out the place where the bodies were said to have been found, drifting in a pool or large eddy on the left bank of the river.

The Magistrate looked up and about, slightly upstream.

"I see dark stains," he announced, "upon that windowsill."

Kasimir could see very little at the distance. But along with the Captain he followed the Magistrate into an old building whose empty windows gaped out over the Tungri.

The three investigators entered the building and climbed to an upper level to find that there were still bloodstains on the worn floor.

"There is no doubt that the fight took place here," mused Wen Chang. "And whoever survived took the trouble to dump the bodies into the river, hoping thereby to postpone their discovery. Ah, if only I had been able to inspect this place sooner! Clues have a way of vanishing quickly with the passage of time."

But Wen Chang soon gave up his lamenting and went to work, examining every centimeter of the scene with a thoroughness Kasimir found surprising—not so Almagro, who had evidently seen similar performances in the past.

Soon the Magistrate was able to discover, on an inner wall of exposed brickwork, a place where Stonecutter had left its distinctive marks. Kasimir could easily imagine the great Sword, swung in combat, taking a small chunk neatly out of the solid wall—and then, its energy unslowed, going on to cut down someone.

Almagro, scowling, looked at the place. He said: "I think you'd better tell me the whole story."

"We shall," Wen Chang promised.

Kasimir asked, "But then who has the Sword now?"

"Someone who was strong and fierce and cunning and lucky enough to survive that meeting yesterday. It seems that our task may be only beginning."

9

STILL standing in the room where the fight had taken place, Wen Chang and Kasimir completed the job of taking Captain Almagro into their confidence regarding the true nature of their mission in Eylau. The Captain, naturally anxious to hear the whole story, listened eagerly.

He had of course heard of the Twelve Swords, and was naturally impressed with the value of such a treasure. "Small wonder, then, that these scum are killing each other over it. And you say the dead man with the red hair was really a foreman on one of the Hetman's stone quarry gangs?"

"I have no doubt that it is the same man. He and a companion brought the Sword here to the city. Doubtless Kovil—that was the foreman's name—expected that his absence from his post would not cause any problems until they had completed the sale—and once he had his fortune in hand it would no longer matter."

The Captain shook his head. "As a rule those convict-labor places are not very well supervised. Not even the ones with the really dangerous people in them. I don't doubt he thought he could get away with it."

"And is the quarry in question populated with really dangerous people, as you call them?"

"Ardneh bless you, Magistrate, that one gets some of the worst. The worst in the line of ordinary, nonpolitical crooks, I mean. I heard a judge tell a convict that hanging was too good for him, and then send him there for ten years—which in the quarry is the same as life."

"And where, I suppose, even the worst offender may be almost forgotten, and ignored." Wen Chang looked worried. "Almagro, I want you to arrest Kovil's hand-picked replacement, Umar, now, and bring him into the city. Preferably to some quiet place where I may be able to question him in privacy, and no one else will pay too much attention. Meanwhile it might be a good idea to preserve the body of the red-haired man, so that Umar can be confronted with it, and shown that at least he has nothing to fear from that quarter any longer. Then, perhaps, he will tell us who Kovil took with him as a companion from the quarry. If Umar still hesitates to tell us the truth about that, a matching of the records at the quarry with the prisoners still actually there may be necessary to tell us who is missing. I want to know the identity of the second man."

"Because he's most likely the one who has the big knife now."

"Exactly. And, by the way, there is something else that you should know, my friend. A large reward has been promised me if my search in this city can be brought to a successful conclusion. You will remember from our past dealings that I am inclined to share such rewards generously."

"I remember that fact very well, Magistrate! And I'll certainly see what I can do about fulfilling all your requests. But reward or not, remember that I can promise nothing."

On leaving the riverside building, the three separated. Almagro had plenty of official work to occupy him. Kasimir had an appointment in the afternoon to meet Natalia, and he did not want to miss it. And Wen Chang was now rather anxious to get back to the inn, fearing that in his absence the elderly caller of yesterday might return, and Lieutenant Komi would after all not detain him.

Kasimir, hearing this fear expressed as the two walked toward the inn, remarked: "You have little faith in Komi, then?"

"I admit that I have some doubts about him." The Magistrate refused to elaborate on that.

As soon as Kasimir and his mentor arrived at the Inn of the Refreshed Travelers, Wen Chang fired questions at Lieutenant Komi, but the replies were disappointing. The Firozpur officer said he had seen nothing of yesterday's elderly visitor. There had been a couple of other people in today asking about antique weapons, but when Wen Chang had heard the details of these inquiries he judged neither of them to be of any importance.

When Kasimir asked Komi a routine question about his men, the lieutenant responded in a satisfied voice that almost all of them had so far kept out of trouble—the one exception was of small moment, involving as it did only one trooper, and a minor altercation in a tavern, which fortunately had been resolved before anyone had called in the Watch.

Wen Chang put in a question: "I don't suppose it had anything to do with the sale or purchase of antique weapons?"

"Nothing whatsoever, sir."

"I thought not. You are continuing to send out winged messengers to your prince?"

"I've dispatched a couple, sir."

"Have any yet returned?"

"No sir." For the first time in Kasimir's experience, Komi looked worried. "They say that there are sandstorms over the desert. Flyers going either way might have trouble getting through."

"Too bad. And are your men all present and ready for duty now?"

"Yes sir. With one exception." The lieutenant went on to assure the Magistrate that the one exception was only a trooper—not the same one who had had the fight—who had relatives in what was called the Desert Quarter of the city. It was called that because of the high proportion of former nomads among its population. That trooper had gone, with Komi's leave, to pay his relatives a brief visit.

Wen Chang ordered the officer to grant no more leaves for the moment—the one already authorized could remain in force—and turned to gaze out the third-floor window. The intermittent rain had now stopped for the time being, leaving picturesque puddles in the courtyard. Now, as the sun emerged briefly from behind a cloud, some of these puddles turned to rainbow pools, stained with spilled dye from the cargo of some merchant's loadbeasts.

Without turning from the window, the Magistrate said to Kasimir: "So far we have observed three different groups in the city, any one of which in my opinion is likely to have the Sword in their possession now, or to very shortly gain possession of it from our mysterious former quarryman. For the time being I intend to concentrate our investigation upon these groups."

Already the sun was gone behind clouds again, and already rain had once more begun to fall, making a steady drip from eaves and gutters just outside the window. Kasimir said: "The first group, I take it, are the authorities at the Red Temple."

"If you wish you may count them as the first—if you include with them the sculptor Robert de Borron."

"Then is it true that you don't think the Red Temple are really the most likely candidates?"

"I did not say that."

Kasimir sighed. "Well, I shall of course find out all that I can about them—and about the sculptor—from Natalia when I see her today."

"Do so by all means. But if she tells you nothing of interest, we may have to institute some stronger measures there—you see, I am interested in the Red Temple. Where and when are you going to meet her?"

"Inside the White Temple, in about an hour and a half." Kasimir at the window tried to judge the height of the clouded sun. "It seemed a good place to arrange a casual encounter."

Wen Chang nodded his approval. "No doubt it will serve."

"So, then, we come to the second group under suspicion. I presume them to be the people at the Blue Temple?"

"Yes. Naturally their leaders would want to gain such a treasure if they could. They have probably already convinced themselves that their organization has an inherent right to possess anything so valuable. And I am sure that Mistress Hedmark would seize any opportunity that might arise to use the Sword in her work. Whether she knows that it is nearby and might be available . . ." Wen Chang shrugged.

"I suppose there's no doubt that Stonecutter would carve a small stone as neatly and easily as a great one?"

"In my mind there is none. It is my understanding that the god Vulcan forged that blade to cut stones, and that is precisely what it will do, with divine power. Though neither of us has ever seen the Sword or handled it, we have now seen enough of its work to feel confident on that point."

"I agree with you that Mistress Hedmark will be trying to get her hands on it if she can."

"Yes . . . Kasimir, I am of two minds about going public with our search. I mean spreading the word as widely as possible that the Sword is lost, and that it is definitely the property of Prince al-Farabi—which is close enough to the exact truth for our purposes. There are certainly difficulties, but still it will be well to have made that point, so that when the Sword is recovered the Prince's claim will be well established."

"You said 'when the Sword is recovered,' Magistrate. I admire your confidence."

Wen Chang smiled dryly. "It is a useful quality."

Kasimir paused for a moment, cleared his throat, and shook his head. "So, after the Blue Temple we come to the third group of suspects, who, I take it, must be the gang—if that is the right word for an organization some of whose members must be quite respectable—associated with the crooked merchant, lately deceased. Judging by what we have heard of them so far, they would cheerfully try to steal the wings off a demon, if they thought they had even the remotest chance of getting away with it."

"You are probably correct. On the other hand, the professional criminals might be easier for us to deal with in one respect at least. They might be willing to collect a ransom and return their loot to al-Farabi or his representatives. And they might even be disposed to be reasonable about the price, considering that the alternative would be severe prosecution—perhaps I mean persecution—by the authorities. We could certainly collaborate with our friend the Captain in an effort to provide that." Wen Chang fell silent, regarding his youngest friend attentively, as if waiting for his reaction.

Kasimir considered. "So, the question becomes, which of these three groups actually has, or is most likely to get, Stonecutter? If Kovil's mysterious bodyguard carried it away from the scene of the fight by the river, has he yet managed to sell it to one of them? Or possibly to someone else altogether?"

The Magistrate's eyes were even narrower than usual. "It would not be wise to dissipate our energies too widely. We will concentrate upon the three groups that I have named."

Kasimir found himself a little irritated by the dogmatic tone of that last sentence. "Of course, you are in charge of the investigation. Though I suppose it is possible that the Sword of Siege *is* really with someone else altogether?"

"Yes, many things are possible." Wen Chang's tone was even; if Kasimir had hoped to provoke an explanation he was disappointed. "Nevertheless, I repeat, we are going to confine our attentions to those three groups, at least for now. So you had better prepare yourself for your meeting with the agent you have recruited to spy on the Red Temple."

The physician needed only a few minutes to complete the few preparations he thought necessary. When he was ready to go, he paused on his way out. "There is one other matter that I cannot stop wondering about: the identity of our original thief, whose body we found buried at the quarry. Perhaps it is only because I actually saw him in the act; I suppose that it hardly matters any longer who he was."

The Magistrate hesitated. Then he said: "On the contrary, I should say that it matters a great deal."

"Eh? Why?"

Wen Chang leaned back in his chair. "There are several interesting points about that man. To begin with, there is the fascinating fact that, as you describe the event, he found it necessary to slit the wall of your tent twice."

"I admit that I puzzled for some time over that detail. But I could see no good reason for it."

"Perhaps you are not approaching the question properly. Of course your attitude may be justified—people sometimes do unreasonable, inexplicable things."

"Yes, they do. You said you found more than one point about the man to be interesting?"

"I consider it also very interesting that the thief was working from the start in accordance with a plan, that the theft was not the mere seizing of an opportunity."

"Well, the only real evidence for his having a plan, it seems to me, is the fact that he brought along an extra riding-beast. Indicating, of course, that he intended to rescue the first prisoner from the road-building gang. But he did not bring along two extra mounts. So we may deduce that the second rescue, that of the prisoner at the quarry, was not planned from the start. It was an improvisation, undertaken perhaps only at the suggestion of the first prisoner to gain the freedom of someone else."

"Very good, Kasimir! We will make an investigator of you yet. What else have you been able to deduce from these facts?"

"Well—nothing as yet."

"As you continue your efforts there are a couple of points you ought to keep in mind. First, no one is likely to steal one of the Twelve Swords with the *sole* object of using it to free a prisoner from that road-building gang. That could be accomplished much more easily . . ." Wen Chang's voice trailed off. His eyes appeared to be gazing at something in the distance, over Kasimir's shoulder.

"Magistrate?"

"A thought has struck me. Never mind, go to your meeting. Learn all that you can from the interesting Natalia. What you learn may be of great importance."

Kasimir set out, pondering the situation as he walked. He had to pay careful attention to where he was going, because his goal this time was in a different part of the city from those which he had previously visited.

The White Temple of Eylau, like most of its kind around the world, was a large, pyramidal building. This example was faced with white marble, while a good many others Kasimir had seen were only painted white. And in this building, as in almost all White Temples everywhere, a good part of its sizable volume was devoted to hospital facilities. Here no one who came seeking food or medical care or emergency shelter would be turned away. Nor would anyone be absolutely forced to pay, though donations were solicited from all who appeared able to give anything at all.

Kasimir's appointment with Natalia was in the Chapel of Ardneh, also a standard feature of most White Temples. Here the chapel was located about halfway up the slopesided structure. It was a white, large room, well lighted by many windows in its slanting outer wall. The room held a number of plain wooden chairs and benches. Above the altar an Old World votive light burned steadily, a pure whiteness without flame or smoke. The altar itself was dominated by a modern image of the ancient god Ardneh. Images of Ardneh as a rule—this one was no exception—were almost always at least partially abstract, in keeping with the idea that the eternal foe of the archdemon Orcus was essentially different from all other gods.

This particular image was an assemblage of bronze blocks and slabs, looking eerily bluish because of some quality in the perpetual glow of the votive light above.

Kasimir took a seat near the middle of the simply furnished chapel and looked around him, at the few others who had come to this place for worship or meditation.

There was one more statue in the chapel, this one of the god Draffut. Carved of some brown stone, it stood in its own niche or grotto off to one side. In this image, as tall as a man, the popular Lord of Beasts and of Healing looked like nothing more, Kasimir thought, than a dog standing on his hind legs. During the last few years a rumor had swept across the land to the effect that Draffut was recently dead; of course a great many people held that the Beastlord, like the other gods, had been

dead for many years. Meanwhile considerable numbers of folk continued to insist that some of the gods or all of them were still alive, and
would come back one day to call people to account for what they had
been doing in the divinities' absence.

Natalia entered the chapel shortly after Kasimir had arrived, and
came quietly to take a chair beside his. She was dressed in a skirt and
blouse and sandals with narrow straps, more citified clothing than when
Kasimir had seen her last, though hardly of any higher quality.

"Hope I'm not late," she whispered demurely.

"Not at all." Actually he had rather enjoyed the interval of waiting,
the chance for peaceful meditation. He might not want to work all day
in a White Temple, but they were good places to visit, havens where you
could sit as long as you wished and not be bothered, unless it might be
by one of your fellow visitors. Street people now and then came in to
take up collections for this or that, or frankly as beggars. None were
ejected, as a rule, unless others complained about them to the White
Guards.

But, back to business. "How did the modeling go?" he asked.

"Not as embarrassing as I had feared—and actually they paid me a
trifle more for it than I had expected."

"That's good. But I suppose you've seen nothing of what I wanted
you to look for?"

"Nothing, I am sorry to say."

"And you go back there tomorrow?"

"That's right. He says he'll want me for several days yet at least. It's
the master himself I'm posing for."

"De Borron, then. Good. What kind of tools is he using to work the
stone?"

She blinked at him solemnly as if she understood this question must
be important but could not think why. "A hammer and a chisel. Several
different chisels actually. Nothing like the special item that you described to me."

"All right. And you haven't mentioned that special item to anyone
else—hey?"

"Not at all. Of course not. You told me not to." Natalia's new lowcut
upper garment showed a lot of pale skin below the former neckline of
the old peasant blouse. Her hair was now worn in a new style too,
Kasimir realized vaguely, though it still looked like strings of dishwa-
ter.

He asked her: "Who else is present in the studio?"

"It's about the same as when you were there, people coming and going. Did you want me to try to keep track of them?"

"Not necessarily. No, you'd better just concentrate on the important thing."

Their conversation about conditions in the Red Temple meandered along, pausing when a stooped old priest in white robes moved close past them on his way to light a candle at the altar.

Kasimir was coming slowly to the realization that he found himself attracted to this woman. Somewhere in his mind, not very far below the surface, he resented the idea of the sculptor and all those red-robes staring at her body. The truth was that he wanted to stare at it himself.

But the purpose of this meeting of course was business. Instead of inviting Natalia to his room, he asked her if she would like something to eat or drink. As before, she accepted, and they moved to a nearby tavern where they enjoyed some food and drink. He also passed over the coins due her for her day's observations and report.

Telling himself it was his duty to become better acquainted with his agent, he justified somewhat prolonging the meeting; and the truth was that they each enjoyed the other's company. They exchanged some opinions upon art, and medicine, and life.

But soon Natalia was growing restless; she had other things to do, she said, and didn't volunteer any hint of what they were. Kasimir didn't volunteer any questions. Instead he went back to the inn alone.

It was near dusk when he arrived again at the sign of the Refreshed Travelers, and he felt somewhat tired. It had been a long and busy day, beginning with his and Wen Chang's visit to the Blue Temple in the morning.

But the long day was not over yet.

As soon as he entered the stable below their rooms, he discovered Lieutenant Komi and his men, fully armed and mobilized. Wen Chang was there too and they were waiting for Kasimir, in fact almost on the point of mounting up and leaving without him. Komi and his men looked ready and willing to say the least; the days of boredom were evidently beginning to tell on them.

Wen Chang said: "Word has just come from Captain Almagro. He has located one of the men who was in the fight yesterday, in which our foreman Kovil was killed. The man we want is hidden in an infamous den of thieves, and Almagro would like our help in digging him out."

The clouds of sleep were cleared in a moment from Kasimir's brain. "Then I am ready!"

10

IN a city with a population the size of Eylau's there would always be large numbers of folk awake and wanting light, and the city would never know total darkness as long as lamps and torches could be made to burn. But night was on the way to enfolding Eylau as completely as it ever did before Wen Chang and Kasimir were ready to mount their riding-beasts. As soon as they were mounted, and Lieutenant Komi and his troop of Firozpur soldiers were in the saddle behind them, their small force set out from the inn. The soldiers' uniforms and some of their weapons were effectively concealed under their desert capes.

Riding close beside Wen Chang at the head of the little column was a sergeant of the city Watch. This was the man who had been sent by Captain Almagro, to inform Almagro's partners that he was about to launch the raid, to request their help, and to guide them to the site as quickly as possible.

Kasimir, riding just behind Wen Chang and their guide, was wide awake now, not tired at all; the excitement of the chase was growing in him. So far their mounts were able to maintain a rapid pace; at this hour the darkened streets of the city held comparatively few people, and those who found themselves in the way of the silent, businesslike procession quickly moved aside.

Streets in the vicinity of the Inn of the Refreshed Travelers were comparatively broad. But it soon became apparent that their guide was leading them into a very different portion of the city. As they approached the district where the raid was to take place, the streets grew narrower and their windings even more convoluted.

This gradual constriction continued for some minutes, during which time the party, now often riding in single file, made the best speed possible. Then their guide signaled them for even slower movement, and less noise.

They had now come in sight of distant lamps, sparkling on a broad expanse of water. Kasimir realized that they were now once more near the bank of the Tungri, which here as elsewhere in the city was lined with docks and warehouses. He had no way to tell how far this site might be from the place where the bodies had been found. Boats bearing lights were passing in the night. Though the sea was thousands of kilometers distant, the river here evidently bore a great volume of local freight and passenger traffic.

In this section of the metropolis the residential area closest to the docks and warehouses was obviously a slum. On both sides of the street, tenements leaned against each other. Few lights showed in these close-packed, ramshackle buildings. The torches carried by a couple of the Firozpur troopers made a moving island of light in the narrow, dusty street.

In this neighborhood the people who appeared in the street were losers, the Emperor's children if Kasimir had ever seen the type. These slum-dwellers were quicker than people in other neighborhoods had been to scramble out of the way of the advancing column. Anonymous voices hidden on roofs and in windows above called out oaths and comments against the mounted men below, whom they took for a patrol of the Watch.

Presently the sergeant who was riding beside Wen Chang pulled his mount to a halt. Close ahead, two figures, one of them carrying a small torch, had just emerged from the mouth of a dark alley. In a moment Kasimir was able to recognize the man holding the torch as Captain Almagro.

The Captain came forward on foot and greeted his two chief colleagues eagerly but quietly as they swung down out of their saddles. Then he led them just inside the mouth of the alley, where he introduced them to his companion, a middle-aged man who tonight would be nameless in the line of duty, a wizard in the employ of the Watch.

"Before we discuss anything else," the Magistrate murmured to his old friend, "tell me whether you have managed to take care of the items I requested at our last meeting."

"I have set things in motion," said Almagro. "That is all I have been able to do so far."

"Then that is all that I can ask."

Next the Captain conducted a low-voiced briefing for the new arrivals, on the subject of the coming action.

The building he meant to raid had been abandoned as a warehouse several years ago, and was now notorious as a den of thieves and cutthroats. On looking out of the mouth of the alley where they now stood they could see it, just visible at the end of the street, less than a hundred meters away. The old warehouse was four or five stories high—depending on how you counted certain irregular additions—and contained perhaps as many as a hundred rooms. Almagro's basic plan was to break into the place through several entrances at the same time.

The Captain had assembled a dozen of his own men here in the alley, and with the reinforcements provided by the Firozpur he planned on being able to conduct the raid with overwhelming force. An attack on such a scale would surprise whatever criminals were in the building, and with any luck at all none of them would be able to get away.

The official wizard followed the Captain's briefing with a reassuring prediction that the gang in the building would be able to mount little or no magical resistance to the raid.

After Wen Chang had approved the plan of attack, the Watch sergeant who had served as guide took over the job of showing Lieutenant Komi exactly where his dismounted men should be deployed. More than a score of feet went shuffling off into the darkness. A couple of other Watch patrolmen were going to remain in this alley, keeping watch over the riding-beasts.

Almagro announced that he himself, with the Watch-wizard beside him, was going to direct operations from street level, while the Magistrate and Kasimir were to accompany the party attacking through the roof. Wen Chang approved this proposal too.

Before leaving his two unofficial colleagues, the Captain cast a worried glance at Kasimir, then shook his head and pronounced a last-minute warning.

"Doctor, there are a good many people in that building who aren't exactly going to welcome us with open arms when they see us. So mind yourself. In fact it might be a good idea if you stayed here, with the men who'll be watching our riding-beasts, until the fighting's done."

"Nonsense, I can take care of myself." Kasimir's tone was a little stiff; perhaps more than just a little. "I carry a dagger. And if one of your men will loan me his cudgel, I am quite prepared to answer for my own safety."

Almagro glanced at Wen Chang, shrugged, and turned to one of his own men nearby to give a quiet order. Kasimir accepted with thanks the oaken cudgel that was handed to him. The weapon was half a meter long, and weighted at one end. At the other end was a leather thong by which the club could be secured to its wielder's wrist. Kasimir had observed that cudgels like this were standard Watch equipment in Eylau, though tonight of course the men embarking upon the raid had equipped themselves with heavier weapons, including swords and axes.

Kasimir tucked the club into his belt, where it rested between two of the bulging pouches of his augmented medical kit. Then he signed that he was ready.

Wen Chang before leaving the inn had buckled on a lovely rapier, and now he was making sure of the fit of this weapon in its sheath. Kasimir had once or twice seen this sword among the Magistrate's belongings, though he had never seen him wearing it until now.

With everything in readiness, Almagro's two unofficial allies followed him through the alley, which was pitch-black except for his small, guttering torch. But the Watch officer seemed to know his way as well as a blind man on a familiar route.

Pausing after they had gone about a hundred meters, the Captain whispered to his companions that they were about to enter a building, another next door to the one they were about to raid. They stood in a doorway of this building, another abandoned-looking warehouse, on the side opposite their target structure. A ruined door on the level of the alley offered a sinister welcome, and once they were inside the building they confronted a tottering, treacherous stairway that Almagro whispered would bring them all the way up to the roof.

The darkness immediately surrounding their torchlight as they climbed was quiet, while crude music and drunken laughter sounded from a few buildings away. The night air smelled of the nearby river, an odor half fresh and half polluted. Kasimir listened in vain for any sounds from elsewhere in the building they had entered, or from the other assault parties, which ought to be getting into position at this moment. If all was going according to the plan Almagro had hastily outlined, two groups would be approaching at street level, and two more through windows on upper floors, one reached by a ladder, one by a low roof. This assault upon the roof would complete the encirclement, and if everything went well the wanted people should be trapped with their loot inside.

The group approaching the front door had the most delicate task. They were mostly Firozpur, on the theory that no one inside would be likely to recognize the desert troopers; but the group included one sergeant of the Watch. It would be his responsibility to raise a loud outcry at the proper moment, signaling the other assault teams that the time had come for them to make their moves.

Meanwhile, Wen Chang, Kasimir, and their group had reached the roof of the warehouse. A moment later they had gained the roof of the target building, equally high, by the simple expedient of stepping over to it across a gap of space less than a meter wide.

The moon had come out clearly now; probably, thought Kasimir, it would soon be obscured again by fast-moving clouds, but meanwhile it was a very useful source of illumination on the open roof, above the narrow, twisting canyons of the streets. Kasimir could see that there were two or perhaps three trapdoors in the roof, which was basically a tarry surface under a layer of light boards. Its contours formed a wilderness of little peaks and gables and ridges, pierced here and there by a skylight. Probably all the skylights had once been covered with oiled skin or paper, but the ones that Kasimir could see were now broken open to the weather. Iron bars, rusted but formidable, still defended these openings against human entry.

Two of the Watch troopers among the assault party on the roof, working under a sergeant's direction, blocked two of the three visible trapdoors closed, wedging them shut with pieces of lumber pulled from the top of the ruined wooden parapet. Then they prepared to break in through the remaining entrance.

Placing themselves one on each side of the third trapdoor, the burly patrolmen hefted their axes and waited for a signal.

Presently it came, in the form of raucous voices raised from street level, loudly demanding to be allowed entrance.

The axes poised over the rooftop fell together. Almost simultaneously there sounded from several directions, near and far, a crashing and splintering of wood, a rending of thin metal. The other entrances to the building were being attacked on schedule.

Kasimir saw now that the onslaught against the roof entrance was being directed not against the trapdoor itself, which was reinforced with metal bars and perhaps with magic as well. Instead the axes fell in a rapid rhythm upon the roof just at one side of the designed entrance. Under their repeated blows a hole had already appeared and was growing rapidly. Doubtless the basic construction of this building had not been particularly sturdy to begin with, and decay had weakened some of the structural members.

While the choppers plied their tools Kasimir, holding one lighted torch, was busy lighting others from it, and handling them out to the members of the attacking party who stood by in readiness.

The roof was quickly pierced, and in a few more moments the hole had been enlarged to the size of a man's head. The sergeant barked an order, and when the axemen paused he went down on his belly beside the hole. Sliding an arm through it, he was able to release the bar that held the trapdoor closed. It fell inside the room below, with the crashing of some homemade alarm system to add to the noise. Only the one fastening had secured the trapdoor, and now it swung up easily.

There were no stairs or ladder inside, but Wen Chang was ready. While others held torches for him, he dropped lithely through. A moment later he called for the others to follow, and the Watch poured in after him, one man at a time. Kasimir, as he had reluctantly agreed, was last. Left alone for a moment on the roof, he sat on the edge of the opening, hung for an instant by one hand from the edge, then let go and dropped.

Landing easily on the bare floor, he found himself still alone. The other members of his party had already hurried ahead, leaving the small unfurnished room through its only other door. Raising his torch, Kasimir saw that this stood at the head of a narrow stairs that led down to the floors below.

Cries of alarm and anger, accompanied by the clash of arms, were resounding from down there now. Holding his torch aloft in his left hand, his right ready to draw a weapon, Kasimir hurried after the Watchmen and Wen Chang.

The stairs went down only one flight, to a flat space with unpromising darkness on every side. Nearby a hole in this floor, with the top of a ladder protruding through it, offered a way to continue the descent. As Kasimir approached the hole he could hear the voices of his comrades, along with other noises, coming from down there. It might be that only the lower levels of this building were inhabited tonight.

When he reached the foot of the ladder, Kasimir could see dim passageways leading off in three directions. At the far end of the passage to his right, he could see torches in rapid motion, as if their holders might be dancing. Kasimir caught a single glimpse of Wen Chang, cloak wrapped around his left arm and rapier active in his right hand, before a door slammed in between, cutting off the physician's view of his partner.

Kasimir ran recklessly toward the action, stumbling through darkness. He burst into the room in which he had seen the Magistrate, to find Wen Chang gone but the situation now well in hand. A lantern burning on a table illuminated the room, and doors in the other walls were standing open. In this room three people remained, two of the Watch having one of their prey boxed into a corner. The man had a blade in each hand, and both were active. But in a moment, after a brief flurry of action, the man resisting arrest was cut down.

Kasimir picked up the lantern from the table and brought it close to the fallen figure. No lengthy examination was needed; the man was obviously dead.

Hurrying on, Kasimir entered a large room where loot that must be the product of a hundred robberies was stacked in several piles. Here were stolen golden candlesticks, over there a collection of silver plate, on the far side of the room a pile of drinking vessels of horn and wood, inlaid with gold and silver, and small open boxes that glinted with precious metals. When he held his torch closer to another pile nearby he could see the wink of gold from the covers and edges of finely bound books. Whether the Sword finally proved to be in this building or not, the Watch would have a goodly profit from their raid, in the form of a haul of loot, at least some of which would presumably find its way back to its rightful owners.

And still shouts and the uproar of conflict sounded from somewhere below. Kasimir found a way down and descended yet another level, estimating as he did so that he must now be very little if at all above the level of the street outside. Here, amid a labyrinth of rooms, torches and lanterns were plentiful. It was obvious that the main drama of the raid was being enacted here.

When the physician entered the next room, it appeared to him for a moment that he had just missed all the excitement. The people here had apparently surrendered just before he entered. Four or five men and a couple of women, one or two of them well-dressed and all of them looking sullenly enraged, were being herded together in preparation for their being searched; one of the women was still screaming insults at the invaders, warning them to keep their hands off her.

Kasimir looked around quickly, then demanded of the room in general: "Where's the Magistrate?"

One of the patrolmen answered with an economical motion of his head. Moving down another passage in the direction indicated, Kasimir felt a momentary sensation, the plucking of some fading defensive magic, a moment of disorientation as he passed through a doorway. It must, he thought, have been only a third-rate defensive spell to begin with, because the moment weapons were drawn it had faded like some night-blooming flower. There would be no point in calling upon Almagro's wizard to deal with anything so trivial.

Looking for the Magistrate, the physician found himself momentarily alone, out of sight of anyone who had come with him.

A faint sound from a dark side passage made Kasimir turn his head. The warning had come just in time; he found himself confronted by a wild-faced man, who struck at Kasimir with a desperate blow. Turning with a simultaneous thrusting motion of the torch in his left hand, Kasimir did his desperate best to parry. The assailant flinched away from the torch at the last moment, and his first stroke at Kasimir missed.

Kasimir swirled his cloak, which was partly wrapped round his left arm, and continued with thrusts and feints of the torch in his left hand to do his best to distract the enemy. The man, who had a long knife in his hand, fell back. A moment later Kasimir had drawn the cudgel from his belt with his right hand.

The two men stalked each other. Kasimir, doubly armed, felt stoutly confident of being able to hold his own.

In this situation time was on Kasimir's side, and he called out for help. As soon as he did this the other man lunged at him again. Kasimir parried with the torch as best he could, stood his ground and swung his club, hitting his assailant on the shoulder. The long knife went clattering to the floor.

A moment later, two Firozpur troopers had materialized in response to the physician's yell, destroying the local darkness with their torches and taking charge of the howling prisoner.

Resenting the time consumed by the scuffle, Kasimir pushed on. He was still trying to locate Wen Chang.

Sounds of another scuffle, in a dim alcove, distracted him. When he held up his torch in that direction, its light gleamed on an arc of startling brightness, the flash of a long blade in deadly motion. One dark figure with a long sword in hand was contending against two others, members of the Watch, more lightly armed. One of these two went down even as Kasimir watched, and the other one dove to the floor a moment later, trying to get out of the way of the long blade.

Could the full-sized sword be Stonecutter? The light was too poor to tell. Shouting again, Kasimir moved forward. The floor here was worse than the stairway, rotten, weakened, and unsafe; suddenly it bent and crackled under his additional weight. The man with the long Sword—Kasimir was suddenly convinced it was indeed Stonecutter that he saw—turned toward him, for the moment sparing his last opponent.

When the stroke of the long blade came Kasimir could do nothing but throw up his right hand holding the cudgel in a sort of defensive reflex, at the same moment casting the rest of his body backward. He felt an impact, but realized that he had survived.

Meanwhile the other surviving opponent, the one who had fallen to the floor unhurt, was not willing to give up the fight. The figure on the floor writhed up to strike at the swordsman with some kind of club.

Before the holder of the Sword could react, the whole treacherous portion of the floor had given way. The people on it, living and dead, were plunged down to the next level, amid a cloud of dust and debris. The collapse was relatively slow, the impact at the end of it somewhat moderated, but it scattered the combatants and put an end to the fight.

Coughing and spitting dust, getting back to his feet as quickly as possible, Kasimir got his back against a wall and looked around for the man with the Sword; but as far as he could tell, he was now quite alone.

The borrowed truncheon in his own hand felt strangely weightless, and he looked down at it. At that point he began to understand how lucky he had been not to lose a hand, or at least several fingers. He had felt the jarring impact between oak and steel, and when he looked down at the club still held to his wrist by a thong he saw that only a wooden stump remained of it. Most of the length of the tough oak had been sheared off neatly, only about two centimeters above his thumb and forefinger.

As far as the physician could tell no magical power had been involved in the blow. Nor had any been needed. Kasimir stood for a moment looking dazedly at the result, understanding now on a deeper level than the intellectual what must be the almost supernatural keenness of a Sword's blade. He could appreciate also the determined strength of the arm that had driven the weighty steel behind that edge.

Undamaged except for a few bruises, he scrambled about on the reassuringly solid surface of the level where he now found himself, looking for any sign of the Sword, or the man who had been carrying it. But both were gone.

More men of the Watch joined him, as well as some Firozpur troopers, and in response to Kasimir's questions reported that the building was being satisfactorily cleaned out.

Not wishing to be delayed by their questions, he said nothing to them about his last skirmish. Instead he asked: "Where's the Magistrate got to now?"

"He's downstairs, sir."

Again Kasimir plunged on, finding a ladder and going down, angry beyond words at having the object of his search almost within his grasp, then seeing it whisked away again. He had risked his life but achieved nothing, nor was he at this moment a centimeter closer to gaining final possession of the Sword.

He had reached what he thought was almost certainly the lowest level of the building—at least it was partially below the level of the ground outside, as he could tell by the view through a barred window—before he again caught sight of Wen Chang. This time he was able to reach the Magistrate's side before anything happened to keep them apart.

He seized him by the sleeve. "Magistrate, I have seen the Sword! For a moment I almost—"

"I, too! The man who has it is down here now. Quickly, go that way! Carefully, for he is deadly dangerous."

With gestures and a few hurried words the Magistrate, rapier in one hand and torch in the other, directed Kasimir down one dim corridor, then turned away and plunged down another himself.

Kasimir, his own torch fallen and extinguished somewhere behind him, moved into dimness as silently as he could. Then he paused, holding his breath to listen.

He could hear only the drip of water somewhere. And farther off, out of sight of the hidden desperation of this struggle, some slum-dweller plunking a stringed instrument.

And now, another sound, also faint, muffled by walls and angles of walls. A muffled pounding . . . Kasimir stalked forward through the dim, half-buried cellar.

Then he was once more taken almost completely by surprise. He caught one bright glimpse of a long blade lifted high, in an energetic arm. In an instant, it was going to swing down directly at him.

In the rush of movement the hood covering the head of this new opponent fell back, momentarily revealing the face. Kasimir had barely the space of a heartbeat in which to recognize that the figure brandishing the sword—or Sword—at him was definitely Natalia. The light was bad, and he had only a brief glimpse, but still the physician felt certain that he was not mistaken.

Again Kasimir could only try to throw himself out of a weapon's path. He might not have succeeded, except that when the blade came swinging at him there was a hesitation, a hitch in the swing that allowed Kasimir to survive.

The enemy rushed past him, and a moment later a heavy door had slammed behind the fleeing figure.

Kasimir allowed himself to remain dazed only for a moment. Then, just as he was scrambling to his feet, a shout in the Magistrate's voice sounded from somewhere behind him.

Let Natalia go—he could not be certain that her weapon was the Sword. In a few moments Kasimir had scrambled halfway across the cellar to join Wen Chang and Captain Almagro, who with some of their men were holding a torchlight meeting in front of a closed and very substantial-looking door.

The Captain appeared to have relaxed a little.

"We've got him, and the Sword too! That's a blind wall on that side of the building. There's no other way out of that room."

But Wen Chang was already stepping back, shaking his head even as he sheathed his rapier. His eye met Kasimir's.

"Come, quickly!" the Magistrate rapped out, and in a moment was running for a stairs that led up to the level of the street.

Kasimir ran after him immediately, ignoring the Captain's startled, querulous call behind them. Already Kasimir thought he understood Wen Chang's haste.

Wen Chang in the lead, with Kasimir continually a step behind him and unable to catch up, the two of them negotiated the tortuous passages of the main floor, and burst out at last into the night. Wen Chang as he ran was able to gather with him a half-comprehending reinforcement of Watch and Firozpur warriors, a group whose footsteps pounded after Kasimir. The moment they were outside, Wen Chang looked back over his shoulder, beckoning to Kasimir.

"The wall of that basement room must give on this alley to our right —quick!"

Kasimir and the Magistrate, a small mob of followers just behind them, thundered around a corner of the building into an alley. There was a heavy thudding sound from somewhere ahead, as if someone, Kasimir thought, were still battering on a door and trying to break it down.

But before they had run halfway down the alley, Kasimir realized that they were already too late. A moment later they had come to the smoothly carved hole in the lower stone portion of the wall. The cut-out pieces of heavy stone were still lying where they had fallen from the touch of the hurrying Sword.

Now someone was coming through the hole. Kasimir stepped back and raised his cudgel. But in a moment the light from the torch he still held in his hand was falling upon the furious, bearded features of Captain Almagro. Understanding had come to the Captain too late, and rage had come with it. He now had a better understanding of Stonecutter's true nature.

But the Sword had now vanished in the night, along with the mysterious person who now possessed it.

11

THE fighting in the old warehouse was over, the last sullen spasms of physical resistance crushed. Now Kasimir the physician was called upon to tend the wounded.

There were not so many of these as he had begun to fear there would be; he estimated now that there must have been about fifteen people in all in the building when the raid began, and more than one had probably escaped, but the great majority had given up without a fight as soon as they became aware of the strength of the attacking force.

Two of the small handful of occupants who had elected to fight, both of them men, were beyond the help of any surgeon, while another had suffered a badly gashed arm. This last man could be expected to live, and even to use his arm again, once Kasimir had stopped the bleeding and administered some stitches. On the other side, one of the Watch had been run through with a long blade and was dying; another had sustained a knife cut on the hand. Casualties among the Firozpur troopers were limited to one, who had hurt his leg, not too badly, falling through a trapdoor between floors in the darkness.

Before Kasimir had finished doing what he could for these people, the swift runners sent out by Captain Almagro in pursuit of the unknown person carrying the Sword had returned to the scene of the raid, reporting that they had failed even to catch sight of their quarry. No one was surprised at their failure. There had been no real hope of overtaking the fugitive in darkness, particularly not in the warren of streets and alleys making up this neighborhood, in which the forces of law and order were at best unwelcome.

The captain cursed his luck, and went on to the next thing. As part of his preparations for the raid, Almagro had arranged to have a couple of heavy wagons, cages on wheels, brought up to the building at the appropriate time. These had now arrived on the scene, and all of the prisoners were bundled into them. Wen Chang gave the catch of captives a cursory looking over, but, having done so, showed no particular interest in any of them.

Kasimir had not yet mentioned to anyone the fact that he had recognized Natalia. But he made the identification now, as soon as he had the chance to pull the Magistrate aside, and make sure that the information reached his ears alone.

Wen Chang stared at him intently in the dim light obtaining in the street. "You are sure?"

"Yes. I am certain it was Natalia."

"The light inside the building was very bad. You say you cannot be sure that the weapon she was holding was Stonecutter."

"True. Nevertheless, I am sure that it was she who held it." Again the moonlight came and went around them, with the passage of a cloud.

"All right." Wen Chang sighed. "Let me call Almagro over here and we will tell him alone before we separate. But say nothing about this identification to anyone else just yet."

"I won't."

In a moment Almagro had joined them. The Captain, not surprised that the Magistrate had chosen to be suspicious of his subordinates, went through the same routine of questioning the certainty of Kasimir's indentification. Kasimir went through the same routine of giving reassurances.

Wen Chang suggested in a low voice: "A matter that calls for thorough questioning of all your prisoners, old friend. To find out which of them might know her."

"Indeed, they shall be questioned. Though most of them may have to wait until tomorrow—I am going to need some sleep."

"And so are we. Good thought is impossible in a condition of great fatigue."

Having seen Almagro off with his pair of cage-topped wagons and their unhappy cargo, Wen Chang, Kasimir, and their mounted Firozpur escort returned to their inn, where they found that the landlord had succesfully guarded their quarters in their absence.

As they were mounting the narrow stairs to their third-floor rooms, the Magistrate suddenly turned to his younger companion and demanded: "Did she say anything to you?"

"Natalia? No. Nor I to her."

When they had entered their suite and closed the door, Wen Chang asked in a low voice: "Do you think she knows that you were able to recognize her?"

Kasimir considered the question very carefully. "I'm not sure," he said at last. "But I don't think so. But I believe that she knew me."

"Why so?"

"Because she might have been able to kill me. But she didn't really try."

"Ah. I see. And you still have, or thought you had, another meeting with her scheduled for today." The time was now so far past midnight as to be obviously morning.

Kasimir sighed wearily. "That is correct."

Wen Chang yawned, and shook his head as if he were now too tired to think effectively.

"What am I to do about the meeting?" Kasimir asked.

"I expect you should try to keep it. But not until you have had some sleep."

Kasimir did not awake, stiff and tired, until well past midmorning. At some time while he slept a screen had been put up in front of his couch, and from beyond this ineffective shield he could hear the energetic voice of the Magistrate. Wen Chang sounded like a man who had been up and about for quite some time as he gave orders to the hotel servants who were just delivering breakfast.

Sitting opposite Kasimir at the breakfast table a few minutes later, Wen Chang reported that more news had just come in from Almagro, who had apparently spent a sleepless night after all. Some of the prisoners who had been taken last night had been persuaded to provide some information about the person who had fled the old warehouse with the Sword.

"Good!"

"I am not so sure it is. There is considerable disagreement among their stories. One prisoner confirms that the person he last saw with the Sword was a woman, another insists he saw a man getting away. But both agree on one thing: that certain criminal elements within the city are developing a plan to rob the Blue Temple. Captain Almagro says he has already sent this information on to the Director of Security there."

"Well," said Kasimir, "that at least ought to confirm your status as a prophet in the eyes of the Blue Temple. But I wonder if the prisoners are just telling the Captain what they think he wants to hear."

"It is quite possible. But there is more. The final element in the Captain's latest communication to us has nothing to do with the interrogation of last night's prisoners, but still I find it the most interesting. It concerns instead prisoner nine-nine-six-seven-seven, the man who was freed from the road gang by the original Sword-thief. Almagro informs me that nine-nine-six-seven-seven was a rural agitator, convicted of minor political offenses—nothing as egregious as those of Benjamin of the Steppe, we may suppose, or he would have been hanged, drawn, and quartered too."

Kasimir waited, but there seemed to be no more. He asked: "And what does that tell us?"

"Do you not find it interesting too? And the squad that is to arrest Umar goes out this morning. By the way, I suppose you are still intending to keep your appointment with the Lady Natalia today?"

"I think I must try to do so, though after last night I have the most serious doubts that she will be there. I suppose you are intending to have the White Temple surrounded, and arrest her if she does show up?"

"On the contrary. If we did that we would have her, but we would not have the Sword. Nor, I think, would we be any closer to getting our hands on it. No, I am willing to gamble on finding a better way."

"Well then, if she appears I will try to open negotiations to get back the Sword, assuming she got away with it last night."

"Do so. And let your behavior be guided by this fact: She will not risk coming to the meeting unless she hopes to gain something of great importance from you."

"What could that be, Wen Chang? In the beginning she must have recognized me as an investigator, and made an agreement with me simply to be able to keep an eye on the course of our investigation. What a fool I was!"

Wen Chang did not dispute the assessment. "Perhaps you should have been a trifle more suspicious of her all along."

"But now what can she and her people hope to gain of great importance? From us?"

"We can hope that she—and the people who are in this with her, as you say—would like to make a deal. An arrangement, whereby we would come into possession of Stonecutter—for a suitable price, of course—after it has filled its purpose in their hands."

"What purpose are they likely to have for it, except to sell it? And why should she not sell it to the highest bidder?"

"With the backing of Prince al-Farabi, we can make our bid sufficiently high."

At this point the conference was interrupted by a tap at the door, followed by the appearance of Lieutenant Komi at the head of the stairs. The officer announced that the Blue Temple's head of security had just arrived at the inn, and was insisting that his business could not wait for even a few minutes. The Director was demanding to see the Magistrate and his associate.

"He'll wait, though, if you tell me that's what you want," Komi added hopefully. No one outside the ranks of its outright worshippers liked the Blue Temple. And even within those ranks, Kasimir had observed, feelings about the upper hierarchy tended to be mixed.

"Keeping the gentleman waiting will serve no purpose." Wen Chang sighed. "Let us hear what he has to say."

Komi saluted and retreated to the room below. The Director's heavy-footed tread could soon be heard climbing the stairs, and in another moment he was in the upper suite. He entered talking loudly, insisting in a domineering voice that something more had to be done to guard the Blue Temple's few remaining assets. He hinted that the Eylau branch at least now tottered upon the brink of bankruptcy; and if such an institution were to be forced into financial failure, the damage done the whole community would be incalculable.

Kasimir noted that here, in a more or less public place, the Director made no direct reference to all to the Orb of Maecenas.

Wen Chang, for the moment all diplomacy, adopted a soothing manner. He suggested the posting of extra guards around the perimeter of the Blue Temple, and also in any of the rooms that were at or below ground level, where thieves armed with the Sword of Siege should be most likely to effect their entrance.

The Director was not soothed, nor reassured. He protested that such measures were easy enough to suggest, but they cost money, a great deal of money. He demanded to know who the Magistrate thought was going to pay for them.

The Magistrate at last allowed some of his disgust to show. "Considering what miserable pay you give the enlisted ranks of your security forces, the men and women who would actually stand guard, such measures would certainly cost you much less than the fee I would charge you, were I willing to act as your consultant."

Kasimir considered that this was a good moment to apply some diplomacy himself. He interrupted to announce his departure, and Wen Chang came partway down the stairs with him to offer a final word of friendly caution.

Today Kasimir had not been sitting for long in Ardneh's chapel before a ragged street urchin approached, tugged at his sleeve, and asked if he were Kasimir the physician. As soon as he had admitted his identity, the boy handed him a folded note.

The physician unfolded the grimy scrap of paper and read its message while the boy stood waiting.

> Kasimir—I am not going to model any longer at the Red Temple. Yet I would like to see you once more. If you would like to see me again, follow the bearer of this message. Believe me, I will be sorry if we can never meet again.
>
> > In friendship,
> > Natalia

Kasimir read the note through twice, then folded it and put it in his pocket. It seemed to him that the wording of the message gave no indication as to whether Natalia knew that he had recognized her last night—or even whether or not she had been able to recognize him.

He asked the urchin: "Who gave you this?"

The child returned no answer, but turned away silently and walked out of the chapel. Kasimir got to his feet and followed, staying close behind his guide.

They descended from the chapel and walked straight out of the White Temple complex. Without ever looking back the urchin entered the bazaar nearby, and moved through it on a zigzag path. Still following, Kasimir suddenly wondered if someone, Wen Chang or an agent of the Watch, might now be following him in turn. If so, it would be easy for anyone loitering in the bazaar to see them and call off the scheduled meeting. Of course if it was Wen Chang himself on Kasimir's tail, he was said to have the capability of making himself invisible . . .

After a few more unhurried and apparently random turns through the marketplace, the ragged child turned suddenly down a side street, one even narrower than most, where he continued to move unhurriedly along. Still the boy did not look back, and Kasimir remained five or six paces behind him.

At last his guide did turn. Stopping at a doorway, the urchin indicated with a brief gesture that Kasimir was to enter it. Then he darted away to vanish in the crowded street.

Kasimir looked the place over; at first glance it appeared quite innocuous, a cheap tearoom three-quarters full of customers. He went in. Seeing no one he could recognize, he took a chair at one of the empty tables and waited for what would happen next.

A waiter came and he ordered tea. Then somehow, before he had any clue that she was near, Natalia was standing at his table, pulling out a chair and sitting down.

She was dressed approximately as he had seen her at their last scheduled meeting, and today she looked tired but still energetic. When their eyes met, Kasimir did his best to look as innocent as he must have been when they first encountered each other.

Natalia's expression was one of calm alertness, which told him nothing. There was a moment of silence, which threatened to stretch out to an awkward length.

"So," Kasimir began at last, clearing his throat. "You have ceased to be a model?"

"I posed this morning. But in another day or two I am going to quit." She paused. Her remarkable eyes flickered, and her husky voice changed. "Kasimir—when did you last see me?"

"At the same moment that you saw me last." His tea had arrived, and he took a deliberate sip, his eyes not leaving hers. "Would you like to order something?"

Natalia's total control of her expression lapsed. "All right. I am very sorry that I almost killed you last night. The moment I realized it was you, I gave up trying to kill you and ran away instead."

"For which I am grateful," Kasimir said. "We both survived last night, and I am glad of it. Where is the Sword now?"

"First I would like some tea." She put out a hand to detain a passing servant, and placed her order. Then she turned back to Kasimir and spoke in a low voice. "I came here today, taking a considerable risk, to talk to you about that."

He said briskly: "It seems we are both accustomed to taking some risks in the course of our jobs. How much do your people want for Stonecutter?"

Natalia shook her head. "I wish you wouldn't be in such a hurry. It's not that easy."

"Why not? This is your business, isn't it? Stealing things and selling them for the best price you can get? Or it's a good part of your business anyway, I should think."

"The idea seems to make you angry, Kasimir."

"Well, I suppose it does. I'm angry that you made a fool of me. But that's beside the point, isn't it?"

"I suppose it is. Well, as for selling you the Sword, I can't quite do that yet."

"What does that mean? We haven't even started haggling about the price."

She turned her head to right and left, as if trying to make sure that they were not being overheard. It seemed highly unlikely that anyone could eavesdrop in the noisy room. Then she said: "It means that the organization I work for has concluded an agreement with the Red Temple. According to the agreement, de Borron must be allowed to use the Sword to finish his work there—he has until the first day of the Festival to complete it. Then the Sword comes back to us, and we are free to make some other disposition of it."

"The Red Temple doesn't mind it being known that they're using stolen property."

"You won't be able to prove it, or do anything about it."

"The Festival begins day after tomorrow."

"Exactly. So you won't have long to wait."

"So in my view right now shouldn't be too soon for us to begin our bargaining."

"It is a little too soon." Her voice was firm.

"I see. Perhaps you'll be able to get in a quick robbery or two, at the Blue Temple, say, before you'll accept our ransom."

Natalia's face was becoming totally unreadable again. "I won't insist on anything like that."

"And when do you want to discuss price? I assume there will be others bidding against us."

"I will tell you when the time has come to discuss price. And now you had better go."

"Just answer me one question first—"

"Now you had better go."

This, he thought, was Natalia's territory. He pushed back his chair and went.

12

IT was a tribute to his sense of direction, Kasimir thought, that he was able to reorient himself, and make his way out of the quarter of extra-narrow streets near the White Temple after making no more than one false start. In a few moments he was in half-familiar thoroughfares again, and heading back in the direction of the Inn of the Refreshed Travelers. He was angry, and thinking furiously as he walked.

When he tried to examine the reasons for his anger he understood that it had several causes. Part of it, he supposed, was a delayed reaction to his being nearly killed, probably by the very weapon he was supposed to be recovering, in the hands of a young woman who had made a fool of him. It did not help a bit to realize that he still found her attractive. And part of his anger was a result of his still being manipulated, largely by the same person—made to attend upon her, until it should be convenient for her to talk business. He was not really in control of anything.

Immersed in gloomy meditations of this kind, he was still at some distance from the inn when he heard his name called, jarring his attention back into focus on the world around him. Looking up he saw one of the Firozpur troopers of Komi's squad, who was standing lounging in front of a tavern as if he had been stationed there simply to watch the street. When Kasimir approached, the man informed him that he was wanted inside the tavern.

When Kasimir demanded an explanation, the trooper only shrugged. Leaving the man in the street, Kasimir entered the tavern, pausing for a moment just past the threshold to allow his eyes to accustom themselves to the relative dimness. The general layout of this place reminded him strongly of the teahouse he had just left, except that here the windows were somewhat smaller and the room as a result notably darker.

Presently Kasimir caught sight of the Captain and the Magistrate, who were established at a table toward the rear of the large room, from which vantage point they were able to observe almost everything that went on inside the tavern, and something of the street outside. The two older men both waved to Kasimir. When he reached their table and pulled out a chair, they both expressed their pleasure that he was still alive.

"You sound surprised to see that I am," he said grimly as he sat down.

Wen Chang shook his head. "Not really that. Come, sit down and tell us of your meeting with the fair Natalia."

"We already know," put in Almagro, "that she arranged for you to be escorted out of the White Temple and through the bazaar. It was there that my people lost sight of you."

"Perhaps," said Kasimir, "it was just as well that they did." He ordered a mug of beer from a passing barmaid, and began to tell his mentors as concisely as possible the details of his meeting with the woman in the teahouse.

The Captain, listening intently, scowled and squinted and tugged at his beard. "So, the lady implies she's willing to make a deal with us—but not just yet, if I understand her. And she's some kind of leader in her gang, or wants to be."

"That was certainly my impression," said Kasimir.

"I'd say she must be fairly new in town, or I'd have run into her somewhere before."

"A most reasonable deduction," agreed Wen Chang. "Though most likely she has associates who are very familiar with the city."

The Captain scowled at him thoughtfully, then faced back to the young physician. "So then, neither of you got down to the real business? I mean, mentioning any specific sums of money?"

"She refused to do so. And I couldn't very well open the bidding, not knowing how much Prince al-Farabi might be prepared to pay to get back his Sword. Also I am generally unfamiliar with this business of paying ransoms."

Wen Chang nodded. "It had seemed to me that the time was ripe for negotiation. But perhaps not. I wonder . . . is it possible that the young lady does not have the Sword in her possession at all?"

"If one of the gang carried it away from the warehouse—"

"One of 'the' gang, you say. But what if there is more than one gang involved?"

The Captain had been listening silently to this last exchange, but it was plain from the expression on his face that the more he thought about the situation, the less he felt he understood it.

"Don't know how much of her story we ought to believe, about an agreement with the Red Temple and all that. It would seem to contradict this talk of a move being planned against the Blue Temple by the people who have the Sword."

Wen Chang took a sturdy draught from his mug, then delicately stroked foam from his black mustache. "The contradiction does not necessarily arise. The more times these enterprising criminals can profit from their loot, the happier they should be. First they rent the Sword to the Red Temple for a high fee; a few days later they use it to break into the Blue Temple; and then lastly they sell it back to its rightful owner for a high price."

"You really think they intend doing all that, Magistrate?" The Captain squinted as if the thought pained him.

"It is certainly a possibility. But what I think most strongly now is that we must contrive somehow to find out whether the Sword is really being used in the Red Temple as the lady said. Is Stonecutter actually there, and under what circumstances? Is it on loan from some gang of criminals? Is it in the hands of Robert de Borron, and is he actually using it in his work?" Wen Chang paused. "If so, what are the chances of our taking it away from him?"

Here the Magistrate broke off to order another round of drinks. As soon as it arrived the two experienced investigators began planning their next move.

Almagro was not optimistic. "If it comes down to our getting into the Red Temple, maybe being able to take the Sword right out of there with us—well." The Captain shook his head and began to spell out some of the difficulties as he perceived them. "If we were just to try to push our way in there, like we did at the old warehouse—well, this is a very different situation. To begin with, there's not much chance that we'd ever get a look at the Sword before it was spirited away somewhere. It'd take an army to search that place—the Red Temple—properly, and I can't order up an army without letting my superiors know what I'm about.

"For another thing, they have their own security force there in the temple—such as it is." Here he paused, and the three men exchanged faint smiles, as at a joke familiar to all. It was received wisdom that Red Temple security people could be counted on for very little, and were more likely than not to show up for duty drunk, or stoned on other drugs than alcohol.

Almagro's smile faded quickly again as he continued. "One thing they do have that works is plenty of political influence. It would probably be more than my badge of office is worth to go barging in there on my own."

Kasimir asked: "Even if you were sure of recovering the Sword of Siege by doing so?"

Almagro rubbed his forehead doubtfully. "Well. That'd certainly make a difference. But I can't be sure of anything like that, can I?"

Wen Chang thought a little, and sighed, and shook his head reluctantly. "No, my friend. Whatever plan we concoct, no one can assure you of its success."

"Well, then." The Captain drank, and ran his fingers through his hair, and drank again, and thought. The impression he gave was that the more he thought about his situation the worse it looked to him. "I wonder if I ought to go to the Hetman himself and tell him at least that the Sword of Siege is here in the city somewhere, and that we're looking for it."

"You know him better than I—"

"Aye, that's why I'm wondering."

"—but it occurs to me that it might be best to tell him only if—or when—Stonecutter has actually been recovered."

"There is something in what you say."

The two older men lifted their mugs simultaneously, as if they were toasting each other, or perhaps harking back to old times, sharing some private joke or ritual.

Then Wen Chang was abruptly serious again. He took the merest sip from his mug, leaned back in his chair again, and said, "Yes, I think we must get someone into the Red Temple to take a look around for us, and do it as soon as possible. Tonight, if we can."

"Tonight?"

"If the sculptor is as desperate to complete his work as everything indicates, then he will be working late, with or without the help of the Sword we are looking for."

"Sculpting after dark?"

"I have no doubt that the Red Temple can provide him with some kind of effective light. I suppose you, the Watch, have no regular agents in place within the temple upon whom you can rely?"

"Hah. The Watch has no agents at all in there that I know of. I wish we did. More likely than not it's working the other way around. Red Temple has a lot more money to spend on bribes than I do."

"Well, then. Do you have anyone available to be sent in? Preferably someone who knows his or her way around inside the temple?"

"Hah! I'd say that most of my men know the public parts of that building only too well. But as for the rest of the place, no, I don't think so. And now that the temple's being remodeled, the layout will be changed anyway. Especially in the parts we most want to see, upstairs where the statues are being carved. No, I can't say that I have anyone I'd want to try sending in there."

Both of the older men turned their heads to gaze at Kasimir. He had been expecting this development for some time now. He drank from his mug and quietly set it down.

"Then I suppose it is up to me to go in again," he said. "If I can. Well, I'm willing."

Wen Chang studied him through narrow appraising eyes.

Almagro looked relieved. "As to simply getting into the place," he offered, "I can be of some help there. I can get the names of some of their security people who are more than ordinarily amenable to bribes, and probably I can find out when and where some of those people are likely to be on duty. I'm afraid, though, that if I were to try to send one of my own people in there the Red priests would know about it before he ever arrived."

Returning to the inn ahead of the others, Kasimir tried to get some rest, and made what other preparations he and Wen Chang thought necessary. Near sunset he held a final conference with the Magistrate, and with Captain Almagro who had come to give him some final directions. Then Kasimir was on his way.

The sun had set before Kasimir arrived in the square in front of the Red Temple, whose façade was aglow with the red of firelight from its numerous torches and iron fire baskets. As usual, nightfall meant an increase in business at the Houses of Pleasure, and as he approached the building he fell in with an almost steady stream of customers, the great majority of them men.

He was within a few meters of the entrance when his eye was caught by a stray gleam of light, coming from above, somewhere within the building, that proceeded from no ordinary fire. When the realization struck him that the source of the peculiar light must be in or very near the artists' studio on the fifth or sixth floor, Kasimir stepped aside from the stream of customers to stand for a moment near the entrance with his head craned back.

He had to find the precisely correct position before he could see the light again. But at last there was the tiny gleam: very steady and bright, pale as daylight. Extraordinary. Even, he thought, unearthly looking. Perhaps, Kasimir thought, the illumination was being produced by some kind of magic. Whatever its ultimate source, the light must be leaking out of the studio through a crevice between some of the draped canvases and drop cloths that shrouded the walls of the sculptor's temporary workshop. And whatever the source, it certainly looked bright enough to allow Robert de Borron and his crew to continue working after dark. Suddenly it occurred to Kasimir that this light had a strong resemblance to the Old World votive lamp on Ardneh's altar in the White Temple.

The intermittent stream of men around Kasimir, intent on thoughts of what they were going to do once they got inside the temple, were ignoring him and the strange light alike. Now more than ever determined to make this mission a success, he rejoined the stream of customers.

Shuffling through the line of impatient customers at the entrance, Kasimir paid his small coin there like everyone else, and as a member of an anonymous throng entered the interior of the temple. At night the public lobbies, lighted by fire, were even redder than during the day. The fires made this part of the building somewhat too warm. Cheerful music throbbed here, played in a rapid tempo by concealed musicians.

On Kasimir's previous visit he had not penetrated this deeply into the public areas. But nothing here was very much different from any other Red Temple that he had ever visited. Signs, well lighted and elaborately designed, relying heavily on iconography as a courtesy to clients who had trouble with their letters, indicated the way to the various Houses contained within the establishment.

Every Red Temple—at least every one Kasimir had ever seen from the inside, admittedly a comparatively small selection—was divided according to the same basic scheme, into interconnected domains devoted to various pleasures. Here as elsewhere there were the Houses of Flesh, of Food, Wine, Chance, Sound or Music, and Heavenly Vapors. The last was a catch-all category for various entertainments, mostly chemical. Kasimir had heard that in other regions of the world the arrangement varied somewhat, but as far as he knew a Red Temple was basically a Red Temple the world around.

Every time you entered a different House you had to pay another fee, though otherwise it was easy and convenient to pass from one to another. The House of Flesh was on the third floor here, the highest level currently open to the public, and for that reason Kasimir had made it his official goal. As soon as he had paid the rather hefty entrance fee, he was free to climb the winding, recursive stairs, liberally provided with landings and chairs for the benefit of the unsteady devotee who might be coming this way from the House of Wine on the ground level. Kasimir's was a popular choice tonight, and he had plenty of company on the stairs.

Once having attained the third level, he entered and passed through a large, softly furnished waiting room. Here youthful servants of the temple, most of them female, all of them provocatively clad, waited to be chosen by customers. From this anteroom corridors branched off, and Kasimir chose one under the icon of a staring eye. Ignoring low-voiced invitations from the employees on the benches, he went that way alone. According to the directions he had received at the last minute from Almagro, his way to the private regions of the temple lay through the Hall of Voyeurs.

The Hall of Voyeurs was almost dark. At regular intervals small, very narrow corridors branched off from it. Closed doors blocked off several of these passages, meaning that they were occupied, each probably by only a single worshipper. Kasimir had never entered a Hall of Voyeurs before, but as he understood the arrangement, the walls of each branching corridor were pierced by numerous peepholes, opening into a selection of lighted rooms. In these rooms servants of the temple, joined sometimes by exhibitionistic customers, were more or less continuously engaged in a variety of sexual performances.

Ignoring the opportunities presented by empty observation posts, Kasimir went straight on to the far end of Voyeurs' Hall. There, in accordance with Almagro's briefing, he discovered a latrine—Kasimir could hear one of the real flush toilets inside working as he approached.

Once inside the dimly lighted and evil-smelling facility, Kasimir fumbled and stalled, feigning intoxication, until other customers moved on and he felt reasonably sure of having a few moments free of observation. Then he hurried to a service door, really only a panel set into a wall, whose lock he had been told was broken.

Actually, as he discovered in a moment, the door or panel was held in place by no lock at all. Typically sloppy Red Temple building maintenance, he thought as he eased the light panel aside, worked his body cautiously through into the dark cavity beyond, and then maneuvered the loose panel as closely as possible back into place.

Now he was standing in a darkness greater than that of the dim latrine, and on an awkward and uneven footing. Kasimir decided to wait, before moving another centimeter, to give his eyes a chance to become adjusted to the gloom.

Soon he was able to discern that he was definitely in an unfinished portion of the building, where he stood surrounded by its darkened skeleton of timbers and stone piers, along with a lot of empty space. There was no real floor anywhere in sight. He was standing on a narrow beam, and even a small step in the wrong direction would earn him a nasty fall. A floor or two below him, the furnished and inhabited rooms were rendered visible in outline by little sparks of light that here and there leaked out through the joints between their walls and ceilings. Also from down there somewhere came loud, drumming music, and wisps of other and more human sounds emanating from the hundreds of occupants.

Looking up, the view was different. A solid roof at about the sixth-floor level blocked out the sky. There was almost no light at all above except for a few more stray gleams of that unearthly looking illumination that had first caught Kasimir's eye when he was still outside the building.

And Robert de Borron—or someone—must indeed be at work up there, three levels above where Kasimir was hiding, for the sounds of the sculptor's studio, an irregular pounding accompanied now and then by voices, came drifting down.

The next thing Kasimir had to do was to get up there.

Some meters distant horizontally from where he stood—it was hard to judge distances in this great darkened cavern where there were only tantalizing hints of light—the light from above was coming down more freely than elsewhere. Traces of the strange illumination shone out through the leaky sides of a large, roughly defined vertical column, that Kasimir presently realized must represent the shaft of the freight elevator used to haul de Borron's heavy blocks of stone up to his studio. That elevator shaft, if he could get into it, certainly ought to offer a way up.

Having got his bearings as well as possible, Kasimir began to work his way in the direction of that vaguely glowing column, two or three meters square and extending its way up from ground level. The task, he discovered almost at once, was even more difficult than it looked. His only means of progress was to edge nervously along a narrow beam, his pathway interrupted at intervals by the thick columns of stone and timber holding up the upper floors. One he had moved away from the paneled rear wall of the latrine, he had only space on right and left.

He had made only a few meters' progress by this means when his way was blocked more substantially, this time by one of the projecting side corridors of the Hall of Voyeurs, complete with its set of performance rooms. The only way to get past this obstacle was to go over the top, and presently Kasimir found himself creeping across the broad upper surface of a thin ceiling. At one point the surface bent alarmingly beneath his weight; he sprawled out flat, as if he were on thin ice, and centimetered his way forward holding his breath.

From inside the lighted room just beneath him there issued moans and rhythmic cries that suggested torture. Of course in a Red Temple other kinds of sensation were more probably the cause. Still, with every movement Kasimir made, the thin panels—and the plastering, if there was any—of the ceiling beneath him threatened to give way. He expected momentarily to go crashing and plunging down amid the bodies mounded on some bed. When that happened, the men with their eyes at peepholes in the lonely adjoining corridors would see a different show than they had expected.

Kasimir surmounted the barrier of the rooms at last. Now, feeling more and more like a beetle burrowing through the woodwork, he was back on his narrow beam again, working his way closer and closer to the silent, faintly glowing elevator shaft. No hoisting was in progress now, he was sure. If it had been, he would be able to hear men or loadbeasts straining at a windlass somewhere, and the creaking of the network of pulleys and cables he had once glimpsed from above. Anyway the sculptor's work was supposed to be nearly done now, and it seemed likely that all his massive workpieces had already been hauled up.

It occurred to Kasimir to wonder briefly why the workshop had not been situated at ground level, and only the finished statues hoisted. But then he supposed that space on the lower levels of the temple would probably be at a premium, already occupied by the various Houses of worship. And then too, secrecy would probably be easier to maintain at the higher level. Might that have been a consideration with de Borron and his employers from the beginning of the project?

Closer and closer Kasimir drew to the enclosed shaft, until at last he reached it. Putting an eye to a chink in one of the roughly enclosed sides, he could see loops of chain as well as lengths of thick rope hanging inside the shaft, whose interior was bathed in near-daylight brilliance falling from above. Kasimir felt sure now that those must be Old World lights up in the studio, relics of the age of technology whose human masters had ruled the world even before Ardneh lived, before Ardneh's Change had come upon the world to restore the dominance of magic.

Right now, as Kasimir had felt sure would be the case, the ropes and chains hung motionless, the hoisting machinery was idle. Not so the workshop above. A number of people were there, he could tell by the intermittent murmur of voices; and at least a few of them were working, as evidenced by the continued sound of tools.

The next step toward reaching the studio was to get inside the elevator shaft. With his eye to a crevice, Kasimir could see that the inner sides were ribbed with cross-bracing that should make an ideal ladder once he got within reach of it.

To get inside that shaft it was necessary to pry one of the ill-fitting side panels loose. That proved to be no great trick once Kasimir had brought his small, sharp-pointed dagger into play. Crude nails loosened quickly. In a few moments the panel was free, and Kasimir was able to slide his body into the shaft, where he clung to the ladderlike sides with a fair degree of security.

Looking up, he could see the big pulleys, wound with chains and ropes, at the top of the shaft. He could see also a part of the overhead of the sculptor's studio, illuminated with that wondrous light, whose source was still invisible.

Before he began to climb the last few meters to his goal, Kasimir, trying to be thorough, moved his loosened panel back as nearly as possible into its proper position. He glanced down once, into darkness —heights had never bothered him particularly—and then started climbing the shaft's ribbed side.

He had about nine or ten meters to ascend, and he moved up as quickly and silently as possible. As he got closer to the top he could see that the head of the elevator shaft was barricaded from the workroom by nothing more than a rude length of rope, stretched as a precaution across the side of the shaft that was open to the room.

As he neared the top of the shaft, he crossed over to the side where the light was dimmest. Even here it was uncomfortably bright for a man who was trying to hide, and he was going to have to be careful to avoid being seen before he had the chance to observe anyone else.

At last, moving very slowly now, Kasimir was able to raise his eyes above the level of the studio floor, and look out into the more distant parts of the big room. Most of it was indeed as bright as day, in the flood of illumination from what Kasimir now saw were indeed two Old World lanterns, each resting on its own small table.

Never before in his life had he seen Old World lights as big as these. But these lamps could hardly be anything else.

And standing between the two lights, almost exactly equidistant from them, with her pale flesh glowing like soft marble in their radiance, her naked back turned toward Kasimir, was Natalia, posing as a model.

13

As a secret observation post, the head of the open elevator shaft suffered from at least two major drawbacks: First, any observer who stationed himself there was far too likely to be seen by the folk he was trying to observe. And second, if he was discovered, he had nowhere to retreat to safety.

But a ready solution was at hand. They empty elevator shaft came up at the edge of the huge workroom, and the three sides of the shaft away from the studio were not tightly enclosed. Kasimir needed only a moment to slip out of the shaft onto the rough floor behind the nearest of the draped canvases that had been hung around the high unfinished walls of the studio. He could see more reason for these hangings now, see them as an effort, not entirely effective, to keep the Old World light from being seen at a distance and arousing people's curiosity. The fewer people who knew about de Borron's efforts here, the fewer would be likely to come around and bother him.

Once Kasimir had established himself behind the canvas, he had only to examine the cloth barrier in front of him, using reasonable caution to keep from moving it very much, until he located a small gap between two imperfectly overlapping pieces. When he put his eye to this aperture, he was able to examine most of the room in front of him while remaining virtually invisible himself.

Now he had a good view, from a different angle, of the two Old World lanterns on their separate tables, seven or eight meters apart. Each light source was a white globe approximately the size of a man's head, almost uncomfortably bright if you looked straight at it. Each globe was supported on a stout dark cylinder with a broadened base, that held it above its table by about half the length of a man's arm.

Ordinarily Kasimir would have found such rare Old World artifacts intensely interesting. But not just now. To begin with, there was Natalia, posing nude halfway between the lights. She was standing in front of a white cloth hung as a backdrop, on a low dais or stand that looked as if it could be rotated on demand.

And there was Robert de Borron, standing with his back turned almost fully to Kasimir. The artist was four or five meters from Natalia, and right beside him was the almost-finished statue he was working on. The statue, larger than life like the others in the studio, was of marble, almost pure white, and it rested on its own small foundation of short but heavy timbers. Close along one side of the marble figure rose a scaffolding, a sort of wide ladder, to enable the artist to reach the upper portions of the work.

Natalia had a robe lying beside her on the rough planks of the floor. She was facing toward both the sculptor's and Kasimir's left. Her pose was erect, standing with hips thrust forward, one foot a little in advance of the other, her arms curved wide as if inviting an embrace. In front of her, and slightly more distant from her than the artist was, a pair of Red Temple security guards in soiled and shabby crimson cloaks had frankly abandoned any pretense of paying attention to their duties, and were devoting themselves to staring at her.

She was managing to ignore them completely.

Beyond both sculptor and model as Kasimir looked at them, far across the broad expanse of the shallowy L-shaped studio space, a handful of other workers were toiling at some tasks that Kasimir did not bother to try to identify exactly. Now and then, out of the relative dimness in which those other people labored, a thin cloud of white stone dust drifted, slight air currents carrying it gradually closer to the lights. But some of the people over there seemed to be working on wood; Kasimir looking at them got the impression that they might be simultaneously demolishing one small scaffold and putting another one together. The sounds of their hammering tried with little success to echo in the large but cloth-draped space.

Besides the statue that de Borron was working on, four or five others were still standing about in the studio. All of these appeared to have been finished by now.

The glow provided by the Old World lights was certainly as strong as daylight in the vicinity of the sculptor and his model, but even at its brightest it was subtly different from the light of day. De Borron's face, plainly visible to Kasimir whenever the sculptor turned his head a little, showed clear as a marble carving in that light. But for once the man's expression was not a study in arrogance. Instead there was something strained and pleading in his look, as if the artist were praying to his Muse.

But none of this, not even the sight of Natalia posing unclothed, claimed Kasimir's attention more than momentarily. Within a few seconds after he had made his peephole in the cloth draperies, Kasimir's attention was entirely riveted upon the object in de Borron's hands.

The sculptor was now indeed working with the Sword of Siege.

The hidden observer could be very sure of this, even though very little of Stonecutter's length was actually visible. Almost the entire weapon was out of sight, sandwiched between a pair of thin, flat boards that were held firmly together with clamps. From one end of this sandwich a dull black hilt protruded, and from the other end, that nearest the work, a few centimeters of bright steel.

Attached at right angles to the flat boards making up this improvised sheath were rounded wooden handles. These offered good grips for the artist, who needed only the few exposed centimeters of the blade to work the stone.

But the most ingenious part of the Sword-holder's design, as Kasimir observed it, was the way in which the whole sandwich of Sword and wood was suspended from overhead, on what looked like a fishing-rod of slender steel, with counterweight attached. By this means the sculptor's arms and hands were freed of the continual burden of the weighty Sword, his muscles were liberated to concentrate upon the demands of art and of the client's deadlines.

Obviously the work was going very swiftly now, and doubtless the artist, despite the occasional expression of anguish that passed across his face, was basically satisfied with how it went. The Sword as he used it to cut stone made little thudding noises. These seemed to have little or no connection with the physical work it was accomplishing, being rather a by-product of its magic. Kasimir needed a minute or two to convince himself that such an inappropriate sound was really coming from the Sword, and was not an echo of the coarse pounding by the workers in the background.

But the dull little thudding sound was proceeding from the Sword, all right. Under the sure control of de Borron's strong hands, Stonecutter's irresistible point was peeling and scooping delicate little chips of stone from the white marble shape. Already the work had taken on at least the crude shape of its model in all its parts, and some of those parts looked completely finished. Only the final stages of carving and smoothing remained to be done.

It was obvious that the work had been going on in this swift fashion for some time. For hours, probably, if the drift of tiny, distinctively shaped chips and shavings around the sculptor's feet offered any reliable indication.

The amplified likeness of Natalia, subtly transformed by de Borron's skill, was rapidly emerging from the stone. But despite the evidence of rapid progress, and the fact that de Borron appeared pleased and fascinated with his new tool, it was apparent to Kasimir that the artist had not yet mastered the Sword to his own satisfaction. Fascination was far from contentment. The artist was intent on learning everything that this magical device would let him do.

He was muttering to himself—or perhaps to his Muse—almost continually as he worked. Kasimir was not quite able to make out any of these comments.

The studio was not as busy as it had been during the day, but a few more people were present, all of them Red Temple personnel of one kind or another. Chief among these, the High Priest himself, now came strolling around the corner of the L, heading in the direction of the laboring artist. The priest had his hands clasped behind his back, and his expression was one of impatience held in check by deliberate toleration; it must appear to him now that his precious deadline was going to be met after all. In no more than a few hours, perhaps, the installation of his precious gambling tables in this space could begin.

The official spoke. "So, it appears that you are going to finish on time, de Borron."

The sculptor, without removing his eyes from his model, muttered something in response. Stonecutter continued to make its dull incongruous noise, and thin stone leaves released by the bright blade fluttered almost continuously to the floor.

"What's that you say, sculptor?"

The man with the Sword in his hands looked up. "I said, 'Yes, if I am not bothered too much by fools.'" This time the answer was spoken with fierce clarity.

The man in the red robes flushed. "One day, stonecutter, you will push your arrogance too far."

But with that the exchange of sharp words died out; de Borron had already turned back to his work and Kasimir, watching, thought it doubtful that he had even heard the priest's reply.

Meanwhile some of the other people in red livery were also strolling closer to where the master artist worked. A couple of them, besides the two enthralled with Natalia, were from security. Two more, women, were probably minor officials, Kasimir thought, come up here to see where the gambling tables were going to be when the remodeling was finished.

The two supposed guards who had abandoned all thoughts of duty in favor of gaping at the model were gaping at her still. Only when one of these moved closer for a better look, actually getting himself into the sculptor's immediate range of vision, did de Borron bark something that sent both men into a hasty retreat.

The High Priest, who had earlier retreated a few steps, said something in a low voice that Kasimir did not catch.

The sculptor heard him, though, and snapped back: "If you want me to finish quickly, then in the name of all the gods get out of my way and let me work!"

Kasimir was just wondering whether he ought to start back down the elevator shaft—he foresaw that getting out of the temple again would take time—and report to Wen Chang as quickly as possible that the Sword was definitely here, when his thoughts were interrupted by a faint and furtive sound coming from somewhere to his right.

Turning his head sharply in that direction, he saw that some of the ropes and chains that hung down into the elevator shaft were stirring slightly, as if someone below were pulling on them or at least had touched them.

While Kasimir had been busy making his own unauthorized entrance into these private parts of the temple, it had not even occurred to him to wonder at how easy it all was. You expected security to be lax in a Red Temple. But now he wondered suddenly whether his entrance had not been suspiciously, ominously easy. Whether a path might not have been deliberately left unguarded; not for him, of course. For someone else, and he had happened to find it.

There were more sounds from the elevator shaft, very faint sounds. Sounds that he would not have heard or noticed if he had not been listening intently for them.

Someone else was coming up to the studio, by the same route Kasimir had taken.

If Kasimir stayed where he was, the new arrival or arrivals would be certain to discover him as soon as they reached the top of the shaft. Maybe it was Red Temple security, after all alert enough to do some checking up on loosened panels. Maybe it was someone else.

As quietly as he could, Kasimir scrambled away from the opening of the shaft, moving into the deeper shadows along the wall of canvas draperies.

From beyond that wall came Natalia's voice, speaking suddenly and clearly. "I need to take a break," she said.

Kasimir, satisfied for the moment that he was safe from discovery, fumbled at the cloth in front of him again until he found another tiny hole, which enabled him to once more look out into the studio. He was in time to see Natalia grabbing up her robe from the floor and pulling it around her, while at the same time she shot a swift glance toward the open elevator shaft. It was not a look of puzzlement, or idle curiosity; instead it was full of calculation. She had heard the sounds there too, and Kasimir got the impression that she had been expecting them.

"Can't you wait?" de Borron barked at her, automatically protesting the interruption of his work.

"No, I can't." Tying the belt of her robe, the tall young woman tossed back her drab hair defiantly. The Old World light did nothing for its color. "We've been at it for hours. I don't know how much longer I'll be able to hold my arms up like that."

"All right, I suppose you're due for a break." The artist's voice was tired. He was rubbing his hands together now, as if to restore circulation in his own tired limbs. He had let go of the apparatus that held the Sword, so that Stonecutter in its odd wooden sheath bobbed lightly in midair, dependent on its fishing-rod support.

Now Kasimir, looking back toward the elevator shaft while holding himself motionless in shadow, could see and hear two people—now three—arriving at the top and climbing out, crouching in the very place where he had been only a few minutes ago. Whoever they might be, they were not Red Temple security. These people were clad in close-fitting dark clothing, including masks. Kasimir saw a long dagger in one hand. He had thought for a moment that the new arrivals were all wearing swords, but when he got a momentary glimpse of them in slightly better light he saw that they were actually wearing swordbelts with long empty sheaths.

And, whoever they might be, Natalia was definitely expecting them. The way she had glanced in their direction and then started a diversion was good evidence of that.

Whoever they were, there was no doubt in Kasimir's mind that they were going for the Sword.

From beyond the wall of fabric Kasimir could hear the sculptor's weary voice: "We can put up a prop for you to rest your arms on." Then de Borron's voice grew louder, barking orders at the people who were still banging away at their work on the other side of the big room.

A moment later all the sounds of hammering had ceased. Kasimir, with his eye again to his latest observation hole, saw that the people on the far side of the room had now put down most of their tools and were coming this way.

The Sword of Siege, with no one very near it at the moment, hung gently bobbing in its homemade tool-holder. A few meters from the Sword, de Borron was pacing back and forth, pushing his hands against the small of his back as if to ease the muscles there.

Natalia was stretching herself too, and rubbing her side under her robe where perhaps the cramp was real. Now, as if following a sudden impulse of curiosity, she moved to stand close beside the low table holding one of the radiant Old World light-globes. Then she reached out one hand to touch the dark material of the lamp's base.

"How does this work?" she asked in a clear, innocent voice. "Why is there no heat?"

"Don't fool around with that light, girl. Stop it, I tell you! That's not your—"

But de Borron's shouted orders were ignored. Natalia's fingers had found the control they sought, and suddenly the lamp went dark.

The other lamp, the one nearest the elevator shaft, was still lighted, flooding the big room with plenty of illumination for everyone to see what happened next. In a moment the remaining lamp had been snatched from its table and extinguished by the first of the three dark-clad figures who now burst out of concealment and came running into the room from that direction.

Kasimir had already made up his mind to act, and when he saw the dark figure running for the one remaining light source he knew that the moment for decisive action had come. The barrier of draped cloth in front of him was no impediment at all. Even as the studio went almost entirely dark, he pushed between the folds of hanging canvas, heading for the Sword.

He was certain that a number of other people would be rushing toward the same goal, but he felt sure of having at least a moment's start on most of them. And when the lights went out he was already moving in the right direction.

As his legs drove him forward the few necessary strides, he heard the blackness around him come alive with oaths, cries of surprise and fear, and sounds as if people were colliding with one another. There was even what sounded like a clash of steel blades; perhaps the Red Temple guards were after all not totally incompetent, or perhaps they had only drawn swords out of fear for their own lives.

The bulk of the unfinished likeness of Natalia, and its scaffolding, loomed up just ahead of Kasimir and to his left, backlighted by the faint red glow that came through crevices from the lights along the front of the temple. The same dim light showed Kasimir something else: Despite the speed with which he was rushing for the Sword, he was not going to be the first to reach it. De Borron was there ahead of him, and the sculptor already had Stonecutter out of its wooden sheath before Kasimir could come to grips with him.

The sculptor had Stonecutter's hilt in his right hand, and was ready to use the Sword as a weapon, when Kasimir crashed into him, determined to wrest the blade away. Kasimir's left hand closed in its hardest grip on de Borron's right wrist.

The physician was no trained warrior, but rough games had been a part of his growing up and of his youth, and he possessed considerable stocky strength. De Borron was perhaps just as strong, but when the two men fell together Kasimir was on top, and most of the sculptor's wind was jarred out of him in the impact.

The Sword fell free. For a moment only it lay unattended on the floor of the studio, almost within reach of the struggling men; and then someone snatched it up. Kasimir had only the impression of a lone running figure, unidentifiable in the near-darkness, grabbing the Sword of Siege in passing, and running with it in the direction of the elevator shaft.

A moment later the wrestling match had reached an end, by common consent. Kasimir and de Borron were both back on their feet, trampling and clawing at each other in an effort to gain some advantage in the pursuit of this most recent Sword-thief.

Around the running pair, other skirmishes were still proceeding under cover of darkness, with oaths and cries and sounds of impact.

Kasimir, glancing to one side caught a glimpse of Natalia, distinguishable by her robe and her pale legs running below it, running in the same direction he was. This time he could be sure it was not she who had seized the Sword and was getting away with it.

This time, he vowed grimly, no one was going to do that, unless it was himself.

Someone was giving the trick a great try, though. The person carrying Stonecutter had now disappeared in the general vicinity of the head of the elevator shaft, and Kasimir assumed that he—or she—must be climbing down the rickety interior sides, or sliding down the chains and cables, in near-total darkness. But how would anyone be able to carry a Sword while doing that? Suddenly Kasimir understood why the latest set of intruders had been wearing empty Sword-sheaths at their belts.

Running up to the shaft himself, the physician in his haste came near diving into it headfirst. His entrance was not quite that precipitate. Having climbed the sides of the shaft before, he was better able to handle it in darkness than most of those pursuing would be.

De Borron, reaching the top of the shaft only a step or two behind him, delayed the start of his own descent briefly. He took time out to bellow uselessly for lights, and for more guards to come and save the Sword.

Then, despairing of any effective help, the sculptor swung out boldly on the chains and ropes. On the end of a loose line he started an almost free-fall plunge into the dark depths below, and had to grab at another chain to save himself.

Meanwhile Kasimir kept doggedly to his own more patient method of getting down, and whoever was carrying the Sword ahead of him and below him still maintained a lead in the descending race. Kasimir looking down could barely see a movement, shadow deeper into shadow, and only some faint sounds, clinking together of the long chains, drifted up.

Now a brief outcry in a familiar voice came from above, and Kasimir glanced in that direction. Something had delayed Natalia, but she had reached the shaft at last, and was struggling with de Borron a couple of meters above Kasimir's head.

In a moment the sculptor was somehow pushed free, or lost his grip on chains and ropes, and started to fall down the shaft. At the last possible moment before disaster he saved himself by regaining his hold on one of the cables or chains.

Once more steel weapons clashed in the near-darkness. The members of the intruding group, one above Kasimir's position and one now somewhere below, had drawn blades to defend the Sword-bearer, and indeed he or she must certainly be using the Sword itself, meanwhile trying to hang on with one hand.

Someone climbing in the gloom nearby lashed out at Kasimir. He stuck to his climbing and succeeded in getting away from this attack. If the attack should be renewed he thought he would have to draw his dagger and try to fight with one hand while he hung on with the other.

With a sharp splintering sound, a loose slat in the wall nearby gave way under someone's grasp. There was a scream and a falling body, followed after a sickeningly long interval by a crash in the darkness far below.

But there was no indication that the person carrying the Sword had fallen.

Scarcely had the sound of that first fall died when de Borron, still a meter or two above Kasimir and just to one side of him, fell again. Someone or something had knocked the artist loose from his grip inside the shaft, and he tumbled past Kasimir, screaming a string of imprecations that were cut short suddenly when he hit the invisible bottom.

And, half that distance below Kasimir, at about the level of the highest inhabited rooms, the vague shadow he had tentatively identified as the Sword-bearer left the shaft, to glide almost silently into some kind of opening in its wall.

Kasimir followed.

His pursuit of the latest thief went on relentlessly, crossing narrow beams and leaping gaps over darkness, going more recklessly with each momentary frustration.

Nor were any of the other pursuers giving up on the confused chase. Rather the number of hounds seemed to be growing, with the guards of the Red Temple forming a gradually increasing presence. However tardily and ineptly they were being mobilized for action, they were everywhere in the building, and they greatly outnumbered all the other participants together.

Kasimir now had lost sight of Natalia completely. But not of his primary quarry, the sinister shape who bore the Sword. The figure tried to lose him and the other pursuers, leaping from one narrow beam to another. But Kasimir, his blood now aroused to the full excitement of the hunt, would not be shaken off. His quarry climbed a stony column, dropped down again, and leaped another gap. But Kasimir stuck with the other as if his teeth were already fastened in his prey's flesh.

They were both centimetering their way across the thin ceiling of one of the orgy rooms on the third floor when Kasimir at last caught sight once more of Natalia's unmistakable bare-legged figure. She was starting to creep toward the quarry too, though holding on with one hand to a solid support. Whether she meant to strike at the Sword-thief or aid him Kasimir could not—

The ceiling underneath them all was giving way.

This time it was really—

The slow-motion sensation of desperate action took over. Kasimir knew a moment of despair, a moment of resignation; there followed in an instant an almost anticlimactic splashdown. He, along with numerous fragments of ceiling, had landed upon what he first took for a gigantic bursting waterbed. But when he went in up to his waist, he realized that the first impact of his fall had been borne by a flimsy raft afloat upon a shallow perfumed pool. Half a dozen naked bodies, looking clinically exposed and vulnerable, were thrashing in the shallow water now, and from the bottom of the tank unsavory things came swirling up. Wine and food, their fragile containers broken, were churning in the water, scattered into garbage.

Whatever performance had been in progress on the raft was over now. Another body, that of a security guard, fell through the ceiling, drenching Kasimir afresh with a great splash as it landed right beside him. The quondam performers were rolling, swimming, scrambling for shelter outside the pool, intent on getting out of any of the target area before more people fell.

An audience, some fifteen or twenty strong, was looking on.

There were two rows of chairs, the rear row elevated, making something like a small grandstand. All of the seats were full. The occupants of the chairs, a jaded-looking and weary crew, brightened enough at the violent innovations to offer a small round of applause, even as the Red Temple guards came crowding in through both doorways.

Kasimir, still waist-deep in the noisome artificial pond, looked round him in despair. There were plenty of blades in sight now, drawn and ready in the hands of the Red Guards who came bursting in the room's doors, and dropping through the newly opened ceiling. Swiftly their attention was concentrated upon Kasimir.

And again the Sword was gone.

14

BOUT an hour after dawn next morning, an elderly and majestic individual, announcing himself as the personal representative of the Hetman, and accompanied by an armed escort that augmented his already formidable dignity, came calling upon Wen Chang and Kasimir at the Inn of the Refreshed Travelers.

Despite the early hour, Wen Chang was wide awake and ready to receive visitors. Kasimir, on the other hand, had to be awakened, a task that was not accomplished without difficulty. The young physician had been intensely questioned by the Red Temple authorities until well after midnight, and then released only on Captain Almagro's written acceptance of responsibility for any further crimes and outrages that this self-proclaimed investigator might commit.

The early-morning business of the Hetman's representative at the inn was soon stated: The Magistrate Wen Chang, and his chief associate, one Kasimir the physician, were courteously but very firmly invited to attend a meeting that was due to begin as soon as they could reach the palace, and was to be presided over by the Hetman himself. The purpose of this meeting was the discussion of certain strange events known to have taken place recently in the city, and the resolution of the resulting problems.

Despite Wen Chang's attempt to question him, the Hetman's representative would be, or could be, no more specific than that.

As the two investigators were concluding their hasty preparations for departure, with the representative of the Hetman waiting in the room just below, Kasimir asked Wen Chang in a low voice: "Shall I tell them everything that happened to me last night?"

The narrowed eyes of the Magistrate widened momentarily. "I presume that you have told *me* everything?"

"Yes, of course."

"Then I see no reason why you should not repeat the same story to the Hetman. Truth is very often an effective weapon; and we mean no harm to anyone in this city except Sword-stealers."

Wen Chang and Kasimir were soon as ready as they could be; they descended to the courtyard and mounted for the ride to the palace. Their escort remained courteous, and the two were not searched, but once in the street they were surrounded continuously by mounted troopers. A light rain was falling again, adding to Kasimir's thoughts of gloom; he took heart from the fact that Wen Chang appeared not at all discouraged.

As their small cavalcade entered the square in front of the Hetman's palace, Kasimir observed that the scaffold that had been erected for tomorrow morning's execution had somehow been severely damaged, and was now undergoing reconstruction. There were signs that fire had destroyed portions of the original wooden structure, while other parts of it had been knocked down and broken. The rebuilding was being carried out under military guard.

Raising his eyes, Kasimir saw that this morning there was a face looking out at one of the small barred windows that here overlooked the square. Looking carefully, he was able to recognize the man he had earlier seen riding in the tumbrel, on the occasion of Kasimir's first visit to this square.

Why should Benjamin of the Steppe, or anyone else, trouble to stand at a window to watch the instrument of his own death take shape? It would seem to indicate a morbid, helpless fascination, certainly. Kasimir gazed up with a kind of sympathy at the face in the small window. But if the prisoner was aware that he had a commiserator, he gave no sign.

Wen Chang, taking in all of this with a glance or two, informed the dignitary in charge of their escort that he intended to pause for a moment. When this was allowed, the Magistrate called over the officer in charge of the military guard, and questioned him.

The officer, of junior rank, plainly enjoyed the chance to be seen talking in public to these important-looking people who were on their way to the palace. He provided what information he could on the situation regarding the scaffold. During the night just past some of those persistent rural protesters had tried to burn the platform down. When rain prevented that, they had mounted the wooden structure with axes and hammers and tried to knock it all apart. The Watch had finally come on the scene and driven them off, but not until the devils had managed to do quite a bit of damage. Never fear, though, the instrument of execution would be ready in time, and this time would be kept under careful guard—there would be a live hanging, drawing, and quartering to begin the Festival tomorrow morning.

Kasimir, who had no intention of attending that kind of a curtain raiser, muttered something about the hopelessness of people who protested by trying to burn a scaffold. Wen Chang was scowling—it was hard to tell just what his reaction was. But as the Magistrate signed that he was ready to ride on again, his eyes twinkled for just a moment.

Their pause in the square had been brief, and only moments later Wen Chang and his associate were being escorted through a rear gate and into a narrow yard behind the palace itself. There all dismounted, leaving their riding-beasts in the care of grooms.

Inside the palace the Hetman was awaiting them in an audience chamber of moderate size, two floors above the ground. A number of other people were also already present, including Captain Almagro, who looked grim and bone-weary.

But most of the small gathering turned actively hostile gazes toward Wen Chang as he entered. The High Priests of both Red and Blue Temples, each accompanied by his own small retinue of advisers, stopped talking and glared at the newcomers on their arrival.

Kasimir was surprised to see that Robert de Borron was also present. Last night Kasimir had reported to Wen Chang that the artist was probably dead following his tumble down the elevator shaft. And indeed, de Borron was in bad shape, with one leg and one arm splinted, and bruises evident on his face.

The silence of the Red Temple's High Priest was only momentary. As soon as that official had recognized Wen Chang and his associate, he immediately accused them in a loud voice of not only taking part in the raid on his establishment the previous night, but of organizing the attack as well.

And of carrying off Stonecutter. "The Sword of Siege is ours by rights, and I demand that you return it to us at once!"

For once the glowering artist gave every evidence of being in complete agreement with what the High Priest said.

That official went on: "I shall make the charges more formal and specific." He grabbed a scroll from an aide and began to read from it. The Magistrate and his associate were accused of conducting a raid last night upon the Temple of Aphrodite and Eros, particularly the House of Flesh, and there conniving in the attempted murder of the sculptor Robert de Borron, and also conspiring with person or persons unknown to steal and sell a treasure of incalculable value.

Wen Chang, who still had not responded, waited calmly until the string of accusations should be finished; this took some time, as the Blue Temple people, unwilling to wait, were trying to get in their own accusations and arguments at the same time.

Meanwhile the Hetman had been sitting silently in his place at the head of the table, evidently willing to let the uproar run its course for a time, in the hope that some facts constituting useful information might emerge. Presently it was evident that nothing of the kind was likely to happen, and he drew his dagger and pounded on the table with the pommel. Almost instantly he was granted the boon of silence.

Kasimir had never heard any personal name for the current ruler of Eylau, and he had gathered that lack was a usage established by tradition as long as the person was in office. The Director of Security at the Blue Temple was operating under a similar rule or tradition.

The present Hetman, whatever his name, was a short, stout man, dressed in an elaborate style that Kasimir considered as bordering on the effeminate. There were rings on almost all his pudgy fingers and his coloring was muddy and unhealthy looking. About forty years of age, he looked as if he might at one time have been very strong physically, but had let himself go to seed. As Kasimir observed him throughout the meeting, the impression he gave was one of fading moral strength as well as physical, of an overriding, undermining insecurity.

Kasimir like all other thinking observers knew that the position of the city-state governed by this man was insecure as well. Eylau was chronically beset and buffeted by the larger powers surrounding it, and sometimes also by international entities like the great and well-nigh universal temples.

The silence obtained by the Hetman's dagger-pounding was of brief duration. He allowed the silence he had won to stretch on a little too long, and the Blue Temple people took advantage of this leniency to burst into verbal action.

What they wanted, they said, was protection against robbers. This danger, they said, had escalated almost infinitely, now that a tool like Stonecutter was in the city, in unknown criminal hands.

"No one's property anywhere will be safe, as long as that Sword is in the hands of irresponsible people!"

Before the Hetman had decided how to respond to that—or Wen Chang could formulate a reply—the Red Temple had seized the floor again, its leaders protesting that they were the ones who had actually been robbed, and had a real grievance to present.

The Hetman, exasperated at last, gave up all effort at a dramatic pause, all pretense at judicial calm, and shouted hoarsely for order. His voice, or something in the way he used it, was even more effective than his earlier dagger-pounding, and he was granted his wish immediately.

This time the silence lasted somewhat longer. As it endured, Kasimir found it possible to hear, faintly, the continual hammering from out in the square where the reconstruction of the scaffold was still in progress.

"Now," said the ruler of the city, looking around the room. He had a bold, commanding voice when he wanted to make it so; but despite the tone and the determined look Kasimir had the definite impression that the Hetman was uncertain of just what ideas he ought to present to the orderly attention of his audience, now that it had been granted him.

It was with a subtle appearance of relief that the Hetman's gaze at last came to rest upon Wen Chang. The voice of practiced boldness asked: "And you are the famed Magistrate?"

"I am, Excellency," replied the lean man, bowing. There was no pretense of any particular modesty in the answer, and the bow was the movement of an experienced diplomat.

"Good." The direction of the Hetman's attention shifted slightly. "And I suppose you are Kasimir the physician?"

"Yes sir, I am." Kasimir bowed in turn.

The stout man sitting in the elevated chair drew in a deep breath. "As you have just heard, it is charged against you both, among other things, that you have conspired to steal a piece of property belonging to the Red Temple. Very valuable property, too, I might add. What have you to say to this accusation?"

Wen Chang replied smoothly. "Only two things, Excellency. In the first place we have stolen nothing, and we do not have the Sword. And in the second place, the property in question—I assume the Sword of Siege, one of the Twelve Swords of the gods, is meant—does not belong to the Red Temple. It never has." Raising his voice, Wen Chang overrode protests from that direction. "Not only are we innocent of the theft of Stonecutter, but we are engaged on behalf of the rightful owner to recover his property for him. The Red Temple has no more legitimate interest in that Sword than does the Blue, or than the people who have it now."

The protests emanating from the Red Temple delegation only increased in violence and noise.

Wen Chang needed help from the Hetman, in the form of more dagger-pounding on the table, before he could regain the floor.

When a semblance of order had been re-established, and the Magistrate granted silence in which to proceed, he said: "It is true that Doctor Kasimir, acting as my agent, was inside the Red Temple last night. He entered legitimately, as a paying customer. He was not trying to kill or injure anyone, or to steal anything. His only purpose—in which, regrettably, he failed—was to recover the Sword for its rightful owner."

"Ah," said the Hetman. "You keep coming to that point. Who is this rightul owner?"

Wen Chang continued smoothly. "My immediate client, Excellency, is Prince al-Farabi of the Firozpur tribe." That created a stir of surprise in the room. The Magistrate went on: "Not many days ago, the Sword we seek was stolen from the Prince's camp in the desert, some three days' journey from Eylau.

"But the Sword of Siege, as Prince al-Farabi will be first to admit, was only his on loan—a matter, I am told, of Stonecutter's powers being needed to root out some bandits from a particularly inaccessible desert stronghold. The true and rightful owner of the blade is Prince Mark of Tasavalta, with whom I am sure Your Excellency is well acquainted, if only by reputation."

"Of course," said the Hetman after a brief pause. He acknowledged some kind of acquaintance with the well-known Prince almost absently, as if his mind were running on ahead already, assessing what the implications of this claim were likely to be if it was true. Tasavalta was not a next-door neighbor, but rather many kilometers to the north of his domain. Nor was it a particularly large country. But the Tasavaltans were said to be formidable in war; the reputation of their ruler had spread farther across the continent than this.

Now there came an interruption. Robert de Borron, refusing to be kept silent by the Red Temple people with him, struggled out of his chair despite his injuries, and came pushing his way forward, leaning on the central table, demanding to be heard.

The burden of his impassioned plea was that a greater matter than treasure or even human lives was here at stake—and that was Art. Now that he had held the Sword in his hands and had begun to discover how much it could do, what marvels a sculptor like himself would be able to accomplish with such an instrument—well, all this talk about property rights and money value was really beside the point.

The Sculptor looked across the table at the Blue Temple people almost as if he really expected them to agree with him. They gazed back. In the face of such heresy their countenance were set like stone beyond the power of any blade to carve.

Meanwhile the Hetman—perhaps from shrewdness, perhaps from chronic indecision—listened to the artist's outburst tolerantly. De Borron grew angry at being tolerated. He had tried to speak respectfully, he said, but perhaps that had been a mistake. Nothing, certainly nothing and no one here in this room, should take second place to Art.

He was silenced at last only by a serious threat from the Hetman to have him removed from the conference chamber and, if even that failed to keep him quiet, locked in a cell.

Next someone in the Blue Temple camp brought up the suggestion that de Borron himself might arranged to have the Sword stolen and spirited away.

Once more a minor outbreak of noise had to be put down.

"Captain Almagro." The ruler's voice was no louder nor bolder than before, but still the Captain blanched. "You are a senior officer in the city Watch. I want you now to tell me in plain words just what did happen inside the Red Temple last night; include everything that your investigations have discovered since the event."

Almagro, who had perhaps been expecting to hear worse from his master, spoke up confidently enough. To begin with, there was no doubt at all that the Sword had been there in the temple, and that it was now missing. But in the Captain's official opinion, there was also no reason to doubt any of the information that had just been provided by the famous Magistrate.

The Hetman nodded, as if he had known that all along. "My own magicians inform me that it is common knowledge, among those in a position to know, that the Prince of Tasavalta has had Stonecutter in his arsenal for some years."

This time the interruption came from the Red Temple representatives. After a hasty consultation among themselves, they put forward a spokesman who protested that, with all due respect to His Excellency's wizards, it was also common knowledge that the Swords, like other pieces of property, changed hands from time to time.

"We maintain, sir, that we were acting in good faith when we, as we thought, recently acquired certain rights to the Sword of Siege."

Wen Chang broke in sharply. "Exactly what rights were those, and from whom did you think you were obtaining them?"

The Red Temple people were still considering what their answer to this ought to be when the meeting was interrupted from outside by the entrance of one of the Hetman's aides. This was a middle-aged woman, who went straight to the ruler's side and imparted some information to him in a very soft whisper.

The Hetman heard the message with no change of expression. Then he nodded, dismissed the messenger with a few quiet words, and turned back to face the assembly at the table.

"Prince al-Farabi himself is now here in the palace," he announced, looking sharply round to gauge his audience's reactions. "And he is coming at once to join our meeting."

A stir ran through the gathering, but Kasimir saw nothing he considered helpful in anyone's reaction. Only Wen Chang, as usual, remained imperturbable.

Within two minutes, amid a flourish of formal announcement at the door, al-Farabi indeed entered the audience chamber. The Prince was wearing what looked like the desert riding costume in which Kasimir had seen him last, and Kasimir noted that his clothing was actually still dusty with traces of the desert.

The two rulers, using one of the short forms of ceremony, exchanged the proper formalities of greeting. As Kasimir watched he was thinking that according to strict protocol the Prince would somewhat outrank or would at least take precedence over the Hetman, though both were heads of state. It seemed unlikely, though, that exact rank was going to be of any practical importance.

After his official welcome by the Hetman, the Prince exchanged brief greetings with all the members of the meeting, taking them generally in order of rank as prescribed by protocol. When he came to Wen Chang, who was well down on the list, Kasimir thought that Prince and Magistrate exchanged significant looks, though he could not tell what the expressions were meant to convey.

As soon as the formal salutations had all been completed, al-Farabi resumed at some length his lamentations for his lost Sword.

Eventually mastering his feelings with an evident effort, he faced the Magistrate again. "I understand that Stonecutter was seen here in the city last night, but that it was impossible to recover it then?"

"That is true, sir."

"Ah, woe is me! My burden of sorrow is great indeed!"

Standing informally now with the two investigators as if they were old friends, the Prince related how, for the past several days, he and several dozen of his tribesmen had been out in the desert, trying in vain to pick up the trail of the villain or villains who had stolen Stonecutter from his camp. But, al-Farabi lamented, he and his trackers had had no success at all—which he supposed was scarcely to be wondered at, considering the nature of the ground and the ferocity of the windstorms that had lashed the area over the past several days.

Wen Chang broke in here to ask if any of the winged messengers dispatched by Lieutenant Komi has managed to reach the Prince.

"Regrettably none of them did." Al-Farabi looked freshly worried. "Is there news I ought to know? On entering the city today I came directly to the palace, feeling that I must consult with my brother the Hetman, and so I have not seen Komi. I have heard nothing."

"There is no news, sir, that is of vital importance for you to learn at this moment—only a few matters relating to the personal affairs of your troops."

With that settled, the Hetman called upon Kasimir to relate his version of events on the night the Sword was stolen from the tent. The ruler listened to the relation with a look of intense concentration. Then he wanted to know Kasimir's version of the events in the Red Temple during the night just passed.

Again Kasimir obliged. From the expression on al-Farabi's face as the Prince listened, Kasimir could tell that he had been expecting to hear nothing like this. As to what he had been expecting to hear, Kasimir could only wonder.

Called upon for comment again when Kasimir had finished, the Magistrate took three or four sentences to say in effect that the situation was indeed most interesting.

The Hetman snorted. "I rejoice to hear that you find it interesting!

But is that all that you can find to tell us? We were hoping for something of more substance from the great Wen Chang."

The Magistrate bowed lightly. "I might of course add that the situation is very serious. But I believe it is far from hopeless."

"I am glad to hear that you think so." The ruler looked round at others in the room as if to sample their reactions. "You see, then, some prospect of eventually being able to recover the Sword?"

Before answering, Wen Chang turned to face the people from the Red Temple. He said: "I must return to an earlier question, one that was never answered. You say you thought you had honestly bought certain rights to Stonecutter, or to its use—with whom did you bargain? Whom did you pay?"

The Red Temple spokesman looked at him haughtily. "As it seems now that we were bargaining in error, I don't see how knowing that is going to help."

"It may be of considerable help in recovering the Sword. Come, who was it? Certain disreputable people of the city, was it not?"

"I fail to understand why—"

"Did you not in fact know that you were dealing with a well-organized criminal gang?"

"Well, and if we were? We had hopes of being able to return the Sword, which we assumed might have been stolen somewhere, to a legitimate use in society."

Robert de Borron was unable to keep himself from bursting forth again, once more putting forth his claim that the demands of Art could justify any such dealings.

Someone from the Blue Temple, not wishing to have fewer words to say than anyone else on this occasion, pronounced: "No one's claims to the Sword are going to mean anything unless it is found. I would like to know how the world-famed investigator we have with us plans to go about recovering it."

The Hetman, determined to assert himself, seized this opportunity. "It does seem," he told Wen Chang, "that so far your efforts have contributed nothing to that end."

"It may seem so, sir."

"What evidence can you give us that you are making progress?"

"At present I can give you none."

Eventually, under pressure, the Magistrate pledged to the Hetman that if given a free hand he would be able to provide some information on the Sword's whereabouts, if he had not succeeded in actually recovering the blade itself, within the next twenty-four hours.

This was taken up by many of the people present as a promise that the Sword would be recovered within a day. All were eager for that—if Stonecutter were to remain in the hands of nameless thieves, it was hard to see how any of the legitimate segments of society could hope to profit from it in any way.

So, Wen Chang could more or less have his way for twenty-four hours. In the meantime, according to the Magistrate's recommendations, the Blue Temple would be more heavily guarded than usual, as would all the city's other main depositories of wealth. And all patrolmen of the Watch, wherever they were on duty, would be alerted to watch for Stonecutter.

With that the meeting broke up.

15

THE Prince was of course invited by the Hetman to partake of the hospitality of the palace. Declining the invitation would have been diplomatically difficult if not impossible, and so al-Farabi was more or less constrained to dine and lodge there, along with the small retinue he had brought into the city with him from the desert.

Though it was plain to Kasimir that the Prince would have preferred to leave the palace at once and have a long talk with Wen Chang, there was no opportunity inside the palace for the two men to converse without a high probability of being overheard. In the brief public exchange of conversation they had before parting, the Magistrate managed to convey to his royal client the idea that things were not really so bad as they might look at present. Wen Chang affirmed earnestly that he still had genuinely high hopes of being able to recover Stonecutter.

Kasimir, listening silently to this reassurance, could only wonder how such hopes might possibly be justified. Reviewing in his mind the situation as it stood, he did not find it promising. The twenty-four hours of Wen Chang's grace period were already passing, and nothing was being accomplished. Of course Wen Chang might have learned something encouraging during the hours he and Kasimir had been separated; the two of them had had no real chance to talk alone since Kasimir had been routed out of bed this morning.

Now, just as Kasimir and Wen Chang were reclaiming their mounts from the palace stables, they were joined by Captain Almagro. The Captain had a meaningful look for each of them, but he delayed saying anything of substance as long as they were still within the palace walls.

The delay, Kasimir discovered, was to be even longer, for as soon as they were outside those walls the Captain left them, with a wink and a wave. Kasimir, not understanding, watched him go.

"He will soon rejoin us, I think," the Magistrate assured him.

"If you say so."

They started for their inn, this time without stopping to watch the rebuilding of the scaffold.

Kasimir had expected the Magistrate himself to have a great deal to say as soon as they were away from the palace. But now, on the contrary, Wen Chang was content to ride along in near silence. Instead of joining Kasimir in trying to plan a last desperate attempt to recover the Sword, he seemed almost to have given up. His precious twenty-four hours were passing minute by minute, and if anything he appeared more relaxed than he had before the meeting at which the deadline had been imposed upon him.

If this was only resignation to the whims of Fate, then in Kasimir's opinion it was carrying that kind of attitude too far. As for himself, he saw no need to carry patience to extremes.

"Well?" he demanded, after they had ridden in silence to a couple of hundred meters' distance from the palace walls. "What are we to do?"

A dark eye gleamed at him from underneath a squinting brow. "Have patience," his companion advised him succinctly.

Kasimir found this, in the circumstances, a thoroughly unsatisfactory answer. But he had to be content with it until they had reached their inn.

There they found Almagro waiting for them in the courtyard, having evidently completed whatever urgent errand had drawn him away. The Captain was impatient too. "Where can we talk? I've got quite a lot to say."

Wen Chang gestured. "Come up to our suite—it is about as secure as any place can be, outside a wizard's palace."

When the three of them were established in the third-floor suite, with Komi and some of his men on watch in the room below, Almagro began to talk, quietly but forcefully.

His pleas that Wen Chang get busy and find the Sword without delay were considerably more urgent than Kasimir's might have been.

"Magistrate, if you know where the damned thing is, or might be, then let's get it and deliver it without delay." The Captain was now obviously worried for himself. "Whatever might or might not happen to you two if you fail, nothing good is going to happen to me. My neck is on the line. I've stuck it way out for you, and His Mightiness the desert Prince is not going to put himself out to protect me."

Wen Chang responded with every appearance of sympathy. "He might very well offer you protection if I ask it of him. And I shall certainly ask it if I think it necessary."

"If? Look here, Magistrate, tell me straight out—do you know where the Sword is now, or don't you?"

"If you mean, can I walk straight to it and put my hand on it—no. Can I send a message from this room, and have it brought here to me within the hour? Again my answer must be no. Nevertheless I do have some definite ideas on the subject of Stonecutter's location."

"Hah! If you have any useful ideas at all, I wish you'd share them with me!"

"The time is not yet right for that . . . look here, old friend. You have trusted me in the past. Can you not trust me once more?"

The Captain blew out a blast of air that made his mustache quiver. "I've seen you act like this before . . . damn it all, I suppose you know what you're doing."

"Thank you. I appreciate the confidence. Now, have the arrangements that I requested been completed?"

"They have." Almagro looked at the room's windows and the closed door. "If you mean about that fellow Umar. We've picked him up, and brought him into the city, as quietly as we could. One of my own men is now temporarily in command out at the quarry."

"Were you able to determine anything from the records out there, about which prisoner or prisoners might be missing?"

"Nah. My people brought in what records they could find, and I've taken a look at them. Hopeless, I'd say. Kept by a bunch of illiterates."

"I feared as much." Wen Chang rubbed his own neck, as if the long strain were beginning to tell on him. "And where are you holding Umar now?"

"At one of our auxiliary Watch-stations. It's a very quiet little place, hardly used for anything anymore, out near the Paupers' Palace. I doubt very much that anyone besides the men I trust know that he's there. The men who took him there and are watching over him are the most trustworthy I have."

"Good." Now Wen Chang was nodding eagerly. "I want to talk to Umar at once."

Kasimir shook off his own recurrent tiredness as well as he could, and made ready to accompany Wen Chang and Almagro through the streets yet once more.

Leaving the inn, they rode through the streets upon a broadly looping course, the Magistrate doubling back and changing his route unpredictably in an efficient effort to determine whether or not they were being followed. At length he was satisfied, and they set out straight for the Paupers' Palace.

Their trip through the streets was somewhat delayed by these precautions, but otherwise uneventful. Presently a familiar landmark came into Kasimir's sight—the isolated, disconnected, crumbling section of high stone wall, with the winged scavengers rising from its top and settling there again, shrieking in their quarrels over food.

At one side of the stretch of barren ground that centered on the wall of exposure stood a small stone building, seventy or eighty meters from the wall and at least half that distance apart from any other structure. This, Almagro indicated, was the Watch-station. The building, Kasimir estimated, looking at it from a distance, could contain no more than two rooms at most. He supposed its chief claim to usefulness, if you could call it that, was its position that would allow the occupants to keep a close eye on the corpse-disposal operation.

They had ridden within fifty meters or so of the building when Almagro abruptly reined in his mount, then just as suddenly spurred forward. Wen Chang was riding at a gallop right beside him.

Kasimir dug his heels into the flanks of his riding-beast and stayed right behind them. He was actually the first off his mount as the three men reached the station. The stout front door of the little building was standing slightly ajar. In the shaded area just inside the entrance, where it would be invisible until you were almost upon it, lay the body of a man in Watch uniform. The man was sprawled on his back in the middle of a considerable pool of blood.

Kasimir took one look at the wound that had opened the man's throat, almost from ear to ear, and forbore to look for signs of life. The blood was starting to dry on the stone floor, and the insects were already busy around the corpse.

Almagro, standing over the dead man now with his short sword drawn, said a name, which Kasimir took to be that of the murdered man; then the Captain and the Magistrate, both with weapons ready, moved farther into the building, toward a doorway leading to the rear.

Once more Kasimir was right behind them.

The second room of the small structure was dim and almost window-less. The heat of the sun upon the thin stone walls was turning the chamber ovenlike; and here was more blood, much more blood, this time spreading out in a fan-shaped, partially dried puddle that had its source inside the single barred cell with which the building was equipped. There was another dead man in there, lying on the floor of the still-locked cell, and in this victim's distorted face Kasimir could recognize the valuable prisoner Umar.

For a few moments the drone of insects, and the cries of those distant, larger scavengers upon the paupers' wall, made the only sounds in that dim room. Then Wen Chang asked his old friend to unlock the door of the cell.

The Captain fumbled at his belt, where there were several sets of keys. He seemed to be having trouble finding the proper one. "How was he killed, in there?" he asked in a querulous voice. "He can't have done it himself, there's no weapon."

The Magistrate shook his head impatiently. "He was lured to the bars, by whoever killed the sentry. Lured by the promise of being set free, I suppose . . . how should I know the details?" Wen Chang was angry at the loss of his witness, perhaps at his own mistakes as well, and disposed to be uncharacteristically surly.

Once Almagro had found the proper key and opened the cell door, Wen Chang and Kasimir went into the cell, both trying to avoid step-ping in the puddled blood. The Magistrate also drew up his trouser legs with a slight fastidious movement.

Soon after Wen Chang had begun his examination of the body, he turned to announce that the man had been attacked from behind, and that his killer was left-handed.

Almagro, his expression at once idle and thoughtful, had been look-ing into the cell from outside, hanging on to the bars of the door. But he reacted sharply to that.

"Left-handed?" His voice rose, in both pitch and volume, from each syllable to the next. The others turned to look at him.

"Left-handed? That tears it, then! About three years ago, right after I came to work for the Hetman, there was a fellow in the city they called the Juggler. Another name he went by was Valamo of the Left Hand. He was the smoothest assassin I've ever run into anywhere. The deadli-est and smartest . . . it was only through a woman that we ever caught him. Even then we knew he'd done a lot of things we couldn't prove. We could prove enough, though. The judge thought that execution was too good for him."

Wen Chang's eyes glittered. "And so he was sent to the quarries?"

"Yes, he was, by all the gods! 'Course I'm not sure it was Kovil's quarry where he ended up. But it might well have been. He was one of the few you don't forget in this business. All this" —and with a savage gesture Almagro indicated the abattoir around them— "this is just the kind of thing he did. He knew, somehow, we had a good witness here, a man who could tell us a lot. And he came to shut him up for good."

"This Valamo, or Juggler, worked alone then, as a rule?"

"In the important things he worked alone as much as possible. Though he could always recruit people in Eylau to work with him, when he thought he needed someone. Had a reputation, that one did. Still has, evidently. I do believe that most of the regular gang leaders were afraid of him . . . so now it looks like the Juggler's back."

"How did he happen to acquire that name?" asked Kasimir.

Almagro's gaze turned toward him. "Nothing very strange about that. It's what he did, they tell me, before he found his real profession. A street performer, doing a little acrobatics, a little sleight of hand, a little juggling. Those people are never very far within the edge of the law anyway."

"True enough," said Wen Chang. "Though there have been times in my own life when I have felt almost completely at home among them . . . but never mind that. What does this Valamo look like?"

Squinting into the air, the Captain took thought carefully. "By now I'd say he must be around forty years old; though by the look of things here he's lost no skill or toughness. Anyone who could survive three years on a quarry gang . . . he's just average height, no taller than the Doctor here. Something of a hooked nose. His hair was dark when he was young, but when I saw him it was going an early gray—so it's likely just about completely white by now. His face would be lined and sunburnt from the quarries, so I'd say he's likely to look a decade or two older than he really is—what's wrong with you, Doctor Kasimir?"

"Tadasu Hazara," said Kasimir, after a pause to swallow. "That was the name he gave when he came to the inn, and talked to me about wanting to buy antique weapons. He must have thought that I was a genuine dealer, and was just making sure. Then he proved to himself that I was a fake." The physician paused and looked at his companions. "How could Kovil have hoped to control such a man?"

"Kovil did not lack in confidence," said Wen Chang dryly. He stood back from the blood and waved a hand about. "Old friend Almagro, this slaughter must of course be reported."

"And am I to report also that Valamo of the Left Hand did it?"

"Yes, I think so. All the pressure that we can put upon that gentleman will not be too much. As for you, Kasimir—"

"Yes?"

"I want you to go back to the inn and rest," said the Magistrate, surprising his hearer. "Rest, but do not sleep too deeply, for this Juggler may even now decide to pay us a visit there. And soon there will be another job for you to do."

16

KASIMIR returned to the inn, where Lieutenant Komi was waiting to greet him with eager questions about the most recent developments. Kasimir, not having been told to keep any secrets, brought the officer up to date as best he could.

Komi shook his head gloomily when he had heard the story of the double murder. "It sounds like bad news; I must find out what the Prince wants me to do now."

"It certainly doesn't sound like good news to me either. But be sure to leave a few reliable men here if you go off to the palace seeking orders."

"I will. Don't worry, my men are all reliable."

Climbing the stairs wearily to his third-floor room, Kasimir lay down on his couch to rest. For a time, the cries of peddlers in the street outside kept him awake.

The peddlers moved on eventually to the next street, but by now Kasimir's thoughts were disturbing enough to prevent his sleeping. He kept seeing the murdered men in the small stone building. Somehow the worst horror was the look of peace upon their faces; even the man in the cell, whose expression was unnatural, seemed to have died calmly. It was as if each of the victims in turn had welcomed the figure in whose guise death came upon them. Neither of them appeared to have taken alarm before the end.

At last Kasimir fell asleep, and with sleep came strange dreams. Someone whose face was hidden in a gray hood was stalking after him with a great steel Sword, trying to coax him to put down his dagger and his cudgel. Then in his dream Kasimir looked down for his right hand, and saw that it was gone, lopped off along with his wooden club.

He awoke sweating and gasping, to find Wen Chang bending over him. For just a moment the horror and strangeness of the dream persisted, and then Kasimir realized that the frightening alteration he perceived in Wen Chang's face was only a result of the Magistrate's just having removed the outer layer of some kind of a disguise.

"What's going on?" Kasimir demanded, almost before he was fully awake. There was something in his mentor's attitude that made him think more action must be imminent.

Wen Chang was standing back now, regarding him calmly. "I have arranged another task for you to perform, my young friend—if you choose. It might help our cause immeasurably, but I must warn you that it is very dangerous."

Kasimir sat up, scratching and rubbing his head. "Now—after we raided that warehouse—after you sent me into the Red Temple—now you think it necessary to warn me that our task is dangerous?"

The Magistrate had seated himself in a nearby chair. "Yes," he said, "I do. There were certainly dangers in those places that you mention. But the risk to be faced now may well be of a different order of magnitude. The fact is that I have been able, through some difficult and indirect negotiation, to arrange a deal with the Watch-station murderer."

Despite himself Kasimir was aware of a chill. "Well, I won't argue that he doesn't require a special warning. I suppose this deal involves the Sword?"

"Of course."

"What makes you think that the Juggler has it now, instead of Natalia and her group?"

"You misunderstand, Kasimir. The fact is that our friend hopes and expects to obtain the Sword from us, in return for a down payment of cash, along with his pledge of cooperation in other matters."

Kasimir, who had just got to his feet, slowly sat down again. "However did he get the idea that we have it?"

"I fear someone must have provided him with misleading information." The Magistrate's eyes twinkled slightly.

"How?"

There was no answer.

"So he wants Stonecutter from us. What do we hope and expect to get from him?"

"I have told him that we want a thousand gold pieces as a down payment, and a pledge, plus his co-operation in future operations."

"And what do we really want?"

"I want his head," said Wen Chang simply.

There was a little silence. "I see what you mean," said Kasimir at last, "about the danger."

"Yes; about that. Understand, Kasimir, that I would not ask this of you if I thought the part I wanted you to play was truly suicidal. But I will think none the less of you if you—"

"Oh, yes, you would." The physician got to his feet. "That's all right. I, on my part, would think something the less of myself if, having come this far, I were to fail to see this matter through to a conclusion. Tell me what you want me to do."

The Magistrate, smiling and obviously relieved, leaned forward to exchange a firm handclasp with his younger associate. Then he sat back in his chair.

"Seldom have I made any plan for the express purpose of killing someone. But I think that in this case it is essential. I have already spoken to Almagro on this matter and he sees no objection. I have spoken also to Lieutenant Komi, as Prince al-Farabi's deputy, and he agrees with me. You and I will have help—but so will the Juggler, who has obviously recruited people from the underworld of Eylau."

"I am sure our allies are at least as capable as his. Tell me what you want me to do."

"You will have a special part to play tonight. You will carry to our meeting with Valamo a wrapped bundle of the proper size and shape to persuade him that we are indeed bringing the Sword. He insists on seeing it at our first meeting, before our negotiations are carried any further. There are good reasons why I cannot undertake to play the part of the Sword-carrier myself, but be assured that I shall be nearby."

"I had assumed you would be."

"Almagro and Komi and myself, with additional help, are going to be as close as we can. But we cannot guarantee your safety should our enemy become suspicious."

"Which he can hardly fail to be. But I understand. I tell you I mean to see this business through."

At this point Lieutenant Komi appeared at the head of the stairs. The officer was carrying under one arm a weighty bundle, definitely the wrong shape for a Sword. When this was placed on a table and unwrapped, it proved to be a mail shirt, the steel links as finely wrought as any Kasimir had ever seen.

"This is for you to wear tonight, sir," Komi informed Kasimir, somewhat grimly.

"Indeed. Under the conditions, I think I will not refuse."

In response to Kasimir's questions, the officer informed him that the garment belonged to Prince al-Farabi himself, but Komi did not think his master would mind its being loaned out in the present circumstances. Komi also stated that the mesh of the shirt, magically reinforced, was so fine and tough that it ought to be able to turn the point of even the sharpest poniard.

While Kasimir was preparing to try the garment on, he asked Wen Chang curiously: "How did you manage to establish communications with Valamo?"

"Only indirectly, and with considerable difficulty." The Magistrate was spreading out a coarsely woven, dull-brown cloth almost the size of a blanket upon the largest table in the apartment. Kasimir's view of this operation was cut off for a moment as Komi helped him pull the mail shirt over his head; then he could see the Magistrate holding up a sword in a plain leather sheath.

"Also borrowed," he said, "from our friend the Prince." The weapon had a brown wooden hilt and an ornate guard; its overall size looked the same as Stonecutter's, but no one able to get a good look could mistake this blade for one of the Twelve forged by a god.

Wen Chang put the sword on the table and began to bundle it up carefully in the brown cloth.

Kasimir asked: "Do we expect the Juggler to accept his treasure without taking a close look at it?"

"We expect, if all goes well, to complete our business with him before he has had a chance to do so." The Magistrate tied his bundle lightly shut and stood back, surveying the effect. Then he hoisted it in one hand, as if testing the weight. "As long as the bundle remains closed the likeness is certainly good enough."

"Where is the meeting scheduled to take place, and when?"

"The time is tonight. The place is the small bazaar at the end of the Street of the Leatherworkers. Rather, that is where you are to carry the Sword, and await further instructions."

"I suppose I am to go alone?"

The Magistrate shot him a glance of amusement, tempered with concern. "You would be willing to do that? No, fortunately our rivals in this matter are too realistic to demand any such foolish behavior on our part. You will have two companions when you arrive at the bazaar, and for some time thereafter. We must expect that at some point an attempt will be made to separate you, the sword-bearer, from your escort."

Kasimir sighed. "Naturally I suppose we must expect treachery from the other side."

No one bothered to answer that. Komi was making certain adjustments in the shirt, which hung with a depressing weight upon Kasimir's shoulders.

"And speaking of treachery," Kasimir insisted, "how do we plan to effect our own?"

"The details of that must wait upon events," said Wen Chang. "Your responsibilities will be, first, to carry this." The brown-cloth bundle was thrust suddenly into Kasimir's grip. "Second, to take direction from me; and third, should that no longer be possible, to use your own wits to the best advantage possible."

Two hours after sunset, flanked by the Magistrate and a sturdy Firozpur sergeant, Kasimir was standing at the south end of the Street of the Leatherworkers, where an intersection with two other busy though narrow thoroughfares had created a square of modest size. One of the city's innumerable open-air markets had grown up in the space thus made available, and was doing a thriving business on this evening, despite the occasional brisk shower and the threat of a real downpour conveyed by heavy background thunder. Again Kasimir found himself in a part of the city no more than a hundred meters, he estimated, from the Tungri and the energetic life that clustered around the river and the docks.

"Why did you decide to give this thing to me to carry?" he asked in a low voice, turning his head slightly toward the Magistrate, who stood at his right hand. "Not that I am unwilling—but I should have thought you'd prefer to have it in hand yourself."

"At the most crucial moments of negotiation," said Wen Chang, "I prefer to have both hands free. Also I chose you because I consider you —after myself—the most quick-witted person available . . . ah. Here, if I am not mistaken, comes our next contact."

An urchin only a little older and bigger than the child who had carried Natalia's message was approaching them steadily through the random traffic of bodies in the bazaar. His eyes were fixed on Kasimir, who held the sword-shaped bundle in his hands. In a moment, as soon as the boy was sure that Kasimir was watching him, he turned sharply and led the way down Leatherworkers' Street.

"Slowly and calmly," said Wen Chang. "After him."

Moving single file with Kasimir in the lead, his bundle held tightly under his left arm, the three men followed.

They were led beneath the flaring oil-lamps of Leatherworkers' Street, and into another bazaar at the other end of the short, crooked thoroughfare. Kasimir, glancing up just as they reached this second marketplace, saw something that almost made him stumble—a small, dark shadow flitting just above the brightness of the nearest lamp. It had to be one of Komi's—or someone's—winged messengers. The lieutenant must be nearby, and must be somehow trying to use one of the creatures to follow their progress through the maze of streets.

On entering the second bazaar their youthful guide had suddenly turned aside, darted under one of the vendors' carts, and in an instant disappeared from view. It was not to be thought of that men of affairs carrying a Sword would follow him in this maneuver; the trio came to an uncertain halt, watching and waiting for further instructions.

The smells of dough frying, and of meat and peppers roasting on a skewer, enlivened the air here. Somewhere in the background, men clapped hands to the rhythm of a drum, and female dancers whirled in torchlight. A small caravan of laden loadbeasts urged other traffic momentarily out of the way of their slow progress.

Then, unexpectedly, their guide was back, walking out of the kaleidoscopic churn of moving bodies, coming from the direction of the dancers. This time the urchin moved past the three men purposefully, and walked straight on through the outer gateway of a low stone building at the start of the next street. Once inside the gate he paused, looking back just long enough to make sure they were following. Then he walked on into the building's courtyard.

The Firozpur sergeant, hand on his swordhilt, followed. At Wen Chang's gesture Kasimir followed two or three paces behind the sergeant; and he could hear Wen Chang's soft footsteps coming along at an equal distance behind him.

The open passage leading into the courtyard went round a right-angled corner, so that now the busy street was out of sight. The torchlit enclosure in which they found themselves was small, no more than five meters square, closed on three sides by the mortared stone walls of a low building, each wall containing one or two heavily barred windows. There was one door, even more impressively fortified, in one of the walls. Save for themselves, the courtyard was empty. Kasimir caught only the briefest glimpse of their guide, small bare feet vanishing onto the roof at the top of a fragile-looking drainpipe.

"Now," said a sepulchral voice, moderately loud, speaking from within the darkness inside the barred window on Kasimir's right. Nerves triggered by the sound, he spun that way.

"Show us," added a tenor from the window that was now behind him. He turned again, seeing Wen Chang and the Firozpur sergeant at his sides turning more slowly.

"The Sword," concluded a voice that Kasimir had heard once before, in the courtyard of his own inn. This time it came from within the window Kasimir had originally been facing.

Kasimir held up the weighty bundle.

"Unwrap it," ordered the central voice, its owner still invisible behind a protective grille.

"Not so fast," interposed Wen Chang. "We should like to know who we are dealing with. And that our path of retreat out of this courtyard is still secure."

"Stay where you are," said the Juggler's voice. "Show me the real Sword, and you will be able to retreat fast enough."

"First you will identify yourself somehow." The voice of the Magistrate sounded as firm as that of a judge seated on the bench. "Or else this dealing proceeds no further."

There was a pause. Then something, a small, harmless-looking object came flying out of the darkness of the barred window to bounce at the feet of Kasimir. Looking down, he saw it was a juggler's ball. The energy of the small sphere's bounces died away, and it came to a full stop almost touching the toe of his right boot.

Kasimir glanced at Wen Chang, who shrugged and with a confident small gesture seemed to indicate that Kasimir should undo the bundle he was carrying. Kasimir hesitated marginally, then set one end of the wrapped sword on the ground, and pretended to be trying to untie the cord that held the wrappings together. He could only assume that Wen Chang would manage some interruption at the last second.

The sounds of the bazaar, the music of people blithely indifferent to villainy, drifted into the three-sided enclosure.

"Hurry, get on with it!" the voice of Tadasu Hazara urged, from out of darkness.

"I'm trying," Kasimir protested, endeavoring to sound irritated rather than frightened. "These knots—"

"Cut them!"

From somewhere, almost lost in the noise of the open street behind Kasimir, a low whistle sounded. In the next instant, as if coincidentally, Wen Chang stepped forward to give Kasimir a hand. "Here, let me."

Kasimir let go and stepped back—and recoiled as from the murderous lunge of a madman. Wen Chang had grabbed up the bundle, still tied shut as it was, and lunged with it straight against the white stone wall in front of him.

There was a minor thunderclap of impact. Wen Chang drew back his arms and thrust again with the concealed blade, slashing and sawing with demonic energy. Stones and their fragments burst from the wall, showering and bruising the astonished Kasimir, while the hammerlike sounds of Stonecutter rose into the night.

Inside each of the three dark rooms behind the window bars, pandemonium burst out. Someone fired a crossbow bolt out of the window at the right, a dart that by some sheer good luck missed the Firozpur sergeant, who was near its line of flight. Kasimir was not quite so lucky. The impact, just under his right armpit, felt like that of an oaken club swung in a giant's fist, and for a moment he staggered off balance.

Now there were cries and the clash of weapons in the rear of the central room, from which the Juggler's voice had sounded. Someone was beating down a door back there, and torchlight shone through, even as a section of the front wall went down before Wen Chang's continuing assault with the Sword. The inside of the room was suddenly open to inspection, but Valamo was gone.

Kasimir looked down at the pavement near his feet; the crossbow bolt was lying there, a wicked-looking dart whose needle point was barely tipped with red. His own red blood. The physician put a hand under his outer shirt and felt the fine mesh of the heavy mail beneath; there in one place the perfect pattern of the links was slightly strained and broken. There was a wound in his bruised flesh, but it was superficial.

And now armed men were swarming everywhere. It appeared that most of Valamo's support had evaporated on the spot. An outcry went up; that gentleman himself had just been spotted trying to get away over the rooftops.

Inside the otherwise barren room from which the Juggler had been speaking, there was a ladder and a trapdoor. Kasimir, halfway up, saw Wen Chang, still on the ground, throw the Sword, still wrapped, up on the roof ahead of him, where presumably some trusted figure was waiting to take it in charge and keep it safe.

And now the Magistrate was on the roof himself, leading the pursuit, shouting: "We must not let him escape!"

The pursuit led in the direction of the river.

The buildings in the neighborhood were mostly low, the streets more often than not mere pedestrian alleys, narrow enough for an active man moving at rooftop level to leap them with a bound. Kasimir's wound did not much trouble him, and he forgot about it once he was caught up in the excitement of the chase.

The moon, perversely from the point of view of the fugitive, was now out, near full and very bright. The broken clouds that would have dimmed its light seemed to avoid it wholly. The figure that must be the Juggler was moving on, leaping and running, in the direction of the river, keeping half a roof ahead of the nearest pursuer.

Kasimir was gaining ground slowly. In a moment the man, one of the Watch, who had been closest to the fleeing Valamo tried to jump too broad a gap, and disappeared with a cry of despair.

Now Kasimir himself was closest to the enemy. Glancing off to one side, he was astounded to catch a glimpse of someone else running in the night, moving away from Valamo rather than toward him, and carrying some object. Light, timing, and distance were all against Kasimir, but he thought that he might have just seen Natalia. Or perhaps it was only that he expected to see her now in every scene of action.

He had no time now to try to puzzle the matter out. The river was very near ahead; the quarry was being brought to bay.

Someone's slung stone whizzed past Valamo's head; the shot had been too difficult in moonlight. The white-haired figure turned on a parapet, two stories above the water's edge. Kasimir, running up, knew that he was going to be too late. There were men rowing a small boat in the stream just under the place where the Juggler perched, men who called up to him with urgent voices.

Valamo turned toward Kasimir, and made a graceful gesture of obscenity. The acrobat's body crouched, then lunged out in an expert dive that ought to land it in the water just beside the boat.

Running out of shadows, the figure of Wen Chang appeared beside the leaping man at the last instant. Moonlight glinted on the faint streak of a bright rapier.

The Juggler's body, pierced, contorted in the air. A choked cry sounded in the night. The graceful dive became an awkward, tumbling splash into the river.

Wen Chang, panting with the long chase, his own sword still in his hand, stood watching beside Kasimir. No one saw the submerged man come up.

17

BEFORE nightfall Wen Chang, Kasimir, and Komi had made their way wearily back to the inn. Kasimir's wound—an ugly bruise, and minor laceration—was throbbing, and at his direction his companions helped him wash it, then took salves from his medical kit and applied them. Wen Chang needed no directions to apply a professional-looking bandage. Kasimir was still functional, doing as well as could be expected.

Meanwhile Komi had retreated below to look after his men, and the Magistrate had ordered food brought to the upper room. While he and Kasimir were eating they conversed.

"I cannot believe that I had Stonecutter in my hand and lost it." Kasimir was loud with growing anger.

Wen Chang did not reply.

"It was you yourself who took it from me. You who passed it on to someone else."

Still no answer.

"Magistrate, I saw you wrap a fake Sword in a bundle. Then you gave the package to me. But later the Sword in the bundle was genuine. I saw it, in your hands, hack to bits a wall of solid stone. I heard the sound of its magic as it did so. The Sword I was carrying was genuine, and I am sure you knew it."

Wen Chang appeared to be meditating.

"I know you are the real Wen Chang, and I cannot believe that the real Wen Chang is a criminal."

At last the narrow gaze turned back to Kasimir. "Thank you." The words sounded sincere, and curiously subdued.

"Then, am I going mad? Or is it not your objective, after all, to get the Sword and return it to its rightful owner?"

"That is my objective," said the Magistrate stiffly, for the first time sounding offended. "I have undertaken it as sincerely as any commitment in my life."

"Then—" Kasimir made a helpless gesture. "Then I am at a loss. If I am to be of any further use to you, I must know what is going on. Was the seeming appearance of the real Sword some result of magic? But no, you do not like to use magic, do you?"

"Magic is not the tool I prefer. Kasimir, if you cannot see what is going on, now is not the time for me to tell you. For your own good, if my efforts should fail."

"Then tell me this at least. Are there magic powers, a curse, arrayed against us? The Sword comes almost into my hands, again and again, and then it flies away—generally into the hands of that woman."

"There is no curse upon us that I know of. We face no overwhelming magic." Wen Chang drank tea from a mug and put it down. "I have heard that the Sword Coinspinner moves itself about freely, refusing to be bound by any merely human attempts at confinement, whether by means of solid walls or of spells. I have not heard that about Stonecutter, or any of the other Swords."

"Then what is the explanation? All I can see clearly is that Stonecutter's gone again," Kasimir declared, in what sounded more like an indictment of Fate than a lament. "You wrapped an imitation in a bundle here; and when I unwrapped the same bundle there, the Sword inside was genuine. I can imagine no nonmagical explanation for that."

Unless, of course, Kasimir's thought went on, *you substituted the real Sword for the imitation by some sleight of hand. You could have done that easily enough. I wasn't really watching. But that means you had the real Sword here, and didn't . . .*

No, Kasimir told himself firmly. That would make no sense at all. The Magistrate himself was trustworthy, if anyone was. He, Kasimir, had committed himself to that.

Unless . . .

"If it was true that we were faced by some overwhelming magic," said Wen Chang, as if he were calmly unaware of all that might be going through Kasimir's mind, "impossible for us to understand or overcome, then there would not be much point in worrying. However that may be,

I am going to get some sleep while I have the chance, and I suggest you do the same."

Kasimir was on the verge of pointing out that more than half of the Magistrate's twenty-four-hour grace period had now elapsed, but he decided that would be useless, and took himself back to his couch. The salves were working, and his wound pained him hardly at all. He dozed off hoping that enlightenment might come in dreams.

But this time there were no dreams. It seemed to Kasimir that he had barely closed his eyes, when he was awakened by a remote pounding, as of mailed fists or heavy weapon-hilts upon some lower portal of the inn. Groaning and cursing his way back to full wakefulness, he rubbed his eyes. By the time the sound of boots ascending the stairs became plain, Kasimir was sitting up and groping for his boots.

A few moments after that, Lieutenant Komi, also freshly awakened, was at the door of the upper suite. "A robbery attempt is reported at the Blue Temple," the officer informed Kasimir tersely. "It seems certain that the Sword of Siege was used."

Kasimir groaned. "An attempt, you say? Was it successful?"

"It doesn't sound like it to me. But the messengers didn't really tell me one way or the other." Komi glanced down the narrow stairs. "Naturally, you and the Magistrate are needed at the Blue Temple at once. The Hetman commands it personally."

"Of course. All right, we'll go. Give us one minute. And get your men up and ready for action. We're probably going to need them again, though for what I don't know."

"They'll be ready before you are."

Wen Chang was sleeping as peacefully as an infant when Kasimir intruded upon the inner chamber to bring him the news. But he woke up with a minimum of fuss, and gave no indication of surprise at this latest development.

Everything was soon in readiness. The trip on riding-beasts through the evening streets was uneventful. This time the Hetman had sent a larger escort, and the level of their courtesy was noticeably less.

When they came in sight of the Blue Temple, Kasimir beheld a swarm of people, many of them bearing torches or lanterns, gathered at one corner of the fortresslike edifice. The High Priest Theodore himself was present, to grab Wen Chang by the sleeve as soon as he had dismounted, and attempt to hustle him forward like a common criminal.

But somehow the hustling was not to be accomplished in that fashion. Wen Chang remained standing where he was, erect and dignified, while the priest stumbled, slightly off balance, as he moved away, and had to recover his own dignity as best he could.

A confused babble of accusing voices rose. Kasimir, now that he could get a good look at the corner of the massive wall, had to admit that it certainly did look as if the Sword had been used on it. Carvings had been made in the stone blocks, deep and narrow cuts that must have required a very sharp, tough tool. And there on the pavement below the cutting were the expected fragments of stone.

Kasimir picked up one of these fragments and held it close to someone's torch. There was no mistaking those smoothly striated markings —yes, the Sword of Siege had really been here, and had been used against this wall.

"It looks," said Kasimir, "as if Natalia's gang isn't going to be easily discouraged."

The Blue Temple priests, as they were not slow in explaining, had an extra reason to be upset. They had been spending time and effort, and presumably even money, in an effort to have their walls rendered proof by opposing magic against the powers of Stonecutter. All this had now proven to have been time and effort—and money—wasted.

Komi said: "The thieves must have been frightened off by a patrol or something, before they could dig in very far."

Wen Chang nodded soberly. "But I wonder how far they fled when they were frightened off?"

"What do you mean?" the Director of Security demanded of him sharply.

"Has it occurred to anyone here that the same band of thieves, armed with the same Sword, might even now be at work beneath our feet? Tunneling out of reach and sight of ordinary patrols, or other defensive measures. Intent upon creating their own entrances to the treasure vaults below?"

This was of course said in full hearing of the High Priest and other Blue Temple officials. They immediately dropped their angry attempt at confrontation with the Magistrate, and began to cast about in search of some way of meeting this new threat. One man immediately went down on all fours to put his ear to the pavement. In a moment almost a dozen people, including the Magistrate himself, were doing the same thing.

Kasimir also gave that tactic a try. But he gave it up in a matter of moments, unable to convince himself that he was really able to hear anything that way.

Others were having more success. One of the relatively minor temple officials was certain that he could detect the sounds of steady digging. Presently two or three others were in agreement with him.

Wen Chang stood up, shaking his head, and said that he could give no firm opinion. His senses were growing old, he said, and were no longer to be absolutely depended upon.

There was some minor excitement as Prince al-Farabi, accompanied by a couple of mounted retainers, came galloping up. He had come, the Prince said, as soon as he had heard the news of the attempted robbery.

He, at least, continued to address Wen Chang with great respect. "What are we to do, Magistrate?"

The investigator stroked his beard. He said, "If it is possible to pin down the direction of these underground sounds more precisely, starting a countermine might be one useful tactic."

Several people took up the suggestion at once. The numbers of low-ranking workers present had been growing steadily, as first one official and then another took it upon himself to order some further mobilization; and now a call went up for digging implements.

Meanwhile the party of dignitaries, some of them keeping an eye on the two investigators as if afraid they might try to escape, adjourned by more or less common consent to inside the temple. There they descended in a body into one of the deeper treasure vaults, and here again there was much listening, with ears now applied to walls.

More lights were called for, and soon supplied, so that even the darker corners of the many underground rooms could be illuminated. More guards were called for too, though it seemed to Kasimir that the place was inconveniently crowded with armed men already.

By this time someone—Kasimir was certain only that it was neither himself nor Wen Chang—had suggested that the robbers' new plan might not be to dig a tunnel at all, but rather to undermine an entire section of the building, so that walls, roof, and everything would collapse suddenly, in a cloud of dust and a pile of rubble. In this disaster and the ensuing confusion, the suggestion was, there would be little to prevent the brigands' bursting up from underground like so many moles, and looting to their hearts' content.

Theodore was trying simultaneously to counter this and other perceived threats. He had another problem, in that his vaults were crowded with authorities and aides from several organizations and of all ranks, from a head of state on down; and each authority, wanting to make his presence known, had something to say. Already a swarm of laborers armed with picks and shovels were—presumably on someone's orders —descending into the lower vaults to begin the task of opening the floors there and getting the countermining under way. Some other leader, driven into a frenzy by this invasion of the sacred precincts, was trying to organize a force of clerks and junior priests to move some of the musty piles of wealth elsewhere. Still others were trying to delay this tactic, until they could come to an agreement on where the treasure would be safest.

In the midst of all this turmoil, Mistress Hedmark and one of her aides appeared. They had come down from their quarters near the gem room to see what was going on; terrible rumors had reached them up there, and there had been nothing to do but see for themselves.

The suspicion crossed Kasimir's mind that Mistress Hedmark might now actually have the Sword in her possession, and that she and the Blue Temple had worked all this wallcarving, and the rumors of tunnels, as a distraction to keep suspicion from themselves. Somehow the situation had that kind of feeling to it. But Kasimir had not a shred of evidence, and he kept his wild theories to himself for the present.

Meanwhile Wen Chang, as might have been expected, was maintaining his calm amid all this confusion. The flurry of accusation against him and his partners had died down now; but when, as still happened now and then, someone blamed him to his face for being responsible, he answered mildly if at all.

As the hours of the night dragged by, nothing at all seemed certain to Kasimir any longer, except that the robbers had not yet managed to cut their way into the temple. Beyond that he had more or less given up trying to keep track of the theories and fears regarding where the blow was likely to fall, and the various efforts to forestall it. Instead he sought out a quiet corner where a pile of empty treasure sacks offered a reasonably soft couch. Relaxing, his back against a wall, the young physician entered a period of intense thought. Or tried to do so; the effort was made no easier by all the noise and activity around him.

When he saw Wen Chang moving quietly toward an exit, he followed. Outside the temple the air was much cooler and easier to breathe. Others, seeing Wen Chang and Kasimir go out, followed suspiciously.

But the Magistrate gave no sign of trying to get away. He looked at the moon, full and near setting now, and breathed of the damp air, and stretched his arms.

Kasimir sat down again, and before he knew it he was drifting into sleep . . .

Something, perhaps it was revelation, came to Kasimir in a dream. And suddenly he understood much that had been hidden from him. He awoke with a start, having the impression that someone had been shaking him. No one had, unless it were possibly his own Muse.

What a damned fool he had been.

Somewhere beyond the tall buildings of the city, the sun had definitely come up.

And, shortly after dawn on this first day of the Festival, another urgent summons arrived for Wen Chang and his associate. This one came directly from the palace, and the face of the messenger who brought it was ashen in the early light. His master the Hetman must indeed be in a rage.

Benjamin of the Steppe had just managed to escape from his cell in the palace. The delegation going to his cell to bring him out for execution had found the chamber empty. A tunnel originating somewhere outside the building had been cut neatly up through the stone floor. There was not the least doubt that the Sword had been used.

The Magistrate, having been apprised of all these facts, turned and repeated them calmly to those who were standing nearest to him—Kasimir, Almagro, and Lieutenant Komi. To Kasimir, Wen Chang's face now appeared wooden with fatigue. With his new insight, he tried but failed to read something more in it than that.

As for Kasimir himself, he did not trouble to hide his feelings particularly. This struck him as the first piece of good news they had heard in some time. Komi appeared to feel the same way.

Almagro on the other hand was professionally cautious and gloomy.

There was no time now for anything like a private conference. The Hetman had sent a carriage for the people he wanted, and the Magistrate and his three associates piled into it.

As the news brought by the Hetman's messenger spread among the dignitaries gathered in and around the Blue Temple, it had the effect of bringing their weary efforts against robbery to a halt. Indeed, it required only a moment of detached thought to see that little or nothing useful was being accomplished anyway. Priests and clerks and guards looked at each other blankly in the dawn, seeking answers that were not to be found in the faces of others as weary as themselves.

Some of the more important of these people found the energy to decide to follow the carriage to the palace.

The High Priest himself did not go to the palace. He was handed a message which he read, frowning with thought, then tucked inside his garments.

He announced that he had too much to do here in trying to put his own house in order, the house of Croesus and the other gods and goddesses of wealth.

Inside the carriage, jolting along swiftly on its way to the Hetman's house, no one had much of anything to say. There were only the sounds of the swift ride.

When their conveyance turned into the square before the palace, Kasimir observed the gallows standing empty in the dawn, the new wood of the construction still damp from the recent rains. The carriage was forced now to slow down, because the plaza was so crowded with people. Of course, a mob would have gathered to see the hanging. Kasimir wondered if now some other victim would have to be found to take the place of Benjamin. He could not entirely avoid the thought that he himself might, before the morning was over, find himself being escorted up those new wooden stairs.

Such was the crush of would-be spectators near the empty scaffold that the carriage had to come almost to a halt. Putting his head out a window, Kasimir got the impression that the crowd was in a light-hearted mood, not too much downcast by the lack of an execution. He supposed that news of the dramatic escape, and the accompanying official discomfiture, provided compensation. Also there might have been an undercurrent of support for Benjamin that would cause people to view this outcome as an even happier one.

Now some mounted patrolmen of the Watch were starting to disperse the throng, and presently the carriage was able to move on. Kasimir, bringing his head in from the window, caught Wen Chang gazing at the scaffold, and there appeared in the Magistrate's eye something of the same faint twinkle Kasimir had noticed when last they passed through this square. This time Kasimir thought he understood, but he said nothing.

The rear gates of the palace opened promptly for the official carriage, and in a few moments its occupants were disembarking within the walls. Very soon thereafter they were all in the main building, being escorted single file up a flight of narrow and very utilitarian stone stairs. The odor of a prison, reminding Kasimir of animal pens and primitive surgery, began to engulf them.

Presently the stairs brought the ascending party to a heavy door, and beyond the door they entered a dark corridor lined with tiny cells. From some of the barred doors the faces of inmates looked out, their expressions variations on madness, fear, and hope.

The four men who had come in the carriage were ushered into one of the cells, already crowded with official bodies. Some already present, who were of lesser ranks, had to vacate the cell before the four newcomers could get in. Voices on all sides demanded that they confront the evidence of their failure.

Now Kasimir was able to see for himself just how the escape had been accomplished. Several officials were pointing out to him and to Wen Chang, as if they might not be able to see for themselves, the fact of a dark, irregular opening in the stone floor. The hole was only half a meter in diameter or a little more, and people getting in and out through it must have undergone something of a squeeze.

The tunnel, as several officials were now explaining simultaneously and unnecessarily, had been started at some distance from the palace, and dug up unerringly to this point through both bedrock and masonry. Actually its other end had already been discovered; the passage had its beginning in the curving wall of one of the great municipal drains that ran right beneath the plaza, a good many meters outside the palace walls.

And there was more the failed investigators had to be shown; the demonstration of outrage was not yet complete. Perhaps, thought Kasimir, it was only getting started. And so far the Hetman himself had not even put in an appearance.

"Look here! Look here!" someone was barking at him.

Now one of the palace officials had brought out an Old World light, a kind of hand lantern, and was directing a bright white beam down into the dark aperture in the floor. In the unwavering brightness Kasimir was easily able to see the distinctive, inescapably familiar little markings left in the freshly carved-out surface of the tunnel's wall. Here was proof—if any proof was needed beyond the mere existence of the tunnel—that Stonecutter must have been used to make it.

For the moment the young man was able to ignore the personal difficulties this tunnel was likely to create for him. He could only marvel, silently but wholeheartedly, at the daring of the project, and at the amount of intense, hurried work it had required.

By now Kasimir had seen enough of the projects accomplished with the Sword to realize that the actual cutting of stone, so easy with the aid of Stonecutter's magic, had been only the beginning of this job. Here all the work had to be done inside a long, narrow tunnel, and all the debris cleared out through the original tunnel entrance, a task that grew more difficult the longer the passage became. The diggers must have shed liters of sweat in the course of this job, and doubtless some blood as well, handling the sharp rock and crawling through piles of it. Pausing for frequent measurements, someone in the rescue party must have known the shape and the dimensions of the prison very well. And they had been working against a deadline.

When had the digging started? Doubtless very soon after the Sword had changed hands there in the Red Temple. Kasimir thought that he could see the history of it now. Right after Natalia and her people had got away with Stonecutter right under the noses of a score or so of guards and priests. Not to mention one very inept young investigator.

Ignoring the continuous babble of accusation that surrounded them both, Kasimir cast a sharp, probing glance at his mentor. Wen Chang's smoothly composed features gave little indication of either the fatigue or the emotions that must be behind them. Still, Kasimir, who was beginning to know his man, thought that he could detect certain subtle signs of—satisfaction.

A hush fell suddenly within the cell. The Hetman himself had come upon the scene at last, and was now standing in the doorway, an aperture so narrow that, even had there been room for him inside the cell, he might have thought twice before attempting to push his corpulent body through.

"What is your answer to this, O great investigator?"

The ruler's question was delivered with what was obviously intended to be scathing sarcasm.

But Wen Chang imperturbably refused to be scathed. "I am not required to have an answer for this, sir. I was never engaged to prevent the prisoner's escaping, therefore his deliverance is not my responsibility."

"Oh, is it not? Well, in any case he is not going to get away for long." The Hetman wiped sweat from his face with a silken cloth. "He could have had at most a few minutes' start before his absence was discovered. And once the discovery was made, the warden acted with commendable speed, notifying the Watch at all the gates of the city by winged messenger. Every man who leaves Eylau is being identified, and every vehicle that departs the city by land or water is being thoroughly searched."

The Magistrate bowed, slightly but graciously. "In that event it would seem that Your Excellency has no cause for concern."

The Hetman's round countenance darkened. But just as it seemed to Kasimir that his learned associate had finally managed to talk himself into serious trouble, a rescuer appeared. The voice of Prince al-Farabi was heard in the corridor outside the cell.

Naturally the Hetman had to turn away from the cell door to greet his peer. Then a moment later he had to move courteously out of the way of the Prince, who was expressing a desire to see the inside of the cell.

A moment later al-Farabi, now accompanied by a couple of his own men as bodyguards, came into the cell loudly proclaiming his wish to behold with his own eyes the evidence that the missing Sword had indeed been here within these very palace walls, only a few hours ago. Perhaps only a single hour!

But the moment his eye fell upon Wen Chang, the Prince broke off these lamentations. In a quite different voice he demanded: "What hope is there of Stonecutter's return?"

The Magistrate began a reassuring answer. But, as soon as it was apparent that the answer would not be simple and direct, half a dozen other voices, angry and weary, broke in on him, and drowned him out. Above all the others rose the near-shout of the Blue Temple's Director of Security.

"If you, O famed Magistrate, who are credited with the power to see into the secret places of the heart, to sift out the honest from the evildoer—if you had recovered the Sword before now, in accordance with your pledge, then this would not have happened!"

Wen Chang faced the man coolly. "As I have said before, sir, this prisoner's escape was not my responsibility."

"But you are responsible for what you promise. And you did promise to have the Sword for us by now, or at the very least to give us some definite word as to its whereabouts. Very well, sir, I now hold you to your word. Where is the Sword?"

"Sir, your demand is premature. I was granted twenty-four hours of free action, and that period is not quite over yet. I still have hopes of being able to recover the Sword—not for you but for the rightful owner —before the time expires."

At these words, calmly uttered, a stir ran through the little crowd filling the cell.

Wen Chang now turned to look out into the corridor, addressing the Hetman directly. "Your Excellency must admit that the objective to which you yourself assigned the highest priority, the safeguarding of the Blue Temple and the other centers of great wealth within the city, has been accomplished."

"You claim credit for that, do you?"

"I neither claim credit nor refuse it, sir. I merely call attention to the fact."

The Hetman glanced toward the Prince. He wiped sweat from his face again. "Yes, I must admit that. And you say there is still hope of recovering the Sword?" The first rush of his anger had passed now, and he sounded wistful, wanting to believe.

"Yes sir, certainly there is at least hope. Perhaps there is even a good chance . . . you have said that you already know where the other end of this tunnel is, gentlemen. I intend to go there myself, without further delay."

In a moment Wen Chang had shed his dignity entirely, and was lowering himself feetfirst into the dark and narrow opening in the floor.

"Hah!" was the comment of the Blue Temple's Director of Security, delivered in a tone of loud derision. But having said that much he did not know what else to add.

Everyone else—except for Kasimir, who was preparing to follow his leader—stood motionless and silent, watching Wen Chang's descent and disappearance. Only a moment after the Magistrate was out of sight, Kasimir was waist-deep in the hole himself, and rapidly working his way lower.

The young man, chin at floor level now, groped below him with his toe for the next foothold—there it was. You really had to go down feetfirst, because climbing down headfirst for any distance would be impossibly awkward. And if the tunnel was this narrow through its whole length, as seemed likely, there wouldn't be any place to turn around.

Now the walls of the tunnel wall had swallowed him completely, the cell he had just left was somewhere overhead. Renewed argument had broken out up there, and now he could hear sounds indicating that someone else was following him down. He trusted that whoever it was would avoid stepping on his head, as he was doing his best to avoid treading on the Magistrate's.

The descent took a long time, and was full of turns and twists, vertical drops alternating with horizontal stretches. That the tunnel was a long one came as no surprise to Kasimir. The diggers would have had to begin operations a fair distance away; they would have needed a secure place, a place where they could drop a lot of displaced rock without hauling it any farther to avoid undue attention.

Now Wen Chang had reached the end. He was calling encouraging words back to his assistant in a soft voice, from somewhere not far ahead. And the darkness in the tunnel around Kasimir was beginning to moderate. In another few moments his feet came out into empty space, and then he had emerged.

He found himself standing on a narrow catwalk, that ran beside a deep drain through a rounded subterranean vault. A steady breeze, cool but decidedly foul-smelling, blew through the larger tunnel. The scene was rendered visible by a wan illumination that washed down through small patches of grillwork set at wide intervals into the stone vaulting overhead. The pattern and spacing of that grillwork was somehow familiar; Kasimir decided that they must be underneath a part of the plaza that surrounded the Hetman's palace.

A rat went scurrying away along the narrow ledge on the far side of the drain. Just at the place where the narrow escape tunnel came out of the wall, the flow in the main drain was partially blocked, so that it ran in a series of miniature waterfalls and rapids. The cause of the blockage was several tons of rock, all in pieces of modest size, an impressive pile of sliced-up and displaced minerals, including building-stone, that had been dumped here by the hurried rescuers.

Wen Chang, standing close beside Kasimir upon the narrow ledge, was squinting thoughtfully up and down the gloomy tunnel of the drain. Now from somewhere in his pockets the Magistrate pulled forth yet another Old World light, this one no bigger than a finger, and began to use it.

"In that direction, of course," he remarked, jiggling his little beam of light downstream, "all of these city drains must empty into the Tungri. And almost directly above us, just over here, must be the palace—yes, I think I am sufficiently well oriented now."

Scraping and grunting noises were issuing from the mouth of the little escape tunnel. In a moment these were followed by a set of legs and feet, garbed in the Hetman's military colors. Soon an officer of the palace guards was standing silently on the ledge, straightening his uniform and looking at Wen Chang and Kasimir with controlled suspicion.

"Ah," said Wen Chang to the newcomer. "You may reassure your master that my associate and I are not trying to escape—far from it. But never mind, here come others to see for themselves."

Another man who had been in the cell above was now grunting his way out through the last meter or two of the constricted tunnel. Scarcely had he found footing on the ledge when another came after him. Soon half a dozen, the most eminent of them Prince al-Farabi himself, were decorously jostling one another for position on the little shelf of masonry, meanwhile watching Wen Chang closely to see what he might be up to now. The group also included the Blue Temple's Director of Security.

"No one was coming down after you, sir?" the Magistrate inquiried of the last arrival, when the tunnel had been silent for a little while. "Good! Then we are ready!" And to Kasimir's surprise Wen Chang relieved the crowling on the ledge by jumping right down into the knee-deep stream. Splashing briskly to the other side in a few quick strides, he went scrambling nimbly up the opposite bank of stone.

· Kasimir, after only the most momentary hesitation, followed. He did his best to look as if he knew exactly what his leader was doing. Privately he wondered, not for the first time, whether his leader might have gone quite mad.

Wen Chang had put away his pocket light. On reaching the catwalk on the other side of the drain, he paused just long enough to glance back once at the assembly he had just left. Then with an air of indifference, ignoring the cries for an explanation that came from behind, he started walking along the new ledge toward an intersection of drains not far away. Again Kasimir followed.

One after another, the other men came after them. It was either that or stand waiting in a sewer for they knew not what, or else make the hard climb through the escape tunnel back to the cell.

Their subterranean progress, lighted by the Magistrate's Old World lamp, continued for some minutes. Then the small party came to an even greater branching of the ways. From here an even larger drain led on in the direction of the river, and a waterfall somewhere in that direction was large enough to sound a note of distant thunder.

Here, on a walkway large enough to accommodate a conference, Wen Chang called a temporary halt.

"From this point forward, gentlemen," he taxed them seriously, "he who accompanies me must remain as quiet as a ghost, say nothing, and follow my orders strictly as regards to noise and movement. He who splashes or mutters, whispers or sneezes—I hereby charge that man with full responsibility for our failure to regain that which we seek.

"Whoever cannot agree to these terms must turn back now."

There was silence as his audience looked at him stubbornly, challenging him to make good on his pledge.

Wen Chang was not perturbed. "Then all of you are with me? Good. Follow where I lead, and be as silent as the grave."

18

A S soon as he had seen the Hetman's carriage depart hastily for the palace, the High Priest Theodore quickly turned away and issued urgent orders to a few of his most trusted associates.

Then he hurried into his temple, where a few necessary personal preparations had to be made. As soon as these had been completed he descended to the lowest level but one of his establishment, then hurried along a half-buried passageway in the direction of the river, passing numerous tired-looking guards as he progressed.

At a dock covered by its own roof and served by an artificial inlet of the river, the High Priest walked past a large ceremonial barge which was used very rarely, and stopped beside a much smaller launch, whose crew, having been sent word of his intentions, was already making ready to put out. Upon the wharf beside this vessel Theodore paced impatiently until a few more people arrived, men he wanted to bring with him on this venture. These sheltered docks were very handy for certain transactions in which the temple sometimes found itself engaged —deals involving some substantial bulk of cargo requiring to be moved in or out. Such goods could be much more readily and unobtrusively transported by water than by moving them in caravans that had to wind their way through all the streets of Eylau.

The Director of Security was notably absent on this occasion, but the High Priest thought that was probably just as well.

The launch had space for only four rowers on a side, and a half deck under which a few more men might lie concealed. Discussing these matters with the captain, Theodore nodded and gestured, and gave more orders.

* * *

A couple of minutes later he was standing near amidships in the launch, gliding across the open surface of the Tungri. River traffic was for the moment comparatively light. The face of the water was spotted with remnants of the morning mist that were rapidly being burned away by the sun. The launch in which he rode was, like the much greater barge, a brightly decorated, somewhat ostentatious craft, and was usually employed only during the Festival and on certain other rare occasions. But it had been the only boat quickly available. The fact that this was the first morning of the Festival might make its presence on the river less surprising to anyone who happened to observe it.

The note that Theodore had received just before the Magistrate's departure was still clutched in his right hand. He stood with eyes shaded under a light gold awning, holding lightly to one of its supports, impatiently scanning the fog-spotted river for any sign that any of the busy vessels in sight had any intention of approaching his launch.

The aide who crouched beside him repeated a doubt, voiced earlier, that the note the High Priest had received was genuine.

On his part the High Priest maintained that he could not afford to ignore any communication like this one. Thieves of some kind were certainly in possession of the Sword of Siege, and what was more logical and natural than that those thieves should seek to sell it at great profit to themselves?

As for taking out the launch in this furtive way, of course it was essential to keep other people, who might take it into their heads to put in their own inconvenient claims, from knowing about the negotiations should the note prove an authentic offer.

Theodore looked down at the note once more, though by now he certainly had it learned by heart. It specified, in crude, block printing, in just what area of the river he was to cruise. He looked up sharply, making sure that the oarsmen were ordered at the proper moment to put about smartly and coast downstream for a while.

Meanwhile the three heavily armed men he had managed to conceal under the half deck were crouching there in awkward patience, now and then shifting their positions stealthily.

The High Priest had also brought with him on this voyage a wizard, the best available at a moment's notice, but a man who was more a specialist in guarding treasure than anything else, so that Theodore had doubts of how useful he was going to be upon this mission.

And now, just when Theodore was beginning to suspect that the note might after all have been a hoax, the officer in command of the launch touched him quietly on the arm to get his attention. "My lord, someone on shore is signaling to us."

The officer was sufficiently discreet to refrain from pointing, but in a moment Theodore, following the man's low-voiced directions, had caught sight of a dark gesturing figure on shore, standing almost out of sight between two low abandoned-looking buildings.

The figure was hooded or masked, and dressed in some loose garment that made even the sex impossible to determine at this distance. He—or she—was standing between two dilapidated buildings, and close above the broken outlet of one of the municipal drains, in such a position as to be practically invisible from anywhere but the narrow strip of water where the launch was cruising.

Farther inland, on the same side of the river, Theodore could see the palace, his own temple, and the tall Red Temple too, somewhat more distant.

Under the officer's direction, the launch was now being rowed toward the dock where the beckoning figure waited. When it had drawn within four or five boatlengths of that goal, the figure on shore suddenly moved a step forward and help up an imperious hand.

"Come no closer!" The voice was deep and throaty, but still, the High Priest thought, it was almost certainly that of a woman. "We must talk first. No closer, I tell you, or you'll not see Stonecutter today!" And the figure held up a Sword-shaped bundle where Theodore could see it.

It took an imperious gesture from the High Priest himself to make the officer and the rowers stop the boat; now the oarsmen were laboring to keep her more or less in the same place in the brisk current. Actually they were doing their job well for men who got so little chance to practice.

Theodore sent his most dominating voice toward the shore. "Is that really a Sword you have there? You must let me see it now, if we are to talk seriously."

Silently the figure holding the bundle shook the wrappings free, and let him see the Sword. Theodore, only a few meters distant, had no doubt that he was seeing the real thing.

But he was not going to admit that right away. "I must see it more closely."

The person who held the bare blade swung it, cutting deeply into the side of a stone bollard. The thudding sound of Vulcan's magic was clearly audible.

The wizard on the launch clutched Theodore by the arm, and spoke into his ear, quietly and unnecessarily affirming the genuineness of the article in question.

Theodore put the man aside impatiently.

"Very well," he called ashore. "I am convinced. Come aboard here and we will talk terms; we cannot treat of a matter so important while shouting back and forth like two street peddlers."

"No, my lord, I think no." Yes, it was definitely a woman's husky voice that issued from behind the mask. "Instead you must come ashore. Bring two men—no more—with you, if their presence will make you feel more comfortable."

"Where ashore?"

"Nowhere, most cautious man, but right here in sight of your boat, though she must retreat and wait for you no closer to the dock than she is now. Come, come, will you do business or not? I am taking a real risk. If you won't accept a tiny one that is no risk at all, I'm sure I can find another buyer who is less timid."

Theodore was frowning, but the offer really seemed fair enough to him. You had to expect that anyone who had the Sword to sell would want to take some precautions. He had to admit that the scoundrels had chosen the place well. Within a few paces of that tantalizing masked figure there could well be a dozen man-sized ratholes, openings in the dock or buildings, into any one of which a thief could easily vanish—or from which other criminals could perhaps come pouring out in case they were intending treachery.

Well, Theodore had some good men with him in the boat, and he would risk it. The sight of Stonecutter, almost within reach, was too much to let him reach any other conclusion.

"I accept your terms," called Theodore. Then, quite openly, he gave some final orders to the men who were to remain aboard the launch, and to the pair, newly emerged from under the half deck, who were going to precede him ashore, telling them to be alert, but to take no action except in case of treachery by the other side. He had already given them their secret orders, by which his own treachery would be implemented if and when he thought the chances of success were good, and the secret signal for which they were to watch.

The boat drew near the dock, and in a moment, the two bodyguards had hopped ashore, their own businesslike weapons drawn and ready. The High Priest followed, and then the launch, according to the agreement, eased out again to her previous position.

Theodore, as was his custom, was carrying with him quite a sizable sum in gold coin, plus a few valuable jewels. Quite likely, he thought, the amount he had with him would be enough to impress a small band of hungry robbers; though of course it was not anywhere near the true value of a treasure like the Blade.

Now he stood on the rough planking of the dock, facing the figure that still held the Sword.

The High Priest was flanked by his two bodyguards, good men both of them. If the slighter figure he confronted had any companions present, they had yet to show themselves.

"Let me hold the weapon myself," said Theodore to his counterpart who faced him. "I must be very sure."

He had expected an argument at least when he made this demand, and indeed the figure opposite seemed to hesitate momentarily. But then the cloth wrapping was cast aside, and the sheathed weapon was proffered hilt first.

Theodore reached for the hilt with both hands, and took the weighty treasure into his possession. He looked at the small white symbol on the hilt, a wedge splitting a block.

And, in that very moment when his full attention was on the Sword, the dark-clad woman who had given it to him turned and darted away, vanishing in an instant into a broken hole in the wooden side of the nearest building.

Theodore's bodyguards started and brandished their weapons—but there was no threat. There was only an empty dock before them, and the High Priest their master left standing with the treasure he had so craved in his hands.

Theodore could not doubt that the weapon he had been given was quite genuine. Then why had it been given him in such a—

There were sounds nearby, a buried stirring, footsteps, careless voices of a different quality than that of the bandit woman who had just left. Someone was about to appear on the scene. No doubt the bandit woman had been first to hear these newcomers approaching, and that explained her sudden disappearance.

Or might she have—

Whatever the reason Theodore now found himself in possession of the Sword, he could not decline the chance to keep it. He had only time to resheathe the blade and muffle Stonecutter under his long blue cape. His right hand was gripping the leather sheath near the middle, so that the pointed end of the blade made a stiff extension of his right arm. It was the best he could do at a moment's notice; no one would be able to see that he had the Sword as long as he could stand still with his long cape furled about him.

Only a heartbeat after Stonecutter had been made to disappear, Wen Chang and his physician-associate, with a surprising escort of notables after them, came popping up out of the opening atop a broken drain nearby. Theodore could only stare without comprehension at the sight of his own Director of Security emerging from the sewers as part of the same group. But the Director was not the highest rank accompanying Wen Chang; Prince al-Farabi himself was in the group as well.

The group appeared on the dock very near the water's edge, so they were actually between Theodore and his waiting boat.

He might call in his launch, but he could not move to get aboard without giving away his secret; so the launch stayed where it was for the moment, the rowers pulling easily to offset the current, some ten or fifteen meters from the dock. The men aboard her could perceive no immediate threat to their master in this arrival of the other eminent folk with whom he had been arguing for the past few days.

In response to something—perhaps a guarded look from the High Priest—they did however begin to ease their craft a little closer to the shoreline.

Before they had closed more than half the distance, however, a somewhat smaller and much shabbier boat appeared just upstream, loaded to the gunwales with armed men. Lieutenant Komi stood in the prow, and in response to his crisp orders his crew propelled their vessel right up to the dock in the launch's way.

"What are you all doing here?" demanded Theodore of Wen Chang and those who had just climbed up onto the dock with him. All of the new arrivals looked more or less wet and bedraggled, especially around the legs and feet, as if they had been wading through noisome waters underground.

"Why," replied one of the unhappier officials reluctantly following the Magistrate, "we are seeking the Sword." The bitter sarcasm in the words was of course directed at Wen Chang. "And I suppose this, in

our leader's estimation, is the very place where we are going to find it."
Then the speaker fell silent, seeing a hard-to-interpret expression pass
over the High Priest's face.

Theodore was never the man to adopt a meekly defensive attitude.
"By following that man you will never find the Sword," he taunted,
putting on his utmost confidence. He sneered openly at Wen Chang.

"I look into your eyes, unhappy Theodore," pronounced the Magistrate in turn, his face contorted in his most theatrical squint, "and I am
persuaded that you lie!"

And on the last word Wen Chang pounced forward, with the speed of
a striking predatory animal, to seize the High Priest. The victim was so
taken by surprise by this direct assault that he made no attempt to
dodge until it was too late; and so astounded were his bodyguards that
they failed to move to their master's defense in time to prevent his being
seized.

A second later the Blue Temple men were galvanized into action. But
one of them was met by Prince al-Farabi, and the other tripped up by
Lieutenant Komi, who reached ashore to thrust a sheathed sword between the guard's legs and send him sprawling. Meanwhile the Prince,
displaying an impressive speed of thought and hand, as well as considerable strength, had knocked down the other bodyguard and stood over
him with drawn blade.

Theodore, the High Priest of the Blue Temple, was a strong man too,
stronger than he looked. And his training in the arts of personal combat
had not been entirely neglected. But neither of those attributes were of
any real service to him now. Wen Chang, displaying a master's skill and
a wiry strength that few would have suspected from his appearance,
needed only a moment in which to overpower the High Priest once they
had come to grips.

From under Theodore's long blue cape there fell out the Sword of
Siege, still sheathed, to land with a muffled metallic sound upon the
worn planks of the dock.

The onlookers gaped at it.

Such was the unexpected suddenness with which the Sword had been
made to appear that for a moment even Kasimir could almost believe
that Wen Chang had produced it through some trick of sleight of hand.
But that was manifestly impossible. There was no conceivable way the
Magistrate could have concealed such a weapon on his person before
his confrontation with Theodore, and no way he could have pulled it

out of the bare planks of the dock. The only place the Sword could possibly have come from was under Theodore's voluminous cape.

An instant after the Sword appeared, the Prince cast aside the more ordinary weapon with which he had been menacing the fallen bodyguard, and pounced upon his treasure. With a great cry of joy he unsheathed Stonecutter, and held up the gleaming blade for all to see.

The High Priest, caught red-handed with another's treasure, refused to blush or even to look uncomfortable. In the space of time needed to draw a full breath he was protesting at the top of his voice the high-handed treatment to which he had been subjected. He announced that all present were witness to his perfect innocence in the face of false accusations—though no accusations, true or false, had yet been voiced.

This was not a good audience for anyone to attempt to deceive with the technique of the big lie. All present were looking at Theodore with guarded expressions, and Kasimir was quite sure that not one of this audience believed him.

For the present, at least, no one was ready to indict him either. Prince al-Farabi, having retrieved Prince Mark's treasure and his own honor, attached the Sword's sheath to a belt at his own waist, and made loud vows of gratitude to everyone who had helped in any way toward Stonecutter's recovery.

Meanwhile the boatload of Firozpur warriors had pulled out of the way of the launch, which was now allowed to dock. Theodore promptly climbed aboard. He was still loudly justifying his possession of the Sword as the launch, in response to his gesture, pulled away again.

And now the Prince no longer delayed a more practical expression of his gratitude. The chief beneficiary of this was of course Wen Chang, to whom al-Farabi promptly handed over his promised reward, in the form of a handful of sparkling, high-grade jewels.

Hardly was the Blue Temple launch out of easy hailing distance when in a small thunder of hoofbeats the Hetman himself arrived at the dock, accompanied by a small mounted escort. How the ruler had learned of the confrontation taking place here was not apparent, but his vast relief at the sight of Stonecutter was. His first glance toward Wen Chang and Kasimir was by far the friendliest he had yet sent their way.

"Where did you find it?" the Hetman inquired eagerly.

The expression on the Prince's face lost some of its happiness. "Hidden under the garments of the High Priest of the Blue Temple."

There was no point in the Hetman's trying to dispute this as unbelievable. Not when he saw confirmation of the unbelievable in every face before him.

"A mistake, on his part," the ruler offered. "Some misunderstanding."

"A mistake, certainly," said the Prince. "To think that he could get away with such a theft."

"A misunderstanding, I am sure," the Hetman said. "I trust that Your Highness has no thought of pressing charges?"

"If you agree," conceded the Prince magnanimously to his fellow ruler, "that no charges of any kind will be pressed against anyone else concerned in this matter—then I will consent to press none against Theodore, or his organization."

"Agreed, with all my heart." Then a slight frown dimmed the Hetman's joy. "Except of course for the escaped prisoner Benjamin, who is already under sentence of death."

"Agreed."

And with that the gathering on the dock split up, the Prince and a few retainers going to a round of rejoicing at their host's palace. The Magistrate most eloquently begged to be excused, and the Hetman did not press him to come along.

Once they were out of sight of the higher authorities, Wen Chang gave a choice jewel to Kasimir, and promptly made good on his promise to Almagro by sharing his reward generously.

"I can use it," the Captain said. "I am very seriously considering retirement."

19

IT was about an hour after dawn on the second day of the Festival, which so far appeared to be making good progress despite the lack of a public execution. Wen Chang, after getting a good night's rest at the inn, had expressed an urge to leave Eylau behind him as quickly as possible. Kasimir, feeling that he could hardly agree with any sentiment more, was going with him. Accordingly the two of them had arisen early, packed up their few belongings at the inn, and paid their bill in full—that was no problem, once a small portion of Wen Chang's reward had been converted into ready cash. Prince al-Farabi had graciously offered, and the Magistrate had accepted, the continued escort of Lieutenant Komi and his small troop as far as the next city.

The Prince himself was not on hand for their departure, having agreed to accept another day or two of the Hetman's grateful hospitality.

Kasimir and the Magistrate, riding their well-rested animals side by side this morning, enjoyed their first real opportunity to talk freely together since the Sword's recovery. Certain hints dropped by Wen Chang had confirmed Kasimir in his opinion that the inn might no longer be a safe place for the frankest sort of conversations; the Blue Temple had been humiliated, if not wounded, and it was notoriously unforgiving of any kind of debt.

"I would like," said Kasimir, after the first few minutes of the morning's ride had passed in silence, "for you to tell me a story."

Wen Chang threw back his head and gave vent to hearty mirth. It was a far more open laughter than any Kasimir had heard from him since their first meeting.

"I fully intend to do so," replied the Magistrate when he had laughed his fill. "I was only wondering how best to begin."

"To begin with, do you believe that the Hetman will ever recapture Benjamin of the Steppe?"

"I hope that he will not," said Wen Chang frankly. "And as a matter of fact I consider the Hetman's chances of success in the matter rather small."

"Oh? I rejoice to hear it. But why is that?"

"Well, in the first place, whoever arranged the prisoner's escape from his cell demonstrated considerable cleverness, and one must expect the same cleverness to be applied to the problem of removing the same prisoner from the city."

"That is true. Well, I have no doubt as to who arranged the escape. And I am still thinking of Natalia. Do you know, in spite of all that has happened, in a way I could wish to see her again."

"You should; were it not for her co-operation in loaning us the Sword for a few hours to trap Valamo, and then returning it honorably when it had served its purpose in the city, you would not have the Prince's jewel in your pocket now. But she is busy, I assume, devoting herself to the survival of her lover. Or perhaps Benjamin is her husband; the rural folk tend to believe strongly in marriage, you know."

"I should have guessed at the connection earlier," Kasimir admitted. "She and Benjamin were even wearing similar clothing when I first saw them. And her hair was styled in the same way as that of those foolish women protesters."

"Perhaps not so foolish. Whether or not they were aware of what part they were playing, they served admirably to distract the authorities from the real rescue effort."

"And their partial destruction of the gallows—"

"Made its rebuilding necessary. And the hammering sounds occasioned by *that* covered the thudding sounds emitted by Stonecutter as the tunnel was dug up to the prisoner's cell. Yes, all in all, a very well-organized escape."

"You implied, earlier, that there was a second reason why the escape might very well succeed?"

"There is. I doubt that the Hetman will push his search for Benjamin as hard as he might, now that the escape is an accomplished fact, and he's had a chance to think matters over."

"And why is that?"

"Of course his pride was touched by the escape. But now that he has at least hints from the Prince that Benjamin's continued survival pleases him, and pleases certain other powerful people as well, it is not an unmixed curse. Perhaps by now al-Farabi has even had time to suggest that allowing poor farmers to vote on matters that concern them greatly might render the task of the radical revolutionary more difficult."

"I can see that this custom of voting might ultimately present a great threat to any ruler."

"Indeed. I am not sure that either of the Princes has thought that far ahead himself . . . in any case, I expect the Hetman is still making a real effort to recapture his victim. He is just not pressing that effort as urgently as he possibly could."

"Well, I repeat that I join you in hoping that he does not succeed."

"We shall see."

"And you are sure that Prince al-Farabi shares our hopes."

"My dear Kasimir, I am very sure of that. Almost from the very beginning I suspected that might be his position. The Prince is a worthy man, though there are times when he displays a lamentable tendency to overact."

"Did you mean to say 'over*react*,' Magistrate?"

"I meant to say just what I said. I only wish that there were many other princes who had no worse faults."

"The implication being, of course, that Prince al-Farabi has been taking a leading role in all this theatrical performance with Stonecutter."

The Magistrate nodded. "Some days ago I became convinced—it was a gradual conviction—that the original theft of the Sword from your caravan's encampment was only a deception, intended to prevent suspicion falling on the two good Princes, Mark and al-Farabi, when it became known that Stonecutter had been used to effect the escape of the prisoner Benjamin."

"My own conviction on that point was much more sudden, but I fear that it took place much later than yours. Tell me, how did yours begin?"

"It began with an oddity. With an event that at first seemed not only inexplicable but meaningless—I refer, of course, to the cutting of the double slit in your tent wall."

"Ah."

"Yes. From the moment you reported that puzzling detail, I suspected that all was not as it seemed regarding the theft of the Sword. Yet the more I talked to you, the more firmly I was convinced that you were telling me the truth as you saw it."

"Indeed I was. I see now that I had been recruited and used without my knowledge; that it was arranged from the start that I should be a witness to the supposed crime."

"And the best kind of witness. Respectable, believable, while at the same time—forgive me, Kasimir—not overly imaginative. Honest and disinterested, a young man who would have no reason to lie about anything he saw or heard. And the plan to use you as a witness of course succeeded—even though the 'thief' had to make more than one slash in the tent wall to wake you up."

"Ah!" said Kasimir, and shook his head, remembering. "But suppose I had wakened at the first whisper of sound inside the tent, and grappled with the intruder?"

"Then there would have ensued noise, shouting, a general alarm. I do not doubt that within moments the tent would have been filled with struggling bodies. Somehow, in the confusion, you would have been pinned down while the thief contrived to make his escape with the Sword. Doubtless his success would have been ascribed to magic."

Kasimir thought about it briefly. "No doubt you are right," he said.

"Yes, I have no doubt of it. If ever we have the chance to talk all this over freely with al-Farabi, he will, I am sure, tell us that the man who took the Sword that night was one of the most trusted members of the caravan, wearing a mask so that you should not recognize him. If you had noticed his absence after the Sword was gone, you would have been told that he was one of the party sent out into the desert to try to track the thief."

"No doubt," said Kasimir again. He let out a faint sigh.

"But as matters actually went, you did not jump up and grapple with the intruder. Instead you watched, still half asleep, as he extracted the Sword from the pile of baggage and made off with it. Moments later the alarm was sounded on schedule. The plan was off to a good start.

"The next step it called for was the freeing of an important prisoner from the road-building gang—I suppose he was someone who knew the layout of the prison cells within the palace, so that a tunnel could be dug out within the narrow compass of the walls. Another person with knowledge just as good must have been found eventually, or the plan could not have succeeded.

"But the prisoner was freed as planned, from Lednik's rather sloppy control. And then things immediately began to go wrong.

"The problem was that the two men who were now carrying the Sword began to improvise. Their next step ought to have been simply to carry Stonecutter into the city and deliver it to Natalia and her people, who were waiting for it. They would have been able to start digging the tunnel at once, with a good margin of spare time before the morning when the execution was scheduled. That would have avoided the need for last-moment heroics, and an escape completed barely minutes before dawn on Festival morning.

"But instead—sudden improvisation. For some reason the two decided to detour to the stone quarry, and release another comrade imprisoned there. There would have been certain advantages in being able to enter the city three strong instead of only two. And perhaps the prisoner at the quarry was a special friend of one or the other of those who were carrying the Sword.

"But those two had not reckoned with Foreman Kovil. That red-haired man was of a very different stamp from the easygoing boss of the road gang. Kovil was not only greedy and ruthless, but treacherous, bold, and resolute as well. When the Sword was shown to him he saw in it a chance to trade the life of a petty prison tyrant for that of a wealthy and successful adventurer; and to seize that chance he did not scruple to commit a double murder.

"He had no real chance, of course, of being able to keep his crime a secret from the other men at the quarry, guards and prisoners alike. But those who knew the secret had no reason to reveal it, and every reason to cooperate with the man who still held their lives in his hands. Mere silence was not enough; Kovil needed a couple of more active accomplices, both in the killing and afterward, when he took the Sword into the city to convert it into more useful wealth.

"He thought his second-in-command, Umar, would do to mind the quarry until the sale of the Sword should have been somehow completed. But he needed and wanted one more man. Someone to stand with him and protect his back while he negotiated the secret sale of a tremendous stolen treasure. And then Kovil made his own fatal mistake. Though probably from the start there was no doubt in his mind as to which man he would choose for a job like that."

"The Juggler," said Kasimir, and shuddered faintly.

"Indeed. Kovil went into the city with Stonecutter in hand, and the

Juggler at his back, and tried to sell the Sword. Whatever might have been the details of that first bloody skirmish on the waterfront, when it was over only one man was left alive—the Juggler, with the Sword of Siege now in his own hands. In one way or another Kovil had fallen victim to the same treachery he had dealt out to others."

"Meanwhile," Kasimir put in, "Natalia and her people had been expecting the Sword to be brought to them. And when it failed to arrive—"

"They became alarmed. Then they heard about the killings on the waterfront, probably from someone who had actually seen the Sword in the Juggler's hands. And they knew that he had it and would almost certainly be trying to sell it quickly."

"And when did you come to an understanding of all this, Magistrate?"

"Alas, with painful slowness! At the start of course I came into the situation by accident, and through your efforts to be helpful. Al-Farabi could scarcely refuse my help, but he sent his most trusted subordinate into the city with us to keep an eye on us.

"As soon as I learned that the prisoner freed from the road gang was political, and that a connection was implied between him and Benjamin of the Steppe, I thought I understood the beginning of the story. After seeing al-Farabi at that conference in the palace, where he seemed more genuinely worried than before, I was sure of it. Since I sympathised with Benjamin, and with Princes Mark and al-Farabi, my task then became not simply to find the Sword, but to cause it to be used according to the original scenario, before being returned to its rightful owner."

"The original plan being of course to free Benjamin."

"Of course."

"And when did you tell the Prince that you had discovered his deception?"

"That came a little later. In beggar's guise I also managed to establish contact with Natalia and her group. I persuaded her to loan me the Sword for a few hours to get rid of Valamo, who had learned of the tunnel into the prison and was threatening to reveal it to the authorities —unless he was paid off very handsomely.

"I dared not try to trick him unless I could have the real Sword in hand to do so—but I could not explain its presence to you ahead of time. Hence my sleight of hand substitution."

"You might have taken me into your confidence completely."

"It is natural that you should be bitter. But I could not be sure of your reaction . . . at any rate, my task became much easier, once we had got Valamo out of the way. There was nothing to do with such a man in such a situation, except to kill him."

Wen Chang looked grim for a long moment, then his features relaxed. "Once the Juggler had been removed from the game board, and the Sword was back in the tunnel-diggers' hands, it was not hard to distract everyone for a few necessary hours with fears of a Blue Temple robbery. In return for my help, Natalia agreed to finally return the Sword to me in the rather impressively dramatic manner that you all witnessed."

"She is a remarkable young woman."

"She is indeed."

And now both men fell silent. The little cavalcade they led was now closely approaching one of the great land gates of the city. It was in fact the same gate by which they had entered Eylau only a few days ago. Just ahead, troopers of the Watch were probing with lances and swords into a wagonload of refuse that was being hauled out of the city.

Kasimir whispered a question. "I wonder—will he manage to get out?"

Wen Chang made no reply. The refuse wagon was moving on, and now it was their turn to ride up to the gate. The Watch officer who was in charge saluted the imposing figure of the Magistrate, held brief conversation with him, and then reached into the guard post at the center of the gateway to get a copy of the roster of recent travelers.

He consulted the list, then once more faced Wen Chang respectfully. "Yes sir, here you are—the merchant Ching Hao and party, fourteen men in all." Swiftly but accurately the officer counted. "Pass on."

Kasimir rode on out through the gate without turning in his saddle to glance behind him. He rode on without looking back, though he could remember perfectly well that when the little column left the inn there had been only ten uniformed troopers riding behind Lieutenant Komi. One man, the lieutenant had said, had fallen ill while visiting his relatives in the Desert Quarter, and would be rejoining his unit later.

So, counting the officer, Wen Chang, and Kasimir himself, that ought to make a company of thirteen men in all. And now there were fourteen. But Kasimir was not going to turn around and look. Not for nothing had he spent the last few days in the company of Wen Chang.